Actual Test

01

中譯與解説

♪ 單題練習版-01

	答對題數	換算分數
聽力		
閱讀		

New TOEIC 第一回

1. `1_01` 美式女聲

(A) He is jotting something down.
(B) He is selecting a notebook.
(C) He is looking through some files.
(D) He is putting on eyeglasses.

(A) 男子正在摘記某些內容。
(B) 男子正在挑選筆記本。
(C) 男子正在瀏覽檔案。
(D) 男子正在戴眼鏡。

正確答案為 **(A)**

看到單人獨照，請注意該人物的動作與衣著特徵。描述男子正在記筆記的 (A) 是最適合的答案。男子雖然戴著眼鏡，但 (D) 的 putting on 使用進行式，指正在戴上眼鏡，而非照片中已經戴著的狀態。男子也不是在挑選筆記本或瀏覽檔案。

字彙　**jot down** 概略寫下、草草記下　**select** 選擇、挑選　**look through** 瀏覽

2. `1_02` 美式男聲

(A) The man is preparing some food.
(B) The woman is pointing to something.
(C) People are helping themselves to some food.
(D) People are placing their orders.

(A) 男子正在準備食物。
(B) 女子正指著某樣東西。
(C) 人們正在幫自己盛裝食物。
(D) 人們正在點餐。

正確答案為 **(C)**

照片男女在自助餐廳盛裝食物。指向物品的人是男子，因此描寫女子指著東西的 (B) 不是答案。**須仔細聆聽主詞性別，避免只聽後面動作的描述就決定答案。**照片也不是男子料理食物或在點餐。

字彙　**point to** 指向　**help oneself to** 自行取用（食物等）　**place an order** 訂購、下單

7. 1_07 美式男聲 / 美式女聲

How can I reach City Hall from here?
(A) City Hall is crowded these days.
(B) A taxi will be the best option.
(C) Yes, he comes from a very rich family.

我該怎麼從這裡到市政府？
(A) 最近市政府人很多。
(B) 計程車是最好的方法。
(C) 是的，他來自一個非常富有的家庭。

正確答案為 (B)

How 疑問句詢問去特定地點的方式，提到交通工具的 (B) 是答案。(A) 是重複題目的 city hall 的陷阱選項。**wh 疑問詞開頭的問句不能以 Yes/No 回答**，因此 (C) 不是答案。

> 字彙　**crowded** 擁擠的　　**option** 選項

8. 1_08 英式男聲 / 美式女聲

Will you attend the workshop, or do you have too much work?
(A) John will finish his work later.
(B) Sorry, but I didn't see it.
(C) I will definitely be there.

你會參加研討會，還是你有很多工作要做？
(A) 約翰晚點會完成工作。
(B) 很抱歉，我沒看到。
(C) 我一定會到場。

正確答案為 (C)

題目問是否會參加，回答一定會到場的 (C) 是答案。(A) 重複題目的 work，是陷阱選項。(B) 的回答是**過去式，與題目問的未來是否參加無關**。

> 字彙　**attend** 參加　　**definitely** 當然、肯定地

9. 1_09 美式女聲 / 美式男聲

Where have you been?
(A) Not really.
(B) It's from New York.
(C) With my friend at the store.

你去哪了？
(A) 不見得。
(B) 它來自紐約。
(C) 和我朋友在店裡。

正確答案為 (C)

Where 疑問句問「在哪裡」，回答地點的 (C) 是答案。(A) Not really. 意思相當於 No. 的否定回答，不可用來回應 wh 疑問詞問句。(B) 雖提到地點，但是**主詞與題目的不一致**。

> 字彙　**so far** 到目前為止、目前

10. 1_10 美式女聲 / 澳式男聲

Which flight are you taking?
(A) Absolutely, I'll take it.
(B) No, are you?
(C) The one at seven.

你打算搭哪班飛機？
(A) 當然，我會搭那班。
(B) 不會，你呢？
(C) 7 點的飛機。

正確答案為 (C)

Which 疑問句問「哪個航班」，(C) 提到特定時間起飛的班機是答案。(A) 用到題目有出現的 take，但 Absolutely. 是相當於 Yes. 的肯定句回答，wh 疑問詞問句不能以 Yes/No 回答，因此不是答案。

> 字彙　**Absolutely.**（表贊同語氣）當然。

11. `1_11` 英式男聲 / 美式男聲

Don't you need this note for your presentation?
(A) No, I don't take notes during the lecture.
(B) I will turn in my paper.
(C) Thanks, I almost forgot it.

你報告不需要這張便條紙嗎？
(A) 不了，上課我不做筆記的。
(B) 我會交論文。
(C) 謝謝，我差點忘了。

正確答案為 (C)

否定疑問句問需不需要這張便條紙，答案是感謝對方提醒的 (C)。(A) 重複使用題目中的 note 誤導作答，(B) 的 paper 是聯想自題目中的 note，但選項與題目無關。

字彙　**presentation** 上台報告　**take notes** 做筆記　**lecture** 講座、講課　**turn in** 繳交

---

12. `1_12` 美式男聲 / 美式女聲

What about playing tennis together?
(A) I don't want to play darts.
(B) He is one of the best tennis players in this country.
(C) This week is full of deadlines.

要不要一起打網球？
(A) 我不想玩飛鏢。
(B) 他是這個國家最好的網球選手之一。
(C) 這禮拜有一堆截止期限要趕。

正確答案為 (C)

本題使用〈what about〉句型提議一起打網球，最適當的**答案是用忙碌間接拒絕的 (C)**。(B) 是重複題目中的 tennis 的陷阱選項，(A) 提到與 tennis 無關的 darts「飛鏢」，皆不是答案。

字彙　**deadline** 截止日、交件日

---

13. `1_13` 英式男聲 / 美式女聲

Have you been to the art gallery yet?
(A) She's a scientist.
(B) No, can we go?
(C) Yes, it is.

你去過畫廊嗎？
(A) 她是個科學家。
(B) 還沒，我們可以去嗎？
(C) 是的，那是對的。

正確答案為 (B)

題目問有無去過某處的經驗，答案是反問要不要一起去的 (B)。說明職業的 (A) 與題目無關，**回答時所用到的代名詞也不對**，因此不是答案。(C) 也與題目無關。

字彙　**art gallery** 畫廊　**yet** 已經（用於疑問句）；還、仍然（用於否定句）

---

14. `1_14` 美式女聲 / 澳式男聲

How long have you been staying in this condominium?
(A) Since I got a new job in this city.
(B) I sold my condominium a long time ago.
(C) My cousin will live in this apartment with me.

你在這間公寓住多久了？
(A) 從我在這個城市找到工作開始。
(B) 很久以前我就把公寓賣掉了。
(C) 我表弟會跟我一起住這間公寓。

正確答案為 (A)

題目是 How long 疑問句，問「期間」，且使用現在完成式 have you been，(A) 使用可以回答現在完成式的〈since ＋過去時間點〉，說明從特定時間點開始居住，是正確答案。(B) 使用過去簡單式，是敘述過去發生的事情，雖用到題目中的 condominium，但與題目無關。(C) 使用到與題目 condominium 有關的 apartment，也與題目無關。

字彙　**condominium** [ˈkɑndə.mɪnɪmən] 公寓　**cousin** 表或堂兄弟

15. `1_15` 美式女聲 / 英式男聲

Why doesn't this printer work?
(A) Ms. Brown asked me to print some documents.
(B) See, you have not pressed the power button.
(C) I don't think the printer is mine.

這台印表機怎麼不動了？
(A) 布朗小姐要我印東西。
(B) 妳看，妳還沒按下電源開關。
(C) 這台印表機不是我的。

正確答案為 (B)

Why 疑問句問「原因」，回答沒有按下開關按鍵的 (B) 是答案。(A) 雖然提到 print，和題目出現的 printer 看似有關，(C) 也重複使用 printer，但都是故意用單字混淆的錯誤選項。

16. `1_16` 美式男聲 / 英式男聲

Would you send our agreement letter with International Tech. to me?
(A) The agreement will be revised soon.
(B) I'll fax it directly after this meeting.
(C) They made a new contract with other company.

你能把國際技術公司的協議書寄給我嗎？
(A) 協議書馬上會更正。
(B) 會議結束後我會立刻傳真給你。
(C) 他們跟其他公司簽了一份新合約。

正確答案為 (B)

題目是要求寄送文件的 wh 疑問句，回答會傳真過去的 (B) 是答案。(A) 重複使用題目中的 agreement，(C) 使用與題目 agreement 意思相近的 contract，都是陷阱選項。此外，(A) 提到協議書會馬上修正，會讓人聯想到尚無法寄送，然而題目是要求寄送協議書，與是否要更正並不相關，因此不是答案。

 字彙　**agreement** 協議、協定　**revise** 修正、修改　**directly** 馬上、立刻　**contract** 合約

17. `1_17` 美式男聲 / 美式女聲

When were the changes to the budget submitted?
(A) To the department mailing list.
(B) They haven't been done yet.
(C) That's what I'd submit.

預算變更是什麼時候提交的？
(A) 寄到部門郵件通訊名單。
(B) 還沒有交出去。
(C) 這就是我提交的東西。

正確答案為 (B)

When 疑問句問的是提交時間，答案是尚未繳交的 (B)。(A) 適合回應 Where 開頭的疑問句，(C) 是利用題目中相同的單字 submit，是陷阱選項。

 字彙　**submit** 提交、繳交

18. `1_18` 英式男聲 / 美式女聲

Who is in the meeting room right now?
(A) The meeting room is being renovated right now.
(B) The shareholders will invite you.
(C) I think I've just seen Monica there.

誰現在在會議室？
(A) 現在會議室正在整修。
(B) 股東將會邀請你。
(C) 我想我剛看到莫妮卡在那裡。

正確答案為 (C)

Who 疑問句問的是誰在會議室，提到特定某人的 (C) 是最合適的答案。(A) 使用到題目出現的 meeting room，故意混淆作答。(B) 提到 shareholders「股東」，看似回應了 Who 疑問句，但回答內容與題目無關。

字彙　**renovate** 改建　**shareholder** 股東

Test 01

19. 1_19 美式女聲 / 美式男聲

He is going to sign a new contract with us, isn't he?
(A) The contract documents are brought by our manager.
(B) I think so. He's satisfied with our presentation.
(C) Our last contract was cancelled.

他打算和我們簽一份新的合約，是嗎？
(A) 這份合約文件是我們經理帶來的。
(B) 我想是的。他對我們的報告很滿意。
(C) 我們的上一份合約已經取消。

正確答案為 (B)

本題是確認是否簽約的附加問句，(B) 除了表示肯定之外，也提到對方對報告感到滿意，因此是正確答案。(A) 和 (C) 的回答都與問題無關，重複使用 contract 誤導作答。

字彙 **sign a contract** 簽訂合約   **cancel** 取消

20. 1_20 美式女聲 / 英式男聲

Can we postpone the deadline for the annual report?
(A) Sure, give me his phone number.
(B) There is a long line.
(C) Yes, for a day or two.

我們可以延後年度報告的截止日期嗎？
(A) 當然可以，給我他的電話號碼。
(B) 隊伍很長。
(C) 可以，大概延長一到兩天。

正確答案為 (C)

本題詢問可否延後截止日期，回答可以延後一到兩天的 (C) 是正確答案。(A) Sure. 雖然是提議疑問句的常見肯定回應，但後面的句子使用了與題目無關的第三人稱 his，**並用發音類似 postpone 的 phone 誤導作答**，(B) 的回答也與題目無關，因此都不是答案。

字彙 **postpone** 延後   **for a day or two** 一到兩天

21. 1_21 英式男聲 / 美式男聲

Have you already prepared the press release?
(A) It will be done shortly.
(B) One of our biggest clients from the UK.
(C) Many journalists will come.

你準備好新聞稿了嗎？
(A) 很快就會完成。
(B) 是我們在英國最大的客戶之一。
(C) 很多記者會來。

正確答案為 (A)

本題問資料是否準備好了，給予肯定回答並表示即將完成的 (A) 是最適合的答案。(B) 的回答與問題無關，(C) 使用了與題目 press release 相關的單字 journalists「記者」，是引起混淆的陷阱選項。

字彙 **press release** 新聞稿、聲明稿   **shortly** 立即、馬上   **journalist** 記者、新聞工作者

22. 1_22 美式男聲 / 美式女聲

How was your previous trip to London?
(A) Have you gone to London before?
(B) No words can describe it.
(C) The trip will be cancelled, I think.

你上次倫敦之行怎麼樣？
(A) 你以前去過倫敦嗎？
(B) 言語無法形容。
(C) 我想這次旅行會取消。

正確答案為 (B)

How 疑問句問對方旅行經驗「如何」，適合的答案為 (B)，回答無法以任何言語形容。注意 No words 是以否定詞 No 開始的句子，很容易誤以為是否定句，請勿掉入陷阱。(A) 和 (C) 都是重複使用題目中的 London 和 trip 誤導作答。

23. 1_23 英式男聲 / 美式女聲

I don't have any appointments tomorrow, do I?
(A) He did it last time.
(B) The results were promising.
(C) No, you're available all day.

我明天沒有任何會面，是吧？
(A) 他上次做了。
(B) 結果蠻有希望。
(C) 沒有，你整天都有空。

正確答案為 (C)

附加問句確認明天是否有行程，回答整天有空的 (C) 是正確答案。(A) 的主詞與題目主詞不一致，(B) 回答也與題目無關。

字彙　**promising** 有希望的、有前途的　**available** 有空的；可用的

24. 1_24 美式女聲 / 澳式男聲

When can I expect to hear from you about the interview?
(A) Within the next few days.
(B) At the end of the street.
(C) I found it right here.

我什麼時候能收到您關於面試的消息？
(A) 就這幾天。
(B) 在這條街的盡頭。
(C) 我就是在這裡找到的。

正確答案為 (A)

When 疑問句問「何時」可以收到通知，答案是回應時間的 (A)。(B) 和 (C) 的回答都是說明地點，適合回應 Where 疑問句，與題目無關。

字彙　**expect** 期待、預期

25. 1_25 美式女聲 / 英式男聲

It's the most unique tower design in this city, isn't it?
(A) None can be compared to this tower, for sure.
(B) This city has a beautiful view.
(C) Did your team design this wide room?

這是這個城市最獨特的高塔設計，不是嗎？
(A) 當然，沒有其他可以與這座塔相比。
(B) 這個城市景色優美。
(C) 這個寬敞的空間是貴團隊設計的嗎？

正確答案為 (A)

本題使用附加問句，確認建築物設計的獨特性，**(A) 間接肯定**沒有其他可以相比，是最適合的答案。(B) 和 (C) 與問題無關，重複使用題目出現過的 city 和 design，是誤導選項。

字彙　**compare to** 與～相比

26. 1_26 美式男聲 / 英式男聲

Have you chosen the new photographer or are you still deciding?
(A) I'll be happy to take a picture of you.
(B) We have two more candidates to interview.
(C) The chief photographer's name is Arthur Gonzalez.

你選好新攝影師了嗎？還是尚未決定？
(A) 我很樂意為你拍張照。
(B) 我們還有兩個應徵者要面試。
(C) 首席攝影師叫亞瑟岡薩雷斯。

正確答案為 (B)

本題是選擇疑問句，問是否已選定攝影師，(B) 回答還要面試應徵者，**等於間接回答尚未決定**，是最適合的答案。(A) 使用了從 photographer 聯想到的 take a picture「拍照」，是陷阱選項，(C) 也使用同樣單字 photographer，但回答內容和題目無關。

字彙　**candidate** 應徵者、候選人　**chief** （階級、職務上）首領、首長

27. 1_27 美式男聲 / 美式女聲

Mr. Miller will be writing the training manual.
(A) They were just hired.
(B) Yes, a few employees did.
(C) I know he'll do a good job.

米勒先生將編寫培訓手冊。
(A) 他們剛被雇用。
(B) 是的,有些員工。
(C) 我知道他會做得很好。

正確答案為 (C)

本題是敘述事實的直述句,最適合的回應是 (C),回答那個人會做得很好。(A) 和 (B) 的主詞與題目的直述句不符,也與題目無關,因此不是答案。

> 字彙　**manual** 使用手冊、說明書

28. 1_28 英式男聲 / 美式女聲

What was the name of the book you recommended?
(A) Thanks, I enjoyed it.
(B) Do you mean the one on proposal writing?
(C) Yes, in the library.

你推薦的那本書叫什麼?
(A) 謝謝,我很喜歡。
(B) 你是說關於寫提案書的那本嗎?
(C) 是的,在圖書館。

正確答案為 (B)

What 疑問句問某書籍的書名,最適合的答案是婉轉反問的 (B)。(A) 的回答與問題無關,(C) 是專門回應 Yes/No 問句的回答句,不適合用於 wh 疑問詞開頭的疑問句。

> 字彙　**recommend** 推薦　**proposal** 提案

29. 1_29 美式女聲 / 美式男聲

Why didn't Brian submit his budget proposal yesterday?
(A) Yes, it's more expensive than I thought.
(B) It's possible that he forgot.
(C) I'll submit the sales figures tomorrow.

為什麼布萊恩不交預算案?
(A) 是的,比我想的還貴。
(B) 他可能忘了。
(C) 我明天將提交銷售數字。

正確答案為 (B)

Why 疑問句詢問沒有提交的理由,答案是回答 Brian 可能忘記的 (B)。wh 疑問句不能用 Yes/No 回答,因此 (A) 不是答案。(C) 重複使用和題目一樣的單字 submit,是陷阱選項。

> 字彙　**budget** 預算　**sales figures** 銷售數字

30. 1_30 美式女聲 / 英式男聲

The facilities manager is out of town for family matters.
(A) That building is empty.
(B) It's fine with me.
(C) Who's covering for her?

設備經理因家中有事出了遠門。
(A) 那個建築物是空的。
(B) 我沒關係。
(C) 誰代理她的工作?

正確答案為 (C)

本題為直述句,轉達設施管理者不在位子上,反問由誰代理其工作的 (C) 是正確答案。(A) 與 (B) 的句意與題目無關,因此都不是答案。

> 字彙　**facility**（常用複數）設備、設施　**out of town**（因出差等）不在、出遠門　**family matter** 家庭事務　**cover** 代理職務

31. 1_31 英式男聲 / 美式女聲

I think you should try a shorter hair cut this time.
(A) Why don't you try this?
(B) Yes, I have been considering that.
(C) One o'clock on Thursday.

我覺得妳這次可以試著剪短髮。
(A) 你為什麼不試試這個？
(B) 是啊，我一直有考慮這樣做。
(C) 星期四 1 點。

正確答案為 (B)

本題是建議對方換新髮型的直述句，正確答案是 (B)，使用 considering「考慮」間接給予肯定回應。(A) 重複使用題目中的 try，誤導作答，(C) 的句意與題目無關。

字彙　**consider** 考慮

Questions 32-34 refer to the following conversation.

W: Matt, I noticed that you were reading this month's issue of *Business Circle* in the staff lounge earlier. Can I have it when you're finished? There's an article that I'd like to look at.

M: Is it the one about the global trade agreement that's currently under negotiation?

W: That's right, if that deal goes through, it's likely to have a major impact on our industry.

M: You're right. We'll need to keep a close eye on the situation as it develops. We want to make plans to try to take advantage of potential opportunities, and we should also be prepared for any negative effects that could result from the deal.

問題 32-34 參考以下對話。

女： 麥特，㉜ 我注意到你在休息室看這個月的《商業圈》，看完之後可以給我嗎？我很想看裡面的一篇文章。

男： ㉝ 是有關目前協商中的全球貿易協定嗎？

女： 沒錯，如果協定通過，會對我們的產業產生重大衝擊。

男： 妳說的沒錯。㉞ 我們必須密切關注這件事情的發展。我們要善用這個機會擬定計畫，另外我們也該做好準備，因應這場交易可能帶來的負面影響。

字彙 **this month's issue** 本月號　　**staff lounge** 員工休息室　　**trade agreement** 貿易協定
under negotiation 談判中、協商中　　**go through** 通過　　**impact** 影響、衝擊　　**keep a close eye on** 密切關注～
take advantage of 善用、利用　　**negative effect** 負面影響　　**deal** 交易

32. What most likely is *Business Circle*?
(A) A trade conference
(B) A Web site
(C) A magazine
(D) A radio program

《商業圈》很有可能是什麼？
(A) 貿易會議
(B) 網頁
(C) 雜誌
(D) 廣播節目

正確答案為 **(C)**

〈注意細節－特定內容〉
須注意聆聽題目關鍵字 *Business Circle*。女子第一段話提到 this month's issue「本月號」的 *Business Circle*，可知這是雜誌。

33. What is the current status of the trade agreement?
(A) It has gone through.
(B) It is being discussed.
(C) It has been suspended.
(D) It will soon expire.

貿易協定目前狀況如何？
(A) 已經通過。
(B) 正在討論。
(C) 已經暫停。
(D) 即將到期。

正確答案為 **(B)**

〈注意細節－特定事項〉
注意聆聽關鍵字為 trade agreement。男子第一段話提到目前全球貿易協定 under negotiation「協商當中」，因此答案是 (B)。

> 字彙 **current** 目前的　**status** 狀態　**suspend** 暫時中止

34. What does the man suggest doing?
(A) Preparing an alternative proposal
(B) Monitoring the situation closely
(C) Advertising job opportunities
(D) Analyzing the negative result

男子建議做什麼？
(A) 準備替代方案
(B) 密切關注情勢
(C) 刊登徵才廣告
(D) 分析負面結果

正確答案為 **(B)**

〈注意細節－提議〉
題目問男子所提議的事項為何，因此須注意男子的談話內容。男子最後一段用 We'll need to 提出建議，說到須密切關注情勢，因此答案是 (B)。

換句話說 **keep a close eye on** 密切注意 → **monitoring the situation closely** 密切關注情勢發展

> 字彙 **alternative** 替代的　**monitor** 監督　**advertise** 刊登廣告、宣傳　**analyze** 分析

Questions 35-37 refer to the following conversation.

W: Did you hear that Jamal is going to be elevated to sales manager soon, and then transferred to our headquarters in Prague next month?

M: Yes, he deserves it. Since joining the company, he's made some outstanding contributions which have helped us become one of the leading pharmaceutical firms in Eastern Europe.

W: That's true. And he's a great team player, so I'm sure that he will be able to lead his own team and deal with them well.

M: Why don't we hold some kind of leaving party for him?

問題 35-37 參考以下對話。

女：㉟ 你有聽説傑莫快要升為銷售經理了嗎？他下個月會調到布拉格總部。

男：有啊，那是他應得的。他加入公司以來，㊱ 做了傑出貢獻，幫助我們成為東歐領先的製藥公司之一。

女：沒錯。他也是個富有團隊精神的人，所以我相信他能夠領導他自己的團隊，並且和他們相處愉快。

男：㊲ 我們何不幫他舉辦個歡送會？

字彙　**be elevated to** 晉升到（某職位）　**be transferred to** 轉調到　**deserve** 應得、值得　**outstanding** 傑出的　**contribution** 貢獻　**pharmaceutical** 製藥的　**firm** 公司

35. What are the speakers mainly talking about?
(A) The advancement of a coworker
(B) The retirement of a manager
(C) A recent business agreement
(D) The relocation of a headquarters

説話者主要在談論什麼？
(A) 同事晉升
(B) 經理退休
(C) 最近的一項商業協定
(D) 總部搬遷

正確答案為 **(A)**

〈掌握基本資訊－主題〉
本題詢問對話主題，對話前半部就能找到線索。女子一開始就提到傑莫晉升為銷售經理的消息，答案是 (A)。

換句話說 **be elevated to** 晉升到（某職位）→ **advancement** 晉升

字彙 **advancement** 晉升　**retirement** 退休　**agreement** 協議　**relocation** 搬遷

36. What type of company do the speakers most likely work for?
(A) A legal office
(B) A marketing firm
(C) A travel agency
(D) A medical firm

説話者最有可能在何種公司工作？
(A) 法律事務所
(B) 行銷公司
(C) 旅行社
(D) 製藥公司

正確答案為 **(D)**

〈掌握基本資訊－場所〉
男子第一段發言提到該同事幫助他們公司成為東歐領先藥廠之一，可見談話者是在製藥公司工作，答案是 (D)。

換句話說 **pharmaceutical firm** 製藥公司 → **medical firm** 製藥公司

37. What does the man suggest?
(A) Leading a workshop
(B) Holding a farewell event
(C) Checking a report
(D) Asking for more information

男子提出什麼建議？
(A) 開設研習會
(B) 舉行歡送會
(C) 確認報告
(D) 要求提供更多資訊

正確答案為 **(B)**

〈注意細節－提議〉
男子在最後一段話說 why don't we 作為提議，並說可舉辦歡送會，因此答案是 (B)。聽到〈**Why not ~?**〉就要聯想到這是「提議」的句子。

換句話說 **leaving party** 歡送會 → **farewell event** 歡送會

Questions 38-40 refer to the following conversation.

M: Glenside Suites. How may I help you?

W: Diego, it's Lisa from housekeeping. Sorry to call you at the front desk, but there's a problem. The guest who just checked in to 709 told me that her room is too cold. It looks like the heater isn't working. I tried calling maintenance but no one answered.

M: Oh, Chris had to go to the hardware store to pick up a few things. I'm afraid he won't be back for a while.

W: Well, what should I tell the guest?

M: Please send her back to the front desk, and we'll put her in a different room.

問題 38-40 參考以下對話。

男：這裡是格蘭賽德豪華套房，我能為您效勞嗎？

女：迪亞哥，我是客房部的麗莎，抱歉打電話到櫃檯，但這裡有問題。38 剛入住 709 的客人告訴我她的房間太冷了。暖氣好像壞了。39 我打電話到維修部，但沒人接。

男：哎呀，39 克里斯去五金行買東西，恐怕他暫時不會回來。

女：40 我該怎麼跟客人說呢？

男：請把她轉接回櫃檯，我們會安排她住另一間房。

字彙 **housekeeping** 客房部、客房服務　**maintenance** 維護　**hardware store** 五金行

38. Why is the woman calling?
(A) To announce a plan
(B) To offer an apology
(C) To request some supplies
(D) To pass along a complaint

女子為何打電話？
(A) 宣布一項計畫
(B) 道歉
(C) 要求補給品
(D) 轉達客訴

正確答案為 **(D)**

〈掌握基本資訊－目的〉
此題問的是此通電話的**目的**，從前半段的**對話就可以找到答案**。男子接到電話後，女子轉達旅客說房間太冷的意見，可能是暖氣故障，因此答案是 (D)。

字彙　**supplies**（固定用複數）補給品、日用品　**complaint** 抱怨

39. In which department does Chris probably work?
(A) Housekeeping
(B) Reception
(C) Maintenance
(D) Security

克里斯最有可能在何種部門工作？
(A) 客房管理部
(B) 接待處
(C) 維修部
(D) 保安部

正確答案為 **(C)**

〈注意細節－提及內容〉
女子第一段話提到曾打電話到 maintenance 維修部，但無人接聽，男子接著表示克里斯去五金行了，由此可見克里斯與維修部有關，答案是 (C)。

40. What will the woman probably do next?
(A) Make some repairs
(B) Speak to a guest
(C) Call a hardware store
(D) Clean a guest's suite

女子接下來會做什麼？
(A) 做一些維修
(B) 與客人談話
(C) 打電話給五金行
(D) 打掃客人的房間

正確答案為 **(B)**

〈注意細節－未來〉
本題問接下來發生的事，通常會在對話後半段提到。女子問了接下來該跟客人說什麼，男子回答 Please send her back to the front desk，將客人電話轉接到櫃檯，因此女子接下來會跟客人談話，答案是 (B)。

Questions 41-43 refer to the following conversation with three speakers.

W: Hi, Peter, you look worried.

M1: I have to get over to Tribien French Restaurant to pick up some food for our party this evening.

M2: You don't have much time. What do you think, Alice?

W: You'll make it. It's only about 5 minutes from here.

M1: Yeah, but that's 5 minutes by car. I rode my bicycle to work today, and I can't carry all that food on my bike. The train doesn't run very often around here.

M2: And it's too far from the station. A lot of their customers complain about it.

W: Why don't you use my car? I was planning to walk home anyway.

M1: Really? Thanks, Alice.

問題 41-43 參考以下三人對話。

女： 嗨，彼得，你看起來有心事。

男1： ④1 我得去廚貝恩法式餐廳拿今晚聚會的餐點。

男2： 你沒有多少時間耶。艾莉絲，妳說呢？

女： 你可以的。④2 從這裡過去只要 5 分鐘。

男1： 沒錯，但那是坐車過去。我今天騎腳踏車上班，而且我無法把所有食物都放在腳踏車上。④3 這裡的火車班次又少。

男2： ④3 而且那裡離車站太遠了，他們很多顧客都抱怨這點。

女： 你開我的車去如何？反正我今天打算走路回家。

男1： 真的嗎？謝謝妳，艾莉絲。

字彙　**get over** 去到（遠方）、跨越～　**run** 行經；營運　**evaluation** 評價、評比

41. Why does Peter want to go to a restaurant?
(A) To meet some clients
(B) To arrange an event
(C) To pick up an order
(D) To book a place

彼得為什麼要去餐廳？
(A) 見客戶
(B) 安排活動
(C) 拿訂購商品
(D) 預約場地

正確答案為 **(C)**

〈注意細節－特定事項〉
這是兩男一女的三人對話，**必須先找出誰是名為 Peter 的男子**。女子和彼得打招呼之後，男 1 開始回應，可見男 1 是 Peter，他去餐廳是為了拿餐點，答案是 (C)。

42. What does the woman mean when she says, "You'll make it"?
(A) She expects a coworker will attend a gathering.
(B) She knows who will prepare a meal.
(C) She thinks a colleague has enough time.
(D) She believes an evaluation will go well.

女子說「你可以的」的意思是什麼？
(A) 她希望有位同事參加聚餐。
(B) 她認識準備餐點的人。
(C) 她認為同事有足夠的時間。
(D) 她相信評估會順利進行。

正確答案為 **(C)**

〈關鍵句－説話者意圖〉
遇到題目詢問説話意圖的題目，必須綜合對話前後句才能選出答案。男 2 説彼得沒什麼時間，女子則表示從這裡到餐廳只要 5 分鐘，可見她想説的是時間還很充裕，答案是 (C)。

43. What do the men imply about the neighborhood?
(A) It has some nice restaurants.
(B) It is inconvenient.
(C) It is growing rapidly.
(D) It was featured in a magazine.

男子對附近有什麼看法？
(A) 有幾家好餐廳。
(B) 不方便。
(C) 發展迅速。
(D) 雜誌曾專題報導。

正確答案為 **(B)**

〈注意細節－提及內容〉
題目與三人對話的共同意見有關，問兩個男子對此地區的共同想法。男 1 提到火車不常行駛到這裡，男 2 也同意從車站過去太遠。兩男子都感覺此地區交通不方便，答案是 (B)。

字彙　**inconvenient** 不便的　　**feature** 專題報導

1_44-46　英式男聲 / 美式女聲

Questions 44-46 refer to the following conversation.

M: I've been reading the reviews of the Finesound car stereo system. Thanks to our campaign, their initial sales were good, but the people who bought them seem really disappointed.

W: So, you mean that our strategy was successful, but the main problem is the client's product quality?

M: That's right. I think it's up to the manufacturer to address the issue.

W: Let's ask the clients to find some time to discuss our concerns. I really believe this product has a lot of potential if they can overcome this problem.

問題 44-46 參考以下對話。

男：我一直在看凡聲汽車音響的評論。44 多虧我們的宣傳活動，他們初步銷售不錯，45 不過購買的人似乎很失望。

女：那麼你是認為我們的策略成功，但問題是出在客戶的產品品質嗎？

男：沒錯。我認為該由製造廠商解決問題。

女：46 我們請客戶抽空一起討論我們的想法。我相信他們若克服這個問題，這個產品會有很大潛力。

字彙　**review** 評論；評價　**campaign** 宣傳活動　**initial** 一開始的、起初的　**strategy** 策略　**manufacturer** 製造商　**address the issue** 解決問題　**potential** 可能性、潛力　**overcome** 克服

44. Who most likely are the speakers?
(A) Potential clients
(B) Car dealers
(C) Product designers
(D) Advertising executives

說話者最有可能是誰？
(A) 潛在客戶
(B) 汽車經銷商
(C) 產品設計師
(D) 廣告執行單位

正確答案為 **(D)**

〈掌握基本資訊－職業〉
題目問到**說話者的職業，通常可以在前半段對話內容找到**。一開始男子提到多虧說話者的宣傳活動，讓音響銷售額增加，由此可知他們是廣告公司的員工，因此答案是 (D)。

字彙 **dealer** 經銷商　　**executive** 執行單位；主管

45. What problems are the speakers discussing?
(A) Sales figures are unimpressive.
(B) Advertising is becoming more expensive.
(C) Customer satisfaction is low.
(D) Production is behind schedule.

說話者討論什麼問題點？
(A) 銷售數字並不突出。
(B) 廣告費用變得更高。
(C) 顧客滿意度低。
(D) 生產進度落後。

正確答案為 **(C)**

〈掌握基本資訊－問題點〉
關於問題點的題目，通常可以在前半段對話找到答案。男子在一開始就提到顧客評價，談到雖然銷售提升但購買者感到失望，因此最適合的答案是 (C)。

換句話說 **disappointed** 失望的 → **satisfaction is low** 滿意度低

字彙 **behind schedule** 進度落後

46. What does the woman suggest?
(A) Reading customer feedback
(B) Reviewing an instruction manual
(C) Reducing prices
(D) Calling a client meeting

女子提出什麼建議？
(A) 閱讀顧客意見
(B) 翻閱使用說明書
(C) 調降價格
(D) 召開客戶會議

正確答案為 **(D)**

〈注意細節－提議〉
女子在最後談話**使用〈Let's ~〉句型提議**抽出時間與客戶討論，答案是 (D)。

字彙 **feedback** 回饋意見

1_47-49　美式男聲 / 美式女聲

Questions 47-49 refer to the following conversation.

M: Excuse me. I'd like to get one of those prepaid lunch cards. I've just joined the company, and a colleague told me to apply for one here at the personnel office.

W: Do you have your employee identification card with you? We can't issue a prepaid card without it.

M: Actually, I just had my photo taken for the ID, and apparently it won't be ready until the end of this week.

W: Well, I'll give you the application form so you can fill that out now. Please return to our office later with your identification card when you get it. The lunch card will be issued within five business days after we receive your application.

問題 47-49 參考以下對話。

男：不好意思，⁴⁸ 我想申請一張午餐預付卡。⁴⁷ 我剛加入公司，我的同事告訴我來人事部申請。

女：你有帶員工識別證嗎？沒有證件我們不能發卡。

男：其實我才剛拍好辦識別證用的照片，看來要到這個週末才能辦好。

女：那麼 ⁴⁹ 我把申請表給你，你可以先填好。拿到識別證以後，把表格和識別證一起繳交回來。收到申請表後 5 個工作天會發出午餐卡。

字彙　**prepaid** 預付的　**colleague** 同事　**apply for** 申請　**personnel** 人事　**identification card** 識別證、身分證　**apparently** 看來、似乎　**not A until B** 直到 B 才 A　**fill out** 填寫　**issue** 發行、發給

47. Who most likely is the man?　　　　　　男子最有可能是誰？
(A) A receptionist　　　　　　　　　　　　(A) 接待員
(B) A new recruit　　　　　　　　　　　**(B) 新進員工**
(C) A store clerk　　　　　　　　　　　　　(C) 商店櫃檯人員
(D) A security officer　　　　　　　　　　　(D) 維安人員

正確答案為 (B)

〈掌握基本資訊－職業〉
題目問的是男子的身分，須注意一開始的對話內容。男子在第一段話表示自己剛加入公司，由此可知他是新進員工，答案是 (B)。

字彙　**recruit** 新成員；招募、招聘

48. Why does the man visit the woman?　　　男子為什麼去拜訪女子？
(A) To get a refund　　　　　　　　　　　　(A) 為了收取退款
(B) To have an interview　　　　　　　　　 (B) 為了面試
(C) To apply for a card　　　　　　　　　**(C) 為了申請卡片**
(D) To pay for items　　　　　　　　　　　 (D) 為了付款

正確答案為 (C)

〈掌握基本資訊－目的〉
題目問的是男子拜訪的目的，從第一段話就可以找到答案。男子在第一段話說明要辦預付卡，因此答案是 (C)。

字彙　**refund** 退款

49. What will the man probably do next?　　　男子接下來可能會做什麼？
(A) Send an application form　　　　　　　　(A) 寄出申請書
(B) Have his photo taken　　　　　　　　　 (B) 拍照
(C) Talk to a colleague　　　　　　　　　　 (C) 與同事交談
(D) Complete the document　　　　　　　**(D) 填寫文件資料**

正確答案為 (D)

〈注意細節－未來〉
題目問的是接下來將會做的事，可以在對話後半段找到答案。女子最後一段話說會給對方申請書，並說可以先填寫申請書，由此可知男子將填寫文件資料，答案是 (D)。

換句話說　**fill the application form out** 填寫申請 → **complete the form** 填寫資料

1_50-52　英式女聲 / 英式男聲 / 澳式男聲

Questions 50-52 refer to the following conversation with three speakers.

W: Chris and Greg! I appreciate the both of you taking time out of your busy schedules today to discuss this consumer survey.

M1: It's no trouble at all.

M2: We know how important the research will be in developing a successful promotional strategy.

W: What do you think of the initial draft of our questionnaire?

M1: Well, the questions are all very good, but some seem a bit repetitive. I'd recommend dropping a few.

M2: That makes two of us. Plus, you'll probably get a lot more responses if the form doesn't take long to complete.

W: Those are convincing points. I'll be sure to pass them along to the project manager at our next meeting.

問題 50-52 參考以下三人對話。

女： 克里斯、古瑞格，⓹⓪ 謝謝你們兩位今天百忙之中抽空討論消費者問卷調查。

男 1： 這沒什麼。

男 2： 我們知道這項研究對擬定成功的促銷策略很重要。

女： 你覺得我們擬的問卷草稿如何？

男 1： 嗯，問題都很好，但似乎有點重複。⓹① 我建議刪去一些。

男 2： ⓹① 我也有同感。另外，如果問卷不用花很多時間完成的話，或許能收到更多回應。

女： 這些建議都很具說服力。⓹② 下次會議時，我一定會把這些想法轉達給專案經理。

字彙　**consumer survey** 消費者問卷調查　**promotional strategy** 促銷策略　**draft** 草稿　**questionnaire** 問卷調查
repetitive 重複的　**drop** 將～排除在外、放棄　**That makes two of us.** 我也是這麼認為。
convincing 有說服力的、令人信服的　**pass along** 傳遞、轉達

50. What are the speakers mainly discussing?　　説話者主要談論內容為何？
(A) A research budget　　(A) 研究預算
(B) A consumer campaign　　(B) 消費者促銷活動
(C) A managerial promotion　　(C) 升管理職
(D) A marketing survey　　**(D) 銷售調查**

正確答案為 **(D)**

〈掌握基本資訊－主題〉
對話主題須從前半段對話找答案。女子一開始感謝兩人在百忙之中抽空來討論問卷調查，因此答案是 (D)。對話中提到的 promotion 是指「宣傳」，(C) 的 promotion 則是指「升職」。

字彙　**promotion** 促銷宣傳；晉升

51. What do the men suggest?　　男子們提出何種建議？
(A) Emphasizing particular points　　(A) 強調特定要點
(B) Shortening a form　　**(B) 縮短表單內容**
(C) Conducting longer interviews　　(C) 進行更長時間的採訪
(D) Extending a deadline　　(D) 延長期限

正確答案為 **(B)**

〈注意細節－提議〉
題目問到在三人對話中說話者的共同意見。對話後半男 1 說問卷調查有重複的部份，建議可以刪減。接著男 2 也說自己同意男 1 的意見。因此答案是 (B)。
換句話說 **drop a few** 刪去一些 → **shorten** 縮短、減少

字彙　**emphasize** 強調　　**conduct an interview** 進行採訪

52. What does the woman decide to do?　　女子決定做什麼？
(A) Make a few revisions to a document　　(A) 修改文件
(B) Find a way to satisfy customers　　(B) 想辦法讓顧客滿意
(C) Alter the schedule for a meeting　　(C) 變更會議日程
(D) Relay some feedback　　**(D) 傳達回饋意見**

正確答案為 **(D)**

〈注意細節－特定事項〉
題目問到女子決定的事項，須聆聽女子說話的內容。女子最後表示會把男子提到的事項轉達給專案經理，答案是 (D)。
換句話說 **pass them along to the project manager** 將它們傳達給專案經理 → **relay some feedback** 轉達回饋

字彙　**relay** 傳達

1_53-55 美式女聲 / 美式男聲

Questions 53-55 refer to the following conversation.

W: Hi, Joseph. Do you have time to go over this press release I just drafted?

M: Certainly. What's it about?

W: It describes some updates that we plan for our Web site.

M: Oh, yeah? I read about that in the company newsletter. I bet a lot of our customers will be making use of the new financial services we'll be offering. So many people are doing their banking online these days.

W: Well, who can blame them? It's so much more convenient than going into a branch.

問題 53-55 參考以下對話。

女：嗨，約瑟夫。 ㊾ 你有空看看我剛擬的新聞稿草稿嗎？

男：當然可以。主題是關於什麼？

女：我們規畫的官網更新內容。

男：這樣啊，我在社內新聞有看過。 ㊾ 我敢說許多客戶一定會使用我們即將上線的新金融服務。現在許多人都在線上辦理銀行業務。

女：誰能怪他們呢？ ㊾ 這比去分行方便多了。

字彙　**newsletter** 時事通訊　**financial** 財務金融的　**do one's banking** 辦理銀行業務　**blame** 責備
branch（公司）分行

53. What does the woman ask the man to do?
(A) **Review her work**
(C) Draft a report
(D) Release some records
(D) Update a Web site

女子要求男子做什麼？
(A) 查看作品
(B) 草擬報告
(C) 發行專輯
(D) 更新網站

正確答案為 (A)

〈注意細節－請求〉

題目問女子的請求事項，須從女子的談話中找線索。女子在第一段話問男子有沒有時間幫她看新聞稿，答案是 (A)。

字彙　**review** 查看、檢閱　　**release** 推出、發行

54. What kind of organization do the speakers work for?
(A) A marketing company
(B) **A banking firm**
(C) A newspaper
(D) A software company

說話者在何種組織工作？
(A) 行銷公司
(B) **金融公司**
(C) 報紙
(D) 軟體公司

正確答案為 (B)

〈掌握基本資訊－場所〉

題目問說話者的工作場合，一般在對話開始就可以找到，但是本題線索出現在對話中間，作答時要特別留意。男子在第二段話提到客戶會利用即將推出的金融服務，這也說明了說話者的業務內容，答案是 (B)。

換句話說　**financial services** 金融服務 → **banking firm** 金融公司

55. What does the woman mean when she says, "who can blame them"?
(A) Customers did not cause the problem.
(B) Customers are likely to make some complaints.
(C) Customers' confusion was expected.
(D) **Customers' behavior is understandable.**

女子說「誰能怪他們呢」是什麼意思？
(A) 顧客沒有製造問題。
(B) 顧客可能會抱怨。
(C) 顧客會困惑是意料之中。
(D) **顧客的行為是可以理解的。**

正確答案為 (D)

〈關鍵句－說話者意圖〉

遇到詢問某句話的意圖時，需綜合聆聽此關鍵句的前後文才能推論。男子先提到許多人會使用網路辦理銀行業務，之後女子說這麼做比較方便，因此答案是 (D)。

字彙　**be likely to** 有可能～　　**behavior** 行為　　**understandable** 可以理解的、合乎情理的

Questions 56-58 refer to the following conversation with three speakers.

W1: Can I ask you guys a favor? I'm scheduled to wait tables on Monday from 7 A.M. to 3 P.M., but I have a doctor's appointment at noon. Could someone possibly cover my breakfast shift?

M: Sorry, Heather, but I can't. I'm off both Monday and Tuesday this week.

W1: Oh, thanks anyway.

M: I wish I could help.

W1: Olivia, do you think you could do it?

W2: Well, I start my shift at 11 A.M. that day. What time do you think you can be here?

W1: I don't expect the appointment to last more than an hour, so I'm sure I'll be in by about 1:30 P.M. Does that work for you?

W2: You bet. Maybe you could cover one of my shifts next month when I go on my camping trip.

問題 56-58 參考以下三人對話。

女1：你們能幫我忙嗎？ 56 我週一早上 7 點到下午 3 點有排班上餐，但我中午要看醫生。 57 有人可以幫我代早餐的班嗎？

男： 很抱歉，海瑟，我幫不上忙，我這禮拜週一週二休假。

女1：噢，無論如何還是謝謝你。

男： 但願我能幫妳。

女1：奧莉薇雅，妳可以嗎？

女2：我那天上午 11 點開始輪班。妳什麼時候能到？

女1：我預計看醫生不會超過一個小時，所以我確定下午 1 點半左右能回來。妳覺得可行嗎？

女2：當然。 58 或許下個月我去露營妳可以幫我代班。

字彙 **schedule** 排定　**wait tables** 餐廳服務生上餐　**shift** 輪班　**You bet.** 當然。（贊同許可之意）

56. What best describes the speakers' jobs?
(A) They are medical staff.
(B) They are cashiers.
(C) They are office employees.
(D) They are restaurant servers.

以下何種敘述最接近說話者的工作？
(A) 他們是醫務人員。
(B) 他們是收銀員。
(C) 他們是辦公室職員。
(D) 他們是餐廳服務生。

正確答案為 (D)

〈掌握基本資訊－職業〉
說話者的職業須從對話前半段聆聽線索。女 1 在第一段話提到星期一要 wait tables「上餐」，答案是 (D)。

57. What does Heather ask the other two people to do?
(A) Assign her different hours
(B) Have breakfast with her
(C) Go on a camping trip with her
(D) Fill in for her at work

海瑟要其他兩人幫她做什麼？
(A) 分配其他時段給她
(B) 和她一起吃早餐
(C) 和她一起去露營
(D) 幫她代班

正確答案為 (D)

〈注意細節－請求〉
三人對話中，請求幫忙是常見題目，必須先掌握誰是題目提到的海瑟 Heather。女 1 在第一段話提到有沒有人可以幫她代班，隨後男子回應時就用這個名字稱呼她，可見女 1 就是海瑟。正確答案是描述女 1 請求內容的 (D)。
換句話說 **cover** 代班 → **fill in for** 替～輪班

58. What does Olivia imply?
(A) She cannot accommodate the request.
(B) She'll be off that day.
(C) Heather should return the favor.
(D) Heather should change her appointment.

奧莉薇亞暗示什麼？
(A) 她無法接受這個請求。
(B) 她那天休假。
(C) 海瑟應該報答她。
(D) 海瑟應該更改預約。

正確答案為 (C)

〈注意細節－提及內容〉
當題目提到第三者名字時，這個人可能出現在對話中或不在對話中，因此必須在對話中尋找題目提及的名字。對話中段女 1 問奧莉薇亞能否幫忙，接著女 2 說話，可見女 2 就是奧莉薇亞。女 2 最後說可以幫忙，並表示希望下個月對方能幫她代班，因此答案是 (C)。

字彙 **accommodate** 接納、容納　**sb. be off** 某人不在、離開的　**return one's favor** 回報某人恩惠

1_59-61　美式女聲 / 英式男聲

Questions 59-61 refer to the following conversation.

W: Thomas, I was wondering if you could help me. I'm thinking of changing my Internet service provider. Could you give me some advice?

M: Which Internet company are you using now? There are several service providers with different packages, depending on both the length of contract and voice service bundles.

W: Actually, high-speed Internet is what I'm considering the most. That's the bottom line. Also I'm being transferred to overseas in about a year so I just want the short-term agreement.

M: Why don't you check an Internet provider comparison Web site? There are a few sites that show the different options and packages.

問題 59-61 參考以下對話。

女： 湯瑪斯，能幫我個忙嗎？ 59 我想換掉我的網路服務供應商。能給我一些建議嗎？

男： 妳現在用的是哪家網路公司？不同服務供應商提供不同服務內容，取決於妳要的簽約期間與語音服務優惠方案。

女： 其實 60 我最重視的是高速網路，這是最低要求。還有，一年之後我就會調到海外工作，所以我只想要短期合約。

男： 61 妳何不看看網路供應商評比網站呢？有幾個網站把各家服務內容跟方案放在一起做比較。

字彙　**Internet service provider** 網路服務供應業者　**advice** 建議　**package** 方案　**depend on** 根據、取決於
bundle 優惠方案　**bottom line** 底線、最重要的點　**overseas** 海外地、海外的

59. Why does the woman ask for advice?　　女子為什麼要徵求意見？
(A) To replace a current service　　**(A) 為了更換目前的服務**
(B) To purchase a computer　　(B) 為了買一台電腦
(C) To provide a new device　　(C) 為了提供新設備
(D) To design a Web site　　(D) 為了設計網頁

正確答案為 **(A)**

〈注意細節－請求〉
女子提出的請求內容必須從女子的談話中尋找。女子一開始表明想更換網路服務供應商，並希望對方提供建議，因此答案是 (A)。

字彙　**purchase** 購買　**device** 裝置

60. Why does the woman say, "That's the bottom line"?　　為什麼女子說「這是最低要求」？
(A) She wants the long-term plan.　　(A) 她要長期方案。
(B) She wants a cheap price.　　(B) 她要便宜的價格。
(C) She uses Internet frequently.　　(C) 她經常使用網路。
(D) She wants fast online access.　　**(D) 她想要高速上網。**

正確答案為 **(D)**

〈關鍵句－說話者意圖〉
本題必須掌握對話前後句脈絡，才能找出女子的意圖。女子說這句話之前提到高速網路是她的最優先考量，因此答案是 (D)。
換句話說 **high speed Internet** 高速網路 → **fast online access** 快速上網

61. What is the woman advised to do?　　女子收到什麼建議？
(A) Transfer to an overseas branch　　(A) 轉調到海外分公司
(B) Get some feedback　　(B) 得到一些反饋
(C) Compare options on the Internet　　**(C) 上網比較不同選擇**
(D) Read some product instructions　　(D) 讀一些產品說明

正確答案為 **(C)**

〈注意細節－提議〉
題目的句型是被動式，等於是問男子提供何種建議，須聆聽後半段男子的說話內容。男子提到可以到網路上看評比網站，答案是 (C)。

1_62-64 美式男聲／美式女聲

Questions 62-64 refer to the following conversation and table.

M: I have received a request from the advertising department for a new printer. They need one that can handle banners and really large posters.

W: Yeah, I spoke with Mr. Warren, their department head, about that yesterday. He said he wants to be able to produce color documents.

M: Hmm... They're not cheap.

W: Well, the most we can afford is $2,000 so get the best one you can within the budget. Do you have the brochure I sent you yesterday?

M: OK. I'm looking at it right now. The next most expensive one only prints black and white.

W: I'll leave it up to you.

Model	Price ($)
Modern 765 (Black and White)	1,530
Solusi 300 (Color)	1,720
Primark 200 (Black and White)	1,940
Allthatprint 500 (color)	2,250

問題 62-64 參考以下對話與表格。

男： 62 我收到廣告部門新印表機的請求。他們需要一台能處理橫布條和超大型海報輸出的印表機。

女： 是的。63 昨天我和他們的主管沃倫先生談過這個問題。64 他說希望能輸出彩色文件。

男： 嗯……它們可不便宜。

女： 是啊，64 我們只能負擔到兩千美元，所以就在預算內買最好的吧。你有我昨天寄給你的小冊子嗎？

男： 有，我正在看。第二貴的那台只能印黑白。

女： 交給你決定。

機型	價格（美元）
Modern 765（黑白）	1,530
64 Solusi 300（彩色）	64 1,720
Primark 200（黑白）	1,940
Allthatprint 500（彩色）	2,250

字彙 **department** 部門　**handle** 處理、負責　**banner** 橫布條、橫幅標語　**afford** 負擔得起

62. According to the man, what has the advertising department requested?
(A) A client list
(B) A customer code
(C) An office device
(D) An e-mail address

根據男子所言，廣告部門的要求為何？
(A) 客戶名單
(B) 客戶代碼
(C) 辦公設備
(D) 電子郵件地址

正確答案為 **(C)**

〈注意細節－請求〉
作答時須注意聆聽關鍵字 advertising department。男子第一段話中表示收到廣告部門新印表機的需求，答案是 (C)。
換句話說 **printer** 印表機 → **office device** 辦公設備

63. Who most likely is Mr. Warren?
(A) A client
(B) A supplier
(C) A manufacturer
(D) A supervisor

沃倫先生最有可能是誰？
(A) 客戶
(B) 供應商
(C) 製造業者
(D) 主管

正確答案為 **(D)**

〈注意細節－提及內容〉
作答時必須掌握關鍵字 Mr. Warren 並仔細聽前後文內容。女子第一句話提到和部門主管 Mr. Warren, their department head 討論過相關問題，head 在這裡指「主管」，因此答案是 (D)。

字彙 **supervisor** 主管

64. Look at the graphic. How much will the company most likely pay for the order?
(A) $1,530
(B) $1,720
(C) $1,940
(D) $2,250

根據圖表，該公司最有可能花多少錢訂購？
(A) 1,530 美元
(B) 1,720 美元
(C) 1,940 美元
(D) 2,250 美元

正確答案為 **(B)**

〈注意細節－圖表相關〉
本題必須掌握選項與圖表的關係。 選項列出產品價格，表示要聆聽每個價格背後代表的各種商品種類。女子中段提到預算是 2,000 美元，必須在預算範圍內購買最好商品，因此符合彩色列印及 2,000 美元以內的印表機是 Solusi 300，正確答案是此商品的對應價格 (B)。

1_65-67 英式男聲 / 美式女聲

Questions 65-67 refer to the following conversation and coupon.

M: How was everything today? Did you enjoy your lunch?

W: Everything was great, and your service was excellent, as always.

M: We really appreciate your repeat business. Can I get you anything else? Dessert perhaps?

W: No, thanks. I'm ready for my check. My lunch break's almost over and I need to head back to the office.

M: All right. I'll be right back.

W: Oh, that reminds me. I have this coupon for a discount. Should I give it to you now?

M: Sure. The coupon's still valid. Let me go calculate your charges and I'll bring you your bill.

Jade's Diner
Present this coupon for
30% **off** Lunch
or
20% **off** Dinner
Valid for parties of up to 3 | Expires June 18

問題 65-67 參考以下對話與優惠券。

男：您今天過得如何？66 午餐吃得開心嗎？

女：一切都很好，你的服務一如往常出色。

男：65 非常感謝您再次光顧。您還需要什麼嗎，或許來份甜點？

女：不，謝了，我準備結帳。66 我的午休時間快結束了，我得回辦公室。

男：好的，我馬上回來。

女：噢，這倒提醒了我。我有一張折價券。我應該現在給你嗎？

男：當然。這張折價券仍然有效。67 我去計算一下您的費用，等一下給您帳單。

翡翠餐廳
出示本優惠券
66 午餐享 **30**% 折扣
或
晚餐享 **20**% 折扣
限三人以下同行 | 優惠至 6 月 18 日截止

字彙 **coupon** 優惠券　**appreciate** 感激　**repeat business** 再次光臨　**check** 帳單　**valid** 有效的　**calculate** 計算
charge 費用　**bill** 帳單

65. What does the man indicate about the woman?　　男子說了關於女子的什麼事？
 (A) She ordered a dessert.　　(A) 她點了一份甜點。
 (B) She is a regular customer.　　**(B) 她是常客。**
 (C) She owns a business.　　(C) 她有自己的事業。
 (D) She works near the restaurant.　　(D) 她在附近餐廳工作。

正確答案為 (B)

〈注意細節－提及內容〉
題目詢問男子談到女子的部份，必須從男子的談話中找答案。男子對用完餐的女子說感謝「再次光臨」repeated business，可見女子常常光顧這家餐廳，因此答案是 (B)。

換句話說 **repeat business** 再次光臨 → **regular customer** 常客

66. Look at the graphic. How much of a discount will the　　根據圖表，女子可以得到多少折扣？
woman receive?　　(A) 5%
 (A) 5%　　(B) 10%
 (B) 10%　　(C) 20%
 (C) 20%　　**(D) 30%**
 (D) 30%

正確答案為 (D)

〈注意細節－圖表相關〉
聆聽對話之前，要先看圖表進行推敲。每個選項都是折扣，而圖表資料優惠券上面也寫著不同用餐種類享有不同折扣，因此答案可能與午餐和晚餐相關。男子第一句話提到午餐，對話中半段女子也提到午休時間快結束，可見此優惠券是用於午餐折價，答案是 (D)。

67. What does the man say he will do?　　男子說他將做什麼事？
 (A) Speak to a manager　　(A) 與經理對話
 (B) Accept a credit card　　(B) 接受信用卡
 (C) Make a calculation　　**(C) 進行計算**
 (D) Fax an invoice　　(D) 傳真發票

正確答案為 (C)

〈注意細節－未來〉
問題問到未來會做的事，可從對話後半部找答案。男子說要去計算費用再把帳單拿過來，因此答案是 (C)。

字彙　**invoice** 發票

1_68-70　美式男聲 / 美式女聲

Questions 68-70 refer to the following conversation and chart.

M: We just got an e-mail from Besthires.com reminding us that our job advertisement is due to be removed from their Web site tomorrow. They asked whether we want to keep it posted for another month.

W: No, we have four strong candidates who all qualify for the position. One of them will certainly get the offer. I just haven't decided which one.

M: Okay, I'll write back to Besthires.com and let them know.

W: Thanks, Dean. I'd appreciate that.

M: No problem. So, is the man you interviewed today among the four you're considering?

W: Yes, he is. Two candidates scored higher on the test than he did, but his interview was the most impressive.

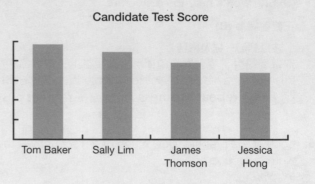

Candidate Test Score

Tom Baker　Sally Lim　James Thomson　Jessica Hong

問題 **68-70** 參考以下對話與圖表。

男： 68 我們剛收到一封來自 Besthires.com 的電子郵件，提醒我們他們即將在明天從網站撤下我們的招聘廣告。他們詢問是否要再張貼一個月。

女： 不用了，有 4 位候選人符合職位條件。他們其中一位會得到這份工作，我只是還沒決定用誰。

男： 好的，69 那我會回信告知 Besthires.com。

女： 謝謝，狄恩。我很感激你這麼做。

男： 沒問題。所以妳今天面試的男士是 4 位的其中一位嗎？

女： 沒錯，他是。70 有 2 個候選人得分比他高，但他的面試最令我印象深刻。

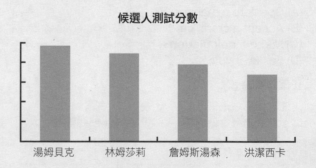

候選人測試分數

湯姆貝克　林姆莎莉　詹姆斯湯森　洪潔西卡

字彙　**remove** 移除　**post** 張貼、告示　**qualify for** 符合資格　**position** 職位

68. How was the job opening probably advertised?　徵才廣告最有可能以何種方式刊登？
(A) In a trade journal　　　　　　　　　　(A) 在貿易雜誌
(B) On some posters　　　　　　　　　　(B) 在海報上
(C) In a newspaper　　　　　　　　　　(C) 在報紙上
(D) On a Web site　　　　　　　　　　**(D) 在網頁上**

正確答案為 **(D)**

〈注意細節－特定事項〉
應掌握關鍵字 Job opening、advertised 等單字，在對話中尋找答案。男子第一段說徵才廣告將從網頁撤下，因此答案是 (D)。

69. What does the man offer to do?　　　男子主動提議做什麼？
(A) Reply to an organization　　　　　**(A) 回覆一家機構**
(B) Screen résumés from applicants　　(B) 篩選應徵者履歷
(C) Write a job description　　　　　　(C) 寫職務說明書
(D) Extend a deadline for a project　　(D) 延長專案期限

正確答案為 **(A)**

〈注意細節－提議〉
由於是男子提議的內容，必須從男子說話的段落找線索。男子在第二次說話時表示會回信給相關業者，因此答案是 (A)。
換句話說 **write back** 回信 → **reply** 回覆、回答

字彙　**applicant** 申請者　**screen** 篩選　**job description** 職務說明

70. Look at the graphic. Who does the woman say gave the most impressive interview?　根據圖表，女子對誰的面試印象最深刻？
(A) Tom Baker　　　　　　　　　　(A) 湯姆貝克
(B) Sally Lim　　　　　　　　　　(B) 林姆莎莉
(C) James Thomson　　　　　　**(C) 詹姆斯湯森**
(D) Jessica Hong　　　　　　　　(D) 洪潔西卡

正確答案為 **(C)**

〈注意細節－圖表相關〉
四個選項都是在圖表橫軸出現的名字，因此圖表縱軸資料就是解題關鍵。縱軸沒有標示數字，就參考長條圖的高低分布，此圖呈現候選人的得分高低。題目關鍵字是 most impressive，須從對話內容尋找此關鍵字。女子在對話最後表示有兩個人得高分，但得分排名第三的人在面試中最令人印象深刻，因此答案是得分第三高的 (C)。

1_71-73 澳式男聲

Questions 71-73 refer to the following advertisement.

Whether you're on the road for work or traveling on vacation, there's a Travel Lodge just where you need it. With over 250 Travel Lodges across the country, we can provide you with a clean, comfortable room nearly anywhere you travel. All locations include free Wi-Fi Internet access, free satellite TV, and complimentary coffee and toast in the morning. Throughout August, if you make a reservation through our Web site at www.travellodge.com, we'll take ten percent off our regular nightly rates. Next time you make travel plans, be sure to include a stay at Travel Lodge.

問題 71-73 參考以下廣告。

無論你是要出差或度假，旅遊舍都在你身邊。**71** **72** 全國超過 250 家的旅遊舍，提供你出遊時乾淨且舒適的房間。所有旅遊舍旗下房間皆提供免費 Wi-Fi 上網、免費衛星電視和免費的咖啡與土司早餐。**73** 整個 8 月透過我們的網站 www.travellodge.com 訂房，我們將提供九折的基本住宿費折扣。下次計畫旅行時，務必考慮旅遊舍住宿。

字彙　**on the road** 旅行或移動途中　**lodge** 小屋、山莊　**satellite** 衛星　**complimentary** 贈送的、免費的　**catering** 餐飲、外燴　**courteous** 彬彬有禮的、謙恭的　**rate** 費用

71. What is being advertised?　　　　　　　　這是什麼廣告？
(A) A tour agency　　　　　　　　　　　　(A) 旅行社
(B) A hotel chain　　　　　　　　　　**(B) 飯店連鎖**
(C) A catering service　　　　　　　　　(C) 外燴餐飲服務
(D) An airline company　　　　　　　　(D) 航空公司

正確答案為 (B)

〈掌握基本資訊－主旨〉
題目問廣告是關於什麼，也就是詢問文章主題，可從文章前半段找答案。內容提到不論到哪裡旅行都能提供乾淨且舒適的房間，由此可知是住宿業者的廣告。答案是 (B)。

字彙 **tour agency** 旅遊業者　　**chain** 連鎖店

72. According to the advertisement, what advantage does　　根據廣告，這家業者提供什麼優勢？
the business offer?　　　　　　　　　　**(A) 方便抵達**
(A) Easy access　　　　　　　　　　(B) 服務親切
(B) Courteous service　　　　　　　　(C) 公司價格
(C) Corporate rates　　　　　　　　　(D) 會員獎金
(D) Membership bonuses

正確答案為 (A)

〈注意細節－特定事項〉
本題是關於廣告的具體內容。文章前半段提到有超過 250 家的住宿設施遍布全國，說明了地點方便抵達，答案是 (A)。

字彙 **advantage** 優點　　**access** 取得、到達

73. What will happen in August?　　　　　　8 月會發生什麼事？
(A) A facility will be expanded.　　　　(A) 擴大設施。
(B) A discount will be offered.　　　**(B) 提供優惠折扣。**
(C) A Web site will be upgraded.　　　(C) 網站升級。
(D) A selection will be widened.　　　(D) 選項變多。

正確答案為 (B)

〈注意細節－時間點〉
須注意聆聽關鍵字 in August。文章後半段提到 8 月期間若透過網站預約，可享 10% 的折扣優惠，因此答案是 (B)。
換句話說 **ten percent off** 折扣 10% → **discount** 折價

Questions 74-76 refer to the following announcement.

Attention, all passengers. On behalf of FlyBE Airlines, I'd like to offer my sincere apologies for the delay. Due to the weather conditions, the runway is extremely crowded. It looks like we won't be able to take off until 6 P.M., 30 minutes after our scheduled time of 5:30 P.M. This means our arrival will also be late. Those of you with connecting flights can speak to our flight crew. We will be serving a meal once we get in the air, but before takeoff, I suggest you read our in-flight magazine that has been recently updated. Once again, I apologize for the inconvenience.

問題 74-76 參考以下廣播。

各位乘客請注意，謹代表 FlyBE 航空公司對這次的延誤表達誠摯歉意。**74** 由於天候因素，飛機跑道相當擁擠。**75** 看來我們要到下午 6 點才能起飛，比預定的下午 5 點半晚 30 分鐘。這意味著抵達時間也會延後，需要轉機的乘客請與機組人員聯絡。飛機一升上高空就會提供餐點，但在起飛前，**76** 建議您閱讀最新的機上雜誌。再次為此不便表示歉意。

字彙　**passenger** 旅客　**on behalf of** 代表　**sincere apology** 誠摯道歉　**runway** 飛機跑道　**extremely** 極度、相當　**take off** 起飛、出發　**connecting flight** 轉機　**flight crew** 機組人員　**in-flight magazine** 機上雜誌

74. Why has the flight been delayed?

(A) **The runway is busy.**

(B) The plane has a mechanical problem.

(C) The fog prevented the plane from departing.

(D) Boarding took a long time.

飛機為何誤點？

(A) **跑道擁擠。**

(B) 飛機有機械故障。

(C) 濃霧讓飛機無法起飛。

(D) 登機花了很多時間。

正確答案為 (A)

〈注意細節－原因〉

須掌握關鍵字 delayed 仔細聆聽飛機誤點的原因。談話前半段有針對誤點道歉，也說明因氣候導致跑道擁擠，因此答案是 (A)。雖然造成跑道擁擠的原因是氣候，但由於無此選項，只能選出最適合的答案 (A)。此外，內容雖提到氣候條件，但並沒有提到是 fog「濃霧」造成，也不能選擇 (C)。

換句話說 **crowded** 擁擠的 → **busy** 繁忙的

字彙　**mechanical** 機械方面的　　**fog** 霧　　**depart** 離開、出發

75. What time will the flight depart?

(A) 5:00 P.M.

(B) 5:30 P.M.

(C) **6:00 P.M.**

(D) 6:30 P.M.

飛機幾點起飛？

(A) 下午 5 點

(B) 下午 5 點半

(C) **下午 6 點**

(D) 下午 6 點半

正確答案為 (C)

〈注意細節－時間〉

題目詢問飛機起飛時間，**應掌握關鍵字 depart「起飛」與同義字 take off**。內容提到下午 6 點才會起飛，答案是 (C)。須注意句型 not A until B「直到 B 才 A」的意義，也不要被其他出現的時間混淆。

76. What does the speaker suggest the listeners do?

(A) Relax in the lounge

(B) **Take a look at some reading materials**

(C) Fill out a form

(D) Revise their schedule

說話者建議聽者做什麼事？

(A) 在休息室放鬆

(B) **閱讀資料**

(C) 填寫表格

(D) 修改行程

正確答案為 (B)

〈注意細節－建議〉

應掌握關鍵字 suggest 並於談話後半部尋找答案。說話者建議聽者可以閱讀機上雜誌，答案是 (B)。

換句話說 **magazine** 雜誌 → **reading materials** 閱讀資料

1_77-79　英式女聲

Questions 77-79 refer to the following telephone message.

Hello, Mr. Aston. My name is Lisa Rodriguez and I represent Dantos Incorporated. We're organizing a five-day seminar on how to maximize employees' potential and we're looking for people with management experience to lead workshops during the event. You were referred to us by Jennifer Ward. She told me that she used to work under you at General Consulting, and said you would be ideally suited to this position. We'd be very interested in having you join us. The seminar runs from Monday, June 18 to Friday 22. If you're interested, please get back to me at your convenience. I can be reached on my cell phone at 303-555-9935. I'm looking forward to hearing from you.

問題 77-79 參考以下電話留言。

你好，安斯頓先生。我是丹托斯公司的代表莉莎羅德里格斯。㊂ 我們正在規劃一場為期 5 天的研討會，主題是發揮員工潛能的方法。我們正在尋找具有管理經驗的人主持這次研討會。 ㊆ 珍妮佛瓦德向我推薦你。她提到以前在傑尼羅顧問公司時曾幫你做事，她說你非常適合這個職務。我們想請您加入我們。研討會在 6 月 18 日星期一至 22 日星期五舉行。㊈ 如果你有興趣，請在您方便時回電給我。我的電話是 303-555-9935。期待你的消息。

字彙　**represent** 代表　　**organize** 組織、籌劃　　**seminar** 研討會　　**be referred to** 被推薦　　**used to** 曾做過～
be suited to 適合　　**get back to** 再聯絡、回覆　　**reach** 聯繫、聯絡

77. Why has the speaker called Mr. Aston?
(A) To ask for some personal information
(B) To solicit his participation
(C) To arrange an interview
(D) To finalize a job offer

為什麼説話者打電話給安斯頓先生？
(A) 詢問個人訊息
(B) 徵求他的參與
(C) 安排訪問
(D) 敲定工作

正確答案為 (B)

〈掌握基本資訊－目的〉
電話的目的須聆聽談話前半段。開頭提到正在準備研討會並尋找活動負責人，談話中段也再次表示希望對方能參與，可見此通電話的目的是勸説對方參與活動，答案是 (B)。由於這是關於此活動的第一通聯絡電話，內容無關提供工作機會或安排面試，應避免選擇其他選項。

字彙　**solicit** 徵求、請求給予

78. What did Jennifer Ward do?
(A) She was Mr. Aston's supervisor.
(B) She recommended Mr. Aston.
(C) She is organizing the seminar.
(D) She founded Dantos Incorporated.

珍妮佛瓦德曾經做了什麼？
(A) 她曾經是安斯頓先生的上司。
(B) 她推薦安斯頓先生。
(C) 她正在規劃研討會。
(D) 她創立丹托斯公司。

正確答案為 (B)

〈注意細節－提及內容〉
注意聆聽關鍵字 Jennifer Ward。説話的人表示 Jennifer Ward 曾經提到 Mr. Aston 並推薦他擔任這項工作，答案是 (B)。

字彙　**found** 創立、建立

79. According to the speaker, what should Mr. Aston do next?
(A) Contact General Consulting
(B) Register for the seminar
(C) Return Ms. Rodriguez's call
(D) Submit the document

根據説話者，安斯頓先生接下來應該做什麼？
(A) 與傑尼羅顧問公司聯絡
(B) 報名研討會
(C) 回覆羅德里格斯小姐的電話
(D) 提交文件

正確答案為 (C)

〈注意細節－請求〉
要求或請求的內容通常出現在談話的後半段。發言者在後半段表示，如果對方也感興趣，煩請致電回覆，答案是 (C)。
換句話說　**get back to** 回覆 → **return a call** 回電

字彙　**register** 報名、註冊

Questions 80-82 refer to the following speech.

I'm very pleased to accept this award for Charity of the Year. After retiring as a chef, I started the Slow Cooker Foundation to promote healthy, economical home-cooked dishes. I asked some of my former colleagues in the restaurant industry to contribute tasty but affordable recipes for a cookbook. They responded with more ideas than one book could hold. So, the Foundation produced a free weekly magazine, *The Slow Cooker Gazette*, which is available in supermarkets throughout the country. This magazine has been a huge hit regionally, so next month we're going to distribute it nationwide. Thank you to everyone who has supported us, and we look forward to your continued support in the years ahead.

問題 80-82 參考以下演說。

我很高興能得到年度慈善獎。⑧ 從廚師退休之後，我創辦了慢廚基金會，推廣健康又實惠的家常菜。我請餐飲業的前同事為一本食譜貢獻美味實惠的食譜。他們回覆的點子比一本書所能收錄的還要多。⑧ 因此，基金會製作了一份免費週刊《慢廚公報》，在全國超市都能取得。這本雜誌在地方很受歡迎，⑧ 所以下個月將會在全國發行。感謝所有支持我們的人，希望各位在未來的日子能繼續支持我們。

字彙　**accept** 接受、同意　　**award** 獎　　**charity** 慈善事業　　**foundation** 基金會　　**economical** 實惠的　　**contribute** 貢獻　**affordable** 價格實惠的　　**regionally** 區域性地　　**distribute** 發行、發放、分配　　**nationwide** 全國性的

80. Who most likely is the speaker?
(A) An author
(B) A food critic
(C) A charity founder
(D) A restaurant manager

講者最有可能是誰？
(A) 作家
(B) 美食評論家
(C) 慈善機構創始人
(D) 餐廳經理

正確答案為 **(C)**

〈掌握基本資訊－說話者〉
說話者的身分通常在談話前半段提到。說話者提到自己從廚師退休之後設立基金會 the Foundation，答案是 (C)。

字彙　**critic** 評論家

81. What has the speaker's organization created?
(A) A documentary film
(B) A complimentary publication
(C) A fundraising competition
(D) A nutrition workshop

說話者的組織製作了什麼？
(A) 紀錄片
(B) 免費刊物
(C) 募款大會
(D) 營養研討會

正確答案為 **(B)**

〈注意細節－特定事項〉
題目問說話者的組織團體製作了什麼，須掌握關鍵字 speaker's organization 並在談話中找答案。談話中提到該基金會創辦免費週刊，由此可知答案是 (B)。
換句話說 **free weekly magazine** 免費週刊 → **complimentary publication** 免費刊物

82. According to the speaker, what will happen next month?
(A) A new product will be developed.
(B) An event venue will change.
(C) A new branch will open.
(D) A project will be expanded.

根據說話者，下個月將發生什麼事？
(A) 將開發新產品。
(B) 活動地點會變更。
(C) 新分店將要開幕。
(D) 將擴大推動專案。

正確答案為 **(D)**

〈注意細節－特定事項〉
應**掌握關鍵字 next month**，仔細聆聽相關內容。談話後半段說到下個月免費雜誌將在全國發行，答案是 (D)。

1_83-85　美式女聲

Questions 83-85 refer to the following radio broadcast.

And for today's weather news. Today marks not only the coldest day we've had so far this month, but the coldest December ever recorded in Ipswich County. We had a high today of two degrees below zero, and a low of minus 18. The second coldest December on record was exactly three decades ago when the high was three degrees above zero and the low hit minus 15. That date was also marked by huge blizzard, which virtually stopped the city for two entire days with 2.5 feet of snow that closed streets, businesses and schools. We don't have the same situation tonight, since there's no moisture in the forecast, but you never know what might happen in such bitter cold. The electrical grid is definitely prone to outages when temperatures get this low. So stay indoors and be sure to listen to our hourly reports.

問題 83-85 參考以下廣播預報。

83 接下來是今日天氣預報。今天不只是本月以來最冷的一天，也是伊普斯維奇地區記錄中最冷的 12 月。本日最高溫零下 2 度，最低溫零下 18 度。而有記錄以來，第二冷的 12 月剛好是在 30 年前，當時最高溫是零下 3 度，最低溫零下 15 度。那天也遇上巨大暴風雪侵襲，讓整座城市停擺兩天，積雪達 2.5 英呎，街道、企業、學校都因此關閉。今晚情況不一樣，天氣預報顯示今天沒有水氣，但你永遠不會知道在這樣寒冷的天氣會發生什麼事。**84** 當氣溫降到這麼低，供電系統容易中斷。**85** 因此請待在家裡，同時務必收聽我們的整點報導。

| 字彙 | mark 標記　　record 創記錄　　degree 度　　minus 零下的　　decade 十年　　blizzard 暴風雪 virtually 事實上、幾乎　　feet 英呎　　moisture 濕氣　　forecast 天氣預報，當動詞時三態同型　　bitter 嚴寒刺骨的 electrical grid 供電系統　　be prone to 易～的　　outage 斷電 |

83. What is true of the weather today?
(A) It is expected to warm up later.
(B) Heavy snowfall is forecast.
(C) It hit a record low temperature.
(D) Heavy rain is expected.

關於今天的天氣何者為真？
(A) 預計天氣稍後會轉暖。
(B) 預報將有大風雪。
(C) 天氣達到了創記錄的低溫。
(D) 預計將降下暴雨。

正確答案為 **(C)**

〈注意細節－特定事項〉

應掌握關鍵字 today 尋找答案。第一句提到今天是最冷的一天，之後的內容也補充說明這一點，答案是 (C)。

84. What potential hazard does the speaker mention?
(A) Loss of power
(B) Lack of fuel
(C) Shortage of supplies
(D) Health issues

說話者提到何種隱憂？
(A) 斷電
(B) 缺乏燃料
(C) 物資短缺
(D) 健康問題

正確答案為 **(A)**

〈注意細節－特定事項〉

此篇為氣象預報，問題是氣候可能引發的危險，須注意聆聽危險的因素 hazard。談話後半段提到溫度過低容易造成供電中斷，答案是 (A)。

換句話說 **electrical grid is prone to outages** 電力供應容易中斷 → **loss of power** 斷電

字彙   **hazard** 隱憂、潛在危險

85. What suggestion does the speaker make?
(A) Listeners should stay home.
(B) Listeners should exercise regularly.
(C) People should drive carefully.
(D) People should purchase supplies.

說話者提出什麼建議？
(A) 聽者應留在家中。
(B) 聽者應定期運動。
(C) 人們應小心駕駛。
(D) 人們應購買物資。

正確答案為 **(A)**

〈注意細節－提議〉

答案會和當天氣候預報有關，並在談話後半段出現。**最後一句使用命令句**，提到應留在室內並收聽氣候預報，答案是 (A)。

`1_86-88` `英式女聲`

Questions 86-88 refer to the following excerpt from a meeting.

We're going to start today with an initial training session for all of you who've just joined our firm. First, you'll view a video detailing the history of the organization, from our founding over fifty years ago up until the present. Then, Mr. Ambrose, who directs our personnel department, will speak with you about some basic company policies and our general expectations from the staff. He'll also issue you each a copy of the employee handbook, which you should take home and try to become familiar with as soon as possible. You will be separated into groups for the afternoon sessions. So, before we break for lunch, make sure to report back to me. I'll need to tell you which group you'll be part of.

問題 86-88 參考以下會會議摘要。

86 今天我們要先幫剛加入公司的各位進行首次培訓課程。首先,各位將觀看一段詳細記錄本組織從 50 多年前成立至今的回顧影片。接著我們的人事主任安布洛斯先生將和各位談談公司基本方針和員工對公司的期許。87 他也會發給各位一人一份員工手冊,請帶回家儘快熟悉內容。下午的課程各位將會分成小組進行。因此在午餐休息時間之前,務必向我回報。88 我會告知各位的小組分配。

字彙 | **session**(一系列)課程 **policy** 政策、方針 **general** 一般的、普遍的 **expectation** 期待、預期
employee handbook 員工手冊 **make sure to** 務必～

86. Who is the speaker addressing?
(A) University instructors
(B) Newly hired employees
(C) Potential clients
(D) Survey participants

說話者在對誰講話？
(A) 大學講師
(B) 新進員工
(C) 潛在客戶
(D) 市場調查參加者

正確答案為 (B)

〈掌握基本資訊－聽者〉
聽者的身分在談話開頭可以找到線索。在介紹今天的活動流程時，提到是為剛進公司的各位安排的，答案是 (B)。

87. According to the speaker, what will Mr. Ambrose do today?
(A) Conduct a series of interviews
(B) Show a video presentation
(C) Introduce the company founder
(D) Distribute guidebooks

根據說話者，安布洛斯先生今天將做什麼？
(A) 進行一連串的面試
(B) 播放一段影片
(C) 介紹公司創立者
(D) 發放參考手冊

正確答案為 (D)

〈注意細節－特定事項〉
注意關鍵字 Mr. Ambrose 安布洛斯先生。談話中段提到這個名字，並說明他將會發給每人員工手冊，答案是 (D)。
換句話說 **handbook** 手冊 → **guidebook** 說明書、手冊

88. What does the speaker mean when she says, "make sure to report back to me"?
(A) She is eager to see some results.
(B) She requires feedback from all attendees.
(C) She wants to give further information.
(D) She works as a department supervisor.

說話者說「務必向我回報」是什麼意思？
(A) 她希望看到一些成果。
(B) 她需要所有參與者的回饋。
(C) 她想提供進一步的資訊。
(D) 她是部門主管。

正確答案為 (C)

〈關鍵句－說話者意圖〉
談話中段提到分小組進行下午課程，並且告知對方分到哪個小組，答案是 (C)，她將告知聽者更進一步的訊息。

字彙 **attendee** 參加者

Questions 89-91 refer to the following announcement.

Hamilton Enterprises today announced that it has decided to purchase the site of the former town center and establish a new manufacturing plant. The work is scheduled to begin as early as April and expected to be completed within two years. The new facility will enable the company to manufacture its complete range of products at just one location, rather than its present three, which will help it distribute its products more promptly. Company spokesperson Ian Douglas has said that the site is the perfect location for Hamilton and that the local community will also benefit from its use.

問題 89-91 參考以下公告。

89 漢密爾頓企業今天宣布買下前市鎮中心的場地，要興建一座新製造工廠。工程預計最早在 4 月展開，預計兩年內完工。**90** 新工廠使該公司得以在同一地點生產全系列產品，不再是分成目前的 3 個地點，這將加速公司配送產品。**91** 公司發言人伊恩道格拉斯表示，這個地點對漢密爾頓企業而言是最佳地點，當地也將因它的啟用而受惠。

字彙　**enterprise** 企業、公司　**establish** 建立、設立　**manufacturing** 製造業　**plant** 工廠　**manufacture** 大量生產、製造　**complete range** 完整產品種類　**promptly** 立即地　**spokesperson** 發言人　**community** 社區　**benefit** 受惠

89. What is the report mainly about?
(A) The renovation of a town center
(B) The construction of a new facility
(C) The introduction of a new product
(D) The relocation of a stadium

這個報導主要內容是什麼？
(A) 市中心的翻新工程
(B) 新設施的建設
(C) 新產品的介紹
(D) 體育場的搬遷

正確答案為 (B)

〈掌握基本資訊－主題〉
談話的主題大部分在前半部就會提到。一開始說明某公司將建立新的製造工廠，因此答案是 (B)。勿將「購買 town center 的地點來建設工廠」與 (A) 選項混為一談。

90. What is an advantage of the plan?
(A) It will accommodate more people.
(B) It will reduce expenses.
(C) It will generate more income.
(D) It will improve delivery times.

這個計畫的優點是什麼？
(A) 將容納更多人。
(B) 將減少開支。
(C) 將產生更多的收入。
(D) 將改善送貨次數。

正確答案為 (D)

〈注意細節－特定事項〉
題目提到的計畫是指興建製造工廠，須從談話內容尋找興建優點。談話中段提到在同一地方生產有助於快速流通銷售，答案是 (D)。

換句話說 **distribute its products more promptly** 更快速配送產品 → **improve delivery times** 改善配送時間

字彙　**expense**（常用複數）支出、開銷

91. Who is Ian Douglas?
(A) A factory manager
(B) A local land owner
(C) A company spokesperson
(D) A real estate agent

伊恩道格拉斯是誰？
(A) 工廠管理者
(B) 當地地主
(C) 公司發言人
(D) 房仲業者

正確答案為 (C)

〈注意細節－特定事項〉
根據關鍵字 Ian Douglas 伊恩道格拉斯尋找答案。談話後半段提到了這個名字及其職務，答案是 (C)。

1_92-94　澳式男聲

Questions 92-94 refer to the following telephone message.

Hello, Mr. Wallace. This is Mavis Stevens at Homeworld Cooling and Refrigeration. I'm returning the message you left earlier regarding your air-conditioning system. Based on your description, you may be able to solve the problem without a technician by resetting the unit manually. Just press the power button for about three seconds. That will shut down the system, and it should restart automatically after about fifteen seconds. The procedure is also explained in the product manual. If you no longer have that, I'd be happy to email a copy of the relevant section. Your unit is still under warranty, so if resetting the system doesn't fix the problem, we'll send a technician to make any necessary repairs at no charge.

問題 92-94 參考以下電話留言。

您好，瓦勒斯先生。我是家世界製冷公司的馬維斯史蒂芬。**92** 我想回覆您留言提到的空調系統。**92** 根據您的描述，您的問題不需要技術人員，手動重置設備就能解決。**93** 只要按下電源鍵大約 3 秒鐘，就能關閉整個系統，**93** 它會在約 15 秒後自動重啟。這個程序在產品說明書中也有說明。如果您沒有說明書，**94** 我很樂意把相關章節用電子郵件寄給您。您的產品還在保修期內，如果系統重置無法解決問題，我們將免費派一位技術人員到府進行必要維修。

字彙　**cooling** 冷卻　**refrigeration** 冷凍、冷藏　**regarding** 關於　**based on** 基於　**technician** 技術人員
unit 小機器、機件　**manually** 手動地　**shut down** 關閉、停工　**automatically** 自動地　**relevant** 相關的
under warranty 保固內　**at no charge** 免費

92. Why is the speaker calling?
(A) A change in schedule
(B) An equipment malfunction
(C) A policy proposal
(D) A revision to a manual

説話者為什麼打電話？
(A) 變更日程
(B) 設備故障
(C) 政策提案
(D) 説明書更正

正確答案為 (B)

〈掌握基本資訊－主題〉
電話留言的主題會在談話的一開始、説話者自我介紹結束後出現。在説明回電的原由是空調系統之後，説話者也對此問題提出解決辦法，因此答案是 (B)。

字彙　**malfunction** 故障

93. Why does the speaker say, "That will shut down the system"?
(A) To upgrade a system
(B) To change a suggestion
(C) To explain a process
(D) To make a complaint

為什麼説話者説「這將關閉整個系統」？
(A) 為了讓系統升級
(B) 為了變更提案
(C) 為了説明程序步驟
(D) 為了提出投訴

正確答案為 (C)

〈關鍵句－説話者意圖〉
須綜合評估該句子前後文，再掌握説話者的意圖。句子前面説到用手動的方式重新啟動冷氣，之後也説明讓系統停止運作的方法，由此可知是在説明重新啟動的程序，因此答案是 (C)。

94. What does the speaker offer to do?
(A) Email a document
(B) Issue a refund
(C) Install a system
(D) Deliver a new unit

説話者提出會做什麼？
(A) 電子郵寄文件
(B) 給予退款
(C) 安裝系統
(D) 運送新機器

正確答案為 (A)

〈注意細節－提議〉
提議與請求事項多半在談話的後半段出現。談話後半段提到説明書上已詳記解決辦法，之後也説，如果手邊沒有説明書，也能以電子郵寄相關內容給對方，答案是 (A)。

1_95-97 英式女聲

Questions 95-97 refer to the following announcement and form.

Thank you for selecting Whiterose! We have everything you need from sturdy plates to wine glasses. Our in-house designers craft quality pieces, made for everyday living. Fill your home with people, laughter, memories and something from Whiterose. We'd like to remind customers with young children that there is a childcare center located on the third level. Children 7 and under may stay in the childcare center for up to two hours. So get ready for a hassle-free shopping experience! And today we have a special event for children — come see dinosaurs from 10 A.M. to 5 P.M. They're on the second level. Reservation forms are available at the information desk by the entrance. Parents, please come 5 minutes before the time of your child's reservation for the smooth running of the event.

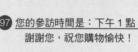

Reservation Slip
See Dinosaurs at Whiterose!

Name of child: _Alex Hunt_
Parent of child: _Susan Hunt_
Age of child: _Six_

Your visit will take place at _1:30 P.M._
Thank you and enjoy your shopping!

問題 95-97 參考以下公告與圖表。

感謝您選擇白羅斯，從耐用的盤子到酒杯，這裡應有盡有。我們專屬的設計師打造日常所需的優質產品。就用人們、笑聲、回憶和白羅斯的產品，豐富您的家吧。提醒有孩童的顧客，三樓有托兒中心。**95** 7 歲及以下的孩童可在托兒中心停留最多兩個小時。所以，準備好好享受一次無憂無慮的購物吧！**96** 今天我們為孩童舉辦一個特別的活動，大家從早上 10 點到下午 5 點可以來看恐龍，就在二樓。預約表格可在入口處服務台索取。**97** 家長請在孩子預約時間前 5 分鐘到場，以便活動順利進行。

預約單
在白羅斯看見恐龍！

孩童姓名：艾力克斯航特
父母姓名：蘇珊杭特
孩童年紀：6

97 您的參訪時間是：下午 1 點 30 分
謝謝您，祝您購物愉快！

 字彙 **sturdy** 結實的、堅固的 **in-house** 公司專屬的 **craft** 精巧地製作、打造 **remind** 提醒 **hassle** 麻煩、麻煩的狀況
smooth running 順利進行 **exclusive** 獨有的、獨家的

95. What is mentioned about the childcare center?
(A) It is on the second floor.
(B) It is exclusive to members.
(C) Children over 7 are not allowed.
(D) Children may stay for a day.

何者是關於托兒中心的內容？
(A) 在二樓。
(B) 會員專屬。
(C) 7 歲以上孩童不得入場。
(D) 孩童可以停留一天。

正確答案為 (C)

〈注意細節－特定事項〉
關鍵字是 childcare center，必須聆聽相關句子。談話中段提到托兒中心，並說 7 歲以下的孩童可停留最多 2 個小時，因此答案是 (C)。

96. What can be found on the second floor?
(A) A reservation form
(B) A special event
(C) A childcare center
(D) An information desk

在二樓可以找到什麼？
(A) 預約表格
(B) 特別活動
(C) 托兒中心
(D) 服務台

正確答案為 (B)

〈注意細節－特定事項〉
關鍵字是 second floor，必須聆聽相關句子。談話中提到專為孩童舉辦的活動位於二樓，因此答案是 (B)。

97. Look at the graphic. By when should Susan arrive at the special event?
(A) 1:20
(B) 1:25
(C) 1:30
(D) 1:35

根據圖表，蘇珊要在幾點前抵達特別活動會場？
(A) 1 點 20 分
(B) 1 點 25 分
(C) 1 點 30 分
(D) 1 點 35 分

正確答案為 (B)

〈注意細節－圖表相關〉
作答時必須先對照圖表與題目選項，再仔細聆聽與圖表有關的元素，拿這題來說，就是注意聽取時間。題目的關鍵字是 Susan，是預約單上的父母姓名，在聽談話時必須確認選項提到的時間。談話後半段說為了讓活動順利進行，請父母在預約時間前 5 分鐘抵達，而預約單上寫著預約時間是下午 1 點 30 分，提早 5 分鐘就是答案 (B)。

1_98-100   英式男聲

Questions 98-100 refer to the following talk and schedule.

Everyone, I want to point out that from here you can see the Goff Bridge to the south in the distance. The bridge is named after Phil Goff, who was elected as Christchurch's first mayor shortly after the founding of the city. Due to its unique architecture, the bridge was considered a marvel of modern engineering at the time of its construction. Before we cross it tomorrow on the way to Mission Bay for our cycling tour, we'll stop so you can see its beautiful features up close and take pictures. Let's pack up our picnic baskets and head to our next activity. Make sure not to leave any beverage containers or food wrappers behind.

Christchurch Tour – Day One		
Time	Location	Activity
09:00-10:30	Waitomo Caves	Morning walk
11:00-12:00	Central Square	Shopping
12:00-14:00	Victoria Park	Afternoon picnic
14:00-17:00	Bay of Islands	Boat ride

問題 98-100 參考以下談話與行程。

各位，請特別看到位於南方遠處的葛夫橋。98 這座橋是以菲爾葛夫的名字命名、葛夫在克里斯特教堂市創立後當選第一任市長。由於其獨特的建築結構，這座橋在建造時被認為是現代工程的奇蹟。99 在明天跨橋去米遜灣騎單車之前，我們會在橋上稍作停留，你們可以近距離欣賞它美麗的風貌並拍照。100 收拾好野餐盒，我們準備進行下一個活動。請務必不要留下任何飲料或食品包裝。

克里斯特教堂市之旅 —— 第一天		
時間	場所	活動
09:00-10:30	維特莫洞穴	早晨散步
11:00-12:00	中央廣場	購物
12:00-14:00	100 維多利亞公園	100 午後野餐
14:00-17:00	100 島嶼灣	搭船

字彙 **point out** 指出   **in the distance** 遠處   **elect** 選舉   **mayor** 市長   **marvel** 奇蹟   **head to** 前往
leave ~ behind 留下~、遺留   **food wrapper** 食品包裝

98. Who most likely is Phil Goff?
(A) A civil engineer
(B) A famous celebrity
(C) A local politician
(D) A renowned architect

菲爾葛夫最有可能是誰？
(A) 土木工程師
(B) 著名人物
(C) 地方政治家
(D) 著名建築師

正確答案為 (C)

〈注意細節－特定事項〉
關鍵字是 Phil Goff 菲爾葛夫，就從這個名字的相關內容找線索。談話前段提到橋名由來是取自克里斯特教堂市首任市長的名字，答案是 (C)。

換句話說 **mayor** 市長 → **local politician** 地方政治家

字彙 **civil engineer** 土木工程師　　**renowned** 知名的

99. According to the speaker, what is the purpose of the trip to Mission Bay?
(A) To ride bicycles
(B) To photograph wildlife
(C) To shop for souvenirs
(D) To visit a castle

根據說話者，米遜灣之旅的目的是什麼？
(A) 騎腳踏車
(B) 拍野生動物照
(C) 購買紀念品
(D) 參觀城堡

正確答案為 (A)

〈注意細節－特定事項〉
關鍵字是 Mission Bay 米遜灣，必須從相關內容尋找答案的線索。在說明明天行程時，提到要去米遜灣騎腳踏車，因此答案是 (A)。

換句話說 **cycling tour** 腳踏車旅行 → **ride bicycles** 騎腳踏車

字彙 **souvenir** 紀念品

100. Look at the graphic. Where will listeners probably go next?
(A) Waitomo Caves
(B) Central Square
(C) Victoria Park
(D) Bay of Islands

根據圖表，聽者接下來會去哪裡？
(A) 維特莫洞穴
(B) 中央廣場
(C) 維多利亞公園
(D) 島嶼灣

正確答案為 (D)

〈注意細節－圖表相關〉
應先掌握選項與圖表之間的關連。四個選項都是圖表中的旅行景點，每個景點後方有不同 Activity「活動」，因此要從活動內容推測答案。談話後半提到收拾野餐以進行下一個活動，由此可知目前聽者所在位置是維多利亞公園，而接下來要去的地方是答案 (D)。

101. Brooks Bookstore can ship an order to your home, business, ------- local post office within 24 hours.
(A) but
(B) that
(C) or
(D) as

布魯克思書店可以在 24 小時之內將訂購商品送到您的家中、公司或當地郵局。

正確答案為 (C)

〈連接詞〉空格位於名詞 business 與名詞 local post office 之間，空格需選擇對等連接詞，與前後句意相符的答案是 (C) or。

> 字彙 　**ship** 配送、運送　**local** 當地的

102. The use of high-quality yet ------- raw materials led to a cost reduction for Mr. Walton's factory.
(A) inexpensive
(B) unhappy
(C) incomplete
(D) undecided

使用優質且低廉的原物料減低了瓦頓先生的工廠成本。

正確答案為 (A)

空格前面的 yet 是對等連接詞，語意是「但是、不過」，帶有轉折的成份，因此適合的答案是相對於 high-quality 的 (A) inexpensive。

> 字彙 　**raw material** 原物料　**lead to** 導致、引起　**cost reduction** 降低成本　**inexpensive** 廉價的
> **incomplete** 不完全的　**undecided** 未定的

103. Jason Flowers is always ------- to deliver nice decorations to your special events.
(A) ready
(B) skillful
(C) complete
(D) delicious

傑森花店隨時準備好為您的特別活動提供精美裝飾。

正確答案為 (A)

空格前面是 be 動詞，後面是 to，語意上合適的是形容詞 (A) ready。

> 字彙 　**decoration** 裝飾　**skillful** 熟練的

104. Kate Vausden was nominated as Best New Artist ------- her elaborate painting now on display at Lindsey Gallery.
(A) about
(B) for
(C) when
(D) since

凱特勞森因其精美畫作被提名為最佳藝術新人，其作品正在琳賽藝廊展出。

正確答案為 (B)

空格後面是名詞 her elaborate painting，根據語意，答案適合選擇表示原因的介系詞 (B) for。

> 字彙 　**be nominated as** 被提名為、獲選為　**elaborate** 精心製作的、精巧的　**on display** 展示中

105. If you want to take advantage of this month's sale, you must do so quickly as ------- ends next week.

(A) it
(B) he
(C) they
(D) your

如果你想利用這個月的折價活動，就必須儘快行動，因為活動將在下週結束。

正確答案為 (A)

〈代名詞格〉空格出現在 as 子句中的主詞位置。as 指「由於～」，帶出必須儘快行動的「理由」。根據語意，空格應指前面出現過的名詞 sale，因此選能代表 sale 的第三人稱單數代名詞 it，答案選 (A)。

字彙　**take advantage of** 利用

106. The ------- of video materials to publication can help companies produce promotional merchandise.

(A) content
(B) addition
(C) pictures
(D) advances

出版品中增加影音資料有助於公司製造宣傳商品。

正確答案為 (B)

句意是指在出版物增加影音資料，因此答案是 (B)。

字彙　**publication** 出版物　**promotional** 促銷的　**merchandise** 商品　**content** 內容　**addition** 添加、增加物

107. Opponents of the city's mayor ------- the claim that she has revived the regional economy.

(A) propose
(B) rely
(C) extend
(D) reject

市長的競選對手反對市長先前振興地區經濟的主張。

正確答案為 (D)

主詞是 Opponents「對手」，空格須填入能帶出「不同意」that 子句的動詞，因此答案是 (D)。

字彙　**opponent** 對手　**claim** 聲稱、主張　**revive** 復興、復甦　**regional** 地區的　**reject the claim** 駁回主張

108. We, Sisco Designs, create a ------- of images that express an individual style suitable for your needs.

(A) frequency
(B) length
(C) shortage
(D) series

我們西思科設計師創作一系列的圖像，能傳達出適合您需求的個人風格。

正確答案為 (D)

空格後面接複數名詞 images，前後又各有 a 和 of，因此適合放入空格的是答案 (D) series，a series of「一系列的、一連串的」。

字彙　**individual** 個人的、個別的　**suitable** 合適的　**frequency** 頻率、次數　**length** 長度　**shortage** 缺乏

109. At Isaac Shoe Store, most customized shoes can be made ------- 2 business days.
(A) since
(B) to
(C) at
(D) within

伊薩鞋店大部分客製化鞋款可於營業日兩天內製成。

正確答案為 (D)

答案要選能表示「在兩天內」的介系詞 (D)。

> 字彙　**customized** 客製化的　**business day** 營業日

110. Mr. Sanders is not checking his voice mail -------, so you can expect a delay in his response.
(A) scarcely
(B) similarly
(C) frequently
(D) partially

山德斯先生不常確認他的語音信箱,所以你可以預期到他的回應會延遲。

正確答案為 (C)

本題要選出適合句意的副詞,合適的句意應為「不常」確認語音信箱,由於前方有否定詞 not,因此答案選 (C) frequently。(A) scarcely「幾乎不」本身帶有否定意義,不與否定詞連用,而 (B) 和 (D) 則是與句意無關。

> 字彙　**scarcely** 幾乎不　**similarly** 相似地　**partially** 部分地

111. To avoid traffic congestion, the ------- of downtown Pleasant Valley requires extensive planning.
(A) restore
(B) restorative
(C) restored
(D) restoration

為了避免交通堵塞,修復普立山市中心需要周全計畫。

正確答案為 (D)

〈詞性〉空格位於定冠詞 the 與介系詞 of 之間,須放入名詞,答案是 (D)。

> 字彙　**traffic congestion** 交通堵塞　**extensive** 整體的、廣泛的　**restore** 修復　**restorative** 恢復的　**restoration** 修復

112. The School Outreach Program honors students ------- volunteer their time to help Twin City.
(A) for
(B) who
(C) those
(D) as

學校關懷計畫是為了表揚那些自願投入時間幫助雙子城的學生。

正確答案為 (B)

〈關代〉空格前後兩個子句,空格前方是結構完整的句子,有主詞、動詞 honors「表揚」與受詞 students。空格後方則有動詞 volunteer「自願去做」跟受詞,但缺少主詞。因此空格中須填入具有「連接詞」與「代名詞」功能的關係代名詞。空格前出現 students,是人,因此選擇修飾人的關係代名詞 who,答案選 (B)。

> 字彙　**outreach** 推廣服務(活動)　**honor** 向～致敬、尊敬　**volunteer** 自願、義務去做

113. The evaluation report will be completed ------- after technicians inspect the lab equipment.
(A) when
(B) only
(C) still
(D) most

評鑑報告要等技術人員檢查實驗室設備之後才會完成。

正確答案為 (B)

空格要強調副詞子句 after 以後的內容，因此答案是 (B) only。因為已經有時間介系詞 after，因此不適合選一樣代表時間的 when。

> 字彙　**evaluation** 評價　**complete** 完成、完畢　**inspect** 檢查　**lab equipment** 實驗室設備

114. The construction of the Grunburg Building ------- because of modifications in the original floor plans.
(A) postponed
(B) has been postponed
(C) will postpone
(D) postponing

古朗堡大樓的建設工程因修改原平面圖而延期。

正確答案為 (B)

〈時態〉空格前有主詞，但缺少動詞，因此要填入動詞。空格後面沒有受詞，因此答案是被動式 (B)。

> 字彙　**modification** 修改　**original** 原本的　**floor plan** 平面圖、藍圖

115. All passengers are advised to check baggage claim tags to verify that retrieved bags are in fact -------.
(A) they
(B) them
(C) theirs
(D) themselves

所有旅客應檢查行李提領標籤，確保取回的行李是自己的。

正確答案為 (C)

〈代名詞格〉空格應完成的句意是「確實是自己的行李」，因此答案應該選能代表 the passengers 的所有格代名詞 (C) theirs = their bags。

> 字彙　**be advised to** 被建議　**baggage claim tag** 行李提領標籤　**verify** 確認　**retrieve** 取回

116. Customers of Charleston Bank can easily transfer funds from one account to -------.
(A) another
(B) either
(C) one
(D) it

查爾斯頓銀行客戶可以輕易將資金從一個帳戶轉到另一個帳戶。

正確答案為 (A)

〈代名詞〉空格接在 one account 後面，由於前面已經使用不定代名詞 one，另一個帳戶也是非特定的，答案選 (A) another，指「任何的另外一個」。

> 字彙　**transfer from A to B** 從 A 轉（帳）到 B

117. Henry Bonaducci's proposal was approved in a ------- short time because of its feasibility.
(A) surprised
(B) surprise
(C) surprisingly
(D) surprising

亨利博努奇的提案因其可行性而出乎意料快速通過。

正確答案為 (C)

〈詞性〉空格位於修飾形容詞 short 的位置，因此答案是副詞 (C)。

字彙　approve 核准、通過　feasibility 可行性

118. Built in 1885, the St. Petersburg Cathedral has been preserved for its historical -------.
(A) signify
(B) significant
(C) significance
(D) significantly

建於 1885 年的聖彼得大教堂因歷史意義而被保存下來。

正確答案為 (C)

〈詞性〉空格位於介系詞 for 和形容詞 historical 之後，因此適合填入的答案是名詞 (C)。

字彙　cathedral 大教堂　preserve 保存　historical 歷史相關的　signify 意味著　significant 重要的
significance 意義、重要性

119. After the ------- improvements have been implemented, the production process should run more efficiently.
(A) suggest
(B) suggested
(C) suggesting
(D) suggests

等提出的改善案實施之後，生產過程就能更有效運作。

正確答案為 (B)

〈分詞〉在限定詞 the 和名詞之間應填入形容詞，因此答案是在 (B) 和 (C) 當中做選擇。名詞 improvement「改善」應使用被動語態的過去分詞修飾，說明該改善案是「被提出的」，因此答案是 (B)。

字彙　improvement 改善　implement 實施、執行　efficiently 有效地

120. Clients should provide both an e-mail address and a telephone number in order to be notified of the most current status of any ------- orders.
(A) dependent
(B) representative
(C) practical
(D) pending

客戶應提供電子郵件及電話號碼，以便收到待辦訂單的最新狀態。

正確答案為 (D)

空格位於修飾名詞 order 的形容詞位置，最貼切句意的單字是「待辦的」訂單，因此答案是 (D) pending。

字彙　notify 通知　current 目前的　status 狀態　dependent 依靠的　representative 有代表性的
practical 實用的、實際的　pending 待辦的、未決定的

121. RT Technology Services will use its training center in Austin ------- preregistered attendees number more than 350.
(A) if
(B) that
(C) either
(D) despite

若提前登記的參加者超過 350 人，RT 科技服務公司就會使用位於奧斯汀的訓練中心。

正確答案為 **(A)**

〈連接詞〉空格之後有主詞 attendee 及動詞 number「多達」，是一個完整子句，因此空格需要選擇可以連接子句的連接詞，答案是 (A)。

> 字彙　**training center** 訓練中心　**preregistered** 提前登記的　**number**（數量）多達　**despite**（介系詞）儘管

122. New customers of Ortega Hardware Store ------- receive a 10 percent discount on their first order.
(A) customarily
(B) perfectly
(C) repeatedly
(D) obediently

照慣例，奧特加五金行的新顧客在第一次訂購可享九折優惠。

正確答案為 **(A)**

空格位於修飾動詞 receive 的副詞位置，符合句意是 (A)。

> 字彙　**customarily** 通常、習慣上、照例　**repeatedly** 反覆地　**obediently** 順從地

123. McAfee Manufacturing is known as a company that makes uniquely ------- tools for the construction industry.
(A) precise
(B) precision
(C) precisely
(D) preciseness

麥克菲製造業者以製作營造業獨特的精密工具而聞名。

正確答案為 **(A)**

空格是位於副詞 uniquely 和名詞 tools 之間的形容詞位置，因此答案是 (A)。

> 字彙　**be known as** 以～著稱、被稱作～　**uniquely** 獨特地　**precise** 精確的　**precision** 精確度、精準　**preciseness** 精確、嚴謹

124. Ms. Hogan, the director of personnel ------- the company's revised manual for recruiting interns at tomorrow's meeting.
(A) had been addressing
(B) is addressing
(C) will be addressed
(D) should be addressed

人事主任霍根小姐將在明天會議上說明修訂過的公司實習生招聘手冊。

正確答案為 **(B)**

〈時態〉空格位於動詞位置，後又有受詞，因此答案是主動式動詞。由於後面提到明天的會議，因此答案不是 (A)。而現在進行式可以用於表示即將到來的未來，因此答案是 (B)。

> 字彙　**personnel** 人事（部）　**revised** 修訂的　**address** 演講、對～說話；處理

125. ------- slow the high-speed printer may be, it is still making copies that are adequate for our purposes.
(A) Rather
(B) Seldom
(C) Thoroughly
(D) However

無論高速印表機再怎麼慢,它依然能夠產出符合我們需求的影印量。

正確答案為 (D)

空格後面是形容詞 slow,之後是主詞 high-speed printer 與動詞 may be,可見這是一個子句,需要一個連接詞。However 指「無論如何、不管怎樣」,是複合關係副詞子句連接詞,因此答案是 (D)。However 另一個常見用法則是當轉折副詞,指「然而、可是」的意思。

字彙　**make a copy** 複製、備份　**adequate** 充足的　**rather** 寧可　**seldom** 幾乎不　**thoroughly** 徹底地

126. Since the Wisconsin Daily is now available digitally, subscribers can read articles one day ------- the general public.
(A) between
(B) during
(C) ahead of
(D) away from

威斯康辛日報推出線上訂閱以來,訂戶可以比一般民眾提早一天閱讀文章。

正確答案為 (C)

〈介系詞〉與 one day 一起使用且貼切句意的答案是 (C) ahead of,形容詞 ahead「在～之前」擺放位置較特別,須放在所修飾的名詞後方。between 指「兩者之間」,與複數名詞一起使用。during「在～期間」,與表示時間的名詞使用。

字彙　**since**（連接詞)自從　**subscriber** 訂戶　**general public** 一般大眾　**ahead of** 提前　**away from** 遠離

127. If the lamp had been damaged during shipment, the company ------- to send Mr. Oakley a replacement.
(A) would have offered
(B) has offered
(C) is being offered
(D) would have been offered

運送期間燈具若遭毀損,公司會寄給奧克利先生替換品。

正確答案為 (A)

〈假設語氣〉這是用過去完成式表示的「與過去事實」相反的假設句,if 子句使用過去完成式 had been damaged,因此主要子句須使用〈過去式助動詞 + have p.p.〉,答案是 (A)。

字彙　**damage** 損害　**replacement** 替換品、替代

128. ------- you have submitted all the required documents for your grant proposal, the decision committee will be convened for evaluation.
(A) Then
(B) Next
(C) Once
(D) Always

一旦你繳交經費補助申請所需的所有文件，決策委員就會召集起來進行評估。

正確答案為 (C)

〈連接詞〉空格是連結兩個句子的副詞子句連接詞位置，選項中唯一的連接詞是 (C) Once，指「一旦～就～」。

字彙 **grant** 補助金 **decision committee** 決策委員會 **convene** 召集

129. Store managers will not ------- approve time off for employees during the peak season.
(A) generalization
(B) generalize
(C) generally
(D) general

商店經理通常不會同意員工在旺季休假。

正確答案為 (C)

〈詞性〉空格前出現助動詞 will not，後方出現一般動詞 approve，空格位於兩者之間，因此須填入副詞，答案是 (C)。

字彙 **time off** 休假 **peak season** 旺季 **generalization** 一般化 **generalize** 使～一般化 **generally** 通常、一般地

130. The decision about company relocation will be ------- until the special meeting scheduled for next month.
(A) deferred
(B) resolved
(C) organized
(D) agreed

公司是否搬遷一事，將延後到下個月的特別會議決定。

正確答案為 (A)

空格挖在被動式的過去分詞位置，與主詞 decision 句意相符且能與 until 做連貫的答案是 (A) deferred。

字彙 **relocation** 搬遷 **defer** 延後、延期 **resolve** 解決

Questions 131-134 refer to the following press release.

For Immediate Release

February 2 — P. H. Manning announces the appointment of Sean Renault as Chief Financial Officer, replacing Sandy Connelly who retired in January.

Prior to ------- P. H. Manning, Mr. Renault worked at KUB Systems. While there, he served in
131.
various accounting and treasury roles, including the role of Chief Financial Officer. He ------- his
132.
career in the audit division of Adams Financial Group.

"Mr. Renault's experience and leadership will be invaluable as we enter our next phase of growth," said Marco Colombo, P. H. Manning's Chief Executive Officer.

Ms. Connelly, the ------- Chief Financial Officer, worked at P. H. Manning for seventeen years.
133.
-------.
134.

問題 131-134 參考以下新聞稿。

快訊

2 月 2 日 —— P. H. 人力公司宣布任命西恩雷諾為首席財務長,接替今年 1 月退休的珊蒂康諾力。

在 ㉛ 加入 P. H. 人力公司之前,雷諾先生在 KUB 系統公司工作。當時他擔任過各種會計和財務職務,包括首席財務長的職務。他的職業生涯 ㉜ 開始於亞當斯金融集團的審計部門。

P. H. 人力公司執行長馬可可倫坡表示:「在我們進入下一個成長階段之際,雷諾先生的經歷與領導能力將十分寶貴。」

㉝ 前任首席財務長康諾力小姐在 P. H. 人力公司工作了 17 年。㉞ 她將繼續留下來擔任董事會顧問。

字彙 **appointment** 任命 **replace** 替代 **prior to** 在～之前 **treasury** 財政部 **audit** 審計
invaluable 貴重的 **phase** 階段

131. **(A) joining**　　　　　　　　　　**(A) 參加**
　　　(B) founding　　　　　　　　　　(B) 創立
　　　(C) promoting　　　　　　　　　(C) 促銷
　　　(D) completing　　　　　　　　(D) 完成

正確答案為 (A)

空格前面是 prior to「在～之前」，空格後面是公司名稱 P. H. 人力公司，接下來的內容是關於雷諾先生過去的經歷，由此可知最適合的答案是表達加入公司之前的單字，因此答案是 (A)。

> 字彙　**join** 加入、參加　　**promote** 推銷；晉升

132. (A) to begin　　　　　　　　　　(A) 要開始
　　　(B) begins　　　　　　　　　　(B) 開始
　　　(C) began　　　　　　　　　　**(C) 過去開始**
　　　(D) will begin　　　　　　　　(D) 即將開始

正確答案為 (C)

這是動詞時態的問題，由於 Adams Financial Group 亞當斯金融集團是雷諾先生過去曾經任職的公司，應使用過去式，答案是 (C)。

133. (A) nearest　　　　　　　　　　(A) 最近的
　　　(B) former　　　　　　　　　　**(B) 前任的**
　　　(C) alternate　　　　　　　　　(C) 替代的
　　　(D) potential　　　　　　　　(D) 潛在的

正確答案為 (B)

在文章一開始提到康諾力已經退休，因此在 Chief Financial Office 首席財務長這個職稱前面適合放 former「前任的」這個單字，答案是 (B)。

134. (A) The accounting team is still hiring new people.
　　　(B) All of our staff members will start work as of tomorrow.
　　　(C) We have made a lot of effort to promote her to CEO.
　　　(D) She will remain as an advisor to the board of directors.

(A) 會計團隊還在招聘新人。
(B) 所有員工將於明天開始工作。
(C) 為了讓她當上執行長，我們做了很多努力。
(D) 她將留下來擔任董事會顧問。

正確答案為 (D)

前面句子提到關於康諾力小姐的部份，因此後面的句子也應選擇跟康諾力小姐相關的敘述，相關敘述有 (C) 與 (D)，就前面敘述來看，符合文意的是 (D)。

> 字彙　**advisor** 顧問

Questions 135-138 refer to the following e-mail.

To: Publishing Department Staff
From: Hans Shuler
Date: February 18
Subject: New Copy Machine

Dear colleagues:

Yesterday a new copy machine was installed in the resource room to replace the one that had ------- broken down. ------- It is an industrial-grade model, so we expect that it will serve us well
135.   **136.**
for several years.

To ensure that the copier remains in working order, keep small objects ------- paper clips and
137.
staples away from the paper feeder.

You may have questions while learning how to operate the new copier. If so, you can ------- the
138.
manual located in the cabinet next to the copier.

Regards,
Hans

問題 135-138 參考以下電子郵件。

收件者：出版部職員
寄件者：漢斯舒勒
日期：2 月 18 日
主旨：新影印機

各位同仁：

為了換掉 135 多次故障的影印機，昨天已在資料室安裝一台新的影印機。 136 我們相信新產品會更可靠。這是一個工業等級機種，我們期待它能為我們效力多年。

為了確保影印機正常運作，137 像是迴紋針、訂書針這類小型物品要遠離送紙匣。

在學習操作這台新影印機時，您可能會有一些問題。那麼您可以 138 查閱位於影印機旁櫃子上的說明書。

漢斯

 字彙   **resource room** 資料室   **break down** 故障   **industrial-grade** 工業等級的   **ensure** 保證
        working order 正常運轉狀態   **object** 物件   **paper feed**（影印機）送紙匣

135. (A) repeats   (A) 重複
     (B) repetition   (B) 重複
     (C) repeated   (C) 重複的
     (D) repeatedly   **(D) 重複地**

正確答案為 (D)

空格位於助動詞 had 與過去分詞 broken 之間，應該填入副詞。因此答案是 (D)。

136. **(A) We trust that the new one will be more reliable.**
     (B) There are several types of copy machines available at the store.
     (C) Please let us know what time you would like to set up an appointment.
     (D) We can give you an accurate estimate later.

     (A) 我們相信新產品會更可靠。
     (B) 店裡提供好幾種類型的影印機。
     (C) 請告訴我們您想約在什麼時候。
     (D) 我們晚一點會給您一份精確的估價單。

正確答案為 (A)

空格前面的句子提到已安裝新的影印機，之後內容提到是工業等級機種，因此可以聯想到空格內應是關於影印機可信度的內容。因此答案是 (A)。

> **字彙**   **set up an appointment** 安排會面   **accurate** 精確的   **estimate** 估價、估計

137. (A) as well   (A) 以及
     (B) such as   **(B) 例如**
     (C) of these   (C) 其中
     (D) sort of   (D) 多少有點

正確答案為 (B)

空格需要的是連接 small objects 和 paper clips and staples 的介系詞。由於是把迴紋針、訂書針當做小型物品的例子，因此答案是 (B) such as。副詞 as well 意思是「也、此外」，而 (C) 和 (D) 不適合接名詞片語。

138. **(A) consult**   **(A) 查閱**
     (B) discard   (B) 扔掉
     (C) approve   (C) 核准
     (D) revise   (D) 修正

正確答案為 (A)

由於空格後面出現 manual，從句意來看，應是請使用者查閱說明書，因此答案是 (A)。

> **字彙**   **consult** 諮詢、查閱   **discard** 丟棄

Questions 139-142 refer to the following article.

February 28 — After two years of construction, the largest hotel in Milwaukee history is almost ready to open. The Mendota Hotel, on the banks of the Cherish River, will have 1,200 rooms for visitors. It will have two conference rooms for groups of up to 300 people. -------. The project is among downtown area hotels currently -------. According to Sanjay Singh, president of Milwaukee Hotel & Lodging Association, these new developments are a -------. "We've had a massive influx of visitors over the past few years," said Mr. Singh. "-------, almost all the hotels in the city are completely full. Clearly, additional hotel rooms are needed."

問題 139-142 參考以下報導。

2 月 28 日 —— 經過兩年的建設，美沃奇地區有史以來最大的飯店即將開幕。位於喬瑞許河畔的麥笛遜飯店有一千兩百間客房，也有兩間大會議室，最多可容納 300 人。 139 第一批客人即將在此參與醫療技術會議。本建案是目前 140 正在建設的市中心飯店之一。麥笛遜飯店兼飯店聯盟總裁桑傑辛格表示，這些新開發是 141 必要的。辛格說：「過去幾年來有大量的遊客湧入這裡。」 142 「結果，城市裡幾乎所有飯店都客滿。顯然我們需要額外的飯店房間。」

字彙　**currently** 目前　　**president** 總裁、董事長　　**development** 開發（案）、發展　　**massive** 大量的
　　　influx 流入

Parker

139. (A) It is unclear whether it will be open to accept reservations or not.
(B) Building renovations will begin next year as originally scheduled.
(C) The first guests will soon arrive as part of a medical technology conference.
(D) There is a speculation that several companies will bid on the project.

(A) 目前還不清楚它是否接受預訂。
(B) 照原定計畫，建築修繕工程將於明年開始。
(C) 第一批客人即將在此參與醫療技術會議。
(D) 據說幾家公司將投標這個項目。

正確答案為 (C)

〈插入句〉
前面句子提到飯店設施即將完成，因此答案是客人將要抵達的 (C)。

字彙　**speculation** 推測、猜測　　**bid on** 投標、競價

140. (A) to construct
(B) are constructing
(C) were constructed
(D) being constructed

(A) 去建設
(B) 正在建設
(C) 曾經被建設
(D) 正在被建設

正確答案為 (D)

句子裡已經有 is 作為動詞，因此 (B) 和 (C) 的一般動詞不適合作為答案，而且空格前面有 hotels，需要分詞修飾。(A) construct 是主動語態，無法在沒有受詞的情況下使用，因此答案是 (D)。

141. **(A) necessity**
(B) nuisance
(C) risk
(D) bargain

(A) 必要之事
(B) 麻煩事
(C) 風險
(D) 交易

正確答案為 (A)

空格後面接的是辛格先生的談話內容，前句提到飯店興建計畫是必須的，原因在於近幾年來有大量的遊客湧入（massive influx of visitors）。因此答案是 (A)。

142. (A) Likewise
(B) Otherwise
(C) Additionally
(D) Consequently

(A) 同樣地
(B) 否則
(C) 此外
(D) 因此

正確答案為 (D)

空格後面是辛格先生說的話，綜合辛格先生說的前後兩句話，需選擇能表達因果關係的副詞，因此適合的答案是 (D)。

Questions 143-146 refer to the following flyer.

Attention, artists and craftspeople!

------- If so, you are encouraged to apply for a chance to display your artwork at the Bloomberg
143.
County Art Fair on May 17.

Applications are available online at www.bloombergfair.org and will be reviewed by several
professors from the art department of our local college. Together with your completed
application document, please upload ------- of your work. The images will aid the judges in their
144.
review process.

The application deadline is February 15, and the judges' decisions will be made by March 30.
------- applicants will have use of a 5 x 5 meter display booth and will be expected to participate
145.
------- the entire day of the fair.
146.

問題 143-146 參考以下傳單。

各位藝術家和工藝家請注意！

143 您有興趣接受一個難得的機會，在我們這裡展示才華嗎？那麼，請您踴躍申請在 5 月 17 日舉辦的布倫堡
郡藝術博覽會展示您的藝術作品。

申請書可上 www.bloombergfair.org 取得，作品由我們地區大學藝術學系幾位教授進行審查。請將您的作
品 144 照片連同填妥的申請文件上傳。這些圖片將有助於審查委員評審。

申請截止日期為 2 月 15 日，審查委員將於 3 月 30 日前做出決定。 145 受邀的申請者可使用 5×5 公尺大小
的展示區，並預計將參與博覽會 146 從頭到尾一整天的活動。

字彙　**craftspeople** 工藝家　**artwork** 藝術作品　**review** 審查　**aid** 幫助、援助

143. (A) If it is possible, we would like to send an invitation to your home to survey the event.
(B) Are you interested in a unique opportunity to showcase your talent in our area?
(C) As a loyal customer, you qualify for extended coverage of six years.
(D) You can see other types of artwork on our Web site.

(A) 如果可以，我們想寄邀請函到您府上進行活動調查。
(B) 您有興趣接受一個難得的機會，在我們這裡展示才華嗎？
(C) 由於您是我們的忠實顧客，您有資格續保 6 年。
(D) 您可以在我們的網站上觀看其他類型的藝術作品。

正確答案為 (B)

〈插入句〉
這是鼓勵參與博覽會的第一個句子，空格後面接著 if so「若是如此，那麼」，因此適合的答案是引起注意力的 (B)。

字彙　　**showcase** 作品展示　　**extended** 延長的　　**coverage**（保險、賠償）涵蓋範圍

144. (A) descriptions
(B) photographs
(C) requirements
(D) developments

(A) 說明
(B) 照片
(C) 要求事項
(D) 發展

正確答案為 (B)

空格後面的句子提到 The image，由此可知必須上傳的是照片。因此答案是 (B)。

145. (A) Inviting
(B) Invites
(C) Invitation
(D) Invited

(A) 邀請中的
(B) 邀請
(C) 請柬
(D) 受邀的

正確答案為 (D)

空格是修飾申請者 applicants 的分詞，從句意上來看，應該填入過去分詞型態的「接受邀請的、被邀請的」，因此答案是 (D)。

146. (A) in
(B) to
(C) through
(D) toward

(A) 在裡面
(B) 去
(C) 從頭到尾
(D) 朝向

正確答案為 (C)

根據題目，答案是強調 the entire day「一整天」的介系詞 (C) through 會最適合。

Questions 147-148 refer to the following advertisement. 廣告

FANCY SKI RESORT
WEEKEND SPECIAL

Fancy Ski Resort is the perfect place for your family or group next weekend vacation.

Spend three nights in a one-bedroom condominium or suite for as low as $240 per person. Our lodgings are conveniently located two miles from scenic Mount Lyon and include an indoor swimming pool, sauna, and ice skating rink. A shuttle service operates between our lodgings and Mount Lyon every half hour from 5 A.M. to 8 P.M.

The Weekend Special price includes two days of skiing on Mount Lyon. This offer is valid from November 11 to February 20, excluding weekdays and holidays. For more information, visit www.skifancy.com.

問題 **147-148** 參考以下廣告。

潮流滑雪場
週末特別活動

潮流滑雪場是家族或團體下週假期的理想場所。

每人只要花 240 美元的低價，就可以連 3 個晚上住在一間公寓房間或套房裡。我們的房舍距離風景優美的里昂山兩英哩遠，交通便利，**148** 有室內游泳池、三溫暖和溜冰場。**147** 每天早上 5 點到晚上 8 點，每隔半小時會有一班接駁車來回行駛於住宿地點與里昂山之間。週末特價包含在里昂山上滑雪兩天。優惠期間從 11 月 11 日到 2 月 20 日為止，工作日和國定假日除外。欲知更多資訊，請參考網站 www.skifancy.com。

字彙　**suite** 套房　　**per person** 每一人　　**lodging** 房舍、住宿的地方　　**scenic** 風景優美　　**valid** 有效的
excluding 不包括

147. How can customers get to Mount Lyon from their lodgings?
(A) By walking
(B) By driving
(C) By taking a taxi
(D) By taking a shuttle bus

顧客如何從住宿房舍去到里昂山？
(A) 走路
(B) 開車
(C) 搭計程車
(D) 搭接駁車

正確答案為 (D)

本題問到交通方式，文章提到 A shuttle service operates between our lodgings and Mount Lyon，shuttle 即「接駁車」，答案是 (D)。

148. What facility is NOT included at the lodgings?
(A) A sauna
(B) A swimming pool
(C) A ski rental service
(D) An ice skating rink

何種設施不包含在住宿設施內？
(A) 三溫暖
(B) 游泳池
(C) 滑雪出租服務
(D) 溜冰場

正確答案為 (C)

可在文章中尋找關鍵字 include，文章第二段提到 include an indoor swimming pool, sauna, and ice skating rink（包含室內游泳池、三溫暖跟溜冰場），因此答案是 (C)。

Questions 149-150 refer to the following information. 資訊

ALTON CITY PARKING GARAGE

Please present this ticket with your payment to the attendant when you return to pick up your vehicle.

Date: *7 March*

Time: *9:15 A.M.*

The attendant can accept only cash and credit card payments.

* Monthly rates are available. Save up to 20%!

To obtain details, call 028-555-3421, or visit our Web site at altoncitygarage.co.uk.

問題 149-150 參考以下資訊。

歐頓市區停車場

149 當您返回取車時，請將此票卡連同您的支付款一起交給服務員。

日期：3 月 7 日
時間：上午 9 點 15 分

服務員只接受現金和信用卡付款。

* 可月租。最多省下 20%！

150 欲獲取詳細內容，請致電 028-555-3421，或上我們的網站 altoncitygarage.co.uk。

字彙   **present** 提出、出示   **payment** 付款   **attendant** 服務員   **monthly rates** 月租

149. How do customers pay for parking?　顧客如何支付停車費？
(A) By depositing money in a parking meter　(A) 把錢投入停車計時器裡
(B) By paying a fee to an attendant　**(B) 把費用交給服務員**
(C) By using a prepaid parking card　(C) 使用預付停車卡
(D) By submitting a payment online　(D) 上網繳交費用

正確答案為 (B)

文章一開始寫著 present this ticket with your payment to the attendant，由此可知答案是 (B)。

字彙　**deposit** 支付押金；存款　**parking meter** 停車計時器

150. Why are customers invited to call the telephone number on the ticket?　為什麼顧客要撥打票卡上的電話？
(A) To request an alternative payment method　(A) 要求用另一種付款方式
(B) To reserve a parking spot for the day　(B) 預訂一個全天停車位
(C) To give feedback about an attendant　(C) 對服務員給予反饋
(D) To get more information about parking fees　**(D) 獲取更多有關停車收費的資訊**

正確答案為 (D)

尋找文章中出現電話的地方，文章最後提到 To obtain details, call 028-555-3421，由此可知答案是 (D)。

字彙　**alternative** 替代的　**reserve** 預約　**parking spot** 停車位

Questions 151-153 refer to the following advertisement. 廣告

Attention!

The Capricorn Library Volunteer Association presents its Used Book Sale for four days only from November 3 through 6. You can browse thousands of books, most in excellent condition! There is something of interest for readers of all ages.

Thursday: Preview Sale
6 P.M. – 9 P.M.
$5 admission fee

Friday: General Sale
6 P.M. – 9 P.M.

Saturday: General Sale
9 A.M. – 3 P.M.

Sunday: Clearance Sale
11 A.M. – 2 P.M.
All books 20% off

Proceeds will benefit the building of an addition to the Capricorn Library.

Location: Capricorn Community Center, Main Event Hall, 15 Harper Street

If you have any questions, contact Leslie Ling, president of the Capricorn Library Volunteer Association at 555-0173

Please note that we are no longer accepting donations of books for the sale.

問題 151-153 參考以下廣告。

注意！

摩羯圖書館志工協會在 11 月 3 日至 6 日期間舉辦二手書拍賣活動，僅此四天。 153B 您可以瀏覽上千本書，大多數都保存完好！ 153A 也有各年齡層的讀者都會感興趣的書。

星期四：預售
下午 6 點～下午 9 點
152 入場費 5 美元

星期五：一般拍賣
下午 6 點～下午 9 點

星期六：一般拍賣
上午 9 點～下午 3 點

星期日：出清拍賣
上午 11 點～下午 2 點
153D 所有書籍八折

所有收入將作為摩羯圖書館的擴建之用。

151 地點：哈潑街 15 號，摩羯社區活動中心大活動廳

若有任何疑問，請聯絡摩羯圖書館志工協會長林雷斯利，聯絡電話 555- 0173。

請注意，我們不再接受書籍捐贈作為活動折扣。

字彙 **in ~ condition** 處在～狀況　　**browse** 瀏覽　　**of interest** 對～感興趣的　　**admission fee** 入場費
proceeds（固定用複數）收入、收益　　**benefit** 對～有幫助

151. Where will the event take place?
(A) **At a community center**
(B) At a local bookstore
(C) At Ms. Ling's residence
(D) At the Capricorn Library

活動地點在哪裡？
(A) **社區活動中心**
(B) 當地書店
(C) 林小姐居住地
(D) 摩羯圖書館

正確答案為 (A)

文章提到 Location: Capricorn Community Center，Location 指「活動地點」，答案是 (A)。

字彙 **take place** 發生　　**residence** 居住地

152. What is stated about Thursday's sales?
(A) Profits from the event will go to a charity.
(B) **An entrance fee will be charged.**
(C) Cash is the only method of payment accepted.
(D) It will run during the whole day.

何者陳述與星期四拍賣相關？
(A) 活動收益將捐給慈善機構。
(B) **將收取入場費。**
(C) 現金是唯一的支付方法。
(D) 活動將進行一整天。

正確答案為 (B)

第一天拍賣日是星期四，內容提到「入場費 5 美元」，由此可知星期四必須支付入場費，答案是 (B)。

字彙 **entrance fee** 入場費

153. What is NOT suggested about the books being sold?
(A) Some of them are suitable for young children.
(B) Many of them are in good condition.
(C) **All of them were donated by library members.**
(D) They will be sold at a reduced price on Sunday.

以下何者與即將出售的書籍無關？
(A) 有些適合兒童。
(B) 許多書籍保存完好。
(C) **所有書籍皆由圖書館會員捐贈。**
(D) 星期日會降價拍賣。

正確答案為 (C)

文章第一段提到 There is something of interest for readers of all ages.，由此推論其中有些是兒童書籍。You can browse thousands of books, most in excellent condition 的內容說明了 (B) 選項。在星期天銷售內容中提到 Sunday: Clearance Sale – All books 20% off，這呼應了 (D) 選項。內容找不到關於 (C) 選項的陳述。

字彙 **reduced price** 優惠價格

Questions 154-155 refer to the following text message chain. 簡訊對話

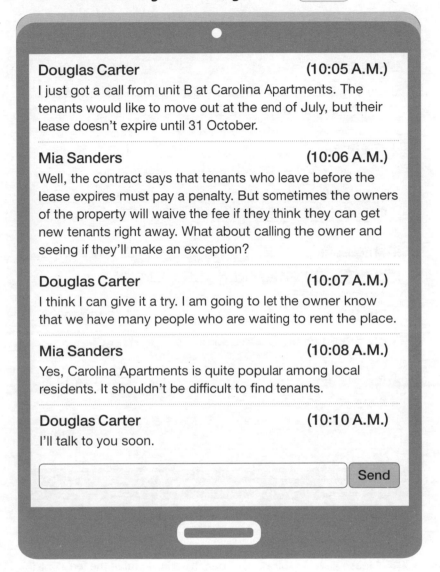

Douglas Carter (10:05 A.M.)

I just got a call from unit B at Carolina Apartments. The tenants would like to move out at the end of July, but their lease doesn't expire until 31 October.

Mia Sanders (10:06 A.M.)

Well, the contract says that tenants who leave before the lease expires must pay a penalty. But sometimes the owners of the property will waive the fee if they think they can get new tenants right away. What about calling the owner and seeing if they'll make an exception?

Douglas Carter (10:07 A.M.)

I think I can give it a try. I am going to let the owner know that we have many people who are waiting to rent the place.

Mia Sanders (10:08 A.M.)

Yes, Carolina Apartments is quite popular among local residents. It shouldn't be difficult to find tenants.

Douglas Carter (10:10 A.M.)

I'll talk to you soon.

Send

問題 154-155 參考以下簡訊對話。

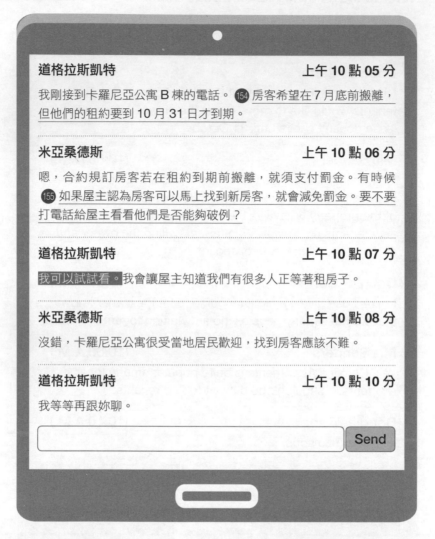

道格拉斯凱特　　　　　　　　　上午 **10** 點 **05** 分

我剛接到卡羅尼亞公寓 **B** 棟的電話。154 房客希望在 **7** 月底前搬離，但他們的租約要到 **10** 月 **31** 日才到期。

米亞桑德斯　　　　　　　　　　上午 **10** 點 **06** 分

嗯，合約規訂房客若在租約到期前搬離，就須支付罰金。有時候 155 如果屋主認為房客可以馬上找到新房客，就會減免罰金。要不要打電話給屋主看看他們是否能夠破例？

道格拉斯凱特　　　　　　　　　上午 **10** 點 **07** 分

我可以試試看。我會讓屋主知道我們有很多人正等著租房子。

米亞桑德斯　　　　　　　　　　上午 **10** 點 **08** 分

沒錯，卡羅尼亞公寓很受當地居民歡迎，找到房客應該不難。

道格拉斯凱特　　　　　　　　　上午 **10** 點 **10** 分

我等等再跟妳聊。

Send

字彙　**tenant** 承租人、房客　**lease** 租約　**expire** 到期　**penalty** 罰鍰　**waive the fee** 減免收費
property 不動產、財產　**make an exception** 破例　**local resident** 當地居民

154. What do the tenants want to do?
   (A) Purchase an apartment
   (B) Rent a different apartment nearby
   (C) Renovate a dining area
   (D) Finish a contract early

房客想做什麼？
   (A) 購買公寓
   (B) 在附近租其他間公寓
   (C) 整修用餐區
   (D) 提早結束合約

正確答案為 **(D)**

在卡特於 10 點 05 分的簡訊提到 The tenants would like to move out at the end of July, but their lease doesn't expire until 31 October.，由此可知答案是 (D)。

字彙　**nearby** 附近的

155. At 10:07 A.M., what does Mr. Carter most likely mean when he writes, "I think I can give it a try"?
   (A) He thinks that the rent is too high.
   (B) He plans to ask the tenants to stay longer.
   (C) He will contact the property owners.
   (D) He is willing to pay a penalty.

凱特於 10 點 07 分的簡訊說「我可以試試看」是什麼意思？
   (A) 他覺得租金太高。
   (B) 他計畫要求房客多住些時間。
   (C) 他會聯絡屋主。
   (D) 他願意支付罰款。

正確答案為 **(C)**

〈推論句意〉
推測說話者的意圖，可從此指定句的前後文做推敲。前一封簡訊桑德斯說 What about calling the owner and seeing if they'll make an exception? 凱特接著表示他願意依建議打電話給屋主，答案是 (C)。

字彙　**rent** 租金　**be willing to** 樂意、願意

Test 01

Questions 156-157 refer to the following notice. 公告

NOTICE

The ticketing machine in the Garland waiting area near Platform 5 has been removed for repairs. We hope to have a new machine in place by Monday, April 14. Until then, railroad passengers may use the machine in the Midvale waiting area near Platform 7 or see one of the ticketing clerks at the counter in the Main Lobby next to the Information Booth. We apologize for the inconvenience. Passengers are reminded that they can save 10 to 20 percent and avoid lines at ticketing machines by purchasing weekly or monthly passes. Passes are only available online at www.fasttrackservice.com.

問題 156-157 參考以下公告。

公告

位於葛蘭地候車區、靠近第 5 月台的售票機已搬離進行維修。我們希望在 4 月 14 日星期一前安裝好新機器。 ⑮⑥ 在此之前，鐵路旅客可以使用靠近第 7 月台位於米韋爾候車區的機器，也可以在服務處旁的主要大廳找櫃檯售票員。我們為所帶來的不便深感抱歉。 ⑮⑦ 提醒各位乘客，購買週票或月票可省下百分之 10 到 20 的費用，也能免去在售票機前排隊。週票或月票只能上網至 www.fasttrackservice.com 網站購買。

字彙   **remove** 移除   **in place** 準備就緒的   **counter** 櫃檯   **apologize** 致歉   **inconvenience** 不便
pass 通行票券

156. Where is the notice most likely posted?
(A) In a movie theater
(B) In a rental car agency
(C) In a train station
(D) In an airport

公告很可能張貼在哪裡？
(A) 電影院
(B) 租車業者
(C) 火車站
(D) 機場

正確答案為 (C)

第三句提到 railroad passengers，由此可知是火車站，答案是 (C)。

157. What is suggested about the ticketing machines?
(A) They do not sell weekly and monthly passes.
(B) They are for credit card customers only.
(C) They provide tickets that are discounted 10 to 20 percent.
(D) They have not yet been installed in Platform 7.

關於售票機，哪些是我們可以知道的？
(A) 不發售週票和月票通行券。
(B) 只有持信用卡顧客能使用。
(C) 提供票價折扣 10 到 20% 的車票。
(D) 第 7 月台還沒安裝。

正確答案為 (A)

最後一句提到 Passes are only available online，因此仕售票機無法購得週票或月票通行券。答案是 (A)。

Questions 158-160 refer to the following letter. 信件

From: Carrie Fenway
To: Harper Randolph
Subject: Keeping on a discussion
Date: December 22

Dear Harper:

It was great to see you at the company's regional managers retreat last week. I wanted to follow up on the discussion we had about your office's upcoming move. The Bristol office's move last year taught me a lot about managing relocation, and I wanted to pass on what I learned to you. –[1]–.

First, I know you are still deciding on whether to close the office for a few days or to keep your office open as usual by moving gradually. I would recommend remaining open if possible. –[2]–. The Bristol office remained open and moved gradually over a period of two weeks, which made the move quite easy. Of course, maintaining the normal work schedule during that time was difficult because some employees had relocated to the new office while their team members remained at the old office. –[3]–. If you choose this approach, I would suggest moving all members of a team at the same time to minimize confusion.

Second, remember that relocation is time-consuming for everyone. Be clear in delivering the message to your employees that you will not be expecting to take on normal workloads during the move. –[4]–. Taking this step ahead of time, as the Bristol office did, greatly improves workflow and reduces stress.

I'll give you a call later this week to talk more about these issues.

Sincerely,

Carrie Fenway
President, Situation Consulting

問題 158-160 參考以下信件。

寄件者：嘉莉芬威
收件者：哈伯蘭道夫
主旨：延續討論
日期：12 月 22 日

親愛的哈伯：

很高興上週在區經理靜修會遇見你。我想接續上次我們討論到貴辦公室即將搬遷的話題。去年布里斯托辦公室搬遷一事讓我學會許多搬遷管理的事，158 我想把我所學轉達給你。-[1]-

首先，我知道你尚未決定是要把辦公室關閉幾天，還是照舊一邊營運一邊搬遷。如果可能的話，我建議照常營運。-[2]- 布里斯托辦公室持續營運並在兩週的時間完成搬遷，這麼做使得搬遷變得容易。當然，159 這段期間很難維持正常的工作進度，因為當時部分團隊成員留在舊辦公室，而部分成員已搬到新辦公室，-[3]- 如果你選擇這種方法，我建議一次遷移團隊所有員工，減少混亂。

其次，記住辦公室搬遷對所有人而言是耗時的。160 要清楚向員工傳達一個信息，那就是在搬遷過程中你不期待大家履行正常的工作量。-[4]- 160 就如同布里斯托辦公室當時一樣，提早採取這一步，將會大幅改善工作流程並減少壓力。

這個星期晚些時候我會打電話給你，進一步討論這些事情。

嘉莉芬威
情境諮商公司總裁

字彙 retreat 靜修會（指工作期間休養生息的聚會）；撤退　follow up 追蹤、繼續進行　pass on 傳承
as usual 照例、一如往常　gradually 逐漸地　approach 方法　minimize 使～降到最低
confusion 混亂　time-consuming 耗時的　deliver the message 傳遞訊息　take on 承擔（工作）
workload 工作量　take a step 採取措施　ahead of time 提早　workflow 工作流程

158. Why is Ms. Fenway writing to Mr. Randolph?
  (A) To offer advice
  (B) To request a document
  (C) To suggest a new project
  (D) To appeal a decision

芬威小姐寫信給蘭道夫的原因是什麼？
  (A) 提供建議
  (B) 申請文件
  (C) 提議新計畫
  (D) 對決定提出訴求、異議

正確答案為 (A)

第一段第三句提到 I wanted to pass on what I learned to you，可見這封信的目的是要提出建言，把自己所知的告訴對方。

> 字彙　**appeal** 提出訴求或異議

159. What did Ms. Fenway think was the error?
  (A) Not closing the office early for a renovation
  (B) Not keeping teams of employees together
  (C) Not giving employees some time off during the move
  (D) Not discussing a new policy with each employee individually

芬威小姐認為之前做錯了什麼？
  (A) 整修期間沒有提早關閉辦公室
  (B) 沒有讓員工一起行動
  (C) 搬遷期間沒有給員工休假
  (D) 沒有和每個員工各別討論新政策

正確答案為 (B)

第二段第三句提到 maintaining the normal work schedule during that time was difficult because some employees had relocated to the new office while their team members remained at the old office，本句使用到過去完成式，說明了當時芬威小姐自己進行搬遷時遇到的問題，因此答案是 (B)。

> 字彙　**individually** 個別地

160. In which of the positions marked [1], [2], [3], and [4] does the following sentence best belong?
  "Instead, talk in detail with each employee about reducing his or her workload during the relocation period."
  (A) [1]
  (B) [2]
  (C) [3]
  (D) [4]

在標示 [1]、[2]、[3]、[4] 的位置中，何者適合放入以下句子？
  「相反地，你應該和每位員工詳細討論在搬遷期間減少工作量的問題。」
  (A) [1]
  (B) [2]
  (C) [3]
  (D) [4]

正確答案為 (D)

〈插入句〉

題目句子以 Instead「相反地」開頭，代表之後的內容跟前一句應該要是「轉折」關係。[4] 前句 you will not be expecting to take on normal workloads during the move 說到要維持正常工作量是很困難的，而後面的句子又接著 this step... greatly improves workflow and reduces stress，剛好也和前一句有轉折關係，因此 (D) 是正確答案。

> 字彙　**in detail** 詳細地

Questions 161-163 refer to the following information on a Web page. 網頁

---

http://www.lowell.edu

⚡ FACULTY PROFILE

Edinburgh Campus

Direction	Home	Contact Us	Faculty

Dr. Margaret Pullman
Business Management
Pullman@lowell.edu

Dr. Margaret Pullman graduated from Arlington University in Manchester with dual degrees in Business and history. She embarked on her career as an educator when, as a graduate student in Duncan University in Liverpool, she tutored students in introductory Business courses. After receiving her doctorate in business management from Duncan University, she joined the business faculty at Lowell University's Edinburgh Campus. She is the author of *How Businesses Succeed* (forthcoming from Lowell University Press). She is also a member of the Great Lake Businesses Council. Currently on leave from Lowell University, Dr. Pullman is conducting a series of international business seminars at the Global Business Affairs Institute in London.

問題 161-163 參考以下網頁。

---

http://www.lowell.edu

⚡ 師資介紹

愛丁堡校區

說明	首頁	聯絡我們	161 師資

瑪格瑞特普曼博士
商業管理
Pullman@lowell.edu

瑪格瑞特普曼博士畢業於曼徹斯特艾林頓大學，擁有商業與歷史雙學位。162 她在利物浦當肯大學當研究生時，就開始教育事業，輔導學生商業入門課程。在當肯大學取得商業管理博士學位之後，她加入洛威大學愛丁堡分校的商學院師資群。她是《企業如何成功》一書的作者（即將由洛威大學出版），也是大湖商業諮商的會員。163 目前普曼博士離開洛威大學休假中，並在倫敦的全球商務機構主持一系列國際商業研討會。

字彙　**faculty** 師資　　**dual** 雙的、雙倍的　　**embark on** 著手、開始　　**introductory course** 入門課程
　　　doctorate 博士學位　　**forthcoming** 即將來臨的　　**on leave** 休假中

161. What is the purpose of the information?
    (A) To announce dates for a business seminar
    (B) To publicize facts about an employee
    (C) To encourage business owners to buy a book
    (D) To provide details about a job applicant

這個資訊的目的為何？
    (A) 宣布商業研討會日期
    (B) 公告職員的實際狀況
    (C) 鼓勵企業主買書
    (D) 提供求職者的詳細資料

正確答案為 (B)

文章目的可以在開頭找到。網頁內容是洛威大學網頁的 faculty「師資」中關於普曼教授的經歷，因此答案是 (B)。

> **字彙**　**publicize** 公布

162. Where did Professor Pullman begin her teaching career?
    (A) In Liverpool
    (B) In Edinburgh
    (C) In Manchester
    (D) In London

普曼教授的教學經歷開始於哪裡？
    (A) 利物浦
    (B) 愛丁堡
    (C) 曼徹斯特
    (D) 倫敦

正確答案為 (A)

根據 She embarked on her career as an educator when, as a graduate student in Duncan University in Liverpool 一句得知，她初次授課地點是在利物浦 Liverpool，動詞片語 embark on 指「開始、著手」，因此答案是 (A)。

163. What is indicated about Professor Pullman?
    (A) She is currently teaching history at a university.
    (B) She applied to be a member of a business council.
    (C) She is working temporarily in London.
    (D) She runs her own business throughout the world.

何者是關於普曼教授的說明？
    (A) 她目前正在一所大學教歷史。
    (B) 她申請成為商業諮商會員。
    (C) 她目前暫時在倫敦工作。
    (D) 她在全球各地經營她的事業。

正確答案為 (C)

在最後句子提到 Dr. Pullman is conducting a series of international business seminars at the Global Business Affairs Institute in London，本句使用到現在進行式，由此可知她目前在倫敦工作，因此答案是 (C)。

Questions 164-167 refer the following advertisement. 廣告

Meyers Complex

Enjoy the scenic beauty of Mendota Bay from the newly renovated Meyers Complex. Formerly a sewing factory, the building has been completely updated to combine modern conveniences and technology with features representative of buildings from the early 1900s. Two years ago Gerund Remodeling Inc., the award-winning architecture firm based in Chicago, undertook the project to convert Fargo's sewing factory to both commercial and residential units. Next month's opening reception will mark the completion of the renovation.

Meyers Complex offers 240 apartments, many of which overlook Fargo Harbor, and 4,500 square meters of commercial space for offices and retail stores. In addition to its sweeping views, it offers beautifully landscaped gardens along the harbor. This appealing, multi-use facility is situated in a prime location. Meyers Complex is just a block away from Fargo's Maple Street, lined with boutique shops, art galleries and restaurants. It also sits at the end of the 23-kilometer Chanda Bay Bicycle Path, which was created from an old railroad line and connects Fargo to Alton City. There are several other well-maintained bicycle trails in the area. To the south, Jacksonville, with all of its attractions, is an easy 30-minute drive away.

To inquire about commercial or residential space, please contact Meyers Complex Property Management at 301-555-3241 or send an e-mail to rentalinfo@meyerscomplex.com. Floor plans for apartments vary. Commercial space can be customized. For more details, visit our Web site, www.meyerscomplex.com.

問題 164-167 參考以下廣告。

梅爾斯複合園區

164 請到全新改裝的梅爾斯複合園區欣賞門多塔灣的美景。園區前身是一家縫紉廠,目前已經全面改建,結合現代的便利與技術,並保有 1900 年代初期的建築特色。165 兩年前,總部位於芝加哥且屢獲殊榮的建築公司古朗德改建公司承接此計畫,將法古縫紉工廠改造成商業與住宅空間。166A 下個月的開幕式將紀念裝修工程的完成。

梅爾斯複合園區提供 240 間公寓,其中許多間可以俯瞰法古港,還有 4,500 平方公尺的商業空間可作為辦公室及零售商店。除了一覽無遺的景色之外,它還提供美麗的港口沿岸花園。這個吸引人的多功能設施位於 167 主要地段。166C 梅爾斯複合園區距離林立精品店、畫廊和餐廳的法古楓葉大街僅一條街。166D 它也剛好位於 23 公里長的昌達灣自行車道盡頭,此自行車道是由一條舊鐵路改造而成,連接法古市和安頓市。這個地區還有幾條維護良好的自行車道。往南走可以到有許多名勝景點的傑克森村,輕鬆駕駛僅需 30 分鐘到達。

如欲詢問商業或住宅空間,請致電 301-555-3241 與梅爾斯複合園區物業管理公司聯絡,或寄電子郵件至 rentalinfo@meyerscomplex.com。公寓平面圖各不相同,商業空間可依照客戶量身訂做。需要更多詳細資訊,請參考我們的網站 www.meyerscomplex.com。

字彙　**complex**（由多種建築物組成）複合園區、多功能建築　**formerly** 過去、以前　**sewing factory** 縫紉工廠
combine 結合~　**features** 特徵　**representative of** 代表~的　**award-winning** 得獎的
undertake 從事、承擔　**convert** 轉換　**commercial** 商業的、營利的　**residential** 住宅的
reception 歡迎會;接受　**mark** 紀念、標記、記號　**completion** 完成　**overlook** 俯瞰、眺望
sweeping 徹底的、廣泛的　**appealing** 吸引人的　**prime** 主要的　**trail** 小徑　**attraction** 觀光景點
inquire about 詢問、打聽　**vary** 多樣　**customize** 量身訂做

164. What is the purpose of the advertisement?
(A) To announce a recently approved project
(B) To promote an architectural awards event
(C) To publicize new office and residential space
(D) To explain a reason for the delay of the opening

廣告的目的為何？
(A) 公告最近通過的專案
(B) 推廣建築大獎活動
(C) 宣傳新的辦公和居住空間
(D) 說明延誤開業的原因

正確答案為 (C)

文章目的可以在開頭找到。 開頭第一句是 Enjoy the scenic beauty of Mendota Bay from the newly renovated Meyers Complex，正是在為建築物做宣傳。

字彙 **approved** 被認可的、獲准通過的

165. What is mentioned about Gerund Remodeling Inc.?
(A) It is a family-owned business.
(B) It has been recognized for its work.
(C) It specializes in commercial properties.
(D) It is known for its unique sewing techniques.

何者陳述與古朗德改建公司有關？
(A) 是家族企業。
(B) 因其作品而被肯定。
(C) 專長商業空間。
(D) 因獨特的縫紉技術而聞名。

正確答案為 (B)

注意關鍵字 Gerund Remodeling，第一段第三句提到 Gerund Remodeling Inc., the award-winning architecture firm，由此可知此建築公司曾經獲獎，因此答案是 (B)。

字彙 **recognize** 認可、肯定　　**specialize in** 擅長、專門做　　**be known for** 因～而聞名

166. What is NOT stated about Meyers Complex?
(A) It will open next month.
(B) It is right next to a subway station.
(C) It is not far from a shopping district.
(D) It is close to bicycle trails.

關於梅爾斯複合園區，何者不在說明之中？
(A) 下個月開幕。
(B) 位於地鐵站旁。
(C) 距離購物商街不遠。
(D) 鄰近自行車道。

正確答案為 (B)

第一段最後一句提到 Next month's opening reception，呼應 (A) 選項，第二段提到 Meyers Complex is just a block away from Fargo's Maple Street, lined with boutique shops，呼應 (C) 選項，而 It also sits at the end of the 23 kilometer Chanda Bay Bicycle Path 的內容也呼應 (D) 選項，內容沒有提到的是 (B) 選項。

167. The word "prime" in paragraph 2, line 4, is closest in meaning to
(A) central
(B) heavy
(C) leading
(D) supreme

第二段第四行的「prime」意義與以下何者相近？
(A) 中心的
(B) 重的
(C) 主導的
(D) 最高層的

正確答案為 (A)

〈推測字義〉
prime location 的 prime 意思是「主要的」，意味著成為中心的重要位置，因此答案是 (A)。

Questions 168-171 refer to the following online chat discussion. 線上聊天室

Rebecca Walton [4:17 P.M.]	Thanks for attending the regional manager meeting earlier this afternoon. Are there any further questions?
Kelly Stevens [4:18 P.M.]	Juan and I are unclear about how the new sales districts affect existing customers. Do the new districts apply only to new customers?
Rebecca Walton [4:20 P.M.]	No, the new districts apply to both new and existing customers.
Kelly Stevens [4:21 P.M.]	So, does that mean I will no longer get incentives from current customers like Perot Publishing?
Rebecca Walton [4:22 P.M.]	Right. All existing clients in District 5 go to Juan.
Juan Rubble [4:23 P.M.]	But what if I agree to let Kelly keep Perot Publishing?
Rebecca Walton [4:25 P.M.]	Perot Publishing is a big client.
Juan Rubble [4:26 P.M.]	Yes, but I'd rather not interrupt a productive relationship. Perot Publishing is not that important to me.
Rebecca Walton [4:27 P.M.]	I don't see it as interrupting, necessarily. However, if you say so, Juan, I might be able to make an exception if our district manager approves it.
Kelly Stevens [4:28 P.M.]	Can I talk to the client in person?
Rebecca Walton [4:30 P.M.]	I don't think that's appropriate.
Kelly Stevens [4:31 P.M.]	I understand.
Juan Rubble [4:32 P.M.]	OK, we'll wait to hear back from you.

Send

問題 168-171 參考以下線上聊天室。

蕾貝卡瓦頓 [下午 04 點 17 分]　⑯感謝大家出席今天下午稍早的區經理會議。還有其他問題嗎？

凱莉史蒂芬 [下午 04 點 18 分]　莊和我不清楚新的銷售區域如何影響現有客戶。新區域是否只適用於新客戶呢？

蕾貝卡瓦頓 [下午 04 點 20 分]　不，新區域適用於新客戶和現有客戶。

凱莉史蒂芬 [下午 04 點 21 分]　那是否表示我再也不能從普洛特出版這類現有客戶獲得獎勵呢？

蕾貝卡瓦頓 [下午 04 點 22 分]　沒錯，第 5 區的所有現有客戶都歸莊。

莊盧保 [下午 04 點 23 分]　⑰但是如果我同意讓凱莉繼續保有普洛特出版呢？

蕾貝卡瓦頓 [下午 04 點 25 分]　普洛特出版是間大客戶。

莊盧保 [下午 04 點 26 分]　是的，但是 ⑯我不想妨礙一段有生產力的關係。普洛特出版對我來說沒有那麼重要。

蕾貝卡瓦頓 [下午 04 點 27 分]　我不認為那一定是妨礙。 ⑰不過，如果你這麼說的話，如果區經理同意，或許我可以破例一次。

凱莉史蒂芬 [下午 04 點 28 分]　我可以跟客戶當面談談嗎？

蕾貝卡瓦頓 [下午 04 點 30 分]　我認為這不適合。

凱莉史蒂芬 [下午 04 點 31 分]　我了解。

莊盧保 [下午 04 點 32 分]　好，我們等候妳的答覆。

Send

字彙　**regional** 地區的　　**be unclear about** 不確定　　**existing** 目前的、現有的　　**district** 區域、地方
apply to 適用於、應用於　　**incentives** 獎勵　　**interrupt** 打斷、中斷　　**productive** 有生產力的、有成效的
in person 親自　　**appropriate** 適當的、恰當的

168. Who most likely is Ms. Walton?　　　　瓦頓小姐可能是什麼人？
(A) A bookstore owner　　　　　　　　　(A) 書店老闆
(B) A sales manager　　　　　　　　　**(B) 銷售經理**
(C) A travel agent　　　　　　　　　　　(C) 旅行社員工
(D) An author　　　　　　　　　　　　　(D) 作家

正確答案為 **(B)**

4 點 17 分 Ms. Walton 瓦頓說參加區經理會議，由此可知答案是 (B)。

169. What is suggested about Ms. Stevens?　　何者陳述與史蒂芬小姐有關？
(A) She has a good relationship with Perot Publishing.　　**(A) 她與普洛特出版關係良好。**
(B) She'd like to transfer to an office in District 5.　　(B) 她想轉調到第 5 區辦公室。
(C) She is very satisfied with the new district assignment.　　(C) 她對新地區的任務感到很滿意。
(D) She was not at the meeting in the morning.　　(D) 她上午沒有參加會議。

正確答案為 **(A)**

下午 4 點 26 分盧保說 I'd rather not interrupt a productive relationship，可見史蒂芬和客戶維持著良好的關係，答案是 (A)。

字彙　**transfer** 調任　**assignment** 分配、任務

170. At 4:25, what does Ms. Walton most likely mean when she writes, "Perot Publishing is a big client"?　　4 點 25 分瓦頓小姐說「普洛特出版是間大客戶」是什麼意思？
(A) She doubts Mr. Rubble can meet Perot Publishing's needs.　　(A) 她懷疑盧保不能滿足普洛特出版的需求。
(B) She believes Mr. Rubble is confused.　　(B) 她認為盧保感到困惑。
(C) She wants Mr. Rubble to visit District 5.　　(C) 她要盧保去拜訪第 5 區。
(D) She thinks Mr. Rubble's idea is surprising.　　**(D) 她對盧保的想法感到訝異。**

正確答案為 **(D)**

〈推論句意〉
前面的句子盧保同意讓凱莉繼續管理普洛特出版，接著瓦頓說這是個大客戶，意味著她對盧保不願接手大客戶的想法感到訝異。因此答案是 (D)。

字彙　**doubt** 懷疑　**meet needs** 滿足需求

171. What will most likely happen next?　　接下來可能會發生什麼事？
(A) Ms. Stevens will review the new map of sales districts.　　(A) 史蒂芬將重新評估新銷售區域地圖。
(B) Ms. Stevens will meet with her client.　　(B) 史蒂芬將與客戶見面。
(C) Ms. Walton will contact the colleague.　　**(C) 瓦頓將與同事聯絡。**
(D) Mr. Rubble will accept a job offer from Perot Publishing.　　(D) 盧保將接受普洛特出版提供的工作。

正確答案為 **(C)**

瓦頓在 4 點 27 分時表示 I might be able to make an exception if our district manager approves it，可見她將與區域經理聯絡，因此答案是 (C)。

Questions 172-175 refer to the following article. 報導

The McClellan Theater is one of Dublin's most treasured historic landmarks and needs to be preserved. The building, constructed almost two centuries ago on Dublin's Central Square, features many striking and unique attributes. –[1]–. The ornate plasterwork of its facade is a magnificent example of architecture of the period in which it was constructed. The walls of the lobby are covered by beautiful murals featuring many famous actors who have performed there over the years, including Wendy Ramsey and Madeline Estes. The theater is not only an architectural gem but also a highly valued entertainment venue for area residents, and it supports the local economy by attracting tourists to the area. –[2]–.

Due to the building's deterioration in recent years, it no longer attracts large theater productions and musical acts. Ensuring the theater's continued use would require extensive restoration. –[3]–. Over the next six months, this committee composed of city residents, local business owners and civic leaders will finalize the restoration plans and raise the capital necessary to complete the project. The committee will also be working to locate corporate and community sponsorships throughout Dublin. –[4]–.

For residents interested in following the restoration efforts, the committee will hold public information sessions on the first Tuesday of each month in the community room of the Dublin Public Library. Detailed plans for the project and information about making a donation to the effort are available at www.restoretheMcClellantheater.com.

問題 172-175 參考以下報導。

(172) 麥克利蘭劇院是都柏林最珍貴的歷史地標之一，需要加以保存。這座建築物位於都柏林中央廣場，距今 200 年前建成，特色是有許多宏偉且獨特的元素。-[1]- 其正面的華麗石膏製品是建造當時的宏偉典範。大廳牆上充滿美麗的壁畫，壁畫特徵是有許多在此表演過的著名演員，包括溫蒂拉姆齊和麥德琳伊斯特。此劇院不僅是建築瑰寶，也是當地居民相當重要的娛樂場所，它吸引遊客到此地區，支持了當地經濟。-[2]-

(172)(173)(175) 近年由於建築物老舊，它不再吸引大型戲劇製作與音樂演出。若要保證劇院能繼續使用，就必須進行全面性整修。-[3]- (175) 接下來 6 個月，由居民、當地企業主和民間領袖所組成的委員會將敲定修復計畫，並籌募完成計畫所需資金。委員會也會在都柏林全區尋求企業與社區贊助。-[4]-

(174) 對重建工作有興趣的居民，委員會將於每月第一個星期二於都柏林公共圖書館社區活動室舉行公共資訊說明會。此專案的詳細計畫和捐款支持這項工作的相關資訊可上 www.restoretheMcClellantheater.com 網站查詢。

字彙　**treasured** 珍貴的　**landmark** 地標、里程碑　**feature** 以～為特色　**striking** 顯著的、突出的
attribute 屬性、特質　**attribute** 特質　**ornate** 華麗的、裝飾的　**plasterwork** 石膏製品
facade 正面、外觀　**mural** 壁畫　**gem** 寶石、珍寶　**venue** 活動地點　**deterioration** 惡化、退化
composed of 由～組成　**civic** 市民的　**resident** 居民　**finalize** 最終確定、定案
raise the capital 籌募資金　**corporate** 企業的　**sponsorship** 贊助、資助

172. What is the article mainly about?
(A) The award received by a town for its architecture
(B) The results of an election for a committee
(C) Information about an upcoming city project
(D) The dates of a theater's performance schedule

這篇報導主要是關於什麼？
(A) 一個城鎮因其建築而獲獎
(B) 委員會的選舉結果
(C) 即將推動的城市計畫
(D) 劇院演出時間表的日期

正確答案為 (C)

主題可在文章開頭找到答案。第一段提到 McClellan 劇院的價值和重要性，第二段說明修復的必要性和設立委員會等相關推動過程。因此答案是 (C)。

字彙　**election** 選舉

173. What is implied about the McClellan Theater?
(A) It is the largest building in Dublin.
(B) It offers discounted tickets to Dublin residents.
(C) It is no longer open to the public.
(D) It once attracted large crowds.

何者與麥克利蘭劇院有關？
(A) 它是都柏林最大的建築。
(B) 它提供都柏林居民優惠票。
(C) 它不再對外開放。
(D) 它曾經吸引大批群眾。

正確答案為 (D)

第二段第一句說到 it no longer attracts large theater productions and musical acts，由此可知過去曾有大規模的公演，答案是 (D)。

174. According to the article, how can people learn more about the changes at the McClellan Theater?
(A) By submitting a request to the city government
(B) By attending monthly meetings
(C) By speaking to Ms. Ramsey in person
(D) By singing up for a monthly newsletter

根據報導，人們怎麼做才能更加了解麥克利蘭劇院的變化？
(A) 向市政府提出申請
(B) 參加每月例會
(C) 直接向拉姆齊小姐說
(D) 申請時事月刊

正確答案為 (B)

第三段第一句提到 For residents interested in following the restoration efforts, the committee will hold public information sessions on the first Tuesday of each month，由此可知在每月一次的會議上將說明詳細狀況，因此答案是 (B)。

字彙　**sign up (for)** 申請、報名　　**newsletter** 新聞通訊

175. In which of the positions marked [1], [2], [3], and [4] does the following sentence best belong?
"For this reason, the McClellan Theater Restoration Committee was formed last month with an ambitious plan for restoring the theater."
(A) [1]
(B) [2]
(C) [3]
(D) [4]

標記 [1]、[2]、[3]、[4] 的位置中，何者是安插下列句子的最佳位置？
「基於這個原因，麥克利蘭劇院修復委員會於上個月成立，並為修復劇院制定了一個遠大的計畫。」
(A) [1]
(B) [2]
(C) [3]
(D) [4]

正確答案為 (C)

〈插入句〉

本句提到成立 committee 一事，因此可尋找相關的句子。[3] 的上一句是 Ensuring the theater's continued use would require extensive restoration，是第一次提到整修的想法。[3] 的下一句提到 this committee，則是首度提及委員會，之前的內容都沒有提到委員會，由此可知適當的安插位置是 [3]，答案是 (C)。

字彙　**ambitious** 有野心的

Questions 176-180 refer to the following article and form. 報導／表格

April 4

The National Association of Plastic Workers (NAPW) will hold its annual conference in Sydney from June 6 to 8. Once again, it will be held at the Stone Conference Center in Sydney's business district. Stan Keating, NAPW President, says that the organization will return to the venue because of its convenient location and the amenities it offers. Says Stan, "The conference center is state-of-the-art, and the staff members are extremely knowledgeable and helpful."

This year's theme is "Emerging Technologies in Plastic Fabrication and Molding." The keynote address on June will be given by Colleen Allen, CEO of Plastigic Innovators, Inc. In addition to Ms. Allen's speech, during the three-day event there will be twenty presentations and a closing address by Mr. Keating.

To register for the conference, visit the NAPW web site (www.napw.com/conference). The cost of the conference is $85 for NAPW members and $120 for nonmembers. Students, please contact your institution for discount information; the NAPW maintains pricing agreements with a number of universities and technical colleges. Hotel reservations can be made through thc Web site as well. Attendees can choose from six area hotels at various price ranges. The NAPW is offering a free shuttle service to and from the participating hotels and conference site.

問題 176-180 參考以下報導與表格。

4 月 4 日

180A 全國塑膠製造業者協會（NAPW）於 6 月 6 至 8 日將在雪梨舉辦年會。它將再次於雪梨商業區的史東會議中心舉行。NAPW 會長史丹基丁表示，組織再次回到該活動會場是因為其地理位置便利且設施齊全。史丹表示：「176 此會議中心是最先進的，而且工作人員見聞廣博，給我們許多幫助。」

今年的主題是「塑膠製造與塑型的新興技術」。177 塑膠科技創新股份有限公司執行長柯林艾倫將在 6 月發表主題演說。除了艾倫小姐的演說之外，在為期三天的活動期間，將有 20 場發表以及基丁先生的閉幕演講。

要註冊參加會議，請至 NAPW 網站（www.napw.com/conference）。180D 會議參加費用是 NAPW 會員 85 美元，非會員 120 美元。178 學生請與所屬院校聯絡，NAPW 與許多大學與科技大學持有價格協議。179 飯店預訂也可透過網站進行。參加者可從不同價位的 6 家地區飯店做選擇。NAPW 提供免費接駁服務，可往返於合作飯店與會議現場。

字彙 **business district** 商業區　　**amenities** 便利設施　　**state-of-the-art** 最先進的　　**extremely** 非常、極其 **knowledgeable** 博學多聞的　　**keynote address** 主題演講　　**CEO** 執行長　　**closing address** 閉幕演講 **register for** 申請　　**institution** 機構　　**maintain** 維持　　**pricing agreement** 價格協議　　**as well** 也、同樣地 **price range** 價位

Mastuki Manufacturing
Expense reimbursement form

Employee name: *Rodney Kruger*
Payroll ID#: *129856*
Manager/supervisor name: *Michelle Robertson*
Purpose: *National Association of Plastic Workers Conference*

Itemized expenses:
Conference fee: $85.00
Bus fare: (round-trip Melbourne/Sydney) $43.34
Accommodation: (1 night at Jefferson Inn on June 6) $126.78

Total: *$255.12*

Attach receipts for all expenses. Allow two to three weeks for processing.

Employee signature: *R. Kruger*
Manager/supervisor signature: *M. Robertson*

Submitted for payment: *June 12*

松木製造業者
費用支出申報表

員工姓名：羅德尼庫魯格
工資單 ID#：129856
經理／主管姓名：米雪兒羅伯森
目的：國際塑膠工會研討會

費用明細：
180D 會議費用：85 美元
180C 公車費：（墨爾本－雪梨往返）43.34 美元
180E 住宿：（6 月 6 日傑佛森客棧住宿一晚）126.78 美元

總計：255.12 美元

請附上所有費用收據。處理時間需要 2 至 3 週。

員工簽名：R. Kruger
經理／主管簽名：M. Robertson

繳交日期：180B 6 月 12 日

字彙　**reimbursement** 核銷、報公帳　**payroll** 工資單　**itemize** 逐條列明　**round-trip** 往返　**fare** 車資
accommodation 住宿　**process** 處理

176. What is stated about the Stone Conference Center?
(A) It is close to the airport.
(B) Its staff is very competent.
(C) It offers a discount on meeting rooms.
(D) It has recently undergone renovation.

何者陳述與史東會議中心有關？
(A) 靠近機場。
(B) 員工很有能力。
(C) 提供會議室折扣。
(D) 最近進行整修。

正確答案為 (B)

關於 Stone Conference Center 可在報導中第一段看到，the staff members are extremely knowledgeable and helpful，可見其員工能力佳，答案是 (B)。

字彙 **competent** 能幹的、稱職的　**undergo** 歷經

177. Who is Ms. Allen?
(A) A guest speaker
(B) A conference organizer
(C) Mr. Kruger's manager
(D) The president of the NAPW

誰是艾倫小姐？
(A) 客座演講者
(B) 會議主辦人
(C) 庫魯格先生的經理
(D) NAPW 總裁

正確答案為 (A)

報導第二段提到 The keynote address on June will be given by Colleen Allen CEO of Plastigic Innovators, Inc.，由此可知柯林艾倫是會議邀請來的演講者。因此答案是 (A)。

178. What does the article suggest about student discounts?
(A) They are given only to graduate students.
(B) They are provided to students working as interns.
(C) They are available through certain schools.
(D) They are available to international students.

關於學生優惠，報導中提到何種陳述？
(A) 只對研究生提供優惠。
(B) 從事實習工作的學生可享優惠。
(C) 特定學校可享優惠。
(D) 國際學生可享優惠。

正確答案為 (C)

可在文章中尋找關鍵字 student 及 discount。報導第三段提到折價優惠的內容，Students, please contact your institution for discount information; the NAPW maintains pricing agreements with a number of universities and technical colleges，可見有提供優惠價給特定學校，答案是 (C)。

179. What can be found on the NAPW Web site?
(A) A shuttle schedule
(B) A list of hotels
(C) A map of the conference center
(D) A description of the presentations

在 NAPM 的網站上可以找到什麼？
(A) 接駁車時間表
(B) 飯店清單
(C) 會議中心地址
(D) 演講內容描述

正確答案為 (B)

報導第三段提到網址，其中 Hotel reservations can be made through the Web site as well.，答案是 (B)。

180. What can be inferred about Mr. Kruger?
(A) He did not listen to the closing speech.
(B) He was reimbursed on June 12 for expenses.
(C) He drove his car to the NAPW conference.
(D) He is not a member of the NAPW.

何者是關於庫魯格先生的推測？
(A) 他沒聽閉幕演講。
(B) 他在 6 月 12 日取得報銷的費用。
(C) 他開車到 NAPW 大會。
(D) 他不是 NAPW 會員。

正確答案為 (A)

〈整合多篇文章資訊〉
根據費用申報表，提出申請的日期是 6 月 12 日，費用明細上有公車費的支出，代表不是自己開車，而會議參加費用是 85 美元，呼應報導第三段提到的 The cost of the conference is $85 for NAPW members，可知庫魯格是 NAPW 會員。費用申報表上顯示只有在活動第一天住宿一晚，而報導內容提到的閉幕演說是在第三天 6 月 8 日，答案是 (A)。

Questions 181-185 refer to the following e-mails. 電子郵件

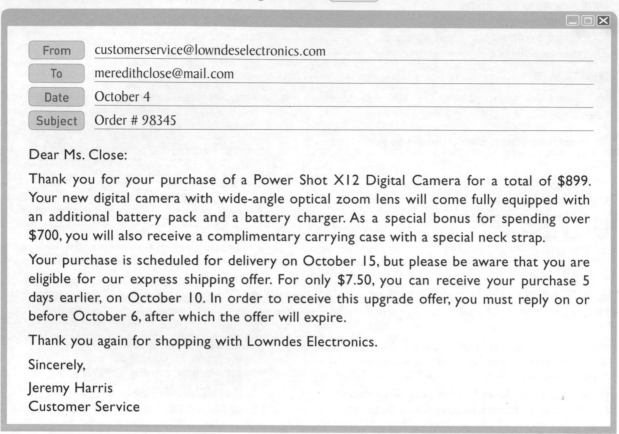

From customerservice@lowndeselectronics.com
To meredithclose@mail.com
Date October 4
Subject Order # 98345

Dear Ms. Close:

Thank you for your purchase of a Power Shot X12 Digital Camera for a total of $899. Your new digital camera with wide-angle optical zoom lens will come fully equipped with an additional battery pack and a battery charger. As a special bonus for spending over $700, you will also receive a complimentary carrying case with a special neck strap.

Your purchase is scheduled for delivery on October 15, but please be aware that you are eligible for our express shipping offer. For only $7.50, you can receive your purchase 5 days earlier, on October 10. In order to receive this upgrade offer, you must reply on or before October 6, after which the offer will expire.

Thank you again for shopping with Lowndes Electronics.

Sincerely,

Jeremy Harris
Customer Service

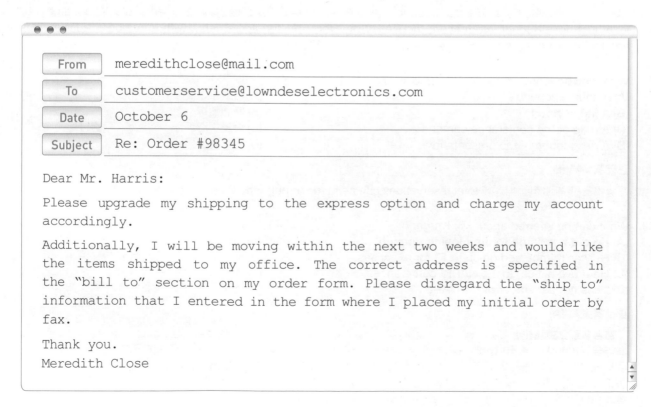

From meredithclose@mail.com
To customerservice@lowndeselectronics.com
Date October 6
Subject Re: Order #98345

Dear Mr. Harris:

Please upgrade my shipping to the express option and charge my account accordingly.

Additionally, I will be moving within the next two weeks and would like the items shipped to my office. The correct address is specified in the "bill to" section on my order form. Please disregard the "ship to" information that I entered in the form where I placed my initial order by fax.

Thank you.
Meredith Close

問題 181-185 參考以下兩封電子郵件。

寄件者	customerservice@lowndeselectronics.com
收件者	meredithclose@mail.com
日期	10 月 4 日
主旨	訂單編號 98345

親愛的克蘿絲小姐：

感謝您購買了一台 Power Shot X12 數位相機，總價 899 美元。您的廣角光學變焦鏡頭數位相機，全配一個額外電池組和電池充電器。 ⑱ 消費超過 700 美元加贈一個配有特殊頸帶的免費手提箱。

⑱ 您購買的商品預計在 10 月 15 日寄送，但請留意您享有快遞方案。只要多支付 7.5 美元，就可以提早 5 天收到訂購商品，也就是 10 月 10 日。 ⑱ 為了獲得此升級優惠，請在 10 月 6 日前回覆，超過期限將不再提供優惠。

再次感謝您購買朗茲電子產品。

傑瑞米哈里斯
客服中心

字彙　**purchase** 購買、購買之物　**optical** 光學的　**equipped with** 配有　**charger** 充電器
complimentary 免費的　**delivery** 運送　**aware** 意識到的、知道的　**express shipping** 快遞
be eligible for 符合～的條件

寄件者	meredithclose@mail.com
收件者	customerservice@lowndeselectronics.com
日期	10 月 6 日
主旨	訂單編號 98345

哈里斯先生您好：

⑱ 請將我的送貨方式升級為快遞，並收取應收費用。

另外，我將在接下來的兩週內搬家，希望商品能寄送到我的辦公室。 ⑱ 正確地址已詳細寫在訂單上的帳單寄送選項。請忽略我在第一次用傳真訂購時 ⑱ 輸入在表格內的送貨地址資料。

謝謝。

梅雷迪斯克蘿絲

字彙　**accordingly** 依照、相應地　**specify** 詳細說明　**disregard** 忽視　**initial** 最初的

181. Why does Mr. Harris write the e-mail?
(A) To inform a customer of an error
(B) To issue an invitation
(C) To apologize for a shipping delay
(D) To present a limited-time offer

哈里斯先生為什麼要寫電子郵件？
(A) 為了通知顧客發生錯誤
(B) 為了寄送邀請函
(C) 為送貨延誤表示歉意
(D) 為了提報限期特惠

正確答案為 (D)

第一封電子郵件第二段提到 In order to receive this upgrade offer, you must reply on or before October 6, after which the offer will expire，當中說明 10 月 6 日的優惠方案，因此答案是 (D)。

182. According to the first e-mail, why will Ms. Close receive a free item?
(A) She opened a business account.
(B) She made a purchase before October 6.
(C) She spent over a stated amount.
(D) She is a returning customer.

根據第一封電子郵件，為什麼克蘿絲小姐將收到免費產品？
(A) 她開了一個商業帳戶。
(B) 她在 10 月 6 日前買了一件東西。
(C) 她消費達一定金額以上。
(D) 她是老客戶。

正確答案為 (C)

在第一封郵件提到 a special bonus for spending over $700，意思是購買達 700 美元以上可以得到一份免費贈品，因此答案是 (C)。

183. What can be inferred about Ms. Close?
(A) She would prefer to upgrade the digital camera.
(B) She is moving to an overseas location.
(C) She would like to cancel two items.
(D) She wants the shipment sent to a different address.

何者是關於克蘿絲小姐的陳述？
(A) 她想幫數位相機升級。
(B) 她要搬到國外。
(C) 她想取消兩樣商品。
(D) 她希望貨物送到不同的地址。

正確答案為 (D)

第二封郵件第二段提到希望能寄送到訂單上的地址，而不是一開始寫在傳真上的地址，因此答案是 (D)。

184. When will Ms. Close most likely receive her order?
(A) On October 5
(B) On October 6
(C) On October 10
(D) On October 15

克蘿絲小姐最可能在什麼時候收到訂購商品？
(A) 10 月 5 日
(B) 10 月 6 日
(C) 10 月 10 日
(D) 10 月 15 日

正確答案為 (C)

〈整合多篇文章資訊〉
第一封郵件提到原本寄送日是 10 月 15 日，但如果在 10 月 6 日前提出申請，就能在 10 月 10 日寄送。第二封郵件中克蘿絲小姐提出了快遞申請，可知她可以在 10 月 10 日收到訂購商品。

185. In the second e-mail, the word "entered" in paragraph 2, line 4, is closest in meaning to
(A) went into
(B) typed
(C) started
(D) thought about

在第二封郵件中，第二段第四行的「entered」與以下何者意義最相近？
(A) 走入
(B) 輸入
(C) 開始
(D) 想到

正確答案為 (B)

〈推論字義〉
句中 entered 是在表格內「輸入資料」的意思，因此答案是 (B)。

Questions 186-190 refer to the following memo, notice, and letter. 內部通知 / 公告 / 信件

from	Thomas Reilly
To	All students
Date	February 26

Welcome to Stein College Residence.

We would like to welcome freshmen and returning students to our residence. We hope that this year will be as good if not better than the last. We have made some renovations to the building that we think you will really enjoy, including a new lounge with four pool tables, and a brand-new dartboard. This lounge will be open from 10 A.M. until 11 P.M. and will be supported by a café that offers a wide range of beverages and snacks for your pleasure.

For all of us to have a fun and safe year, it is important to set up some ground rules for your behavior. It is very important to note that breaking three rules can result in suspension of privileges, eviction from the residence, and possibly expulsion from school. In addition, you are responsible for the action of any guest that you bring into the residence. This means that upon entry and exit, any guest that you wish to stay with you MUST sign in and out. The maximum number of guests per person is two.

For further details of the residence rules and by-laws of the residence, refer to the notice on the bulletin board in the lobby.

Stein College Residence Rules

1. Drinking in the common spaces — for example, outside of your room — is prohibited.

2. Illegal drugs of any kind are banned.

3. Violence of any kind is prohibited.

4. Damage to the property is not tolerated.

5. Smoking inside the building is not allowed.

6. Noise in the hallways after 10 P.M. is prohibited.

We hope that these main rules will help everyone have a safe and educational year at Stein College.

If you have any questions, please ask the Resident Tutor, Thomas Reilly, in Room 102.

問題 186-190 參考以下內部通知、公告與信件。

寄件者	湯馬斯萊力
收件者	全體學生
日期	2 月 26 日

歡迎來到史坦大學宿舍。

歡迎各位新生和同學來到我們的宿舍。我們期許今年即使不比去年好，也會和去年一樣好。我們對這棟建築做了一些整修，你們應該會非常喜歡，包括一個新的休息室，裡面有 4 張撞球桌以及一個全新的飛鏢靶。這間休息室將從早上 10 點開放到晚上 11 點，並由一家簡餐店提供各種飲料和零食供各位取用。

186 190 為了讓所有人都能度過愉快又安全的一年，制定基本行為規範相當重要。注意，違反以下規則中的 3 條，可能會導致 187 取消特權、逐出宿舍，甚至退學。此外，您也需要為您帶來的訪客的行為負責。這意味著任何您希望留下陪伴您的訪客，進出宿舍時都必須簽名。每人一次最多可有 2 名訪客。

詳細的住宿規則和住宿章程，請參閱大廳布告欄上的通知。

字彙 **memo** 備忘錄、內部通知　　**returning student** 在學生，泛指新生之外的在學生　　**café** 簡餐廳
wide range of 各式各樣的　　**set up** 建立、設立　　**ground rule** 基本法則　　**suspension** 暫停、中斷
privilege 特權　　**eviction** 逐出　　**expulsion** 開除、退學　　**by-law** 章程、細則　　**bulletin board** 公布欄

史坦大學住宿規定

1. 189B 禁止在公共空間飲酒，例如自己房間以外的場所。
2. 禁止任何非法毒品。
3. 禁止任何形式的暴力。
4. 不許毀損建築物。
5. 大樓內禁止吸菸。
6. 189B 晚上 10 點以後走廊禁止噪音。

我們希望這些規則能幫助每個人在史坦大學度過既安全又具教育意義的一年。

如果您有任何疑問，請諮詢 102 號房的 189A 住宿輔導老師湯馬斯萊力。

字彙 **common space** 公共空間　　**prohibit** 阻止、禁止　　**illegal** 非法的　　**ban** 禁止　　**violence** 暴力
tolerate 忍受、默許

May 1

Dear Mr. Smith:

This letter is being sent to formally notify you that you are being summoned to the residence committee meeting this Friday, May 6. The actions of your guests on the night of April 21 were not in line with our rules, and you, as stated in the memo, are responsible.

Allegedly, your guests were involved in drinking and fighting in the hallway of the 12th floor at 1 o'clock in the morning. Upon arrival of the resident tutor, they were disrespectful and began shoving him around. This is completely unacceptable and requires us to take action. You will have to attend this meeting on the 11th floor of Johnson Hall with the Residence Board of Directors and committee. They will decide your ultimate fate.

Sincerely,

Vanessa Burkowitz
Residence Manager

---

5 月 1 日

親愛的史密斯先生：

188 本函旨在正式通知您，您將於 5 月 6 日本週五接受召集參加住宿委員會會議。您的訪客在 4 月 21 日晚上的行為不符合校舍規定，如內部通知上所聲明的，必須由您負責。

據說您的訪客們 **189B** 與凌晨 1 點在 12 樓走廊喝酒打架一事有關。**189A** 當宿舍輔導老師抵達時，他們對老師無禮並開始推他。這是完全無法接受的事，我們必須採取行動。這次會議在強森大樓的 11 樓，您必須同宿舍董事會及委員會一起出席。**190** 他們將決定您的最終命運。

凡妮莎貝爾柯維琪
宿舍經理

字彙 **formally** 正式地、形式上　　**summon** 召集　　**in line with** 與～一致　　**as stated** 如上所示、按照規定
allegedly 據說　　**be involved in** 涉及到～　　**disrespectful** 無禮的、不敬的　　**shove around** 推來推去
unacceptable 不能接受的　　**take action** 採取行動　　**ultimate** 最終的

186. Why was the memo sent?
(A) To ask the students to complete the form
(B) To remind the students to follow the rules
(C) To remind the students to attend the committee meeting
(D) To tell the students how to get into the residence

為什麼要發送這則內部通知？
(A) 要求學生完成表格
(B) 提醒學生遵守規定
(C) 提醒學生參加委員會會議
(D) 告訴學生如何進入宿舍

正確答案為 (B)

在備忘錄第二段提到 It is very important to note that breaking three rules can result in suspension of privileges, eviction from the residence, and possibly expulsion from school.，內容再次強調規則的重要性，因此答案是 (B)。

187. In the memo, the word "suspension" in paragraph 2, line 2, is closest in meaning to
(A) delay
(B) interruption
(C) trial
(D) difficulty

內部通知第二段第二行的「suspension」與何者意義最相近？
(A) 延後
(B) 中斷
(C) 審判
(D) 困難

正確答案為 (B)

〈推測字義〉
句中「suspension」是指宿舍住宿生的特權被終止，因此答案是意為「中斷」的 (B)。

字彙　**interruption** 中斷　**trial** 審判、試驗

188. What is most likely the purpose of the letter?
(A) To announce the closure of the residence
(B) To suggest moving out of the residence
(C) To invite Mr. Smith to a community event
(D) To call Mr. Smith to a committee meeting

信件的目的是什麼？
(A) 宣布宿舍關閉
(B) 建議搬離宿舍
(C) 邀請史密斯先生參加社區活動
(D) 通知史密斯先生參加委員會會議

正確答案為 (D)

信件第一句提到 you are being summoned to the residence committee meeting.，答案是 (D)。

189. What is indicated about Mr. Smith's guests?
(A) They were approached by Thomas Reilly.
(B) They broke ground rules 3 and 5.
(C) They had visited the residence before April 21.
(D) They were supposed to leave the residence before 9.

何者陳述與史密斯先生的訪客有關？
(A) 湯馬斯萊力曾與他們接觸。
(B) 他們違反了基本規則第 3 條和第 5 條。
(C) 他們在 4 月 21 日之前拜訪過宿舍。
(D) 他們應該在 9 點前離開宿舍。

正確答案為 (A)

〈整合多篇文章資訊〉
根據信件第二段，可知訪客違反了第 1 條、第 6 條與第 3 條規定。同時帶出這些人曾與宿舍輔導老師 resident tutor 碰面。從第二篇文章可以知道 resident tutor 是萊力先生，因此答案是 (A)。

190. What can be inferred about the meeting on Friday?
(A) Whether Mr. Smith can stay in the residence will be determined.
(B) It is open to all Stein college students.
(C) It is regularly scheduled to be held on Fridays.
(D) Mr. Smith will attend the meeting to select the board members.

從星期五的會議可以推測出什麼？
(A) 將決定史密斯先生是否能繼續留在宿舍。
(B) 對史坦大學所有學生公開。
(C) 每週五定期舉辦。
(D) 史密斯先生將出席會議挑選董事會成員。

正確答案為 (A)

〈整合多篇文章資訊〉
內部通知提到 breaking three rules can result in suspension of privileges, eviction from the residence，信件提到 They will decide your ultimate fate.，綜合前後文可以得知答案是 (A)。

Questions 191-195 refer to the following Web page, flyer, and e-mail. 網頁 / 傳單 / 電子郵件

---

http://www.communityboard.com/housing

Name: Donovan Swayze

Date: January 23

I accepted a new position in Kensington and need to relocate near the downtown area before my start date on May 15. I'm seeking a simple, clean, one-bedroom rental or larger, depending on the price. A relaxing location with outdoor seating for entertaining friends or family would be a plus. I do have a car, but I'd appreciate having good access to public transportation. I have a budget of around £1,200 monthly to cover all housing costs, including utilities.

問題 191-195 參考以下網頁、傳單與電子郵件。

---

http://www.communityboard.com/housing

姓名：多納萬史偉茲

日期：1 月 23 日

⑲ 我接受了一份在肯辛頓的新工作，需要在 5 月 15 月日開始工作之前搬到市中心附近。我想租一間簡單、乾淨，有一間臥房或更大的地方，視價格而定。如果位於令人放鬆的地方並擁有戶外座位可以招待親朋好友會更好。我有一部車，但我希望地點能方便搭乘大眾交通工具。 ⑲ 我每個月的預算約 1,200 英鎊，可支付包括公共設施在內的所有住房費用。

字彙　**relaxing** 令人放鬆的　　**seating** 座席、座位　　**have good access to** 接近～　　**housing cost** 住屋費用
utility 公共設施（水電等）相關費用

RELAX AT YOUR OWN PLACE IN KENSINGTON

Be the first to rent this two-bedroom apartment upon completion of extensive renovation. This property will be move-in ready on May 1. It will feature a clean modern look, new floors throughout, and all new appliances. It is situated downtown, and students are welcome as it is less than 10 minutes by bus to Trinity University from the City Transportation office. Cats and small dogs are potentially permitted but with conditions, so please inquire. £1,200 also pays for water, sewer, garbage pick-ups, and general upkeep of the property. The electricity and natural gas will be the responsibility of the tenant. A one-time security deposit equal to one month's rent should be paid upon signing the rental agreement.

If you are interested, please email us at nancyphan@kensingtonpalace.com.

在肯辛頓找到屬於你休息的家

請成為第一個租到這間即將全面裝修完工的兩房公寓的人。 195 5 月 1 日可以搬進這間公寓。它的特色是乾淨的現代化外觀，全面鋪設新地板與全新家電。位於市中心，從城市交通中心搭公車到聖三一大學不到 10 分鐘，因此歡迎學生入住。 193 可養貓和小型狗但有附加條件，詳細內容請洽詢。 192 1,200 英鎊也包含水費、下水道、垃圾車和建築物的日常維護費。電力和天然氣由房客負擔。簽訂租賃契約時，應繳納相當於一個月租金的一次性保證金。

如果您感興趣，請寄電子郵件至 nancyphan@kensingtonpalace.com。

字彙	**throughout** 遍及；從頭到尾　　**appliance** 家電　　**situated** 位於～的　　**permit** 許可、准許
	with conditions 有條件地　　**sewer** 下水道　　**garbage pickup** 收垃圾　　**upkeep** 維修保養
	security deposit 保證金　　**rental agreement** 租賃合約

To: Nancy Phan
From: Donovan Swayze
Date: January 24
Subject: Apartment

Dear Ms. Phan:

I happened to see your rental advertisement flyer. From the description, it sounds as if it may be just what I've been looking for. I'm eager to look over the apartment, and I am going to be in Kensington all this week for work. My last day in town will be Sunday, January 30. If the place suits me, I'd want to move in the same day that it's expected to be available. The timing would be perfect! I hope to hear from you soon.

Thank you.
Donovan Swayze

收件人：潘南西
寄件人：多納萬史偉茲
日期：1 月 24 日
主旨：公寓

潘小姐您好：

我碰巧看到您的租屋廣告傳單。從敍述看來，這裡似乎是我一直尋找的房子。 ⑲⑷ ⑲⑸ 我非常想看看這間公寓，本週一整週我將會到肯辛頓出差。1 月 30 日星期日是我停留的最後一天。如果這個地方適合我，我希望在開放入住的當天就可以入住。時間配合得剛剛好！希望很快能收到您的回信。

謝謝。

多納萬史偉茲

字彙　**happen to** 偶然　**description** 說明　**suit** 適合

191. For what reason is Mr. Swayze relocating?
(A) To launch his own business
(B) To return to his hometown
(C) To work in a new place
(D) To begin his retirement

史偉茲先生搬遷的原因為何？
(A) 開創自己的事業
(B) 重返故鄉
(C) 在新的地方工作
(D) 開始他的退休生活

正確答案為 **(C)**

網頁第一句提到 I accepted a new position in Kensington and need to relocate，也就搬家的理由，因此答案是 (C)。由於使用了 accept「接受」這個字，因此 (A) 不是答案。

192. What aspect of the property does NOT match Mr. Swayze's preferences?
(A) The location
(B) The utility costs
(C) The size
(D) The available date

房子哪一點不符合史偉茲先生的喜好？
(A) 地點
(B) 公共設施費用
(C) 面積大小
(D) 可入住日期

正確答案為 **(B)**

〈整合多篇文章資訊〉
網頁最後一句史偉茲先生提到 £1,200 monthly to cover all housing costs, including utilities，但傳單上寫著 The electricity and natural gas will be the responsibility of the tenant.，因此答案是 (B)。

193. Why does Ms. Phan mention that she will need additional information?
(A) For needed changes to the décor
(B) For a tenant who does not pay a security deposit
(C) For remodeling of the apartment
(D) For someone who wants to keep a pet

為什麼潘小姐提到她會需要附加說明？
(A) 為了要改裝潢
(B) 為了不繳交保證金的承租人
(C) 為了重新裝修公寓
(D) 為了要養寵物的人

正確答案為 **(D)**

傳單上提到 Cats and small dogs are potentially permitted but with conditions, so please inquire.，此外，傳單上留下的電子郵件是 Phan 潘小姐，可知潘小姐是房仲。答案是 (D)。

194. What is the purpose of the e-mail?
(A) To agree to the terms of the contract
(B) To change the details of a residential advertisement
(C) To inquire about the features of the apartment
(D) To make an arrangement to view the property

電子郵件的目的是什麼？
(A) 同意契約條件
(B) 更改租屋廣告的細節
(C) 詢問公寓特色
(D) 安排預約看房

正確答案為 **(D)**

郵件裡提到 I'm eager to look over the apartment，等同 I hope to hear from you soon，表示希望對方跟他聯絡，答案是 (D)。

字彙　**terms of the contract** 合約條件

195. When does Mr. Swayze want to start living in the residence?　　史偉茲先生希望何時能入住？

(A) January 24　　(A) 1 月 24 日

(B) January 30　　(B) 1 月 30 日

(C) May 1　　**(C) 5 月 1 日**

(D) May 15　　(D) 5 月 15 日

正確答案為 (C)

〈整合多篇文章資訊〉

傳單上面寫著可以從 5 月 1 日開始入住，而 Swayze 史偉茲先生的郵件上寫著 I'd want to move in the same day that it's expected to be available，意思是希望能在可以入住的日期當天入住，因此答案是 (C)。

Questions 196-200 refer to the following e-mails and newsletter. 電子郵件 / 內部通訊報

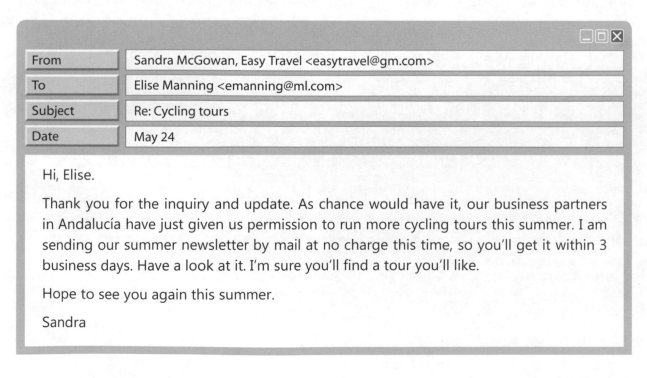

E–Mail Message

From: Elise Manning <emanning@ml.com>
To: Sandra McGowan, Easy Travel <easytravel@gm.com>
Subject: Cycling tours
Date: May 23
Attach: photo (scan #1)

Hi, Sandra.

Well, I'm ready to travel with you again to Andalucía. This time, I want to try one of your cycling tours if you plan on offering them. I'd love to have another look at Almeria Falls from a bike, but I am a beginning cyclist and am not ready for any tough tours. I would also like to take the train rather than the plane back to Valencia this year. Honestly, though, I'm not up to that long journey from Huelva! Would there be any suitable tours for me to join this summer?

I look forward to hearing from you.

Elise

P.S. I've enclosed an updated photo for my Andalucía travel visa, just so you have it on file when I apply for a tour.

From   Sandra McGowan, Easy Travel <easytravel@gm.com>
To   Elise Manning <emanning@ml.com>
Subject   Re: Cycling tours
Date   May 24

Hi, Elise.

Thank you for the inquiry and update. As chance would have it, our business partners in Andalucía have just given us permission to run more cycling tours this summer. I am sending our summer newsletter by mail at no charge this time, so you'll get it within 3 business days. Have a look at it. I'm sure you'll find a tour you'll like.

Hope to see you again this summer.

Sandra

問題 196-200 參考以下電子郵件與內部通訊報。

E-Mail Message

寄件人： 艾莉絲曼妮 <emanning@ml.com>
收件人： 山卓麥高萬，易遊網 <easytravel@gm.com>
主旨： 自行車之旅
日期： 5 月 23 日
⑲⑺ 附加檔案： 照片 (scan#1)

山卓妳好：

我已經準備好要跟妳再次同遊安達盧西亞。這次如果你們有打算推出自行車之旅的話，我想試試。我很想再騎腳踏車欣賞一次阿爾梅里亞瀑布，⑲⑼ 但我是個腳踏車新手，還沒準備好迎接困難的行程。 ⑲⑼ 今年回瓦倫西亞時，我希望能坐火車而不是飛機。不過說實話，我不怎麼喜歡從韋爾瓦出發的長途旅行！ ⑲⑹ 不知道今年夏天有沒有適合我的旅行團呢？

期待您的回信。

艾莉絲

附註： ⑲⑺ 我隨信附上了我的最新照片，好申辦我的安達盧西亞的旅遊簽證，隨信附上以便申請旅行團時需要。

字彙 **tough** 困難的　　**rather than** 寧可～也不願　　**be up to** 準備好～　　**enclose** 隨信附上

寄件人　山卓麥高萬，易遊網 <easytravel@gm.com>

收件人　艾莉絲曼妮 <emanning@ml.com>

主旨　回覆：自行車之旅

日期　5 月 24 日

您好，艾莉絲：

感謝您的查詢與更新。碰巧的是，我們在安達盧西亞的商業夥伴剛剛同意我們在夏天辦更多的自行車之旅。 ⑳⓪ 這次我會把我們的夏季社刊免費郵寄給您，這麼一來您可以在 3 個工作天之內收到。請您看一下，相信您可以找到喜歡的旅行方案。

希望今年夏天能再見到您。

山卓

字彙 **as chance would have it** 湊巧、碰巧　　**permission** 許可

EASY TRAVEL NEWSLETTER new cycling tour opportunities in Andalucía!

After celebrating our 20th anniversary at the Amalia Hotel during last week's National Day tour, EASY TRAVEL secured the rights to once again become the world's only tour company to offer cycling tours in the remote Andalucía area. Our tours are a good value at 1,100 Euros and include all meals, plane/train transport to/from Valencia, and use of mountain bikes. Note that we can now accommodate vegetarian dietary requests.

DATES AND ITINERARIES

TOUR A
July 3-8
Cadiz – Darya – Lenza – Slakotov – Cadiz
Level of difficulty: easy (exit Andalucía by plane only from Cadiz)

TOUR B
July 3-8
Cadiz – Darya – Lenza – Almeria Falls – Cadiz
Level of difficulty: challenging (exit Andalucía by plane or train from Cadiz)

TOUR C
July 3-8
Cadiz – Darya – Almeria Falls – Huelva
Level of difficulty: moderate (exit Andalucía by train from Huelva)

TOUR D
July 3-8
Cadiz – Darya – Almeria Falls – Cadiz
Level of difficulty: easy (exit Andalucía by plane or train from Cadiz)

NOTE: All of our tours rated "easy" and "moderate" offer a combination of light cycling and vehicle transport. If you are a keen cyclist, you should take a tour rated "challenging."

易遊網社刊　全新安達盧西亞單車之旅！

上週國慶之旅期間，我們在阿曼里亞飯店慶祝 (196B) 我們成立 **20** 週年，之後易遊網再次得到授權，(198C) 成為全球唯一一家在偏遠的安達盧西亞地區提供自行車之旅的旅行業者。我們的旅行商品價值 **1,100** 歐元，很划算，包含所有餐點、來回於瓦倫西亞的飛機／火車，以及登山自行車的使用費。(198D) 提醒您，我們現在也接受素食者的餐飲需求。

日期與活動日程

TOUR A
7 月 3 日－8 日
卡地斯－塔亞－蘭沙－史拉柯托夫－卡地斯
難度：簡易（從卡地斯搭飛機離開安達盧西亞）

TOUR B
7 月 3 日－8 日
卡地斯－塔亞－蘭沙－阿爾梅莉亞瀑布－卡地斯
難度：具挑戰性（從卡地斯搭飛機離開安達盧西亞）

TOUR C
7 月 3 日－8 日
卡地斯－塔亞－阿爾梅莉亞瀑布－韋爾瓦
難度：中等（從韋爾瓦搭火車離開安達盧西亞）

(195) TOUR D
7 月 3 日－8 日
卡地斯－塔亞－阿爾梅莉亞瀑布－卡地斯
(199) 難度：簡易（從卡地斯搭飛機或火車離開安達盧西亞）

注意：所有標示「簡易」和「中等」的旅行方案是安排輕度單車加車輛移動的方式。如果您是一名敏捷的自行車手，請選擇難度「具挑戰性」的旅行方案。

字彙　**secure the right to** 確保權利　**remote** 偏遠的　**a good value at** 價格划算　**transport** 移動、運送
accommodate 容納　**dietary request** 餐飲要求　**itinerary** 活動日程表　**rate** 評等、評價
moderate 溫和的、中等的　**combination** 組合　**keen** 敏捷的、敏銳的　**challenging** 具挑戰性的

196. What is the purpose of the first e-mail?
(A) To schedule a meeting
(B) To request some information
(C) To make hotel reservations
(D) To announce a change in plans

第一封電子郵件的目的是什麼？
(A) 確定開會日期
(B) 要求資訊
(C) 預約飯店
(D) 告知計畫變更

正確答案為 **(B)**

第一封信件提到 Would there be any suitable tours for me to join this summer? 是為了詢問旅遊商品，答案是 (B)。

197. Which has Ms. Manning attached with her e-mail?
(A) A project proposal
(B) A photo for visa
(C) A travel itinerary
(D) A tour application form

曼妮小姐在她的電子郵件附加了什麼檔案？
(A) 計畫提案書
(B) 簽證用照片
(C) 旅行日程表
(D) 旅行申請表

正確答案為 **(B)**

在第一封信的附註中提到 I've enclosed an updated photo，因此答案是 (B)。

198. What is NOT mentioned about EASY TRAVEL?
(A) It runs a chain of hotels.
(B) It has been operating for 20 years.
(C) It has exclusive rights to some tours.
(D) It provides riding equipment on some of its tours.

何者陳述與易遊網無關？
(A) 經營連鎖飯店。
(B) 已經營運 20 年。
(C) 部分旅遊商品擁有獨家授權。
(D) 部分旅遊商品提供騎乘工具。

正確答案為 **(A)**

在社刊第一段提到 our 20th anniversary，是指答案 (B)，once again become the world's only tour company to offer cycling tours 是指答案 (C)，use of mountain bikes 是指答案 (D)。因此沒有提到的 (A) 是正確答案。

字彙 **exclusive right** 獨家授權

199. Which tour plan is Ms. Manning most likely choose to join?
(A) Tour A
(B) Tour B
(C) Tour C
(D) Tour D

曼妮小姐可能會選哪一個旅行計畫？
(A) A 方案
(B) B 方案
(C) C 方案
(D) D 方案

正確答案為 **(D)**

〈整合多篇文章資訊〉
曼妮小姐在第一封信件裡提到希望是搭火車以及難度較低的自行車旅行，因此 Tour A 和 Tour B 不是答案。此外也提到不喜歡從韋爾瓦出發，因此她會喜歡的旅行方案是 (D) Tour D。

200. What can be implied about Ms. Manning?
(A) She has visited Huelva before.
(B) She likes to travel in winter.
(C) She works as a real estate agent.
(D) She does not subscribe to the Easy Travel newsletter.

何者說明與曼妮小姐有關？
(A) 她去過韋爾瓦。
(B) 她喜歡在冬天旅行。
(C) 她在不動產仲介公司上班。
(D) 她沒有訂閱易遊網社刊。

正確答案為 **(D)**

在第二封信件裡，山卓說這次會免費寄送社刊給曼妮小姐，代表曼妮小姐沒有定期訂閱社刊，因此答案是 (D)。

Actual Test

02

中譯與解說

♪ 單題練習版-02

	答對題數	換算分數
聽力		
閱讀		

1. 2_01 美式女聲

(A) She's putting on glasses.
(B) She's putting a sign on the wall.
(C) She's connecting a cable.
(D) She's plugging in a copier.

(A) 她正戴上眼鏡。
(B) 她把指示牌掛到牆上。
(C) 她在連接電纜線。
(D) 她在幫影印機插上電源。

正確答案為 **(C)**

出現一人獨照時應注意人物的動作與特徵。描述女子正在幫電腦接上纜線的 (C) 是答案。女子雖然有戴眼鏡，但 (A) 的 putting on 是描寫戴上的動作，因此不是答案。指示牌和影印機都沒有出現在照片，(B) 和 (D) 不是答案。

 put on 穿戴上　　**connect** 連結　　**plug in** 插上電源

2. 2_02 美式男聲

(A) They're walking alongside one another.
(B) They're waiting to cross the street.
(C) They're facing in opposite directions.
(D) They're headed into the building.

(A) 他們並肩走路。
(B) 他們等著穿越街道。
(C) 他們朝著相反方向。
(D) 他們正要進去建築物裡。

正確答案為 **(A)**

答案是男子與女子並肩一起穿越街道的 (A)。兩人並非朝著不同方向，且已經橫越到道路中間，(B) 和 (C) 都不是答案。

 alongside 並肩、在旁邊　　**one another** 彼此、互相　　**opposite** 相反的、對面的　　**head** 前往

3. 2_03 英式男聲

(A) A plane is about to land on the runway.
(B) Passengers are checking their baggage.
(C) Mechanics are working on an engine.
(D) A vehicle is parked next to an aircraft.

(A) 一架飛機即將降落在跑道上。
(B) 旅客們正在託運行李。
(C) 技師們正在修理引擎。
(D) 一輛汽車停在一架飛機旁邊。

正確答案為 (D)

看到出現多樣事物的照片，應注意聆聽各選項的主詞。停機坪的飛機旁邊有一台車輛的 (D) 是最適當的答案。飛機已經停在跑道上，因此 (A) 不是答案。照片中沒有旅客也沒有技師，因此主詞是旅客和機師的 (B) 和 (C) 都不對。

字彙 **land** 降落　**runway** 跑道　**check** 託運行李　**mechanic** 技師　**vehicle** 車輛　**aircraft** 飛機

4. 2_04 美式女聲

(A) Baked goods have been put in the boxes.
(B) The woman is tying her apron.
(C) Some baskets are being cleared.
(D) The customer is being served at the counter.

(A) 盒子裡裝了烘焙食物。
(B) 女子正在綁圍裙。
(C) 一些籃子正被清理中。
(D) 客人在櫃檯接受服務。

正確答案為 (D)

遇到有多名人物的照片，須注意每個人物的動作。麵包店員工服務客人用 serve 一字，(D) 是正確答案。圖中麵包是放在籃子裡，不是放在盒子裡，也沒有清理籃子的動作，因此 (A) 和 (C) 不是答案。此外，穿上圍裙的是男子，(B) 的主詞錯誤。

字彙 **baked** 烘焙的　**apron** 圍裙　**serve** 招待、服務、供應

5. `2_05` `英式男聲`

(A) Some armchairs are being occupied.
(B) Books have been arranged on multiple shelves.
(C) There is a lamp beneath the door.
(D) A rug has been placed on the floor.

(A) 部分扶手椅正在使用中。
(B) 書本陳列在多個書架上。
(C) 門下方有一盞燈。
(D) 地板鋪了一塊地毯。

正確答案為 **(B)**

這是典型的事物照，須注意所有物品的位置與狀態。答案是書架上有排列書籍的 (B)。事物照中沒有人物，可排除與人有關的單字以及描述動作的現在進行被動式（be being p.p.）。椅子上沒有人，照片裡沒有地毯，門與燈的位置也無相關。

字彙　**occupied** 使用中的　**multiple** 多數的　**beneath** 在～下方　**rug** 小地毯、踏墊

6. `2_06` `澳式男聲`

(A) The building is located behind an open-air market.
(B) A vendor is unfolding a large parasol.
(C) Some goods are being packed into a basket.
(D) A price tag is being attached to the box.

(A) 建築物位於露天市場後面。
(B) 一名小販正打開一把大陽傘。
(C) 一些貨物正被裝入一個籃子裡。
(D) 一個價格標籤正被貼到盒子上。

正確答案為 **(A)**

同時出現人事物的照片，除了注意人的動作，人與事物的關係以及背景也須確認。照片看到建築物位於露天市場後方，因此答案是 (A)。雖然有看起來是小販的人，但他並沒有打開陽傘，物品也沒有被裝入籃子裡，因此 (B) 和 (C) 不是答案。照片無法確認價格標籤，(D) 也不是答案。

字彙　**be located** 位於　**open-air** 戶外的、露天的　**unfold** 打開　**parasol** [ˈpærə͵sɔl] 陽傘　**attach to** 連接、使附著
　　　price tag 標價

7. 2_07 美式男聲 / 美式女聲

Where are the best available seats for tonight's play?
(A) Yes, they are the best.
(B) It's Mr. Monroe.
(C) There are some in the second row.

今晚比賽還有剩下最好的座位嗎？
(A) 是的，他們是最棒的。
(B) 是孟路先生。
(C) 第二排還有座位。

正確答案為 (C)

這是詢問座位位置的 Where 疑問句，答案是使用〈介系詞＋場所〉的 (C)。**wh 疑問詞開頭的疑問句不能用 Yes/No 回答**，因此 (A) 不是答案。(B) 是回答人物，與題目無關。

> 字彙　**available** 可購買的、可使用的　　**row**（劇院座位）排

8. 2_08 英式男聲 / 美式女聲

Isn't Mr. Chan on vacation?
(A) Actually his trip was cancelled.
(B) He's from Zurich.
(C) No, she still has some.

陳先生不是正在休假嗎？
(A) 其實他的旅行已經取消了。
(B) 他來自蘇黎士。
(C) 不，她還有一些。

正確答案為 (A)

這題是否定疑問句，要確認「是否正在休假」，答案是 (A)。(B) 提到特定都市，沒有回答到題目。(C) 的主詞與題目不一致，因此都不是答案。

> 字彙　**cancel** 取消

9. 2_09 美式女聲 / 美式男聲

When will dessert be served?
(A) Right away.
(B) The head chef.
(C) It was a week ago.

甜點什麼時候上？
(A) 馬上。
(B) 主廚。
(C) 一個禮拜以前。

正確答案為 (A)

When 疑問句問甜點什麼時候上，答案是回答時間點的 (A)。(B) 回答人，與詢問時間的題目無關。(C) 回答過去的時間點，與詢問未來時間點的題目不一致，也不是答案。**選擇 When 疑問句的答案時，時態是否一致是重要線索，作答須特別注意。**

> 字彙　**right away** 立即、馬上

10. 2_10 美式女聲 / 英式男聲

Are you satisfied with your new car?
(A) Sorry, I can't.
(B) They're very sophisticated.
(C) Yes, it runs well.

你對你的新車滿意嗎？
(A) 抱歉，我沒辦法。
(B) 它們非常精緻。
(C) 是的，它運作相當順利。

正確答案為 (C)

be 動詞疑問句問對新車的滿意度，先給予肯定回答再附加說明車子運轉狀況良好的 (C) 是答案。(A) 使用助動詞 can 回答，答非所問。(B) 使用與題目的 satisfied 發音相似的 sophisticated，是陷阱選項。

> 字彙　**be satisfied with** 對～感到滿足的　　**sophisticated** 精密的；老練的　　**run** 運作

Test 02

11. 2_11 英式男聲 / 美式男聲

Why did he leave the office so early?
(A) By taxi.
(B) Didn't he tell you?
(C) In an hour or so.

他為什麼這麼早就離開辦公室？
(A) 搭計程車。
(B) 他沒告訴你嗎？
(C) 大概一個小時。

正確答案為 (B)

Why 疑問句問提早下班的原因，反問提早下班的人沒有告知對方的 (B)。(A) 適合回答 How 疑問句，(C) 使用〈介系詞 + 時間〉，適合回答問時間的 When 疑問句。

字彙　**leave the office** 下班、離開辦公室　　**or so** 大約

12. 2_12 美式男聲 / 美式女聲

Wasn't Bruce at the sales conference in Dallas last week?
(A) Yes, I'm in excellent health.
(B) I didn't see him there.
(C) Where is Conference Room C?

布魯斯上禮拜沒去達拉斯的銷售會議嗎？
(A) 是的，我身體非常健康。
(B) 我在那裡沒看見他。
(C) 會議室 C 在哪裡？

正確答案為 (B)

否定疑問句問第三者是否有參加會議，，回答沒看見並**婉轉說明**那個人沒參加的 (B) 是答案。(A) 雖用 Yes 回答，但後面是不相關的內容。(C) 重複使用問題中的 conference，是陷阱選項。

字彙　**conference** 會議

13. 2_13 英式男聲 / 美式女聲

Who is helping Mr. Winslow schedule the night shifts?
(A) He's doing it by himself.
(B) From 9 A.M. to 6 P.M.
(C) Visitors are welcome.

是誰幫溫斯洛先生安排夜班的？
(A) 他自己。
(B) 從上午 9 點到下午 6 點。
(C) 我們歡迎訪客。

正確答案為 (A)

Who 疑問句問誰幫溫斯洛先生，答案是回答當事人自己的 (A)。(B) 回答時間點，與題目無關。(C) 故意用 visitor 回答 Who 疑問句，聽起來似乎合理，但回答內容與題目無關，因此不是答案。

字彙　**night shift** 夜班　　**by oneself** 獨自、親自

14. 2_14 美式女聲 / 美式男聲

Why isn't Helena working on the newspaper advertisement?
(A) I thought she was.
(B) On the last page.
(C) Next Thursday, I think.

海蓮娜為何沒在做報紙廣告？
(A) 我想她有。
(B) 在最後一頁。
(C) 我想是下週四。

正確答案為 (A)

Why 疑問句詢問海蓮娜不做事的理由，答案是回答她有做的 (A)。(B) 適合回答 Where 疑問句，(C) 的答案適合 When 疑問句。

字彙　**work on** 從事；對～起作用

15. `2_15` 美式女聲 / 英式男聲

The managers are taking a long time to come to a decision.
(A) I'll ask for directions.
(B) Within a month.
(C) I wonder why.

經理們正在花很多時間做出決定。
(A) 我來問路。
(B) 一個月內。
(C) 我想知道是什麼原因。

正確答案為 (C)

直述句提到經理花很多時間做出決定，婉轉表示想知道原因的 (C) 是答案。(A) 是在迴避回答時常用的〈ask+ 人〉句型，試圖用 ask 造成混淆，但答非所問。(B) 回答需要花費的時間，也是想造成混淆，但回答並不相符，因此也不是答案。

> 字彙　**come to a decision** 做出決定　　**direction** 方向、路線　　**wonder** 想知道

16. `2_16` 美式男聲 / 英式男聲

When will we release the updated software?
(A) It's too early to tell.
(B) At least six.
(C) At the auditorium.

我們何時會發布更新的軟體？
(A) 現在說還太早。
(B) 至少 6 個。
(C) 在禮堂。

正確答案為 (A)

When 疑問句問發布軟體的時間，答案是婉轉表示還無法確定的 (A)。(B) 使用數字表示個數，但缺少了時間介系詞，容易誤以為是答案，(C) 適合回答地點，因此不是答案。

> 字彙　**release** 公開、發布　　**auditorium** 禮堂

17. `2_17` 美式男聲 / 美式女聲

Should I send the contract now or after the workshop?
(A) I believe there is.
(B) Wait until after.
(C) Both of the pages.

我該現在寄出合約，還是等研討會結束後？
(A) 我相信有。
(B) 等（研討會結束）之後吧。
(C) 兩頁都是。

正確答案為 (B)

選擇疑問句問寄合約的時間，答案是等結束之後再寄的 (B)。(A) 與題目無關，(C) 使用選擇疑問句的典型答案 both 想造成混淆，但回答內容與題目無關。

> 字彙　**contract** 合約

18. `2_18` 英式男聲 / 美式女聲

I'm just reviewing the quarterly sales report.
(A) How do the figures look?
(B) Sara will be leading it.
(C) After reviewing it.

我正在看季度銷售報告。
(A) 這些數字看起來怎麼樣？
(B) 莎拉會負責。
(C) 在評估之後。

正確答案為 (A)

直述句說正在看銷售報告，反問數字看起來如何的 (A) 是答案。(B) 與題目無關，(C) 重複使用題目中的 review，但不是答案。

> 字彙　**review** 查看；評估、檢討　　**quarterly** 季度的　　**figures** 數據、數字　　**lead** 指揮、帶領

Test 02

19. 2_19 美式女聲 / 美式男聲

Would you be interested in designing our in-house newsletter?
(A) Online research.
(B) Yes, I use several.
(C) When do you need it done?

你有興趣設計我們的內部通訊嗎？
(A) 線上研究。
(B) 是的，我用好幾個。
(C) 你需要什麼時候完成？

正確答案為 (C)

助動詞疑問句問對方有無興趣參與特定業務，反問應該在何時完成任務的 (C) 是答案，表示有意願參與。(A) 與題目無關。(B) 回答 Yes，表示對提問的內容感興趣，但後面回應與題目無關，因此不是答案。

 字彙   **in-house** 內部的、公司專屬的   **newsletter** 時事通訊   **research** 研究、調查   **several** 幾個的

20. 2_20 美式女聲 / 英式男聲

How much will it cost to reprint the brochures?
(A) There should be twelve.
(B) To make it easier to print.
(C) It depends on the design.

重印冊子要花多少錢？
(A) 應該有 12 個。
(B) 為了更容易印刷。
(C) 這取決於設計。

正確答案為 (C)

How much 疑問句問費用問題，答案是**典型的迴避式回應**，表示需視設計而定的 (C)。(A) 提到數量而非費用，想造成混淆，但內容與題目無關。(B) 的答案適合用來回答問原因的 Why 疑問句。

 字彙   **brochure** （廣告）小冊子   **depend on** 視～而定、取決於～

21. 2_21 英式男聲 / 美式男聲

Which train goes to the Natural History Museum?
(A) About a mile.
(B) The green line stops there.
(C) Yes, we saved them for large events.

哪班火車開往自然歷史博物館？
(A) 約一英哩。
(B) 停在那裡的綠線。
(C) 是的，我們把它們存下來用在大型活動上。

正確答案為 (B)

Which 疑問句問哪班火車開往博物館，答案是回答特定路線的 (B)。(A) 回答距離，與題目無關。(C) 是 Yes/No 答句，不適用於疑問詞引導的疑問句。

22. 2_22 美式男聲 / 美式女聲

This eatery has a wireless Internet connection, doesn't it?
(A) A reservation for three.
(B) Of course, and it's free for customers.
(C) In a connecting flight.

這間餐飲店有無線網路，不是嗎？
(A) 3 個人的訂位。
(B) 當然有，顧客可以免費使用。
(C) 在轉機航班上。

正確答案為 (B)

這題是確認餐廳是否有無線網路服務的附加問句，答案是用 Of course 給予肯定答覆並附帶說明免費的 (B)。(A) 使用與題目的 eatery「餐飲店」有關的 reservation，但回答訂位人數與題目無關。(C) 重複使用題目的 connection 來誤導作答，內容也與題目無關。

字彙   **eatery** 餐飲店、飯館   **wireless Internet connection** 無線網路連接   **connection flight** 轉接班機

23. `2_23` 英式男聲 / 美式女聲

What are you bringing in to the celebration event?
(A) I won't be attending.
(B) I had some already.
(C) Yes, I went there last year.

你會帶什麼來參加慶祝會？
(A) 我不會參加。
(B) 我已經有一些了。
(C) 是的，我去年去過。

正確答案為 (A)

What 疑問句問對方會帶什麼物品去活動會場，**間接表示不會出席活動的 (A) 是答案**。(B) 的回答與題目無關，(C) 使用 Yes/No 答句，不適合回應由 wh 疑問詞引導的疑問句，因此都不是答案。

字彙 celebration 慶祝   attend 出席

24. `2_24` 美式女聲 / 美式男聲

Who is the director of your firm?
(A) You'll be meeting her at noon.
(B) You're welcome to sit here.
(C) Herbert Foster will order it.

你公司的主管是誰？
(A) 你會在中午見到她。
(B) 你可以坐在這裡。
(C) 赫伯佛斯特會訂。

正確答案為 (A)

Who 疑問句問公司主管是誰，回答在中午就會見到那個人的 (A) 是答案。(B) 適合回應徵詢同意的問句，與題目無關。(C) 雖然提到人名，看似可以回答 Who 疑問句，但由於內容與題目無關，也不是答案。**Who 疑問句容易出現以「姓名、職位」作為回應的陷阱選項，須先掌握題目再進行作答。**

字彙 director 總監、主管

25. `2_25` 美式女聲 / 英式男聲

Did you send them the notice about the project timeline?
(A) I'll go look for a projector.
(B) I thought Rio was going to do it.
(C) To save money.

你把企劃時程表通知寄給他們了嗎？
(A) 我會去找一台投影機。
(B) 我以為里歐會做。
(C) 為了省錢。

正確答案為 (B)

助動詞開頭的疑問句問是否寄出通知，**答案是間接回應以為是第三者負責的 (B)**。(A) 使用與題目中 project 發音類似的 projector「投影機」造成混淆，但回應內容與題目無關。(C) 說明原因，適合回應 Why 疑問句。

字彙 notice 公告、通知   timeline 時間表   save 節省、儲蓄

26. `2_26` 美式男聲 / 英式男聲

Would you like some help with the presentation or can you finish it by yourself?
(A) I'm almost done.
(B) She is a good speaker.
(C) Yes, I can see it.

你的報告需要幫忙嗎，還是你可以獨自完成？
(A) 我快完成了。
(B) 她是名很棒的講者。
(C) 是的，我看得到。

正確答案為 (A)

本題是選擇疑問句，問需要幫忙還是可以獨自完成，答案是表示幾乎快完成的 (A)，婉轉說明自己來就可以。(B) 故意使用與題目 presentation 相關的 speaker 試圖誤導，(C) 與題目完全無關，因此都不是答案。

字彙 presentation 上台報告

Test 02

27. 2_27 美式男聲 / 美式女聲

How can I change the password?
(A) I don't have any change, sorry.
(B) Chris will show you later.
(C) Whenever you like.

我該如何變更密碼？
(A) 我沒有任何零錢，很抱歉。
(B) 克里斯等等會跟你說。
(C) 任何時間都可以。

正確答案為 (B)

How 疑問句問方法，答案是表示另一個人會告知的 (B)。**回答第三者會告知是在 How 疑問句題目中常見的婉轉回應。**(A) 重複使用題目中的 change「更改」，利用同音異義的 change「零錢」來造成混淆，作答應留意。(C) 的回答與題目不相關。

 字彙　**password** 密碼

---

28. 2_28 英式男聲 / 美式女聲

Let's try the new deli that opened near the office.
(A) I've already eaten lunch.
(B) The office is closed today.
(C) It's by the copier.

我們去試看看公司附近新開的那家熟食店吧。
(A) 我已經吃過午餐了。
(B) 辦公室今天不營業。
(C) 在影印機旁邊。

正確答案為 (A)

說話者提議去吃辦公室附近新開的一家熟食店，**答案是間接回答已經吃過午餐作為拒絕的 (A)**。(B) 重複題目中的 office，也用了從 open 會聯想到的 close，企圖造成混淆，但回答內容與題目無關。(C) 也是和題目無關的回應。

字彙　**deli** 是 **delicatessen** 的縮寫，指販售三明治、潛艇堡等速食料理的熟食店

---

29. 2_29 美式女聲 / 美式男聲

Where did you learn to make such delicious meatballs?
(A) I'd like the pasta, thanks.
(B) My aunt showed me her recipe.
(C) I saw you at the restaurant.

你在哪裡學會做這麼好吃的肉丸子的？
(A) 義大利麵，謝謝。
(B) 我阿姨給我看她的食譜。
(C) 我在餐廳看到你。

正確答案為 (B)

Where 疑問句問對方在哪裡學會這道料理，答案不是地點而是提到資訊來源的 (B)。**Where 疑問句除了用地點回應，也可以回答資訊來源的人或職稱。**(A) 用了與題目 meatballs 有關的 pasta 回應，但內容與題目無關，(C) 雖然回答地點，但內容與題目無關，因此都不是答案。

---

30. 2_30 美式女聲 / 英式男聲

Do you know whether our Monday meeting is still on?
(A) No, it's been called off.
(B) Because she didn't have enough time.
(C) That doesn't work for me.

週一會議是否仍然照計畫進行？
(A) 不，已經取消了。
(B) 因為她沒時間。
(C) 那對我沒用。

正確答案為 (A)

間接疑問句問對方週一會議還開不開，答案是用 No 給予否定回應並附帶說明已經取消的 (A)。(B) 回答內容與問題無關，(C) 的回應雖然相當於否定句，但與題目完全無關。

字彙　**call off** 取消、撤回

31. 2_31 美式男聲 / 英式男聲

Because of the rain, we've rescheduled the company picnic for next Friday instead.
(A) It sure was a lot of fun.
(B) Okay, I'll change the date on my calendar.
(C) I loved meeting everyone there.

因為下雨的緣故，公司野餐計畫改到下星期五。
(A) 這真的很有趣。
(B) 好的，我會更改我行事曆上的日期。
(C) 我喜歡在那裡見到每個人。

正確答案為 (B)

直述句告知對方野餐日期因天氣因素而改期，答案是表示自己接下來會在月曆上註明的 (B)。(A) 的時態與題目不一致，內容也沒有任何關連。(C) 提到很高興見到面，但使用過去式，與題目時態不符。

字彙　**reschedule** 重新安排　　**instead** 作為替代

2_32-34 美式女聲 / 英式男聲

Questions 32-34 refer to the following conversation.

W: Excuse me. I really like the pattern on this scarf. Are there any other color variations in the same style? I looked, but I didn't see any on display.

M: Yes, actually, there are several color combinations that all have the same pattern. But I'm afraid we've already sold out of nearly everything from our original order. We have more on the way, though. The complete selection will be back in stock by the end of this week.

W: Great. Well, I guess I'll go ahead and take this one today. I'll stop by again this weekend to look at the others once they've arrived.

M: That sounds reasonable. I'll wrap it up for you.

問題 32-34 參考以下對話。

女：不好意思。32 我很喜歡這條圍巾上的圖案。這種圖案還有出別的顏色嗎？我看了展示品，都沒有看到。

男：是的，這個圖案我們有出好幾種顏色。但我們初期訂的貨幾乎都賣完了。33 不過我們有追加貨品，正在運來的路上。齊全的款式將在本週末到貨。

女：太好了。34 我今天就先買這個。等這個週末商品到貨，我會再過來看看。

男：聽起來不錯。我幫您包起來。

字彙 **variation** 變化、差異 **pattern** 圖案、圖樣 **combination** 組合 **though** 然而、不過 **selection** 選擇、挑選 **in stock** 在貨的、有庫存的 **go ahead** 著手進行；前進 **stop by** 順道拜訪 **reasonable** 合理的 **wrap** 包裝

32. Who is the woman talking to?
(A) A graphic designer
(B) A patron
(C) A sales clerk
(D) An interior decorator

女子正在和誰交談？
(A) 平面設計師
(B) 老顧客
(C) 售貨員
(D) 室內設計師

正確答案為 **(C)**

〈掌握基本資訊－職業〉
題目問說話者的職業，是屬於基本資訊，通常在對話開始就會出現。女子第一句話說她喜歡圍巾的樣式，並詢問有沒有其他顏色，由此可知男子是售貨員，答案是 (C)。

字彙　**patron** 老主顧　　**interior decorator** 室內設計師

33. What does the man expect to happen by the end of this week?
(A) An order will be placed.
(B) A range of new patterns will be designed.
(C) Some supplies will run out.
(D) Additional merchandise will be delivered.

男子預計這週末會發生什麼事？
(A) 會有訂單。
(B) 一系列新的圖案將被設計出來。
(C) 補給品將會用完。
(D) 追加商品將被送來。

正確答案為 **(D)**

〈注意細節－特定事項〉
應掌握關鍵字 by the end of this week 提到本週末的地方尋找線索。對話中段，男子提到追加商品正在運來的路上，所有商品在週末會到齊，答案是 (D)。

字彙　**supplies**（常用複數）補給品、日用品　　**merchandise** 商品　　**deliver** 運送、投遞

34. What will the woman probably do next?
(A) Visit a different store
(B) Make a purchase
(C) Call a regular customer
(D) Look at color samples

女子接下來很可能會做什麼？
(A) 逛另一家商店
(B) 買下商品
(C) 打電話給一名常客
(D) 看顏色樣品

正確答案為 **(B)**

〈注意細節－未來〉
題目問未來會發生的事情，可以在對話後半段找到線索。女子最後一段話表示週末會再過來看看，今天先只買眼前的商品，答案是 (B)。

字彙　**make a purchase** 購物　　**regular customer** 常客

2_35-37 [美式男聲 / 美式女聲]

Questions 35-37 refer to the following conversation.

M: Hi, Nancy. This is Alex Park from the sales department. Has production started on the jerseys for the Brighton hockey team yet?

W: No, it's not scheduled to start until tomorrow. We need to finish making the new uniforms for Elias Diner first. Why do you ask?

M: A team representative called me this morning and asked if it was too late to alter the design. He sent me the new specifications by e-mail, and the changes look pretty minor.

W: Well, go ahead and forward the new specifications to me right away. I'll take a look and see whether we can make the changes without affecting the production schedule.

問題 35-37 參考以下對話。

男：喂，南西，我是銷售部的艾力克斯帕克。㉟ 布萊頓曲棍球隊的球衣開始生產了嗎？

女：還沒，預定明天才開始。我們必須先完成製作伊力絲餐館的新制服。你為什麼問這個？

男：㊱ 今天早上球隊代表打電話給我，問我還來不來得及修改設計。他用電子郵件寄給我新的規格，要改的部份看起來很少。

女：嗯，㊲ 那現在就把新規格轉寄給我。我看看是否可以在不影響生產時程的情況下更改。

字彙　**jersey** 球衣、隊服　**not A until B** 直到 B 才 A　**representative** 代表人　**alter** 更改、修改　**specification** 規格　**minor** 少的；次要的　**forward** 轉寄、轉達　**affect** 影響

35. Where do the speakers probably work? 　說話者可能在哪裡工作？

(A) **At a manufacturing company** 　(A) **製造公司**
(B) At a hockey field 　(B) 曲棍球場
(C) At a department store 　(C) 百貨公司
(D) At a storage facility 　(D) 倉儲設施

正確答案為 **(A)**

〈掌握基本資訊－地點〉

題目問說話者的工作地點，可以在**對話開頭找到答案**。男子第一段話說想確認衣服是否開始製作，由此可知這裡是製造衣服的工廠，最適當的答案是 (A)。

字彙　**manufacturing** 製造業　**storage** 儲藏　**facility** 設施

36. According to the man, what did a representative ask to do? 　根據男子所言，代表人要求做什麼？

(A) Increase an order 　(A) 增加訂貨量
(B) Delay a shipment 　(B) 延後送貨
(C) **Revise a design** 　(C) **更改設計**
(D) Reschedule a visit 　(D) 重新安排拜訪日程

正確答案為 **(C)**

〈注意細節－特定事項〉

掌握題目關鍵字 representative「代表人」，並從男子提到此字的段落尋找線索。男子第二段話提到球隊代表打電話來要求變更設計，答案是 (C)。

換句話說 **alter the design** 修改設計 → **revise a design** 變更設計

37. What does the woman want the man to do? 　女子要男子做什麼？

(A) Draft another design 　(A) 另起草設計
(B) Arrange a meeting 　(B) 安排會面
(C) **Send some information** 　(C) **寄發資訊**
(D) Change a plan 　(D) 改變計畫

正確答案為 **(C)**

〈注意細節－請求〉

題目問女子對男子提出什麼要求，須在女子所說的話找線索。女子最後要求對方轉寄設計變更說明給她，答案是 (C)。

換句話說 **forward the specifications** 轉寄規格 → **send some information** 寄發資訊

字彙　**draft** 草擬；草稿

2_38-40 · 英式男聲 / 美式女聲

Questions 38-40 refer to the following conversation.

M: Hi, Ms. Kammerick. My name is Brad Simon and I'm from the Westside Theater in London. I enjoyed your company's performance of *The Phantom of the Opera* last month.

W: Thanks for coming. I've produced several plays in London in the past. I'm sure we've met before.

M: Well... I'm not sure because I recently moved there from Manchester. By the way, I'd like to invite you to London with your cast and crew. The Westside Theater is very interested in hosting you for two or three months.

W: That sounds wonderful but we've just made an agreement with a theater in New York. Our schedule is full until the end of this year.

問題 38-40 參考以下對話。

男：您好，卡麥理可小姐，我是布萊德西蒙，來自倫敦西區劇院。㊳ 上個月我欣賞了貴公司《歌劇魅影》的演出。

女：感謝蒞臨觀賞。㊳ 我過去曾在倫敦製作過幾部戲，我相信我們以前見過面。

男：嗯……㊴ 我不確定，因為我最近才從曼徹斯特搬到那裡。順道一提，我想邀請您和您的劇組人員到倫敦來。西區劇院想在這兩三個月請你們主演。

女：㊵ 聽起來很不錯，但我們已經和紐約一家劇院簽訂合約。我們的行程到今年年底已經滿檔。

字彙 **cast** 卡司、演員群　**crew** 工作人員　**be interested in** 感興趣、有意願　**host** 主演；款待

38. Who most likely is Ms. Kammerick?
(A) An actor
(B) A writer
(C) A producer
(D) A critic

卡麥理可小姐很可能是誰？
(A) 演員
(B) 作家
(C) 製作人
(D) 評論家

正確答案為 (C)

〈注意細節－特定內容〉
題目關鍵字是人名，就仔細聆聽該名字。第一句話男子提到此人名並問候對方，可知 Kammerick 卡麥理可小姐就是對話中的女子，男子接著說自己看過女子公司所製作的《歌劇魅影》，再加上女子說自己過去多次在倫敦製作影片，可知答案是 (C)。

字彙 | **critic** 評論家

39. What does Mr. Simon say about London?
(A) He will meet a publisher there.
(B) He went to university there.
(C) He recently moved there.
(D) He used to work there.

西蒙先生說倫敦如何？
(A) 他會在那裡跟一名出版商碰面。
(B) 他在那裡讀大學。
(C) 他最近搬到那裡。
(D) 他之前在那裡工作。

正確答案為 (C)

〈注意細節－特定內容〉
須注意聆聽 Mr. Simon 西蒙先生和 London 倫敦兩個關鍵字。男子第一段話自我介紹，說自己是來自倫敦的 Simon。之後男子提到最近才從 Manchester 曼徹斯特搬到倫敦，因此答案是 (C)。

40. What problem does Ms. Kammerick mention?
(A) The cost of living is too high.
(B) Her schedule is full.
(C) The theater is fully booked.
(D) She cannot meet a deadline.

卡麥理可小姐提到什麼問題點？
(A) 生活費太高。
(B) 她的行程滿檔。
(C) 劇院已經客滿。
(D) 她無法按時完成任務。

正確答案為 (B)

〈注意細節－問題點〉
從第 38 題可以知道卡麥理可小姐是對話中的女子，因此必須注意女子說話的內容。針對男子的提議，女子在最後表示，今年底前的行程都已經排滿，因而拒絕男子的邀請，所以答案是 (B)。**對話出現轉折語氣 but、however、actually、unfortunately 的地方常是重要的出題線索，須留意。**

2_41-43 美式女聲 / 美式男聲

Questions 41-43 refer to the following conversation.

W: Frank, I got your e-mail with the materials you've created for our presentation to the board of directors next week. You asked me to get back to you with my opinions. Do you have a moment now?

M: Sure, Annabel. I've been looking forward to hearing from you.

W: Well, for the most part, everything looks good. But I would recommend including some graphs.

M: Oh, that sounds good. What type of graphs?

W: I'll leave that to you. Whatever you think will make it easier to understand the figures we'll be reporting.

問題 41-43 參考以下對話。

女：法蘭克，我收到你的電子郵件了，裡面有你幫我們在下週董事會上報告做的素材。㊶你要我把我的意見告訴你。你現在有空嗎？

男：當然，安娜貝爾。我一直在等妳的回覆。

女：嗯，大部分看起來都很好。㊷但我會建議再添加一些圖表。

男：噢，聽起來很棒。哪種圖表？

女：交給你了。㊸任何讓報告數據更容易理解的圖表都可以。

字彙　**material** 材料、素材　**board of directors** 董事會　**opinion** 意見　**look forward to** 期待
recommend 推薦　**graph** 圖表

41. What did the man ask the woman to do in his e-mail?　男子在電子郵件裡要求女子做什麼？
(A) Confirm the length of a presentation　(A) 確認演講長度
(B) Provide some feedback on his work　**(B) 對他的工作提供回饋意見**
(C) Offer some presentation materials　(C) 提供演講素材
(D) Contact the board of directors　(D) 聯絡董事會

正確答案為 **(B)**

〈注意細節－請求〉
本題應掌握 e-mail 這個關鍵字，仔細聽其前後文的內容。題目出現 ask 一字，是詢問男子要求的事情，答案通常會出現在男子說的話。但是這個題目的關鍵字 e-mail 是女子所說的，須多加留意。女子表示已經看過男子寄的電子郵件，並提到男子需要女子回覆意見，因此答案是 (B)。

換句話說 **get back to you with my opinions** 把意見告訴你 → **provide some feedback** 提供回饋意見

42. What does the woman suggest?　女子的建議為何？
(A) Contacting a coworker　(A) 聯絡一名同事
(B) Increasing a budget　(B) 增加預算
(C) Adding a visual aid　**(C) 添加視覺輔助圖表**
(D) Shortening a document　(D) 精簡內容

正確答案為 **(C)**

〈注意細節－提議〉
題目問女子提議的內容，應注意女子說的話。女子在第二段話建議添加圖表，答案是 (C)。

換句話說 **including some graphs** 包含圖表 → **adding visual aid** 增加視覺資料

字彙 **budget** 預算　**visual aid**（圖表等）視覺輔助

43. What does the woman mean when she says, "I'll leave that to you"?　女子說「交給你了」是什麼意思？
(A) She plans to give an item to the man.　(A) 她打算給男子一樣產品。
(B) She does not intend to stay for much longer.　(B) 她不打算再待下去。
(C) She will not accompany the man.　(C) 她不會與男子同行。
(D) She will allow the man to make a decision.　**(D) 她讓男子做決定。**

正確答案為 **(D)**

〈關鍵句－說話者意圖〉
本題須綜合女子相關反應與前後文脈絡才能回答。男子問女子應加上哪種圖表後，女子才說這句話，並附加說明無論是哪種圖表，重點是能幫助理解報告中的數字即可。因此答案是讓男子自行決定的 (D)。

字彙 **accompany** 陪同、伴隨

2_44-46 英式男聲 / 美式女聲

Questions 44-46 refer to the following conversation.

M: Hi, Ashley. Did you order the additional boxes? We're almost out of stock.

W: I was going to, but I noticed that the price has gone up by about 20% from the last time we ordered.

M: Oh, is that true?

W: Yeah. And the discount rates for bulk orders have gone down as well.

M: We can't afford to spend more than what we're paying now. We should definitely start looking for a different company.

W: I think so. I'll get some price estimates from several suppliers and make a list. Let's think about all the possibilities.

問題 44-46 參考以下對話。

男：嗨，艾希莉，妳有加訂箱子嗎？我們庫存快沒了。

女：我打算要訂，44 但是我發現價格比我們上次訂貨時漲了 20%。

男：噢，真的嗎？

女：是的，而且大宗訂單的折扣也下降了。

男：44 我們沒辦法負擔比現在更高的金額。45 我們要開始找其他廠商。

女：我也這麼認為。46 我會向幾家供應商要估價，再做成清單。我們要考慮所有的可能性。

字彙	additional 額外的　　out of stock 無庫存、缺貨　　bulk order 大宗訂單、大量訂購　　afford 買得起、負擔得起
	definitely 明確地、肯定地　　estimate 估價單　　supplier 供應商

44. What are the speakers concerned about?
(A) Defective items
(B) Wrong orders
(C) Lack of staff
(D) Rising expenses

説話者擔心什麼？
(A) 不良品
(B) 錯誤訂單
(C) 員工短缺
(D) 費用增加

正確答案為 **(D)**

〈注意細節－擔心〉

男子問目前訂購狀況時，女子表示本來打算訂購，但因價格上漲而作罷，在説明理由之後，男子也表示無法再增加支出金額，因此答案是 (D)。

字彙　**defective** 有缺損的

45. What does the man suggest?
(A) Changing a supplier
(B) Checking the order form
(C) Reporting to a manager
(D) Discussing a problem

男子建議什麼？
(A) 更換供應商
(B) 檢查訂單
(C) 向經理報告
(D) 討論問題

正確答案為 **(A)**

〈注意細節－提議〉

題目詢問男子提出何種建議，須從男子談話中尋找答案。男子第二段話提到目前交易公司提高價格，就應該尋找其他公司合作，因此答案是 (A)。

換句話說 **looking for a different company** 找一家不同的廠商 → **changing a supplier** 更換供應商

46. What does the woman decide to do?
(A) Cancel orders
(B) Work overtime
(C) Get some price quotes
(D) Help her coworker

女子決定做什麼？
(A) 取消訂單
(B) 超時工作
(C) 取得估價單
(D) 幫忙她的同事

正確答案為 **(C)**

〈注意細節－特定事項〉

題目是有關女子的決定，須從女子的談話內容尋找答案。女子最後談話時說會向幾家供應商索取估價單，再做成清單，因此答案是 (C)。

換句話說 **get some price estimates** 索取估價單 → **get some price quote** 取得估價單

字彙　**price quote** 報價單

Questions 47-49 refer to the following conversation.

W: Excuse me. I'm looking for journals on agriculture. Could you tell me where they are?

M: Ah, sure. They're in aisle 2, next to the sale items display. Unfortunately, our selection is quite small at the moment; the publisher has been having trouble with shipping.

W: I see. I suppose that could be a result of the terrible weather in the East Coast.

M: That's probably the case. Anyway, we hope to be getting more journals next week. If you'd like to leave your name and number, I can give you a call as soon as they come in.

問題 47-49 參考以下對話。

女： 打擾了。我正在找農業方面的期刊，你能告訴我在哪裡嗎？

男： 當然。它們在 2 號走道，特價品展示區旁邊。遺憾的是，47 目前的選擇非常少，出版商在送貨時出了狀況。

女： 原來如此。48 我想那可能是東岸的惡劣氣候造成的。

男： 可能是這樣。不管怎樣，我們希望能在下週拿到更多的期刊。49 如果您留下姓名與電話，一到貨我就可以打電話通知您。

字彙 **journal** 期刊、學術刊物　**agriculture** 農業　**aisle** 走道　**publisher** 出版商　**ship** 運送、送貨　**suppose** 猜想、認為

47. What is the problem?
(A) The store is under construction.
(B) Only a few items are available.
(C) Some equipment is not working.
(D) A sale has just ended.

問題點是什麼？
(A) 商店正在施工。
(B) 只有少數商品有貨。
(C) 有些設備壞了。
(D) 特價活動剛結束。

正確答案為 (B)

〈注意細節－問題點〉

此題型是詢問某個問題點，需要注意細節，通常在對話前半段就會提供相關線索。男子對正在找期刊的女子說明所在位置之後，也告知目前商品運送出現問題導致顧客選項不多，因此答案是 (B)。

換句話說 **selection is quiet small** 選擇相當少 → **only a few items are available** 只提供一些商品

字彙 **under construction** 施工中

48. Why does the man say, "That's probably the case"?
(A) He agrees with the woman.
(B) He is searching in a display case.
(C) He hopes the weather will clear up.
(D) He is offering his idea.

為什麼男子說「可能是這樣」？
(A) 他同意女子的看法。
(B) 他正在一個陳列櫃上找東西。
(C) 他希望天氣好轉。
(D) 他提出他的想法。

正確答案為 (A)

〈關鍵句－說話者意圖〉

題目問說話者的意圖，應掌握前後文脈絡才能得出男子說話的本意。女子最後說出版商運送出問題應是東岸惡劣氣候造成，隨後男子表示認同，因此答案是 (A)。

字彙 **agree with** 同意～看法　　**the weather clears up** 天氣好轉

49. Why does the man request the woman's personal information?
(A) To give her details of another location
(B) To tell her about upcoming sale
(C) To offer a membership discount
(D) To notify her when more stock arrives

為什麼男子要求女子提供個人資料？
(A) 要告訴她另一個地點的細節
(B) 要告訴她即將舉行的特價活動
(C) 要給她會員折扣
(D) 當更多商品抵達時能通知她

正確答案為 (D)

〈注意細節－特定事項〉

掌握 personal information 這個關鍵字，在同義詞出現的地方尋找線索。對話最後男子說若留下姓名與電話，期刊一到就會電話通知，因此答案是 (D)。

換句話說 **name and number** 姓名與電話號碼 → **personal information** 個人資料

字彙 **notify** 通知

2_50-52 美式女聲 / 英式女聲 / 英式男聲

Questions 50-52 refer to the following conversation with three speakers.

W1: Hey, Charles. I just heard about your art exhibition opening this weekend. You must be excited.

W2: What's this? Charles, I didn't know you were an artist.

M: It's just a hobby, really. In fact, this will be my first time to exhibit my art in public.

W1: Are you nervous?

M: I hate to admit it, but I'm very nervous.

W2: What type of artwork do you do? Paintings or photographs?

M: No, sculpture. I make all my pieces out of recycled material.

W2: Sounds very interesting.

M: Why don't you guys come to the gallery and check it out? It'd be nice to have some coworkers show up to give me some emotional support.

問題 50-52 參考以下三人對話。

女 1： 嗨！查理斯，我剛聽說你的藝術展在本週末開幕。你一定很興奮。

女 2： 什麼？查理斯，我不知道你是個藝術家。

男： 只是興趣，真的。(50) 事實上這是我第一次公開展出我的藝術創作。

女 1： 你會緊張嗎？

男： 我很不想承認，但我真的很緊張。

女 2： 你創作的藝術品是什麼種類？繪畫還是攝影？

男： 不，是雕塑。(51) 我的所有作品都是用再生材料製成。

女 2： 聽起來很有意思。

男： (52) 妳們何不來藝廊看看呢？有同事來給我情感上的支持是件很棒的事。

字彙 **exhibition** 展覽　**exhibit** 展出　**in public** 公開　**admit** 承認　**sculpture** 雕塑　**recycle** 回收利用、再生　**gallery** 畫廊　**emotional** 情感上的

50. What is the man nervous about?
(A) Making a public speech
(B) Showing his work
(C) Entering a competition
(D) Leading a discussion

男子在緊張什麼？
(A) 公開演講
(B) 展示作品
(C) 參加比賽
(D) 帶領討論

正確答案為 (B)

〈注意細節－特定事項〉

男子感到緊張的原因須從男子的談話當中找答案。男子說這是他第一次舉辦作品展時，女 1 問他是否緊張，他表示很緊張，答案是 (B)。

換句話說 exhibit one's art in public 公開展示藝術創作 → show one's work 展示作品

51. What does the man say about his work?
(A) It is made from recycled material.
(B) It is being sold at an auction.
(C) It consists mainly of paintings.
(D) It has recently won an award.

男子怎麼說他的作品？
(A) 由再生材料製成。
(B) 在拍賣會上販售。
(C) 主要由繪畫組成。
(D) 最近獲獎。

正確答案為 (A)

〈注意細節－提及內容〉

必須注意聆聽男子對於自己作品的說明。男子說自己創作的是雕塑，而且所有作品都是利用再生材料製成，答案是 (A)。

字彙 **auction** 拍賣 **award** 獎項

52. What does the man suggest the women do?
(A) Collaborate on a design
(B) Support an artist
(C) Attend an exhibition
(D) Cast a vote online

男子建議女子們做什麼？
(A) 合作一項設計
(B) 支持藝術家
(C) 參加展覽
(D) 上網投票

正確答案為 (C)

〈注意細節－提議〉

對於男子向兩個女子做出的提議，應從男子的談話內容尋找線索。在談話的最後，男子建議她們可以直接到場參觀展覽，因此答案是 (C)。

字彙 **collaborate** 合作 **cast a vote** 投票

2_53-55 美式女聲 / 美式男聲

Questions 53-55 refer to the following conversation.

W: Welcome back to the lunch hour show here on Radio Five. Today we're talking with documentary filmmaker Ernest Schmidt, who's just come back from an excursion to Congo. Tell us about that, Ernest.

M: It was a thrilling experience. I went rafting on the River Ivindo. It's even more thrilling than any other places. Of course, my favorite thing was interacting with the locals, although it can be challenging when few people speak English.

W: Sounds interesting! Can you tell us little more about what's in your upcoming film?

M: Well, it'll feature a lot of interviews, mostly with very low-income people. There's still a lot of poverty even as the government and economy improve.

問題 53-55 參考以下對話。

女： 歡迎回到第五廣播電台的午餐時間節目。(53) 今天我們要採訪的是紀錄片導演厄尼斯特施密特，(54) 他才剛從剛果旅行回來。和我們談談這趟旅行吧，厄尼斯特。

男： 那是一次激動人心的經驗。我去伊溫多河泛舟。這比去任何地方都還刺激。當然，我最喜歡的事情是和當地人交流，儘管很少人說英文這件事並不容易。

女： 聽起來很有趣！你能跟我們多談談關於你即將上映的電影嗎？

男： 嗯，(55) 電影特色是有大量的採訪，受訪者多半是低收入者。即使政府和經濟有所改善，仍然存在許多貧窮人口。

字彙
documentary 紀錄片 **filmmaker** 電影製作人或公司 **excursion**（團體）短程出遊、遠足
thrilling 令人興奮的、激勵人心的 **challenging** 有挑戰性的、困難的 **upcoming** 即將到來的
feature 以～為特色 **interview** 訪談 **low-income** 低收入的 **poverty** 貧窮 **improve** 改善

53. What type of business does the man work for?　男子從事什麼工作？
(A) A tour service　(A) 旅遊服務
(B) A film production company　**(B) 影片製作公司**
(C) A radio station　(C) 廣播電台
(D) An airline company　(D) 航空公司

正確答案為 **(B)**

〈掌握基本資訊－地點〉

題目問的是男子**工作的地點，應注意開頭的談話內容**。女子一開始介紹男子，並預告今天將與 documentary filmmaker 紀錄片導演 Ernest Schmidt 厄尼斯特施密特在節目中聊聊，答案是 (B)。

54. What has the man recently done?　男子最近做了什麼？
(A) Written a book　(A) 寫一本書
(B) Attended an international seminar　(B) 參加一場國際研討會
(C) Returned for a trip abroad　**(C) 從國外旅遊返國**
(D) Started his own business　(D) 開始自己的事業

正確答案為 **(C)**

〈注意細節－特定事項〉

男子最近做的事情可以從女子介紹男子時的談話內容尋找線索。應掌握關鍵字 recently，並從同義字出現的部份找答案。女子使用 just 和現在完成式進行說明的地方就是答案所在。女子說 who's just come back from an excursion to Congo「男子才剛從剛果旅行回來」，答案是 (C)。

換句話說 **come back from an excursion to Congo** 從剛果旅行回來 → **return for a trip abroad** 從國外旅行回來

字彙 **seminar** 研討會

55. Who does the man say he talked with?　男子說他和誰談話？
(A) Volunteer aid workers　(A) 志願救援人員
(B) Government officials　(B) 政府官員
(C) Many poor people　**(C) 許多窮人**
(D) Newspaper journalists　(D) 新聞記者

正確答案為 **(C)**

〈注意細節－特定事項〉

男子最後談話時提到紀錄片大部份的受訪者是低收入戶，答案是 (C)。

換句話說 **low-income people** 低所得的人 → **poor people** 貧窮的人

2_56-58 英式男聲 / 美式女聲 / 澳式男聲

Questions 56-58 refer to the following conversation with three speakers.

M1: We need to get the rest of these packages sent out today. I'll check that each box's contents are correct, and Melissa, you tape them shut.

W: Okay, I'll get the tape.

M1: Jack, will you check the address labels?

M2: You bet. I have the final list right here.

W: What time does the post office close today?

M1: At 6. Don't worry, we've still got two hours until then, and we only have 6 more boxes to do. We've got lots of time.

M2: Brian, we have to finish more than 6. There's a big stack of them over there too.

W: Really? Let's get on with it, then.

問題 56-58 參考以下三人對話。

男1： 56 我們得在今天把剩下的包裹寄出去。我會檢查每個盒子裡的東西是否正確，玫麗莎，妳用膠帶把它們封起來。

女： 好的，我去拿膠帶。

男1： 傑克，請你檢查一下地址標籤好嗎？

男2： 當然可以。我這裡有最後底定的清單。

女： 今天郵局幾點結束營業？

男1： 57 6點。別擔心，在那之前我們還有兩個小時的時間，而且我們只剩下 6 個箱子要處理。時間很充裕。

男2： 布萊恩，58 我們要完成的不只 6 個，那邊還有一堆。

女： 真的嗎？那我們開始吧。

字彙 **rest** 剩餘　**content** 內容　**tape ~ shut** 用膠帶密封~　**label** 標籤　**stack** 堆

56. What activity are the speakers participating in?　　説話者正參與什麼活動？
　　(A) Driving to the post office　　(A) 開車到郵局
　　(B) Operating some office equipment　　(B) 操作辦公設備
　　(C) Placing an order of supplies　　(C) 訂購民生用品
　　(D) Preparing parcels to mail　　**(D) 準備要寄的包裹**

正確答案為 (D)

〈注意細節－特定事項〉

題目問說話者正在參與什麼活動，而答案正好就出現在對話的第一句。男 1 第一句話就說今天必須寄送包裹，答案是 (D)。

換句話說 **send out a package** 寄出包裹 → **mail a parcel** 郵寄包裹

字彙　　**participate in** 參加　　**operate** 操作；經營　　**parcel** 包裹　　**place an order** 訂購

57. At what time does the conversation most likely take place?　　對話可能發生在幾點？
　　(A) 2:00　　(A) 2 點
　　(B) 3:00　　(B) 3 點
　　(C) 4:00　　**(C) 4 點**
　　(D) 5:00　　(D) 5 點

正確答案為 (C)

〈注意細節－特定事項〉

應留意提到時間的內容。女子問男子郵局關門的時間，男 1 回答 6 點，並說還有兩個小時的時間可以工作，由此可知對話當時是 4 點，答案是 (C)。

58. What does the woman mean when she says,　　女子說「那我們開始吧」是什麼意思？
　　"Let's get on with it, then"?　　**(A) 每個人都應該加速工作。**
　　(A) Everyone should work faster.　　(B) 標籤已經準備好了。
　　(B) The labels are all ready.　　(C) 還剩下很多時間。
　　(C) There is plenty of time left.　　(D) 他們現在必須出發。
　　(D) They need to leave right now.

正確答案為 (A)

〈關鍵句－說話者意圖〉

綜觀題目提及的句子前後文內容，男 1 說時間還很充裕，但男 2 回應男 1 還有很多箱子堆在一旁等待處理，緊接著女子就說出題目中的句子，可見在時間有限但工作量大的情況下，女子想表達的是大家動作要加快，答案是 (A)。

字彙　　**plenty of** 充裕的～

2_59-61 美式女聲／英式男聲

Questions 59-61 refer to the following conversation.

M: Hi, Naomi. Has there been any progress on the year-end function?

W: Actually, yes. We've booked the Kingston Auditorium.

M: That big place?

W: That's right. To be honest, it's a little expensive to rent, but it has enough space to accommodate the large numbers we're expecting, as well as plenty of free parking.

M: Great! We had some problems with last year's venue, especially the fact that it wasn't easily accessible. A lot of people have told me Kingston is very easy to get to. Have the tickets gone on sale yet?

W: They went on sale yesterday. I heard around 35% have already been sold. We've managed to keep prices the same as last year, which is proving to be attractive.

M: Wow, that's a very good idea.

問題 59-61 參考以下對話。

男：嗨，直美，59 年底活動有任何進展嗎？

女：有的。我們已經預訂了金士頓禮堂。

男：那個大場地嗎？

女：沒錯。老實說租金有點貴，但它有足夠空間容納我們預期的大量人數，還有很多免費停車位。

男：太好了！60 去年的活動場地我們遇到了一些問題，特別是不便抵達的問題。很多人都告訴我金士頓地點便利。已經開始賣票了嗎？

女：昨天開賣。61 我聽說已經售出大約三成五。我們設法維持住去年的價格，證明這活動很具吸引力。

男：哇，這真是個很好的點子。

字彙 **progress** 進展、進步、發展 **year-end function** 年尾活動、尾牙（指公司舉辦來犒賞員工一年辛勞的活動） **to be honest** 老實說 **accommodate** 容納 **venue** 活動場地 **accessible** 易接近的；可進入的 **attractive** 有吸引力的

59. What is the conversation mainly about?
(A) Preparation for an award ceremony
(B) Plans for an event
(C) The cost of supplies
(D) Directions to a venue

對話主要內容為何？
(A) 準備頒獎典禮
(B) 活動策劃
(C) 供應成本
(D) 活動地點路線

正確答案為 **(B)**

〈掌握基本資訊－主題〉

題目問對話的主題，通常在對話的前半段就有線索。男子第一次說話時提到年底活動，因此答案是 (B)。

60. What does the man say about the previous year's event?
(A) It had enough space.
(B) It was hard to get to.
(C) It was expensive to rent.
(D) It had free parking.

關於去年活動，男子說了什麼？
(A) 有足夠的空間。
(B) 很難抵達。
(C) 租金很貴。
(D) 可免費停車。

正確答案為 **(B)**

〈注意細節－提及內容〉

應掌握關鍵字 previous year's event，並留意提到同義詞的談話內容。對話中段男子說去年的活動場地有些問題，並附加說明了不易抵達的狀況，因此答案是 (B)。

換句話說 It wasn't easily accessible. 不容易抵達 → It was hard to get to. 很難到達

61. What is indicated about the tickets?
(A) They are quite expensive.
(B) They have already sold out.
(C) The prices are lower than before.
(D) They are selling well.

關於入場票的說明為何？
(A) 相當昂貴。
(B) 已經售罄。
(C) 價格低於以往。
(D) 賣得很好。

正確答案為 **(D)**

〈注意細節－提及內容〉

可在有關票券的對話內容找到線索。對話後半段男子問票是否已經開賣，女子回答從昨天開始販售，並且已經售出約 35% 的票，因此答案是售票狀況很好的 (D)。

2_62-64　美式女聲 / 英式男聲

Questions 62-64 refer to the following conversation and floor plan.

W: Thanks for coming so quickly.

M: Not at all. Actually I was working on the renovation on an apartment a couple of blocks away.

W: I see. Well, I'd like to get an estimate on some remodeling work. Do you think it would be possible to remove this wall between the workroom and the living room?

M: That should be a simple job.

W: Great. Also the bathroom is far from the workroom. I'd like to put it next to where the workroom is now.

M: Good idea. I should tell you that this will take around five weeks to complete though. There is a lot of plumbing and electrical work to do. That kind of work is quite expensive, too.

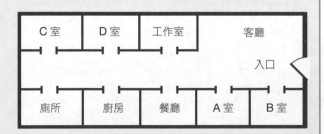

Room C	Room D	Workroom	Living room
			Entrance
Bathroom	Kitchen	Dining room	Room A	Room B

問題 62-64 參考以下對話與樓層平面圖。

女：謝謝你這麼快過來。

男：不客氣。㉒ 我正好在裝修距離這裡幾條街的一間公寓。

女：原來如此。是這樣的，我想整修，請你做個報價。你覺得我可以把工作室和客廳之間的牆拆掉嗎？

男：那應該很簡單。

女：太好了。㉓ 另外，廁所距離工作室很遠。我希望把它改到現在工作室的隔壁。

男：好主意。㉔ 我必須告訴妳，這大約需要 5 個星期的時間才能完工。有許多水管和電力工程要做，工程費用也蠻高的。

C 室	D 室	工作室	客廳
			入口
廁所	廚房	餐廳	A 室	B 室

字彙 | **renovation** 裝修、整修　**remodeling** 整修　**plumbing** 水管設施、管道工程　**electrical work** 電力作業

62. Who most likely is the man?
(A) A plumber
(B) An electrician
(C) A real estate agent
(D) A builder

男子可能是什麼人？
(A) 水管工
(B) 電工
(C) 不動產仲介
(D) 建築商

正確答案為 **(D)**

〈掌握基本資訊－職業〉
題目問男子的職業，應於對話的前半段找答案。女子對男子的到來表達感謝，男子說正在附近進行 renovation 裝修工程，因此男子的工作與 renovation 有關，最適合的答案是 (D)。

字彙 **electrician** 電工　　**real estate agent** 不動產仲介

63. Look at the graphic. Where does the woman say she would like to put the bathroom?
(A) Room A
(B) Room B
(C) Room C
(D) Room D

根據圖表，女子說希望把廁所放在哪裡？
(A) A 室
(B) B 室
(C) C 室
(D) D 室

正確答案為 **(D)**

〈注意細節－圖表相關〉
聽對話前，應先看過題目和圖表以預測答案線索。由於是與配置相關的問題，線索可能與位置的相對關係有關。女子說目前的廁所和工作室的距離很遠，希望能把廁所移到工作室旁邊，工作室旁邊的位置就是答案 (D)。

64. What does the man say about the project?
(A) It will take a long time.
(B) It requires a lot of travel.
(C) It will be started next week.
(D) It will be cheap to complete.

男子說這個案子怎麼樣？
(A) 將會花很多時間。
(B) 需要經常出差。
(C) 可以在下個禮拜開始。
(D) 用便宜的費用就能完成。

正確答案為 **(A)**

〈注意細節－提及內容〉
應從男子提及裝修工程的內容尋找答案。在談話最後，男子說因為管道工程和電力作業的緣故，費用會較高，也需要 5 個禮拜的工作天才能完工，因此答案是 (A)。

2_65-67 美式女聲 / 美式男聲

Questions 65-67 refer to the following conversation and schedule.

W: Hi, Martin. I'm wondering when we should hold the welcoming reception for Ms. Sato.

M: Her first day here will be on Tuesday, but I don't think we should hold it then because people will be too tired to work the next day.

W: Besides, the financial reports are due then so we'll probably have to work until late.

M: Yeah, and some of the staff members have to take a trip to inspect the factory in Portland on the seventh and eighth.

W: And they won't want to go out on the evening they get back.

M: Right, so the day of the product release is our only option. Would you mind making a reservation at a local restaurant — for twenty people, I guess.

W: Sure, I'll see if Gino's can accommodate us.

SCHEDULE	
Tuesday, October 6	Financial Reports Due
Wednesday, October 7	Plant Inspection
Thursday, October 8	Plant Inspection
Friday, October 9	New Item Introduction

問題 65-67 參考以下對話與行程表。

女：嗨，馬丁。⑥⑤ 我想知道我們什麼時候為佐藤小姐舉辦歡迎會。

男：她第一天來這裡是星期二，但我認為不應該在那天辦，因為第二天大家會累到不能工作。

女：而且那一天是財務報告截止日，我們可能要工作到很晚。

男：是啊，7 號和 8 號有些員工必須去波蘭視察工廠。

女：而且他們回來的那天晚上不會想出去。

男：對，⑥⑥ 所以產品發布日是我們唯一的選擇。⑥⑦ 妳能幫忙在當地餐廳訂位嗎？我猜大概 20 個人吧。

女：沒問題，⑥⑦ 我來看看吉諾餐館能不能容納得下我們。

日程安排	
10 月 6 日星期二	財務報告截止日
10 月 7 日星期三	工廠視察
10 月 8 日星期四	工廠視察
⑥⑥ 10 月 9 日星期五	⑥⑥ 新產品介紹

字彙 **welcome reception** 歡迎會 **financial report** 財務報表 **inspect** 視察、檢查

65. What is the main topic of the conversation?
(A) A guest speaker
(B) A sporting competition
(C) A welcome event
(D) A local festival

對話主題是什麼？
(A) 客座演講者
(B) 運動競賽
(C) 歡迎活動
(D) 地方節慶

正確答案為 **(C)**

〈掌握基本資訊－主題〉
對話主題必須仔細聽前半段的對話。對話第一句，女子問在什麼時候舉辦歡迎會，因此答案是 (C)。

66. Look at the graphic. When most likely will the event be held?
(A) On Tuesday
(B) On Wednesday
(C) On Thursday
(D) On Friday

根據圖表，活動可能在什麼時候舉辦？
(A) 星期二
(B) 星期三
(C) 星期四
(D) 星期五

正確答案為 **(D)**

〈注意細節－圖表相關〉
題目選項與圖表中皆出現活動的舉辦日期和星期，因此應預先想到答案與行程有關。對話後半段，男子說唯一能選擇的是產品發布當天，也就是新產品介紹日，答案是星期五 (D)。

換句話說 **product release** 發布產品 → **New Item introduction** 新品介紹

67. What does the woman say she will do?
(A) Attend a conference
(B) Book a venue
(C) Prepare an inspection
(D) Reserve a hotel room

女子說她將會做什麼？
(A) 出席會議
(B) 預訂場地
(C) 準備檢驗
(D) 預訂飯店房間

正確答案為 **(B)**

〈注意細節－未來〉
對話之後即將發生的事情，應在對話後半段尋找答案。男子請女子幫忙預約餐廳後，女子最後提到特定地點 Gino's 吉諾餐館，並表示將確認該場地能否容納活動人數，可見她將會預約場地，答案是 (B)。

換句話說 **make a reservation at the restaurant** 預約餐廳 → **book a venue** 預約場地

2_68-70　英式男聲 / 美式女聲

Questions 68-70 refer to the following conversation and bill.

M: Thank you for calling the Union Town Dental Clinic. How may I help you?

W: Hello. This is Joyce Hahn. I'm a patient of Dr. Betts. I just received the bill for my visit last Wednesday, and it looks like I've been charged twice for the same treatment. Dr. Betts just filled a cavity in one tooth during my visit, but my bill shows the cost for two fillings.

M: Oh, I'm terribly sorry, Ms. Hahn. We recently installed new accounting and billing software. The error must have been made when I transferred your information into the new system. I'll make the correction to your records and issue a new bill right away.

Name: Joyce Hahn Patient# 002875	
Date:	Wednesday 9/13
Examination	$ 40.00
2x Gum Treatment	$ 200.00
2x Dental Filling	$ 260.00
Toothpaste	$ 10.00
Balance Due	$510.00

問題 68-70 參考以下對話與帳單。

男：感謝您打電話到統一城鎮牙醫診所。能為您服務嗎？

女：你好，我是喬伊斯韓。我是貝茲醫師的病人。我剛收到上週三的就診帳單，看來我因為同樣的治療被收取兩次費用。**68** 看牙當天貝茲醫生幫我補了一顆蛀牙，但是我的帳單顯示補了兩顆牙。

男：噢，真是抱歉，韓小姐。**69** 我們最近安裝了新的會計和計帳軟體。在我把您的資訊轉進新系統時一定發生了錯誤。**70** 我會修改您的紀錄並馬上開一張新的帳單。

姓名：喬伊斯韓 患者編號：002875	
日期：	星期三 9/13
檢查	40 美元
2× 牙齦治療	200 美元
2× 補牙	260 美元
牙膏	10 美元
支付額	510 美元

字彙 | **clinic** 診所　**patient** 病人　**charge** 收費；費用　**treatment** 診療　**cavity** 蛀牙　**bill** 帳單、請款單　**install** 安裝、設置　**transfer** 移轉　**correction** 改正、修正　**issue** 發行、發放　**gum** 牙齦

68. Look at the graphic. Which charge on the bill is incorrect?
(A) $10
(B) $40
(C) $200
(D) $260

根據表格，帳單上哪筆收費錯誤？
(A) 10 美元
(B) 40 美元
(C) 200 美元
(D) 260 美元

正確答案為 **(D)**

〈注意細節－圖表相關〉
應該先掌握題目選項和表格之間的關係，由於選項都是價格，應從對話中提到的看診種類尋找答案線索。根據女子所言，醫生只補了一顆牙，但是帳單上顯示補了兩顆牙，可知補牙的收費錯誤，答案是 (D)。

字彙　**incorrect** 錯誤的

69. What does the man say about the clinic?
(A) It changed its phone number.
(B) It installed a new program.
(C) It hired new staff members.
(D) It purchased new equipment.

關於診所，男子說了什麼？
(A) 更改了電話號碼。
(B) 安裝新程式。
(C) 聘僱新員工。
(D) 添購新設備。

正確答案為 **(B)**

應從男子提到診所的內容中尋找答案。男子說最近安裝了新程式，因此答案是 (B)。

70. What does the man say he will do?
(A) Upgrade a system
(B) Issue a refund
(C) Update software
(D) Send another statement

男子說他會做什麼？
(A) 升級系統
(B) 予以退款
(C) 更新軟體
(D) 寄送另一張帳單

正確答案為 **(D)**

〈注意細節－未來〉
關於未來的問題應從對話後半段的男子談話尋找答案。男子最後提到會修改記錄並重寄新帳單，答案是 (D)。
換句話說 **issue a new bill** 寄送新帳單 → **send another statement** 寄送另一張結算單

字彙　**statement** 帳單、清單

2_71-73 英式男聲

Questions 71-73 refer to the following announcement.

This is the Metropolitan Express bound for Watford and Amersham stations. The next stop is Pinner station. There will be a five-minute stop while the train is separated into two sections. Cars one through five will then proceed to Watford, and cars six through twelve will continue on to Amersham. Please check your car number to ensure that you are in the right section. Once again, the front sections, cars one through five, are bound for Watford. The rear sections, cars six through twelve, are bound for Amersham.

問題 71-73 參考以下公告。

71 本車是開往沃特福和阿默舍姆站的特快地鐵列車。**72** 下一站是品諾站。火車將停靠 5 分鐘,並在此分成兩段。第 1 到第 5 車廂將繼續開往沃特福站,第 6 到第 12 車廂將開往阿默舍姆站。**73** 請核對您的車廂號碼,確保您在正確的列車區間。再次提醒您,前段火車,也就是第 1 到第 5 車廂將開往沃特福站。後段火車,也就是從第 6 到第 12 車廂將開往阿默舍姆站。

字彙　**bound for** 開往　**car**（列車)車廂　**proceed to** 前往~　**ensure** 保證、確保　**rear** 後方的、後面的、後門的

71. Where does the announcement take place?
(A) In a train station
(B) At an airport
(C) On an express train
(D) At an express bus terminal

這份廣播是在何處公告？
(A) 火車站
(B) 機場
(C) 特快列車上
(D) 特快巴士轉運站內

正確答案為 **(C)**

〈掌握基本資訊－地點〉
地點的線索通常在對話的前半段出現。廣播第一句說明這是開往特定目的的特快列車，因此答案是 (C)。

72. Why is the announcement being made?
(A) To provide information on destinations
(B) To explain a schedule change
(C) To ask passengers to start boarding
(D) To apologize for a delay

為什麼會發布這個廣播？
(A) 提供有關目的地的資訊
(B) 解釋行程變更
(C) 請求乘客開始上車
(D) 因延遲而表示歉意

正確答案為 **(A)**

〈掌握基本資訊－目的地〉
廣播內容提到火車下一個停靠站，並提到火車將分段行駛。因此這個廣播的目的是為了告知乘客，不同車廂將開往不同目的地，答案是 (A)。

字彙 **board** 搭乘（車、船、飛機） **destination** 目的地

73. What are listeners asked to do?
(A) Proceed to a different platform
(B) Present their documents
(C) Wait for more instructions
(D) Confirm they are in the correct place

聽者被要求做什麼？
(A) 前往不同月台
(B) 出示文件
(C) 等待進一步指示
(D) 確認他們在正確的地方

正確答案為 **(D)**

〈注意細節－要求〉
與要求相關的答案常出現在談話內容後半部，和 please、make sure 等用詞一起出現。內容提到要乘客再次確認車廂號碼，以確保位於正確的列車區間，因此答案是 (D)。

換句話說 **in the right section** 在正確區間 → **in the correct place** 在正確的地方

字彙 **platform** 月台 **instruction** 指示；指導 **confirm** 確認

2_74-76 英式女聲

Questions 74-76 refer to the following announcement.

Fifteen years ago this week, the Ormer Mayfair restaurant opened its doors to the public and has been a proud member of the Kensington community ever since. To mark the occasion, we're inviting our patrons to join us for a special anniversary celebration. This coming Friday we'll present live band performances from open to close in our courtyard dining area. In addition, we'll be preparing a special menu selection just for the event. As always, we'll be using only the finest quality, locally grown vegetables in all of the dishes we serve. Join us this Friday at Ormer Mayfair. Located at 8 Patriot Square, Kensington.

問題 74-76 參考以下公告。

15 年前的這個星期，歐默梅菲爾餐廳對大眾開放，從此成為肯欣頓社區引以為傲的一員。為了紀念這個日子，74 我們邀請我們的老主顧一同參與這個特別的週年慶典。75 本週五從開始營業到打烊，我們在庭院用餐區將有現場樂團演奏。此外，我們將為這次活動專門準備特別菜單。一如以往，76 我們只使用最優質、本地栽種的蔬菜。請在本週五共襄盛舉。歐默梅菲爾餐廳位於肯欣頓愛國者廣場 8 號。

字彙　**be opened to the public** 對大眾開放　**community** 社區　**mark** 紀念　**occasion** 特殊場合或活動
anniversary 紀念日　**courtyard** 庭院、院子　**located** 位於～的

74. What is being celebrated?
(A) An opening of a new branch
(B) A business anniversary
(C) A retirement ceremony
(D) A special award

正在慶祝什麼？
(A) 新分店開張
(B) 公司週年慶
(C) 退休典禮
(D) 一個特別獎項

正確答案為 **(B)**

〈注意細節－特定事項〉
掌握關鍵字 celebrated 並注意提到相關單字的部份。談話前半段邀請顧客參加一場特別的紀念活動，可知答案是 (B)。

75. What is the restaurant planning to do on Friday?
(A) Extend its hours of operation
(B) Offer musical entertainment
(C) Provide complimentary meals
(D) Discount certain items

這家餐廳星期五打算做什麼？
(A) 延長營業時間
(B) 提供音樂娛樂節目
(C) 免費提供食物
(D) 特定產品特價優惠

正確答案為 **(B)**

〈注意細節－特定事項〉
應掌握關鍵字 Friday 來回答問題。內容提到週五將有現場樂團表演，答案是 (B)。
換句話說 **live band performances** 現場樂團表演 → **musical entertainment** 音樂娛樂節目

字彙 **extend** 延長 **complimentary** 免費的

76. What does the speaker say about the restaurant?
(A) It uses local produce.
(B) It hired a renowned chef.
(C) It has multiple locations.
(D) It is under new ownership.

關於餐廳，說話者提到了什麼？
(A) 使用當地農產品。
(B) 聘僱著名的主廚。
(C) 有多家分店。
(D) 所有權易主。

正確答案為 **(A)**

〈注意細節－提及內容〉
應從介紹餐廳的部分尋找答案線索。談話後半部提到此餐廳提供的所有餐點都是使用當地優質蔬菜，答案是 (A)。
換句話說 **locally grown vegetables** 當地栽種的蔬菜 → **local produce** 當地農產品

字彙 **produce** 農產品 **renowned** 著名的 **under new ownership** 換人經營，**ownership** 指經營權

2_77-79 美式男聲

Questions 77-79 refer to the following talk.

Good afternoon, and welcome to the future site of Walton electronics' newest production facility. As you can see, construction work is ongoing but nearing its completion. In fact, installation of our assembly equipment is scheduled to begin in just one month, and we expect production to begin by early next month. As investors, you'll be happy to know that everything about this facility has been designed to maximize efficiency and reduce costs. The lighting system, for example, will consume about twenty percent less energy than those at our other plants. For your own safety, I'd like to remind everyone to keep your hardhats on at all times as we tour the site. Now, let's get started.

問題 77-79 參考以下談話。

午安，歡迎來到瓦頓電子未來最新的生產工廠現場。**77** 如您所見，建築工程正在進行中，近日即將完工。事實上，我們的裝配設備預定在一個月內開始安裝，並預期在下個月初開始生產。**78** 身為投資人，您會很高興得知這個設施的所有設計都是為了將效率提升到最高並降低成本，如照明系統所消耗的能源比其他的工廠少 20%。為了您的自身安全，**79** 在此提醒大家，參觀現場時，全程請戴著安全帽。現在開始吧。

字彙　**production facility** 生產設備　**construction work** 施工工程　**ongoing** 持續進行的　**installation** 安裝　**assembly** 裝配　**investor** 投資者　**maximize** 最大化　**efficiency** 效率、效能　**consume** 消耗　**reduce costs** 降低成本　**hardhat** 安全帽

77. Where is the talk probably taking place? 　　　這段談話很可能發生在哪裡？
(A) At an electronics store 　　　(A) 電子用品店
(B) In a research center 　　　(B) 研究中心
(C) In a conference room 　　　(C) 會議室
(D) At a construction site 　　　**(D) 施工現場**

正確答案為 **(D)**

〈掌握基本資訊－地點〉
地點的線索一般會出現在談話前半段。開場提到歡迎大家來到未來的工廠現場，也提到目前正在施工中 construction work is ongoing，因此答案是 (D)。

78. Who most likely are the listeners? 　　　聽者很可能是誰？
(A) New employees 　　　(A) 新進員工
(B) Company investors 　　　**(B) 公司投資人**
(C) Store patrons 　　　(C) 商店顧客
(D) Factory workers 　　　(D) 工廠工人

正確答案為 **(B)**

〈掌握基本資訊－聽者〉
聽者的身分大多會出現在談話前半部。不過這段談話的前半段並沒有特別提到，反而在中間才提到身為投資人會感到開心，作答時應特別留意。答案是 (B)。

79. What does the speaker mean when he says, "let's get started"? 　　　説話者説「開始吧」是什麼意思？
(A) A tour is about to begin. 　　　**(A) 參觀即將開始。**
(B) Some delivery is ready to be shipped. 　　　(B) 有些貨已經備妥等待運送。
(C) Listeners should go back to work immediately. 　　　(C) 聽者應立即回去工作。
(D) Listeners should fill out some forms. 　　　(D) 聽者應填寫一些表格。

正確答案為 **(A)**

〈關鍵句－説話者意圖〉
説話者意圖須綜合聆聽前後文才能掌握。談話後半提到參觀工廠要一直戴著安全帽 hardhat，之後就出現此句，可知參觀活動即將開始，答案是 (A)。

2_80-82 美式女聲

Questions 80-82 refer to the following recorded message.

You have reached Domus Design Institute's administration office. Due to the approaching blizzard, all morning classes today have been canceled. The National Weather Service has issued a severe weather alert for the Florence metropolitan area. Our school's policy is to cancel morning classes when a severe weather alert is in effect for the region as of 6 A.M. If this alert is still in effect at 10:30 A.M., afternoon classes will be canceled as well. Look for updates on our Web site at www.domusdesign.com, or call this number again for the latest news.

問題 80-82 參考以下錄音留言。

⑧⓪ 這裡是多摩斯設計學院行政辦公室。 ⑧① 由於暴風雪即將到來，今天上午課程全部取消。國家氣象局對佛洛倫斯大都會區發布惡劣氣候警報，本校政策是地區惡劣氣候警報於上午 6 點生效時，上午課程就會取消。如果警報持續至上午 10 點半，下午課程也會取消。 ⑧② 請在本校網站 www.domusdesign.com 查看最新訊息，或再次撥打這個電話獲取最新消息。

字彙 **institute** 教育機構、學院 **administration** 管理、行政業務 **approaching** 接近的 **blizzard** 暴風雪
metropolitan area 大都會區 **severe** 嚴重的、劇烈的 **alert** 警報 **in effect** 生效

80. What type of organization recorded this message?
(A) A radio station
(B) A transportation service
(C) The National Weather Service
(D) A local school

何種組織錄製了這段訊息？
(A) 廣播節目
(B) 交通運輸服務
(C) 國家氣象局
(D) 地方學校

正確答案為 (D)

〈掌握基本資訊－說話者〉
題目問此訊息是由何種機構錄製，從開場打招呼的內容就能聽到機構名稱。談話一開始的介紹是 Design Institute 設計學院，institute 指「學院」，因此答案是 (D)。

81. What does the speaker say about Florence?
(A) Its roads have been repaved.
(B) It will experience a snowstorm.
(C) Its schools will all be closed.
(D) It is the largest city in the region.

關於佛洛倫斯，說話者說了什麼？
(A) 道路已經重新鋪設。
(B) 將經歷一場暴風雪。
(C) 所有學校都將關閉。
(D) 是地區內最大城市。

正確答案為 (B)

〈注意細節－提及內容〉
關鍵字是地名 Florence 佛洛倫斯。談話主題是因天候取消課程，因此在提到 Florence 之前就能猜到答案與天氣有關。此外，內容也提到氣象廳已對 Florence 大都會區發布惡劣氣候警報，因此答案是 (B)。
換句話說 **blizzard** 暴風雪 → **snowstorm** 暴風雪

字彙 **repave** 重鋪

82. What are listeners asked to do?
(A) Attend the afternoon classes
(B) Check for updated information
(C) Design a new Web site
(D) Listen to an upcoming broadcast

聽者被要求做什麼？
(A) 參加下午課程
(B) 查看更新資訊
(C) 設計新網站
(D) 收聽下一段廣播

正確答案為 (B)

〈注意細節－要求〉
談話中的要求多半在後半段出現。談話最後要聽者在網站查詢更新消息，因此答案是 (B)。

字彙 **broadcast** 廣播

Test 02

2_83-85 澳式男聲

Questions 83-85 refer to the following talk.

Good afternoon, everyone. First, I regret to inform you that Jacob Lansing is retiring at the end of the month, ending his 25 years of service at Dover Sport Equipment. Jacob originally joined us as a sales assistant, and over the years he's demonstrated outstanding ability. In the past five years as a project director, he has led many projects to success. Especially successful was his recent advertisement which gained widespread media attention. I'll send you an e-mail shortly with details of a farewell ceremony we're planning. Please attend if you can.

問題 83-85 參考以下談話。

大家午安。83 首先很遺憾通知大家，約伯藍辛將在本月底退休，結束他在多佛運動器材公司 25 年以來的服務生涯。約伯最初是以業務助理加入我們公司，多年來他展現出色的能力。過去 5 年他作為專案經理，帶領許多專案成功。84 其中最成功的是他最近得到大批媒體關注的廣告。85 我稍後會寄出一封簡短的電子郵件給各位，內容包含我們規畫的歡送會細節。請各位盡可能參加。

| 字彙 | **regret** 遺憾；後悔 **inform** 通知 **retire** 退休 **assistant** 助理 **demonstrate** 展示、證明 **project director** 專案經理 **widespread** 大批的、廣泛的 **farewell ceremony** 歡送會 |

83. What is the purpose of the talk?
    (A) To introduce a new employee
    (B) To reschedule a farewell party
    (C) To explain about new policy
    (D) To announce the resignation of an employee

這篇談話的目的為何？
(A) 介紹新員工
(B) 重新安排歡送會
(C) 說明新政策
(D) 宣布一位員工辭職

正確答案為 (D)

〈掌握基本資訊－目的〉
對話的目的通常出現在談話的前半段。內容是通知某位特定人士即將退休，因此答案是 (D)。
換句話說 **retire** 退休 → **resignation** 辭職

84. What has Mr. Lansing recently done?
    (A) Accepted a promotion
    (B) Created an advertisement
    (C) Submitted a report
    (D) Attended a seminar

藍辛先生最近做了什麼？
(A) 接受晉升
(B) 製作廣告
(C) 提交報告
(D) 參加研討會

正確答案為 (B)

〈注意細節－特定事項〉
本題問 Lansing 藍辛先生的介紹，關鍵字是 recently。談話的後半段說最近受媒體關注的廣告非常成功，答案是 (B)。

字彙 **promotion** 升官

85. What will the speaker probably do next?
    (A) Join a conference
    (B) Talk to a supervisor
    (C) Receive an electronic mail
    (D) Send detailed information

說話者接下來很可能做什麼？
(A) 參加會議
(B) 和主管談談
(C) 接收電子郵件
(D) 寄出詳細資訊

正確答案為 (D)

〈注意細節－未來〉
題目詢問未來，**通常在對話後段出現，須注意聆聽使用到未來時態的句子。**談話最後，說話者說將會用電子郵件寄送送別會的詳細內容，答案是 (D)。

2_86-88 英式女聲

Questions 86-88 refer to the following telephone message.

Mr. Gupta, this is Tammy Hughes from Meyer Estate about a location for your office in Lancaster. We've just listed a commercial space on the second floor of Acton Building, on Abbey Road. This business center has recently been refurbished. It offers fully-furnished, immediately operational space for between 5 and 18 work stations. Also, it is equipped with a cutting-edge office technology system and high-speed Internet, which is something you said you'd wanted. This luxury serviced office is set in a spacious modern building and offers a comfortable business environment. This property is quite popular on the market, so if you're interested in seeing it, please let me know as soon as possible. Thank you.

問題 86-88 參考以下電話留言。

古普塔先生，我是馬亞不動產的塔咪休葛絲，回應您在藍克斯特的辦公室地點。我們剛剛聽說艾比路上的艾可頓大廈 2 樓有個商業空間。86 這個商業中心最近剛整修完畢，它有 5 到 18 個工作站，全套裝潢，可以立即使用。87 而且它配備最先進的辦公技術系統與高速網路，是您先前說過想要的。這個豪華的辦公室位在一個寬敞的現代建築內，能提供舒適的辦公空間。88 這個房地產物件在市場上很受歡迎，如果您有興趣看看，請儘快告訴我。

字彙		
commercial space 商業空間	**refurbish** 翻新、整修	**fully-furnished** 全套裝潢的
cutting-edge 先進的、尖端的	**spacious** 寬敞的	**property** 不動產、財產

86. What is mentioned about the property?
(A) It's newly renovated.
(B) It is for up to 15 persons.
(C) It offers on-site parking.
(D) It is close to the station.

關於這個房地產物件，談話提到什麼？
(A) 已全新改裝。
(B) 最多可讓 15 人使用。
(C) 提供免費停車場。
(D) 距離車站很近。

正確答案為 (A)

〈注意細節－提及內容〉
此談話是不動產仲介說明建築物件的電話留言。說話者提到這棟商業中心最近已經重新整修，因此答案是 (A)。

換句話說 **recently refurbished** 最近重新整修 → **newly renovated** 全新改裝

87. According to the message, what feature is Mr. Gupta looking for?
(A) A fully-furnished office
(B) A convenient location
(C) Modern equipment
(D) Adequate parking

根據留言，古普塔先生在找什麼？
(A) 完全裝潢好的辦公室
(B) 方便的地點
(C) 現代化設備
(D) 空間充足的停車場

正確答案為 (C)

〈注意細節－特定事項〉
電話留言提到的名字通常不是留言者，就是接聽者。談話第一句就提到 **Mr. Gupta** 古普塔先生，由此可知 Gupta 是聽留言的人，之後談話內容就不再提到名字，而是用 **You** 來稱呼對方。對話中段提到這個辦公室具備最先進的辦公室系統和高速網路，而這些也都是接聽留言者要求的條件，因此答案是 (C)。

字彙 **adequate** 充足的

88. Why does the speaker recommend viewing the building as soon as possible?
(A) It will rent out quickly.
(B) Its price will go up soon.
(C) It will be renovated shortly.
(D) It will be advertised on TV.

為什麼說話者建議儘快去看這個建築物？
(A) 它很快就會出租出去。
(B) 它的價格將調漲。
(C) 它即將進行整修。
(D) 它將在電視上做廣告。

正確答案為 (A)

〈注意細節－建議〉
本題與提案、要求有關，應從談話後半尋找線索。後半段提到此房地產很受歡迎，有興趣要趕緊打電話，答案是 (A)。

Questions 89-91 refer to the following talk.

Welcome to the organizing committee for the 2018 Memorial Golf Tournament. Male golfers from all over the country will be competing in this tournament, and you are all here to help things run smoothly over the next five days. You and your fellow student volunteers from Cleveland High School will make certain the golfers and caddies have everything they need, so they can focus on the competition. Remain on the sidelines and be alert at all times, but unless specifically asked, please stay off the fairways. You must remain silent while play is in progress, and don't talk to the golfers or caddies unless they speak to you first. Keep up with your assigned athlete as he progresses through the course. And, last but not least, let's hope for sunny skies over these next five days.

問題 89-91 參考以下發言。

歡迎來到 2018 年高爾夫紀念錦標賽組織委員會。 90 來自全國各地的男性高爾夫選手將會參加此次賽事，接下來的 5 天，各位將協助比賽順利進行。 89 各位以及身為同事的克里佛蘭高中的學生志工們，要確保高爾夫選手和球童能獲取所需，如此才能專注於比賽。請站在場外，並隨時保持警覺， 91 除非有特別要求，否則請遠離球道。比賽進行時，務必保持安靜，除非高爾夫選手和球童主動與你交談，否則不要和他們說話。整個比賽進行過程中，請跟緊你的指定選手。最後，讓我們期望未來 5 天都是晴朗的好天氣。

字彙　**committee** 委員會　**tournament** 錦標賽　**compete** 競爭　**volunteer** 志工；志願做　**caddie** 高爾夫球童　**sideline**（運動場地）邊線　**unless** 除非　**stay off** 遠離　**fairway**（高爾夫球場開球區和果嶺之間的）球道　**in progress** 進行中　**course** 高爾夫球場　**athlete** 運動員、選手　**progress** 前進、進行

89. Who is the intended audience for this talk?
(A) Golfers
(B) Caddies
(C) Teachers
(D) Volunteers

這次談話的聽眾是誰？
(A) 高爾夫選手
(B) 高爾夫球童
(C) 教師
(D) 志工

正確答案為 **(D)**

〈掌握基本資訊－聽者〉
關於聽者的資訊一般都出現在談話的前半部。談話前半部提到「各位以及與你們同事的學生志工們將確保高爾夫球手和球童們取得一切所需」，因此答案是 (D)。

90. What is mentioned about the tournament?
(A) It is a national competition.
(B) It will last three days.
(C) It is an annual event.
(D) It will be rescheduled.

關於比賽，談話提到了什麼內容？
(A) 這是個全國賽事。
(B) 活動將連續舉辦 3 天。
(C) 這是一年一度的活動。
(D) 日程將重新安排。

正確答案為 **(A)**

〈注意細節－提及內容〉
應掌握關鍵字 tournament「錦標賽」之後再仔細聆聽內容。談話一開始就提到 tournament，因此作 89 題同時也要聆聽本題該注意的內容。一開始句子說「來自全國各地的男性高爾夫球手將參加這次比賽」，因此答案是 (A)。
換句話說 **all over the country** 遍及全國 → **national** 全國的

91. What is one instruction given to the listeners?
(A) Speak loudly during play
(B) Stay off the greens
(C) Ask questions to the athletes
(D) Check out the schedule

聽者收到何種指示？
(A) 比賽時大聲說話
(B) 遠離草皮
(C) 向運動員提問
(D) 確認行程

正確答案為 **(B)**

〈注意細節－要求〉
與要求或請求相關的線索會在後半段，與 **please**、**be sure to** 等用法一起出現。內容提到要求大家遠離球道 please stay off the fairways，因此適當的答案是 (B)。

2_92-94　英式男聲

Questions 92-94 refer to the following news report.

Hello. I'm Kevin Taylor with your seven o'clock business news update. United Textiles announced today that it intends to open a new factory in New Delhi. Jack Wentworth, the company CEO, said that United Textiles will transfer its central operation to the new factory. He also said that the new factory will help United Textiles to continue growing on sales, which have more than tripled over the last three years. Industry insiders say the local government has encouraged the project. That would make perfect sense. The factory will help ease local unemployment while bringing in much-needed hard currency.

問題 92-94 參考以下新聞。

您好，我是卡文泰勒，為您播報 7 點整的商業新聞。92 聯合紡織公司今天宣布要在新德里開設一家新工廠。93 公司首席執行長傑克文沃斯表示，聯合紡織公司會將核心營運業務轉移到新工廠。他還説，新工廠將提昇聯合紡織公司的銷售，而過去 3 年來，該公司的銷售已經成長超過 3 倍。94 業界相關人士表示，地方政府鼓勵這項計畫。這是再合理不過的事。在這家工廠帶來極需的強勢貨幣的同時，也將有助於緩解當地的失業率。

字彙　**announce** 宣布、公布　　**textile** 紡織品　　**intend** 打算、計畫　　**triple** 成長三倍　　**insider** 內部人員、知情者
ease 減輕、緩和　　**unemployment** 失業率　　**hard currency** 強勢貨幣

92. What is the report mainly about?
(A) A planned closure of a facility
(B) An acquisition of two companies
(C) A new line of product
(D) A company's expanded operation

這篇報導主要關於什麼？
(A) 設施的關閉計畫
(B) 收購兩家公司
(C) 新的產品線
(D) 公司擴張事業

正確答案為 **(D)**

〈掌握基本資訊－主題〉

與主題相關的題目線索通常在談話一開始就能找到。第一句報導了某特定公司將在 New Delhi 新德里開新工廠，因此答案是換另一種方式描述的 (D)。

換句話說 **open a new factory** 開設新工廠 → **expand one's operation** 擴張事業

字彙　**acquisition** 收購

---

93. Who is Jack Wentworth?
(A) A company spokesperson
(B) A corporate executive
(C) A broadcast reporter
(D) A news reader

傑克文沃斯是什麼人？
(A) 公司發言人
(B) 企業主管
(C) 廣播記者
(D) 新聞主播

正確答案為 **(B)**

〈注意細節－提及內容〉

應在名字出現的地方找答案。由於提到此名字的內容介紹他是公司首席執行長，因此答案是 (B)。

字彙　**spokesperson** 發言人　　**executive** 主管

---

94. What does the speaker mean when he says, "That would make perfect sense"?
(A) United Textiles is an international company.
(B) Any local government would favor such a plan.
(C) Textile sales are strong in the local area.
(D) United Textiles is famous in the region.

說話者說「這是再合理不過的事」是什麼意思？
(A) 聯合紡織公司是國際企業。
(B) 任何地方政府都會贊同這樣的計畫。
(C) 紡織品銷售在當地表現強勁。
(D) 聯合紡織公司在該地區相當有名。

正確答案為 **(B)**

〈關鍵句－說話者意圖〉

談話後半段引用業界相關人士的話，轉達地方政府也相當鼓勵這個計畫，之後便接著說題目當中的這句話，因此最適當的答案是 (B)。

字彙　**favor** 贊同、青睞

2_95-97 英式女聲

Questions 95-97 refer to the following talk and graph.

Everyone, I would like to thank all of you for coming here today. I know that I asked you here on short notice. The board of directors went over last year's management report and unfortunately I can't say they were altogether happy with it. Specifically, they weren't pleased with the area where we performed the worst. They want us to develop a strategy as to how we're going to do better in this area and they want it by Thursday morning. That means that we're probably going to spend the next three days here in the office. We'll spend a lot of time brainstorming this issue and draw up some proposals. After that Ashley Gallagher will write up a final submission.

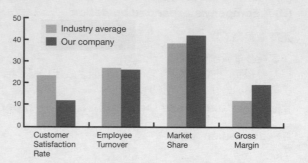

問題 95-97 參考以下談話與圖表。

各位，我要感謝你們今天來到這裡。95 我知道我是臨時通知你們過來的。董事會審查了去年的管理報告，不幸的是，我不能説他們完全滿意。96 具體來説，他們對我們表現最差的部分感到不滿。至於我們如何在這方面做得更好，他們要我們制定對策，並希望在週四上午以前知道結果。這代表接下來 3 天我們可能必須待在辦公室裡。我們將花很多時間針對這個議題集思廣益並擬出一些提案。97 之後，艾絲莉加拉赫將撰寫最終提交報告。

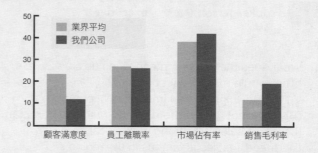

字彙 **short notice** 臨時通知　　**go over** 仔細檢查　　**specifically** 明確地、具體來說　　**strategy** 策略　　**as to** 至於、說到　　**brainstorming** 腦力激盪、集思廣益　　**draw up** 草擬、起草　　**submission** 提案書

95. Why does the speaker thank the listeners?
(A) They formed a committee.
(B) They finished a quarterly report.
(C) They distributed a notice.
(D) They gathered quickly.

為什麼說話者要感謝聽者？
(A) 他們組織了委員會。
(B) 他們完成了季度報告。
(C) 他們發出了通知。
(D) 他們迅速集合起來。

正確答案為 **(D)**

〈注意細節－特定事項〉
一開場說話者表達感謝，因為說話者承認是臨時通知大家聚集。答案是換了另一種方式說明的 (D)。

96. Look at the graphic. What area does the board of directors most want to improve?
(A) Customer satisfaction rate
(B) Employee turnover
(C) Market share
(D) Gross margin

根據圖表，哪個領域是董事會最希望改善的？
(A) 顧客滿意度
(B) 員工離職率
(C) 市場佔有率
(D) 銷售毛利率

正確答案為 **(A)**

〈注意細節－圖表相關〉
掌握選項和圖表的關係是解題關鍵。橫座標的項目分別為四個題目選項，因此可推測縱座標的數值與答案有關，業界平均和該公司的最低或最高表現都可能是答案線索。由於說話者提到董事會對公司表現最差的領域感到不滿意，並希望針對這個項目提出對策，而圖表顯示出公司表現低於業界平均的是顧客滿意度，因此答案是 (A)。

字彙　**satisfaction rate** 滿意度　**turnover** 離職率　**market share** 市佔率　**gross margin** 毛利

97. What will Ms. Gallagher have to do?
(A) Use a different facility
(B) Create a document
(C) Report a current issue
(D) Contact a manager

加拉赫小姐必須做什麼？
(A) 使用不同的設施
(B) 製作文件資料
(C) 報告目前議題
(D) 與管理者聯絡

正確答案為 **(B)**

〈注意細節－特定事項〉
應注意聆聽提到 Ms. Gallagher 加拉赫小姐的段落。後半段說話者提到將由 Gallagher 加拉赫小姐寫出最終報告書，因此答案是 (B)。

換句話說 **write up a final submission** 寫出最後報告書 → **create a document** 製作文件資料

2_98-100 澳式男聲

Questions 98-100 refer to the following talk and table.

Welcome to Alice Spring Desert Park. We'll be covering over eight kilometers today, so I hope you all remembered to bring plenty of water and wear practical shoes. Today we'll see wild native animals and plants that have made the park famous. It also offers us the opportunity to experience the variety of the deserts of central Australia, exploring the inter-relationships between the plants, animals and people. By the way, a cloudy day like today is rare for this area and provides a great opportunity for us. The highly reflective surfaces of some areas in the park make photographing the plants from certain angles difficult when it's sunny. Make sure to take advantage of the cloud cover by getting plenty of pictures during today's hike.

Alice Spring Regional Weather Report		
Day	Skies	Temperature
Tuesday	Sunny	Hot
Wednesday	Sunny	Warm
Thursday	Sunny	Warm
Friday	Cloudy	Cool

問題 98-100 請參考以下對話與表格。

歡迎來到愛麗斯泉沙漠公園。我們今天要走 8 公里以上，因此希望各位都記得攜帶足夠的水，穿著實用的鞋子。98 今天我們將會看到這個公園遠近馳名的本地野生動植物，也有機會體驗澳大利亞中部沙漠的多樣性，探索動植物與人類之間的相互關係。順道一提，99 像今天這樣多雲天氣在這個地區很少見，為我們提供了一個很好的機會。公園有些區域是高反光表面，使得在陽光下從特定角度拍攝植物時會變得困難。100 務必在今天的長途健行過程中，充分利用雲層，多拍些照片。

Alice Spring 地區天氣預報		
日期	天氣	溫度
星期二	晴天	熱
星期三	晴天	溫暖
星期四	晴天	溫暖
星期五	陰天	冷

字彙　**cover** 行走　**practical** 實際的、實用的　**native** 本地的、土生土長的　**inter-relationship** 相互關係　**rare** 稀有的、罕見的　**reflective** 反射的　**surface** 表面、地面　**angle** 角度　**take advantage of** 利用　**exotic** 異國的

98. According to the speaker, what is the park known for?
(A) Impressive rock formations
(B) Native species
(C) Exotic flowers
(D) High numbers of visitors

根據說話者，這個公園以什麼聞名？
(A) 令人印象深刻的岩層
(B) 當地的野生物種
(C) 異國風情的花
(D) 大量訪客

正確答案為 (B)

〈注意細節－特定事項〉
應注意與關鍵字 be known for 同義的談話內容。談話一開始提到將會看到讓這個公園遠近馳名的野生動物和植物，因此答案是 (B)。

換句話說 **wild native animals and plants** 本土野生動植物 → **native species** 本土物種

99. Look at the graphic. When does the talk probably take place?
(A) On Tuesday
(B) On Wednesday
(C) On Thursday
(D) On Friday

根據圖表，談話大概發生在星期幾？
(A) 星期二
(B) 星期三
(C) 星期四
(D) 星期五

正確答案為 (D)

〈注意細節－圖表相關〉
在聆聽談話內容以前，請事先看過題目選項和天氣預報表。選項都是星期，可推測答案線索應該與氣象或溫度有關。對話後半段提到天氣雖然是多雲，但是卻提供了拍照的絕佳機會，因此答案是天氣呈現陰天的星期五 (D)。

100. What does the speaker advise listeners to do?
(A) Take a lot of photographs
(B) Draw some pictures
(C) Wear sunglasses
(D) Stay on the hiking trail

說話者建議聽者做什麼？
(A) 拍攝很多照片
(B) 畫一些圖
(C) 戴太陽眼鏡
(D) 繼續留在徒步旅行的路線上

正確答案為 (A)

〈注意細節－要求〉
遇到邀請或要求的問題，答案線索往往和後半段提到 please、make sure 等字一起出現。說話者建議大家可以利用陰天的優點，多拍一點照片，因此答案是 (A)。

換句話說 **get plenty of pictures** 拍很多照片 → **take a lot of photographs** 拍很多照片

101. Bergeson's began as a small retail store, but ------- transitioned into a large wholesaler.
(A) quickly
(B) well
(C) quite
(D) highly

伯格洋行原本是間小零售店,但很快就變成一個大批發商。

正確答案為 (A)

空格位於修飾動詞 transitioned 的副詞位置,答案是 (A)。其他三個副詞 quite、well、highly 只修飾形容詞,不修飾動詞。

字彙 **retail store** 零售商店　　**transition** 轉變　　**wholesaler** 批發商

102. The open-access database can be used to search ------- job opportunities at Jefferson Electronics.
(A) for
(B) up
(C) as
(D) to

開放存取資料庫可用來搜尋傑佛森電子的工作機會。

正確答案為 (A)

search 後面固定接介系詞 for,指「搜尋」的意思,答案是 (A)。

字彙 **open-access** 開放存取的　　**job opportunity** 工作機會

103. It is ------- that managers be made aware of a shortage of supplies when it occurs.
(A) sudden
(B) actual
(C) eventful
(D) critical

重要的是,當供應出現短缺時,管理者們必須意識到這一點。

正確答案為 (D)

〈特殊詞類〉that 子句後方使用原形動詞 be,可推測出前方助動詞 should 被省略,也就是要選擇有「要求、主張、堅持、提議」意涵的形容詞,答案是 (D) critical。在〈It is important / imperative / essential that〉的句子當中,that 子句要使用 should 被省略的原形動詞。

字彙 **aware of** 意識到　　**a shortage of** 短缺～的　　**occur** 發生　　**sudden** 突然的　　**eventful** 多事的、特別的　　**critical** 重要的

104. Most of the employees at the company have work experience, but only a handful of ------- can see the future importance of current trends.
(A) we
(B) us
(C) our
(D) ourselves

多數公司員工具有工作經驗,但僅有少數人能看出當前趨勢對未來的重要性。

正確答案為 (B)

〈代名詞格〉介系詞 of 後面須使用受格代名詞,因此答案是 (B)。

字彙 **a handful of** 少數的　　**current** 目前的

105. Please read through ------- page of the contract carefully before signing on the final page.
(A) all
(B) each
(C) whole
(D) complete

在最後一頁簽名前，請仔細閱讀合約的每一頁。

正確答案為 (B)

〈數量詞〉空格後面的 page 是單數，因此答案是可以表達單數的數量詞 (B) each。(C) whole 與 (D) complete 是一般形容詞，前面要加冠詞。如果要用 (A) all，則要把可數名詞 page 改為複數型。

 read through 看完　**complete** 完全的

106. A ------- shopping bag is a necessary item for someone who does not like the ordinary plastic bags from the grocery store.
(A) rigorous
(B) comparable
(C) durable
(D) vigorous

對那些不喜歡雜貨店塑膠袋的人，耐用的購物袋是必需品。

正確答案為 (C)

適合修飾 bag 的形容詞是 (C) durable。

字彙　**ordinary** 普通的　**plastic bag** 塑膠袋　**rigorous** 嚴格的　**comparable** 可比較的、相當的　**durable** 耐用的　**vigorous** 活力充沛的

107. The judges for this year's debate competition include ------- from a broadcasting station.
(A) represents
(B) representatives
(C) represented
(D) represent

今年辯論賽的評審委員包含廣播電台代表。

正確答案為 (B)

〈詞性〉include 是及物動詞，需要接名詞，而 representative 可作為形容詞和名詞使用，因此答案是 (B)。

字彙　**judge** 評審委員　**debate** 辯論　**competition** 競賽　**include** 包括　**broadcasting station** 廣播電台　**representative** 代表人；代表的

108. The filters of your Total Water Purifier must ------- at least once a month to keep the appliance functioning properly.
(A) be cleaned
(B) cleaning
(C) have cleaned
(D) clean

為了讓設備保持正常運作，全面水淨化的濾心必須一個月至少更換一次。

正確答案為 (A)

〈時態〉空格位於助動詞 must 後面，空格後面也沒有受詞，因此答案是被動加原形動詞形式的 (A) be cleaned。

字彙　**water purifier** 淨水器　**appliance** 家電　**function** 運作　**properly** 適當地、正確地

109. Mr. O'Neil ------- his speech when he realized that he hadn't printed out the draft.
(A) achieved
(B) improvised
(C) commanded
(D) officiated

當歐尼爾先生發現自己沒有印出草稿時，便進行即興演說。

正確答案為 (B)

沒把草稿列印出來，表示演說必須在沒有講稿的情況下進行，因此答案是進行即興演說的 (B)。

字彙　**draft** 草稿　**achieve** 達成　**improvise a speech** 進行即興演說　**command** 命令　**officiate** 主持、行使職務

---

110. Varner Bank works ------- with customers to establish long-term partnerships.
(A) nearly
(B) recently
(C) closely
(D) newly

瓦諾銀行與客戶密切合作，以建立長期的合作關係。

正確答案為 (C)

從句意來看，應放入能表達與客戶關係密切的單字，答案是 (C) closely。

字彙　**establish** 建立、創造　**long-term** 長期的　**nearly** 幾乎　**closely** 緊密地

---

111. The updated safety analysis report is limited to site supervisors ------- the Russell Software System.
(A) within
(B) until
(C) during
(D) since

最新的安全分析報告僅限羅素軟體系統內部的現場主管可看。

正確答案為 (A)

空格後面的 Russell Software System 是表示公司名稱的專有名詞，因此表示「公司內部」的 (A) within 是答案。until 跟 since 作為介系詞使用時，需與時間連用，因此不是答案。

字彙　**analysis report** 分析報　**be limited to** 僅限於　**site supervisor** 現場主管

---

112. ------- needs to be highlighted is the area of agriculture and natural resources.
(A) What
(B) Which
(C) Whichever
(D) Whose

需要強調的是農業和天然資源領域。

正確答案為 (A)

〈關代〉空格前方沒有主詞，後面出現兩個動詞 needs 和 is，因此空格的答案必須是可以同時扮演主詞角色和連接詞角色的 (A) What。(B) Which 是關係代名詞，前面需要與主詞連用。(C) Whichever 是帶有讓步意思的「無論哪個」，不是合適的答案。(D) Whose 是關係代名詞所有格，前面也需要出現主詞才能使用。

字彙　**highlight** 強調　**agriculture** 農業　**natural resources** 天然資源

113. San Remo Lemonade maintained ------- sales all year around though promoted as a summertime drink.
(A) final
(B) correct
(C) steady
(D) seasoned

聖里默檸檬水雖是以夏季飲品作為宣傳，但一整年都維持穩定銷售。

正確答案為 (C)

從 all year around「一整年」可得知要表達持續銷售的意思，因此答案是 (C) steady。

字彙　**maintain** 保持　**all year around** 一整年　**promote** 促銷、宣傳　**steady** 穩定的　**seasoned** 經驗豐富的、老練的

114. Morrison Electronics is acquiring Yearwood Tech. for ------- $35 million in stocks and cash.
(A) approximates
(B) approximation
(C) approximately
(D) approximate

默里森電子用股票和現金共值約 350 萬美元的價格併購宜爾伍科技。

正確答案為 (C)

〈詞性〉空格是修飾數字 $35 million 的副詞位置，答案是 (C)。

字彙　**acquire** 併購　**approximate** 大約的　**approximation** 近似值　**approximately** 大約地

115. The building may be accessed only by personnel ------- have attended the employee orientation.
(A) must
(B) since
(C) who
(D) some

只有參加過員工職前訓練的人員才能進入大樓。

正確答案為 (C)

〈關代〉答案是可以連接名詞 personnel 和動詞 have attached 的關係代名詞主格 (C) who。

字彙　**access** 使用　**personnel** 人員、職員　**employee orientation** 員工訓練

116. New technologies have ------- Poland Cell Tech. to expand its network and explore sales opportunities.
(A) emerged
(B) improved
(C) introduced
(D) enabled

新技術使波蘭細胞科技公司能夠擴大其網絡並開發銷售機會。

正確答案為 (D)

受詞 Poland Cell Tech 後面有不定詞 to，因此答案是 (D) enabled，片語 enable to 指「有能力去做某事」。

字彙　**expand** 擴張　**explore** 尋找、探索　**sales opportunity** 銷售機會　**emerge** 浮現、顯現　**enable** 使能夠

117. Mr. Long repaired the fax machine ------- last Friday because the maintenance department was short on staff.
(A) his
(B) his own
(C) himself
(D) him

上週五龍先生自己修理了傳真機，因為維修部人手不足。

正確答案為 (C)

〈代名詞格〉構成句子的基本元素主詞、受詞都已經齊全，空格應填入的是用來強調的反身代名詞 (C) himself。

字彙　**maintenance** 管理、維護　**short on** 短缺

118. You can have fun at our indoor waterpark all through the year, ------- of the season.
(A) regardless
(B) regarded
(C) regarding
(D) regard

一年四季您都可以在我們的室內水上樂園遊玩。

正確答案為 (A)

從空格到 of the season 是一個片語，因此答案是可以完成片語的 (A) regardless，regardless of 指「無論」。

字彙　**regardless of** 不管、無論

119. A panel may begin to review the entries ------- the deadline for submitting designs has passed.
(A) how
(B) nor
(C) whether
(D) now that

評審團可能會開始審查參賽作品，因為繳交設計的截止日期已經過了。

正確答案為 (D)

〈連接詞〉整個句子有兩個動詞 may being 和 has passed，從空格開始是副詞子句，因此答案是副詞子句連接詞 (D) now that。

字彙　**panel** 評審團　**entry** 參賽作品　**now that** 由於

120. For results to be convincing, the temperature and humidity in the laboratory must remain ------- the same throughout the experiment.
(A) exacted
(B) exactness
(C) exact
(D) exactly

為了使結果具有說服力，實驗室的溫度和濕度必須在實驗過程保持完全相同。

正確答案為 (D)

〈詞性〉構成句子的基本元素都已經齊全，答案是副詞 (D) exactly。

字彙　**convincing** 有說服力的　**humidity** 濕度　**laboratory** 實驗室　**exact** 確實的　**exactness** 正確、精確
exactly 確切地、完全正確地

121. ------- Ms. Motohashi missed her train, she was fortunately still on time for the awards ceremony.

(A) Though
(B) Despite
(C) As if
(D) Just as

雖然本橋小姐沒趕上火車，但幸運的是她仍準時參加頒獎典禮。

正確答案為 (A)

沒趕上火車和準時參加頒獎典禮是相反的內容，因此答案要選表達轉折的字詞，(A) 與 (B) 都符合，但空格後面是句子，因此要選擇連接詞 (A) Though。

字彙　**awards ceremony** 頒獎典禮　**despite**（介系詞）儘管

122. Karl Byquist at Gordon Architecture, a British Company, is the ------- of this year's Master Architects Award.

(A) receiving
(B) received
(C) recipient
(D) receipt

英國葛登建築公司的卡羅拜奎斯特是今年建築大獎的得獎人。

正確答案為 (C)

〈詞性〉空格前面有冠詞 the，後方沒有名詞，可見答案是名詞。從句子脈絡來看，空格是可作為主詞 Karl Byquist 補語的 (C) recipient。

字彙　**architecture** 建築　**architect** 建築師　**recipient** 受獎人、接受者　**receipt** 收據

123. Results of the two audit findings report ------- the director's expectations.

(A) surpassed
(B) surpassing
(C) to surpass
(D) having surpassed

這兩份審計報告的結果超出主管預期。

正確答案為 (A)

〈時態〉句中缺少動詞，答案是過去式動詞 (A) surpassed。

字彙　**audit findings report** 審計結果報告　**surpass** 超乎　**expectation** 預期

124. If you have not visited the Valley Restaurant recently, you may be ------- to see how the interior has changed.

(A) pleasing
(B) pleased
(C) please
(D) pleaser

如果你最近沒有去過河谷餐廳，你可能會很高興看到內部陳設的改變。

正確答案為 (B)

空格前面有 be 動詞，後面有 to 不定詞，適合的答案是 be pleased to，意思是「樂於～」，因此答案是 (B)。

字彙　**be pleased to** 樂於、對～感到高興

125. A nine-mile ------- of Fosberg Road between Norview Road and Harriot Avenue will be resurfaced in September.
(A) journey
(B) duration
(C) stretch
(D) instance

介於挪賓路和哈略特大道之間長達 9 英哩的福斯伯格路將在 9 月重鋪路面。

正確答案為 (C)

可以讓形容詞 nine-mile 修飾，且適合當 resurface「重鋪路面」的主詞是 (C) stretch。

字彙 resurface 重鋪路面　between A and B 介於 A、B 之間　duration 期間　stretch 一段路　instance 實例

126. Article submissions to Journal Explore Nature must not exceed 2,000 words, ------- references.
(A) exclude
(B) excluding
(C) exclusive
(D) exclusion

不含參考文獻在內，探索自然期刊投稿的文章，不得超過兩千字。

正確答案為 (B)

〈詞性〉空格前面是一個完整的句子，因此答案是可以接受詞 references 的介系詞 (B) excluding。

字彙 submission 提交　exceed 超過　exclude（動詞）排除　exclusive 獨家的、專屬的　exclusion（名詞）排除

127. Registration for the community programs will start with residents, ------- are students.
(A) inasmuch as
(B) the reason being
(C) because of them
(D) most of whom

社區課程的註冊將從居民開始，其中多數都是學生。

正確答案為 (D)

〈關代〉空格後面的句子結構是從 are 開始，缺少主詞與連接詞，因此答案是同時有主詞和連接詞的 (D) most of whom。

字彙 registration 登記、註冊　resident 居民　inasmuch as（連接詞）由於、因為

128. The board meeting ended so ------- that few members had an opportunity to comment on the proposed road construction project.
(A) abruptly
(B) broadly
(C) practically
(D) obviously

董事會會議結束如此突然，幾乎沒有成員有機會就擬議中的道路建設計畫發表評論。

正確答案為 (A)

空格必須是修飾動詞 ended 的副詞，並能同時銜接 that 子句後方內容，因此適合句意的答案是 (A) abruptly。

字彙 few 很少、不多　comment on 對～發表評論　proposed 提出的　abruptly 突然地　broadly 概括地
practically 實際上　obviously 顯然地

129. Because of her lack of experience, Ms. Abraham was ------- to volunteer for the astronaut training.

(A) reluctance
(B) more reluctantly
(C) reluctance
(D) reluctant

亞柏拉罕小姐由於缺乏經驗，不願意自願參加宇宙航行訓練。

正確答案為 (D)

〈詞性〉空格位於 be 動詞後面的補語位置，答案要選形容詞 (D) reluctant「不情願的」。

> 字彙　**astronaut** 宇宙航行員　　**reluctance**（名詞）不情願　　**be reluctant to** 不願意、不情願做～

130. In order to make an official purchase agreement, a manager must submit ------- from at least three qualified experts.

(A) combinations
(B) appointments
(C) estimates
(D) comprises

為了達成正式採購協議，經理必須提交至少三位合格專家的估價單。

正確答案為 (C)

空格前方提到 purchase agreement「採購協議」，符合句意的是 (C) estimates「估價單」。

> 字彙　**make an agreement** 達成協議　　**official** 正式的　　**qualified** 合格的　　**expert** 專家　　**estimate** 估價單
> **comprise** 包含、由～組成

Questions 131-134 refer to the following memo.

To: All staff

The Light Cloud Airlines' board of directors is pleased to announce that board chair Mathew Mavens has been appointed the new interim president of the foundation ------- the departure of
131.
Roberto Rinaldi. -------. We also wish him the best in his future endeavors. In the meantime, the
132.
committee for the new permanent president has been formed. Mr. Mavens will resume his duty as board chair ------- the new president of the organization is chosen.
133.
If you have any questions or concerns, please feel free to contact me while we ------- the
134.
transition in leadership.

Thank you.
Rajiv Shrestha
Communication Director

問題 131-134 參考以下備忘錄。

致全體員工：

輕雲航空董事會很高興宣布，在羅伯特里納爾迪離職 ⑬ 之後，董事會主席馬修馬文斯被任命為基金會新任臨時主席。 ⑬ 董事會和工作人員感激羅伯特先生在過去 7 年為我們的任務所做的付出。我們也祝福他在未來一切順利。在此同時，新的常任主席委員已經成立。馬文斯先生 ⑬ 將在組織選出新主席期間，繼續擔任董事會主席。

如果您有任何問題或疑慮，請在 ⑬ 進行交接期間隨時與我聯繫。

謝謝。

羅吉夫許瑞沙
通訊長

 字彙　**board chair** 董事會主席　　**appoint** 任命　　**interim** 中間的、暫定的　　**foundation** 基金會　　**departure** 離開　　**endeavor** 努力　　**in the meantime** 同時間　　**permanent** 永久的、常任的　　**resume** 重新開始、恢復　　**transition** 過度、轉變

131. (A) following
(B) follow
(C) follows
(D) followed

(A) 之後
(B) 跟隨
(C) 跟隨
(D) 跟隨了

正確答案為 (A)

空格後方是名詞 the departure of Roberto Rinaldi，因此要選擇介系詞，答案是 (A)。following 除了可以當作動詞 follow 的進行式，在此則是當作介系詞，意思是「在～之後」。

132. (A) I am happy to inform you that we have found the product he is looking for and have placed an order.
(B) I forgot to tell you that I would not be able to make it to the meeting because I have to meet some board members.
(C) Let me know if there's anything I can do for you to make the hiring process run smoothly.
(D) The board and staff greatly appreciate Mr. Rinaldi's commitment to our mission over the past seven years.

(A) 很高興通知你，我們已經找到他想要的產品，也下了訂單。
(B) 忘了告訴你，我沒辦法去那個會議了，因為我要去見一些董事。
(C) 如果我能為你做些什麼使招聘過程順利，請告訴我。
(D) 董事會和工作人員非常感謝羅伯特先生在過去 7 年為我們的任務所做的付出。

正確答案為 (D)

〈插入句〉
空格前面的內容首度提到 Rinaldi 先生，空格後面 We also wish him the best in his future endeavors，繼續是關於 Rinaldi 的內容，因此答案是 (D)。

字彙　**commitment** 付出

133. (A) so
(B) when
(C) because
(D) although

(A) 所以
(B) 當
(C) 因為
(D) 雖然

正確答案為 (B)

空格是連接兩個句子 Mr. Mavens will resume his duty as board chair 和 the new president of the organization is chosen 的副詞子句連接詞位置，兩個句子的動詞分別是 will 和 is，根據前後語意，適合選擇表示時間的副詞子句連接詞 (B) when，後一句是用現在式代替未來式的用法。

134. (A) question
(B) reconsider
(C) undergo
(D) avoid

(A) 質疑
(B) 再考慮
(C) 經歷
(D) 避免

正確答案為 (C)

符合句意的是 (C) undergo「經歷」。

Questions 135-138 refer to the following announcement.

Qualified candidates are now being considered for the position of lead web designer at Gibson Ltd.

A well-known advertising firm, Gibson Ltd. provides businesses with the innovative technical resources that are ------- of dramatically increasing a company's presence on the Internet. As
135.
demand for this unique service continues to grow, so does the number of Gibson Ltd.'s -------. In
136.
fact, new offices have recently opened as far away as Berlin, Tokyo, and Abu Dhabi.

As a member of Gibson Ltd.'s production division, the new lead Web designer ------- the efforts
137.
of a team responsible for developing and maintaining client Web sites. -------.
138.

問題 135-138 參考以下公告。

吉伯森有限公司現正招聘符合資格的網頁設計主管。

吉伯森是一家知名廣告公司,它為企業提供創新的技術資源,135 能夠顯著提高公司在網路上的影響力。隨著這種獨特服務的需求不斷增長,吉伯特有限公司的 136 分公司數量也不斷增加。事實上,最近也在柏林、東京、阿布達比等遙遠地區設置了新的辦公室。

作為吉伯特有限公司製作部門的一員,新的網頁設計主管 137 將管理開發兼維護客戶網站的團隊工作。138 完整的工作內容與其他資訊可在 www.gibson.com/jobs 取得。

字彙 **be considered** 被納入考慮 **innovative** 創新的 **dramatically** 劇烈地、顯著地 **presence** 存在
demand 需求 **division** 部門

135. (A) capably
(B) capabilities
(C) capability
(D) capable

(A) 能夠地
(B) 能力
(C) 能力
(D) 能夠的

正確答案為 **(D)**

空格出現在 be 動詞後面、介系詞 of 前面，因此要選擇形容詞 capable，答案是 (D)。be capable of 指「能夠做～」。

字彙　**be capable of** 有能力去～的、能勝任～的　**capability** 能力

136. **(A) locations**
(B) instructions
(C) reports
(D) schedules

(A) 辦公室
(B) 指示
(C) 報告
(D) 時程

正確答案為 **(A)**

下一句提到 new offices have recently opened，因此答案是 (A) locations，指「辦公室、分公司」。

137. (A) had overseen
(B) will oversee
(C) was overseen
(D) has been overseeing

(A) 已經管理
(B) 將管理
(C) 被管理
(D) 已經開始管理

正確答案為 **(B)**

由於 the new lead Web designer「新網頁設計主管」還沒有決定是誰，所以要選擇符合未來要做的工作，答案選未來式 (B)。

字彙　**oversee** 監督、管理

138. (A) Thank you for your e-mail and for sharing the positive feedback from your clients.
(B) A full job description and other information for applicants are available at www.gibson.com/jobs.
(C) It has been a great pleasure working with you and the entire Gibson staff.
(D) If our work doesn't meet your standards, we will honor our guarantee.

(A) 感謝您的來信並與我們分享來自貴客戶的正面回饋。
(B) 完整的工作說明與其他資訊可在 www.gibson.com/jobs 取得。
(C) 很高興能和你以及吉伯特全體員工共事。
(D) 如果我們的工作不符合您的標準，我們將履行我們的保證。

正確答案為 **(B)**

〈插入句〉

前面提到新網頁設計主管的工作內容，因此正確答案是進一步說明具體招聘內容的 (B)。

字彙　**positive feedback** 正面回饋　**job description** 職務內容　**applicant** 申請者　**meet the standard** 達到標準
honor 尊重、遵守　**guarantee** 保證（書）

Questions 139-142 refer to the following article.

November 29 — Jake's Restaurant on Sheboygan Street recently submitted an application for an entertainment permit. If ------- , the permit will enable the restaurant to host live musical performances nightly.
139.

The restaurant is located in what is primarily a residential area, and some neighbors are concerned that they will be exposed to loud music ------- a regular basis. Others don't think that it will be a major ------- , "We won't have a problem," said resident Beth Martinez.
140. **141.**

------- . However, the decision ultimately lies with the staff in the city licensing office.
142.

問題 139-142 參考以下報導。

11 月 29 日──位於西伯伊根街上的傑克餐廳最近提交了娛樂許可申請書。如果 ⑬⑨ 獲得批准，該許可證將使餐廳可以在晚上舉辦現場音樂表演。

這家餐廳位在住宅區，部分鄰居擔心他們將會 ⑭⓪ 經常聽到吵鬧的音樂。其他人不認為這是個大 ⑭① 問題。居民貝絲馬丁尼斯說：「我們沒差。」

⑭② 居民依然可以聯絡市議會表達擔憂。然而，最終決定仍取決於市府牌照辦公室的官員。

字彙　**entertainment** 娛樂、消遣　**permit** 許可證、執照　**primarily** 主要地　**residential area** 住宅區　**be exposed to** 暴露於～　**major** 主要的、大的　**ultimately** 最終、最後　**lie with** 取決於　**licensing office** 牌照辦公室

139. (A) approved

(B) approving

(C) approves

(D) approval

(A) 被核准

(B) 正在核准

(C) 核准

(D) 許可

正確答案為 (A)

空格位於 if 子句後面,缺少主詞,所以是分詞構句句型。真正的主辭是後方子句的主詞 the permit「許可證」,approve 是及物動詞,但空格後面沒有受詞,由此可知要使用表達被動的過去分詞,指「被核准」,答案是 (A)。

140. (A) at

(B) on

(C) from

(D) among

正確答案為 (B)

空格是要選擇能配合後面名詞 basis 的介系詞。「on a regular basis」是「定期、經常」的意思,答案是 (B)。

141. (A) investment

(B) issue

(C) deadline

(D) act

(A) 調查

(B) 問題

(C) 截止日

(D) 法案

正確答案為 (B)

前一句提到有些居民會擔心,但其他居民表示不是個大問題,從句意來看最適合的答案是 (B) issue,意思是「議題、問題」。

142. **(A) Residents may still contact the town council to voice their concerns.**

(B) We are looking for some volunteers to help perform at the restaurant.

(C) To make the transition go faster, please remove your personal items.

(D) This is one of the changes the management plans to implement.

(A) 居民依然可以聯絡市議會表達擔憂。

(B) 我們正在尋找志工在餐廳幫忙演出。

(C) 為了加速轉換,請移除個人用品。

(D) 這是經營團隊計畫要執行的改變之一。

正確答案為 (A)

〈插入句〉

空格之後是用 However 來連結句子 the decision ultimately lies with the staff in the city licensing office,與此互為對照的 (A) 是正確答案。

字彙　**council** 議會　**voice** 表達、發言　**implement** 實行、實施

Questions 143-146 refer to the following e-mail.

To: Fred Jaspers <fjaspers@westfordmarketing.com>
From: Winnie Price <WPrice@lapimaelectronics.com>
Date: April 8
Subject: New Marketing Campaign
Attachment: Electronics

Hello, Fred.

Lapima Electronic Store will receive its summer inventory shortly. -------, I would like to begin

143.

another print and online advertisement campaign to promote our new products.

I would like to feature Mason's new home appliance line, which is made from 100 percent

recycled materials. Lapima Electronic Store is ------- of only two local retailers to offer this line,

144.

so we want it ------- in our ads. -------. You may use these images at will.

145.   **146.**

Thank you.

Winnie Price
Vice President of Sales, Lapima Electronic Store

問題 143-146 參考以下電子郵件。

收件者：佛萊德賈司柏 <fjaspers@westfordmarketing.com>
寄件者：維尼普林司 <WPrice@lapimaelectronics.com>
日期：4 月 8 日
主旨：新行銷活動
附件：電子產品

佛萊德，你好：

拉普瑪電子商店近期會收到夏季產品目錄。**143** 因此，我想開始另一波平面與線上行銷活動來宣傳新產品。

我想主打曼森的新家電產品線，它是由百分之百的回收材料製成。拉普瑪電子商店是當地僅有的兩家有提供此產品線的零售商 **144** 之一，所以我們希望在廣告中 **145** 強調這一點。**146** 我附上電子產品的照片給你。你可以隨意使用這些圖像。

謝謝。

維尼普林司
拉普瑪電子商店營業副理

字彙　　**campaign** 宣傳活動　　**inventory** 產品目錄　　**shortly** 很快地　　**promote** 宣傳　　**print** 書面、平面
feature 主打、以～為特色號召　　**retailer** 零售商　　**at will** 隨意

143. (A) Accordingly
(B) Likewise
(C) Moreover
(D) Nevertheless

(A) 因此
(B) 同樣地
(C) 此外
(D) 然而

正確答案為 **(A)**

空格是位於兩個句子之間的連接副詞位置，根據前後語意，適合選擇表達「因果」關係的 (A)。

144. (A) some
(B) both
(C) one
(D) other

(A) 一些
(B) 兩者都
(C) 其一
(D) 其他

正確答案為 **(C)**

指的是兩家零售商之一，答案是 (C)。

145. (A) emphasis
(B) emphasizes
(C) emphasized
(D) emphasizing

正確答案為 **(C)**

空格前方的代名詞 it 指前面提到的事情，即拉普瑪電商是唯二有販售該商品的店家如事實，因此動詞 want 後面必須使用被動，表達「此事在廣告上被強調」，答案是過去分詞的 (C)。

> 字彙　**emphasis**（名詞）強調　　**emphasize**（動詞）強調

146. (A) I would like to know what is going on with the order.
(B) I just wanted to remind you that we're meeting before the ceremony.
(C) I ordered a heater from your online store last Friday.
(D) I have attached some photos of the electronics for you.

(A) 我想知道訂單的狀況。
(B) 我只是想提醒你，我們會在典禮前見面。
(C) 上週五我在貴網站訂購一台暖氣。
(D) 我附上一些電子產品照給你。

正確答案為 **(D)**

〈插入句〉
下一句提到 these images，these 指示代名詞，表示前一句應該會用到相關的敘述，(D) 提到能與 image 連結的 photos，是正確答案。

> 字彙　**attach** 隨信附上

Questions 147-148 refer to the following text message. 簡訊

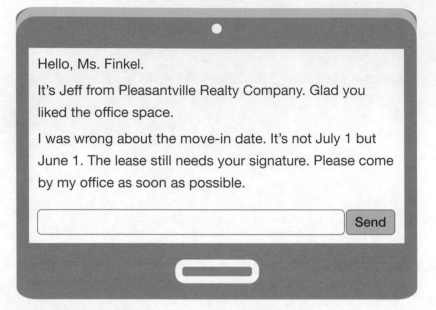

Hello, Ms. Finkel.

It's Jeff from Pleasantville Realty Company. Glad you liked the office space.

I was wrong about the move-in date. It's not July 1 but June 1. The lease still needs your signature. Please come by my office as soon as possible.

Send

問題 147-148 參考以下簡訊。

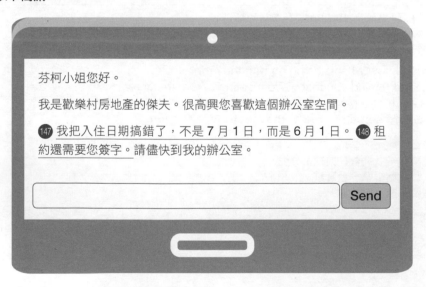

芬柯小姐您好。

我是歡樂村房地產的傑夫。很高興您喜歡這個辦公室空間。

147 我把入住日期搞錯了，不是 7 月 1 日，而是 6 月 1 日。 148 租約還需要您簽字。請儘快到我的辦公室。

Send

字彙　**realty** 房地產　**lease** 租約　**come by** 順道過來

147. What is the purpose of the message?
(A) To purchase an apartment
(B) To introduce a moving company
(C) To give directions to an office
(D) To correct some information

此訊息的目的是什麼？
(A) 為了購買一間公寓
(B) 為了介紹搬家公司
(C) 為了告知前往辦公室的路
(D) 為了更正一些資訊

正確答案為 **(D)**

從 I was wrong about the move-in date. It's not July 1 but June 1. 可以得知是為了更正搬遷日期。

148. What is Ms. Finkel asked to do?
(A) Sign a document
(B) Mail a package
(C) Make a donation
(D) Pay some fees

芬柯小姐被要求做什麼？
(A) 在文件上簽字
(B) 寄送包裹
(C) 捐贈
(D) 支付一些手續費

正確答案為 **(A)**

內文提到 The lease still needs your signature，希望她在文件上簽名，因此答案是 (A)。

Questions 149-150 refer to the following Web page. 網頁

---

http://www.sanremowellbeingfoundation.com

San Remo Well-being Foundation is pleased to announce that we are now accepting applicants for our annual grants. Each year, we provide four grants to projects throughout the world that are committed to improving the health and well-being of a community.

The award amounts are detailed below.

◇ First place ￡2,000
◇ Second place ￡1,500
◇ Third place ￡1,000
◇ Fourth place ￡500

Only not-for-profit entities are eligible for our grants; for-profit businesses are ineligible. Previous years' winners include an adult swim program, a lunch program for schoolchildren, and a series of pet care workshops.

Click this link to download grant application forms.

問題 149-150 參考以下網頁。

---

http://www.sanremowellbeingfoundation.com

聖雷默福利基金會高興宣布,現在起受理申請我們的年度獎助金。我們每年提供四項獎助金給世界各地致力於改善社區健康和福祉的專案計畫。

獎勵金額如下。

◇ 第一名 2,000 英鎊
◇ 第二名 1,500 英鎊
◇ 第三名 1,000 英鎊
◇ 第四名 500 英鎊

只有非營利組織才有資格獲得我們的獎助金,營利性企業不符合條件。

往年的獲獎者有成人游泳計畫、學童午餐計畫,以及 150 一系列的寵物照護工作坊。

請按此連結下載獎助金申請表。

 字彙 **well-being** 福祉、福利　**annual** 年度　**grant** 獎助金　**be committed to** 致力於　**not-for-profit** 非營利的
entity 團體、組織　**be eligible for** 有～資格的、符合～的條件　**ineligible** 沒有資格的　**pet care** 寵物照護

149. What is the purpose of the Web page?
(A) To solicit a government grant
(B) To announce the winner of a sports event
(C) To encourage participation in an event
(D) To remind people that a new school has opened

網頁的目的為何？
(A) 請求一項政府補助
(B) 宣布體育活動優勝者
(C) 鼓勵參與活動
(D) 提醒人們一所新學校已經開學

正確答案為 (C)

從第一句 we are now accepting applicants for our annual grants 可以得知這篇文章的目的是為了鼓勵獎助金的申請者參與，答案是 (C)。

字彙　**solicit** 請求、懇請

---

150. What have San Remo Well-being grants been used for in the past?
(A) Educating people on how to take care of pets
(B) Organizing singing contests for children
(C) Purchasing medical equipment for community hospitals
(D) Holding an international conference on health

過去聖雷默福利基金會獎助金的用途為何？
(A) 教育人們照顧寵物
(B) 舉辦孩童歌唱大賽
(C) 為社區醫院購買醫療設備
(D) 舉辦健康相關國際會議

正確答案為 (A)

在第三段 Previous years' winners include an adult swim program, a lunch program for schoolchildren, and a series of pet care workshops 一句中提到過去優勝者如何使用獎助金，答案 (A) 提到其中之一。

Questions 151-152 refer to the following text message chain. 線上聊天室

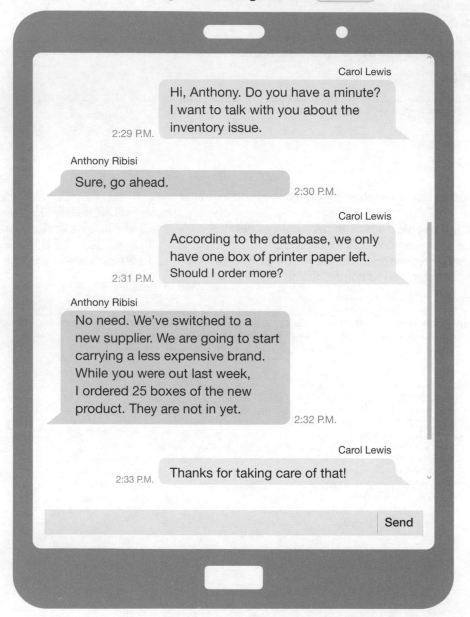

Carol Lewis
Hi, Anthony. Do you have a minute? I want to talk with you about the inventory issue.
2:29 P.M.

Anthony Ribisi
Sure, go ahead.
2:30 P.M.

Carol Lewis
According to the database, we only have one box of printer paper left. Should I order more?
2:31 P.M.

Anthony Ribisi
No need. We've switched to a new supplier. We are going to start carrying a less expensive brand. While you were out last week, I ordered 25 boxes of the new product. They are not in yet.
2:32 P.M.

Carol Lewis
Thanks for taking care of that!
2:33 P.M.

Send

問題 151-152 參考以下線上群組聊天。

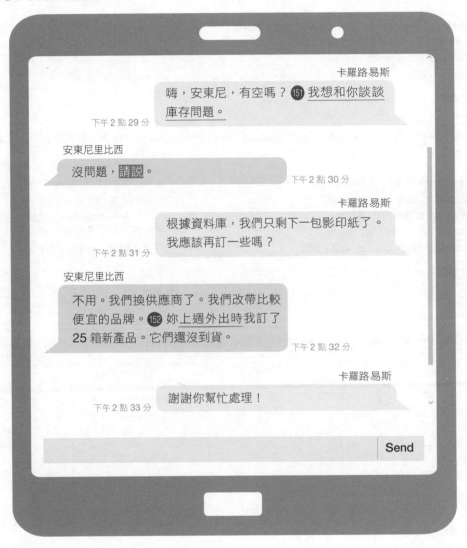

| 字彙 | **inventory** 存貨清單　　**switch** 更換 |

151. At 2:30 P.M., what does Mr. Ribisi most likely mean when he writes, "go ahead"?
(A) He has time to answer Ms. Lewis' questions.
(B) He did what Ms. Lewis requested.
(C) He agrees to meet with Ms. Lewis.
(D) He gave Ms. Lewis permission to work on a project.

下午 2 點 30 分，里比西先生說「請說」是什麼意思？
(A) 他有空回答路易斯小姐的問題。
(B) 他做了路易斯小姐要求的事。
(C) 他同意和路易斯小姐見面。
(D) 他允許路易斯小姐著手一項計畫。

正確答案為 (A)

〈推測句意〉

這是針對下午 2 點 29 分 I want to talk with you about the inventory issue 的回應。答案是表示「繼續說下去」的 (A)。

152. What is mentioned about Ms. Lewis?
(A) She created a new database.
(B) She received a delivery today.
(C) She placed an order last week.
(D) She recently took some time off.

何者是有關路易斯小姐的說明？
(A) 她建立了新資料庫。
(B) 她今天收到一份快遞。
(C) 她上星期下了訂單。
(D) 她最近休假一陣子。

正確答案為 (D)

下午 2 點 32 分尼里比西先生說 While you were out last week，答案是 (D)。

Questions 153-155 refer to the following information. 資訊

Thank you for purchasing a brand-new Cosmos 7 cell phone. An additional battery pack is included in your purchase. All kinds of cellphone accessories can be purchased directly from Cosmos at our online store, www.cosmoscellphone.com. We guarantee that you will receive your order within seven working days or the order is free of charge.

As a preferred customer, you will receive a 20 percent discount off your first purchase of cellphone accessories. Simply type in promo code BHURRY when placing your order. If you would rather purchase accessories through a retail location, our cellphone accessories are available at all leading electronics stores. Please note that most retailers do not honor our corporate discount.

Questions or feedback about your new cell phone? Call 800-555-9876 24 hours a day for technical support, or 800-555-9878 Monday through Friday 7 A.M to 8 P.M. for sales and accounts.

問題 153-155 參考以下資訊。

(153) 感謝您購買全新的 Cosmos 7 手機，您購買的產品包含一個額外電池組。您可以直接在我們的網路商店 www.cosmoscellphone.com 購買各式手機配件。(154) 我們保證您將在 7 個工作天內收到訂購商品，否則您訂購的商品將完全免費。

(155) 您是我們的優惠客戶，第一次購買手機配件可享有八折的折扣，只需在訂購時輸入優惠代碼 BHURRY 即可。如果您想在零售商店購買配件，我們的手機配件在各大電子商店也可以買到。請注意，多數零售商店不配合我們的公司折扣。

您對於新手機有什麼問題或意見嗎？撥打 24 小時電話 800-555-9876 尋求技術支援，或在週一至週五上午 7 點到下午 8 點撥打 800-555-9878 到銷售或會計部門。

字彙   **accessory** 配件   **free of charge** 免費   **preferred customer** 貴賓客戶   **promo code** 優惠代碼
do not honor 不配合特定行銷行為   **corporate** 企業的、公司的   **technical support** 技術支援

Test 02

153. For whom was the notice written?
(A) Technical support professionals
(B) Product designers
(C) Owners of new mobile phones
(D) Research workers

此訊息的對象是誰？
(A) 技術支援專家
(B) 產品設計師
(C) 有新手機的人
(D) 研究員

正確答案為 (C)

文章訴求對象通常在開頭就會提及。第一段提到 Thank you for purchasing a brand-new Cosmos 7，答案是 (C)。

154. What can be inferred from the information?
(A) There is no charge for the order if delivery is late.
(B) Sales representatives are available at all times.
(C) The product is under warranty for a full year.
(D) Technicians will return calls as soon as possible.

從這篇資訊可以知道什麼？
(A) 交貨延遲將不收取任何費用。
(B) 銷售人員隨時待命。
(C) 產品保固一年。
(D) 技術人員將儘快回電。

正確答案為 (A)

在第一段提到 We guarantee that you will receive your order within seven working days or the order is free of charge，答案是 (A)。

字彙　**at all times** 隨時　　**under warranty** 保固內

155. What is recommended to receive a discount?
(A) Calling customer service
(B) Entering a word on a Web site
(C) Visiting any electronics store
(D) Mailing in a coupon

內容建議要怎樣享有優惠？
(A) 打電話到客服中心
(B) 在網站輸入一個字
(C) 前往任何電子商店
(D) 郵寄優惠券

正確答案為 (B)

可在文章中尋找有關 discount 的關鍵字或同義字。第二段提到 you will receive a 20 percent discount off your first purchase of cellphone accessories. Simply type in promo code BHURRY when placing your order，答案是 (B)。

Questions 156-157 refer to the following notice. 通知

Easton's Books is pleased to host a public reading by writer Annette Lyons on Wednesday, August 12, from 3 P.M. to 5 P.M. A two-time winner of the prestigious Reily Award for best science fiction, Ms. Lyons will read excerpts from *Behind the Doors*. This fiction book, the fifth and final installment in her *Kingdoms of the Unknown* series, has topped the best-selling lists and earned enthusiastic praise from book reviewers. Don't miss an opportunity to hear one of the most popular SF authors of the last decade read from her latest work.

Tickets are $5 and can be purchased at Easton's Books, 27 Grey Lane, Memphis, or by calling the store's customer service line at 080-555-4834.

問題 156-157 參考以下通知。

伊斯頓書店很高興在 8 月 12 日下午 3 點到 5 點舉辦一場由 156 作家安娜坦里昂絲主講的公開朗讀會。里昂絲小姐曾兩度獲得頗富盛名的雷利最佳科幻小說獎，她將朗讀小說《門後》的摘錄內容。這本小說是她的 157《未知王國》系列第 5 部，也是最後一部，在暢銷書排行榜上高居榜首，贏得書評家的熱情讚揚。不要錯過聆聽一位近 10 年來最受歡迎的科幻小說作家朗讀她最新作品的機會。

門票售價 5 美元，可以在孟菲斯葛雷巷 27 號的伊斯頓書店購買，或撥打書店客服電話 080-555-4834。

字彙　**public reading** 公開朗讀會　**prestigious** 頗富盛名的　**excerpt** 摘錄、節錄　**installment**（系列中的）部分　**enthusiastic** 熱情的　**praise** 讚許　**book reviewer** 書評家　**SF** 科幻小說，**science fiction** 的縮寫　**decade** 十年

Test 02

156. Who is Ms. Lyons?
 (A) A librarian at a famous university
 (B) The owner of Easton's Books
 (C) A literary critic from a publishing company
 (D) The author of a popular book

里昂絲小姐是誰？
 (A) 知名大學的圖書館員
 (B) 伊斯頓書店的老闆
 (C) 出版公司的文學評論家
 (D) 暢銷書的作者

正確答案為 (D)

第一段提到 a public reading by writer Annette Lyons，可知她是一位作家，答案是 (D)。

> **字彙** **librarian** 圖書館員 **critic** 評論家

157. What is mentioned about *Behind the Doors*?
 (A) It was written over a ten-year period.
 (B) It received an important award.
 (C) It is the last book in a series.
 (D) It sold more than half a million copies.

關於《門後》，本文提到什麼內容？
 (A) 超過十年的時間寫成。
 (B) 得到重要的獎項。
 (C) 是系列作品的最後一部。
 (D) 已經銷售超過 50 萬冊。

正確答案為 (C)

在第一段提到 the fifth and final installment in her Kingdoms of the Unknown series，答案是 (C)。作家 Lyons 里昂絲雖然得過獎，但無法得知是否因《門後》一書而得獎，因此 (B) 不是答案。

Questions 158-160 refer to the following article. 報導

New Take Off for Edgerton

Vernon City, September 2 – Revised plans for the Edgerton International Airport were presented to the Vernon City Transportation Board by Nina Grant, the project's chief engineer, on August 30. –[1]–.

Plans for the new airport, to be located just west of Vernon City, were first approved three years ago. However, a study commissioned by the Transportation Board last year concluded that the number of passengers traveling by air to the region is expected to increase substantially within the next few years. –[2]–. This is largely a result of the decision by Marcus Hotel Ltd. to open a large beach resort about twenty kilometers north of Vernon City. –[3]–.

Proposed changes include lengthening the runways to accommodate the large-capacity planes, expanding the passenger waiting areas, and adding shopping areas to the passenger terminal. –[4]–.

Board chairperson Jenny Mason noted that the board is likely to approve the revised plans within the month, which will allow the first of four construction phases for the airport to begin in January as originally scheduled.

問題 158-160 參考以下報導。

艾杰頓再起飛

維農市，**9 月 2 日** ── 158 8 月 30 日艾杰頓國際機場專案總工程師尼那葛蘭特向維農市交通董事會提交修改後的計畫。–[1]–

159 位於維農市西部的新機場計畫在 3 年前獲得批准。然而，交通委員會去年委託進行的一項研究結果顯示，未來幾年搭乘飛機前往該地區的乘客預計將大幅增加。–[2]– 這主要是因為馬可斯飯店決定在維農市以北約 20 公里處開設一個大型海灘度假村的緣故。–[3]–

159 160 計畫包括以下更動：延長跑道容納大型飛機、擴大旅客等候區，以及在客運轉運站增加購物區。–[4]–

董事會主席珍妮馬森指出，董事會可能會在本月批准修改後的計畫，這將使原計畫機場 4 個建築階段的第一階段可於明年 1 月開始進行。

字彙 **revised plan** 修正的計畫 　**commission** 委託、委任 　**region** 地區 　**substantially** 大量地 　**resort** 度假村 　**capacity** 容量 　**terminal** 終點站；航廈 　**chairperson** 主席、議長 　**phase** 階段

158. What is the reason for the meeting of Ms. Grant and board members?
(A) To request that research be conducted
(B) To announce an appointment of her company's new president
(C) To keep them updated about design plans
(D) To explain why construction work will start later than expected

葛蘭特小姐和董事會成員見面的原因為何？
(A) 要求進行研究
(B) 宣布公司新總裁的任命
(C) 讓他們了解最新的設計計畫
(D) 解釋為何建築工程延後開工

正確答案為 **(C)**

本題詢問文章主旨，並提到關鍵字 Ms. Grant 與 board，第一段提到 Revised plans for the Edgerton International Airport were presented to the Vernon City Transportation Board by Nina Grant, the project's chief engineer, on August 30，由此可知在 8 月的時候葛蘭特小姐向董事會提交了修正的計畫，答案是 (C)。

159. What is suggested about the Edgerton International Airport?
(A) It will be able to accommodate large-capacity planes.
(B) It will be located to the north of Vernon City.
(C) It will have three passenger terminals.
(D) It will have the largest shipping area of any airport in the region.

關於艾杰頓國際機場，我們知道些什麼？
(A) 它將能容納大型飛機。
(B) 它位於維農市的北方。
(C) 它將有 3 個乘客轉運站。
(D) 它將擁有該地區最大的航運區域。

正確答案為 **(A)**

第三段提到 Edgerton International Airport 修改後的建築計畫，包括 lengthening the runways to accommodate the large-capacity planes，答案是 (A)。第二段提到 to be located just west of Vernon City，所以 (B) 錯誤，(C) 與 (D) 文章中無提及。為了爭取時間，這種找出正確選項的問題不須看完全部選項才作答，只要找到對的選項就可以作答。

160. In which of the positions marked [1], [2], [3], and [4] does the following sentence best belong?
"Plans for the design of the airport cargo terminal, already on track to be the largest in the region, remain unchanged."
(A) [1]
(B) [2]
(C) [3]
(D) [4]

在標示 [1]、[2]、[3]、[4] 的位置中，何處適合放入以下句子？
「機場貨運站的設計維持不變，該機場貨運站即將成為該地區最大的貨運站。」
(A) [1]
(B) [2]
(C) [3]
(D) [4]

正確答案為 **(D)**

〈插入句〉
本句提到機場設施的設計內容，與機場設施有關的內容是在第三段，因此答案是 (D)。

字彙　**cargo terminal** 貨運轉運站　**on track** 進行中的

Questions 161-164 refer to the following letter. 信件

Whitfield Grocery

July 1

Dear Customer:

Exciting changes are happening at Whitfield Grocery! We hope you will visit us later this month and see the improvements we are making in order to enhance your shopping experience.

As you may know, we have been undergoing a significant renovation that is adding about 8,000 square meters to our store. Beginning on July 10, our produce section will be nearly twice as big, which will allow us to offer a variety of fruits and vegetables and allow you to move around the store with ease. We are also expanding our bakery section to provide you with freshly baked bread.

We will be celebrating the renovations on Saturday, July 20. There will be cooking demonstrations and free food tastings. In addition, we will start opening on Saturdays at 6 A.M. instead of 7 A.M.

To encourage you to visit the new Whitfield Grocery, we have enclosed discount coupons. The coupons are good until July 31. You will also find a calendar indicating special sale days.

Sincerely,

Ann O'Connor
Store manager

問題 161-164 參考以下信件。

威菲路雜貨店

7 月 1 日

親愛的顧客：

令人興奮的改變正在威菲路雜貨店發生！161 衷心希望您能在本月中旬後光顧本店，看看我們為了提高顧客購物體驗所做的改善。

162B 如您所知，我們正在進行重大整修工程，店面會增加約 8,000 平方公尺的面積。從 7 月 10 日開始，我們的農產品區將擴大將近一倍，162A 提供您各式各樣的新鮮果，並讓您可以在店裡輕鬆走動。我們也擴大了烘焙區，提供您新鮮出爐的麵包。

我們將在 7 月 20 日星期六慶祝改裝，會有烹飪示範與免費食物試吃。另外，162C 我們星期六早上將改為 6 點開始營業，而不是早上 7 點。

為了鼓勵您參觀全新的威菲路雜貨店，隨信附上折扣券。優惠券 164 有效期限到 7 月 31 日為止。163 您也會看到一張標註特價日期的月曆。

店經理安歐康納

字彙　**improvement** 改進、發展　**enhance** 加強、提昇　**significant** 重大的　**free food tasting** 免費食物試吃
enclose 附上、把～裝入信封　**coupon** 優惠券　**good** 有效的　**indicate** 表明、指出

161. What is the purpose of the letter?
(A) To publicize the completion of a store renovation
(B) To advertise custom-made baking goods
(C) To announce a change in a store's ownership
(D) To promote a new store location

信件的目的為何？
(A) 宣傳店面裝修已完工
(B) 宣傳客製化烘焙產品
(C) 宣布商店所有權的變更
(D) 推廣新的店面位置

正確答案為 (A)

文章目的通常能在第一段看到，本文第一段提到 We hope you will visit us later this month and see the improvements we are making in order to enhance your shopping experience，可知這是封通知裝修完工的信件，答案是 (A)。

> **字彙** **completion** 完成　**custom-made** 客製化的　**ownership** 物主、所有權

162. What is NOT mentioned in this letter?
(A) A wider selection of products
(B) Increased floor space
(C) Extended hours of operation
(D) Additional cashiers

這封信沒有提到什麼？
(A) 產品選擇更廣
(B) 樓層空間增加
(C) 營業時間延長
(D) 收銀員增加

正確答案為 (D)

第二段提到 adding about 8,000 square meter to our store「增加店面」，符合選項 (B)。offer a variety of fruits and vegetables「商品更多樣化」，符合選項 (A)。we will start opening on Saturdays at 6 A.M. instead of 7 A.M.「提早營業」，符合選項 (C)，因此答案是 (D)。

163. What is included in the letter?
(A) A questionnaire
(B) A schedule of events
(C) A list of products
(D) A product sample

信件裡包含以下何者？
(A) 問卷調查
(B) 活動日程表
(C) 產品目錄
(D) 產品樣品

正確答案為 (B)

本題詢問是否還有其他附件，通常能在最後一段找到答案。本文最後一段提到 You will also find a calendar indicating special sale days，可知信件裡含有告知優惠活動日期的日曆，答案是 (B)。

164. In the letter, the word "good" in paragraph 4, line 2, is closest in meaning to
(A) enough
(B) valid
(C) kind
(D) efficient

信件第四段第二行的「good」與以下何者的意思最相近？
(A) 足夠的
(B) 有效的
(C) 親切的
(D) 有效率的

正確答案為 (B)

〈推測字義〉

在 The coupons are good until July 31 整句意思是「到 7 月 31 日為止前可以使用」，good 也常作「有效的」之意，因此答案是 (B)。

Questions 165-167 refer to the following memo. 備忘錄

MEMO

To: Clarion Market Project Team Members
From: Marijus Fitzgerald
Date: September 4
Subject: Project Results

First, I would like to thank everyone for their hard work with the Clarion Outdoor Market held over the weekend at Jefferson Park. The event was a success overall, raising a large amount of proceeds for the medical center like we had hoped, and will definitely be continued. Nevertheless, we will need to improve a few areas before conducting the second installment of the event the month after next.

The main concern is inclement weather. As many of you noticed, despite the rain on Sunday, we still had a large turnout of guests, which was fantastic. Sadly, we had not prepared for this, and received a number of complaints from both merchants and customers about not having protective coverings on the booths. I have discussed this with staff at the park, and they are willing to provide us with several large tents for future markets.

On another note, we may also want to consider eliminating the registration fee, since some of the merchants complained about a lack of sales. Instead, we could consider collecting a percentage of what they earn in transactions. I would like for everyone to propose another suggestion to alleviate this problem, or perhaps methods that could be used to implement this idea without making the process unnecessarily difficult. If you have any ideas, please send them to Adam Mosley, the outdoor market coordinator.

Marijus Fitzgerald
Director, Clarion Market Project

問題 165-167 參考以下備忘錄。

備忘錄

收件者：號角市場專案小組成員

寄件者：馬留費茲傑羅

日期：9 月 4 日

主旨：專案結果

首先，我要感謝大家上週末努力協助在傑佛森公園舉辦的號角戶外市場。這次活動整體而言很成功，正如我們所希望的，該活動為醫療中心募集到大量資金，未來肯定也能繼續下去。儘管如此，⑯⑤ 在下下個月進行第 2 梯次的活動之前，我們還需要改進一些地方。

惡劣天氣是主要擔憂。正如許多人注意到的，儘管週日下雨，振奮的是仍然有許多顧客到場。但可惜我們並沒有為此做好準備，因而收到許多商家與顧客投訴，⑯⑥ 他們抱怨我們的展位沒有遮雨措施。我已經和公園工作人員討論過，他們願意為我們接下來的展場提供幾個大帳棚。

另一方面，我們可以考慮不收註冊費，因為有些商家抱怨銷售欠佳。相反地，我們可以從商家的收入收取一定比例的費用。⑯⑦ 我希望各位都要提出相關建議來改善這個問題，或者提供能更快落實此提議的方法。有任何想法，請寄信給戶外市場調查員亞當摩斯利。

馬留費茲傑羅
號角市場專案召集人

字彙　**proceeds** 收益，特別指從某種活動獲得的收入　　**definitely** 肯定地　　**installment** 分次、分期
the month after next 兩個月後　　**inclement weather** 險惡天氣　　**turnout** 參加人數　　**merchant** 商人
covering 帷幕、遮棚　　**on another note** 另一方面　　**eliminate** 排除、消除
registration fee 註冊費、登記費　　**transaction** 交易　　**alleviate** 減輕、緩解

165. What can be inferred about the Market Project?

(A) **It has only been held one time.**
(B) It takes place once a month.
(C) It was canceled due to weather.
(D) It will be changing locations.

關於市場專案，從短文可以推斷出什麼？

(A) **只舉辦了一次。**
(B) 一個月舉辦一次。
(C) 因為天氣因素而取消。
(D) 將變更場地。

正確答案為 (A)

第一段的 we will need to improve a few areas before conducting the second installment of the event the month after next 說到第二梯次活動，由此可知這次是第一次，答案是 (A)。第二梯次將是在下下個月後舉辦，可推斷活動是兩個月舉辦一次。

166. What did the customers complain about?

(A) The expensive registration fee
(B) **The lack of protection from rain**
(C) The small number of merchants
(D) The low amount of product variety

顧客抱怨什麼？

(A) 登記費昂貴
(B) **缺乏避雨設施**
(C) 商人數量少
(D) 產品種類少

正確答案為 (B)

可在文章中尋找關鍵字 complain。第二段提到 not having protective coverings on the booths，可知答案是 (B)。

167. What does Mr. Fitzgerald ask the members of the project to do?

(A) Organize a new event
(B) Contact park officials
(C) **Submit some suggestions**
(D) Speak with the merchants

費茲傑羅先生要求專案成員做什麼？

(A) 企劃新活動
(B) 聯絡公園職員
(C) **提交建議**
(D) 和商人談話

正確答案為 (C)

第三段 I would like for everyone to propose another suggestion to alleviate this problem, or perhaps methods that could be used to implement this idea 的內容表示希望大家提出建議，答案是 (C)。

Questions 168-171 refer to the following article. 報導

THIS MONTH'S HIGHLIGHT

Susie Murray, who plans to step down as chief accountant in May, has served Harrison Accounting Firm in many capacities for 32 years. –[1]–. The president of the firm, Mario Vinchenso, said, "It's rare to find anyone who has the range of experience at Harrison that Susie has."

Ms. Murray began her career in accounting as a temporary receptionist at Miller Creek Accounting in Milwaukee. –[2]–. She was then hired as a full-time receptionist at Harrison's Norfolk branch. After two years of answering telephones and directing customers' calls, Ms. Murray was hired as a manager at Harrison Accounting's Richmond branch, and in less than a year was promoted to head manager.

–[3]–. Ms. Murray's promotions did not end there, however. She recounted, "I enjoyed working with numbers and wanted to move into the accounting department. My manager at the Richmond branch, Galen Broadbent, gave me advice on how I could achieve my goal. On Galen's recommendation, I decided to pursue an accounting degree at Whitney College in Norfolk, just as Galen had done some years before. –[4]–. By applying for a student loan and continuing to work as a part-time employer, I was able to complete the accounting program in five years."

Once she had received her degree from Whitney College, Ms. Murray joined the accounting department at Harrison Accounting's headquarters. Three years later, she was appointed assistant to Chief Accountant Jeanne Archer, and when Ms. Archer transferred to the commercial accounting division, Ms. Murray was chosen to fill the position. "Just think about that," Ms. Murray said, "I started out handling telephone calls, and I ended up as chief accountant at the firm's headquarters."

問題 168-171 參考以下報導。

本月最精采

蘇西墨瑞計畫今年 5 月辭去會計主任一職，她在哈里遜會計師事務所擔任多種職務已 32 年之久。–[1]– 事務所總裁馬力歐文森索說：「在哈里遜很難再找到像蘇西這麼有豐富工作經驗的人。」

171 墨瑞小姐是從美沃奇的米勒克里克會計公司擔任臨時接待員開始其會計職涯。–[2]– 171 後來她被聘為哈里遜諾福克分公司的正職接待員。經過兩年的電話接聽和引導客戶電話，墨瑞小姐被哈里遜會計的里蒙分公司聘為經理，不到一年的時間就升為總經理。

–[3]– 然而，墨瑞小姐的升職並未就此結束。她說：「我很喜歡和數字打交道，想進入會計部門。169 里蒙分公司經理高倫布洛本給了我實現目標的建議。在高倫的推薦下，我決定像高倫幾年前做過的一樣，去諾福克的惠特尼大學攻讀會計學位。–[4]– 靠著學生貸款和兼職工作，我在 5 年內完成了會計學程。」

墨瑞小姐取得惠特尼大學學位後，加入哈里遜會計總部的會計部門。3 年後，她被指派為當時會計主任潔安亞契的助理。170 亞契小姐轉調到商業會計部門後，墨瑞被選為該職位的負責人。墨瑞小姐說：「想想看，我一開始只是處理電話業務，結果成了公司總部的會計主任。」

 字彙　**step down** 辭職、退位　**accountant** 會計師　**capacity** 能力　**temporary** 臨時的　**full-time** 正職的　**receptionist** 接待員　**recount** 詳述　**pursue** 追求　**student loan** 就學貸款　**headquarters** 總部　**fill the position** 遞補職缺　**end up** 最終成為

168. What is the article mainly about?
(A) An announcement of a result from a customer survey
(B) A variety of open positions at a bank
(C) A reason for holding special training programs
(D) A profile of an employee at an accounting firm

這篇文章的主要內容是什麼？
(A) 宣布顧客調查結果
(B) 銀行的各種空缺職位
(C) 舉辦特別培訓課程的原因
(D) 一名會計師事務所員工的簡介

正確答案為 (D)

文章整體內容都是關於 Susie Murray 的經歷，因此答案是 (D)。

字彙　**profile** 簡介

169. What is indicated about Mr. Broadbent?
(A) He is a part-time worker at Harrison.
(B) He was interviewed for the article.
(C) He studied accounting.
(D) He has experience as a professor.

何者是關於布洛本先生的描述？
(A) 他是哈里遜的兼職員工。
(B) 他接受這篇文章採訪。
(C) 他攻讀過會計。
(D) 他當過教授。

正確答案為 (C)

第三段提到 I decided to pursue an accounting degree at Whitney College in Norfolk, just as Galen had done some years before，由此可知 Broadbent 布洛本先生也曾攻讀過會計，答案是 (C)。

170. What is suggested about Harrison Accounting?
(A) Its headquarters are in Richmond.
(B) It has a commercial accounting division.
(C) Its employees can receive a discount on college tuition.
(D) It recently merged with Miller Creek Accounting.

何者是關於哈里遜會計的描述？
(A) 總部位於里蒙。
(B) 設有商業會計部門。
(C) 員工享有大學學費折扣。
(D) 最近和米勒克里克會計合併。

正確答案為 (B)

第四段提到 Ms. Archer transferred to the commercial accounting division，由此可知答案是 (B)。

字彙　**tuition** 學費

171. In which of the positions marked [1], [2], [3], and [4] does the following sentence best belong?
"She found the work to be very rewarding and, when her contract ended, began searching for a permanent position in the industry."
(A) [1]
(B) [2]
(C) [3]
(D) [4]

在標示 [1]、[2]、[3]、[4] 的位置中，何者適合放入以下句子？
「她發現這份工作相當有意義，於是當她的合約到期時，她開始在這個行業尋找正職工作。」
(A) [1]
(B) [2]
(C) [3]
(D) [4]

正確答案為 (B)

〈插入句〉

題目句子和之前的工作經驗有關，因此適合放在 [2] 的位置，也就是之前曾任臨時員工的句子 Ms. Murray began her career in accounting as a temporary receptionist 和成為正職的句子 She was then hired as a full-time receptionist 之間，答案是 (B)。

字彙　**rewarding** 有意義的、值得做的

Questions 172-175 refer to the following online chat discussion. 線上聊天室

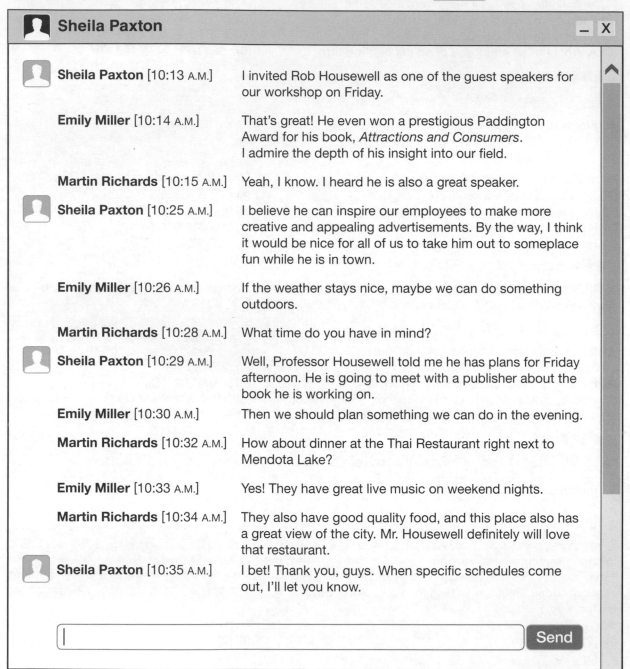

Sheila Paxton   —   X

Sheila Paxton [10:13 A.M.]   I invited Rob Housewell as one of the guest speakers for our workshop on Friday.

Emily Miller [10:14 A.M.]   That's great! He even won a prestigious Paddington Award for his book, *Attractions and Consumers*.
I admire the depth of his insight into our field.

Martin Richards [10:15 A.M.]   Yeah, I know. I heard he is also a great speaker.

Sheila Paxton [10:25 A.M.]   I believe he can inspire our employees to make more creative and appealing advertisements. By the way, I think it would be nice for all of us to take him out to someplace fun while he is in town.

Emily Miller [10:26 A.M.]   If the weather stays nice, maybe we can do something outdoors.

Martin Richards [10:28 A.M.]   What time do you have in mind?

Sheila Paxton [10:29 A.M.]   Well, Professor Housewell told me he has plans for Friday afternoon. He is going to meet with a publisher about the book he is working on.

Emily Miller [10:30 A.M.]   Then we should plan something we can do in the evening.

Martin Richards [10:32 A.M.]   How about dinner at the Thai Restaurant right next to Mendota Lake?

Emily Miller [10:33 A.M.]   Yes! They have great live music on weekend nights.

Martin Richards [10:34 A.M.]   They also have good quality food, and this place also has a great view of the city. Mr. Housewell definitely will love that restaurant.

Sheila Paxton [10:35 A.M.]   I bet! Thank you, guys. When specific schedules come out, I'll let you know.

| | Send |

問題 172-175 參考以下線上聊天室。

詩莉亞派西頓   — X

詩莉亞派西頓 [上午 10 點 13 分]　173 我邀請了羅伯豪斯威爾作為我們週五研討會的演講嘉賓之一。

愛蜜莉米勒 [上午 10 點 14 分]　太好了！他的書《吸引力與消費者》甚至幫他贏得著名的帕丁頓獎。我欽佩他對我們這個領域的深刻見解。

馬丁李察斯 [上午 10 點 15 分]　是的，我知道。我聽說他也是一個了不起的演說家。

詩莉亞派西頓 [上午 10 點 25 分]　172 我相信他能激發我們的員工製作更有創意和吸引力的廣告。順便說一下，我們大家在他還待在這裡的時候，可以帶他去個好玩的地方，我想這麼做應該很棒。

愛蜜莉米勒 [上午 10 點 26 分]　如果天氣好，也許我們可以做一些戶外活動。

馬丁李察斯 [上午 10 點 28 分]　妳想什麼時候去？

詩莉亞派西頓 [上午 10 點 29 分]　173 豪斯威爾教授告訴我他星期五下午有事。他要去見一個和他正在寫的書有關的出版商。

愛蜜莉米勒 [上午 10 點 30 分]　那麼，我們就應該計畫一些可以在晚上做的事情囉。

馬丁李察斯 [上午 10 點 32 分]　174 要不要去門多塔湖旁邊的泰式餐廳？

愛蜜莉米勒 [上午 10 點 33 分]　好啊！他們在週末晚上有很棒的現場音樂。

馬丁李察斯 [上午 10 點 34 分]　他們有高品質的食物，也可以看城市的美景。175 豪斯威爾先生一定會喜歡那家餐廳。

詩莉亞派西頓 [上午 10 點 35 分]　肯定會的！謝謝大家。具體的日程安排出來後，我會通知你們。

[   ]　**Send**

字彙　**insight** 洞察力　**inspire** 激發靈感　**appealing** 吸引人的　**have in mind** 考慮、想到
publisher 出版業者　**specific** 具體的

172. At what kind of company do the writers most likely work?
(A) An advertising firm
(B) An accounting office
(C) A publishing company
(D) A catering service

訊息撰寫者很可能在哪種公司工作？
(A) 廣告公司
(B) 會計事務所
(C) 出版公司
(D) 外燴餐飲服務

正確答案為 (A)

上午 10 點 25 分派西頓說 I believe he can inspire our employees to make more creative and appealing advertisements，可知是廣告公司員工。

173. What can be inferred about Mr. Housewell?
(A) He teaches management at a local university.
(B) He has written several award-winning books.
(C) He has a meeting and a speech on the same day.
(D) He has met with all of the writers before.

何者是關於豪斯威爾先生的推測？
(A) 他在地方大學教管理學。
(B) 他寫了很多得獎著作。
(C) 他在同一天開會並演講。
(D) 他以前見過所有簡訊對者。

正確答案為 (C)

上午 10 點 13 分訊息中提到邀請 Rob Housewell 羅伯豪斯威爾作為週五研討會的演講嘉賓之一。10 點 29 分的訊息中提到豪斯威爾先生星期五下午要和出版業者見面，因此答案是 (C)。內容雖然提到有本書獲獎，但沒有提到有很多獲獎作品，因此 (B) 不是答案。

174. What is suggested about the Thai Restaurant?
(A) It is located on the top floor of a building.
(B) It is a waterfront restaurant.
(C) It has music performances every night.
(D) It is open for dinner by reservation only.

何者陳述與泰式餐廳有關？
(A) 它位於大樓最頂層。
(B) 它是一家水岸餐廳。
(C) 它每晚都有音樂演出。
(D) 它的晚餐只接受預訂。

正確答案為 (B)

上午 10 點 32 分李察斯提到 Thai Restaurant right next to Mendota Lake，因此答案是 (B)。

> 字彙 **waterfront** 水畔

175. At 10:35 A.M., what does Ms. Paxton mean when she writes, "I bet"?
(A) She thinks the restaurant is fully booked on Friday.
(B) She is confident that Mr. Housewell will like the place.
(C) She will contact Mr. Housewell in person.
(D) She needs to be in a hurry to organize a workshop.

上午 10 點 35 分派西頓小姐寫道「肯定會的」是什麼意思？
(A) 她認為星期五餐廳已經訂滿了。
(B) 她相信豪斯威爾先生會喜歡這個地方。
(C) 她會親自聯絡豪斯威爾先生。
(D) 她必須趕快規劃研討會。

正確答案為 (B)

〈推測句意〉

她想對上午 10 點 35 分的 Mr. Housewell definitely will love that restaurant 表示贊同，因此寫 I bet.「肯定如此。」，答案是 (B)。

Questions 176-180 refer to the following memo and form. 備忘錄 / 表格

To	All staff
From	Cathy Pinkerton, Vice President of Operations
Date	October 2
Re	Equipment Refresh

Please be reminded that it is again time to place orders for office equipment. Company policy states that standard equipment, such as computers, telephones and fax machines, is eligible for replacement after five years. To replace an item that is any newer, it must be determined that the cost of repair exceeds the cost of replacement. The staff in Purchasing Department will be happy to assist you in researching these costs.

Please use the attached form to list equipment requests. Photocopies of this form may be made as needed. All requests must have the signature of your department manager indicating his or her approval. Note that the Purchasing Department will return the form to its sender if any information is omitted. Make sure that a serial number or ID number appears for the items listed. Forward the completed form to Frank Wong, Purchasing Department, Building C, by October 14. Requests received after that date will be considered in the following quarter.

Thank you for your consideration.

CONNOR CHEMICALS
OFFICE EQUIPMENT ORDER FORM

Employee Name: <u>Martin Jacobs</u>
Title and Department: <u>Quality Control Inspector, Production Department</u>

Equipment Description	Serial Number	Age (years)
Photo Jet Printer	8 HDQ5	5
Computer Monitor		7
Power Cable	PH-3 AL	4

Approved by <u>Daniel Donaldson</u>

Date <u>October 15</u>

176-180 參考以下備忘錄與表格。

收件者	全體員工
寄件者	凱西品克頓，營運副總
日期	10 月 2 日
主旨	汰換設備

⑯ 提醒您，現在又到訂購辦公設備的時候。公司政策規定，電腦、電話、傳真機等一般設備可在使用 5 年後更換。⑱ 若要更換使用期間低於 5 年的設備，必須確定其維修成本是超過換新的成本。採購部的員工會很樂意協助您研究這些支出。

請使用附件表格列出設備要求。如果需要，可以影印這個表格。⑰ ⑲ 所有要求都必須有部門經理的簽字，表示經過他或她的批准。⑳ 請注意，如果遺漏任何訊息，採購部門將會把表單退回寄件者。請確認已標示在目錄上的用品序號或 ID 編號。填妥表格後，請在 10 月 14 日或之前寄發完成的表格給 C 棟大樓採購部的王法蘭克。在該日期之後收到的請求將在下個季度審理。

感謝您的關注。

字彙 equipment 設備　be eligible for 有資格的　determine 決定　exceed 超出
assist sb. in sth. 協助某人做某事　photocopy 影印　signature 簽名　approval 許可　omit 遺漏
serial number 產品編號、序號　forward A to B 轉寄或轉交 A 給 B

康諾化學
辦公室設備訂購單

員工姓名：馬丁雅各
職稱與單位：⑲ 生產部門品管檢驗員

設備說明	序號	使用年數
照片噴墨印表機	8 HDQ5	5
⑳ 電腦監視器		7
⑱ 電力纜線	PH-3 AL	4

同意者：⑲ 丹尼爾唐納森

日期：10 月 15 日

字彙 inspector 檢查員

176. Why is the memo being sent?
(A) To notify staff about a budget reduction for office equipment
(B) To describe how the cost of office equipment is calculated
(C) To explain the process of new office equipment requests
(D) To revise the manual for the office equipment setup

為什麼要寄出此備忘錄？
(A) 通知員工辦公室設備的預算減少
(B) 描述如何計算辦公室設備的成本
(C) 解釋辦公設備的申請流程
(D) 修訂辦公設備的安裝手冊

正確答案為 (C)

詢問目的的答案通常可在文章第一段找到。備忘錄的第一句提到 Please be reminded that it is again time to place orders for office equipment，由此可知答案是 (C)。

字彙　**notify** 通知　**budget reduction** 預算刪減　**calculate** 計算　**setup** 安裝

177. What is mentioned about the forms?
(A) They are reviewed by the operation department once every five years.
(B) They should include the signature of department managers for submission.
(C) They must be submitted to the purchasing office by October 15.
(D) They have been issued in a variety of formats.

關於表格，短文提到什麼內容？
(A) 營運部門每 5 年檢查一次。
(B) 提交時應包含部門經理的簽名。
(C) 必須在 10 月 15 日前交到採購辦公室。
(D) 以各種形式印發。

正確答案為 (B)

備忘錄的第二段提到 All requests must have the signature of your department manager indicating his or her approval，由此可知答案是 (B)。提交日期是 10 月 14 日，因此 (C) 不是答案。

178. What is suggested about the power cable?
(A) Its purchase price is less than the repair costs.
(B) Its production was discontinued last year.
(C) It comes with an extended warranty.
(D) It is not compatible with the company's computers.

何者陳述與電力纜線有關？
(A) 購買費用比修理費用低。
(B) 去年停止生產。
(C) 有延長保固期。
(D) 與公司電腦無法相容。

正確答案為 (A)

〈整合多篇文章資訊〉
備忘錄第一段提到若要更換使用期間低於 5 年的設備，必須確定其維修成本是超過換新的成本。在設備訂購表裡，電力纜線只使用四年卻仍申請更新，代表其購買費用比維修費用低，答案是 (A)。

字彙　**discontinue** 中斷　**be compatible with** 與～相容

179. What staff position does Mr. Donaldson most likely hold?
(A) Purchasing director
(B) Repair technician
(C) Production manager
(D) Administrative assistant

唐納森先生的職位很可能是什麼？
(A) 採購部負責人
(B) 維修技師
(C) 生產部經理
(D) 行政助理

正確答案為 (C)

〈整合多篇文章資訊〉
備忘錄第二段提到若要提交申請表，必須有部門經理的簽名，而申請表的申請員工是來自生產部的員工，由此可知在申請表上簽名的 Donaldson 唐納森先生是生產部經理。

Test 02

180. Why would Mr. Jacobs most likely have the form returned to him?
(A) Because he submitted a photocopy of the form
(B) Because he left out some necessary information
(C) Because he listed equipment for his personal use
(D) Because he needed to obtain Ms. Pinkerton's signature

為什麼雅各提交的表格很可能被退回？
(A) 他提交的是表格影本
(B) 他漏填必要資料
(C) 他列出的是個人使用設備
(D) 他需要得到品克頓小姐的簽名

正確答案為 **(B)**

〈整合多篇文章資訊〉

備忘錄第二段提到申請表格須知 Make sure that a serial number or ID number appears for the items listed，但申請表上並沒有填上電腦監視器的 serial number 序號。在有漏填訊息的情況下，採購部門將會把表單退回寄件者，因此答案是 (B)。

字彙 **leave out** 遺漏　　**obtain** 取得

Questions 181-185 refer to the following Web page and e-mail. 網頁 / 電子郵件

www.tartanairlines.com

| Tartan Airlines | New Services and Special Offers | Reservations | Tartan Airlines Plus Program |

Tartan Airlines is proud to offer new services from the Nashik Airport to the following destinations.

Kolkata - September 5
Agra - September 20
Chennai - September 15
Mumbai - September 25

Book a flight now and save money! Members of the Tartan Airlines frequent-flyers program, Tartan Airlines Plus, who book a flight for one of the above inaugural flights, will receive a 25% discount.

Click on Reservations to book a flight now.

Restrictions and other Reminders

** This offer is valid for one-way or round-way travel for flights originating from the Nashik Airport only on the dates specified above.

** Frequent Flyers can receive a 25% discount by using the Tartan Airlines Plus Membership number when reserving their flights.

** Tartan Airlines is no longer issuing paper tickets. Upon purchasing their tickets, passengers receive e-mails confirming their reservations. This includes an 8-digit confirmation number. Please, keep this number handy to speed your check-in process; passengers are asked to enter it at one of the self-check-in stations.

** In order to offer the lowest possible airfares, Tartan Airlines no longer offers free newspapers, magazines, or headsets and no food or snacks are served during flights. Each passenger is entitled to one complimentary beverage; beverage choices include fruit juice, coffee, tea or water.

問題 181-185 參考以下網頁與電子郵件。

---

www.tartanairlines.com

| 韃坦航空 | 新服務與優惠活動 | 預約 | 韃坦航空 Plus 計畫 |

韃坦航空公司很榮幸提供從那須克機場飛到以下地點的新服務。

181A 184 加爾各達 – 9 月 5 日
阿格拉 – 9 月 20 日
金奈 – 9 月 15 日
孟買 – 9 月 25 日

現在就訂購機票省下更多錢！韃坦航空公司常客飛行計畫「韃坦航空 Plus」的會員若訂購上述首飛航班，將享有七五折的折扣。

請立即點擊「預約」預約航班。

限制與其他注意事項

** 此優惠只適用於上述日期由那須克機場出發的單程或往返機票。

** **182** 常飛旅客使用韃坦航空 Plus 會員號碼預約班機時，可享有七五折折扣。

** **181C** 韃坦航空不再發行紙本機票。購買機票時，乘客會收到確認預約的電子郵件。裡面包含一組 8 位數字的確認號碼。請將這個號碼帶在身邊，以便加速辦理登機手續。乘客須在自助檢票站輸入號碼。

** 為了盡可能提供最低廉的機票價格，韃坦航空不再提供免費報紙、雜誌，或耳機，飛航期間也不提供食物或零食。**181D** 每位旅客可免費享用一杯飲料，選擇包括果汁、咖啡、茶或水。

字彙　destination 目的地　　frequent-flyer program 常客飛行計畫　　inaugural 開幕的　　restriction 限制
valid 有效的　　round-way 往返的　　originate 起始、發源　　specified 詳細說明的、具體列出的
issue 發行　　confirmation 確認　　keep ~ handy 隨身攜帶~　　airfare 飛機票價
be entitled to 有~的資格　　beverage 飲料

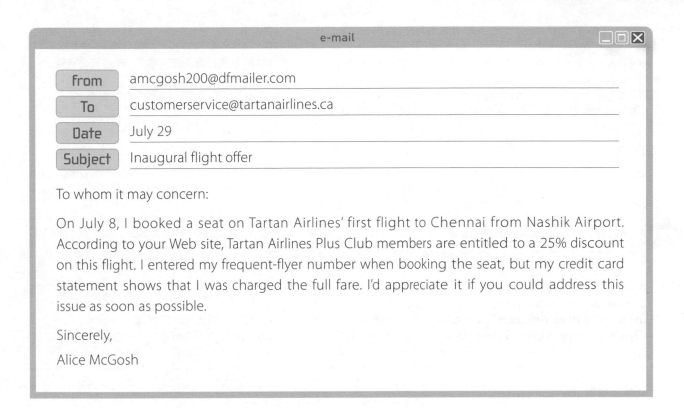

e-mail

from	amcgosh200@dfmailer.com
To	customerservice@tartanairlines.ca
Date	July 29
Subject	Inaugural flight offer

To whom it may concern:

On July 8, I booked a seat on Tartan Airlines' first flight to Chennai from Nashik Airport. According to your Web site, Tartan Airlines Plus Club members are entitled to a 25% discount on this flight. I entered my frequent-flyer number when booking the seat, but my credit card statement shows that I was charged the full fare. I'd appreciate it if you could address this issue as soon as possible.

Sincerely,

Alice McGosh

e-mail

寄件者	amcgosh200@dfmailer.com
收件者	customersieveice@tartanairlines.ca
日期	7 月 29 日
主旨	首航優惠活動

敬啟者：

184 7 月 8 日我預定了韃坦航空從那須克飛往金奈的首發航班座位。根據你們的網站，韃坦航空 Plus 會員搭乘此航班可享七五折扣。183 預約座位時，我輸入了我的常客飛行號碼，但我的信用卡帳單顯示我已付了全額票價。如果您能儘快 185 處理這個問題，我將不勝感激。

艾莉絲麥高許

字彙 **To whom it may concern** 敬啟者，用於未指定收信者的正式開頭　　**statement** 清單　　**full fare** 全額票價

Test 02

181. What is NOT mentioned about Tartan Airlines?
(A) It is offering service to four new destinations.
(B) It charges customers a penalty of $25 to change itinerary.
(C) It has stopped providing customers with paper tickets.
(D) It currently provides one soft drink at no charge during flights.

關於韃坦航空，文章沒有提到下列何者內容？
(A) 提供 4 個新目的地的飛行服務。
(B) 向變更行程的旅客收取 25 美元的罰款。
(C) 已停止發行紙本機票。
(D) 目前飛行期間免費提供一杯飲料。

正確答案為 **(B)**

網站上標示 Kolkata、Agra、Chennai、Mumbai 等 4 個新目的地，符合選項 (A)。後半提到 Tartan Airlines is no longer issuing paper tickets，符合選項 (C)。最後一段提到 Each passenger is entitled to one complimentary beverage，符合選項 (D)。答案是文章內容沒有提到的 (B)。

字彙 **penalty** 罰款　　**itinerary** 旅行計劃

182. According to the information, what must customers do to receive the advertised discount?
(A) Supply their frequent-flyer program number
(B) Make a reservation at least two weeks in advance
(C) Apply for membership in the frequent-flyer program
(D) Purchase tickets to any two of the featured destinations

根據訊息，顧客必須做什麼才能得到廣告中的折扣？
(A) 提供常飛旅客計畫號碼
(B) 至少提前兩週預約
(C) 申請加入常客飛行計畫的會員
(D) 購買任 2 個主打目的地的機票

正確答案為 **(A)**

網站上的 Frequent Flyers can receive a 25% discount by using the Tartan Airlines Plus Membership number，說明使用會員號碼可享有折扣優惠，答案是 (A)。

字彙 **in advance** 預先、提前　　**apply for** 申請

183. Why did Ms. McGosh send the e-mail?
(A) To complain about delays she experienced on a recent trip
(B) To make a change to her departure date
(C) To ask for a replacement confirmation number
(D) To report a billing mistake with her reservation

為什麼麥高許小姐寄出這封電子郵件？
(A) 客訴最近一次的班機延誤
(B) 更改出發日期
(C) 索取更新確認號碼
(D) 告知帳單出現預訂錯誤

正確答案為 **(D)**

電子郵件裡提到 my credit card statement shows that I was charged the full fare，答案是 (D)。

字彙 **complain about** 抱怨　　**departure** 出發　　**billing mistake** 帳單錯誤

184. When is Ms. McGosh scheduled to depart?
(A) On September 5
(B) On September 15
(C) On September 20
(D) On September 25

麥高許小姐從那須克機場出發的預定日是何時？
(A) 9 月 5 日
(B) 9 月 15 日
(C) 9 月 20 日
(D) 9 月 25 日

正確答案為 **(B)**

〈整合多篇文章資訊〉

電子郵件提到 I booked a seat on Tartan Airlines' first flight to Chennai from Nashik Airport，要去金奈，若參考網站上新目的地航班的首航日期，可以得知出發日是 9 月 15 日，答案是 (B)。

185. In the e-mail, the word "address" in paragraph 1, line 4, is closest in meaning to
(A) speak
(B) remark
(C) deal with
(D) write

電子郵件第一段第四行的「address」意思與以下何者最相近？
(A) 說
(B) 談論
(C) 處理
(D) 寫

正確答案為 **(C)**

〈推測字義〉

address this issue 意思是「解決問題」，address 在這裡有「處理」之意。

字彙　**remark** 談論　　**deal with** 處理

Questions 186-190 refer to the following article, advertisement, and Web page. 文章／廣告／網頁

Vancouver (March 10)

✖ Regina Regency Resorts Get Bigger ✖

The Seattle-based Regina Hotel Group has acquired Orchid Inc., a small but exclusive locally owned hotel chain. With the addition of the Orchid properties, Regina now operates 11 hotels in the Vancouver area with more than 800 guest rooms.

Prior to the acquisition, Regina had been best known for its Regina Travel Suites, smaller hotels designed with business travelers in mind. Orchid's four properties include the luxurious Grand Hall Hotel, built in 1924, and the Hotel Olivia, a high-end hotel that opened just last year.

The Orchid Hotels are a very welcome addition to the Regina Brand, said Regina spokesperson Douglas Wong. Orchid has a solid reputation in Vancouver, and with accommodations that appeal especially to tourists, they are a perfect complement to Regina's existing hotels.

Regina loyalty-club members can now earn points when they stay at any of the former Orchid Hotels.

問題 186-190 參考以下文章、廣告與網頁。

溫哥華（3 月 10 日）

✖ 日益壯大的瑞根納雷根西度假村 ✖

(186) 總部位於西雅圖的瑞根納飯店集團收購當地一家規模較小但擁有獨家經營權的連鎖酒店蘭花股份有限公司。加上蘭花的所有權之後，目前瑞根納在溫哥華經營 11 家飯店，超過 800 間客房。

進行收購之前，瑞根納最著名的是專為商務旅客設計的小型飯店瑞根納旅遊套房。蘭花旗下的 4 個飯店包含建於 1924 年的豪華大廳飯店以及去年才剛開幕的奧利維亞高級飯店。

瑞根納發言人翁道格拉斯表示，蘭花飯店是瑞根納品牌中相當受歡迎的新成員。(187) 蘭花在溫哥華享有良好聲譽，特別吸引遊客住宿，將使瑞根納現有飯店更為完善。

即日起，瑞根納忠實顧客會員入住任一家蘭花飯店，皆可獲得點數。

字彙　**exclusive** 獨家的　**property** 所有權　**operate** 營運　**prior to** 在～之前　**acquisition** 收購　**luxurious** 豪華的　**high-end** 高階的、高級的　**spokesperson** 發言人　**solid** 堅固的、堅硬的　**appeal to** 有吸引力，吸引～　**complement** 補足　**loyalty-club member** 忠實顧客會員　**former** 以前的

Your Home in Vancouver City Center

Visiting Vancouver? Want to be in the heart of the city? Choose Regina Hotel. Our hotel family now includes the popular Orchid Hotels. Below are a few of our most popular hotels in the downtown area.

▪Moon Hotel

From complimentary wireless Internet service to deluxe bed, large-screen TVs and an indoor swimming pool. This hotel has something for everyone. Great for families!

▪Hotel Fantastic Plaza

"Fantastic" does not begin to describe this hotel! Enjoy our newly refurbished luxurious guest rooms, fine dining at our recently remodeled restaurant, and convenient access to theaters, shopping and sightseeing.

▪Hotel South

With free transportation to the airport and a fully equipped business center, this is the perfect hotel for business travelers. It features conference rooms and complimentary wireless Internet service. This hotel makes it easy to work while traveling.

▪Cozy Inn

An old-fashioned inn with modern conveniences such as microwaves and hair dryers in every room. With its charming decor, tasty complimentary breakfast, and proximity to public transportation, this is a wonderful place to stay during your Vancouver holiday.

Or choose one of our many other hotels in the Vancouver region. When you choose Regina, you choose the best!

---

http://vancouverdays.com/review

| RESTAURANTS | HOTELS | ATTRACTIONS | TRANSPORTATION |

I really enjoyed my recent stay at the Hotel Fantastic Plaza. My room was comfortable and well furnished, and all my meals at the hotel restaurant were expertly prepared. The hotel staff provided outstanding service as well. I only wish there had been a shuttle service. I had a difficult time getting a taxi to the airport, and it was expensive. Aside from that minor inconvenience, I enjoyed my stay very much.

Shirley Rogers
London

您在溫哥華市中心的家

您要前往溫哥華嗎？(188)想住在市中心嗎？請選擇瑞根納飯店。我們的飯店集團現在包含了廣受歡迎的蘭花飯店。以下是幾間位於市中心最受歡迎的旗下飯店。

■ 月亮飯店
從免費無限網路到豪華床鋪、大螢幕電視以及室內游泳池，這間飯店能滿足所有旅客需求。非常適合家庭訪客！

■ 夢幻購物飯店
用「太棒了」也無法形容這家飯店。請盡情享受我們重新整修的豪華客房，在近期全新布置的餐廳享用精緻美食，還有(190)便利通道可前往電影院、商店街和觀光勝地。

■ 南方飯店
對商務旅客而言，這是一間完美的飯店，它擁有免費前往機場的交通接駁，以及一應俱全的商務中心。它具備會議室和免費無線網路。這間飯店能讓您在旅行期間更輕鬆地工作。

■ 舒適客棧
這是一間老式旅館，所有房間都有微波爐和吹風機等現代便利設施。因其吸引人的室內裝飾、免費提供的美味早點、(189)接近大眾交通工具的地理位置，這裡將是您在溫格華度假期間美好的住宿地點。

或者您也可以選擇我們位於溫哥華地區的其他飯店。瑞根納將是您最佳的選擇！

字彙 deluxe bed 豪華雙人床　　fine dining 精緻餐飲　　decor 室內裝潢　　proximity 鄰近

---

http://vancouverdays.com/review

| 餐廳 | 飯店 | 觀光景點 | 交通 |

(190)我最近在夢幻購物飯店的住宿經驗非常愉快。我的房間很舒適，家具擺設得宜，我在飯店餐廳享用的所有餐點都經過精心準備。飯店員工也提供傑出的服務。我唯獨希望那裡若能提供接駁服務就好。我叫計程車到機場的過程感到困難，而且很昂貴。除了這點小小的不便之外，我非常享受我這次的住宿經驗。

雪莉羅傑斯
倫敦

字彙 well furnished 家具陳設得當　　expertly 熟練地、專業地　　outstanding 出色的　　as well 也、同樣地
have a difficult time + Ving 做～經歷困難　　aside from 除～以外

186. What is the article mainly about?
(A) New trends in the hotel industry
(B) The results of a committee election
(C) The merger of two businesses
(D) Announcement of a new construction site

這篇文章主要是關於什麼？
(A) 飯店產業新趨勢
(B) 委員會選舉的結果
(C) 兩家業者合併
(D) 新建築工地的公告

正確答案為 **(C)**

文章的第一句 The Seattle-based Regina Hotel Group has acquired Orchid Inc. 提到了兩家業者的合併，答案是 (C)。**多益文章常出現 acquire 與 merger**，指「合併、併購」，務必記住。

> 字彙　**merger** 合併　**construction site** 建築工地

187. What can be inferred about Regina Regency Resorts?
(A) It is relocating its headquarters.
(B) It has discontinued its membership program.
(C) It specializes in luxury hotels.
(D) It attempts to draw a wider variety of customers.

關於瑞根納雷根西度假村，我們可以知道什麼？
(A) 它的總部將搬遷。
(B) 它的會員活動已中止。
(C) 它專營高級飯店。
(D) 它試圖吸引更廣泛的顧客。

正確答案為 **(D)**

文章的第三段提到 accommodations that appeal especially to tourists, they are a perfect complement to Regina's existing hotels，可以看出瑞根納飯店正努力吸引更多樣的遊客，答案是 (D)

> 字彙　**specialize in** 專精於　**attempt to** 試圖　**draw** 吸引

188. What is indicated about the hotels in the advertisement?
(A) They all have swimming pools.
(B) They were first built in 1920.
(C) They are centrally located in downtown.
(D) They offer discounts to business travelers.

從廣告可以得知關於飯店何種資訊？
(A) 全部都有游泳池。
(B) 1920 年開始興建。
(C) 位於市中心。
(D) 提供商務旅客折扣。

正確答案為 **(C)**

廣告一開始提到 Want to be in the heart of the city? Choose Regina Hotel，可知廣告出現的 4 個飯店都是位於溫哥華的市中心，答案是 (C)。

> 字彙　**downtown** 市中心（的）

189. In the advertisement, the word "proximity" in paragraph 5, line 2, is closest in meaning to
(A) subsequence
(B) approximation
(C) nearness
(D) possibility

廣告第五段第二行的「proximity」意思最接近以下何者？
(A) 接續
(B) 近似值
(C) 接近
(D) 可能性

正確答案為 **(C)**

〈推測字義〉
proximity to 是「接近、鄰近」的意思，答案是 (C)。

> 字彙　**subsequence** 接續、持續

190. What is mentioned about the hotel in which Ms. Rogers has stayed?
(A) It is not far from the shopping place.
(B) Its restaurant recently hired a new chef.
(C) It is wheelchair-accessible.
(D) It offers free admission to the hotel facilities.

關於羅傑斯小姐下塌的飯店，以下何者有提及？
(A) 飯店距離購物場所不遠。
(B) 飯店餐廳最近聘用新主廚。
(C) 輪椅可進出飯店。
(D) 飯店設施提供免費使用。

正確答案為 (A)

〈整合多篇文章資訊〉
從網頁可以得知羅傑斯小姐入住的是 Hotel Fantastic Plaza，廣告中提到這家飯店的特色是 convenient access to theaters, shopping and sightseeing，由此可知飯店距離購物場所不遠，答案是 (A)。

字彙　**admission** 入場、入會

Questions 191-195 refer to the following notice, schedule, and e-mail. 通知 / 行程表 / 電子郵件

International Auto Trade Fair

This year's International Auto Trade Fair will be held at the MXFM Convention Center in Detroit from August 6th through 13th, and we will have some of the hottest cars and trucks you've ever seen – all under one roof! More sneak peeks, more new production models, and more concept vehicles than ever before. This year only, Cervi Automotive will be showcasing all of its vehicles from director Meredith Grazinski's blockbuster movie *Before the Sun Goes Down*. Stars of that movie, Peter Wiseman and Alicia Michel, will be on hand on August 11th and 12th to demonstrate some of the vehicles' super effects.

La Siesta

NINTH INTERNATIONAL AUTO TRADE FAIR IN DETROIT

• **Public Show Dates**
Friday, August 6th through Friday, August 13th
11:00 A.M. – 10:30 P.M. (Sunday: 10:00 A.M. – 7:30 P.M.)

• **Special Public Sneak Preview**
Friday, August 6th: 11:00 A.M. – 10:30 P.M.

• **Official Opening Day**
Saturday, August 7th
Festivities begin at 9:00 A.M.
The showroom floor opens at 11:00 A.M.

• **Press Preview**
Wednesday, August 11th & Thursday, August 12th
Media credentials required

• **Dealer Preview**
Thursday, August 12th from 4:00 P.M. – 10:00 P.M. (by invitation only)
Credentials required

Test 02

問題 191-195 參考以下通知、行程表與電子郵件。

國際汽車貿易博覽會

(191) 今年的國際汽車貿易博覽會將於 8 月 6 日至 13 日在底特律的 MXFM 會議中心舉辦,屆時我們將在同一個地方展出一些您從未見過的熱門款轎車和卡車。今年展出將有更多的搶先看,更多的新產品模型,更多的概念車款。今年獨家,Cervi 汽車將展出在導演梅雷迪斯葛藍辛基的電影鉅片〈在太陽下山之前〉中出現的所有車款。(195) 這部電影的主要演員彼得懷思曼與愛莉西亞米雪兒將於 8 月 11 日和 12 日蒞臨現場,展示汽車的驚人特效。

拉席薇斯塔

字彙 **sneak peek** 搶先看、先睹為快　　**showcase** 展示　　**on hand** 方便的、在手邊、在場　　**blockbuster** 賣座電影

第九屆底特律國際汽車貿易博覽會

- **公開展演日**
8 月 6 日星期五至 8 月 13 日星期五
上午 11 點 – 下午 10 點 30 分(星期日:上午 10 點 – 下午 7 點 30 分)

- (192) **特別公開先睹為快**
8 月 6 日星期五上午 11 點 – 下午 10 點 30 分

- **正式開幕日**
8 月 7 日星期六
活動開始於上午 9 點
展館於上午 11 點開放

- **媒體搶先看**
8 月 11 日星期三與 8 月 12 日星期四
需媒體識別證

- (193) **經銷商搶先看**
8 月 12 日星期四下午 4 點 – 下午 10 點 (193)(僅受邀者參加)
需資格證

字彙 **festivity** 慶祝活動　　**credential** 資格證

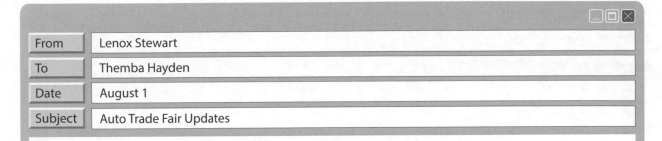

From	Lenox Stewart
To	Themba Hayden
Date	August 1
Subject	Auto Trade Fair Updates

Dear Themba,

I am sorry I couldn't meet with you yesterday. I was busy meeting representatives from the various automakers that will be participating in this year's show. Today, I am meeting with the publicist from Zen Motors at one of its dealerships in the area.

There are a few things I need to talk to you about. The first is that Ms. Michel will not be able to attend the show because of scheduling conflicts with another film she's making. Her agent, Charles Levingston, called yesterday to inform me.

Another problem, and one that could potentially have a more damaging effect, is something that Ms. Woodward in admissions brought to my attention. Apparently all orders for advance tickets were supposed to be accompanied by a certificate that would be good for discounts at area hotels. Unfortunately, only about a third of the people who bought advance tickets received these certificates in time. Ms. Woodward wants to know if we can work out a system where we give the certificates to the people when they arrive for the show, to be retroactively applied to their hotel bills. I like this idea, but let me know what you think.

Sincerely,

Lenox Stewart
Public Relations Manager

寄件者	里諾克斯史都華
收件者	森巴海頓
日期	8 月 1 日
主旨	汽車貿易博覽會最新

森巴你好：

很抱歉昨天無法和你碰面。當時我正忙著會見各個汽車製造商的代表，他們將參加今年的車展。今天我要和 Zen Motors 的宣傳人員在他們其中一家地區經銷商見面。

我有幾件事情需要和你談談。195 首先，米雪兒小姐無法參加活動演出，因為活動和她正在拍攝的另一部電影檔期有衝突。她的經紀人查理斯萊文斯頓昨天打電話通知我。

還有一個可能會造成較大影響的問題，是負責入場的伍德華小姐提醒我的。顯然所有購買預售票的人都應得到一張可在當地飯店享有折扣的禮券。不幸的是，只有約三分之一的預售票購買者能及時收到這些禮券。194 伍德華小姐想知道我們能否做出一套系統，在顧客進場時發放禮券，讓他們之後能用在飯店帳單上。我喜歡這個主意，但也請告訴我你的想法。

里諾克斯史都華
公關經理

字彙　**publicist** 宣傳人員　**dealership** 經銷商　**schedule conflict** 行程衝突、撞期　**damaging** 有破壞性的
advance ticket 預售票　**be supposed to** 應該　**accompany** 伴隨、陪同　**certificate** 禮券、證明
be good for 利於、有益於　**in time** 及時　**retroactively** 事後追補、溯及既往

191. What is the purpose of the notice?
(A) To explain the details of a new policy
(B) To promote an upcoming event
(C) To advertise a new line of products
(D) To raise money for an organization

這份公告的目的為何？
(A) 解釋新政策的詳細內容
(B) 宣傳即將舉行的活動
(C) 宣傳新系列產品
(D) 為組織籌集資金

正確答案為 **(B)**

公告的第一句提到 This year's International Auto Show will be held at the MXFM Convention Center in Detroit from March 6th through 15th，可知答案是 (B)。

192. What is mentioned about the event?
(A) Registration is required to attend.
(B) People can attend before the official opening.
(C) Invitations have been sent to only the media.
(D) A local industry will be hosting it.

關於活動，文章提到什麼內容？
(A) 必須報名才能參加。
(B) 在正式開幕之前人們可以參加。
(C) 邀請函只寄給媒體。
(D) 當地業者將主持活動。

正確答案為 **(B)**

根據活動日程表，8 月 7 日正式開幕日之前，8 月 6 日也有舉辦開幕前活動 Special Public Sneak Preview，因此答案是 (B)。

193. Who is allowed to attend the Dealer Preview?
(A) All certified dealers
(B) All press officials
(C) Anyone who has paid for advance tickets
(D) People who are invited to come

誰能參加經銷商搶先看？
(A) 所有認證的經銷商
(B) 所有媒體工作者
(C) 凡購買預售票者
(D) 受邀入場者

正確答案為 **(D)**

活動日程表中，8 月 12 日的經銷商搶先看規定是 by invitation only，因此答案是 (D)。

字彙　**certified** 有資格的、被證明的　**press official** 媒體工作者

194. What does Ms. Woodward suggest doing?
(A) Issuing certificates at the convention center
(B) Mailing out letters of apology
(C) Contacting each customer as soon as possible
(D) Waiting to see if there are any complaints

伍德華小姐提議做什麼？
(A) 在會議中心發放禮券
(B) 寄送致歉函
(C) 儘快與每個顧客聯繫
(D) 等等看是否有什麼不滿

正確答案為 **(A)**

電子郵件第三段提到 Ms. Woodward wants to know if we can work out a system where we give the certificates to the people when they arrive for the show，建議在入場時發放禮券，展場地點在 convention center，因此答案是 (A)。

195. Who will probably attend the event on August 12?
(A) Mr. Granzinski
(B) Mr. Wiseman
(C) Ms. Michel
(D) Mr. Levingston

誰可能會參加 8 月 12 日的活動？
(A) 葛藍辛基先生
(B) 懷思曼先生
(C) 米雪兒小姐
(D) 萊文斯頓先生

正確答案為 **(B)**

〈整合多篇文章資訊〉
公告最後一句寫著 Peter Wiseman and Alicia Michel, will be on hand on August 11th and 12th，但在電子郵件第二段提到 Ms. Michel will not be able to attend the show，可見只有 Wiseman 懷思曼先生會參加，答案是 (B)。

Questions 196-200 refer to the following advertisement and e-mails. 廣告／電子郵件

Reporter Wanted

Daily Indiana, a leading publishing company, is seeking a reporter to join our team at our location in downtown Bloomington. The successful candidate will have previous experience as a reporter, preferably in a high-profile publishing company. Responsibilities include reading opinions from subscribers, contacting correspondents, processing mail, and other clerical work. This part-time position is 20 hours a week including evening and Saturday hours, which are paid at our overtime rate. Interested individuals should send résumés to hr@dailyindiana.ca.

E-Mail Message

To: hr@dailyindiana.ca
From: lstein@gmail.com
Date: August 8
Subject: Reporter position
Attachment: Stein_résumé; Stein_samples

Dear Human Resources,

I'm writing to express my interest in the reporter position. Though I'm a professional photographer, I have four years of experience working in office settings. While in art school, I worked for three years as an editor at a university newspaper. I also worked in a mailroom of a large corporation. In addition, I'm proficient at several software programs that can be used in editing articles.

Currently, I work as a reporter and photographer at a magazine. Since I only work three mornings a week, I want additional work to fill out my schedule. Though this would be my first job in a newspaper company, I'm willing to learn new skills, and the skills I have would be an asset to you. I'm sending my résumé and my sample work when I worked as an editor in a university newspaper. They demonstrate my writing and interview skills. I look forward to hearing from you and appreciate your consideration.

Sincerely,

Lucy Stein

問題 196-200 參考以下廣告與兩封電子郵件。

招募記者

頂尖的出版公司《印第安那日報》現正招募一名記者，加入我們在布魯明頓市中心的團隊。成功的申請者應具有記者工作經驗，最好是曾在知名出版公司工作。職責包括 ⑲⑥ 閱讀訂閱者的意見、聯絡撰稿記者、處理郵件和其他文書工作。⑲⑦ 此兼職職位每週工作 20 小時，其中包含支付加班費的晚上和星期六工作時間。有意者請將履歷表寄到 hr@dailyindiana.ca。

 字彙　**reporter** 記者　　**seek** 尋找　　**candidate** 應徵者、候選人　　**preferably** 偏好地
high-profile 知名度高的、高調的　　**subscriber** 訂閱者　　**correspondent** 撰稿人、外派記者
clerical work 文書工作　　**overtime rate** 超時工作費、加班費

E–Mail Message

收件者：　　hr@dailyindiana.ca
寄件者：　　lstein@gmail.com
日期：　　　8 月 8 日
主旨：　　　記者職位
附加檔案：　Stein_ 履歷表；Stein_ 作品樣本

致人資部門：

我寫這封信是為了表達我對記者一職的興趣。雖然我是專職攝影師，但我有 4 年在辦公室工作的經驗。就讀藝術學校時，我在大學報社做了 3 年編輯。我還在一家大公司的收發室工作過。此外，我還精通一些文章編輯軟體程式。

目前我在一家雜誌社擔任記者和攝影師。⑲⑦ 因為我一週只工作 3 個上午，我想要額外的工作來充實日程安排。⑲⑧ 雖然這將是我在報社的第一份工作，但我願意學習新的技能，我所擁有的技能將是貴公司的財富。㉒⓪ 我寄了履歷表和在大學報社擔任編輯的作品。它們展示了我的寫作和採訪技巧。期待您的回覆，感謝您的考慮。

露西史坦

字彙　**human resource** 人資　　**setting** 環境　　**mailroom** 收發室　　**proficient** 精通的　　**currently** 目前
asset 資產　　**demonstrate** 展示、證明

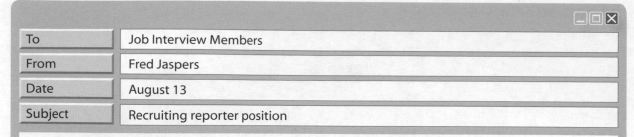

To	Job Interview Members
From	Fred Jaspers
Date	August 13
Subject	Recruiting reporter position

Hello, everyone.

Our final interview will take place tomorrow at 9:30 A.M. We will be interviewing Ms. Stein. Please read the materials that she submitted so that the information is fresh in your mind during the interview. I know that some of you are concerned about her qualifications, but she could be easily trained to do routine office tasks. In my opinion, she offers much more. In fact, the materials she submitted demonstrate a creativity that could really spice up our marketing materials. If you would like to discuss anything before the interview, please contact me.

Fred

寄件者	工作面試官
寄件者	福瑞德賈斯伯
日期	8 月 13 日
主旨	招聘記者職位

大家好，我們的最後一次面試將在明天上午 9 點 30 分舉行。我們將面試史坦小姐。199 請仔細閱讀她提交的資料，以便在面試過程中能清楚想起這些資訊。我知道你們有些人擔心她的資歷條件，但要訓練她到能勝任辦公室的日常工作是很簡單的。在我看來，她能貢獻的反而更多。200 事實上，她提交的資料展現了創造力，可以為我們的行銷資料增添趣味。如果您在面試前有什麼問題想要討論，請與我聯絡。

福瑞德

字彙 **take place** 發生、舉辦　**qualification** 資格條件　**routine** 日常的　**creativity** 創造力、創意
spice up 增添趣味

196. According to the advertisement, what is a duty of the reporter position?
(A) **Reviewing feedback**
(B) Scheduling board meetings
(C) Writing editorials
(D) Calling subscribers

根據廣告，記者的職務內容是什麼？
(A) 審閱意見回饋
(B) 安排董事會日程
(C) 寫社論
(D) 打電話給訂閱者

正確答案為 (A)

廣告裡針對職務內容提到 reading opinions from subscribers, contacting correspondents, processing mail, and other clerical work，符合職務說明的是 (A)。

字彙 **editorial** 社論

197. What aspect of the position is likely the most appealing to Ms. Stein?
(A) The newspaper's reputation
(B) The downtown location
(C) The job responsibilities
(D) **The work schedule**

此職位的哪一方面最吸引史坦小姐？
(A) 報紙的名聲
(B) 市中心地理位置
(C) 工作職務內容
(D) 工作時程

正確答案為 (D)

〈整合多篇文章資訊〉
廣告中提到 This part-time position is 20 hours a week，而史坦小姐的電子郵件中提到 Since I only work three mornings a week, I want additional work to fill out my schedule，由此可知她是因為工作時間符合需求而應徵這份工作。答案是 (D)。

198. What is indicated about Ms. Stein?
(A) She is currently writing for a newspaper company.
(B) She will enroll as an art student.
(C) **She has never worked for a newspaper before.**
(D) She will relocate to Bloomington.

何者是有關於史坦小姐的陳述？
(A) 她目前在一家報社工作。
(B) 她將註冊為一名藝術學校的學生。
(C) 她從未在報社工作過。
(D) 她將搬到布魯明頓。

正確答案為 (C)

在第一封電子郵件提到 this would be my first job in a newspaper company，可知答案是 (C)。

字彙 **enroll** 入學

199. What is the purpose of the second e-mail?
(A) To encourage more interviewers to participate in the board
(B) **To ask the job interview members to review some materials**
(C) To remind staff members that an interview has been canceled
(D) To inform new employers about an orientation session

第二封電子郵件的目的為何？
(A) 鼓勵更多面試官參加董事會
(B) 要求面試成員閱覽資料
(C) 提醒員工面試已經取消
(D) 通知新雇主關於培訓的事宜

正確答案為 (B)

此郵件的第二句提到 Please read the materials that she submitted，因此答案是 (B)。

200. What does Mr. Jaspers think makes Ms. Stein a good candidate for the position?

(A) Her experience as an editor
(B) Her availability for extended work hours
(C) Her expertise in dealing with clients
(D) Her skills as a computer programmer

什麼因素讓賈斯伯先生認為史坦小姐適合此職位？

(A) 她身為編輯的經驗
(B) 她可以配合延長工時
(C) 她處理客戶的經驗豐富
(D) 她身為電腦程式設計師的技術

正確答案為 **(A)**

〈整合多篇文章資訊〉

Jaspers 賈斯伯先生提到 the materials she submitted demonstrate a creativity，可見他對 Stein 史坦小姐的資料很滿意。在第一封史坦小姐寫的郵件裡，第二段提到 I'm sending my résumé and my sample work when I worked as an editor in a university newspaper。由此可知她寄的資料是過去在報社擔任編輯的相關經歷，答案是 (A)。

Actual Test

03

中譯與解說

	答對題數	換算分數
聽力		
閱讀		

1. 3_01 美式女聲

(A) She is holding a book in her hands.
(B) She is reclining in a field.
(C) She is reading to his companion.
(D) She is writing a book outdoors.

(A) 她手上拿著一本書。
(B) 她在草地上斜靠。
(C) 她正讀書給他的同伴聽。
(D) 她正在戶外寫書。

正確答案為 (B)

單人照片應注意人物的動作與特徵。照片裡女子斜靠著樹並看著 notebook 筆記型電腦，最恰當的答案是 (B)。(A) 和 (D) 提到的書在照片看不到，也看不到 (C) 所描述的其他人，因此都不是答案。

字彙　**recline** 斜躺、倚靠　　**companion** 同伴、朋友

2. 3_02 美式男聲

(A) The man is browsing in a camera shop.
(B) The man is posing for a photograph.
(C) The man is kneeling down to take a picture.
(D) The man is placing his camera on the sidewalk.

(A) 男子正在一家相機店裡瀏覽商品。
(B) 男子正在擺姿勢照相。
(C) 男子正跪蹲著拍照。
(D) 男子正將相機放在人行道上。

正確答案為 (C)

描述男子跪蹲著拍照的 (C) 是最適當的答案。(A) 說背景是商店，但照片是在戶外。(B) 描述男子正在擺姿勢，但男子正在拍照。男子的照相機是拿在手上，(D) 也不是答案。

字彙　**browse** 瀏覽　　**kneel down** 跪下、跪坐　　**sidewalk** 人行道

3. `3_03` 澳式男聲

(A) The meeting has gotten underway.
(B) The participants are sitting near the windows.
(C) Some of the seats are occupied.
(D) Identical chairs surround the table.

(A) 會議已經開始進行。
(B) 參加者坐在窗戶附近。
(C) 有些座位有人坐。
(D) 相同的椅子圍繞著桌子。

正確答案為 (D)

沒有人物出現的照片，應注意聽各種物品的名稱。在空無一人的會議室裡，描述相同椅子圍繞著桌子的 (D) 是最符合的答案。(A) 描寫會議正在進行，(B) 提到參加會議的人，(C) 說有些椅子有人在使用，都不是正確答案。

> 字彙　**underway** 進行中的　**participant** 參加者　**occupy** 佔據、佔用　**identical** 同樣的、完全相同的

4. `3_04` 英式美聲

(A) Rows of shelves hold various products.
(B) The top rows are empty of merchandise.
(C) Shoppers are selecting different types of tea.
(D) All of the products are the same size.

(A) 一排排的貨架上擺著各式各樣的產品。
(B) 最上面一排沒有商品。
(C) 購物者正在選購不同種類的茶。
(D) 所有產品大小一樣。

正確答案為 (A)

這是沒有人物的商店內部照片。描寫多層貨架擺著不同物品的 (A) 是答案。每排貨架上都有物品，因此 (B) 不是答案。(C) 描寫購物者的動作，但照片沒有人不是答案。物品大小並沒有一模一樣，因此 (D) 不是答案。

> 字彙　**row** 列、排　**various** 各種各樣的　**empty of** 缺乏　**merchandise** 商品

Test 03

5. 3_05 美式女聲

(A) Passengers are unpacking some suitcases.
(B) People are facing a baggage carousel.
(C) Travelers are pushing carts along the floor.
(D) People are checking in their luggage.

(A) 旅客正在打開手提箱。
(B) 人們正面對行李傳送帶。
(C) 旅客正在推手推車。
(D) 人們正在託運行李。

正確答案為 (B)

這張照片是出現許多人的室內照,須注意聆聽各人物的動作描述。描寫人們看著行李傳送帶並等待行李的 (B) 是最適當的答案。照片裡看不到人們打開行李;照片裡雖然可以看到手推車,但沒有人推動著它;(D) 描述人們辦理託運行李,不符合照片內容,因此都不是答案。

字彙 **passenger** 乘客 **unpack** 打開包裹 **baggage carousel** 機場行李傳送帶 **check in** 報到、登記、辦理手續

6. 3_06 英式美聲

(A) The bedcover has been straightened.
(B) There are two pictures hung above the bed.
(C) Reading material has been placed on a couch.
(D) There are lamps on both sides of the desk.

(A) 床罩被平整攤開。
(B) 床頭上掛著兩幅圖畫。
(C) 閱讀資料放在沙發上。
(D) 桌子兩側都有燈。

正確答案為 (A)

這是沒有人物的事物照片,應仔細聽照片裡面事物的位置或狀態。答案是床罩平整攤開的 (A)。(B) 的描述不符合床頭上圖畫數量。(C) 提到的沙發並不存在於照片中。(D) 雖然看得到燈,但燈的敘述位置不符,因此不是答案。

字彙 **straighten** 整平 **reading material** 讀物、閱讀資料 **couch** 長沙發

7. 3_07 英式男聲 / 美式男聲

When do you move to the new building?
(A) Jade has the schedule.
(B) The regional office is in Delhi.
(C) Into the financial district.

你什麼時候搬進新大樓？
(A) 潔德有時間表。
(B) 地方辦事處在新德里。
(C) 進入金融區。

正確答案為 (A)

When 疑問句問搬家的時間點，答案是指明第三人知道時間表的 (A)。(B) 和 (C) 適合回答 Where 問句。**作答時請不要將 When 問句混淆聽成 Where。**

> 字彙 **regional** 地區的、局部的　**financial** 金融的　**district**（行政）地區、區域

8. 3_08 美式男聲 / 美式女聲

Does your manager use the company's intranet system?
(A) No, on the Internet.
(B) Yes, every day.
(C) Check the access code.

你的經理使用公司內部通訊網嗎？
(A) 不，在網路上。
(B) 是的，每天。
(C) 請檢查通行碼。

正確答案為 (B)

題目問經理是否使用內部通訊網，最適合的答案是表示肯定的 (B)。(A) 回答 No，表示不使用，但接下來回應的內容與問題無關，(C) 的回答也是與問題無關。

> 字彙 **intranet** 內部通訊網　**access** 存取、接近、使用

9. 3_09 英式男聲 / 美式男聲

Kyle Hanagami is the choreographer of this performance, isn't he?
(A) Yes and it's perfectly done.
(B) No, it's their performance reviews.
(C) He is a world-famous writer.

凱爾哈馬葛尼是這次表演的編舞家，不是嗎？
(A) 是的，而且編得很棒。
(B) 不，那是他們的績效考核。
(C) 他是世界知名的作家。

正確答案為 (A)

問題問某人是否為編舞家，給予肯定回應並表示稱讚的 (A) 是最適合的答案。(B) 使用與題目出現的 performance 相關的 reviews 做聯想，但回答的內容與問題無關，因此不是答案。(C) 提到特定的職業，但與問題無關。

> 字彙 **choreographer** [ˌkɔrɪˋɑgrəfə] 編舞家　**performance review** 績效考核

10. 3_10 美式男聲 / 美式女聲

Would you like me to bring copies of the customers' feedback for the meeting or email it to everyone?
(A) Listen to the customers.
(B) About two thousand Euros next year.
(C) We'll have to hand them out to everyone.

我是要帶顧客意見影本去開會，還是寄電子郵件給大家？
(A) 請聆聽顧客的意見。
(B) 明年大約兩千歐元。
(C) 我們要把它們發給每個人。

正確答案為 (C)

問題問該把資料直接帶去開會還是用電子郵件寄給大家，最適合的答案是 (C)，回答發給大家，相當於**間接回答帶影本**。(A) 重複使用題目中出現的 customer，是陷阱選項，(B) 的回應與問題完全無關。

> 字彙 **customer** 顧客　**feedback** 回饋意見　**hand out** 分發

Test 03

11. 3_11 英式男聲 / 美式男聲

How many times have you relocated for work?
(A) Yes, I live in Berlin now.
(B) You should make twenty-five signs.
(C) This is my third move.

你為了工作搬過幾次家？
(A) 是的，我現在住在柏林。
(B) 你應該做 25 個標誌。
(C) 這次是第三次。

正確答案為 (C)

How many 疑問句問次數，回答這次是第三次的 (C) 是答案。(A) 的答覆不適合，因為 wh 疑問句不能以 Yes/No 回答。(B) 提到數字作為陷阱選項，但回應內容與問題無關，因此不是答案。

字彙　**relocate** 搬遷

12. 3_12 美式男聲 / 美式女聲

Didn't you say you were a vegetarian?
(A) Yes, all my family is.
(B) Not too salty.
(C) Fresh fruits and vegetables.

你不是説你吃素嗎？
(A) 是的，我全家都是。
(B) 不要太鹹。
(C) 新鮮的蔬果。

正確答案為 (A)

問題是確認對方是否為素食者的否定疑問句，答案是表示認同且進一步説明的 (A)。(B) 適合回應對食物做評論或點菜時的要求。(C) 刻意使用了從題目 vegetarian 聯想到的 vegetables，但內容與題目無關。**注意，無論問句是否帶有否定詞，思考回覆的時候一律以拿掉否定詞進行思考。**

字彙　**vegetarian** 素食者

13. 3_13 英式男聲 / 美式女聲

Why has the construction been delayed?
(A) A two-story building.
(B) We still need Mr. Marble's approval.
(C) I've read the introduction.

工程為什麼延期？
(A) 兩層樓高的建築。
(B) 我們還需要馬伯先生的批准。
(C) 我已經看過説明書。

正確答案為 (B)

Why 疑問句問延後的原因，答案是説明還在等候批准的 (B)。(A) 的回答與問題無關，(C) 使用了跟題目的 construction 發音相似的 introduction，是陷阱選項。

字彙　**construction** 建設、工程　**delay** 延期、耽擱　**story** 樓層　**approval** 許可、贊成　**introduction** 説明書、介紹

14. 3_14 美式女聲 / 美式男聲

Which attendees are missing from the guest list?
(A) Yes, I'm ready to leave.
(B) They're staying for a while.
(C) The new hires still haven't been added.

賓客名單上少了哪些人？
(A) 是的，我準備要離開了。
(B) 他們會停留一段時間。
(C) 新進員工還沒有加進去。

正確答案為 (C)

Which 疑問詞問名單上遺漏了哪些人，答案是回答少了新進員工的 (C)。(A) 不是答案，因為疑問詞的問句不能以 Yes/No 回答。(B) 的回應與題目無關。

字彙　**attendee** 參加者　**for a while** 暫時、一會兒　**hire** 雇用者；聘用

15. 3_15 美式女聲 / 英式男聲

Will you continue to work here or move to the head office?　你打算繼續在這裡工作還是搬到總公司？
(A) I'm planning on staying.　**(A) 我打算留下來。**
(B) The boxes are in storage.　(B) 那些箱子在倉庫裡。
(C) I can work until 6.　(C) 我可以工作到 6 點。

正確答案為 (A)

選擇疑問句問工作地點，答案是回答繼續留在原地工作的 (A)。(B) 的回應與問題無關，(C) 是說明時間，不適合用來回答地點問題。

字彙　**head office** 總公司　　**storage** 儲藏室、倉庫、儲存

16. 3_16 美式男聲 / 英式男聲

I've completed all my assignments.　我已經完成所有工作。
(A) Friday at noon.　(A) 在星期五中午。
(B) I missed Dane's signature.　(B) 我漏了丹恩的簽名。
(C) Could you help Aaron then?　**(C) 那你可以幫艾隆的忙嗎？**

正確答案為 (C)

直述句說明自己的工作已經做完，答案是請對方協助他人的 (C)。(A) 回答時間點，與題目無關。(B) 使用與題目中 assignments 產生聯想的 signature，但回應與題目無關。

字彙　**assignment** 任務、作業　　**signature** 簽名

17. 3_17 美式男聲 / 美式女聲

Who is the magazine targeted at?　這本雜誌鎖定的讀者是誰？
(A) It's aimed at journalism experts.　**(A) 它的目標是新聞專家。**
(B) I write for magazines.　(B) 我為雜誌撰文。
(C) I didn't attend, but Mary did.　(C) 我沒去，但瑪麗有去。

正確答案為 (A)

Who 疑問句問雜誌的目標客群，答案是提到特定職業族群的 (A)。(B) 是重複使用 magazine 的錯誤答案，(C) 提到第三者的名字，乍聽之下是 Who 疑問句的典型回答，但內容與問題無關，因此不是答案。

字彙　**target** 把～視為目標、瞄準（某群體）　　**aim at** 瞄準　　**journalism** 新聞業　　**expert** 專家

18. 3_18 英式男聲 / 美式女聲

Can anyone take these cylinders to the laboratory?　有人能把這些量筒拿到實驗室嗎？
(A) I can do it in a minute.　**(A) 我馬上就做。**
(B) Look in those cabinets.　(B) 請看這些陳列櫃。
(C) No, I didn't take them.　(C) 不，我沒有拿。

正確答案為 (A)

請求別人帶走特定物品的疑問句，最適合的答案是回答馬上可以去做的 (A)。(B) 使用了與題目的 laboratory 做聯想的 cabinet，但並不是答案。(C) 重複使用題目中的 take，但答非所問。

字彙　**cylinder** 圓筒、圓柱體　　**laboratory** 實驗室　　**in a minute** 立即、馬上　　**cabinet** 陳列櫃、櫥櫃

Test 03

19. `3_19` 美式女聲 / 美式男聲

Are you looking for a full-time or part-time position?
(A) I can work two days a week.
(B) We've been looking forward to it.
(C) I found it on my desk.

你要找的是全職還是兼職？
(A) 我一週可以工作兩天。
(B) 我們期待很久了。
(C) 我在我的書桌上找到的。

正確答案為 (A)

選擇疑問句詢問對方所找的工作性質，適當的答案是間接表示想做兼職工作的 (A)。(B) 是重複使用 looking 的誤導選項，(C) 同樣也是誤導選項，使用可從 looking for 聯想到的 found，故意混淆作答。

 字彙　**look forward to** 期待

20. `3_20` 美式女聲 / 英式男聲

Weren't you expecting more people to come to the product demonstration?
(A) I received it yesterday.
(B) In the auditorium.
(C) No, this is everybody.

你沒預期到會有更多人來產品展示會嗎？
(A) 我昨天收到了。
(B) 在禮堂。
(C) 沒有，這裡就是全部人了。

正確答案為 (C)

否定疑問句再次確認對方是否期待會有更多人來參加，答案是 (C)，表示目前到場的人就是全部會參加的人。(A) 使用 received，是因為題目 expecting 會常聯想到這個單字，但回答與題目無關。(B) 提到活動場地，與題目無關。

 字彙　**expect** 預期、期待　　**receive** 接收　　**demonstration** 示範、展示　　**auditorium** 禮堂

21. `3_21` 英式男聲 / 美式男聲

This year's award ceremony is being held in Singapore.
(A) We plan to board on time.
(B) Yes, a rewarding occupation.
(C) I didn't know they decided to move it.

今年的頒獎典禮在新加坡舉行。
(A) 我們打算準時搭乘。
(B) 是的，是個收入不錯的職業。
(C) 我不知道他們決定換地方。

正確答案為 (C)

直述句傳達頒獎典禮的地點，最適合的回應是婉轉表示不知道在該地舉行的 (C)。(A) 使用從題目 Singapore 聯想的 board「搭乘飛機」誤導作答。(B) 使用發音與題目 award 相似的 rewarding 誤導作答。

 字彙　**award ceremony** 頒獎典禮　　**rewarding** 值得的、有所收獲的　　**occupation** 職業

22. `3_22` 美式男聲 / 美式女聲

Could you tell me whether the marketing director can see me this morning?
(A) The interview went well.
(B) Take a left at the intersection.
(C) Certainly, she can meet with you at 10.

你能告訴我行銷總經理今天早上能不能見我？
(A) 面試很順利。
(B) 請在十字路口左轉。
(C) 當然，她 10 點可以和你見面。

正確答案為 (C)

間接疑問句問見面的可能性，答案是給予肯定答覆的 (C)。(A) 適合回答是否能面試的問句，與本問句沒有關係。(B) 的答案與題目無關。

 字彙　**interview** 面試　　**go (on) well** 很順利　　**intersection** 交叉路口、十字路口　　**certainly** 當然、無疑地

23. `3_23` 英式男聲 / 美式女聲

How did you hear about the job?
(A) The volume is too high.
(B) Yes, I believe he started last week.
(C) It was advertised on the Web site.

你是怎麼聽説這份工作的？
(A) 音量太大。
(B) 是的，我猜他是上週開始。
(C) 網站上刊登了廣告。

正確答案為 (C)

How 疑問句詢問對方如何得知工作消息，答案是回答看到網站廣告的 (C)。(A) 使用與題目 hear 相關的 volume 誘導作答，但內容與題目無關。(B) 的答覆與題目無關。

字彙 **volume** 音量　　**advertise** 刊登廣告

24. `3_24` 美式女聲 / 美式男聲

Have you seen the agenda?
(A) No, does it look interesting?
(B) To meet with an agent.
(C) Yes, generally it does.

你看過議程了嗎？
(A) 還沒，看起來有趣嗎？
(B) 為了和代理人見面。
(C) 是的，通常是這樣。

正確答案為 (A)

助動詞疑問句問對方是否看過議程，答案是反問是否有趣的 (A)。(B) 適合回答 Why 疑問詞的問句，且選項中使用與題目 agenda 發音相似的 agent 誤導作答。(C) 回答 Yes，表示自己曾經看過，但後面內容與問句無關，因此不是答案。

字彙 **agenda** 議程　　**agent** 代理人、仲介

25. `3_25` 美式女聲 / 英式男聲

Should we start the meeting now or wait for Ms. Lee?
(A) I don't know until tomorrow.
(B) I'm waiting for the 210 train.
(C) We have a lot to get through, so let's begin.

我們應該現在來開會，還是要等李小姐？
(A) 我明天才知道。
(B) 我在等 210 車次的火車。
(C) 我們還有很多事要做，所以我們先開始吧。

正確答案為 (C)

選擇疑問句問應該馬上開會還是要再等另一個人，最適合的答案是 (C)，表示因為還有很多事要做，提議現在就開始。(A) 是迴避回答的常用句，但內容與題目無關。(B) 重複使用題目的 wait，但內容與題目無關。

字彙 **get through** 處理

26. `3_26` 英式男聲 / 美式男聲

How often do you work overtime?
(A) Hardly ever.
(B) We're extremely busy.
(C) For a week or so.

你多久加班一次？
(A) 幾乎沒有。
(B) 我們非常忙碌。
(C) 長達一個星期左右。

正確答案為 (A)

How often 疑問句問加班「頻率」，答案是表示幾乎不加班的 (A)。(B) 與題目無關，(C) 適合回答 How long「時間有多長」疑問句。

字彙 **overtime** 加班　　**hardly ever** 幾乎不　　**or so** 大約、左右

27. 3_27 美式男聲 / 美式女聲

When was Ernest transferred to the Jakarta office?
(A) I opened before he started working.
(B) At least six years ago.
(C) Even I've never been there.

厄尼史特什麼時候調到雅加達辦公室的？
(A) 我在他工作前打開的。
(B) 至少 6 年前。
(C) 即使我從沒去過那裡。

正確答案為 (B)

When 疑問詞問調職時間點，答案是提到過去時間點的 (B)。(A) 使用 before，看起來像回答 When 疑問句，但內容與題目無關。(C) 的回覆也與題目無關。

字彙　**transfer** 轉調

28. 3_28 英式男聲 / 美式女聲

The price of stamps is going up next month, isn't it?
(A) No, she'll be back next week.
(B) A thousand-dollar prize.
(C) Not until next year, I think.

下個月郵票價格要上漲，是嗎？
(A) 不，她下禮拜就會回來。
(B) 獎金一千美元。
(C) 我想要等到明年吧。

正確答案為 (C)

附加疑問句想確認郵票價格是否上漲，答案是提到調漲時間點的 (C)。(A) 重複使用題目的 next，是陷阱選項。(B) 使用從題目的 price 聯想到的 a thousand dollar，並使用發音相近的 prize 誤導，但內容與題目無關。

字彙　**go up** 上漲、漲價　　**prize** 獎金

29. 3_29 美式女聲 / 美式男聲

What percentage of sales comes from advertising on the Internet?
(A) Around a third.
(B) They sell a lot of groceries.
(C) I sent several e-mails.

銷售額有多少百分比是來自網路上的廣告？
(A) 三分之一左右。
(B) 他們賣很多食品雜貨。
(C) 我寄了好幾封電子郵件。

正確答案為 (A)

What 疑問句問來自網路廣告的獲利占比，答案是回答占 1/3 的 (A)。(B) 使用從題目的 sales 聯想到的 sell，(C) 則使用從題目的 Internet 聯想到的 e-mails，但內容皆與題目無關。

字彙　**grocery** 食品雜貨　　**several** 數個的

30. 3_30 美式女聲 / 英式男聲

Where should I put all this paper?
(A) Just by the copier is fine.
(B) By Friday at the latest.
(C) I think it was Troy.

我該把這份文件放哪？
(A) 放在影印機旁邊就可以了。
(B) 最晚星期五以前。
(C) 我覺得是托瑞。

正確答案為 (A)

Where 疑問句問位置，答案是回答特定位置的 (A)。(B) 回答特定時間點，(C) 回答特定人物，皆答非所問。

字彙　**copier** 影印機　　**at the latest** 最遲、最晚

31. `3_31` 美式男聲 / 英式男聲

The keynote speaker hasn't arrived yet, has he?
(A) It shouldn't last more than two hours.
(B) No, apparently his plane was delayed.
(C) I'll check the microphone.

專題主講人還沒到，對吧？
(A) 不應該超過兩個小時。
(B) 還沒，看來他的飛機誤點了。
(C) 我會檢查麥克風。

正確答案為 (B)

附加問句想確認第三者是否已經抵達，**答案是回答尚未抵達並進一步說明原因的** (B)。(A) 回答特定期間，與題目無關。(C) 使用從題目的 keynote speaker 聯想到的 microphone，但內容與題目無關。

字彙	**keynote speaker** 專題主講人	**apparently** 似乎、看來

Questions 32-34 refer to the following conversation.

M: Hello. I'm calling about the high-speed color copier listed in your online ad. The advertisement said the device is only a year old. Is that right?

W: Yes, and it's in perfect working condition. It's a great piece of equipment: it's fast and the image quality is exceptional. We're only selling it because our company is relocating overseas next month.

M: I see. Well, how soon could I drop by your office to take a look?

W: If you could come sometime after 6 o'clock today, I'd be happy to stay past the end of my shift to meet you. By the way, we also have some nice desks and drawers for sale if you're interested.

問題 32-34 參考以下對話。

男：你好，㉜我打電話是要問網路廣告的高速彩色影印機。上面說這款裝置只用了一年，對嗎？

女：是的，而且它的功能狀態相當好。這是款很棒的設備，速度快，圖像品質也非常出色。我們出售它只是因為㉝我們公司下個月要搬到海外。

男：我明白了。那麼我最快什麼時候可以到你們辦公室看一看？

女：如果你今天能在 6 點以後來，㉞我很樂意在下班後留下來和你碰面。順便，如果你感興趣，我們也有一些不錯的桌子和抽屜要賣。

字彙　**advertisement** 廣告，簡稱 ad　　**equipment** 設備、裝置　　**exceptional** 非凡的　　**overseas** 海外地、海外的　**drop by** 順道拜訪

32. What item does the man ask about?　　　　　男子詢問何種商品？
(A) A color printer　　　　　　　　　　　　(A) 彩色印表機
(B) A copy machine　　　　　　　　　　**(B) 影印機**
(C) A laptop　　　　　　　　　　　　　　　(C) 筆記型電腦
(D) A scanner　　　　　　　　　　　　　　(D) 掃瞄機

正確答案為 (B)

〈注意細節－特定事項〉
男子提到的商品應該從男子的談話找答案。男子第一句話提到因為高速彩色影印機而打這通電話，因此答案是 (B)。
換句話說 copier 影印機 → copy machine 影印機

33. What does the woman say will happen next month?　　　女子說下個月會發生什麼事？
(A) New equipment will be purchased.　　　　(A) 將採購新設備。
(B) She will resign from her company.　　　　(B) 她將從公司辭職。
(C) A new model will be released.　　　　　　(C) 新機種即將上市。
(D) Her work location will change.　　　　**(D) 她的工作地點將會改變。**

正確答案為 (D)

〈注意細節－特定事項〉
問題關鍵字是 next month，應從女子提到 **next month** 的段落找答案。女子說明出售影印機的原因是下個月公司要遷移到海外，因此答案是 (D)。
換句話說 The company is relocating 公司將搬遷 → Her work location will change 她的工作場所將改變

字彙 **location** 地點、位置　　**resign** 辭職

34. What does the woman offer to do for the man?　　　女子提議為男子做什麼？
(A) Remain after work　　　　　　　　　**(A) 下班後留下來**
(B) Discount a price　　　　　　　　　　　(B) 價格折扣
(C) Speak with a seller　　　　　　　　　　(C) 和銷售員談話
(D) Arrange a delivery　　　　　　　　　　(D) 安排送貨

正確答案為 (A)

〈注意細節－提議〉
女子提議願意為男子做的事情可在後半部女子的談話尋找答案。男子說想去辦公室看看，女子說若是約在工作結束之後，她可以留下來和男子見面。因此答案是 (A)。

Questions 35-37 refer to the following conversation.

W: Hi, Real Power Company. How can I help you?

M: Hello. I'd like to discuss my electricity account with someone.

W: Would you mind giving me your account information?

M: My name's Charles Tran, and my account number is, hold on a second... got it, it's CA56398, I think I've been overcharged.

W: Okay, let me have a look. I'm looking at your account now. I see what's happened. You've been charged at the commercial rate rather than the residential rate. It must've been caused by the system upgrade last month.

M: That's understandable.

W: I'm sorry about the mistake. Would you like a refund, or shall I give you a credit on your next month's bill?

M: Actually, I'd prefer a refund, please.

問題 35-37 參考以下對話。

女：您好，㊱ 這裡是瑞爾電力公司，有什麼能為您效勞的嗎？

男：您好，㉟ ㊱ 我想討論一下我的電費問題。

女：能告訴我您的帳戶資料嗎？

男：我的名字是查理斯川恩，我的帳號是，等一下……找到了，是 CA56398，我想我被超收費用了。

女：好的，我看一下。我正在看您的帳戶，我知道發生什麼事了。您被依商業價格收費，而不是依住宅價格收費，這一定是上個月系統升級引起的。

男：我可以理解。

女：我為這個錯誤感到抱歉。㊲ 您希望退款，還是用在下個月帳單做扣抵？

男：我比較希望退款，謝謝。

字彙　**electricity** 電、電力　**account** 帳戶、帳單　**overcharge** 超收費用　**commercial** 商業的、營利的
residential 住宅的　**understandable** 可以理解的、無可厚非的　**refund** 退款　**credit** 貸款

35. What is the purpose of the man's call?
(A) To request a discount
(B) To make a payment
(C) To inquire about a bill
(D) To open an account

男子打電話的目的是什麼？
(A) 要求折扣
(B) 付費
(C) 詢問帳單問題
(D) 開設帳戶

正確答案為 (C)

〈掌握基本資訊－目的〉
詢問目的的問題大部分在對話開始就能找到線索。男子向接電話的小姐表示希望能找人談談自己的電費帳單，因此最適合的答案是 (C)。

 字彙 　**request** 請求　　**inquire** 詢問

36. What type of business is the man calling?
(A) A bank
(B) An Internet service provider
(C) An electric company
(D) An insurance company

男子打電話到何種公司？
(A) 銀行
(B) 網路服務業者
(C) 電力公司
(D) 保險公司

正確答案為 (C)

〈掌握基本資訊－職務〉
與職務相關的內容也通常會出現在對話前半段，因此 35 和 36 題的答案會出現在前半段，聆聽時須一併注意。第一句是女子接電話並說明自己是電力公司，接下來男子表示希望談談電費帳單，可知答案是 (C)。

37. What does the woman offer to do?
(A) Give a discount
(B) Fix some device
(C) Provide new service
(D) Return a payment

女子提議要做什麼？
(A) 給予折扣
(B) 修理一些機器設備
(C) 提供新服務
(D) 退費

正確答案為 (D)

〈注意細節－提議〉
應從女子的談話內容找答案。男子提出被超收費用，而女子**使用〈Would you ~?〉句型，提出退費的建議，**因此答案是 (D)。

Questions 38-40 refer to the following conversation with three speakers.

W: That representative from Mitchell Cleaning was quite persuasive about the benefits of his cleaning service.

M1: I know the price they charge is attractive, too.

M2: That's right. It's considerably lower than what we're paying for the service we're using now.

W: Do you think we should switch, Oscar?

M1: Hmm... But we haven't had any problems with our current service. They're very reliable and do a good job.

W: What about you, Frank?

M2: I think we should go with Mitchell Cleaning. They have a good reputation, and we'd save our expenses.

W: In that case, let's think it over for a while.

問題 38-40 參考以下三人對話。

女： ㊳ 米契爾清潔公司代表提出的清潔服務優點相當具說服力。

男1：我知道他們的價格也很有吸引力。

男2：沒錯，比我們現在使用的服務要低得多。

女： ㊴ 你覺得我們應該換一家嗎，奧斯卡？

男1：嗯……但是目前的服務沒有任何問題。㊴ 他們很可靠，工作也很出色。

女： 那你的想法呢，法蘭克？

男2：我覺得我們應該採用米契爾清潔公司。他們信譽良好，我們也能節省開銷。

女： ㊵ 既然這樣，那我們再考慮一下。

字彙 representative 代表、負責人　persuasive 有說服力的　benefit 利益、好處　attractive 吸引人的、有魅力的
considerably 相當地、大幅地　reliable 可靠的、可信賴的　reputation 聲望、名譽　expense 費用、開銷

38. What does the woman say about the employee from Mitchell Cleaning?
(A) He was late for the meeting.
(B) He offered a persuasive deal.
(C) He left a product pamphlet.
(D) He will stop by the next day.

關於米契爾清潔公司的員工，女子說了什麼？
(A) 他開會遲到。
(B) 他提出了具說服力的交易案。
(C) 他留下了一本產品小冊子。
(D) 他明天會順道過來一趟。

正確答案為 (B)

〈注意細節－提及內容〉
應從女子談及該公司的談話中找答案。女子說的第一句話提到 Mitchell Cleaning 米契爾清潔公司的服務具有說服力，因此答案是 (B)。

39. What does Oscar say about the company's current cleaning service?
(A) It is highly dependable.
(B) It charges less money.
(C) It has an international reputation.
(D) It offers a discount.

奧斯卡如何評價公司目前的清潔服務？
(A) 它非常可靠。
(B) 它的費用較低。
(C) 它有國際聲譽。
(D) 它提供折扣。

正確答案為 (A)

〈注意細節－提及內容〉
這是典型的三人對話題型，**應先確認題目中提到的 Oscar 奧斯卡是參與對話的其中一人，還是談話提到的第三者**。女子第二次說話時叫 Oscar 的名字並請他說自己的意見，之後接著是男 1 的回答，可見男 1 就是 Oscar。男 1 認為目前使用的服務並沒有大問題而且很可靠，因此答案是 (A)。
換句話說 reliable 可靠的 → **highly dependable** 相當可靠的

40. What does the woman suggest?
(A) Keeping the current service
(B) Negotiating better service
(C) Postponing a decision
(D) Searching for a different service

女子提出什麼建議？
(A) 繼續目前的服務
(B) 商議出更好的服務
(C) 延後決定
(D) 找尋不同的服務

正確答案為 (C)

〈注意細節－建議〉
這個題目問女子提議的事項，應從女子的談話中找答案。女子在最後使用〈Let's ~〉提議句型，讓大家再考慮一下，因此答案是 (C)。
換句話說 **think it over for a while** 再仔細考慮一下 → **postponing a decision** 延後決定

字彙 **negotiate** 協商、談判

Questions 41-43 refer to the following conversation.

M: Jasmine, just to remind you that I'm off to London tomorrow to attend a COMDEX convention next Monday. I won't be back until Friday.

W: Yes, that'll be no problem at all. I arranged a taxi service from Heathrow airport but I haven't made a hotel reservation yet.

M: Don't worry. I'm planning to stay with a friend of mine for the whole week. He's lived there for more than five years now and he's going to show me around for a day or two once the convention is over.

W: Sounds nice. I'm sure there's so much to see.

問題 41-43 參考以下對話。

男：茉莉，提醒一下，㊷ 我明天要去倫敦參加下週一的 COMDEX 會議。我星期五才會回來。

女：是的，㊶ 完全沒有問題。我已經在希斯羅機場安排計程車，不過尚未訂飯店。

男：不用擔心。㊸ 我打算在我朋友那裡待一個星期。他在那裡住了 5 年多。大會結束後，他會帶我到處參觀一兩天。

女：聽起來很棒。我相信那裡有很多地方可以看看。

字彙　**sb. be off** 某人離開、不在的　　**convention** 會議　　**remind** 提醒　　**arrange** 安排、處理、整理
make a reservation 預約

41. Who most likely is the man talking to?　　　男子很可能在和誰說話？
    (A) A tour conductor　　　　　　　　(A) 導遊
    (B) A secretary　　　　　　　　　　**(B) 祕書**
    (C) A manager　　　　　　　　　　　(C) 經理
    (D) A taxi driver　　　　　　　　　　(D) 計程車司機

正確答案為 (B)

〈注意細節－職業〉
這是與女子職業有關的題目，應從對話前半段尋找答案。男子在一開始對話時表示自己要出差，女子隨後說已經安排計程車並準備預定飯店，可知女子是負責男子出差相關業務的祕書，答案是 (B)。**職業的問題應注意題目問的是男子還是女子的職業。**

> 字彙　　**tour conductor** 領隊、導遊

42. What will the man do next Monday?　　　下週一男子將會做什麼？
    (A) Tour the city　　　　　　　　　　(A) 城市旅遊
    (B) Attend a convention　　　　　　**(B) 參加會議**
    (C) Meet his friend　　　　　　　　　(C) 和他的朋友見面
    (D) See a client　　　　　　　　　　(D) 拜訪一名客戶

正確答案為 (B)

〈注意細節－特定事項〉
應從男子提到 Monday 的談話中找答案。男子在第一句話提到為了參加下週一的會議明天必須去倫敦，因此答案是 (B)。**題目的關鍵字是星期幾或是時間，應特別注意關鍵字的前後內容。**

43. How long will the man be away?　　　男子將離開多久？
    (A) About three days　　　　　　　　(A) 約三天
    (B) About a week　　　　　　　　　**(B) 約一週**
    (C) More than two weeks　　　　　　(C) 兩個禮拜以上
    (D) More than a month　　　　　　　(D) 一個月以上

正確答案為 (B)

〈注意細節－特定事項〉
題目使用未來式，請在對話中尋找使用未來式的句子。男子提到將和朋友待一個禮拜，因此男子的出差期間約一週左右。答案是 (B)。

3_44-46　英式男聲／美式女聲

Questions 44-46 refer to the following conversation.

M: Good afternoon, Ms. Bridges. This is Hugh Blair from Jade Architectural Design. I'm calling to see if you'd seen the layout of your new store. I sent it to your office by express mail last week.

W: Yes, I received it yesterday, and I really liked what you did. However, there is just one thing that worries me. Do you think there are enough fitting rooms available? We expect a deluge of customers every weekend, so we need to avoid the clutter. Can you increase the number of changing rooms?

M: Certainly, no problem. I'll send you the revised version as soon as I make the change.

W: That sounds perfect. I'll give you my feedback once I get it.

問題 44-46 參考以下對話。

男：午安，布里姬小姐。我是寶玉建築設計的修布萊爾。㊹ 我致電是想知道你們是否已經看過新店的設計圖。我上週用快遞寄到你們辦公室了。

女：是的，我們昨天收到了，我相當喜歡。不過有件事我有點擔心。㊺ 你覺得試衣間足夠嗎？我們預計每個週末會有大批顧客，我們得避免混亂擁擠。你能增加更衣間數量嗎？

男：當然沒問題。㊻ 修改之後我會立即寄出修改後的版本。

女：聽起來很棒。我一收到會立即告訴你我的想法。

字彙　**architectural** 建築學的　**layout** 平面圖、格局　**express mail** 快遞　**fitting room** 試衣間　**a deluge of** 大量的　**clutter** 混雜、壅塞　**increase** 增加　**revise** 修改、變更

44. What most likely did the man do last week?　　男子上個禮拜很可能做了什麼？
(A) He emailed a document.　　　　　　　　(A) 他用電子郵件寄出一份文件。
(B) He sent a floor plan.　　　　　　　　**(B) 他寄出一份平面圖。**
(C) He changed the schedule.　　　　　　　(C) 他更改行程。
(D) He analyzed the sales data.　　　　　　(D) 他分析銷售數據。

正確答案為 (B)

〈注意細節－特定事項〉
應從男子說到 last week 的對話內容找答案。男子第一次說話時提到上週郵寄出一份商店的平面圖，因此答案是 (B)。

換句話說 **layout** 配置圖 → **floor plan** 樓層平面圖

字彙　　**analyze** 分析

45. What does the woman mean when she says,　　女子說「有件事令我擔心」是什麼意思？
"there is just one thing that worries me"?　　(A) 預算可能不夠。
(A) The budget may not be sufficient.　　　(B) 資料可能遺失。
(B) Information could have been missing.　　**(C) 可能需要調整格局。**
(C) The layout might need adjusting.　　　(D) 員工人手可能不足。
(D) There may be a shortage of staff.

正確答案為 (C)

〈關鍵句－說話者意圖〉
仔細聆聽該句的前後文脈絡，才能推敲出說話者意圖。女子說完這句話之後，就問對方覺得試衣間是否足夠，可見女子擔心的是與試衣間數量有關的問題，因此答案是 (C)。

字彙　　**sufficient** 足夠的　　**adjust** 調整　　**shortage** 短缺、不足

46. What does the man say he will do?　　　男子說他將會做什麼？
(A) Send the woman the modified document　　**(A) 把修改後的文件寄給女子**
(B) Call the woman later in the day　　　　(B) 當天稍晚再打電話給女子
(C) Give the woman his feedback　　　　　(C) 告訴女子他的意見
(D) Visit the woman's office　　　　　　　(D) 拜訪女子的辦公室

正確答案為 (A)

〈注意細節－未來〉
應在對話後半段男子的談話內容找答案。男子最後說會把修改後的版本寄給女子，因此答案是 (A)。

換句話說 **revised version** 修改後的版本 → **modified document** 修改後的文件

3_47-49　美式男聲／美式女聲

Questions 47-49 refer to the following conversation.

M: Joyce, can I ask you something? I've heard that there are two management workshops. One is for beginners and the other is at an advanced level. Someone told me that you've attended both since you became a manager. Which one would you suggest for me?

W: With your management experience, the beginner's course would be too basic for you. I'm sure you'll get more out of the advanced one.

M: Thanks for your advice. I'll attend the advanced one then.

W: You should also speak to Ian Kline. He's the organizer of both workshops, so he should be able to tell you more information.

問題 47-49 參考以下對話。

男：喬伊絲，我可以問妳一個問題嗎？我聽說有兩場經營管理工作坊。**48** 一個是專為初學者開設的，另一個是進階的。我聽說 **47** 妳當上經理以後這兩場都參加過。**48** 妳建議我參加哪一場？

女：47 以你的管理經驗，初階課程對你來說可能過於基礎。我相信進階場你會獲得更多。

男：謝謝妳的建議，那我會參加進階場。

女：49 你也應該和伊恩克藍談談。他是這兩場工作坊的承辦人，應該可以告訴你更多資訊。

字彙 **management** 經營管理　　**workshop** 工作坊　　**advanced** 高級的、進階的　　**organizer** 主辦者、承辦人

47. Who most likely are the speakers?
(A) Company executives
(B) Business consultants
(C) New interns
(D) Seminar organizers

説話者很可能是誰？
(A) 公司主管
(B) 企業顧問
(C) 新實習人員
(D) 研討會主辦人

正確答案為 (A)

〈注意細節－職業〉
關於説話者的職業，應仔細聽對話的前半段。男子一開始提到有經營管理工作坊，接下來是關於參加的內容，可見説話者的職務與經營管理相關，因此答案是 (A)。

換句話說 **manager** 經理、管理者 → **executive** 經理主管

字彙 **executive** 主管 **consultant** 顧問、諮商師 **intern** 實習生

48. What does the man want to know about the workshops?
(A) The dates
(B) The registration fees
(C) The levels
(D) The attendees

關於研討會，男子想知道什麼？
(A) 日期
(B) 註冊費
(C) 級別
(D) 參加者

正確答案為 (C)

〈注意細節－特定事項〉
應仔細聽男子談話中提到關鍵字 workshop 的內容。男子一開始談話時提到工作坊分成兩個級別，並請女子給予建議，因此答案是 (C)。

49. What does the woman tell the man to do?
(A) Apply for the position
(B) Organize the event
(C) Speak to a manager
(D) Contact the person in charge

女子告訴男子做什麼？
(A) 應徵職位
(B) 主辦活動
(C) 和經理交談
(D) 聯絡負責人

正確答案為 (D)

〈注意細節－提議〉
女子在最後建議男子可以和承辦人 Ian Kline 談談，最適合的答案是 (D)。

換句話說 **organizer** 主辦人 → **person in charge** 負責人

字彙 **organize** 組織、主辦

3_50-52　美式女聲 / 英式男聲

Questions 50-52 refer to the following conversation.

W: Trevor, I just learned about your transfer to our Berlin branch. What will the company have you doing there?

M: Mostly the same type of work I do here. We'll be introducing our new menswear line throughout Europe starting this fall. My project team has had a lot of success promoting the line here, so the company assigned me to oversee our European marketing efforts as well.

W: That's great. Congratulations. That sounds very interesting. Have you arranged for a place to live yet?

M: Actually, someone I used to work with teaches at a university in Berlin. He invited me to stay with him and offered to help me find an apartment once I get there.

問題 50-52 參考以下對話。

女：崔佛，我剛聽説你要調到柏林分公司。公司要你在那裡做什麼？

男：基本上跟我在這裡做的一樣。50 今年秋天開始，我們將在全歐洲推出新的男裝系列。51 我的專案小組在這裡促銷這系列的產品很成功，因此公司也委任我管理歐洲市場行銷工作。

女：太棒了，恭喜你。聽起來很有趣。你已經安排好住處了嗎？

男：事實上，52 我以前的同事在柏林一所大學教書。他邀請我暫住他那裡，過去之後他就會幫忙我找公寓。

字彙　**branch** 分公司　　**throughout** 遍及；自始自終　　**promote** 宣傳促銷；升遷　　**assign** 指派　　**oversee** 監督、管理　　**used to**（表示過去經驗）曾經做～

50. What will the speakers' company do in Europe during the fall?

(A) Conclude a research study

(B) Launch a product line

(C) Construct a new facility

(D) Open a new branch

秋天時說話者的公司將在歐洲做什麼？

(A) 總結一項研究

(B) 推出新產品系列

(C) 建造新設施

(D) 開設新分店

正確答案為 (B)

〈注意細節－特定事項〉

應注意尋找關鍵字 in Europe during the fall 的前後內容。男子提到秋季期間公司在歐洲會推出男裝產品，答案是 (B)。

> 字彙　**conclude** 總結、下結論　**launch** 新發表、新推出　**construct** 建設

51. Why does the woman say, "That's great. Congratulations"?

(A) The man was promoted to an executive position.

(B) The man finished a project ahead of schedule.

(C) The man enrolled in a well-known university.

(D) The man was given an important assignment.

為什麼女子說「太棒了，恭喜你」？

(A) 男子升為管理職。

(B) 男子提前完成一個專案計畫。

(C) 男子考上一所知名大學。

(D) 男子被指派一項重要任務。

正確答案為 (D)

〈關鍵句－說話者意圖〉

應掌握關鍵句前後文句的脈絡，以了解女子說話意圖。男子說自己因在國內成功促銷產品，因此被派任負責歐洲市場行銷的工作，接著女子就說了這句話，因此答案是 (D)。

> 字彙　**ahead of schedule** 提前　**enroll in** 報名參加、註冊入學

52. According to the man, what will a former coworker help him do?

(A) Locate a residence

(B) Arrange transportation

(C) Prepare for a course

(D) Make professional contacts

根據男子所言，他的前同事會幫他做什麼？

(A) 尋找住處

(B) 安排交通

(C) 準備課程

(D) 與專業人士聯繫

正確答案為 (A)

〈注意細節－特定事項〉

應仔細聽男子提到關鍵字 former coworker「前同事」的內容。男子最後提到曾經共事的人將協助他尋找公寓，因此答案是 (A)。

換句話說　**find an apartment** 找公寓 → **locate a residence** 尋找住處

3_53-55 美式女聲 / 美式男聲

Questions 53-55 refer to the following conversation.

W: Hi. Could you tell me how far it is from here to the city center? This is my first time in Hanoi on business.

M: Well, it's not too far. If you take a taxi, you'll probably get there in about half an hour. The airport shuttle bus takes almost twice as long, but it's considerably cheaper.

W: If you say so, I'll take the shuttle bus. Do you know how often it goes?

M: It departs every half hour from outside door B, which is at the end of the terminal by the foreign exchange counter.

問題 53-55 參考以下對話。

女：嗨，㊋ 你能告訴我從這裡到市中心有多遠嗎？我第一次來河內出差。

男：嗯，不會很遠。如果妳搭計程車，大約半個小時就能到那裡。㊋ 機場接駁巴士要花近乎兩倍的時間，不過便宜許多。

女：既然你這麼說，㊌ 那我就搭接駁巴士。你知道多久一班嗎？

男：㊎ 每半個小時從 B 門口發車，B 門就在轉運站的盡頭，外幣兌換處旁邊。

---

 take 搭乘；花時間　**half an hour** 半小時　**shuttle bus** 接駁公車　**depart** 出發、離開　**terminal** 轉運站；航廈　**foreign exchange** 外幣兌換

53. Where does the conversation most likely take place?
(A) At a bus stop
(B) On a plane
(C) At an airport
(D) At a city center

對話最有可能發生在什麼地方？
(A) 公車站牌
(B) 飛機上
(C) 機場
(D) 市活動中心

正確答案為 **(C)**

〈掌握基本資訊－地點〉
題目問對話發生的地點，答案大部分出現在對話的前半段。女子第一次說話時是在問路，並表示自己是第一次到 Hanoi 河內，加上中間男子提到可以搭乘 airport shuttle bus，答案是 (C)。

54. What will the woman probably do next?
(A) Take a shuttle bus
(B) Purchase a ticket
(C) Exchange money
(D) Take a taxi

女子接下來可能會做什麼？
(A) 搭乘接駁巴士
(B) 購票
(C) 換錢
(D) 搭計程車

正確答案為 **(A)**

〈注意細節－未來〉
關於未來會發生的事，答案的線索通常在對話的後半段，可注意未來式的句子。女子在最後的談話中提到自己會搭乘接駁巴士，答案是 (A)。

字彙 **purchase** 購買

55. How many shuttle buses run per hour?
(A) One
(B) Two
(C) Three
(D) Four

接駁巴士每小時來幾班？
(A) 1 班
(B) 2 班
(C) 3 班
(D) 4 班

正確答案為 **(B)**

〈注意細節－特定事項〉
應仔細聽關鍵字 shuttle bus 出現的前後句子。女子問接駁巴士發車間隔，男子回答說每 30 分鐘一班車，也就是一小時兩班。答案是 (B)。

Test 03

3_56-58　英式男聲 / 美式女聲 / 美式男聲

Questions 56-58 refer to the following conversation with three speakers.

M1: Angela, there are left-over materials after we've remodeled our office. It's a shame to get rid of them. Can we use them somehow?

W: Well, we could use this paint to redo the sign on the entrance. It's just about the right color.

M2: You did a good job thinking it out, and we could put the extra cabinets in the staff lounge.

M1: Yeah! Smart thinking, Nathan! That would finally give us a place to store our clean cups and plates. Dealing with that tiny, cluttered area — it drives me up the wall.

W: The sign on the entrance won't take long. I could do it tomorrow.

M2: Then I'll go and ask Ms. Morris to put the cabinets in the lounge.

M1: It's great that we can make good use of these things.

問題 56-58 參考以下三人對話。

男1：安潔拉，辦公室裝修後還剩下一些材料，丟掉很可惜。我們可以設法利用它們嗎？

女：嗯，56 我們可以用這種油漆來重做入口處的招牌。顏色剛好是對的。

男2：這個點子很棒，然後我們可以把多出來的櫥櫃放在員工休息室。

男1：耶！聰明的想法，納桑！這樣我們就有地方存放乾淨的杯盤。那裡又小又亂，讓我很火大。

女：57 入口處的招牌不會花很久的時間，我可以明天處理。

男2：58 那麼我會去和莫里絲小姐商量把櫥櫃放在休息室裡。

男1：能好好利用這些東西真是太棒了。

字彙　**left-over** 剩下的　**remodel** 改建　**it's a shame** 可惜～　**get rid of** 擺脫　**redo** 重做　**entrance** 入口
staff lounge 員工休息室　**tiny** 很小的　**cluttered** 雜亂的　**It drives sb. up the wall.** 使某人大怒。

56. What does Angela suggest doing?　　安潔拉建議做什麼？
(A) Remodeling the office　　(A) 重新裝修辦公室
(B) Repainting a sign　　**(B) 重漆招牌**
(C) Selecting colors　　(C) 選擇顏色
(D) Buying more paint　　(D) 購買更多油漆

正確答案為 (B)

〈注意細節－特定事項〉
對話第一句男子說出關鍵名字 Angela，並問她如何使用剩下的材料，接著便是女子的回答，由此可知對話裡的女子就是 Angela，她提議可以用油漆重漆門口的招牌，因此答案是 (B)。

57. What will most likely happen tomorrow?　　明天很可能會發生什麼事？
(A) Angela will use the paint.　　**(A) 安潔拉會使用油漆。**
(B) Nathan will throw away the materials.　　(B) 納桑會把材料丟掉。
(C) Ms. Morris will install the shelves.　　(C) 莫里絲小姐會安裝架子。
(D) They will go to the head office.　　(D) 他們會去總公司。

正確答案為 (A)

〈注意細節－特定事項〉
應仔細聽關鍵字 tomorrow 出現的前後內容。對話中段女子表示做招牌不會花很多時間，可以在明天處理，因此最適合的答案是 (A)。

58. What does the man say he will do?　　男子說他將會做什麼？
(A) Consult with his colleague　　**(A) 和同事商量**
(B) Hire a professional　　(B) 聘請專家
(C) Attend a workshop　　(C) 參加研討會
(D) Renovate a staff lounge　　(D) 整修員工休息室

正確答案為 (A)

〈注意細節－未來〉
三人對話中，需分清楚每個角色所說的話，這段對話有兩名男子，由於本問題使用到未來式，所以要注意使用未來式說話的男子。在男 2 談話的後半段，說到自己將會去和 Ms. Morris 談談放置櫃子的事，因此答案是 (A)。

字彙　**consult with** 和～商量　**colleague** 同事　**renovate** 整修

Test 03

3_59-61　美式男聲 / 英式女聲

Questions 59-61 refer to the following conversation.

M: Excuse me. We've just arrived on a flight from Scotland but my son's suitcase is missing. We had four checked bags, but only three of them are here.

W: Oh, have you checked the area thoroughly? Sometimes the attendants take bags off the carousels and place them over by that wall.

M: Yes, we've looked everywhere but it's just not here. I wonder if another passenger took it by mistake. So many suitcases look alike these days.

W: That's possible, but more likely it got misdirected somehow. I'll start looking into it. Here's a form for you to fill out. And can I have your baggage claim checks, please?

M: Sure, here they are.

問題 59-61 參考以下對話。

男：打擾一下，我們剛從蘇格蘭搭乘飛機過來，但是 59 我兒子的手提箱不見了。我們有 4 件託運行李，但只有 3 件在這裡。

女：噢，這個區域你都找過了嗎？有時候服務人員會把行李從傳送帶上取下來放在那面牆邊。

男：是的，我們到處都找過了，就是沒找到。我在想會不會是其他乘客拿錯了。最近很多行李箱看起來都很像。

女：這是有可能的，60 但更有可能是不知怎麼地被放錯地方。我會開始調查。60 這裡有張表格請你填一下。61 可以給我您的行李提取單嗎？

男：當然，它們在這裡。

字彙　**thoroughly** 徹底地　　**attendant** 服務員　　**by mistake** 錯誤地　　**alike** 相似的、相同的　　**misdirect** 放錯地方
somehow 不知何故、不知怎麼地　　**fill out** 填寫　　**baggage claim check** 行李提領單

59. What are the speakers mainly talking about?　　談話者主要在討論什麼？
(A) A missing flight　　(A) 錯過的班機
(B) A lost item　　**(B) 遺失的物件**
(C) A delayed flight　　(C) 誤點的班機
(D) A rude passenger　　(D) 無禮的乘客

正確答案為 (B)

〈掌握基本資訊－主題〉
對話的主題會出現在前半段。男子在第一句話就告訴對方自己兒子的旅行箱遺失，因此答案是 (B)。

60. What does the woman mean when she says,　　女子說「我會開始調查」是什麼意思？
"I'll start looking into it"?　　**(A) 她將展開調查。**
(A) She will start an investigation.　　(B) 她將確認一些資訊。
(B) She will check out some information.　　(C) 她將預約班機。
(C) She will book a flight.　　(D) 她將聯絡同事。
(D) She will contact a colleague.

正確答案為 (A)

〈關鍵句－說話者意圖〉
與說話者意圖相關的關鍵句問題，必須掌握關鍵句的前後文句脈絡。女子說這句話之前，提到旅行箱很可能被送到其他地方，並要對方填寫調查時需要的資料。因此答案是 (A)。

字彙　**investigation** 調查

61. What does the woman ask the man to give her?　　女子請男子給她什麼？
(A) Some traveler's checks　　(A) 一些旅行支票
(B) His boarding pass　　(B) 他的登機證
(C) His passport　　(C) 他的護照
(D) Some documents　　**(D) 一些文件**

正確答案為 (D)

〈注意細節－請求〉
女子最後談話時跟男子要他的 baggage claim check「行李提取單」，換句話說，最適當的答案是 (D)。
換句話說 **your baggage claim checks** 你的行李提取單 → **some documents** 一些文件

字彙　**boarding pass** 登機證

3_62-64 美式女聲 / 英式男聲

Questions 62-64 refer to the following conversation and building directory.

W: Hi, Jeff. It's a shame that Mark & Spencer has moved out of the building. It was really convenient having a law firm on the floor right above us.

M: Yeah, and I was a good friend with Charles, the lawyer. I'll miss having lunch with him. He said that they didn't like having their offices on the top floor so they'd been searching for a right office for a while.

W: They're right across 5th Street now. I hear they've settled in nicely.

M: Why don't we take a walk over there at lunchtime and say hello? I want to talk with Charles about a few things while we're there.

The Triumph Building Directory

5th floor	Mark & Spencer Advisers
4th floor	L&D Service
3rd floor	Green Fingers Magazine
2nd floor	Twingle Advertising
1st floor	Lobby

問題 62-64 參考以下對話與樓層指示。

女：嗨，傑夫。62 63 真遺憾，馬克＆史賓瑟搬走了。以前律師事務所就在我們樓上，真的很方便。

男：是啊，我和查理斯律師是好朋友，我會想念和他一起吃午飯的日子。63 他說他們不喜歡辦公室位在頂樓，所以他們花了些時間尋找適合的辦公室。

女：他們現在就在第五街對面。聽說他們已經安頓好了。

男：64 我們何不在午餐時間散步過去打聲招呼呢？我想和查理斯談談幾件事情。

凱旋大廈樓層說明

5 樓	馬克＆史賓瑟顧問團
4 樓	L&D 服務
3 樓	綠手指雜誌
2 樓	雙角廣告公司
1 樓	大廳

字彙 **law firm** 法律事務所   **settle** 定居、安頓

62. What kind of company has moved out of the building?
(A) An accounting company
(B) A legal office
(C) An advertising agency
(D) A publishing company

何種公司搬出了這棟大樓？
(A) 會計公司
(B) 法律事務所
(C) 廣告公司
(D) 出版公司

正確答案為 (B)

〈注意細節－特定事項〉
應仔細聽關鍵字 moved out 出現的段落。女子一開始表示以前樓上就有法律事務所真方便，但很可惜現在他們已經搬走了，因此正確答案是 (B)。

換句話說 **law firm** 法律事務所 → **legal office** 法律事務所

63. Look at the graphic. At what company do the speakers most likely work?
(A) Mark & Spencer Advisers
(B) L&D Service
(C) Green Fingers Magazine
(D) Tingle Advertising

請看圖表，說話者最可能在哪個公司上班？
(A) 馬克＆史賓瑟顧問團
(B) L&D 服務
(C) 綠手指雜誌
(D) 雙角廣告

正確答案為 (B)

〈注意細節－圖表相關〉
必須交叉確認對話內容與圖表資料，由於選項出現公司名稱，所以須注意聽對話裡提到樓層的部份。法律事務所搬家的原因在於位在頂樓，由此可知 Mark & Spencer 馬克＆史賓瑟位在 5 樓，在女子第一次談話時提到律師事務所就在他們公司樓上，因此答案是 (B)。

64. What does the man suggest?
(A) Reviewing a document
(B) Planning an event
(C) Visiting a friend
(D) Hiring a lawyer

男子建議做什麼？
(A) 檢查文件
(B) 企劃活動
(C) 拜訪朋友
(D) 招聘律師

正確答案為 (C)

〈注意細節－建議〉
仔細聽男子最後的談話。男子最後談話時使用〈Why not?〉句型提議在中午用餐時間去拜訪已搬遷到新地方的律師朋友，答案是 (C)。

3_65-67　美式男聲／美式女聲

Questions 65-67 refer to the following conversation and program.

M: Hello, I'm calling about the management and marketing conference being held at the Town Events Center in July. I'm very interested in Dr. Hillary Palin's presentation. Is there any way for me to attend without registering for the entire conference?

W: I'm sorry sir, but you cannot. In fact, due to limited seating, even conference attendees aren't guaranteed admission to every presentation. If you really want to see Dr. Palin, you should probably register and reserve a seat as soon as possible.

M: Okay, can you let me know how to do that?

W: We can do it right now if you have a credit card handy, or you can register online through our Web site.

Management & Marketing Conference Presentations in July
Dr. Edward Williamson, Risk Management
Dr. Raymond Gomez, Time Management
Dr. Hillary Palin, Decision Making
Dr. Jina Hong, Group Working

問題 65-67 參考以下對話與節目表。

男：您好，我打電話是想問一下 7 月在市區活動中心舉辦的經營管理與市場行銷會議。❻❺ 我對希拉蕊帕林博士的講座有興趣。請問我可以只參加這場但不報名所有會議嗎？

女：對不起，先生，不行。事實上由於座位有限，即使是大會參加者也不保證每場講座都能入場。❻❻ 如果您真的想見帕林博士，您應該儘快報名登記並預約座位。

男：好，可以告訴我怎麼做嗎？

女：如果您手邊有信用卡，我們現在就可以辦理，或者 ❻❼ 您可以透過我們的網站報名。

7 月經營管理與市場行銷會議講座
愛德華威廉森博士，危機管理
雷蒙葛摩絲博士，時間管理
希拉蕊帕林博士，決策制定
洪吉納博士，團隊工作

字彙　**conference** 會議　**presentation** 上台報告、講座　**register** 登記、註冊　**entire** 全部的、整個的　**limited** 有限的　**guarantee** 保證、擔保　**admission** 入場　**handy** 手邊的、方便的

65. Look at the graphic. Which presentation is the man most interested in seeing?
(A) Risk Management
(B) Time Management
(C) Decision Making
(D) Group Working

請看圖表，男子最感興趣的是哪場講座？
(A) 風險管理
(B) 時間管理
(C) 決策制定
(D) 團隊工作

正確答案為 (C)

〈注意細節－圖表相關〉
選項是各講座主題，對照節目表後，必須注意對話當中提到的主講者名字。男子在第一句談話中提到對 Dr. Hillary Palin 的講座有興趣，因此正確答案是該主講者對應的主題，答案是 (C)。

66. What does the woman advise the man to do?
(A) Arrive at the venue early
(B) Make a reservation
(C) Contact a presenter
(D) Create a credit card

女子建議男子做什麼？
(A) 提早抵達會場
(B) 預約
(C) 聯絡講者
(D) 辦一張信用卡

正確答案為 (B)

〈注意細節－建議〉
應在女子對男子提出建議的部份找答案。在對話中間的部份，女子告訴男子若想參加講座，應儘快報名登記並預約座位，因此答案是 (B)。

換句話說 **reserve a seat** 預約座位 → **make a reservation** 預約

字彙 **venue** 活動場地

67. According to the woman, what can the man do at the Web site?
(A) Sign up for the conference
(B) Access research data
(C) Check out the schedule
(D) Confirm the credit card number

根據女子所言，男子可以在網站上做什麼？
(A) 報名參加會議
(B) 使用研究數據
(C) 確認日程表
(D) 確認信用卡卡號

正確答案為 (A)

〈注意細節－特定事項〉
應注意聽女子提到關鍵字 Web site 的對話內容。女子在最後一句建議男子可以透過網站報名登記，因此答案是 (A)。

換句話說 **register** 報名登記 → **sign up** 報名登記

字彙 **sign up for** 登記、報名　　**confirm** 確認

Questions 68-70 refer to the following conversation and map.

W: This is the layout of the factory we're supposed to install the solar panels in, right?

M: That's right. The company that owns the factory is trying to reduce energy costs. That's a near-term target for them.

W: I see. Well, just looking at things, the locations seem ideal. It looks like we could do the installation almost anywhere. I mean, the roof is so flat and everything.

M: Yes, but they only want us to cover the closest building to Stockwell Avenue, and it's right next to the lake. That catches the highest amount of average sunlight during the day year-round.

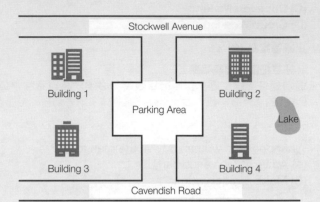

問題 68-70 請參考以下對話與地圖。

女：這是我們要安裝太陽能板的那間工廠平面圖，對嗎？

男：是的。68 擁有這家工廠的公司正試圖降低能源成本。這是他們的近期目標。

女：我明白了。嗯，從各方面來看，69 這些地點似乎都很理想。看起來在任何地方都可以進行安裝。我是說，屋頂很平坦、還有各方面等等。

男：是的，70 但是他們只要我們安裝在最靠近史塔克韋爾街的大樓、位於湖邊的那一棟。這是全年白天平均日照量最高的地方。

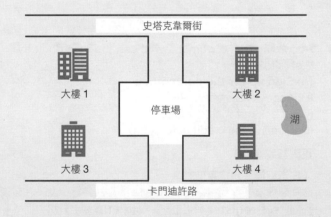

字彙 **layout** 設計、格局 　**be supposed to** 應該 　**install** 安裝、設置 　**solar panel** 太陽能板 　**own** 擁有、持有
reduce 減少、降低 　**near-term** 近期的 　**ideal** 理想的 　**installation** 安裝、裝置 　**flat** 平坦的 　**average** 平均的
year-round 整年的

68. What does the man say is a near-term goal of the company?
(A) **Reducing expenses**
(B) Producing more energy
(C) Opening a new branch
(D) Completing a project

男子說公司近期的目標是什麼？
(A) 減少開支
(B) 生產更多能源
(C) 開設新分店
(D) 完成專案

正確答案為 (A)

〈注意細節－特定事項〉
應從男子提到關鍵字 near-term goal 的談話部分找答案。男子第一句台詞說公司的短期目標是減少能源成本，因此答案是 (A)。

換句話說 **reduce costs** 減少成本支出 → **reducing expenses** 減少開銷

69. What does the woman say is ideal?
(A) The amount of sunlight
(B) Weather condition
(C) **The worksite**
(D) The work hours

女子說什麼東西很理想？
(A) 日照量
(B) 氣候狀況
(C) **工作場所**
(D) 工作時間

正確答案為 (C)

〈注意細節－特定事項〉
女子提到關鍵字 ideal 並表示 location「位置」很理想，因此答案是 (C)。

70. Look at the graphic. Where will the installation be done?
(A) On building 1
(B) **On building 2**
(C) On building 3
(D) On building 4

請看圖表，裝置會被安裝在哪裡？
(A) 大樓 1
(B) **大樓 2**
(C) 大樓 3
(D) 大樓 4

正確答案為 (B)

〈注意細節－圖表相關〉
選項出現平面圖上的大樓，應從平面圖上的其他資訊，如道路名稱、停車場、湖等單字尋找線索。男子最後提到該公司希望安裝在最靠近 Stockwell 史塔克韋爾街並且位於湖邊的大廈上，因此答案是 (B)。

Test 03

3_71-73 美式男聲

Questions 71-73 refer to the following excerpt from a meeting.

As you all know, it is very crucial that we make a good impression at the presentation tomorrow. If the clients accept our proposal, it'll have a positive impact on our financial situation for years to come. Their building is at 247 Brompton Road, just down the street from Hyde Park. Our appointment is at 1:00 P.M., but let's all try to get there early. We'll meet up at the coffee shop next door and then go in together as a group. For those of you who will drive there, there's a pay garage on the corner across from Hyde Park.

問題 71-73 參考以下會議摘要。

各位都知道，(71) 我們要在明天的簡報上留下好印象，這至關重要。如果客戶接受我們的提案，對我們今後幾年的財務將有正面影響。他們的大樓位在布朗普頓路 247 號，就在海德公園那條街上。我們會面時間是下午 1 點，但 (72) 請各位提早到達。(73) 我們先約在隔壁的咖啡店，再一起進去開會。開車的人，海德公園對面的轉角處有個付費停車場。

字彙 **excerpt**（演說、書籍或影片）節錄 **crucial** 重要的、決定性的 **impression** 印象 **positive** 積極的、肯定的 **impact** 影響、衝擊 **financial situation** 財務狀況 **garage** 車庫、停車場

71. What is the purpose of the talk?
(A) To prepare for a meeting
(B) To vote on a proposal
(C) To change a presenter
(D) To appoint a project manager

談話的目的是什麼？
(A) 為會議做準備
(B) 投票表決一項提案
(C) 更換簡報者
(D) 指定專案經理

正確答案為 (A)

〈掌握基本資訊－目的〉
談話目的會出現在談話一開始。談話一開始強調在明天的簡報中必須留下好印象，並且提到這次的簡報所帶來的正面影響，可知正在準備與客戶開會的會議，答案是 (A)。

字彙 **appoint** 指定　**presenter** 做簡報的人

72. What does the speaker suggest?
(A) Arriving ahead of time
(B) Postponing a meeting date
(C) Making a presentation
(D) Cutting a budget

説話者提出什麼建議？
(A) 提前到達
(B) 延後開會日期
(C) 做簡報
(D) 削減預算

正確答案為 (A)

〈注意細節－建議〉
在談話的中間説話者使用〈Let's ~〉句型提議大家盡量提早到，因此答案是 (A)。
換句話說 **get there early** 早一點到 → **arriving ahead of time** 提早到達

73. Where are listeners asked to meet tomorrow morning?
(A) At a café
(B) In a parking lot
(C) At the park
(D) In a seminar room

明天早上聽者被要求在哪裡見面？
(A) 咖啡廳
(B) 停車場
(C) 公園
(D) 會議室

正確答案為 (A)

〈注意細節－特定事項〉
説話者最後要大家在隔壁的咖啡廳見面，因此答案是 (A)。

Questions 74-76 refer to the following excerpt from a meeting.

There is something all of you need to do before returning to your workstations. The new packaging machine arrived here at our factory yesterday and was installed by our technicians last night. The new machine is capable of packaging our products at about twice the speed of our former equipment, but it's operated differently and uses a different system of mechanical processes. It won't take long, but everyone needs to learn how to use it. My assistant, Ms. Miller, is now going to hand out copies of the machine's instruction manual to everyone, and then we'll proceed to the packaging department and I'll demonstrate how to use it.

問題 74-76 參考以下會議提要。

在返回各自的工作之前，所有人都需要做一件事。**74** 新的包裝機昨天送到工廠，昨晚技術人員已經安裝完畢。**75** 這台新機器能夠以舊有設備約兩倍包裝速度包裝產品，但是它的操作方式不同，使用了不同的機械程序系統。每個人都需要學習操作方法，這不會花很長的時間。**76** 我的助理米勒小姐正準備把這台機器的使用說明書發給各位，然後我們會前往包裝部門，我將示範如何使用。

| 字彙 | **workstation** 個人工作站　**packaging** 包裝　**capable of** 有能力做～　**operate** 操作；運轉 **instruction manual** 使用說明書　**demonstrate** 示範、展示 |

74. Who most likely are the listeners?
    (A) Office workers
    (B) Computer technicians
    (C) Packaging designers
    (D) Factory workers

聽者很可能是什麼人？
(A) 辦公室員工
(B) 電腦技術人員
(C) 包裝設計師
(D) 工廠作業員

正確答案為 (D)

〈掌握基本資訊－聽者〉
關於聽者的基本資訊通常出現在對話前半段，前面談話提到昨天工廠進了新機器並且已經安裝完畢，因此答案是 (D)。

75. What is an advantage of the new machine?
    (A) It uses less power.
    (B) It requires fewer operators.
    (C) It performs more quickly.
    (D) It is easier to maintain.

這台新機器的優點是什麼？
(A) 更省電。
(B) 需要更少操作員。
(C) 執行工作更快速。
(D) 更容易維護。

正確答案為 (C)

〈注意細節－特定事項〉
在說明新機器的內容當中提到包裝速度比原有的機器快兩倍，由此可知答案是 (C)。

76. According to the speaker, what will Ms. Miller do next?
    (A) Distribute some documents
    (B) Contact another department
    (C) Give a demonstration
    (D) Install some equipment

根據說話者的陳述，米勒小姐接下來會做什麼？
(A) 分發文件
(B) 聯絡其他部門
(C) 親自示範
(D) 安裝機器

正確答案為 (A)

〈注意細節－特定事項〉
應掌握關鍵字 Ms. Miller 並仔細聽前後文。在提到此名字的內容中說到她將發給每個人使用說明書，因此答案是 (A)。

換句話說 **hand out the instruction manual** 分發使用說明書 → **distribute some documents** 分發一些文件

字彙   **distribute** 分發、分配

Test 03

3_77-79 美式女聲

Questions 77-79 refer to the following telephone message.

Hello. This is Juliet Holton from Astoria Event Agency. I'm calling to let you know that I've finished the outline for the *Discovering the Collection* event to be held at the Piccadilly Art Gallery. I've signed the contracts you faxed me, and we mailed them this afternoon. So that'll be all. I think everything is ready for us to start. I'd like to test the equipment and the designs at your gallery one day next week. I'm quite flexible with the time and date. So if you would contact me with a time that is suitable for you, I'll go there with my team and make sure everything works.

問題 77-79 參考以下電話留言。

您好,我是安斯托里亞活動經紀公司的茱麗葉荷頓。我打電話是想告訴你 77 我已經完成在皮卡迪里畫廊舉辦的〈發現展覽〉活動概要。你傳真來的合約我都簽好了,今天下午已經寄出。就這些了。 78 我想一切都已經準備就緒。 79 我想在下週的某一天到你的畫廊測試設備和設計。我的時間和日期都很彈性,如果你能告知我適合的時間,我會和我的團隊一起過去,確保一切正常運作。

字彙 **outline** 大綱、概要 **gallery** 畫廊 **contract** 合約 **flexible** 有彈性的、靈活的

77. What kind of business is Ms. Holton calling?
(A) An architectural firm
(B) An art gallery
(C) An event agency
(D) A real estate agency

荷頓小姐打電話到什麼公司？
(A) 建築公司
(B) 畫廊
(C) 活動經紀公司
(D) 房地產仲介公司

正確答案為 **(B)**

〈掌握基本資訊－聽者〉
題目問說話者打電話到什麼公司，因此必須找出聽者的上班地點。談話前半段提到打這通電話是為了通知已經完成了在 Piccadilly 皮卡迪里畫廊舉辦的〈Discovering the Collection〉活動概要，由此可知答案是 (B)。要小心別與說話者 Ms. Holton 的公司 (C) An event agency 混淆了。

78. What does the speaker mean when she says, "that'll be all"?
(A) She thinks the event will finish soon.
(B) She has completed preparations.
(C) She bought new equipment.
(D) She has found what she was looking for.

說話者說「就這些了」，她想表達什麼？
(A) 她覺得活動很快就會結束。
(B) 她已經準備完畢。
(C) 她買了新設備。
(D) 她已經找到了她要的東西。

正確答案為 **(B)**

〈關鍵句－說話者意圖〉
應掌握關鍵句的前後文脈絡，才能掌握說話者的意圖。在關鍵句之後，說話者表示一切已經準備就緒，因此答案是(B)。

79. What does Ms. Holton say she will do next week?
(A) Sign a contract
(B) Contact a manager
(C) Visit a client
(D) Revise an estimate

荷頓小姐說她下週將會做什麼？
(A) 簽合約
(B) 聯絡經理
(C) 拜訪客戶
(D) 修改估價單

正確答案為 **(C)**

〈注意細節－特定事項〉
注意聽說話者提到關鍵字 next week 的部份。說話者表示下週想過去聽者的畫廊，答案是 (C)。

3_80-82 英式女聲

Questions 80-82 refer to the following news report.

These are WTSZ evening updates. We have some good news for Wimbledon commuters. The construction work on the Tower Bridge is nearly complete and all four lanes will be open starting tomorrow morning. Workers began resurfacing the bridge in June, and the project was expected to take seven weeks. However, the heavy rainfalls the city experienced this summer slowed the pace of the work dramatically. Having only two lanes on the bridge open in each direction caused traffic congestion for miles during rush hour. The city has been under pressure to finish the work in time for the Wimbledon Tennis Tournament, which begins in two weeks and is expected to bring thousands of sports fans to the city.

問題 80-82 參考以下新聞報導。

這裡是 WTSZ 晚間新聞。我們為溫布頓的通勤族帶來一些好消息。⑧ 倫敦塔橋的工程已接近完工，全部 4 條車道將於明天早上通車。工人從 6 月開始重新舖設橋樑路面，當初工程預計為期 7 週。⑧ 然而本市在今年夏天所經歷的暴雨嚴重延誤到工程進度。橋上只能開放兩條車道通行，造成顛峰時間交通堵塞數英哩。為了及時完成工程，本市一直處於壓力之下，因為 ⑧ 溫布頓網球公開賽即將於兩週後開打，預計將有數千球迷來到這個城市。

字彙　**commuter** 通勤者　**resurface** 重鋪路面　**pace** 步調、進度　**dramatically** 顯著地、劇烈地
traffic congestion 交通堵塞、交通擁擠　**rush hour** 尖峰時間

80. What is main topic of this report?
(A) The results of a sports match
(B) The completion of roadwork
(C) The expansion of a stadium
(D) The construction of a tennis court

報導的主題是什麼？
(A) 運動賽事結果
(B) 道路完工
(C) 體育場擴建
(D) 蓋網球場

正確答案為 (B)

〈掌握基本資訊－主題〉

報導的主題會在前半段出現。談話的一開始，說話者就告知大橋的工程已經完工，因此答案是 (B)。

81. According to the report, what caused the delay?
(A) Insufficient funding
(B) A legal dispute
(C) A supply shortage
(D) Inclement weather

根據報導，是什麼造成延誤？
(A) 資金不足
(B) 法律糾紛
(C) 供應不足
(D) 惡劣氣候

正確答案為 (D)

〈注意細節－特定事項〉

談話的中段提到因為夏季暴雨而導致工程作業極度緩慢，工程受到拖延，因此答案是 (D)。

換句話說 **heavy rainfalls** 暴雨 → **inclement weather** 惡劣的氣候

字彙 **insufficient** 不足、缺乏 **dispute** 辯論、爭論 **inclement** 惡劣的

82. What does the speaker say about the Wimbledon Tennis Tournament?
(A) It will attract many people to the area.
(B) It will not start on schedule.
(C) It is causing some traffic detours.
(D) It is held on a regular basis.

關於溫布頓網球公開賽，說話者提到什麼？
(A) 它將吸引許多人來這個地區。
(B) 它將不會如期舉行。
(C) 它導致交通改道通行。
(D) 它定期舉行。

正確答案為 (A)

〈注意細節－提及內容〉

必須仔細聽說話者提到關鍵字 Wimbledon Tennis Tournament 的前後文。報導提到兩週後舉行的 Wimbledon 溫布頓網球公開賽將吸引成千球迷前往，因此答案是 (A)。

換句話說 **bring thousands of sports fans** 帶來數千名的球迷 → **attract many people** 吸引許多人

字彙 **on schedule** 如期地 **detour** 改道 **on a regular basis** 定期地、經常地

3_83-85　澳式男聲

Questions 83-85 refer to the following telephone message.

Hi, Emma. It's Jason. I just wanted to make sure you haven't forgotten about your appointment with Oliver Smith on Friday morning. He just called me to say that he expects to be here sometime between ten and eleven, depending on when he finishes another sales call he's making. He wanted me to mention that he has some samples from a new line that he's excited about showing you on Friday. By the way, I've really got to hand it to you. The new store display you put together yesterday looks wonderful. I'm sure it's been attracting a lot of people into the shop.

問題 83-85 參考以下電話留言。

嗨，艾瑪，我是傑森。84 我只是想確定妳沒忘記跟奧利佛史密斯週五早上有約。他剛才打電話給我，說他預計在 10 點到 11 點之間到，要看他何時結束另一通業務通話而定。83 他希望我跟妳說，他有些新產品的樣品想在週五給妳看。對了，我真的很佩服妳。85 昨天的新店布置展示看起來棒極了。我敢說那一定吸引很多人光臨。

字彙　**make sure** 確認、確保　　**expect** 期待、預期　　**depend on** 取決於　　**have got to hand it to** 相當佩服～
put together 裝配、組合、擺設

83. What will the listener most likely do on Friday morning? | 聽者星期五早上很可能要做什麼？
(A) View product samples | **(A) 看產品樣品**
(B) Reserve a place | (B) 訂場地
(C) Make a phone call | (C) 打電話
(D) Create a window display | (D) 製作櫥窗展示

正確答案為 (A)

〈注意細節－特定事項〉
掌握關鍵字 Friday morning，仔細聽相關內容。說話者在一開始幫忙提醒對方星期五早上與 Oliver Smith 奧利佛史密斯有約，中間提到會面者將展示樣品，因此答案是 (A)。

84. Why is the speaker calling? | 說話者為什麼打電話？
(A) To report an error | (A) 為了報告一個錯誤
(B) To reschedule an appointment | (B) 為了更改約會行程
(C) To give a reminder | **(C) 為了提醒對方**
(D) To make a sale | (D) 為了銷售

正確答案為 (C)

〈掌握基本資訊－主題〉
關於談話主題通常會出現在前半段。說話者一開始提醒對方與 Oliver Smith 在星期五上午有約，因此答案是 (C)。**詢問主題或主旨的問題雖然放在第二題，但在聆聽談話內容時，就應事先知道在一開始就會提到相關內容。**

85. What does the speaker mean when he says, "I've really got to hand it to you"? | 說話者說「我不得不佩服妳」是什麼意思？
(A) He wants to give an item to the listener. | (A) 他想給聽者一樣東西。
(B) He needs to rearrange the window display. | (B) 他需要重新布置櫥窗展示。
(C) He wants to offer the listener help. | (C) 他想為聽者提供協助。
(D) He thinks the listener deserves praise. | **(D) 他認為聽者值得讚許。**

正確答案為 (D)

〈關鍵句－說話者意圖〉
應掌握關鍵句的前後文脈絡，再推測出這句話的背後意圖。關鍵句後面一句是在稱讚聽者的商品展示，因此答案是 (D)。

字彙　**deserve** 值得　**praise** 稱讚

Questions 86-88 refer to the following radio broadcast.

Welcome back to Developing Yourself. I'm Jack Dawson. You are listening to the program for people who are eager to get ahead in the corporate world. Today's guest is Sarah Parker, the former president of Metropolitan University's School of Business. Ms. Parker will tell us how furthering your education can improve your career. She'll look through some of the options that are available, such as attending short-term classes, taking online courses at a local community college, or even taking a break from work for a year or two to get an advanced degree. At the end of the show, we'll open the phone lines so you can ask Ms. Parker questions about education and training.

問題 86-88 參考以下廣播節目。

歡迎回到〈自我發展〉，我是傑克道森。**86** 您收聽的節目是為那些渴望在工作上晉升的人所準備。　**87** 今天的來賓是大都會大學商學院前任院長沙拉帕克。帕克小姐將告訴我們持續受教育如何改善職業生涯。她將仔細分析一些可行的選擇，例如參加短期課程、社區大學線上課程，甚至是暫停工作一兩年去追求更高學位。**88** 節目最後，我們將開放專線電話，讓各位問帕克小姐有關教育和培訓的問題。

字彙　**eager** 渴望的、熱切的　　**corporate** 企業的、公司的　　**further** 更進一步、更深入　　**improve** 改善、提升
advanced degree（碩博士等）高等學歷

86. What type of information does Developing Yourself probably focus on?
(A) Developing new products
(B) Fashion trends
(C) Technological innovations
(D) Career advice

〈自我發展〉會關注何種資訊？
(A) 開發新產品
(B) 流行趨勢
(C) 科技革新
(D) 職涯建議

正確答案為 **(D)**

〈注意細節－特定事項〉
談話一開始就提到題目的關鍵字 Developing Yourself，接下來說明此 program 廣播節目是專為想在公司出人頭地的人而準備，因此最適合的答案是 (D)。

87. According to the broadcast, what has Sarah Parker done?
(A) She published a book.
(B) She ran a school.
(C) She took an online course.
(D) She owned a company.

根據廣播節目，沙拉帕克做了什麼？
(A) 她出版過書籍。
(B) 她經營過學校。
(C) 她上過網路線上課程。
(D) 她擁有一家公司。

正確答案為 **(B)**

〈注意細節－特定事項〉
掌握關鍵字 Sarah Parker 沙拉帕克並仔細聽前後文內容。說話者介紹今天的來賓是 Sarah Parker，她是 Metropolitan 大都會大學商學院前任院長，因此答案是 (B)。

88. What will Ms. Parker do at the end of the show?
(A) Take calls from listeners
(B) Introduce another guest
(C) Attend the educational training
(D) Make a questionnaire

帕克小姐在節目最後將會做什麼？
(A) 接聽聽眾打來的電話
(B) 介紹另一個來賓
(C) 參加教育培訓
(D) 製作一份問卷

正確答案為 **(A)**

〈注意細節－特定事項〉
掌握關鍵字 end of the show，說話者表示為了可以向 Parker 小姐提問，將開放電話專線，因此答案是 (A)。
換句話說 **open the phone lines** 開放專線電話 → **take calls from listeners** 接聽聽眾的電話

3_89-91　英式女聲

Questions 89-91 refer to the following talk.

Let me take this opportunity to introduce you all to Brian Price. He's replacing Glen Keys as a director of research and development department. Mr. Price comes to us from Warwick University, where he's been teaching business management for last fifteen years. He has worked in the industry far longer than any of us here in our company and won countless awards. As you can imagine, many companies want to work with him. So, we're lucky! Before I ask him to talk about himself and his vision for us, I'd like you to stand up one by one and tell Mr. Price your name and the position in the company.

問題 89-91 參考以下談話。

89 讓我藉此機會向大家介紹布萊恩普萊斯。他將接替葛藍奇斯擔任研發部主任。普萊斯先生來自瓦韋克大學，他在那裡已經教了 15 年的商業管理。他在這個行業工作的時間比我們公司的任何人都還久，並且贏得無數獎項。如同各位可以想像的，90 有許多公司想和他合作。因此我們非常幸運！在請他談談自己和對我們的看法之前，91 請各位逐一站起來向普萊斯先生自介姓名與所擔任的職位。

字彙　**opportunity** 機會　**research and development** 研究開發　**industry** 產業、工業　**countless** 無數的、數不盡的　**personnel** 員工、人事

89. What is the purpose of the talk?
(A) To announce a new policy
(B) To introduce a new employee
(C) To plan a company event
(D) To inform about a business hour

此談話的目的是什麼？
(A) 宣布新政策
(B) 介紹新員工
(C) 策劃公司活動
(D) 告知營業時間

正確答案為 **(B)**

〈掌握基本資訊－主題〉
談話主題通常在談話開頭就會出現。本談話的第一句就介紹了特定人物，因此最適合的答案是 (B)。

90. What does the speaker mean when she says, "So, we're lucky"?
(A) The company has received the media attention.
(B) Brian Price has accepted the job offer.
(C) Glen Keys will join the company.
(D) The company has been highly ranked in the industry.

說話者說「因此我們非常幸運」是什麼意思？
(A) 這家公司受到媒體關注。
(B) 布萊恩普萊斯已經接受了這份工作。
(C) 葛藍奇斯將加入這家公司。
(D) 這家公司在業界名列前茅。

正確答案為 **(B)**

〈關鍵句－說話者意圖〉
應綜合掌握關鍵句的前後文，以了解說話者的意圖。關鍵句之前，說話者提到許多公司想和他合作，因此能到我們公司上班是我們的榮幸。可知答案是 (B)。

字彙　**highly ranked** 名列前茅的

91. What will most likely happen next?
(A) The employees will introduce themselves.
(B) There will be a discussion session.
(C) The staff will submit the forms.
(D) Mr. Price will speak about the company's future.

接下來很可能會發生什麼事情？
(A) 員工將自我介紹。
(B) 將舉行討論會。
(C) 工作人員將提交表格。
(D) 普萊斯先生將談論公司未來。

正確答案為 **(A)**

〈注意細節－未來〉
接下來將發生的事情會出現在談話最後。談話最後說話者請聽者逐一起身自我介紹，因此答案是 (A)。

3_92-94 美式男聲

Questions 92-94 refer to the following telephone message.

Hi, Ivan. It's Jonathan. I got your message. Thanks for inviting me to dinner, but I don't think I can make it. My laptop froze just as I was finishing my report this morning. Since only half of the data was recovered, a lot has to be done over and over again. That's not the end because the department manager called today asking for some last-minute changes to the sales figure. It is a terrible day. All this is gonna keep me up at night, so going out for dinner is out of the question. Let's try to get together soon, though. Bye!

問題 92-94 參考以下電話留言。

嗨，伊凡，我是強納森，我收到訊息了。92 謝謝你邀請我吃晚餐，但我無法過去。今天早上我快完成報告時，我的筆記型電腦突然當機。93 由於只復原了一半的數據，有許多部分我必須一次又一次重做。 還不止如此，94 部門經理今天打電話來要求對銷售數字做最後的修改。真是糟透的一天。這一切將讓我無法入眠，所以出去吃飯是完全不可能的事。不過，我們儘快想辦法再聚一聚吧。再見！

字彙 **freeze** 當機　**last-minute** 最後一刻的、緊要關頭的　**recover** 復原　**keep sb. up** 讓某人保持清醒、無法睡覺　**out of the question** 絕不可能的

92. Why is the speaker calling?
(A) To congratulate on the success
(B) To complete the sales report
(C) To decline an invitation
(D) To confirm a meeting agenda

說話者為什麼打電話？
(A) 為了祝賀成功
(B) 為了完成銷售報告
(C) 為了回絕邀請
(D) 為了確認開會議題

正確答案為 **(C)**

〈掌握基本資訊－主題〉
題目問電話留言主題，注意談話的第一句。說話者提到感謝對方的邀請但無法前往，可知答案是 (C)。

字彙　**decline** 婉拒、謝絕

93. What does the speaker mean when he says, "A lot has to be done over and over again"?
(A) He bought several computers.
(B) He lost some of his work.
(C) He attended a variety of workshops.
(D) He needed to call a manager repeatedly.

說話者說「有許多部分我必須一次又一次重做」，他的意思是什麼？
(A) 他買了幾台電腦。
(B) 他遺失一些工作成果。
(C) 他參加各種工作坊。
(D) 他需要不停打電話給經理。

正確答案為 **(B)**

〈關鍵句－說話者意圖〉
須從關鍵句前後脈絡找出答案。關鍵句之前，男子提到自己的筆電當機，遺失的數據只有一半復原成功，答案是 (B)。

94. According to the speaker, what did a department manager ask for?
(A) A deadline extension
(B) A personal visit
(C) Modification of information
(D) Completion of a questionnaire

根據說話者，一名部門經理要求什麼？
(A) 延後交期
(B) 親自拜訪
(C) 修改資訊
(D) 完成問卷調查

正確答案為 **(C)**

〈注意細節－特定事項〉
應掌握關鍵字 department manager「部門經理」並仔細聽其前後文。談話最後提到部門經理打電話來要求做最後修改，換句話說，最適合的答案是 (C)。

換句話說 **changes to the sales figure** 修改銷售數字 → **modification of information** 修改資訊

3_95-97 澳式男聲

Questions 95-97 refer to the following talk and floor plan.

Before we start, I want to pass on to you a message from our customer Maggie Clarkson. Actually, she left some instructions for where to put some of the things we're moving to her new home. She said the green boxes should be placed in the bedroom in the back of the house, the one with access to the garden. And the rear door to the home connects directly with the living room. Plus, it's a lot wider than the front entrance, so it'll be easier if we bring the living room furniture in through the back. Ms. Clarkson said she'd leave the gate to the fence unlocked for us.

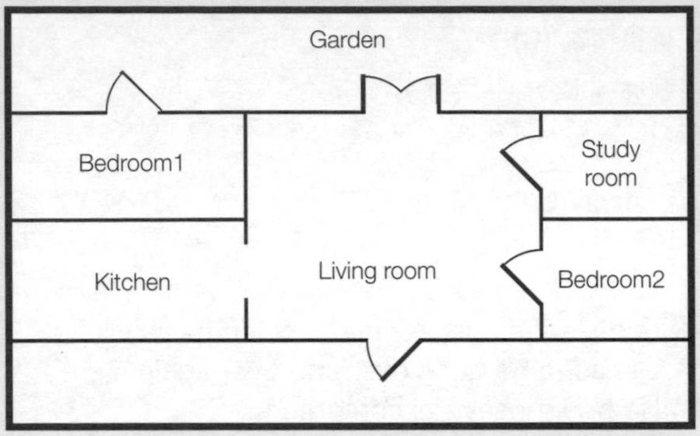

問題 95-97 參考以下發言與樓層平面圖。

在我們開始之前，我想把客戶瑪姬克拉森的留言轉達給各位。事實上，(95) 她留言指示我們把搬到新家的東西放到該放的地方。(96) 她說綠色的箱子應該放在房子後方的寢室，也就是通往庭園的那間。住家的後門直接與客廳相通，而且也比前門寬多了，因此我們從後門把客廳家具搬進來會比較方便。(97) 克拉森小姐說她不會鎖上柵欄的門。

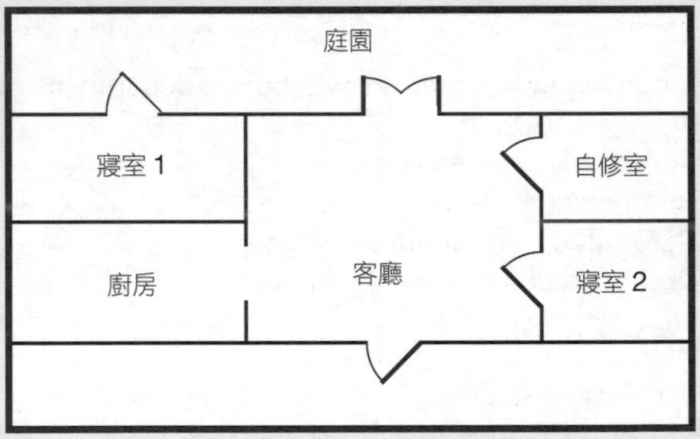

字彙 **instruction** 說明、指示 **rear** 後面的 **directly** 直接地、正好地

95. What type of business do the listeners probably work for?
(A) A furniture dealer
(B) An interior design agency
(C) A cleaning service
(D) A moving company

聽者很可能從事什麼類型的行業？
(A) 家具公司
(B) 室內設計代理商
(C) 清潔服務
(D) 搬家公司

正確答案為 **(D)**

〈掌握基本資訊－場所〉

關於聽者的工作場所，線索通常會在對話的前半部出現。說話者在談話一開始提到客人留下指示，告訴大家應該把搬到新家的物品放在什麼地方，因此答案是 (D)。

96. Look at the graphic. Where should the green boxes be placed?
(A) Bedroom 1
(B) Bedroom 2
(C) The study room
(D) The living room

請看圖表，綠色箱子應該放在什麼地方？
(A) 寢室 1
(B) 寢室 2
(C) 自修室
(D) 客廳

正確答案為 **(A)**

〈注意細節－圖表相關〉

在聽對話之前，應先預測出題目與圖表之間的關係。**與平面圖相關的問題，答案通常會出現在有關位置的描述。**應掌握關鍵字 green box 並對照平面圖的位置與談話。內容提到綠色箱子應放在可以通往庭園的後方寢室，因此答案是靠近庭園的寢室 (A)。

97. What does the speaker say Ms. Clarkson will do?
(A) Leave the entrance open
(B) Unpack some boxes
(C) Clean up the new home
(D) Lock up some valuable items

說話者提到克拉森小姐將會做什麼？
(A) 讓大門開著
(B) 打開一些箱子
(C) 清潔新家
(D) 將貴重物品鎖上

正確答案為 **(A)**

〈注意細節－未來〉

應掌握關鍵字 Clarkson 克拉森小姐並仔細聽最後的部份。說話者在最後一句提到 Clarkson 小姐將會為了聽者不鎖柵欄的門，因此答案是 (A)。

3_98-100 英式男聲

Questions 98-100 refer to the following excerpt from a meeting and map.

Unlike in previous years, we're encouraging all of you to bring along a family member to this year's company banquet. This means we'll need a larger venue to accommodate more than 200 guests. Have a look at this map, which shows four potential locations. I'd like to get your input before making a final decision. Personally, I think this one on the corner of Leman Avenue and Prescot Street is the best option. It's close to our office so we won't need to pay for parking and it's the cheapest one of the four, too. We don't have any time to discuss this now, so if you have any thoughts, send me a text later this afternoon.

問題 98-100 參考以下會議摘要與地圖。

與往年不同，98 我們鼓勵大家都能帶一名家人來參加今年的公司宴會。這意味我們需要更大的場地來容納 200 多位客人。看看這張地圖，它標出 4 個可能的地點。在做最後決定以前，我想聽聽各位的意見。就我個人而言，99 我認為這家位在拉曼大道和普瑞斯卡特街轉角的是最佳選擇。它距離辦公室很近，我們不需支付停車費，也是 4 家當中最便宜的一家。我們現在沒有時間討論這個問題，如果有任何想法，100 請在今天下午發簡訊給我。

字彙　**previous** 以前的　**encourage** 鼓勵、獎勵　**bring along** 帶～來、攜帶～　**banquet** 晚宴　**accommodate** 容納　**potential** 潛在的、可能的　**input** 意見、想法　**option** 選項

98. What kind of event is going to be held?
(A) A product launch
(B) A business gathering
(C) A sales workshop
(D) A special dinner

即將舉辦什麼活動？
(A) 產品發表會
(B) 商務聚會
(C) 銷售工作坊
(D) 特別晚餐

正確答案為 **(D)**

〈注意細節－特定事項〉
說話者在談話一開始提到公司鼓勵大家都能帶一位家人來參加公司宴會，因此最適合的答案是 (D)。

字彙　**gathering** 聚會

99. Look at the graphic. Which venue does the speaker recommend?
(A) Lloyds Building
(B) Wallace Center
(C) Mansion House
(D) Duke Hall

請看圖表，說話者推薦的是哪個場地？
(A) Lloyds 大樓
(B) Wallace 中心
(C) Mansion 公館
(D) Duke 宴會廳

正確答案為 **(B)**

〈注意細節－圖表相關〉
地圖上列出大樓名稱，因此在聽談話前就應該預測到會提及道路名稱。說話者推薦位於 Leman 拉曼大道和 Prescot 普瑞斯卡特街轉角處的場所，大樓名稱是 Wallace Center，因此答案是 (B)。

100. How can the listeners contact the speaker?
(A) By text message
(B) By electronic mail
(C) By fax
(D) By extension phone

聽者要如何與說話者聯絡？
(A) 利用文字簡訊
(B) 利用電子郵件
(C) 利用傳真
(D) 利用電話分機

正確答案為 **(A)**

〈注意細節－特定事項〉
談話最後，說話者提到有任何想法都可以 sent a text 發簡訊給他，因此答案是 (A)。

字彙　**extension phone** 分機電話

101. ------- new dental office will occupy the third floor of the new building on Mason Street.

(A) We
(B) Our
(C) Ours
(D) Us

我們新的牙醫辦公室將進駐曼森街新大樓的 3 樓。

正確答案為 **(B)**

〈代名詞格〉空格後面的名詞 office 缺少適合的限定詞,因此選擇所有格 (B) Our。

> 字彙　**occupy** 佔據

102. Bus passengers ------- bicycles are responsible for securing them appropriately.

(A) with
(B) over
(C) of
(D) from

攜帶腳踏車上公車的乘客有責任妥善保管它們。

正確答案為 **(A)**

〈介系詞〉根據語意,應是 passenger 擁有腳踏車,因此答案是介系詞 (A) with。

> 字彙　**be responsible for** 對～負責　**secure** 保護　**appropriately** 適當地

103. The advance deposit is ------- refundable as long as the rental car is returned without damage.

(A) full
(B) fully
(C) fuller
(D) fullest

只要出租的車輛完好無損歸還,押金可以全額退還。

正確答案為 **(B)**

〈詞性〉空格位於 be 動詞與形容詞之間,因此要填入副詞,答案是 (B) fully。

> 字彙　**advance deposit** 預繳押金　**refundable** 可退費的　**as long as**（連接詞）只要　**without damage** 沒有損壞
> **fully** 充分地、完全地

104. ------ has worked harder than Lisa Stanley to market New Skin's new line of hair treatment products.

(A) Whoever
(B) Nothing
(C) Nobody
(D) Any

沒有人比麗莎史丹利更努力行銷新肌護髮系列新產品。

正確答案為 **(C)**

〈單複數〉空格位於主詞位置,句意上須能搭配動詞 has worked,因此答案是 (C) Nobody。

> 字彙　**hair treatment** 頭髮護理

105. The ------- of the construction project was covered by a generous donation from some local entrepreneurs.
(A) currency
(B) benefit
(C) account
(D) cost

建築工程費用是透過當地幾位企業家的慷慨捐贈支付。

正確答案為 (D)

空格位於 the construction of the project「建案」之前，答案要選擇能表達「建案費用」的名詞 cost「花費」，答案選 (D)。currency 指「貨幣」，benefit 當名詞時指「福利」，都不適合本句語意。

字彙　**generous** 慷慨大方的　　**donation** 捐贈　　**entrepreneur** 企業家　　**currency** 貨幣

106. Please remember to double-check the spelling of Mr. Prichard's name when ------- the document.
(A) revising
(B) revises
(C) revised
(D) revise

修改文件時，請記得再次檢查普林查德先生的名字拼寫。

正確答案為 (A)

〈分詞構句〉副詞子句連接詞 when 原本是接〈主詞＋動詞〉的完整句，但本句省略主詞，可見是分詞構句。此處的動詞要使用能夠主動執行修改文件的現在分詞 (A) revising。

字彙　**double-check** 再三確認　　**revise** 修改

107. Recruiting interns is a ------- solution to filling entry-level positions eventually at Cypher Bank.
(A) talented
(B) various
(C) willing
(D) sensible

招聘實習生終究是填補希佛銀行初階職的一個合理解決方案。

正確答案為 (D)

空格要放能修飾名詞 solution 的形容詞，因此答案是符合句意的 (D) sensible，意思為「合理的」。

字彙　**recruit** 招聘　　**intern** 實習生　　**eventually** 終究、最終　　**talented** 有才華的　　**various** 多樣的　　**sensible** 合理的

108. Delegates visited the mayor to ask ------- developers will preserve the work of ancient artisans.
(A) although
(B) since
(C) whether
(D) both

代表們拜訪市長，詢問開發商是否會保留古代工匠們的作品。

正確答案為 (C)

〈連接詞〉空格位於 ask 後方作為後方子句的一部分，答案是能當受詞的名詞子句連接詞 (D) whether。Although 跟 since 是副詞子句連接詞。both 不符合句意。

字彙　**delegate** 代表　　**preserve** 保存　　**ancient** 古代的　　**artisan** 工匠

109. Workers now send in travel requests electronically ------- submitting a paper form.
(A) instead of
(B) because of
(C) through
(D) which

現今員工透過電子方式寄發出差申請書，而非提交書面表格。

正確答案為 (A)

空格之後是動名詞片語，表示空格須填入介系詞，且要帶出 paper form 和 electronically 的對比語意，答案是 (A) instead of。

字彙　**submit** 提交　**instead of** 代替、而不是～　**through** 透過

110. Tenants who are ------- in renewing their lease should follow the process outlined on the Lakeview Apartments Web site.
(A) interest
(B) interests
(C) interested
(D) interesting

有意續約的房客應按照湖景大廈網站上的流程辦理。

正確答案為 (C)

〈詞性〉空格位於 be 動詞後方的補語位置。根據語意，答案是形容詞 (C) interested，表「感到有興趣的」，用來修飾前方的先行詞 Tenants「房客」。

字彙　**tenant** 承租人、房客　**renew** 更新　**lease** 租約　**follow the process** 依照程序

111. Juan Reyes, the newest employee of the Manheim Film Production, ------- worked in London for eight years.
(A) consequently
(B) always
(C) still
(D) previously

朱雷耶斯是曼海姆電影公司的最新員工，之前曾經在倫敦工作 8 年。

正確答案為 (D)

空格位於修飾動詞過去式 worked 的副詞位置，符合句意的答案是 (D) previously。

字彙　**consequently** 結果、因此　**previously** 以前

112. ------- Ms. Jenkins wrote her thesis on housing markets, she knew how to make profitable property investments.
(A) Either
(B) Rather
(C) Unless
(D) Because

傑金絲小姐寫的論文與住宅市場有關，因此她知道如何進行能獲利的房地產投資。

正確答案為 (D)

〈連接詞〉空格要填入副詞子句連接詞，依照句意，可以表示「原因、理由」的答案是 (D) Because。

字彙　**thesis** 論文　**housing** 住宅　**profitable** 有利潤的　**property** 不動產、資產　**investment** 投資
　　　rather（副詞）寧可

113. At the Board meeting, it was mentioned that there is a slight ------- that the Carmichael Arts Center will be closed.
(A) possible
(B) possibility
(C) possibly
(D) possibilities

董事會會議上有人提到查米雪兒藝術中心有關閉的可能性。

正確答案為 (B)

〈**詞性**〉空格位於冠詞 a 與形容詞 slight 的後面，須放入單數名詞，答案是 (B)。

字彙　**slight** 些微的

114. ------ receiving the prestigious Evangeline Award, Ms. Mehta made a point of thanking her long-time colleagues.
(A) Onto
(B) Unlike
(C) About
(D) Upon

瑪塔小姐一拿到享有盛名的伊凡葛林獎，就特地感謝她長久以來的共事同仁。

正確答案為 (D)

〈upon + Ving〉指「一～就～」，答案是 (D)。

字彙　**prestigious** 享有盛名的　　**make a point of** 重視、強調　　**colleague** 同事　　**unlike** 和～不同、不像

115. Because the rates for the Wellington Hotel were very high, Logisoft Inc. will hold a workshop ------- this year.
(A) seldom
(B) recently
(C) somewhat
(D) elsewhere

由於威靈頓飯店費用相當高昂，羅技軟體有限公司今年將在別的地方舉辦工作坊。

正確答案為 (D)

seldom「鮮少」是頻率副詞，必須放在動詞前面，recently「最近」必須與過去式一起使用，somewhat 是修飾形容詞的副詞，因此答案是 (D) elsewhere。

字彙　**rate** 費用　　**seldom**（否定頻率副詞）很少、幾乎不　　**somewhat**（副詞）多少、有點　　**elsewhere** 在別處

116. Dr. Di Scala indicates that important shopping trends become ------- with the use of data analysis.
(A) predict
(B) prediction
(C) predictable
(D) predictably

迪史卡拉博士指出，利用數據分析可以預測重要的購物趨勢。

正確答案為 (C)

〈**特殊動詞**〉become 是連綴動詞，為了說明主詞 trends，空格要填入形容詞 (C) predictable。

字彙　**indicate** 表明、指出　　**data analysis** 數據分析、資料分析

Test 03

117. ------- to Braxton Drive will be limited to one side of the street after the road work begins next month.
(A) Access
(B) Accesses
(C) Accessible
(D) Accessing

下個月道路工程開始之後，通往布萊斯頓車道的道路將限制為單側道路。

正確答案為 (A)

〈詞性〉空格位於句子的主詞位置，答案要選名詞 (A)，access to 指「通往～的途徑或路線」。access 是不可數名詞，因此無法使用 (B) Accesses。

118. Professor Hillsman's ------- for teaching at Malkin College remains still strong at the age of 65.
(A) enthusiasm
(B) assortment
(C) likeness
(D) inclusion

摩金大學希斯曼教授的教學熱忱即使到 65 歲依舊很強烈。

正確答案為 (A)

空格是主詞位置，需要與 for teaching 和動詞片語 remain strong 相呼應，因此答案是 (A) enthusiasm。

字彙　**enthusiasm** 熱情　　**assortment** 分類、各種各樣　　**likeness** 相似之處　　**inclusion** 包含

119. To be eligible for the Jessie's Electronics discount, you must submit the coupon ------- in the mail.
(A) has sent
(B) have to send
(C) that was sent
(D) for sending

要獲得傑喜電子的產品折扣，您必須提交透過郵件發送的優惠卷。

正確答案為 (C)

〈主被動〉(A) has sent 和 (B) have to send 是主動時態，無法在沒有連接詞的情況下使用。(D) for sending 因為空格後面沒有受詞而無法使用。答案是包含關係代名詞 that 在內的被動式型態 (C)。

字彙　**be eligible for** 符合～的資格　　**submit** 繳交、提交

120. With the rainy season, Faye's Bicycle Rentals will most likely have ------- customers this month.
(A) neither
(B) every
(C) fewer
(D) higher

雨季到來，菲腳踏車出租店這個月的客人很有可能會減少。

正確答案為 (C)

選項的形容詞當中，可以用在複數型 customers 之前的數量形容詞是 fewer，因此答案是 (C)。every 必須與單數名詞一起使用。

121. ------- all interview processes have been completed, the top three candidates for the advertising director position will be contacted.
(A) Compared to
(B) As soon as
(C) So that
(D) Not only

所有面試流程一結束，我們就會和廣告總監一職的前 3 名候選人聯絡。

正確答案為 (B)

〈連接詞〉逗點前後各別是完整的句子，表示空格要填入能連接兩個子句的連接詞。四個連接詞選項中最符合面試流程一結束就會馬上聯絡的句意是 (B) As soon as。

字彙 **process** 流程　　**complete** 完成　　**contact** 聯絡　　**compared to** 與～相比　　**as soon as** 一～就～　　**so that** 以便～

122. ------- the assigned speaking time not work for you, please let Ms. Everett know, so she can rearrange the presentation schedule.
(A) Whenever
(B) Anywhere
(C) As well as
(D) Should

如果指定的演講時間不適合您，請告知艾弗雷特小姐，她會重新安排演講時間。

正確答案為 (D)

〈假設語氣〉從空格到 for you 是一個子句，並使用否定詞 not，但沒有看到助動詞，因此句子需要助動詞和連接詞。在假設語氣中，如果省略連接詞 if，助動詞 should 可以倒裝放至句子開頭，因此答案是 (D)。

字彙 **assigned** 指定的、分配的　　**rearrange** 重新安排　　**as well as** 也

123. The hiring committee will ------- an offer of employment to Dwan Willis next Monday.
(A) extend
(B) assign
(C) displace
(D) commit

招聘委員會將在下週一向杜旺威力斯公司開放一個職缺。

正確答案為 (A)

空格前面是助動詞，因此空格要填入原形動詞，句意最適合的是 extend an offer「提供」，答案是 (A)。

字彙 **hiring committee** 招聘委員會　　**assign** 分配、派指　　**displace** 取代、代替

124. If you lose your identification card, the security manager will deactivate it and issue -------.
(A) other
(B) other one
(C) one another
(D) another

如果遺失識別證，保安經理將會停用原卡，再發放另一張。

正確答案為 (D)

〈代名詞〉空格位於動詞 issue「發行」的受詞，暗示著會有其他的身分證，因此答案是可以當不定代名詞 (D) another。**other** 是指定指示詞，後面必須接名詞。

字彙 **identification card** 識別證、身分證　　**security** 保安　　**deactivate** 使失效　　**issue** 發行　　**one another** 彼此、互相

125. City inspectors will evaluate every office on 5th floor next week ------- determine how to best reduce energy usage.
(A) even if
(B) in order to
(C) after all
(D) given that

下個星期，城市稽查員將針對 5 樓每間辦公室進行評估，決定最佳減少能源使用的方法。

正確答案為 (B)

空格位於動詞 determine 前面，答案是可以置於動詞前面的 (B) in order to。

 字彙　**inspector** 檢查員　**evaluate** 評估　**determine** 決定、確定　**energy usage** 能源使用
　　in order to 為了～　**after all** 畢竟、終究　**given that** 考慮到～

126. To select its Audit Committee members, Blake Techline Ltd. ------- employees who are ready for a challenge.
(A) seeking
(B) is seeking
(C) are sought
(D) have been sought

為了遴選出審計委員會成員，布萊克科技有限公司正在尋找準備好迎接挑戰的員工。

正確答案為 (B)

〈主被動〉空格要放入動詞，而且後方有受詞 employees，因此答案要選主動語態 is seeking。

字彙　**select** 挑選　**audit committee** 審計委員會　**challenge** 挑戰　**seek** 尋找

127. Ms. Perone provided an explanation of recent changes to keep the funding arrangement process as ------- as possible.
(A) interested
(B) forceful
(C) transparent
(D) remarkable

佩羅內小姐解釋，最近的變革是為了使資金安排過程盡可能透明。

正確答案為 (C)

動詞 keep 的受詞 funding arrangement process 需要形容詞作為受詞補語，因此答案是可以修飾過程的 (C) transparent。

 字彙　**explanation** 說明　**funding arrangement** 資金安排　**forceful** 強而有力的、有魄力的　**transparent** 透明的
　　remarkable 非凡的

128. The workplace safety at Glaxton-Jenner Company is something ------- will never be compromised.
(A) where
(B) that
(C) when
(D) then

葛拉斯頓－珍妮爾公司在職場安全上永遠不會妥協。

正確答案為 (B)

〈關代〉答案是可以連結名詞 something 和助動詞 will 的關係代名詞 (B) that。where、when 是關係副詞，then 是沒有代名詞功能的一般副詞。

字彙　**safety** 安全　　**compromise** 妥協、讓步

---

129. Relevant documents are ------- delivered to the lawyer's office by our secretary from the Legal Department.
(A) timely
(B) identifiably
(C) highly
(D) typically

相關文件一般是由我們法務部的祕書送到律師辦公室。

正確答案為 (D)

空格要放入適合修飾動詞 delivered 的副詞，答案是最符合句意的 (D) typically。

字彙　**relevant** 相關的　　**timely** 及時地　　**identifiably** 可辨識的　　**highly** 非常　　**typically** 通常、一般來說

---

130. Technicians will inspect the historic Karen Marx Building next week to ------- the building is still architecturally sound.
(A) ensure
(B) measure
(C) modify
(D) accept

下週技術人員將針對歷史悠久的凱倫馬克思大樓進行檢查，以確保大樓的建築結構依舊完整。

正確答案為 (A)

空格後面是一個完整句，選項當中符合句意，且可以接句子當受詞的動詞是 (A) ensure「確保」。

字彙　**inspect** 檢查　　**historic** 具歷史意義的　　**sound** 健全的、堅固的　　**measure** 測量　　**modify** 修改

Questions 131-134 refer to the following memo.

From: Jin Li Zhang
To: All staff
Date: April 10
Subject: Natalie Albright

As some of you know, Natalie Albright, our head landscaper, will soon be leaving our company.

She has ------- a position in residential construction industry. Natalie has been interested in that
      131.

field for some time. -------. Even so, we are ------- sorry to see her go.
      132.   133.

Natalie's last day with us is Friday, 25, April. At 2:30 P.M., on that day, we have a farewell

gathering in company cafeteria ------- her ten year service with us. We look forward to seeing you
      134.

all.

Marry Rogers
Facilities Director

問題 131-134 參考以下備忘錄。

寄件者：張景禮
收件者：全體員工
日期：4 月 10 日
主旨：納塔莉艾伯特

有些人已經知道，我們的首席景觀設計師納塔莉艾伯特即將離開公司。

她已經 ⑬¹ 接受住宅建築業的一個職位。納塔莉一直對該領域感興趣。⑬² 她的新工作更符合她成為建築工程
師的最終目標。儘管如此，看著她離開，我們感到 ⑬³ 非常不捨。

納塔莉和我們在一起的最後一天是 4 月 25 日星期五。當天下午 2 點 30 分我們會在公司自助餐舉行歡送會，
⑬⁴ 表揚她這十年來與我們一起服務。期待到時候能看到大家。

瑪麗羅傑斯
設施管理經理

 字彙　**landscaper** 景觀設計師　**residential** 住宅的　**be in line with** 符合、適合　**ultimate** 最終的、終極的
farewell gathering 歡送會

131. (A) advertised　　　　　　　　(A) 刊登
(B) supported　　　　　　　　　(B) 支持
(C) accepted　　　　　　　　　**(C) 同意**
(D) indicated　　　　　　　　　(D) 提出

正確答案為 (C)

空格後方有受詞 a position，且句意是關於 Natalie 接受的職務內容，因此答案是 (C)。

> 字彙　**advertise** 刊登廣告、宣傳

132. **(A) Her new job is more in line with her ultimate goal of becoming construction engineer.**
(B) Managers meetings will move from 10 A.M. to 2 P.M. starting next Monday.
(C) The human resources director will explain health insurance offered by the company.
(D) Employees are required to arrive at work at least five minutes before 9 A.M. every day.

(A) 她的新工作更符合她成為建築工程師的最終目標。
(B) 下週一起，經理會議從上午 10 點改到下午 2 點。
(C) 人力資源部經理將說明公司提供的健康保險。
(D) 員工每天至少要比早上 9 點提早至少 5 分鐘到公司。

正確答案為 (A)

〈插入句〉
前句的內容是關於納塔莉要到新公司上班，因此對新工作做附加說明的 (A) 是正確答案。

> 字彙　**human resources** 人力資源　　**health insurance** 健保　　**be required to** 被要求、必須

133. **(A) very**　　　　　　　　　　**(A) 非常**
(B) rather　　　　　　　　　　(B) 頗
(C) too　　　　　　　　　　　(C) 也
(D) such　　　　　　　　　　(D) 如這類

正確答案為 (A)

空格要放入修飾形容詞 sorry 的副詞，正確答案是 (A)。rather 通常用在負面語氣，such 是形容詞，不適合放入空格。

134. (A) has recognized　　　　　　　(A) 已經表揚
(B) is recognizing　　　　　　　(B) 正在表揚
(C) would recognize　　　　　　(C) 會表揚
(D) to recognize　　　　　　　**(D) 為了表揚**

正確答案為 (D)

句中缺少連接詞，空格前面有動詞 have，因此選項 (A)、(B)、(C) 的動詞型態都不適合，(D) 是正確答案。

> 字彙　**recognize** 表揚、嘉獎；認可、承認

Test 03

Questions 135-138 refer to the following brochure excerpt.

-------. Sponsored by the Bronxville Visitor Bureau, each tour is led ------- a knowledgeable guide
   135.   **136.**
and features a unique area of town.

The most popular focuses on Cyrus Square are the town's theater -------.
                                                       137.

In addition to three playhouses and two music halls, Cyrus Square includes an opera house and
several historic hotels that represent a range of architectural styles. The tour lasts approximately
two hours and ------- with a delicious meal at the Waterfront Café, one of Bronxville's best known
                138.
dining establishments.

To register for the Cyrus Square tour or learn about the other tours, call the Bronxville Visitor
Bureau at 555-0114.

問題 135-138 參考以下手冊節錄。

⑬⑤ 從 4 個常規健走行程中，擇一探索布朗克斯小鎮吧。每個行程皆有布朗克斯小鎮觀光局贊助，⑬⑥ 由知識淵博的導遊帶領，並以小鎮的獨特區域作為特色。

賽諾斯廣場上最受歡迎的焦點，就是城鎮的劇院 ⑬⑦ 區。

除了 3 個劇場和 2 個音樂廳，賽諾斯廣場還包括 1 個歌劇院和幾個代表各種建築風格的歷史悠久飯店。行程大約持續兩個小時，⑬⑧ 最後會到小鎮上最著名的餐廳，水畔咖啡館享用一頓美味佳餚做為旅程的結束。

欲報名賽諾斯廣場之旅或了解其他旅遊項目，請致電布朗克斯小鎮觀光局 555-0114。

字彙	
sponsor 贊助 **Visitor Bureau** 觀光局 **tour** 旅遊行程 **knowledgeable** 博學多聞的 **feature** 以～為特色	
in addition to 此外 **playhouse** 劇場 **approximately** 大約、大概 **best known** 最知名的	
dining 用餐的	

135. (A) Customers waited in line for six hours to purchase new guide books and city maps.
(B) Explore the town of Bronxville through one of our four regularly scheduled walking tours.
(C) The city gallery will feature relics about the Tang Dynasty in its spring exhibit.
(D) We think it's a great idea that will generate more revenue from the sale of food and beverages.

(A) 顧客排隊排了 6 個小時購買新的導遊手冊和城市地圖。
(B) 從 4 個常規健走行程中，擇一探索布朗克斯小鎮吧。
(C) 城市畫廊將在春季展覽展出唐代文物。
(D) 我們認為這想法很棒，透過販售食物和飲料能獲得更多收入。

正確答案為 (B)

空格後面提到 Sponsored by the Bronxville Visitors Bureau, each tour...，因此答案是提到 Bronxville 及 tour 的 (B)。

> 字彙　**relic** 遺跡、文物　**exhibit** 展覽　**generate** 產生　**revenue** 收入　**beverage** 飲料

136. (A) for　　　　　　　　　　　(A) 為
(B) by　　　　　　　　　　**(B) 由**
(C) during　　　　　　　　　(C) 在～期間
(D) behind　　　　　　　　　(D) 在之後

正確答案為 (B)

空格前面是被動式 is led，因此答案是能放在執行動作者前面的介系詞 by (B)。

137. (A) actors　　　　　　　　　(A) 演員
(B) programs　　　　　　　　(B) 節目
(C) district　　　　　　　　**(C) 區域**
(D) school　　　　　　　　　(D) 學校

正確答案為 (C)

相當於本句主詞 the most popular focuses「最受歡迎的焦點」的補語，要選擇場所 (C)。

138. (A) exits　　　　　　　　　　(A) 離去
(B) orders　　　　　　　　　(B) 訂
(C) reserves　　　　　　　　(C) 保留
(D) concludes　　　　　　　**(D) 作結**

正確答案為 (D)

空格是位在主詞 The tour 後面的動詞位置，表達用晚餐結束行程的 (D) 是正確答案。

Test 03

Questions 139-142 refer to the following memo.

From: Gabrielle Rothschild, Building Manager
To: All employees
Date: Thursday, August 9
Re: Construction work

As you are -------, renovations to our office building will begin on Monday, August 13, and
    139.
continue until the end of the day on Friday, August 17. As a result, you may experience some

-------.
140.

-------. Employees who regularly use this elevator should take the stairs or use the elevator on
141.
the south side of the building.

-------, the entrance on the northwest side of the building facing Ali Avenue will be closed on
142.
Tuesday through Thursday. All other entrances to the building will be open as usual during this

time.

問題 139-142 參考以下備忘錄。

寄件者：蓋比爾羅斯凱爾，大樓管理者
收件者：全體員工
日期：8 月 9 日星期四
主旨：工程作業

如各位 **139** 所知，我們辦公大樓的裝修工程將於 8 月 13 日星期一開始，持續到 8 月 17 日星期五結束。因此
各位可能會遇到一些 **140** 不便。

141 北側電梯一整週將停止運作。經常使用此電梯的員工應走樓梯或使用位於大樓南側的電梯。

142 此外，大樓西北側面向阿里大道的入口也將在週二到週四封閉。在此期間，大樓的所有其他入口將照常
開放。

字彙　　renovation 整修　　**as a result** 因此　　**elevator** 電梯　　**take the stairs** 使用樓梯

139. (A) helpful
(B) aware
(C) informing
(D) famous

(A) 有幫助的
(B) 清楚知道的
(C) 通知
(D) 有名的

正確答案為 (B)

答案是 (B)，aware 的意思是「清楚知道後面所提到的內容」。

140. **(A) inconvenience**
(B) assignment
(C) addition
(D) interference

(A) 不便
(B) 任務
(C) 增加
(D) 干擾

正確答案為 (A)

句意想表達因施工而面臨不便，答案是 (A) inconvenience。

141. (A) Noise levels must be kept at a minimum at all times.
(B) Please dispose of garbage in the proper receptacles.
(C) The north-side elevator will be out of service for the entire week.
(D) Employees are forbidden from entering private area designated for CEO.

(A) 任何時候都必須把噪音級數降到最低。
(B) 請把垃圾放在適當的容器裡。
(C) 北側電梯一整週都將停止運作。
(D) 員工禁止進入執行長專屬區域。

正確答案為 (C)

〈插入句〉

後面的句子提到 this elevator「電梯」，因此本句應與電梯相關，說明電梯使用事項的 (C) 是正確答案。

 字彙 **at a minimum** 最低限度 **at all times** 任何時候 **dispose of** 丟棄 **proper** 適當的 **receptacle** 容器 **out of service** 停止運行 **forbid** 禁止 **designated** 指定的 **CEO** 即 **chief executive officer**，執行長

142. (A) However
(B) Instead
(C) Previously
(D) Also

(A) 然而
(B) 而非
(C) 先前
(D) 此外

正確答案為 (D)

空格是連結前後句子的連接副詞位置，由於後面是對前面句子的進一步說明，因此答案是 (D)。

Test 03

Questions 143-146 refer to the following news article.

July 1 – Beginning in September, the South Central School District will rely ------- on Chester **143.** Educational Publishing Group for health-related learning and teaching materials. -------. **144.**

As of July 30, the school board ------- its contracts with the other two vendors. This decision **145.** was based on a survey of teachers and school nurses, who attested to the superior quality of Chester's products. ------- the cost of Chester's textbooks is high, its workbooks, models, **146.** and teacher's guides are less expensive than those of its competitors, helping to keep overall expenditures within budget.

問題 143-146 參考以下新聞文章。

7 月 1 日——自 9 月起，南部中央學區的健康相關學習與教學教材將 ⑭ 完全仰賴雀思特教育出版集團。⑭ 從歷史上來看，雀思特是供應這類內容的 3 大供應商之一。

從 7 月 30 日起，學校董事會 ⑭ 將終止與另外 2 家供應商的合約。這個決定是基於對學校老師和學校護理人員做的問卷調查，他們證實雀思特的產品品質優良。⑭ 儘管雀思絲特的教科書價格昂貴，但它的練習本、模型、教師手冊都比競爭對手便宜，有助於將總支出控制在預算以內。

字彙　**as of** 自～起　**attest to** 證實　**superior quality** 卓越品質　**competitor** 競爭對手　**expenditure** 支出、費用

143. (A) formally   (A) 正式地
     (B) periodically   (B) 定期地
     (C) initially   (C) 最初
     (D) solely   **(D) 唯一地**

正確答案為 (D)

空格是修飾動詞 rely on 的副詞位置，句子後面的意思是決定只向 Chester 雀思特採購，因此答案是 (D)。

144. (A) Thank you for your cooperation in abiding by all the teaching rules.
     (B) Users of the Web site will be able to download the files for teaching.
     (C) Chester also work closely with teachers to provide bilingual assistance if necessary.
     (D) Historically, Chester was one of three preferred vendors for such content.

     (A) 感謝您遵守所有的教學規則。
     (B) 網站的使用者可下載教學檔案。
     (C) 雀思特也與教師緊密合作，在需要的時候提供雙語支援。
     (D) 從歷史上來看，雀思特是供應這類內容的 3 大供應商之一。

正確答案為 (D)

〈插入句〉
前句提到 health-related learning and teaching materials，與選項 (D) 的 content 相符，因此答案是 (D)。

> 字彙   **cooperation** 合作   **abide by** 遵守   **bilingual** 雙語的   **assistance** 協助   **preferred** 優先的、首選的
>   **vendor** 供應業者；攤販

145. (A) was discontinuing   (A) 過去正在終止
     (B) is discontinued   (B) 正在終止
     (C) will discontinue   **(C) 將會終止**
     (D) would have discontinued   (D) 早已終止

正確答案為 (C)

文章寫的日期是 7 月 1 日，合約終止日是在 7 月 30 日，因此答案是未來時態的 (C)。(D) 是假設語氣。

> 字彙   **discontinue** 中斷、停止

146. **(A) Even though**   **(A) 儘管**
     (B) Unless   (B) 除非
     (C) Because   (C) 因為
     (D) As soon as   (D) 一旦

正確答案為 (A)

空格後面有兩個子句，是相互對比的內容，因此答案選可以呈現轉折語氣的 (A)。

Questions 147-148 refer to the following tag. 標籤

JUNG & JO APPAREL
MEDIUM

100% wool

Wash by hand or by machine on gentle cycle with similar colors.
Wash in cold water only.
Machine dry on coolest setting.

Please note that variations in color are an intended feature of this fabric.
With repeated washing, texture also may alter further.

Made in Italy

問題 147-148 參考以下標籤。

JUNG & JO 服飾
中尺寸

100% 羊毛

手洗、或與顏色相近的衣物以柔和運轉的方式機洗。
147 只能以冷水洗淨。
最低溫烘乾。

請注意，顏色的變化是此種織物可預期的特性。
148 反覆洗滌也可能造成質感改變。

義大利製

字彙　**tag** 標籤　**apparel** 服裝、服飾　**gentle** 柔和的　**setting** 設定　**variation** 變化
intended feature 預期的特性、原來的特性　**fabric** 織物　**texture** 質感、質地　**alter** 變化

147. According to the tag, how should the item be care for?
(A) By washing it at a low temperature
(B) By drying it for a specific time
(C) By soaking it in warm water
(D) By wiping it with a damp cloth

根據標籤說明，該如何保養此物品？
(A) 以低溫清洗
(B) 在特定時間烘乾
(C) 用溫水浸泡
(D) 用濕布擦拭

正確答案為 (A)

文章提到 Wash in cold water only，因此答案是 (A)。

字彙　**specific** 特定的　**soak** 浸泡　**wipe** 擦拭　**damp** 潮溼的

148. What is stated about the item?
(A) It was made by hand.
(B) It will shrink after washing.
(C) It may change in texture.
(D) It was produced in France.

何者是關於此物品的說明？
(A) 是手工製品。
(B) 清洗後會縮小。
(C) 質感可能改變。
(D) 在法國生產。

正確答案為 (C)

文章提到 With repeated washing, texture also may alter further，因此答案是 (C)。

字彙　**shrink** 縮小、縮水

Test 03

Questions 149-150 refer to the following advertisement. 廣告

Major Technical Institute

Are you considering returning to school? Education can be an important part of your career path, and Major Tech. is pleased to offer a variety of continuing-education courses for the busy professional. In addition to our regular daytime course offerings, we now offer classes online that conveniently fit into anyone's schedules.

Choose from many training programs, including computer networking, food preparation, and medical technology. Consult our Web site www.majortech.edu for a complete list of courses available.

For detailed information regarding our certification programs, please contact admission at 090-555-7890 or send an e-mail to info@majortech.edu.

問題 149-150 參考以下廣告。

梅傑技術學院

您正考慮重返校園嗎？教育可以是您職業生涯的重要部分，梅傑技術很高興為忙碌的專業人士提供各種進修教育課程。除了定期的白天課程之外，149 我們現在還提供線上課程，便於符合任何人的日程安排。

請從電腦網路、食品準備、醫療技術等許多訓練課程中做選擇。150 請洽詢我們的網站 www.majortech. edu 以獲得可選課程的完整清單。

150 有關於我們的檢定課程詳細資訊，請致電 090-555-7890 或寄電子郵件到 info@majortech.edu 與招生部門聯絡。

字彙　**institute** 教育機構、學院　　**consider** 考慮　　**continuing-education** 進修教育　　**offer** 提供
fit into 適合、符合　　**consult** 諮詢、洽詢　　**regarding** 關於　　**certification** 資格、檢定
admission 招生、入學、入會

149. According to the advertisement, what is a recent development at Major Tech.?

(A) Courses over Internet

(B) Free consultation for graduates

(C) A revised admission policy

(D) Brand-new computers and monitors

根據廣告，梅傑技術最近發展是什麼？

(A) 網路課程

(B) 畢業生免費諮詢

(C) 入學政策變更

(D) 全新電腦和監視器

正確答案為 (A)

在第一段提到 we now offer classes online that conveniently fit into anyone's schedules，可知答案是 (A)。

字彙　**consultation** 諮詢　**graduate** 畢業生

150. What is NOT stated as a way to learn more about Major Tech.?

(A) Making a phone call

(B) Sending an e-mail

(C) Visiting the Web site

(D) Going to the campus

若想了解更多梅傑技術的事情，以下哪個方法是內文沒有提到的？

(A) 打電話

(B) 寄電子郵件

(C) 進入官網

(D) 前往校園

正確答案為 (D)

在第二段提到網站 Consult our Web site www.majortech.edu for a complete list of courses available，符合 (C)，第三段提到電話與電子郵件 please contact admission at 090-555-7890 or send an e-mail to info@majortech.edu，符合 (A) 與 (B)，沒有提到的是 (D)。

Questions 151-153 refer to the following Web page. 網頁

http://fantasticspain.com

Fantastic Spain Travels

| HOME | DESTINATIONS | REVIEW | CONTACT |

Recently, a colleague and I were on business in Madrid and had a free day for sightseeing. On advice from the clerk at the front desk of our hotel, we booked a tour of the royal palace through Fantastic Spain Travels (FST). It was my colleague's first chance to see this attraction and my second. The first time I visited, though, I was with a large group. I felt very rushed and was not able to really appreciate the palace or take as many photos as I would have liked. This time, I was happy to book a pricier private excursion, led by guide Juan Dominguez.

In contrast to my last tour, which did not include transportation, Mr. Dominguez took us to the palace by car. We could tell that Mr. Dominguez's historical knowledge was extensive. Since my colleague and I were his only clients, we were able to ask a lot of questions and took our time.

I was pleased that the entrance fees were covered by the excursion price, and that FST obtained our tickets in advance, so that we would not have to wait in line when we arrived. Lunch at a delicious local restaurant was provided, so we didn't even have to spend time looking for a good place to eat.

This tour is a great value and much more worth the price.

Jane Weatherly (Calcutta, Australia)

問題 **151-153** 參考以下網頁。

---

http://fantasticspain.com

神奇西班牙旅遊

首頁	目的地	評論	聯絡我們

最近我和一名同事到馬德里出差，有一天可以自由觀光。⑮ 依照飯店櫃檯人員的建議，我們透過神奇西班牙旅遊（FST）預約皇家宮殿之旅。⑮ 我同事是第一次參觀這個景點，而我是第二次。不過我第一次參觀是和一群人去的，非常匆忙，無法真正欣賞這座宮殿，也無法隨意多拍照片。這次我很開心能訂到價格稍高的私人導覽，由導遊朱安多明格思領團。

⑮ 跟我上次沒包交通工具的旅行不同，多明格思先生開車帶我們去宮殿。我們看得出來多明格思先生的歷史知識非常豐富，因為我和我同事是他唯一一組客人，所以我們可以問他很多問題並慢慢參觀。

⑮ 我很高興入場費已經包含在導覽費裡，而且 FST 還提前取票，這樣我們抵達時就不需排隊購票。⑮ 午餐是由當地一家美味的餐廳提供，我們甚至不需要花時間去找好吃的地方。

這趟旅行真的很值得，而且是物超所值。

珍維瑟利（澳大利亞喬可達）

字彙　**clerk** 櫃檯人員　**royal palace** 皇宮　**attraction** 觀光景點　**appreciate** 欣賞、感激　**pricey** 昂貴的　**excursion** 短程旅行、遠足　**in contrast to** 與～做對照　**extensive** 廣泛的、大量的　**entrance fee** 入場費　**cover** 包含　**much more worth the price** 物超所值

151. Who introduced FST to Ms. Weatherly?
(A) A travel agent
(B) A business associate
(C) A hotel employee
(D) A local friend

誰將 FST 介紹給維瑟利小姐？
(A) 旅行社職員
(B) 生意夥伴
(C) 飯店員工
(D) 當地朋友

正確答案為 (C)

在第一段提到 clerk「櫃檯人員」：On advice from the clerk at the front desk of our hotel, we booked a tour of the royal palace through Fantastic Spain Travels (FST)，因此答案是 (C)。

152. What was NOT covered in the price of tour?
(A) A souvenir photograph
(B) A meal
(C) Transportation
(D) Admission charges

導覽費用裡不包含什麼？
(A) 紀念照片
(B) 餐點
(C) 交通
(D) 入場費

正確答案為 (A)

文章的第三段提到 Lunch at a delicious local restaurant was provided「午餐」，第二段提到 Mr. Dominguez took us to the palace by car「交通工具」，第三段提到 the entrance fees were covered by the excursion price「入場費」，因此答案是 (A)。

153. What is suggested about Ms. Weatherly?
(A) She travels often for business.
(B) She is Mr. Dominguez's colleague.
(C) She has visited Madrid before.
(D) She is interested in Spanish history.

以下哪個陳述與維瑟利小姐有關？
(A) 她常出差。
(B) 她是多明格思先生的同事。
(C) 她曾經去過馬德里。
(D) 她對西班牙歷史很感興趣。

正確答案為 (C)

第一段提到 It was my colleague's first chance to see this attraction and my second，由此可知她以前曾去過 Madrid 馬德里，答案是 (C)。

Questions 154-155 refer to the following text message chain. 線上聊天串

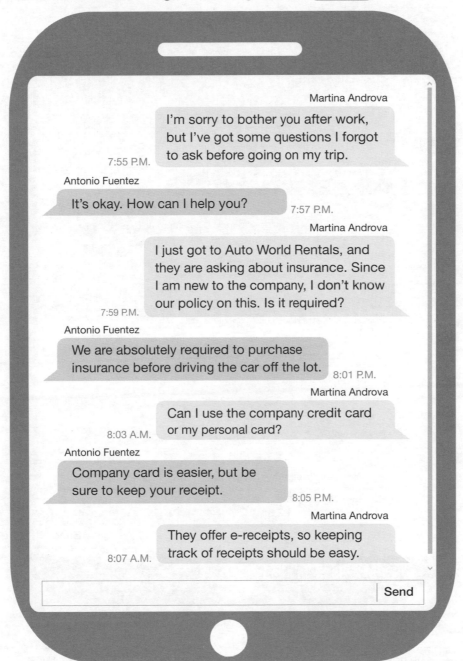

Martina Androva

I'm sorry to bother you after work, but I've got some questions I forgot to ask before going on my trip.

7:55 P.M.

Antonio Fuentez

It's okay. How can I help you?

7:57 P.M.

Martina Androva

I just got to Auto World Rentals, and they are asking about insurance. Since I am new to the company, I don't know our policy on this. Is it required?

7:59 P.M.

Antonio Fuentez

We are absolutely required to purchase insurance before driving the car off the lot.

8:01 P.M.

Martina Androva

Can I use the company credit card or my personal card?

8:03 A.M.

Antonio Fuentez

Company card is easier, but be sure to keep your receipt.

8:05 P.M.

Martina Androva

They offer e-receipts, so keeping track of receipts should be easy.

8:07 A.M.

Send

Test 03

問題 154-155 參考以下線上聊天串。

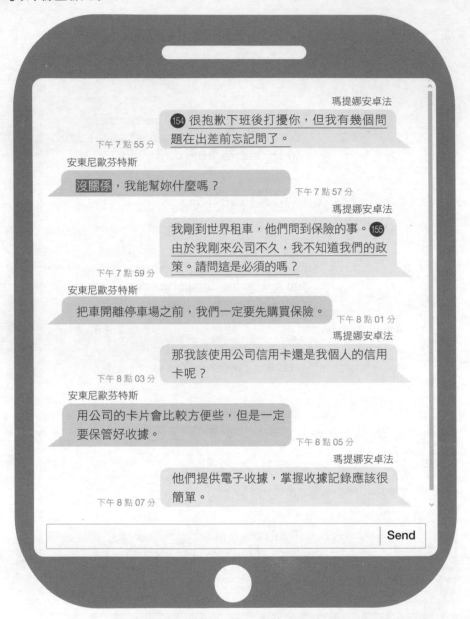

瑪提娜安卓法

154 很抱歉下班後打擾你，但我有幾個問題在出差前忘記問了。

下午 7 點 55 分

安東尼歐芬特斯

沒關係，我能幫妳什麼嗎？

下午 7 點 57 分

瑪提娜安卓法

我剛到世界租車，他們問到保險的事。**155** 由於我剛來公司不久，我不知道我們的政策。請問這是必須的嗎？

下午 7 點 59 分

安東尼歐芬特斯

把車開離停車場之前，我們一定要先購買保險。

下午 8 點 01 分

瑪提娜安卓法

那我該使用公司信用卡還是我個人的信用卡呢？

下午 8 點 03 分

安東尼歐芬特斯

用公司的卡片會比較方便些，但是一定要保管好收據。

下午 8 點 05 分

瑪提娜安卓法

他們提供電子收據，掌握收據記錄應該很簡單。

下午 8 點 07 分

Send

字彙　**bother** 打擾　**be new to** 新來的　**insurance** 保險　**required** 必要的　**off the lot** 離開停車場　**receipt** 收據

154. At 7:57 P.M., what does Mr. Fuentez mean when he writes, "It's okay"?
(A) Ms. Androva can submit proof of purchase electronically.
(B) Information on company travel is easy for Ms. Androva to obtain.
(C) He suggests that Ms. Androva not purchase insurance.
(D) He is willing to answer Ms. Androva's questions.

下午 7 點 57 分芬特斯先生說「沒關係」是什麼意思？
(A) 安卓法小姐可透過電子方式提交購買證明。
(B) 安卓法小姐很容易取得公司差旅資訊。
(C) 他建議安卓法小姐不要購買保險。
(D) 他將回答安卓法小姐的問題。

正確答案為 (D)

〈推測句意〉

推測句意的題目要檢視本關鍵句的前後脈絡。前一段簡訊，Androva 安卓法小姐提到 I'm sorry to bother you after work, but I've got some questions I forgot to ask before going on my trip，之後 Fuentez 芬特斯才回答「沒關係」，因此答案是 (D)。

字彙　**proof of purchase** 購物證明　**obtain** 獲得　**be willing to** 樂意做～

155. What is indicated about Ms. Androva?
(A) She has applied for a credit card.
(B) She is recently hired at the company.
(C) She would like a refund for travel expenses.
(D) She needs transportation to an airport.

以下何者陳述與安卓法小姐有關？
(A) 她申請了一張信用卡。
(B) 她最近被公司錄用。
(C) 她要求退還出差費。
(D) 她需要交通工具前往機場。

正確答案為 (B)

下午 7 點 59 分 Androva 安卓法小姐提到 Since I am new to the company，由此可知答案是 (B)。

字彙　**travel expenses** 差旅費、出差費

Questions 156-157 refer to the following notice. 通知

Ranger Carpet Store

2389 Market Street

Laramie, WY 39877

902-555-0145 www.rangercarpet.ca

Don't miss out our special event on October 2!

As one of our best customers, you are invited to a special event marketing the introduction of Comfortzone, a new line of carpets featuring a revolutionary new carpet fiber. Factory tests show that Comfortzone carpets trap up to 25 percent less dirt and last longer than comparably priced carpets. And if you purchase a Comfortzone carpet at our store on October 2, you can save up to 40 percent off the regular price. Simply bring this notice to our store on October 2 and show it to a store employee to gain admission to the Comfortzone show room. We look forward to seeing you!

問題 **156-157** 參考以下通知。

蘭傑地毯商店

39877 懷俄明州拉勒米

市場街 2389 號

902-555-0145 www.rangercarpet.ca

請勿錯過我們 10 月 2 日的特別活動！

您是我們的模範顧客，我們邀請您參加一個特別活動，推廣介紹 Comfortzone， 此新品的特色在於具有革命性的新地毯纖維。工廠測試顯示 Comfortzone 地毯比同等價位的地毯少 25% 的髒污，且使用壽命更長。157 如果您在 10 月 2 日於我們店內購買一張 Comfortzone 地毯，可省下定價 40% 的金額。您只需在 10 月 2 日攜帶此通知函到我們商店並出示給員工看，即可享有 Comfortzone 展館的入場資格。我們期待與您見面！

 字彙　　**miss out** 錯失　　**be invited to** 受邀出席　　**revolutionary** 革新的　　**trap up** 捕捉、陷入
comparably priced 同等價格的　　**regular price** 定價

156. What is indicated about Comfortzone carpets?
(A) They come in a variety of colors.
(B) They are produced with a special new material.
(C) They last 40% longer than more expensive carpets.
(D) They can be delivered complimentarily.

以下何者是關於 Comfortzone 地毯的說明？
(A) 它們有出各種顏色。
(B) 它們是用特殊的新材料製成。
(C) 它們比更貴的地毯還耐用 40%。
(D) 它們可免費宅配。

正確答案為 (B)

文章提到 Comfortzone, a new line of carpets featuring a revolutionary new carpet fiber.，因此答案是 (B)。

| 字彙 | **material** 材料　**complimentarily** 免費地 |

157. How can a customer quality for a discount on a Comfortzone carpet?
(A) By ordering the carpet online
(B) By participating in a store event
(C) By presenting a document
(D) By completing a customer survey

顧客如何才能享有 Comfortzone 地毯的折扣資格？
(A) 線上購買地毯
(B) 參加商店活動
(C) 出示文件
(D) 填寫顧客意見調查

正確答案為 (B)

文章提到 if you purchase a Comfortzone carpet at our store on October 2, you can save up to 40 percent off the regular price，可知只要在 10 月 2 日參加活動並購買地毯，就能享有折扣，因此答案是 (B)。

| 字彙 | **qualify for** 有～資格　**participate in** 參加　**present** 出示　**customer survey** 顧客意見調查 |

Questions 158-160 refer to the following article. 報導

May 10 – Media Tree, the company that contributed to artwork for the popular Look at Others billboard campaign, has been nominated for the prestigious Malta Award, which has been recognizing innovation in published artwork and illustration for 40 years. Selected from almost 2,000 entrants, Media Tree is the first Taipei-based illustration studio to be nominated for the artwork. –[1]–. All of this year's Malta Award winners will be announced on June 15 during a ceremony in London.

"We are very excited about this nomination, which is a testament to the high level of skill, expertise, and creativity of our staff," said Melinda Bonner, founder and CEO of the company.

–[2]–. The Malta Award judges, a group of twelve leading art executives from museums and galleries across the globe, noted that Media Tree was nominated based on the diversity, quality, and sophistication of its portfolio of art. "We illustrate everything from magazines and children's literature to cosmetics and food packaging," noted Ms. Bonner, "and we work closely with our clients to ensure the end product exceeds their expectations."

–[3]–. Since the names of the nominees were released, the studio has seen a large increase in the number of requests for its services. "There is no way we can meet the growing demand unless we hire more illustrators and project managers. Of course, that's exactly what we are going to do now," said Ms. Bonner.

More information about Media Tree can be found at www.mediatree.co.in. Details about the Malta Award are at www.maltaaward.org. –[4]–.

問題 158-160 參考以下報導。

5 月 10 日—— 媒體樹，一家致力於藝術創作的公司，為知名藝術作品〈請看看他人〉所製作的廣告看板獲得了享譽盛名的 158 瑪塔獎提名，此獎 40 年以來持續肯定藝術作品與插圖的出版創新。媒體樹從將近兩千名參賽者中脫穎而出，成為台北第一個作品獲得提名的插圖工作室。–[1]– 今年將於 6 月 15 日於倫敦頒獎典禮上頒布瑪塔獎的所有得獎者。

公司創辦人兼執行長米蘭達伯諾表示：「今年獲得提名我們感到相當興奮，這證明了我們員工的高水準技巧、專業知識和創意。」

–[2]– 瑪塔獎的評審委員是由世界各地博物館與畫廊的 12 位主要藝術主管組成，他們指出，媒體樹的提名是基於其作品集的多樣性、品質和成熟度。伯諾小姐表示：「從雜誌、兒童文學到化妝品和食品包裝，我們替各種產品製作插圖，我們與客戶密切合作，確保最終產品超乎期待。」

–[3]– 160 自從公布提名者名單以來，這間工作室的服務需求量大增。伯諾小姐表示：「159 除非我們聘請更多的插圖家和產品經理，否則我們無法滿足持續增加的需求。當然，這正是我們即將要做的。」

更多關於媒體樹的資訊，可至 www.mediatree.co.in 查詢。關於瑪塔獎的詳細內容在 www.maltaaward.org。–[4]–

字彙

contribute to 致力於、貢獻　　**billboard** 看板　　**campaign** 宣傳活動　　**nominate** 提名
illustration studio 插圖工作室　　**entrant** 參賽者　　**testament** 證明　　**expertise** 專業
creativity 創造力、創意　　**founder** 創建者　　**sophistication** 熟練　　**portfolio** 作品集
end product 成品　　**exceed one's expectation** 超乎～的期待　　**nominee** 被提名者　　**release** 發表
growing demand 持續增加的需求

158. What is suggested about the Malta Award?
(A) It was established by a single individual.
(B) It has been awarded to advertising companies before.
(C) It gives cash prizes to its recipients.
(D) It was first awarded forty years ago.

關於瑪塔獎，以下何者正確？
(A) 它是由一個人獨力創辦的。
(B) 它以前曾經頒獎給廣告公司。
(C) 它給獲獎者現金作為獎勵。
(D) 該獎項是在 40 年前首次頒發。

正確答案為 **(D)**

關於 Malta Award 的介紹可以看到第一段，其中提到 Malta Award, which has been recognizing innovation in published artwork and illustration for over 40 years. ，因此答案是 (D)。

字彙　**establish** 設立　**prize** 獎金　**individual** 個人　**recipient** 獲獎者、接受者

159. According to the article, what does Ms. Bonner plan to do?
(A) Recruit new employees
(B) Open a second branch
(C) Decrease the publicity budget
(D) Attend a ceremony in Taipei

根據報導內容，伯諾小姐計畫做什麼？
(A) 招募新員工
(B) 開第 2 間分公司
(C) 減少宣傳預算
(D) 參加台北頒獎典禮

正確答案為 **(A)**

談及未來的事情，多數可以在文章後段找到線索。第四段 Bonner 伯諾提到 There is no way we can meet the growing demand unless we hire more illustrators and project managers，可知答案是 (A)。

字彙　**publicity** 宣傳、輿論關注

160. In which of the positions marked [1], [2], [3], and [4] does the following sentence best belong?
"Apart from the honor, the nomination has produced publicity and increased business for Media Tree."
(A) [1]
(B) [2]
(C) [3]
(D) [4]

在標示 [1]、[2]、[3]、[4] 的位置中，何者適合放入以下句子？
「除了得到榮耀，獲得提名也為媒體樹帶來輿論關注與業務成長。」
(A) [1]
(B) [2]
(C) [3]
(D) [4]

正確答案為 **(C)**

〈插入句〉
此句提到提名所帶來的好處，文章的第四段也提到因提名而業務量增加，適合放在第四段，答案是 (C)。

字彙　**apart from** 除～之外、此外　**honor** 名譽

Questions 161-164 refer to the following report. 報告

PERFECT HEALTH AND FITNESS CENTER

Notes from the Board Meeting

■Financial

Last year ended with a surplus of £3,100. This year's budget is estimated to have a surplus of £6,291.

■Membership/Retention

This year is starting off strong in terms of membership numbers. January's New Year's Bash brought in 176 new members.

Not including the New Year's Bash, Fitness Center memberships were up 8% in January. In an effort to continue increasing membership, we are implementing a free one-week trial period.

Total membership is up from January last year, reflecting new membership sales as well as an increased percentage of renewing members. Membership usage has increased, which has caused some concern especially in the facilities located near office parks. We will need to address parking and locker availability in the near future.

問題 161-164 參考以下報告。

完美健身中心

董事會會議記錄

■ 財務

去年年底盈餘 3,100 英鎊。161 今年預算估計有 6,291 英鎊的盈餘。

■ 會員資格／續留

會員數量今年一開始表現強勁。1 月份的新年派對帶來了 176 名新成員。

不包括新年派對在內的話,健身中心會員人數在 1 月分增加了 8%。為了繼續增加會員,162 我們正實施為期一週的免費試用期。

會員總數比起去年 1 月呈現成長,164 顯示新會員銷售量以及續約會員比例增加。會員使用量增加已引發擔憂,特別是辦公園區附近的地點。163 近期內我們必須解決停車和置物櫃數量的問題。

字彙　**surplus** 盈餘　**estimate** 預測、預估　**retention** 保留　**in terms of** 在～方面　**bash** 派對　**bring in** 帶來
in an effort to 致力於　**implement** 實施　**trial period** 試用期　**address** 處理　**availability** 可用、可取得

161. What is stated about the coming year's budget?
(A) It is estimated to have a surplus.
(B) Several programs will need to be cut.
(C) Membership sales account for 60% of the budget.
(D) It is balanced for the first time in five years.

關於今年的預算，何者正確？
(A) 預估將會有盈餘。
(B) 必須刪除幾項計畫。
(C) 會員銷售佔預算的 60%。
(D) 這是 5 年來首次達到收支平衡。

正確答案為 (A)

第一段提到 This year's budget is estimated to have a surplus of £6291.，由此可知答案是 (A)。

> 字彙　**balance** 收支平衡

162. What is Perfect Health and Fitness Center offering?
(A) Free fitness tests
(B) A week-long trial period
(C) Three free training sessions
(D) One-time payment for individual classes

完美健身中心提供什麼？
(A) 免費健身測試
(B) 一週免費試用期
(C) 3 堂免費訓練課程
(D) 個別課程的一次性付款

正確答案為 (B)

第三段提到 we are implementing a free one-week trial period，可知答案是 (B)。

163. What will Perfect Health and Fitness Center need to address in the future?
(A) Extending the center's operating hours
(B) Adding more fitness classes and equipment
(C) Opening new centers closer to downtown
(D) Making more storage space available at centers

完美健身中心未來必須處理什麼事情？
(A) 延長運動中心的營運時間
(B) 增加更多健身課程與器材
(C) 在鄰近市鎮開設新健身中心
(D) 為健身中心提供更多儲物空間

正確答案為 (D)

最後一句提到 We will need to address parking and locker availability in the near future.，答案是 (D)。

> 字彙　**operating hours** 營業時間

164. The word "reflecting" in paragraph 4, line 1, is closest in meaning to
(A) showing
(B) concerning
(C) returning
(D) wondering

第四段第一行提到的「reflecting」與以下何者的意思最為相近？
(A) 顯示
(B) 關於
(C) 歸還
(D) 想知道

正確答案為 (A)

〈推測字義〉
內容是會員總數提升顯示出新會員的銷售量以及續約會員的比例增加，因此答案是 (A)。

Questions 165-167 refer to the following memo. 備忘錄

A Memo from the Editor

This November issue of *Cuisine in New Orleans* marks the magazine's first anniversary. Just one year ago, we distributed our first issue, and since then we have become one of the area's most widely read magazines on regional cooking. Our circulation recently reached 50,000, and the number continues to climb. Local food enthusiasts have praised our publication, and at last month's New Orleans Food Fest we became the proud recipient of an award for best new culinary magazine. As editor-in-chief, I would like to share my appreciation for our hardworking staff, our contributors, our advertisers, and our expanding community of readers, all of whom have played an important part in our success.

Colin Green

問題 165-167 參考以下備忘錄。

編輯備忘錄

這次《紐澳良美食》11 月號紀念雜誌創刊滿一週年。一年前我們發行了創刊號,從那時起,我們便成為本地最為廣泛閱讀的地區烹飪雜誌之一。166 我們的發行量在最近達到 5 萬份,而且數字還在持續攀升。當地的美食愛好者稱讚我們的刊物,在上個月的 167 紐澳良美食節中,我們成為最佳烹飪雜誌新刊獎的榮譽獲獎者。165 作為總編輯,我要對我們辛勤工作的員工、撰稿人、廣告商,以及我們不斷擴大的社區讀者們表達感謝,你們在我們的成功當中扮演了重要的角色。

柯林葛林

 字彙　**issue**(雜誌、書籍)期號　**mark** 紀念　**widely** 廣泛地　**regional** 地區的　**circulation**(新聞雜誌)發行量
reach 達到　**enthusiast** 愛好者　**publication** 出版　**culinary** 烹飪的　**editor-in-chief** 總編輯
contributor 撰稿者;捐助者

165. What is the purpose of the memo?
(A) To express gratitude
(B) To extend an offer
(C) To introduce a contributor
(D) To send an invitation

這個備忘錄的目的是什麼？
(A) 為了表達感謝
(B) 為了擴大提議
(C) 為了介紹貢獻者
(D) 為了寄送邀請函

正確答案為 (A)

文章提到 I would like to share my appreciation，可知答案是 (A)。

166. What is mentioned about *Cuisine in New Orleans*?
(A) It is seeking additional writers.
(B) It will soon be distributed internationally.
(C) It is growing in popularity.
(D) It has increased its advertising rates.

關於《紐澳良美食》何者正確？
(A) 它正在尋找更多作家。
(B) 它很快就會在國際上發行。
(C) 它越來越受歡迎。
(D) 它提高廣告費。

正確答案為 (C)

文章提到 Our circulation recently reached 50,000, and the number continues to climb.，因此答案是 (C)。

> **字彙**　**popularity** 受歡迎　**advertising rates** 廣告價格

167. Why does Mr. Green mention the New Orleans Food Fest?
(A) To give a cooking demonstration there
(B) To recruit staff members to volunteer there
(C) To indicate that the magazine sponsored the event
(D) To note that the magazine was honored at the event

為什麼葛林先生提到紐澳良美食節？
(A) 為了在那裡做烹飪示範
(B) 為了招募工作人員在那裡做志工
(C) 為了表明雜誌贊助了這次活動
(D) 為了表示雜誌在這次活動中獲得榮譽

正確答案為 (D)

文章提到 at last month's New Orleans Food Fest, we became the proud recipient of an award for best new culinary magazine，因此答案是 (D)。

Questions 168-171 refer to the following online chat discussion. 線上聊天室

Lydia Johnson [11:30 A.M.]	Marie and I are grabbing a bite to eat for lunch around 12:30. Anyone wants to join us?
Joanie Lockhart [11:31 A.M.]	Maybe. I still have some work to do on the mid-year report. Where are you planning to go?
Lydia Johnson [11:32 A.M.]	We're thinking of trying the new Thai restaurant on Rexington Road. It's called Erawan Hit.
John Randolph [11:33 A.M.]	You're out of luck. That place closed a few days ago.
Lydia Johnson [11:34 A.M.]	Sorry to hear about that. People said great things about it.
John Randolph [11:36 A.M.]	How about Kaosan Road around the corner? They always have a special menu on Fridays.
Lydia Johnson [11:37 A.M.]	That would be great. Do you guys want to go Kaosan Road?
Joanie Lockhart [11:38 A.M.]	OK. But I won't be able to get there until about one.
Marie Cantanzaro [11:39 A.M.]	Sounds good to me. Joanie, I just sent you the updated figures for the report.

Send

問題 **168-171** 參考以下線上聊天室。

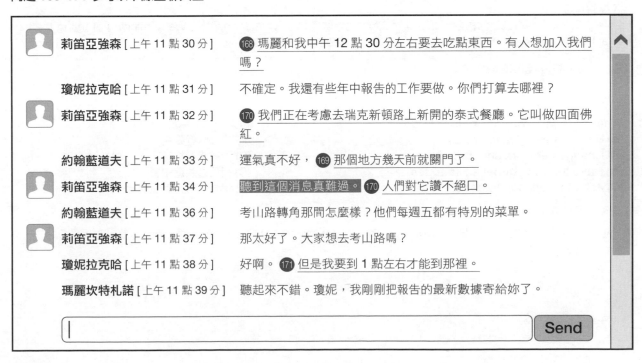

莉笛亞強森 [上午 11 點 30 分]	(168) 瑪麗和我中午 12 點 30 分左右要去吃點東西。有人想加入我們嗎？
瓊妮拉克哈 [上午 11 點 31 分]	不確定。我還有些年中報告的工作要做。你們打算去哪裡？
莉笛亞強森 [上午 11 點 32 分]	(170) 我們正在考慮去瑞克新頓路上新開的泰式餐廳。它叫做四面佛紅。
約翰藍道夫 [上午 11 點 33 分]	運氣真不好，(169) 那個地方幾天前就關門了。
莉笛亞強森 [上午 11 點 34 分]	聽到這個消息真難過。(170) 人們對它讚不絕口。
約翰藍道夫 [上午 11 點 36 分]	考山路轉角那間怎麼樣？他們每週五都有特別的菜單。
莉笛亞強森 [上午 11 點 37 分]	那太好了。大家想去考山路嗎？
瓊妮拉克哈 [上午 11 點 38 分]	好啊。(171) 但是我要到 1 點左右才能到那裡。
瑪麗坎特札諾 [上午 11 點 39 分]	聽起來不錯。瓊妮，我剛剛把報告的最新數據寄給妳了。

Send

字彙 **grab a bit** 吃點東西　　**out of luck** 運氣不好　　**figures** 數據

168. What are the people discussing?
(A) The place to hold an award ceremony
(B) The best restaurant in the area
(C) Today's special at Erawan Hit
(D) The place for lunch

這些人在討論什麼？
(A) 頒獎典禮的場地
(B) 該地區最好的餐廳
(C) 四面佛紅的今日特餐
(D) 午餐地點

正確答案為 (D)

本題問對話主旨，通常可以在一開始找到答案。上午 11 點 30 分強森說 Marie and I are grabbing a bite to eat for lunch around 12:30. Anyone wants to join us?，因此對話主旨是在討論午餐。

169. What information does Mr. Randolph provide about Erawan Hit?
(A) It has a good reputation for seafood.
(B) It usually closes on Sundays.
(C) It offers food at a low price.
(D) It does not operate any more.

藍道夫先生提供有關四面佛紅的何種資訊？
(A) 它以海鮮聞名。
(B) 通常在星期日休息。
(C) 它以低價提供食物。
(D) 它已經不再營業。

正確答案為 (D)

上午 11 點 33 分提到 That place closed a few days ago，close 指「關店、停止營業」，因此答案是 (D)。

170. At 11:34 A.M., why most likely does Ms. Johnson write, "Sorry to hear about that"?
(A) She wanted to try a new place.
(B) Mr. Randolph cannot complete a project.
(C) A restaurant is too small for everyone.
(D) She has a scheduling conflict.

上午 11 點 34 分強森小姐說「聽到這個消息真難過」的原因可能是什麼？
(A) 她本來想去新餐廳吃吃看。
(B) 藍道夫先生無法完成專案。
(C) 餐廳太小無法容納所有人。
(D) 她的日程安排有衝突。

正確答案為 (A)

〈推測句意〉

推測句意的題目要檢視該句的前後語意進行推敲，上一個簡訊，Lydia Johnson 說 We're thinking of trying the new Thai Restaurant on Rexington Road，可知她本來想去新餐廳吃吃看，因此答案是 (A)。

> 字彙　**scheduling conflict** 行程衝突

171. What does Ms. Lockhart decide to do?
(A) Browse nearby restaurants
(B) Change her work shift tomorrow
(C) Have lunch with her colleagues
(D) Ask Ms. Johnson to get some sandwiches

拉克哈小姐決定做什麼？
(A) 逛逛附近餐館
(B) 更改明天排班
(C) 與同事共進午餐
(D) 請強森幫忙買三明治

正確答案為 (C)

上午 11 點 38 分她提到 OK. But I won't be able to get there until about one，可見雖然會晚一點但仍會過去，因此答案是 (C)。

Questions 172-175 refer to the following letter. 信件

IOFF

International Office Furnishing Foundation
40 Block Road
Bloomington, IN 01398

May 4

Risa Daniels
Taylor Office Furniture
14 Pine Street
Belleville, IL 80214

Dear Ms. Daniels,

On behalf of the IOFF board, I thank you for your early registration for the IOFF trade show in Bloomington this summer. We are confident that this year's event will be our best ever. Not only are we moving to a more spacious venue but the keynote speaker for the convention will be renowned furniture designer Lisa DeNoble.

As always, IOFF wishes to provide an enjoyable atmosphere where the top furniture designers can exhibit their works and develop professional relationships with high-end retailers throughout Bloomington. –[1]–. To accommodate a growing number of exhibitors, this year's event will be held at the Lafayette Convention Center. The center has over 70,000 square meters for exhibition and meeting spaces, and is located only minutes from Bloomington's central commercial area with easy access to restaurants, shops, and theatres. –[2]–. To help you prepare for participation in the convention, please read carefully the enclosed brochure.

One of our goals is to facilitate your installation in the exhibition hall. –[3]–. Please note the time and dates for exhibitor check in, set up, teardown for the trade show. IOFF volunteers will process on-site registration, check in registered exhibitors and hand out name badges at the registration desk outside Hall A, starting at noon, Sunday, August 24. Hall A and Hall B will be open on that day for installation from noon to 7 P.M. Teardown will be on Thursday, August 28 from 1 P.M. to 6 P.M. IOFF volunteers will be available to assist you on both days for set up and teardown.

The convention brochure has a complete event calendar and a map of the Convention Center including designated unloading areas. –[4]–. If you have questions beyond the scope of this letter and brochure, our special support staff are on site to help you with any matters. Just call us at 033-555-0011.

We are really honored to be having you at our convention and wish the event to be the most successful one.

Sincerely,

John Ellsworth
Senior Event Manager

問題 **172-175** 參考以下信件。

IOFF

國際辦公家具基金會
01398 伊利諾州布魯明頓布洛克路 40 號

5 月 4 日

理莎丹妮爾
泰勒辦公室家具
80214 伊利諾州貝爾韋爾松木街 14 號

丹妮爾小姐您好：

謹代表 IOFF 董事會感謝您提前報名參加今年夏天在布魯明頓舉行的 IOFF 貿易展。我們有信心今年的活動將是我們有史以來最好的一次。**172** 我們不僅會搬到一個更寬敞的場地，而且請到著名家具設計師麗莎迪諾貝爾擔任大會的主題演講者。

一如既往，IOFF 希望讓各位頂尖家具設計師在愉快的氛圍中展示作品，並與整個布魯明頓的高階零售商發展專業關係。–[1]– 為了容納越來越多的參展商，**173** 今年的活動將在拉非特會議中心舉行。該中心有超過 70,000 平方公尺的展覽和會議空間，**173** 地點距離布魯明頓中心商業區只有幾分鐘的車程，方便前往餐廳、購物和劇院。–[2]– 為了方便您準備這次大會，請詳細閱讀隨信附上的小冊子。

我們的目標之一是協助您完成展場設置。–[3]– 請注意參展商的登記、入場、與拆除展位的時間和日期。**174A** **174B** 8 月 24 日星期日從中午開始，IOFF 志工將在 A 館外的登記處進行現場登記，登記參展商並發放名牌。A 館和 B 館將於當日中午至晚間 7 點開放設置。拆除時間為 8 月 28 日星期四下午 1 點到 6 點。**174C** IOFF 志工將在這兩天協助您安裝與拆除。

大會手冊有完整的活動日程表和會議中心地圖，其中包含指定卸貨區。–[4]– **175** 如果您有任何超出這封信和小冊子範圍的問題，我們的特別支援小組會在現場協助您解決。請致電 033-555-0011。

我們非常榮幸能邀請您來參加我們的大會，並預祝這次活動圓滿成功。

謹上

約翰艾力斯沃斯
資深活動經理

 字彙　**on behalf of** 代表～　**spacious** 寬敞的　**keynote speaker** 專題演講者　**renowned** 著名的
high-end 高階的　**exhibitor** 參展者　**enclosed** 隨函附上的　**facilitate** 幫助、使容易　**teardown** 拆除
process 處理　**on-site** 現場的　**set up** 安裝　**unloading area** 卸貨區　**beyond the scope of** 超出～範圍
be honored to 很榮幸～

172. According to the letter, what is a new feature of the IOFF convention?
(A) It will include entertainment performances.
(B) It will start at an earlier time.
(C) It will provide a wider range of events.
(D) It will take place at a bigger venue.

根據這封信，IOFF 大會的新特色是什麼？
(A) 它將包含娛樂表演。
(B) 它將在更早的時間開始。
(C) 它將提供更廣範圍的活動。
(D) 它將在更大的地點舉行。

正確答案為 (D)

第一段提到 we moving to a more spacious venue，因此答案是 (D)。

173. What is indicated about the Convention Center?
(A) The building was recently renovated.
(B) It is near Bloomington's business district.
(C) It has the latest technological equipment.
(D) The building includes restaurants and shops.

關於會議中心，以下何者正確？
(A) 大樓最近整修過。
(B) 靠近布魯明頓商業區。
(C) 擁有最新的科技設備。
(D) 大樓包含餐廳與商店。

正確答案為 (B)

在第二段提到 this year's event will be held at the Lafayette Convention Center，由此可以得知活動的場所。接下來的句子提到 is located only minutes from Bloomington's central commercial area with easy access to restaurants, shops, and theatres，答案是 (B)。

174. What is NOT mentioned as one of the ways IOFF volunteers will help at the convention?
(A) Registering participants
(B) Handing out badges
(C) Assisting with exhibits
(D) Answering phones

關於 IOFF 志工在大會提供的協助，以下何者信中沒有提到？
(A) 登記參加者
(B) 發放名牌
(C) 協助展品
(D) 接聽電話

正確答案為 (D)

信件內容第三段提到 IOFF volunteers will process on-site registration, check in registered exhibitors，符合 (A)。後面提到 hand out name badges at the registration desk 符合 (B)。第三段最後提到 IOFF volunteers will be available to assist you on both days for set up and teardown，符合 (C) 的內容。因此答案是信件未曾提到的 (D)。

175. In which of the positions marked [1], [2], [3], and [4] does the following sentence best belong?
"A list of frequently asked questions with responses are also included."
(A) [1]
(B) [2]
(C) [3]
(D) [4]

在標記 [1]、[2]、[3]、[4] 的位置當中，何者是安插下列句子的最佳位置？
「還包括一份附上回答的常見問題清單。」
(A) [1]
(B) [2]
(C) [3]
(D) [4]

正確答案為 (D)

〈插入句〉
關鍵句提到 questions 問題與解答，[4] 後面的句子提到超出信件和小冊子範圍的問題將由特別支援小組提供協助，因此前後有相關，答案選 (D)。

Questions 176-180 refer to the following announcement and notice. 通知 / 公告

May 1st

Aberman Books Announces New Young Authors Titles

Don't Look Back in Anger by Gabr Alfarsi

With a storm brewing off the coast and a newcomer in town, this gripping mystery set in a lighthouse is full of surprising twists. This is also the first of the enchanting series.

The Visigoths the Western Goths by Kenneth Ling

In this anthology of essays, world traveler Kenneth Ling recounts his expeditions to the Iberian Peninsula in a way that reads like delightful fiction. Includes a classroom discussion guide.

All the Way Up by Ricardo Gomez

No one knows what to expect when the queen of Geizan disappears and her young daughter inherits the throne. This humorous look at royal life is comedy writing at its best.

Sit Next to Me by Joseph Gustaferro

A group of acquaintances vacationing in a quiet, seaside town learn about each other's past. This tale, from the winner of the Lennox Fiction Prize, deftly analyzes the power of friendship.

For immediate release contact:

Grover Misra at (212) 555-0130

Upcoming Events in Woodward Bookstore

Saturday, July 12

Woodward Bookstore (455 Mason Avenue) will host a panel discussion moderated by Sanjay Dellegrio, associate editor of Writing & Publishing Magazine. Authors Gabr Alfarsi, Kenneth Ling, Ricardo Gomez whose first books were released by Aberman Books earlier this year, will speak about how they became published authors. They'll answer questions and give advice to those hoping to do the same. A book signing will take place after the event. Call (212) 555-0187 for more information.

問題 176-180 參考以下通知與公告。

5 月 1 日

(176) 亞伯拉罕圖書出版公司介紹新銳年輕作家作品

(180) 賈柏阿法契的《勿懷抱憤怒回首》

一場風暴在岸邊醞釀的同時,一名新訪客來到鎮上,這部扣人心弦的懸疑推理小說以燈塔為背景,充滿意想不到的轉折。這也是此迷人系列故事的第一集。

(180) 林肯尼的《西哥德人的西哥德》

在這本文選集中,世界旅行家林肯尼描述了他在伊比利亞半島的探險, (177) 敘述的方式就像讀一本愉閱的小說。內容包含課堂討論導讀。

(180) 理查德葛梅茲的《一路向上》

葛桑女王失蹤、由她的稚女繼承王位,沒有人知道接下來會發生什麼事。這本幽默看待皇室生活的寫作是喜劇的顛峰之作。

(180) 喬瑟夫古斯坦費羅的《伴我左右》

一群熟識的人在安靜的濱海小鎮度假,過程中漸漸了解彼此的過去。這個故事出自尼諾克斯小說獎的得主,他巧妙分析了友誼的力量。

即時出版書刊洽詢專線:
(212) 555-0130 負責人員古佛密斯拉

字彙 **brew** 醞釀、形成　**off the coast** 鄰近海岸　**gripping** 扣人心弦的　**lighthouse** 燈塔　**twist** 轉折　**enchanting** 迷人的　**anthology** 選集　**recount** 詳述、敘述　**expedition** 探險　**delightful** 令人愉快的　**inherit** 繼承　**throne** 王位　**royal** 皇家的　**acquaintance** 熟識的人　**deftly** 熟練地、巧妙地

伍德瓦書店活動預告

7 月 12 日星期六

伍德瓦書店(曼森大道 455 號)將主辦座談會,由寫作與出版雜誌副編輯 (179) 山傑迪勒葛里歐主持。今年初,阿伯曼圖書出版了 (178) (180) 賈柏阿法契、林肯尼、理查德葛梅茲等作家的第一本著作,活動將講述他們是如何成為出版作家。他們將回答問題並提供建議給有相同夢想的人。 (180) 活動結束後將舉行新書簽名會。更多資訊請電洽 (212) 555-0187。

字彙 **panel** 座談小組　**moderate** 主持　**associate editor** 副編輯　**book signing** 簽書會

176. What do all of the books in the announcement have in common?
(A) They are all mystery books.
(B) They are being published at the same time.
(C) They are intended for young adults.
(D) They are written by young writers.

公告中的所有書籍有什麼共通點？
(A) 都是懸疑推理小説。
(B) 在同時間出版。
(C) 都是為年輕人設計的。
(D) 都是由年輕作家寫的。

正確答案為 (D)

公告的第一句提到 Aberman Books Announces New Young Authors Titles，因此答案是 (D)。

> 字彙　**have ~ in common** 有～的共同點

177. In the announcement, the word "recounts" in paragraph 3, line 1, is closest in meaning to
(A) describes
(B) calculates
(C) estimates
(D) returns

公告的第三段第一行提到的「recounts」與以下何者的意思最接近？
(A) 描述
(B) 計算
(C) 估計
(D) 返回

正確答案為 (A)

〈推測字義〉
recounts his expeditions 意思是「描述他的探險」，答案是 (A)。

178. What is the topic of the July 12 event?
(A) How bookstores can attract customers
(B) How aspiring writers can get published
(C) How to become a magazine editor
(D) How to write lesson plans for a class

何者是 7 月 12 日的活動主題？
(A) 書店如何吸引顧客
(B) 有抱負的作家如何出版創作
(C) 如何成為雜誌編輯
(D) 如何擬定課程計畫

正確答案為 (B)

要從文章中找到有關活動主題的訊息，活動預告上提到 will speak about how they became published authors，答案是 (B)。

> 字彙　**aspiring** 有抱負的

179. What will Mr. Dellegrio do at the event?
(A) Sign a book for fans
(B) Give teaching advice
(C) Lead a group discussion
(D) Serve refreshments

迪勒葛里歐先生將在活動上做什麼？
(A) 幫粉絲簽書
(B) 提供教學建議
(C) 帶領團體討論
(D) 供應點心和飲料

正確答案為 (C)

活動預告上提到 a panel discussion moderated by Sanjay Dellegrio，由此可知他將主持座談會，因此答案是 (C)。

> 字彙　**refreshment** 點心

180. What book will NOT be signed by its author at the event?
    (A) *Don't Look Back in Anger*
    (B) *The Visigoths the Western Goths*
    (C) *All the Way Up*
    (D) *Sit Next to Me*

活動中哪本書將不會有作者簽名？
    (A)《勿懷抱憤怒回首》
    (B)《西哥德人的西哥德》
    (C)《一路向上》
    (D)《伴我左右》

正確答案為 **(D)**

〈整合多篇文章資訊〉

活動預告中提到 Authors Gabr Alfarsi, Kenneth Ling, Ricardo Gomez 這三人會出席活動，並表示 They'll answer questions and give advice to those hoping to do the same. 可見不會來活動現場的是 Joseph Gustaferro，答案是其作品 (D)。

Test 03

To	Keith Blanchett
From	Sam Brewer
Subject	The Audit Schedule
Date	June 10

Dear Mr. Blanchett:

Thank you for contracting with Environment Safe. We are proud to be your choice for corporate environmental standards certification of your company and look forward to working with you.

As we discussed, the audit will determine whether your company is in compliance with government regulations regarding clean air, clean water, and waste disposal. It will cover four main categories: general practices, the quality of discharged air, the quality of discharged water, and waste removal and recycling. Ratings for each category will be included in the report along with an overall rating of your business. We will perform separate audits and ratings for your manufacturing facility, warehouse and shipping center.

As you know, the audit period lasts two weeks and must occur when all operations are running normally. On your enrollment application, you requested that the audit occur during the last two weeks of August. This time frame works well for us. Unless I hear from you otherwise, I will assume that this is the best time to schedule environmental assessment of your company. Please contact me at your convenience to go over the details of how to prepare for the audit.

Thank you,

Sam Brewer
Public Relations Manager
Environment Safe

問題 181-185 參考以下兩封電子郵件。

收件人	奇斯布來契
寄件人	山姆布魯爾
主旨	審查日程
日期	6 月 10 日

布來契先生您好：

感謝您與環境安全簽約。我們很榮幸成為貴公司企業環境標準認證的選擇，期待與您的合作。

⑱ 正如我們所討論的，審查將決定貴公司是否符合政府有關乾淨空氣、乾淨水和廢物處理的規定。它包含 4 個主要類別：一般規範、排出空氣的品質、排出水的品質，以及廢棄物的清理與回收。每個類別的評分將連同您的企業整體評分一起納入報告。⑱ 我們將對你們的生產設施、倉庫、運輸中心分別進行審查與評分。

如您所知，審查期間持續兩週，必須在所有運作正常的情況下進行。⑱ 在您的登記申請書中，您要求審查在 8 月份的最後兩週進行。這個時間範圍也適合我們。除非我們收到您的回覆，不然我將認為這是對貴公司進行環境評估的最佳時間。請您在方便的時候與我聯絡，以便詳細說明如何準備審查。

謝謝。

山姆布魯爾
環境安全公關經理

字彙	
audit 審查 **standard** 標準 **certification** 認證 **in compliance with** 符合 **regulation** 規定 **govern** 管理、控制 **discharge** 排放、流出 **waste removal** 清除垃圾 **rating** 評價、評分 **separate** 各自的、單獨的 **occur** 發生 **time frame** 時間範圍 **otherwise** 否則、不然 **assume that** 假設、假定 **assessment** 評定、評估 **at one's convenience** 在某人方便的時候 **go over** ——討論、仔細檢查

To	Keith Blanchett
From	Tom McKnight
Subject	Schedule for 3rd quarter
Date	June 12
Attachment	schedule.pdf

Dear Keith,

I have attached the current draft of the company schedule for July, August and September. Please note that the warehouse staff will most likely need to work additional hours during these months depending on the Roberts Plumbing orders. We expect the orders to come in by the end of this week, at which point we should be able to finalize the schedule. All other existing orders have been finalized and entered into the schedule.

At our last meeting, you mentioned that we might add to the schedule. I have entered the July safety training sessions on it already, but could you let me know what else I should add? I'd like to send the schedule to the regional managers by the beginning of next week.

Tom

收件者	奇斯布來契
寄件者	湯姆麥奈
主旨	第三季日程表
⑱ 日期	6 月 12 日
附加檔案	schedule.pdf

奇斯你好：

⑱ 附件是目前公司 7 月、8 月、9 月的日程安排草案。⑱ 請注意，倉庫工作人員很可能要在這幾個月加班，這必須視羅伯斯水管工程的訂單量而定。我們希望這週末能收到訂單，屆時我們應該就能確定日程。其他現有訂單都已經確定並已進入日程安排。

⑱ 上次會議你提到我們可以增加行程。我已經加入了 7 月份的安全訓練，你能告訴我還有什麼需要補充的嗎？⑱ 我想在下週一前把日程表寄給區經理。

湯姆

字彙 | **current** 目前的　　**draft** 草案　　**warehouse** 倉儲　　**plumbing** 水管工事　　**finalize** 定案
existing 現存的、目前的　　**enter into** 輸入、進入　　**add to** 加入

181. According to the first e-mail, what service does Environment Safe provide?
(A) Hiring of manufacturing and warehousing staff
(B) Preparing financial reports for companies
(C) Recycling of paper and other materials
(D) Rating companies' compliance with government rules

根據第一封電子郵件，環境安全提供什麼樣的服務？
(A) 雇用製造和倉儲人員
(B) 為企業準備財務報告
(C) 回收紙類與其他材料
(D) 對企業是否遵守政府規定進行評鑑

正確答案為 (D)

第一封電子郵件第二段的最後提到 We will perform separate audits and ratings for your manufacturing facility, warehouse and shipping center，這是呼應第二段第一句的內容，為了確認業者是否遵守政府規定，答案是 (D)。

182. According to the second e-mail, what will likely happen next month in the warehouse?
(A) Some employees will be working extra hours.
(B) Some advanced equipment will be serviced.
(C) Waste materials will be collected for reprocessing.
(D) The revised company policy will be posted.

根據第二封電子郵件，下個月倉庫很可能將發生什麼事？
(A) 一些員工將加班工作。
(B) 一些高級設備將進行維修。
(C) 收集廢物進行再處理。
(D) 將公告修訂後的公司政策。

正確答案為 (A)

第二封電子郵件提到 I have attached the current draft of the company schedule for July, August and September. Please note that the warehouse staff will most likely need to work additional hours during these months，這封信是在 6 月份寫的，預計在 7 月可能要加班，因此答案是 (A)。

183. What does Mr. McKnight hope to do by the end of this week?
(A) Evaluate Environment Safe's offer
(B) Complete the company's calendar
(C) Begin an environmental standards assessment
(D) Order supplies from Roberts Plumbing

麥奈先生希望這週前能完成什麼事？
(A) 評估環境安全的提案
(B) 完成公司日程安排
(C) 開始環境標準評估
(D) 向羅伯斯水管工程訂購物品

正確答案為 (B)

問到未來相關的事情，通常會在文章後半段提及，麥奈所寫的第二封信的第二段最後提到 I'd like to send the schedule to the regional managers by the beginning of the next week，因此答案是 (B)。

184. In the second e-mail, the word "note" in paragraph 1, line 2 is closest in meaning to
(A) write down
(B) pick up
(C) take out
(D) bear in mind

第二封信第一段第二行提到的「note」與下列何者的意思最接近？
(A) 寫下
(B) 撿起
(C) 帶走
(D) 記住

正確答案為 (D)

〈推測字義〉
句型 Please note that「請注意」是提醒對方注意接下來的內容，相當於 (D) bear in mind「牢記在心、記住」。

185. What will Mr. Blanchett probably say in his response to the second e-mail?

(A) Manufacturing facilities must prepare for increased business.

(B) An audit of the company must be added to the calendar.

(C) A safety training session must be arranged for September.

(D) The method for updating the calendar must be revised.

布來契先生很可能如何回覆第二封信件？

(A) 生產設備必須為增加的業務量做好準備。

(B) 公司審查必須加入日程安排。

(C) 9 月份必須安排一次安全訓練課程。

(D) 日程表的更新方式必須修改。

正確答案為 (B)

〈整合多篇文章資訊〉

第二封信最後一段，McKnight 麥奈希望 Blanchett 布來契告訴他 7、8、9 月份有無需要增加的日程安排，而第一封信中提到已定在 8 月的最後兩週進行審查，因此答案是 (B)。

> **字彙**　**manufacturing facilities** 生產設備

Questions 186-190 refer to the following advertisement, e-mail, and text message. 廣告／電子郵件／簡訊

CRESTPORT DANCE ACADEMY

Crestport Dance Academy is pleased to announce its next season of performances. From modern dance and hip-hop to classical ballet — come and see all that we have to offer! You can purchase tickets for the entire season or for single performances. Season ticket subscribers also receive 50 percent off same-day ticket purchases.

January 18 - 22
• The Shelburne Group comes with hip-hop music.

February 7
• Catelynn Martin performs her award-winning dance.

February 15-21
• The Strauss Trio puts on an amazing ballet performance.

February 22-27
• Zachary Keaton dances while accompanied by live piano.

問題 186-190 參考以下廣告、電子郵件與簡訊。

傑斯堡舞蹈學院

傑斯堡舞蹈學院很高興宣布下一季的演出。186 從現代舞、嘻哈到古典芭蕾，請來看看我們所提供的所有一切！您可購買季票或單場門票。190 季票訂購者還可享有當日購票五折。

1 月 18 日 – 22 日
• 雪爾布納團體帶來嘻哈音樂。

2 月 7 日
• 凱特林馬丁表演獲獎舞蹈。

188 2 月 15 日 - 21 日
• 188 斯特勞斯三人組帶來精采的芭蕾舞表演。

2 月 22 日 – 27 日
• 札查瑞基頓搭配現場鋼琴伴奏表演舞蹈。

字彙　**be pleased to** 樂意　**announce** 宣布　**classical** 古典的　**subscriber** 訂戶　**award-winning** 獲獎的
put on 上演　**accompany** 伴奏；陪伴、伴隨　**live** 現場的

To: Tara Craft
From: Jeanne Harris
Cc: Ben Springer
Subject: Your Visit to Belle Systems
Date: December 29

Dear Ms. Craft:

On behalf of Belle Systems, I would like to let you know how much we are looking forward to adopting the document maintaining project you will teach us about on February 21 and 22. I reserved a room, laptop, projector, and microphone as you requested. Please let me know if you need further assistance with your presentation.

Our department head, Ben Springer, has made a special plan to express our gratitude and make your visit more enjoyable. He has planned dinner with you at an acclaimed local restaurant on the first evening of your visit, followed by an outing to a dance performance offered by Crestport Dance Academy.

Sincerely,

Jeanne Harris
Marketing Manager
Belle Systems

收件者：塔拉克拉芙特
寄件者：珍娜哈里斯
副本：班史普林納
主旨：您到訪貝拉系統公司
日期：12 月 29 日

克拉芙特小姐您好：

187 謹代表貝拉系統公司向您傳達，我們相當期待採用您在 2 月 21 日和 22 日即將教導我們的文件維護計畫。我已按照您的要求，預定一間房間、一台筆記型電腦、一台投影機和一支麥克風。如果您的演講還需要更多協助，請告訴我。

我們的部門主管班史普林納規劃一個特別行程來表達我們的感激，希望能讓您的到訪更加愉快。187 188 他計畫在您到訪的第一天晚上，邀您在當地廣受歡迎的餐廳共進晚餐，接著去看場由傑斯堡舞蹈學院提供的舞蹈表演。

珍娜哈里斯
貝拉系統行銷經理

字彙　**adopt** 採用　　**maintain** 維持、保養　　**request** 請求　　**acclaimed** 受到讚揚的　　**followed by** 隨後、接著

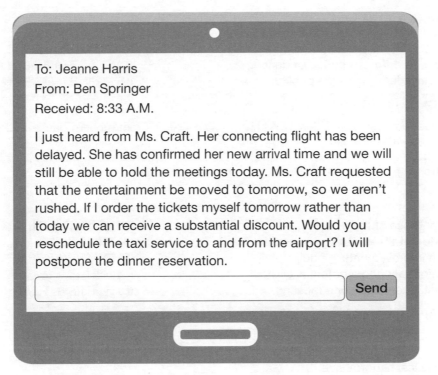

To: Jeanne Harris
From: Ben Springer
Received: 8:33 A.M.

I just heard from Ms. Craft. Her connecting flight has been delayed. She has confirmed her new arrival time and we will still be able to hold the meetings today. Ms. Craft requested that the entertainment be moved to tomorrow, so we aren't rushed. If I order the tickets myself tomorrow rather than today we can receive a substantial discount. Would you reschedule the taxi service to and from the airport? I will postpone the dinner reservation.

Send

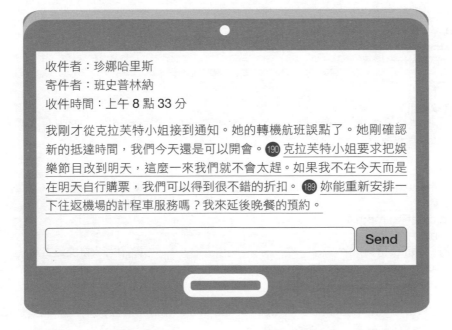

收件者：珍娜哈里斯
寄件者：班史普林納
收件時間：上午 8 點 33 分

我剛才從克拉芙特小姐接到通知。她的轉機航班誤點了。她剛確認新的抵達時間，我們今天還是可以開會。⑲⓪ 克拉芙特小姐要求把娛樂節目改到明天，這麼一來我們就不會太趕。如果我不在今天而是在明天自行購票，我們可以得到很不錯的折扣。⑱⑨ 妳能重新安排一下往返機場的計程車服務嗎？我來延後晚餐的預約。

Send

字彙　**connecting flight** 轉機航班　**confirm** 確認　**rush** 勿促　**rather than** 而不是　**substantial** 相當大的、可觀的

186. What is suggested about Crestport Dance Academy?
(A) It has been in operation over the past 20 years.
(B) It is now recruiting dance instructors.
(C) It showcases different styles of dance.
(D) It offers dance lessons to the public.

關於傑斯堡舞蹈學院，以下何者正確？
(A) 它營運超過 20 年。
(B) 它正在招募舞蹈老師。
(C) 它展示不同風格的舞蹈。
(D) 它對大眾提供舞蹈課程。

正確答案為 (C)

Crestport Dance Academy 的介紹可以看到廣告，第一段提到 From modern dance and hip-hop to classical ballet，可知答案是 (C)。

> 字彙　**in operation** 營運　**instructor** 講師、指導者　**showcase** 展示、展現

187. What is the purpose of the e-mail?
(A) To provide details about the schedule
(B) To explain improvements in equipment
(C) To give information to a potential client
(D) To suggest a new date for a meeting

電子郵件的目的是什麼？
(A) 提供行程細節
(B) 說明設備的改進狀況
(C) 向潛在客戶提供資訊
(D) 建議新的會議日期

正確答案為 (A)

電子郵件第一段提到「日期」you will teach us about on February 21 and 22，在第二段提到「行程細節」He has planned dinner with you at an acclaimed local restaurant on the first evening of your visit, followed by an outing to a musical performance，可知答案是 (A)。

188. What performance was Ms. Craft originally scheduled to attend?
(A) The Shelburne Group
(B) Catelynn Martin
(C) The Strauss Trio
(D) Zachary Keaton

克拉芙特小姐原本計畫看哪場表演？
(A) 雪爾布納團體
(B) 凱特林馬丁
(C) 斯特勞斯三人組
(D) 札查瑞基頓

正確答案為 (C)

〈整合多篇文章資訊〉

信件中提到 Craft 克拉芙特小姐的訪問日期是 2 月 21 日與 22 日，並計劃於第一天欣賞舞蹈表演。廣告中 21 日的表演是 The Strauss 斯特勞斯三人組，因此答案是 (C)。

189. According to the text message, what does Mr. Springer ask Ms. Harris to do?
(A) Reserve a meeting room
(B) Prepare dinner
(C) Rearrange transportation
(D) Cancel a performance

根據文字簡訊，史普林納先生要求哈里斯小姐做什麼？
(A) 預約會議室
(B) 準備晚餐
(C) 重新安排交通工具
(D) 取消表演

正確答案為 (C)

簡訊最後面提到 Would you reschedule the taxi service to and from the airport? 因此答案是 (C)。

190. What can be inferred about Mr. Springer?
(A) He has not confirmed Ms. Craft's schedule yet.
(B) He is not sure whether Ms. Craft will like the performance.
(C) He will soon be able to get a credit for the old tickets.
(D) He has a subscription to Crestport Dance Academy.

關於史普林納先生，以下說明何者正確？
(A) 他尚未確認克拉芙特小姐的行程。
(B) 他不確定克拉芙特小姐是否喜歡表演內容。
(C) 他很快就能得到以前入場票的信用點數。
(D) 他有傑斯堡舞蹈學院的長期票。

正確答案為 **(D)**

〈整合多篇文章資訊〉

文字簡訊提到 If I order the tickets myself tomorrow rather than today we can receive a substantial discount，由此可知 Springer 史普林納先生若購買明天的票，即可享有折扣。廣告提到 Season ticket subscribers also receive 50 percent off same-day ticket purchases，由此可知享有折扣的史普林納是季票訂購者。答案是 (D)。

字彙　**get a credit for** 獲得信用（點數）　　**subscription**（文化活動的）長期票

Questions 191-195 refer to the following advertisement, Web page and review. 廣告 / 網頁 / 評論

Zentron Systems Inc.

At Zentron Systems Inc., our product testers' opinions are a key part of our market research work. We are one of the best-known research centers in the city, and we are now expanding our staff and product testers to meet higher demand. We help companies develop new and innovative products — from food to toys to electronics. We also follow rigorous quality standards. By becoming a product tester for Zentron Systems Inc., you can earn cash and even great prizes. Just click www.zentronsystems.org/tester and refer to our "Rewards program."

http://www.zentronsystems.org/tester/register

HOW TO BECOME A PRODUCT TESTER

THE FIRST STAGE

Complete our "new tester" registration form (click here), and then create a password that you will use every time you log on from this Web site. This registration places you on a list of available product testers.

THE SECOND STAGE

As product tests arise, you will be informed via phone or e-mail. Some people get called more than others; it all depends. However, we do not call any of our registered testers more than once a month.

THE THIRD STAGE

When you have expressed interest in a product test, our recruitment specialist will ask you some questions about your product preferences to see if you are a good match for the research study.

THE FOURTH STAGE

When chosen for a product test, the recruitment specialist will inform you how much it pays. Most tests take about 1 hour and pay $30 to $40 cash.

REWARDS PROGRAM

All product testers who register with us for the first time will automatically be entered into a random drawing to win $100 or a brand-new digital camera. No entry form is required. Current product testers who refer a friend to Zentron Systems Inc. will receive $25 when that person completes his/her first study. For more information on the program, click here.

問題 191-195 參考以下廣告、網頁與評論。

禪純系統

在禪純系統中心，產品測試人員的意見是我們市場研究工作的關鍵。我們是本市最著名的研究中心之一，我們正在擴編員工和產品測試人員，以滿足更多需求。我們協助企業開發新穎和創新的產品，從食品、玩具到電子產品應有盡有。我們也遵循嚴格的品質標準。成為禪純系統的產品測試員，您可以賺取現金，甚至獲得大獎。請至 www.zentronsystems.org/tester 並點閱「獎勵計畫」。

字彙　**meet a demand** 滿足需求　**electronics** 電子產品　**rigorous** 嚴格的

http://www.zentronsystems.org/tester/register

如何成為產品測試員

第一階段
完成我們的「新進測試人員」註冊表（點擊這裡），接著建立一組密碼，未來每次登入網站時會使用到。此註冊會將您列入可參與產品測試人員的名冊當中。

第二階段
當有產品測試需求時，您會透過電話或電子郵件收到通知。有些人收到的通知會比其他人多，要視情況而定。不過 ⑲⑭ 我們每個月撥給任何註冊測試員的電話次數不會超過一次。

第三階段
如您對產品測試有興趣，我們的招聘專員將會詢問您關於產品偏好的問題，以確認您是否適合該項研究。

第四階段
當您獲選參加產品測試時，招聘專員會告知您報酬。多數測試需要一個小時，⑲⑤ⒸⓄ 報酬為 30 美元到 40 美元。

獎勵計畫
⑲① 所有首次在此網站註冊的產品測試員將自動進入隨機抽獎，有機會贏得 100 美元或一台全新數位相機。不需額外填寫參加申請書。⑲② 介紹朋友到禪純系統的現任產品測試員，可在此人完成第一項研究時獲得 25 美元。更多詳細資訊請點擊這裡。

字彙　**registration form** 註冊表　**place on a list** 列入清單　**arise** 發生　**via** 經由　**specialist** 專家
preference 偏好、傾向　**match for** 與～匹配　**random** 隨機的　**drawing** 抽出、抽籤
entry form 參加申請表　**refer A to B** 介紹 A 給 B

http://www.zentronsystems.org/tester/register

Date: October 29th
Sandra Stable

Being a tester at Zentron Systems Inc.

I joined Zentron Systems Inc. as a product tester last year, and since then I've gotten paid to try beverages, soda, and much more. Registering is easy — you simply complete an online application and make a password — and the tests are fun and interesting. I usually get paid $40 cash for just one hour of testing each time I visit, but they call a lot! I received 5 to 6 calls a week during a month when I was out of the country, and my voicemail was full. It's a good way to earn money, but they do ask a number of questions about what products you like. That's part of the qualifying process for tests.

To participate as a product tester, just sign up here: www.zentronsystems.org.

I recommend joining! The testing facility, in Napa Valley, is near a city bus stop and there is also plenty of free parking in the lot in front of the building.

---

http://www.zentronsystems.org/tester/register

日期：10 月 29 日
珊卓史坦堡

成為禪純系統的測試員

❶❾❸ 我去年加入了禪純系統中心擔任產品測試員，從那時起，我開始領取酬勞試喝飲料、汽水和其他更多東西。註冊很簡單，只需要完成一個線上申請表，並設置密碼即可，而且測試好玩又有趣。每次通常花 1 個小時的測試就能得到 40 美元的現金，但是 ❶❾❹ 他們經常打電話給我！在我出國的一個月裡，我接到 5、6 通電話，我的語音信箱都滿了。這是個賺錢的好方法，但是他們的確會問你很多關於你喜歡什麼產品的問題。這是資格審核的一部分。

想參與產品測試，只要到這裡註冊：www.zentronsystems.org。

我推薦加入！❶❾❺Ⓐ ❶❾❺Ⓑ 測試地點位於納帕鎮，靠近市公車站，大樓前的停車場也有很多免費停車位。

字彙　**application** 申請（表）　　**qualifying** 具資格的　　**sign up** 註冊、登記

191. How most likely would a new registrant win $100 from Zentron Systems Inc.?
(A) By conducting a customer survey
(B) By doing two product tests
(C) By completing an entry form
(D) By being selected randomly

新註冊者很可能從禪純系統贏得 100 美元的方法是什麼？
(A) 執行消費者意見調查
(B) 進行兩項產品測試
(C) 完成參加申請表
(D) 隨機選出

正確答案為 (D)

網頁最後一段的 REWARDS PROGRAM 當中提到 All product testers who register with us for the first time will automatically be entered into a random drawing to win $100 or an MP3 player，因此答案是 (D)。

192. The word "refer" in paragraph 5, in line 3 of the Web page, is closest in meaning to
(A) address
(B) guide
(C) promise
(D) transport

網頁的第五段第三行提到的「refer」意思與以下何者最接近？
(A) 演說、處理
(B) 介紹
(C) 約定
(D) 運送

正確答案為 (B)

〈推測字義〉
網頁提到 refer a friend to Zentron Systems 是指介紹朋友給禪純系統的意思，因此答案是 (B)。

193. What can be inferred about Ms. Stable?
(A) She used to be a recruiter for Zentron Systems Inc.
(B) She heard about Zentron Systems Inc. from a friend.
(C) She has tested various drinks in the past.
(D) She does not usually qualify for product tests.

關於史坦堡小姐的描述，以下何者正確？
(A) 她曾經是禪純的招聘負責人員。
(B) 她從一個朋友那裡聽說了禪純系統公司。
(C) 過去曾試喝過各種飲料。
(D) 她常不符合產品測試的資格。

正確答案為 (C)

在感想文的第一句提到 I joined Zentron Laboratory as a product tester last year, and since then I've gotten paid to try beverages, soda, and much more，由此可知她在 1 年當中參與多次的測試，因此答案是 (C)。

194. Based on the review, which part of the Web page is most likely not accurate?
(A) The first stage
(B) The second stage
(C) The third stage
(D) The fourth stage

根據評論，網頁的哪一部分很可能不正確？
(A) 第一階段
(B) 第二階段
(C) 第三階段
(D) 第四階段

正確答案為 (B)

〈整合多篇文章資訊〉
網頁提到 we do not call any of our registered testers more than once a month，但在 Stable 史坦堡的評論中提到 I received 5 to 6 calls a week during a month when I was out of the country，因此答案是 (B)。

195. What is NOT mentioned about Zentron Systems Inc.?
(A) They are conveniently located in a city.
(B) They have free parking available.
(C) They give cash payments to product testers.
(D) They visit you in person with the product.

關於禪純系統，文章沒有提到以下何者？
(A) 位於都市的便利位置。
(B) 有免費的停車位。
(C) 支付給產品測試者現金。
(D) 帶著產品親自到訪。

正確答案為 (D)

評論提到 The testing facility is near a city bus stop 符合 (A)。there is also plenty of free parking in the lot 符合 (B)。I usually get paid $40 cash for just one hour of testing 符合 (C) 選項。因此答案是沒有提到的選項 (D)。

Questions 196-200 refer to the following e-mail, schedule, and news article. 電子郵件 / 行程表 / 新聞報導

To	Terzo Ventimiglia
From	Augustine Liu
Date	June 25
Subject	Events for Summer Interns
Attachment	Event Schedule

Hello, Terzo.

I have been asked to plan the summer events for our interns. Because there are far fewer interns in the research department than in product development, I want to invite your interns to join ours for some weekend and evening activities we will be offering. The experience will be very meaningful, and they will feel that being an intern gives them a chance to develop first-hand experience by participating in the events.

I'd like to introduce a new recreational opportunity I read about in the online edition of the Brandington Daily News. Here's the link to the article with information about the location of this year's new event: www.brandingtondailynews.com/mtduncan.

I am excited about the event, but I have some concerns and value any input you can offer me. Please let me know what you have in your mind for the events. Thank you in advance for any advice you can offer. Attached is this year's schedule.

Warm regards,

Augustine Liu
Product Development Manager

SUMMER CAMP SCHEDULE

July 6	Agricultural Fair at the Corners Farms in East Pleasantville
July 28	Day at the Topenski Amusement Park
August 14	Movie Night featuring Great Skies
September 10	Outdoor Hiking Day Trip

Please note that this year's schedule of activities is slightly different from that of previous years.

Test 03

問題 196-200 參考以下電子郵件、行程表與新聞報導。

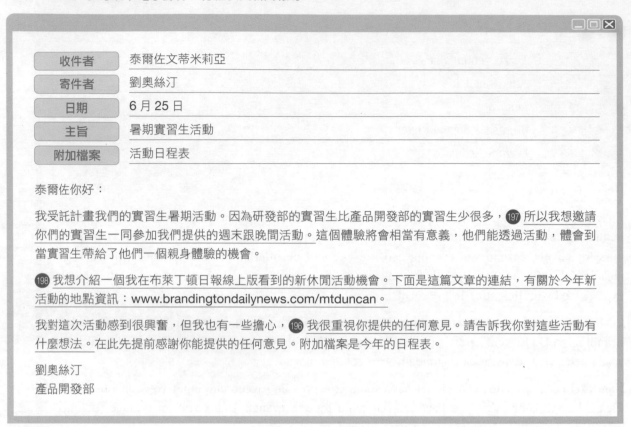

收件者　泰爾佐文蒂米莉亞
寄件者　劉奧絲汀
日期　6 月 25 日
主旨　暑期實習生活動
附加檔案　活動日程表

泰爾佐你好：

我受託計畫我們的實習生暑期活動。因為研發部的實習生比產品開發部的實習生少很多，197 所以我想邀請你們的實習生一同參加我們提供的週末跟晚間活動。這個體驗將會相當有意義，他們能透過活動，體會到當實習生帶給了他們一個親身體驗的機會。

198 我想介紹一個我在布萊丁頓日報線上版看到的新休閒活動機會。下面是這篇文章的連結，有關於今年新活動的地點資訊：www.brandingtondailynews.com/mtduncan。

我對這次活動感到很興奮，但我也有一些擔心，196 我很重視你提供的任何意見。請告訴我你對這些活動有什麼想法。在此先提前感謝你能提供的任何意見。附加檔案是今年的日程表。

劉奧絲汀
產品開發部

字彙　recreational 休閒的、娛樂的　edition 出版版次、號　value 重要性　in advance 事先、提前
attached 附加的

暑期營隊日程表

7 月 6 日	農業博覽會，位於東歡樂谷的康納斯農場
7 月 28 日	多芬司基遊樂世界一日遊
8 月 14 日	大天空電影之夜
198 9 月 10 日	戶外遠足一日遊

請注意，今年的活動安排與往年略有不同。

字彙　agricultural fair 農業博覽會

Brandington Daily News

Improved Trails on Mount Duncan to Open Next Week

June 23 – Park officials announced on Friday that three new hiking trails will be open to the public on July 1. Construction began on the trails last autumn. Work on the trails, which had been suspended from December through March due to winter weather, has been ongoing throughout April and May. The new trails are designed for beginners and will not require participants to have any experience and expertise.

Park and Recreation Director Nancy Phan said she is "thrilled" by the new opportunities the trails offer for recreation in the area. "Mount Duncan has always been a beloved local landmark," Ms. Phan said, "but it was previously accessible only to experienced hikers. Now, everyone in our community will be able to enjoy it." Ms. Phan added that she hopes the trails will increase tourism and create future business opportunities by providing a desirable location for corporate excursions and families on vacation.

布萊丁頓日報

198 改良後的都肯山步道將於下週開放。

6 月 23 日 —— 公園管理員於星期五表示，有三條新的登山步道將於 7 月 1 日對外開放。這些步道從去年秋天開始建設。199 由於冬天氣候因素，去年 12 月到今年 3 月暫停施工的步道工程持續在整個 4 月和 5 月進行。200 新步道是專為初學者而設計，參加者不須具備相關經驗或專業知識。

公園兼休閒娛樂總監范南西說，她對新步道替這一帶提供新的休閒活動機會「感到興奮不已」。范小姐表示：「都肯山一直是當地人喜愛的地點，但以前只有有經驗的登山者才能進入，如今我們社區的每個人都能享受它。」范小姐補充，她希望這些步道能成為企業出遊與家庭度假的理想地點，進而發展旅遊業並創造商機。

字彙　**trail** 小徑、步道　**the public** 公眾　**suspend** 停擺、中斷　**ongoing** 不間斷的、進行的　**thrilled** 興奮不已的、萬分激動的　**beloved** 心愛的　**landmark** 地標　**accessible** 容易到達的　**desirable** 令人滿意的

196. What is the main purpose of the e-mail?　　電子郵件的主要目的是什麼？
(A) To request feedback from a coworker　　**(A) 請同事給予意見**
(B) To inquire about organizing a workshop　　(B) 詢問如何企劃一場研討會
(C) To correct an event schedule　　(C) 更正活動行程
(D) To cancel a product demonstration　　(D) 取消產品示範

正確答案為 (A)

在電子郵件第二段提到 Please let me know what you have in your mind for the events. Thank you in advance for any advice you can offer，因此答案是 (A)。

197. What does Ms. Liu suggest in the e-mail?　　劉小姐在電子郵件中建議什麼？
(A) Increasing the number of interns hired in the Research Department　　(A) 增加研究部門的實習生數量
(B) Planning a joint summer camp between two departments　　**(B) 計畫兩個部門合辦夏令營**
(C) Decreasing the number of social gatherings to save money　　(C) 減少聯誼會以節省經費
(D) Appointing one of the interns to organize the event　　(D) 指定其中一名實習生企劃活動

正確答案為 (B)

信件的第一段提議 I want to invite your interns to join ours，由此可知答案是 (B)。

字彙　joint 共同的、聯合的　　social gathering 聯誼會

198. What date does Ms. Liu suggest for this year's new activity?　　以下何者是劉小姐提議的今年新活動日期？
(A) July 6　　(A) 7 月 6 日
(B) July 28　　(B) 7 月 28 日
(C) August 14　　(C) 8 月 14 日
(D) September 10　　**(D) 9 月 10 日**

正確答案為 (D)

〈整合多篇文章資訊〉
電子郵件中提到 I'd like to introduce a new recreational opportunity I read about in the online edition of the Brandington Daily News，報導中提到 Improved Trails on Mount Duncan，因此答案是在日程表中進行戶外活動的日期 (D)。

199. What was the reason for construction being halted?　　造成施工停擺的原因是什麼？
(A) Weather conditions　　**(A) 天氣狀況**
(B) Budgetary considerations　　(B) 預算考量
(C) A delay in obtaining city permits　　(C) 延後取得市府許可
(D) A lack of experienced workers　　(D) 缺乏有經驗的工人

正確答案為 (A)

報導的第一段提到 Work on the trails, which had been suspended... due to winter weather，因此答案是 (A)。

200. What can be suggested about Mount Duncan?　　關於都肯山，以下何者的描述正確？
(A) Several sports competitions are scheduled to take place.　　(A) 有幾項運動競賽打算在此舉行。
(B) Experienced hikers now enjoy the challenge to climb there.　　(B) 經驗健行者現在喜歡去那裡挑戰登山。
(C) It becomes easily accessible to the general public.　　**(C) 變得讓大眾也能輕鬆使用。**
(D) Its construction has been completed ahead of schedule.　　(D) 其工程建設已經提前完工。

正確答案為 (C)

在報導的第二段訪問中提到 it was previously accessible only to experienced hikers. Now, everyone in our community will be able to enjoy it，因此答案是 (C)。

Actual Test

04

中譯與解說

♪ 單題練習版-04

	答對題數	換算分數
聽力		
閱讀		

New TOEIC 第四回

1. `4_01` `美式女聲`

(A) She is making a photocopy.
(B) She is posting a notice on the board.
(C) She is operating a machine.
(D) She is holding some wires.

(A) 女子正在影印。
(B) 女子在公布欄張貼公告。
(C) 女子正在操作一台機器。
(D) 女子手正握著一些電線。

正確答案為 (C)

本題為單人照片，請留意人物的動作或狀態。女子正在操作設備，因此答案要選 (C)。(A) 女子使用的機器並非影印機；照片中並未出現公布欄和電線，因此 (B) 和 (D) 皆不正確。

> **字彙** **make a photocopy** 影印　**post a notice** 張貼公告　**board** 公布欄　**operate** 操作（機器）　**wire** 電線、鐵絲

2. `4_02` `英式男聲`

(A) A cyclist has pulled ahead of the bus.
(B) A cyclist and a bus have collided.
(C) A group of cyclists is traveling along the street.
(D) A cyclist is riding alongside a vehicle.

(A) 一名腳踏車騎士騎在公車前方。
(B) 一名腳踏車騎士和公車相撞。
(C) 一群腳踏車騎士沿著街道騎車。
(D) 一名腳踏車騎士騎在車輛旁。

正確答案為 (D)

(D) 描寫騎士沿著車輛旁騎腳踏車，為最適當的答案。照片中並未出現腳踏車和公車相撞、也沒有出現一群人騎著腳踏車，因此 (B) 和 (C) 皆不正確。

> **字彙** **cyclist** 單車騎士　**pull ahead of** 領先　**collide** 相撞、碰撞　**travel along** 沿著～行走
> **alongside** 在旁邊、並排地　**vehicle** 車輛

3. `4 03` 美式女聲

(A) **Merchandise is being displayed outside a shop.**
(B) Postcards are being selected from a pair of racks.
(C) A cabinet has been stocked with supplies.
(D) Some items are being put onto hangers.

(A) **商品陳列於商店外。**
(B) 有人從架上挑選明信片。
(C) 有人在補貨上架。
(D) 有人把一些商品掛上衣架。

正確答案為 **(A)**

(A) 描寫商品陳列於商店外，為最適當的答案。**請熟記〈be being displayed/shown/exhibited〉的用法，以被動進行式表示「正在被陳列、擺設」的狀態**，可以作為無人照片的答案。(B) 和 (D) 皆以物品當作主詞，使用被動進行式，此類敘述不適用於無人照片；(C) 照片中並未看到櫃子（cabinet），因此不是答案。

字彙　**merchandise** 物品、商品　　**rack** 掛物架　　**stock** 進貨　　**hanger** 衣架

4. `4_04` 美式男聲

(A) Workers are emptying a trash can.
(B) Visitors are enjoying an outing.
(C) **A path winds through a park.**
(D) Plants are being planted along the path.

(A) 工作人員們正在清空一個垃圾桶。
(B) 遊客們正在享受郊遊。
(C) **公園內小徑蜿蜒。**
(D) 有人正沿著小徑種植植物。

正確答案為 **(C)**

照片中只有一個人在走路，最適合的答案是 (C)。而 (A) 和 (B) 皆針對數個人進行描寫，**主詞數量錯誤**；(D) 以物品當作主詞，使用被動進行式 be being planted，表示有人正在進行此動作，但是照片中並未出現種植物的人，因此不是答案。

字彙　**empty** 清空　　**outing** 短程旅遊、郊遊　　**wind**（道路或河川）蜿蜒、曲折前進

Test 04

5. `4_05` `美式女聲`

(A) A clerk is stationed behind a sales counter.
(B) A woman is handing a card to a cashier.
(C) An employee is stocking a store shelf.
(D) A woman is trying on necklaces.

(A) 一名店員站在櫃檯後方。
(B) 一名女子把卡片遞給收銀員。
(C) 一名員工正在將商品上架。
(D) 一名女子正在試戴項鍊。

正確答案為 (A)

本題為多個人物的室內照片，須留意各個人物的動作。(A) 正確描寫商店店員站在櫃檯後方，為正確答案。(B) 和 (D) 針對女子的動作進行描寫，但與照片不符；(C) 上架的動作與店員的動作不符，因此不是答案。

> **字彙**   **station** 配置、位於   **employee** 員工   **try on** 試戴、試穿

6. `4_06` `英式男聲`

(A) A shelter has been erected by the water.
(B) Cargo ships are lined up at the docks.
(C) A container is suspended from a crane.
(D) Sailors are about to board a vessel.

(A) 水邊建造了一個遮蔽處。
(B) 碼頭邊有一排貨船停靠。
(C) 起重機吊著一個貨櫃。
(D) 船員們正準備要上船。

正確答案為 (A)

題目為無人的物品照或風景照時，須認真聆聽各物品的名稱。(A) 描寫岸邊建造了遮陽的地方，為最適當的答案。(B) 遠方有貨船，但是並未排成一列，因此該敘述不正確；(C) 和 (D) 提到照片中沒有出現的物品（container）和人物（sailors），因此不是答案。

> **字彙**   **shelter** 遮蔽處   **erect** 設立、建立   **cargo ship** 貨船   **dock** 碼頭   **container** 貨櫃   **suspend** 懸掛、吊
> **crane** 起重機   **vessel**（大型）船、艦

7. 4_07 美式男聲 / 美式女聲

Which of these pictures would look better in the brochure?
(A) Thanks, I feel better.
(B) I got it in the mail.
(C) I don't like either one.

這些照片中，哪一張適合用在手冊上？
(A) 謝謝，我覺得好多了。
(B) 我收到郵寄來的東西了。
(C) 兩張我都不喜歡。

正確答案為 (C)

本題為 Which 開頭的問句，詢問哪一張照片比較好。(C) 的回答表示當中沒有好的照片，為最適當的答案。(A) 重複使用題目中的 better，屬於陷阱選項；(B) 的回答答非所問。

> 字彙　**brochure**（廣告）冊子　**mail** 郵件

8. 4_08 英式男聲 / 美式女聲

Is Mr. Kline back from his appointment yet?
(A) Are you all ready?
(B) Yes, he gave it back.
(C) I'm not certain.

克萊恩先生已經結束約會回來了嗎？
(A) 你準備好了嗎？
(B) 對，他把東西歸還了。
(C) 我不太確定。

正確答案為 (C)

本題為 be 動詞開頭的問句，詢問 Mr. Kline 是否已經回來，**(C) 表示不太清楚，為常見的間接回答**，為正確答案。(A) 的內容與題目無關，且**主詞有誤**；(B) 回答 Yes 表示 Mr. Kline 已經回來，但後方為不相干的內容，因此不能作為答案。

> 字彙　**yet**（用於問句）已經　**certain** 確信、無疑的

9. 4_09 美式女聲 / 美式男聲

What type of firm are you working for?
(A) We provide a variety of financial services.
(B) Mostly during our regular office hours.
(C) Actually, I'm still working on it.

你任職於什麼類型的公司？
(A) 我們公司提供各式各樣的金融服務。
(B) 大多在我們辦公時間內。
(C) 事實上，我還在處理它。

正確答案為 (A)

本題為 What 開頭的問句，詢問對方在什麼類型的公司工作。(A) **並非以簡答回應，而是進一步具體説明工作內容**，為最適當的回答。(B) 應搭配以 How long 開頭的問句，詢問多久時間較為適當；(C) 重複使用 working，但題目的 working for 指「從事的工作」，選項 (C) 的 working on 則是指「處理工作事項」。

> 字彙　**firm** 公司　**a variety of** 各式各樣的　**financial service** 金融服務　**office hours** 營業時間、辦公時間

10. 4_10 美式女聲 / 英式男聲

Do you think the guests would prefer Italian or Thai food?
(A) I'll just have a dessert.
(B) It's probably more popular.
(C) Why don't you ask them?

你覺得客人比較喜歡義大利菜還是泰國菜？
(A) 我只吃甜點。
(B) 這個可能更受歡迎。
(C) 為何不直接問他們？

正確答案為 (C)

本題為選擇疑問句，詢問客人喜歡哪一種食物。(C) 建議對方直接問他們，屬於反問回答法，最為適當。回答〈ask ＋人物〉為常見的非正面回答。(A) 試圖使用會聯想到題目食物的 dessert「甜點」，試圖誤導，但答非所問；(B) 的回答也是答非所問。

Test 04

11. `4_11` 英式男聲 / 美式男聲

Can you call to see if the accounts office received the report we sent?
(A) In the phone directory.
(B) Here's Tran's office.
(C) I'll do it right away.

你可以打電話給會計事務所確認是否收到我們寄送的報告書嗎？
(A) 在電話簿上。
(B) 這裡是特蘭辦公室。
(C) 我馬上去做。

正確答案為 (C)

本題以問句要求對方確認，(C) 採肯定答覆，表示馬上去做，故為最適當的回答。(A) 適合回應詢問地點的問句；(B) 重複使用題目的 office，為陷阱選項。

字彙 **accounts office** 會計事務所 　**phone directory** 電話簿

12. `4_12` 美式男聲 / 美式女聲

How late will you be working at the office today?
(A) Tomorrow morning instead.
(B) I plan to leave within a couple of hours.
(C) As long as I finish on time.

你今天會在辦公室工作到多晚？
(A) 改成明天上午。
(B) 我預計於 2 小時內離開。
(C) 只要能準時完成。

正確答案為 (B)

本題為 How late 開頭的問句，詢問對方預計工作到多晚。(B) 明確回答時間，為正確答案。(A) 答非所問。值得留意的是，請勿將此句誤解成「我要工作到明天上午（until tomorrow morning）」。(C) 提出條件，不適合用來回答本題問句。

字彙 **instead** 作為替代 　**as long as** 只要

13. `4_13` 英式男聲 / 美式女聲

Whose turn is it to clean the staff lounge?
(A) Rachael already placed that order.
(B) The company's new internship program.
(C) I'll have to check the schedule.

輪到誰打掃員工休息室？
(A) 瑞秋已經下訂單了。
(B) 公司新的實習課程。
(C) 我需要確認一下排班表。

正確答案為 (C)

本題為 Whose 開頭的問句，詢問輪到哪個人。(C) **採間接回答**，回應要先確認排班表，為最適當的回答。Whose 問句可以用第三者的名字作為回應，(A) 選項雖回答姓名，但內容與題目無關；(B) 用與題目 staff 有關的 internship「實習」試圖造成誤導。

字彙 **turn** 依次、照順序 　**staff lounge** 員工休息室 　**place the order** 下單、購買

14. `4_14` 美式女聲 / 美式男聲

You discussed the marketing campaign with the supervisor, didn't you?
(A) Some of the new employees.
(B) I'm meeting with him later this afternoon.
(C) Certainly, whenever you'd like.

你和主管討論過促銷活動一事，對吧？
(A) 幾名新進員工。
(B) 我今天下午會和他碰面。
(C) 當然，看你何時方便。

正確答案為 (B)

本題為附加問句，向對方確認是否有跟主管討論。答案選 (B)，說明預計下午和主管碰面討論。(A) 使用與題目 supervisor 有關的 employees 作為誤導；(C) 先回答 Certainly. 表示已經討論過，但是後方內容與題目無關，因此並非答案。

字彙 **supervisor** 主管、監督人

15. 4_15 美式女聲 / 英式男聲

Who'll be representing our firm at the seminar?
(A) With a marketing manager.
(B) Ms. Brenner will.
(C) That's a good idea.

誰即將代表我們公司出席研討會？
(A) 和行銷經理一起。
(B) 布倫納小姐將出席。
(C) 這個點子不錯。

正確答案為 (B)

本題為 Who 開頭的問句，詢問誰是代表。(B) 提出第三者的名字，表示由此人代表，故為最適當的回答。(A) 提到職稱，乍看像是 Who 問句的答案。但是當中並未明確提到誰和經理一起，因此並不適合；(C) 適合回應建議，不適合作為 wh 問句的回答。

字彙　**represent** 代表

16. 4_16 美式男聲 / 英式男聲

Will anyone accompany you to the convention, or are you going on your own?
(A) Yes, until I start my own company.
(B) A colleague is coming along with me.
(C) It's an amazing invention.

有人跟你一起參加會議嗎？還是你自己一個人去？
(A) 對，直到我的公司開業為止。
(B) 我同事會跟我一起去。
(C) 這是很棒的發明。

正確答案為 (B)

本題為選擇疑問句，詢問對方是獨自一人、還是和別人一起參加會議。(B) 表示要和同事一起去，為最適當的回答。(A) 提到時間點，答非所問；(C) **使用與 convention 的發音相似的** invention 讓人產生混淆，回答與題目毫無關聯。

字彙　**convention** 會議　**accompany** 陪同、同行　**on one's own** 獨自、獨立地　**invention** 發明

17. 4_17 美式男聲 / 美式女聲

Why didn't you visit our plant in Cyprus?
(A) To visit with my nephew.
(B) We ran out of time.
(C) It went very well.

為何你不去參觀塞普勒斯的工廠？
(A) 為了去拜訪我的姪子。
(B) 我們的時間不夠。
(C) 一切進展得很順利。

正確答案為 (B)

本題為 Why 開頭的問句，詢問對方不參觀工廠的原因。(B) 說他們沒有時間，為最適當的回答。(A) 使用 to 不定詞表示原因，但內容與題目無關。且重複使用題目句中的 visit，為陷阱選項；(C) 適合回應以 How 開頭、詢問進展狀況的問句。

字彙　**nephew** 姪子、外甥　**run out of** 用完、耗盡　**go well** 進展順利

18. 4_18 英式男聲 / 美式女聲

We aren't allowed to park here, are we?
(A) Not at this time of day.
(B) It seems extremely long.
(C) The park used to be there.

我們不能把車停在這裡，對吧？
(A) 這個時段不能停車。
(B) 似乎非常長。
(C) 那裡以前是公園。

正確答案為 (A)

本題為附加問句，向對方確認是否可以停車。(A) 表示現在不能停車，為最適當的回答。(B) 答非所問；(C) **故意使用一字多義的詞彙 park 讓人產生混淆**。題目的 park 指「停車」，選項的 park 指「公園」，兩者沒有關聯，請特別留意。

字彙　**extremely** 極端地、極其

Test 04

19. 4_19 美式女聲 / 美式男聲

When will the new safety guidelines take effect?
(A) Very safe, in my opinion.
(B) Not according to the new tour guide.
(C) The date hasn't been announced yet.

新的安全方針何時開始實施？
(A) 我認為非常安全。
(B) 不符合新的旅遊指南。
(C) 尚未公布日期。

正確答案為 (C)

本題為 When 開頭的問句，詢問實施的時間點。(C) 採間接回答的方式，表示還沒決定好日期，為最適當的回答。(A) 故意使用題目中 safety 的字首 safe，(B) 則使用與題目 guidelines 相似的 guide，讓人產生混淆，皆非答案。

 字彙　**take effect** 生效、實施　　**in one's opinion** 某人覺得　　**guideline** 方針、規範

20. 4_20 美式女聲 / 英式男聲

I hope the board meeting doesn't run late.
(A) It usually doesn't.
(B) He runs in the evening on most days.
(C) I was there until the end.

我希望董事會會議不要開到太晚。
(A) 通常不會開到太晚。
(B) 他大多會在傍晚跑步。
(C) 我在那裡待到結束。

正確答案為 (A)

本題為直述句，表示希望董事會會議不會開到太晚。(A) 採肯定回答，表示通常不會發生這樣的事，為最適當的回答。(B) 使用同音異義字 run 讓人產生混淆，題目的 run 指「進行」，選項的 run 則是指「跑步」；(C) 使用 the end，僅與題目句的 late 有所關聯，不能作為答案。

字彙　**board meeting** 董事會會議　　**run** 跑步；經營、進行　　**on most days** 大多時候、一般而言

21. 4_21 英式男聲 / 美式男聲

Didn't Mr. Palo make a copy of the sales report for the staff?
(A) Sales were higher than expected.
(B) He's buying a lot of stuff.
(C) No, I'm afraid we have to share.

帕洛先生沒有影印銷售報告給員工嗎？
(A) 銷售量高於預期。
(B) 他要買很多東西。
(C) 沒有，我們恐怕得共用。

正確答案為 (C)

本題為否定疑問句，詢問第三者是否有幫員工影印資料。(C) 回答要共用，表示沒有影印足夠的量，故為最適當的回答。(A) 重複使用題目句中的 sales，並非答案；(B) **stuff 與題目句中 staff 的發音相似**，並使用同樣的主詞讓人產生混淆，但內容與題目毫無關聯。

 字彙　**stuff** [stʌf] 東西、物品

22. 4_22 美式男聲 / 美式女聲

Has the board of directors reviewed the contract yet?
(A) Yes, I saw it last night.
(B) I'll have them contact you right away.
(C) They'll discuss it tomorrow.

董事會已經看過合約內容了嗎？
(A) 是，昨晚我有看到。
(B) 我馬上請他們聯絡你。
(C) 他們預計明天討論。

正確答案為 (C)

本題詢問董事會是否已經研究過合約。**(C) 表示預計明天討論，等於尚未研究，是間接回應**，為最適當的回答。(A) 回答 Yes 表示已經研究過，但是後方句子中的主詞並不正確；(B) 使用了和題目句 contract「合約」發音相似的字 contact「聯絡」，請勿被誤導。

字彙　**review** 查看、檢閱

23. 4_23 英式男聲 / 美式女聲

I heard that Steve is being promoted next month.
(A) Yes, his secretary said so.
(B) He should be proud of you.
(C) No, he didn't do it.

我聽說史提夫下個月會升官。
(A) 對，他的祕書有說過。
(B) 他一定會為你感到驕傲。
(C) 不，他沒有做過。

正確答案為 (A)

本題以直述句告知對方第三者升遷的消息。(A) 回答第三者的祕書曾說過，表示同意這句話，為最適當的回答。(B) 使用 be proud of，但這句子應該是為 Steve 感到驕傲比較合理，並非答案；(C) 回答 No，表示那個人沒有獲得升遷，但是後方補充說明的內容與題目句無關，因此不能作為答案。

> 字彙　**promote** 升遷；促銷

24. 4_24 美式女聲 / 美式男聲

When do you think we should start preparing presentation slides?
(A) I'll be in the office then.
(B) By next Thursday, at the latest.
(C) We already have enough materials.

你覺得我們應該要何時開始著手作簡報？
(A) 到時候我會在辦公室裡。
(B) 最晚在下週四以前。
(C) 我們已有充分的資料。

正確答案為 (B)

本題為 When 開頭的問句，詢問開始準備的時間，回答某時間前會做的 (B) 是答案，〈by + 時間〉指「～時間之前」。(A) 適合回答 Where 開頭的問句；(C) 使用與題目句 presentation 有關的 materials，但整句話答非所問。

> 字彙　**slide** 投影片　　**at the latest** 最晚　　**material** 資料、材料

25. 4_25 美式女聲 / 英式男聲

We've run out of envelopes.
(A) I'll get some more letters.
(B) Have you look in the stationery cabinet?
(C) You should do some exercise.

我們的信封用完了。
(A) 我再去拿一些信。
(B) 你確認過文具櫃了嗎？
(C) 你應該做一些運動。

正確答案為 (B)

本題為直述句，告知對方沒有信封一事。(B) 採反問方式，詢問對方是否確認過放置信封的地方，故為最適當的回答。(A) 使用 letters 讓人產生混淆，僅與題目句中的 envelopes 有所關聯；(C) 使用 exercise 讓人產生混淆，僅與題目句中的 run 有所關聯，不能作為答案。

> 字彙　**envelope** 信封　　**stationery** 文具

26. 4_26 英式男聲 / 美式男聲

How's the discussion coming along?
(A) It'll be finished shortly.
(B) We'll talk about it later.
(C) They've been waiting a long time.

討論進行得如何？
(A) 很快就會結束。
(B) 我們打算稍晚再談。
(C) 他們等了很長一段時間。

正確答案為 (A)

本題為 How 開頭的問句，詢問討論的進展狀況。(A) 表示很快就結束，為最適當的回答。(B) 使用 talk 讓人產生混淆，僅與題目句中的 discussion 有關。(C) long 與題目句中 along 的發音相似，為常見的答題陷阱。

> 字彙　**come along** 發展　　**shortly** 很快地

Test 04

27. `4_27` 美式男聲 / 美式女聲

Shouldn't you be attending the management workshop this afternoon?
(A) I was told to work on this analysis instead.
(B) Yes, I've been there last night.
(C) It's in Meeting Room 102.

你不是應該要參加今天下午的管理研討會？
(A) 我先前被告知要改做分析工作。
(B) 對，我昨晚一直在那裡。
(C) 在 102 會議室。

正確答案為 (A)

本題為否定疑問句，確認對方是否會參加研討會。(A) 表示他被告知不用參加，並説明不參加的理由，為最適當的回答。(B) 回答 Yes 表示會參加，但是後方説明與題目無關；(C) 使用 Meeting Room 讓人產生混淆，僅與題目句中的 workshop 有所關聯。

> **字彙** **management** 管理　**be told to** 被告知　**analysis** 分析

28. `4_28` 英式男聲 / 美式女聲

What was your hotel like in Milan?
(A) Sure, I made a reservation.
(B) Sounds like a good plan.
(C) The rooms were tidy and spacious.

你在米蘭住的飯店如何？
(A) 當然，我預約好了。
(B) 聽起來是個不錯的計畫。
(C) 房間乾淨又寬敞。

正確答案為 (C)

本題為 What 開頭的問句，詢問對方對飯店的感想。(C) 描述飯店房間，故為正確答案。**wh 問句不能使用 Yes 或 No 回答**，(A) 的 sure 表示肯定之意，因此不能作為答案。(B) 適合回答詢問建議的問句。

> **字彙** **tidy** 整潔、整齊的　**spacious** 寬敞的

29. `4_29` 美式女聲 / 美式男聲

Did the camera you bought include batteries?
(A) No, they were extra.
(B) I'll take them, thank you.
(C) Yes, because it was full.

你買的相機有附電池嗎？
(A) 沒有，要另外購買。
(B) 我買了，謝謝。
(C) 有，因為已經充滿了。

正確答案為 (A)

本題詢問對方買的相機是否有附電池。(A) 提到要另外花錢買，故為最適當的回答。(B) 買東西時經常會用到此句。但是本題是針對已經購買的東西提問，此回答答非所問；(C) Yes 表示有附電池，但是後方回應與題目無關。

> **字彙** **extra** 額外的、另外收費的

30. `4_30` 美式女聲 / 英式男聲

Were you on vacation last week?
(A) I'll be back on Monday.
(B) I went up to Castalian Spring.
(C) I'll make sure to be on time.

你上週去度假了？
(A) 我下週一回來。
(B) 我去了希臘聖泉。
(C) 我一定會準時到。

正確答案為 (B)

本題詢問對方上週是否去度假。(B) 回答去了特定地點，為最適當的回答。(A) **時態與題目句不一致**，不能作為答案；(C) 的回答答非所問。

> **字彙** **Castalian Spring** 希臘聖泉　**on time** 準時

31. 4_31 英式男聲 / 美式男聲

Where did Mr. Williams say the training would be held?
(A) There are enough seats for everyone.
(B) Anytime would be great with me.
(C) Hasn't it been postponed until tomorrow?

威廉斯先生說訓練在哪裡舉行？
(A) 座位足以容納所有的人。
(B) 任何時間我都可以。
(C) 不是延到明天了嗎？

正確答案為 (C)

本題為 Where 開頭的問句，詢問訓練的地點。(C) 反問對方不是延期了嗎，自然延續對話，故為正確答案。此處以時間點 tomorrow 表示原因，乍看之下像是回覆 When 問句的內容，請特別留意。(A) 提到座位的內容、(B) 說明有空的時間，皆與題目內容無關。

字彙　**postpone** 延期、推遲

4_32-34 英式男聲 / 美式女聲

Questions 32-34 refer to the following conversation.

M: Hello. Can I speak to Ernest Ferrel?

W: I'm afraid he is not in at the moment. He should be here later on this afternoon. Can I take a message and ask who is calling, please?

M: Yes, this is Andy Hunt from City Weekly Deliveries. I sent Mr. Ferrel an e-mail last night regarding changes that need to be made to the clients' delivery list. I've just received the updated version from him in the mail, but three new clients still haven't been added to it.

W: Oh, I'm sorry to hear that, Mr. Hunt. I'll let Ernest know as soon as possible and ask him to call you back.

問題 32-34 題參考以下對話。

男：您好，我想找歐內斯特費瑞爾。

女：㉜ 抱歉，他現在不在位子上，下午才會進來。您要留言給他嗎？請問您尊姓大名？

男：好的，我是城市週刊快遞的安迪亨特。我昨晚寄了一封電子郵件給費瑞爾先生，內容是關於客戶配送清單需要更動的事項。㉝ 稍早我收到他回覆給我的最新版本，但是清單上遺漏了 3 名新客戶。

女：噢，我對此感到遺憾，亨特先生。㉞ 我會盡快告知歐內斯特，並請他回電給您。

字彙 **regarding** 關於 **client** 客戶 **deliver** 遞送 **updated version** 最新版本

32. Who most likely is the woman?　　女子最有可能是誰？
(A) An instructor　　(A) 教師
(B) A customer　　(B) 顧客
(C) A personal assistant　　**(C) 私人祕書**
(D) A delivery person　　(D) 送貨員

正確答案為 **(C)**

〈確認基本資訊─職業〉
本題詢問說話者的職業，因此請從對話開頭找出線索。男子想要跟特定人士通話，女子告知對方此人不在位子上，以及方便通話的時間，可以由此推測出女子為特定人士的祕書，因此答案選 (C)。

字彙　instructor 講師、教師

33. According to the man, what is the problem?　　男子提出什麼問題點？
(A) A manager is not available.　　(A) 經理不在位子上。
(B) A list of customers is incomplete.　　**(B) 客戶清單不完整。**
(C) A document has been misplaced.　　(C) 找不到文件。
(D) A meeting was postponed.　　(D) 會議時間延期。

正確答案為 **(B)**

〈注意細節─問題點〉
本題詢問男子提出的問題，因此請從男子所說的話中找出線索。男子對話中段提到他收到郵件，但是當中有缺漏。(B) 採換句話說的方式，故為最適當的答案。告知歐內斯特不在位子上的人為女子，不要選 (A)。

字彙　misplace 亂放、放錯地方

34. What will the woman do next?　　女子接下來會做什麼事？
(A) Contact the relevant person　　**(A) 聯絡相關人士**
(B) Check the customer list　　(B) 確認客戶清單
(C) Search the Internet　　(C) 上網搜尋
(D) Provide an e-mail address　　(D) 提供電子郵件地址

正確答案為 **(A)**

〈注意細節─未來〉
本題針對未來提問，因此答題線索會出現在後半段對話中，並且注意使用未來式的句子。女子的最後一句對話提到她會告知歐內斯特，並請他聯絡對方，因此答案為 (A)。
換句話說　let someone know 讓某人知道 → contact a relevant person 聯絡相關人士

4_35-37　美式女聲 / 美式男聲

Questions 35-37 refer to the following conversation.

W: Hello. I'm a guest in the room 802 who checked in this morning. I'm calling because I found a leak in the bathroom. When I ran the shower, the floor got all wet. I turned it off right away but the whole area is totally soaked.

M: I apologize, ma'am. Unfortunately, our repair person has left for the day. Why don't I change your room to another? We have some vacant rooms on the second floor.

W: That would be nice. But that's six stories below where I'm staying now, and I have some heavy suitcases. Is there anyone who can help me?

M: Sure, we'll be glad to do that. I'll call someone at once.

問題 35-37 題參考以下對話。

女：您好，㊱ 我是今天上午入住 802 號房的房客，㉟ 我打電話是因為我發現浴室會漏水。我一打開蓮蓬頭，整個地板都是水。雖然我馬上關掉，但水已經淹得整間都是。

男：我向您致歉，小姐。遺憾的是我們的維修人員已經下班。請問方便幫您換到別的房間嗎？㊱ 2 樓還有一些空房。

女：太好了。㊱ 不過那跟我現在住的房間差了 6 層樓，㊲ 我有幾個行李箱特別重，請問可以派人來幫我搬嗎？

男：沒問題，我們十分樂意。我現在就派人過去。

字彙　**leak** 漏水　**leave for the day** 下班　**vacant** 空的　**story** 樓層　**at once** 馬上、立即

35. What does the woman complain about?　　女子抱怨什麼事？
(A) A water leakage　　　　　　　　　　(A) 漏水
(B) A broken electrical wire　　　　　　(B) 電線斷掉
(C) A cracked bathtub　　　　　　　　(C) 浴缸破裂
(D) A locked door　　　　　　　　　　(D) 門被鎖住

正確答案為 (A)

〈注意細節―問題點〉
本題詢問女子抱怨的內容，因此從女子開頭所說的話推測出答案。開頭女子提到她發現浴室會漏水，因此答案為 (A)。
換句話說 **a leak in a bathroom** 浴室漏水 → **a water leakage** 漏水

36. What floor is the woman staying on?　　女子住在哪一層樓？
(A) The second floor　　　　　　　　　(A) 2 樓
(B) The fourth floor　　　　　　　　　(B) 4 樓
(C) The sixth floor　　　　　　　　　(C) 6 樓
(D) The eighth floor　　　　　　　**(D) 8 樓**

正確答案為 (D)

〈注意細節―特定事項〉
女子開頭便提到自己入住的房號，可以由此得知她入住的樓層。另外，對話中段男子告訴她 2 樓還有空房，接著女子提到有 6 層樓之差，也可以由此推測出答案。綜合上述，答案要選 (D)。

37. What does the woman ask the man to do?　　女子要求男子做什麼事？
(A) Give her a wake-up call　　　　　　(A) 電話晨間叫醒服務
(B) Bring her some refreshments　　　　(B) 提供茶點
(C) Assist her with the luggage　　　**(C) 幫她搬行李**
(D) Pick up her laundry　　　　　　　(D) 取回送洗的衣物

正確答案為 (C)

〈注意細節―要求〉
本題詢問女子要求男子的事情，因此請從女子所說的話中找出答案。女子在對話最後請男子派人幫她搬行李，因此答案為 (C)。

字彙　**refreshment** 茶點、小點心　　**laundry** 待洗衣物；洗衣店

Questions 38-40 refer to the following conversation.

W: Mr. Cole, this is Naomi Grant from Walton Commercial. I noticed your résumé on a professional marketing communication, and I'm calling about an opening at our firm. We're looking for someone to help manage our design team, and your experience as both a public relations manager and instructor makes you ideal.

M: I'm certainly interested in hearing more, but unfortunately I'm in a rush. I'm conducting a workshop at the community center in just under an hour, and I'm a bit behind schedule. Can I call you back afterwards?

W: I'll be out of town on business this afternoon, so how about tomorrow instead? In the meantime, I'll email some details about the position for you to look through. It's a great opportunity for someone with your background.

問題 38-40 題參考以下對話。

女：科羅先生，我是沃爾頓商業的娜歐米格蘭特。我看了您的履歷表，注意到您擁有專業行銷溝通的能力，**38** 因此來電告知您本公司在徵才。我們正在尋找負責管理設計部門的人，而您過去曾任公關活動經理和講師，我們認為您是相當合適的人選。

男：我真的很想繼續聽妳說下去，**39** 但遺憾的是我正在趕時間。我要到社區活動中心主持一個工作坊，剩不到一個小時的時間，而我已經比預定時間晚到了。我可以稍晚再回電給妳嗎？

女：我今天下午要出差，方便改成明天通話嗎？**40** 我會將職缺的細節寄給您過目。我認為以您的資歷來說，這是一個極佳的工作機會。

字彙　**commercial**（電視或廣播）廣告　**résumé** 履歷表　**opening** 職缺　**public relations** 公關活動
in a rush 趕時間　**conduct** 帶領；執行　**behind schedule** 比預定時間晚　**afterwards** 之後
out of town 出遠門、出差　**on business** 出差　**in the meantime** 同時　**look through** 瀏覽

38. What is the woman calling to discuss?　　　　女了致電討論什麼事？
　　(A) An open position　　　　　　　　　　**(A) 職缺**
　　(B) A university program　　　　　　　　　(B) 大學課程
　　(C) A marketing proposal　　　　　　　　　(C) 行銷提案
　　(D) A fashion magazine　　　　　　　　　　(D) 時尚雜誌

正確答案為 (A)

〈確認基本資訊—目的〉
本題詢問來電的**目的**，因此前半段對話中會出現答題線索。第一段女子提到來電的原因為告知對方公司職缺，因此答案為 (A)。

39. What does the man tell the woman?　　　　男子告訴女子什麼事？
　　(A) He is out of town.　　　　　　　　　　(A) 他人在外地。
　　(B) He is on another line.　　　　　　　　 (B) 他正在講電話。
　　(C) He has a flexible plan.　　　　　　　　(C) 他的計畫有彈性。
　　(D) He is in a hurry.　　　　　　　　　　**(D) 他在趕時間。**

正確答案為 (D)

〈注意細節—提及內容〉
本題詢問男子提到的內容，因此從男子所說的話推測出答案。男子提到他很想繼續通話，但是他的行程延誤，正在趕時間，答案為 (D)。**當對話中出現轉折語如 But、However、Unfortunately、I'm sorry、I'm afraid，後方通常會是答題重點，請留意。**
換句話說 **in a rush** 匆忙地 → **in a hurry** 匆忙地

40. What does the woman want the man to review?　　女子希望男子檢閱什麼東西？
　　(A) A detailed résumé　　　　　　　　　　(A) 詳細的履歷表
　　(B) A job description　　　　　　　　　　**(B) 職務說明**
　　(C) A business report　　　　　　　　　　(C) 商務報告
　　(D) A magazine article　　　　　　　　　　(D) 雜誌報導

正確答案為 (B)

〈注意細節—建議〉
本題的關鍵字為 review「檢視」，詢問女子希望男子做的事，請仔細聆聽女子要求男子檢閱什麼東西。女子在最後一段提到她會將職缺相關細節寄給男子，方便他檢閱，因此答案為 (B)。
換句話說 **details about the position** 職缺相關細節 → **job description** 職務說明

Test 04

599

Questions 41-43 refer to the following conversation.

M: You have a much larger number of finance books and journals than I'd thought. In fact, I was thinking I'd actually join the library membership since I plan on moving around this area.

W: We do have a pretty extensive collection. I could sign you up right away, if you'd like. All you need to do is fill out this form and then pay a five dollar registration fee.

M: Just five dollars? Is that all? I saw an ad in a brochure indicating there is a $15 fee. I think it was something about the library membership program.

W: Oh, that's right. That's kind of like a special program. It allows you to borrow double the number of books, up to 20 at a time instead of the usual 10 under the standard card. One thing that's great about either card, though, is that it never expires.

問題 41-43 題參考以下對話。

男： ㊶ 這裡的金融書籍和期刊遠比我想像中還多。其實我在思考要不要加入圖書館會員，因為我打算搬到這一區。

女： 我們這裡擁有大量的藏書。如果你願意的話，我現在就能幫你加入會員。只要填寫這個表格，繳交 5 美元的申請費用，就可以加入了。

男： 只要 5 美元？就這樣？我看到手冊廣告上寫要 15 美元。那應該是指圖書館的某種會員制度。

女： 喔，沒錯。那算是一種比較特殊的會員制度。㊷ 普通會員一次只能借閱 10 本書，但是如果加入特殊會員，一次則能借閱 20 本。㊸ 兩種會員卡的共同優點是都沒有使用期限。

字彙　**extensive** 廣闊（廣大的）、大規模的　**sign up (for)** 報名　**fill out** 填寫　**registration fee** 報名費　**expire** 到期

41. Why is the man impressed with the library?
(A) The membership fee is free.
(B) The library is open all year round.
(C) The library's selection is broad.
(D) The library is open until late.

為何圖書館令男子印象深刻？
(A) 可以免費加入會員。
(B) 圖書館全年開放。
(C) 圖書館擁有各式各樣的藏書。
(D) 圖書館開放到很晚。

正確答案為 (C)

〈注意細節－特定事項〉
本題詢問令男子印象深刻的原因，因此請注意聆聽男子所說的話。第一段男子提到他對於圖書館擁有的藏書量感到驚訝，(C) 的描述最為適當。

字彙 **all year round** 全年無休的 **broad** 廣大的

42. How many books can the man borrow if he has a regular card?
(A) 5 books
(B) 10 books
(C) 15 books
(D) 20 books

若男子持有一般會員卡，他可以借閱幾本書？
(A) 5 本書
(B) 10 本書
(C) 15 本書
(D) 20 本書

正確答案為 (B)

〈注意細節－特定事項〉
本題關鍵字為 regular card，聆聽對話時，請務必注意此詞彙。後半段對話中，女子針對圖書館的會員制度進行說明，當中提到一般會員和特殊會員的差異。持有一般會員卡者可以借閱 10 本書，因此答案選 (B)。**當選項出現數字，對話就可能會提及多個數字故意誤導，請特別留意。**

換句話說 **standard** 標準、普通的 → **regular** 普通的

43. What does the woman say is special about the library card?
(A) It requires no payment.
(B) It can be used indefinitely.
(C) It expires every 10 months.
(D) It can be replaced with an ID card.

女子提到圖書館卡片有什麼特點？
(A) 不需要支付費用。
(B) 可以無限期使用。
(C) 期限為 10 個月。
(D) 可以使用身分證代替。

正確答案為 (B)

〈注意細節－提及內容〉
本題關鍵字為 library card，請特別留意女子所說的話。最後一段女子提到圖書館發行的兩種卡片都沒有使用期限，因此答案為 (B)。

換句話說 **never expire** 不會到期 → **indefinitely** 無限期

Questions 44-46 refer to the following conversation.

W: Jason, can you check the number of attendees we'll have tomorrow? And find out if the local brasserie prepared the appropriate number of croissants and beverages.

M: Julie told me that she's already taken care of it.

W: That's wonderful. Do you know how many croissants she's ordered exactly?

M: Thirty, I heard, because we are expecting 25 guests.

W: I'm concerned that won't be enough. I've heard that about 12 more guests have registered because the managing director has been invited as one of the presenters.

M: Really? I'll check the list of attendees, and alter the order accordingly. Do you want me to arrange the delivery? I'm sure the brasserie will provide us the delivery service.

問題 44-46 題參考以下對話。

女： 傑森，⑭ 你可以幫我確認明天的出席人數嗎？順便也確認一下當地餐館是否準備好與人數相符的可頌麵包和飲料。

男： 茱莉跟我説她已經都處理好了。

女： 太好了。那你知道她訂了多少個可頌麵包嗎？

男： 聽説是 30 個，因為預計會有 25 名賓客前來。

女： ⑮ 我很擔心數量會不夠。聽説還有多 12 名賓客報名，因為總經理受邀擔任其中一名報告人。

男： 真的嗎？那我再確認一遍出席者名單，並依照人數修改訂購數量。⑯ 妳覺得我要改成外送嗎？我相信餐館會提供外送服務。

字彙 **attendee** 出席者　**brasserie** [ˋbræsərɪ] 小餐館　**croissant** 可頌　**register** 登記、紀錄　**presenter** 上台報告人　**alter** 改變　**accordingly** 相應地　**arrange** 安排　**delivery** 外送

44. What are the speakers discussing?
(A) The number of participants
(B) A registration fee
(C) Enrollment in a course
(D) The process of a survey

説話者在討論什麼事？
(A) 參加人數
(B) 報名費
(C) 報名課程
(D) 調查過程

正確答案為 **(A)**

〈確認基本資訊―主旨〉
本題詢問對話主旨，因此請留意對話開頭。女子第一句話要求男子確認出席人數，因此答案為 (A)。

換句話說 **attendee** 出席者 → **participant** 參加者

字彙 **enrollment** 註冊、入學

45. What information does the woman give the man?
(A) A location of a brasserie
(B) Details of the delivery
(C) An updated number of guests
(D) The name of managing director

女子提供男子什麼資訊？
(A) 餐館位置
(B) 外送細節
(C) 更新賓客人數
(D) 總經理名字

正確答案為 **(C)**

〈注意細節―特定事項〉
本題詢問女子告知男子的資訊，因此請從女子所説的話推測出答案。女子在對話中段提到因為賓客人數增加，她擔心食物數量會不夠，因此答案為 (C)。

46. What does the man ask the woman about?
(A) If the woman has spoken with the managing director
(B) Whether food will be delivered
(C) Whether the woman has gotten any messages
(D) If the woman contacted a guest

男子向女子詢問什麼事？
(A) 女子是否與董事總經理談話
(B) 是否要外送食物
(C) 女子是否有收到訊息
(D) 女子是否有聯絡賓客

正確答案為 **(B)**

〈注意細節―提問〉
請特別留意男子向女子提問的內容。對話最後男子詢問女子是否要請餐館外送食物，因此答案為 (B)。

Test 04

4_47-49 | 美式女聲 / 美式男聲 / 英式男聲

Questions 47-49 refer to the following conversation with three speakers.

W: I'm so pleased that our sales have doubled since our store was featured in the local newspaper.

M1: That's right, Jessica. But on the other hand, our workload has increased too because we're shorthanded.

M2: I agree. I wonder if we can afford to hire a few more employees.

M1: I believe that we can, Frank. How about putting it on our next meeting's agenda?

W: Well, before that, let me talk directly to the regional manager for permission.

M2: As soon as we get permission, I'll contact Steve to arrange job advertisements to be sent out.

問題 47-49 題參考以下三人對話。

女： 自從我們商店被地方報紙大幅報導後，銷售量增加了兩倍，這讓我非常開心。

男1： 沒錯，潔西卡。 **47** 但是從另一個角度來看，人手不足導致我們的工作量大增。

男2： 我同意你的看法。我想知道我們能否再多雇用幾名員工。

男1： 我想應該沒問題，法蘭克。何不把這件事放進下次的會議議程中？

女： 嗯， **48** 在此之前，我得先徵求地區經理的同意。

男2： 一旦獲得同意， **49** 我就聯絡史提夫，請他準備刊登徵才廣告。

字彙 **be featured in** 刊登～為特集　**on the other hand** 另一方面　**workload** 工作量　**shorthanded** 人手不足的
can afford to 能負擔～　**agenda** 議程　**permission** 許可、允許　**as soon as** 一旦

47. What are the speakers concerned about?
　(A) The size of the workforce
　(B) New regulations
　(C) The newspaper subscription
　(D) The store location

說話者擔心什麼事？
　(A) 人力規模
　(B) 新規定
　(C) 訂閱費用
　(D) 商店位置

正確答案為 (A)

〈注意細節―特定事項〉

說話者們擔心的事通常會出現在前半段對話中，並與主旨相扣，因此請留意前半段對話的內容。對話開頭，女子提到她對於銷售量增加感到開心，接著男子表示他認同銷售量增加一事，但是員工數量不足導致工作量大增，答案選 (A)。

> 字彙　**workforce** 人力　**regulation** 規定　**subscription** 訂閱（費用）

48. What does the woman offer to do?
　(A) Contact an executive
　(B) Place an order
　(C) Speak with a customer
　(D) Give a raise

女子主動提出做什麼事？
　(A) 聯絡主管
　(B) 下訂單
　(C) 和客人談話
　(D) 加薪

正確答案為 (A)

〈注意細節―主動提出〉

本題詢問女子主動提出做什麼事，因此從女子所說的話中找出答題線索。最後一段女子提到她要直接詢問經理取得同意，因此 (A) 為最適當的答案。

換句話說 **regional manager** 地區經理 → **executive** 主管

49. Why will Frank contact Steve?
　(A) To correct an error
　(B) To set up a meeting
　(C) To create an advertisement
　(D) To conduct an interview

為何法蘭克要聯絡史提夫？
　(A) 為了修正錯誤
　(B) 為了安排會議
　(C) 為了製作廣告
　(D) 為了進行面試

正確答案為 (C)

〈注意細節―特定事項〉

對話中段，男子 2 提出建議，接著男子 1 在回答中叫他法蘭克，表示男子 2 為法蘭克。而後在對話最後，男子 2 提到他會聯絡史提夫，請他準備徵才廣告，因此答案要選 (C)。**三人對話經常會提及數個人名，若題目的關鍵字為人名時，請務必要確認該人名為該對話中的人物、還是對話之外的第三者。**

Test 04

4_50-52 美式女聲 / 英式男聲

Questions 50-52 refer to the following conversation.

W: Hey, Oliver, I'm glad you're finally here. I can't access the Internet, and I have an e-mail I need to send by 2 o'clock. Could you please help me out?

M: Certainly. Ashley, let me have a look. Ah, you're connected to the wrong network. You have to use the one named "real-time-connection."

W: So that's all! It kept asking for a password, and I couldn't figure out why, since the office computers all connect automatically. How can I fix it?

M: Do you see this icon? Click on that, and then click on "real-time-connection." That's all you should do. You're now online.

問題 50-52 題參考以下對話。

女：終於找到你了，奧力佛。(50) 我連不上網路，可是我得在 2 點以前寄出一封郵件，你可以幫幫我嗎？

男：沒問題，艾許莉，我來看看。噢，(51) (52) 妳連錯網路了。妳應該要連接「即時連線」這個名稱。

女：原來如此！我不懂它為什麼要一直問我密碼，辦公室的電腦明明都會自動連線。我該怎麼搞定它？

男：妳看到這個圖示了嗎？點選圖示後，再選取「即時連線」就可以了，現在就連上網了。

字彙　**access** 存取　**figure out** 想出、理解　**automatically** 自動地　**So that's all.** 原來如此。

50. What is the man asked to do?
(A) Provide a new password
(B) Help writing an e-mail
(C) Assist with getting online
(D) Analyze some data

男子被要求做什麼事？
(A) 提供新的密碼
(B) 協助撰寫郵件
(C) 幫忙連接網路
(D) 分析一些數據

正確答案為 (C)

〈注意細節—要求〉
本題詢問男子被要求什麼事，因此請從女子所說的話中找出答題線索。女子在第一句話中提出無法連線的問題，並請求對方幫忙，因此答案為 (C)。請特別留意，當題目使用被動語態時，答案並不是出現在題目主詞所說的話，而是出現在另一方所說的話。

51. What was the issue?
(A) The computer was broken.
(B) The password had been changed.
(C) The e-mail address was wrong.
(D) The connection was wrong.

發生了什麼問題？
(A) 電腦故障。
(B) 密碼有所更動。
(C) 電子郵件地址有誤。
(D) 連線有問題。

正確答案為 (D)

〈注意細節—問題點〉
女子向男子請求協助，男子向她說明因為連錯網路才無法順利連線，因此答案要選 (D)。

字彙 **issue** 議題

52. Why does the woman say, "So that's all!"?
(A) She found an e-mail address.
(B) She understood the problem.
(C) She fixed the laptop.
(D) She had to restart the computer.

為何女子會說「原來如此！」？
(A) 她找到電子郵件地址。
(B) 她找出問題所在。
(C) 她修好了筆電。
(D) 她得重新啟動電腦。

正確答案為 (B)

〈關鍵句—說話者意圖〉
碰到詢問關鍵句的說話者意圖時，務必仔細聆聽關鍵句的前後句。關鍵句前面一句，男子告知女子引發問題的原因，接著女子說出該句話，並表示辦公室的電腦都會自動連線，所以自己並沒有發現問題。由此可以得知女子聽完男子的話後，便明白問題的起因，因此答案為 (B)。

Test 04

Questions 53-55 refer to the following conversation.

M: How is the new Brewer Street property coming along?

W: Well, everything is going okay. The electricians should finish updating the wiring in three of the condominiums by Wednesday. After that, they'll need painting. You called the painters, right?

M: Yeah, they're coming next week on Tuesday. I have the carpet layers scheduled to come in on the following Thursday. That should be enough time for the paint to dry. Have all of the units been rented?

W: Renters have signed contracts for five of them. The other three are still listed on our Web site, but I'm also going to place an ad all next week in the *Sun Daily*.

問題 53-55 題參考以下對話。

男： 新的布魯爾街房屋目前進展如何？

女： 一切都很順利。㊾ 電力工程人員會在週三前完成其中 3 間套房的線路更新作業。接著再進行粉刷。你聯絡好油漆工人了吧？

男： ㊿ 對，他們下週二會過來。我請地毯安裝工人下週四再來，中間預留的時間應該足以讓油漆變乾。所有房間都租出去了嗎？

女： 其中 5 間房已經跟房客簽約了，還有 3 間仍刊登在我們的網站上。㊿ 不過我打算下週在〈太陽日報〉上刊登廣告。

字彙 **property** 財產、房地產　**electrician** 電工技師　**condominium** 公寓　**carpet layer** 舖設地毯人員
unit（公寓大樓的）單間套房　**renter** 房客、承租人

53. What work will be finished by Wednesday?　　週二前將會完成什麼工作？
(A) Wall painting　　(A) 牆壁粉刷
(B) A floor plan　　(B) 平面圖
(C) Electrical construction　　**(C) 電路施工**
(D) A promotional campaign　　(D) 宣傳活動

正確答案為 (C)

〈注意細節一特定事項〉
本題關鍵字為 Wednesday，請注意聆聽出現該詞彙的句子。女子的第一句中提到電力工程人員會在週三前完成公寓的線路更新作業，因此答案為 (C)。

換句話說 updating the wiring 線路更新作業 → electrical construction 電路施工

字彙　**floor plan** 平面圖

54. What does the man say about the painting?　　針對粉刷工作，男子提到什麼？
(A) The cost is reasonable.　　(A) 價錢合理。
(B) The work takes a long time.　　(B) 工作十分耗時。
(C) The painters delayed the schedule.　　(C) 油漆工人延宕時程。
(D) The work will commence next Tuesday.　　**(D) 預計於下週二開始進行。**

正確答案為 (D)

〈注意細節一提及內容〉
請從男子的對話中，找出提及關鍵字 paining 的片段。女子向男子詢問是否聯絡好油漆工人，男子回答下週二油漆工人會過來，因此答案要選 (D)。男子在第二句對話有提到粉刷油漆後需要足夠的時間變乾，所以請地毯安裝人員週四再過來。請注意千萬不要因而判定粉刷工作相當耗時，而誤選成 (B)。

字彙　**commence** 開始

55. How does the woman say she will find more tenants?　　女子提到她將如何找到更多房客？
(A) By passing out leaflets　　(A) 發傳單
(B) By designing a new Web site　　(B) 設計新的網站
(C) By advertising in a newspaper　　**(C) 在報紙上刊登廣告**
(D) By talking to other tenants　　(D) 告知其他房客

正確答案為 (C)

〈注意細節一提及內容〉
請從女子的對話中找出提及關鍵字 tenants 的片段。女子在最後的對話中提到她和數名房客簽約，並計劃於下週刊登廣告在 *Sun Daily*〈太陽日報〉上，因此答案為 (C)。

字彙　**tenant** 房客、承租人　　**pass out** 分發　　**leaflet** 傳單

4_56-58 美式女聲 / 英式男聲

Questions 56-58 refer to the following conversation.

W: Kevin, I tried to get you a Monday flight to Bangkok, but there are no seats on any flights from Boston, even in first class. You'll either have to leave on Thursday if you want to fly direct, or you can depart on Tuesday afternoon with a five-hour layover in San Diego.

M: I can't leave on Thursday. I need to lead a workshop on Friday morning Bangkok time, and that wouldn't get me there by then.

W: You are right. You'll lose 11 hours just with the time change, plus you'll be exhausted when you finally get there.

M: Well, I hate stopovers but I don't see any other alternative. I guess I'll have to take the Tuesday flight.

問題 56-58 題參考以下對話。

女： 凱文，我原本要幫你預訂週一飛往曼谷的班機，56 但是從波士頓出發的班機都沒有位子了，甚至連頭等艙也是。如果你要直飛的班機，得改成週四出發，或是週二下午出發，在聖地牙哥停留 5 小時轉機。

男： 57 我沒辦法等到週四才出發。我在曼谷時間的週五上午得主持一個研討會，如果週四出發的話，來不及在時間內抵達。

女： 你說得對，因為時差關係，你會少掉 11 個小時。加上你飛到那裡後一定會相當疲憊。

男： 嗯，雖然我很討厭轉機，但看來沒有其他替代方案了。58 我想我得搭乘週二的班機。

 字彙 **fly direct**（班機）直飛的　　**depart** 離開、出發　　**layover** 飛行中途短暫停留　　**exhausted** 精疲力竭的
stopover 飛行中途停留　　**alternative** 替代方案

56. Which city does the man probably work in?　　　　男子可能在哪一個城市工作？
(A) Bangkok　　　　　　　　　　　　　　　　(A) 曼谷
(B) Boston　　　　　　　　　　　　　　　　**(B) 波士頓**
(C) San Diego　　　　　　　　　　　　　　　(C) 聖地牙哥
(D) Los Angeles　　　　　　　　　　　　　　(D) 洛杉磯

正確答案為 **(B)**

〈注意細節―特定事項〉
開頭女子告知男子預訂機票一事，當中提到從波士頓出發的班機都沒有位子了，因此答案選 (B)。**當選項列出特定地點、時間等簡短的回答內容時，通常對話中會出現好幾個同性質的陷阱，因此請務必仔細聆聽對話中提及各選項詞彙的內容，以免誤選。**對話提到曼谷為目的地、聖地牙哥為轉機停留的地方。

57. Why can't the man leave on Thursday?　　　　為何男子無法於週四出發？
(A) He has other plans.　　　　　　　　　　(A) 他有其他計畫。
(B) He can't afford the price.　　　　　　　(B) 他無法負擔費用。
(C) He doesn't like a layover.　　　　　　　(C) 他不喜歡轉機。
(D) He would arrive too late.　　　　　　**(D) 他會太晚抵達。**

正確答案為 **(D)**

〈注意細節―特定事項〉
本題關鍵字為 Thursday，請特別留意男子提到該詞彙的片段。男子在對話中段提到週五要在曼谷開研討會，週四才出發會來不及，因此 (D) 為最適當的答案。

58. What decision does the man make?　　　　男子做了什麼決定？
(A) To postpone his workshop　　　　　　(A) 延後研討會時間
(B) To pay for first class　　　　　　　　　(B) 購買頭等艙
(C) To depart on Tuesday　　　　　　　**(C) 於週二出發**
(D) To arrive on Friday　　　　　　　　　(D) 於週五抵達

正確答案為 **(C)**

〈注意細節―特定事項〉
本題詢問男子所做的決定，因此要從男子的對話中推測答案。男子在最後提到由於沒有其他方案，他只好選擇搭乘週二的班機，因此答案為 (C)。

Test 04

Questions 59-61 refer to the following conversation.

W: Hello, Dr. Leon's office. How can I help you?

M: Hi. My name is Timothy Johnson, and I have an appointment with Dr. Leon tomorrow at 3 P.M., but unfortunately something has come up and I won't be able to make it by then. Does Dr. Leon have anything else open — say later tomorrow or the next day?

W: Well, let me check his schedule. It looks like he's fully booked tomorrow, and the next day is Saturday, so he doesn't work. Oh, wait! It looks like he has an opening at five-twenty tomorrow. Does it work for you?

M: Certainly, yes. That works for me. I could make it by then. Thanks for your help.

W: See you tomorrow, Mr. Johnson.

問題 **59-61** 題參考以下對話。

女：喂，這裡是里昂診所，請問需要什麼幫忙？

男：妳好，我是帝莫西強森。59 我原本預約明天下午 3 點看診，但不幸我臨時有事，沒辦法過去。請問里昂醫生是否有其他看診時段呢？比方說明天稍晚或者後天？

女：好的，我確認一下時間表。60 61 明天的預約全滿，接著隔天是週六，他沒有看診。噢，等等！61 明天 5 點 20 分還有空檔，那個時間你方便嗎？

男：沒問題，那個時間我可以。我會準時抵達，感謝妳的幫忙。

女：那麼明天見，強森先生。

字彙 **say**（口）假設、舉例來說

59. What is the purpose of the man's call?
(A) To reschedule a visit
(B) To change his physician
(C) To get a prescription
(D) To make an appointment

男子打電話的目的為何？
(A) 更改拜訪時間
(B) 更換醫生
(C) 取得處方簽
(D) 預約

正確答案為 **(A)**

〈確認基本資訊—目的〉
本題詢問打電話的目的，前半段對話中通常會出現答題線索。女子接了電話後，向對方簡單問候，接著男子說明無法配合原本約診的時間，因此答案為 (A)。

字彙　　**reschedule** 更改行程　　**physician**（內科）醫生　　**prescription** 處方簽

60. What does the woman mean when she says, "the next day is Saturday"?
(A) Dr. Leon usually works on weekends.
(B) The office is closed on weekends.
(C) Saturday is available for a reservation.
(D) Mr. Johnson is fully booked on Saturday.

女子說「隔天是週六」是什麼意思？
(A) 里昂醫生週末通常會工作。
(B) 診所週末休息。
(C) 週六可以預約。
(D) 強森先生週六預約全滿。

正確答案為 **(B)**

〈關鍵句—說話者意圖〉
須仔細聆聽關鍵句的前後文內容掌握女子的意圖。對話中段男子詢問預約是否能改成明天或後天，接著女子提到明天的預約全滿，隔天又是週六，醫生沒有看診，因此答案為 (B)。

61. On what day will the man visit the office?
(A) Tuesday
(B) Thursday
(C) Friday
(D) Saturday

男子將會在哪一天造訪診所？
(A) 週二
(B) 週四
(C) 週五
(D) 週六

正確答案為 **(C)**

〈注意細節—特定事項〉
第 60 題已經確認男子想更改約診時間，女子告訴他明天的預約已滿，而後天為週六沒有看診，其中便釋出了答題線索 —— 明天為週五。再來，對話中女子表示明天 5 點 20 分可以預約，男子同意這個時間前往診所，因此答案選 (C)。

4_62-64 美式女聲 / 英式男聲

Questions 62-64 refer to the following conversation and coupon.

W: Can you tell me where I can find the clothing department here? I'm looking for it because I saw an ad about a sale on skirts in a magazine.

M: It's behind the escalators, and yes, we're currently offering great savings on some items. If you'd like to stop by our customer help desk, they'll give you all sorts of coupons you can use.

W: Oh, sounds great. Thanks. I wonder if there are any coupons for skirts. There's a certain one I'd like to buy. I remember it sells for €60.

M: Of course, I know we've definitely got discounts on skirts, but I suggest you hurry. They're going pretty fast. We're down to about half of the inventory we started with before the sale.

Harvey Nichols Department Store
Clothing Department
€10.00 OFF
Any piece of clothing priced over €50
Expires Oct 19

問題 62-64 題參考以下對話和優惠券。

女： 62 請問你知道服飾專櫃在哪裡嗎？我在雜誌上看到裙子的促銷廣告，所以正在尋找該櫃位。

男： 服飾專櫃位在手扶梯後方。您說的沒錯，目前正提供部分商品的促銷優惠。63 方便的話您可以先前往客服櫃檯，索取各種優惠券使用。

女： 噢，太好了，謝謝你。不曉得有沒有裙子的優惠券，64 我想買某件裙子，印象中是 60 歐元。

男： 當然有，據我所知也有提供裙子的優惠。但我建議您動作要快一點，服飾販售速度很快，在特惠正式開始前就只剩下一半左右的存貨而已。

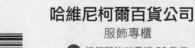

哈維尼柯爾百貨公司
服飾專櫃
64 任何服飾消費滿 50 歐元
折抵 10 歐元
有效期限 10 月 19 日

字彙 **escalator** 手扶梯 **currently** 現在、當前 **definitely** 明確、清楚地 **discount** 折扣 **inventory** 存貨清單、庫存

62. What does the woman ask the man about?
(A) The hours of operation
(B) The price of a certain item
(C) The duration of a sale
(D) The location of a section

女子向男子詢問什麼？
(A) 營業時間
(B) 特定商品的價格
(C) 優惠期間
(D) 櫃位的位置

正確答案為 **(D)**

〈注意細節—特定事項〉
女子在第一句話便詢問服飾專櫃的位置，因此答案為 (D)。

字彙 **operation** 營業、運作、操作

63. Where does the man suggest the woman go?
(A) To a staff lounge
(B) To a fitting room
(C) To a service desk
(D) To the main entrance

男子建議女子去哪裡？
(A) 員工休息室
(B) 試衣間
(C) 服務台
(D) 正門

正確答案為 **(C)**

〈注意細節—建議〉
對話中段男子建議她前往顧客服務櫃檯索取優惠券，因此答案為 (C)。
換句話說 **stop by** 順道前往 → **go** 去

64. Look at the graphic. How much would the woman have to pay for the skirt?
(A) €50
(B) €60
(C) €70
(D) €80

觀看圖表，女子買裙子應該要付多少錢？
(A) 50 歐元
(B) 60 歐元
(C) 70 歐元
(D) 80 歐元

正確答案為 **(A)**

〈注意細節—圖表相關〉
請同時確認對話提及的內容和圖表資訊，再選出答案。選項列出了價格，因此請特別留意對話中提及價格之處。女子提到她想買一件 60 歐元的裙子，符合優惠券上的條件「消費滿 50 歐元，折抵 10 歐元」，因此女子可以用 50 歐元買到原價 60 歐元的裙子，答案選 (A)。

Test 04

615

4_65-67 美式男聲 / 美式女聲

Questions 65-67 refer to the following conversation and map.

M: Hi. I've been offered a position here at Karachi Education Center next month, but I'd like to take a look around the facilities before I start the job. Is it possible?

W: I'm sorry but no one is available to show you around right now. I recommend you make an appointment and come back another day.

M: Hmm, but I don't live in this town and I'm not sure when I'll be able to come back this month.

W: In that case, why don't I give you this map? You should be able to find your way easily. Remember to take this guest pass with you. Also, there's no point going down Ranston Road. The only building there is closed for renovation.

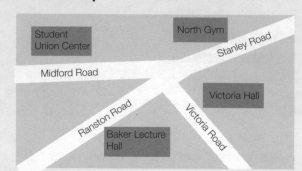

問題 65-67 題參考以下對話和地圖。

男：妳好，我下個月會在卡拉奇教育中心工作，⑥⑤ 在正式工作之前，我可以先參觀一下周邊設施嗎？

女：⑥⑥ 我很抱歉，現在沒有人手能為你導覽。我建議你先預約，然後下次再過來。

男：嗯……可是我不住這裡，也不確定我這個月有沒有時間再來這裡。

女：這樣好了，我給你地圖好嗎？這樣你就能輕鬆找到路。記得隨身攜帶訪客證。另外，⑥⑦ 不要走到蘭斯敦路，那裡只有一棟大樓，目前因裝修而關閉。

字彙　**facility** 設備、設施　**available** 可得到、可利用、在手邊的　**recommend** 推薦、建議　**pass** 通行證
no point + Ving 做～沒有意義的　**renovation** 翻修、整修

65. What does the man ask the woman to do?
(A) Take a map
(B) Make an appointment
(C) Arrange a tour
(D) Apply for a position

男子要求女子做什麼事？
(A) 索取地圖
(B) 預約
(C) 安排參觀
(D) 應徵工作

正確答案為 (C)

〈注意細節—要求〉
本題詢問男子要求的事，因此請從男子所說的話中找出答題線索。男子在第一句話提到他想參觀此處，徵求對方的許可，因此答案為 (C)。

66. What most likely is the problem?
(A) An interview has been postponed.
(B) Some people do not like a tour.
(C) A guide is not available.
(D) There will not be another meeting.

問題最有可能是什麼？
(A) 面試時間延後。
(B) 有些人不喜歡參觀行程。
(C) 導覽員沒空。
(D) 沒有其他的會議。

正確答案為 (C)

〈注意細節—問題點〉
第 65 題中已經確認男子要求參觀教育中心，但女子回答今天沒有人能為他導覽，因此答案選 (C)。

67. Look at the graphic. Which building is under construction today?
(A) North Gym
(B) Student Union Center
(C) Baker Lecture Hall
(D) Victoria Hall

請看圖表，哪一棟大樓今天正在施工？
(A) 諾斯體育館
(B) 學生會館
(C) 培克演講廳
(D) 維多利亞禮堂

正確答案為 (C)

〈注意細節—圖表相關〉
選項列出了地圖中的建築物名稱，因此可以推測出對話中應該會提到道路名稱，請仔細聆聽該答題線索。另外，本題詢問施工的地點，關鍵字為 under construction，請一併留意相關答題線索。對話最後女子提到 Ranston Road 蘭斯敦路，並告知男子那裡的大樓正在翻修，目前關閉中，建議他不要走到哪裡。由此話可以得知蘭斯敦路上的培克演講廳正在施工，答案為 (C)。

換句話說 renovation（建築物）翻修 → **under construction** 施工中

Test 04

4_68-70 英式男聲／美式女聲

Questions 68-70 refer to the following conversation and list.

M: Good afternoon. I'm here to perform some maintenance work for your department. Mr. Rodriguez dispatched me here as soon as he received your list. Apparently, there's quite a bit of work to be done.

W: That's right. Thanks for coming so quickly. I sent him an e-mail with the things that should be fixed. Do you have a copy as well?

M: Yes, and I'll get started right away. I've already prepared the right equipment, so it shouldn't take me long to finish.

W: Wonderful! We'd like to make one slight change, though. Is it possible for you to switch the times of the first and last items on the list? That way, we can start using the most important ones more quickly.

Items for repair		
Item	Quantity	Time
Fax machines	2	1:00 P.M.
Photocopiers	2	2:00 P.M.
Scanners	3	3:00 P.M.
Color printers	4	4:30 P.M.

問題 68-70 題參考以下對話和清單。

男：午安，⑥⑧ 我來這裡幫您部門內的物品進行維修。羅德里格斯先生收到清單後，馬上派我來這裡，看來有很多工作等著我去做。

女：沒錯，謝謝你這麼快過來。我把維修品項用電子郵件傳給他了，你也有拿到清單嗎？

男：有，我現在可以馬上開始做。⑥⑨ 我已經準備好維修用的工具，應該不會花太多時間完成。

女：太好了！不過，有個地方想要做調整。⑦⓪ 請問可以調換清單上第一個品項和最後一個品項的維修時間嗎？這樣我們才能盡快使用最重要的機器。

維修品項		
品項	數量	時間
傳真機	2	下午 1 點
影印機	2	下午 2 點
掃描器	3	下午 3 點
彩色印表機	4	下午 4 點

字彙　**perform** 執行、履行　**maintenance work** 維修工作、設備保養　**dispatch** 派遣、發送　**apparently** 似乎、看來　**quite a bit of** 相當多的　**equipment** 設備、用具　**slight** 少量、微小的　**switch** 更換

68. Who most likely is Mr. Rodriguez?
(A) A client
(B) An accountant
(C) An assistant
(D) A supervisor

羅德里格斯先生最有可能是誰？
(A) 客戶
(B) 會計師
(C) 助理
(D) 主管

正確答案為 (D)

〈注意細節—特定事項〉

請先抓出關鍵字 Mr. Rodriguez 再找出答案。男子在第一句話告知來訪目的，他提到羅德里格斯先生派他來此地進行維修工作。由此話可以得知他是收到羅德里格斯先生的指示來此工作，因此答案為 (D)。

69. What does the man say he has already done?
(A) Sent some tools
(B) Brought items for repair
(C) Purchased new equipment
(D) Contacted a manager

男子提到他已經做好什麼事？
(A) 寄送工具
(B) 帶來維修要用的工具
(C) 購買新設備
(D) 聯絡經理

正確答案為 (B)

〈注意細節—特定事項〉

本題關鍵字為 already，因此請特別留意男子提及該詞彙的片段。對話中段，男子提到他已經準備好會用到的工具，所以不會花太多時間在維修上，因此答案選 (B)。

70. Look at the graphic. What items will be repaired first?
(A) Fax machines
(B) Photocopiers
(C) Scanners
(D) Color printers

根據圖表，最先維修的是哪一個品項？
(A) 傳真機
(B) 影印機
(C) 掃描器
(D) 彩色印表機

正確答案為 (D)

〈注意細節—圖表相關〉

請務必先掌握選項和圖表間的關係。選項列出了品項，由此可以推測出對話中應該會提到時間或數量，請仔細聆聽該答題線索。對話最後，女子詢問男子是否能調換清單上第一個品項和最後一個品項的維修時間。維修清單表中第一個品項為傳真機、最後一個品項為彩色印表機，因此可以得知最先維修的是 (D) 彩色印表機。

Questions 71-73 refer to the following talk.

Thank you all for joining us this afternoon. We're conducting this session to get consumer reviews on various aspects of our new mobile device. Feedback from previous groups has already helped us to improve the product. We've made it even easier to use its basic features and built-in apps. Today, we're going to concentrate on topics related to the eventual marketing of the product. We'll start by looking over some preliminary ideas for the package design. After that, we'll show you some sample layouts and different versions of copy for commercial advertisements, and then we'll go over a few survey questions.

問題 71-73 題參考以下談話。

感謝各位今天下午蒞臨現場。71 我們舉辦這場活動，是為了取得用戶在使用我們的新行動裝置過程中的各方面使用評價。先前的團體回饋意見幫助我們改善產品，72 基本功能和內建應用程式在使用上也變得更加容易。今天，我們會將重點放在最終階段的產品行銷。73 首先，我們會讓各位看看幾個包裝設計的初步構想，接著展示樣品設計和不同版本的廣告文案，最後再針對問卷調查進行討論。

字彙 **session** 會議、集會　**consumer review** 用戶評價　**mobile device** 行動裝置　**aspect** 方面　**built-in** 內建的　**app** 應用程式　**concentrate on** 集中、全神貫注　**related to** 與～有關　**eventual** 最終的　**preliminary** 初步的、預備的　**layout** 設計

71. What is the purpose of today's session?
(A) To evaluate staff performance
(B) To conduct an interview
(C) To gather opinions
(D) To explain a company regulation

今天的活動目的是什麼？
(A) 評估員工表現
(B) 進行面試
(C) 收集意見
(D) 說明公司規定

正確答案為 (C)

〈確認基本資訊─目的〉
本題詢問目的，開頭處會出現相關答題線索。說話者簡單問候完後，告知舉辦活動的目的為取得消費者的評價，因此答案要選 (C)。

換句話說 **get reviews** 取得評價 → **gather opinions** 收集意見

字彙 **evaluate** 評價

72. According to the speaker, how has the new device been improved?
(A) It performs more easily.
(B) It is light-weight.
(C) It is faster to use.
(D) It is a cost-effective product.

根據說話者，新的行動裝置改善了什麼？
(A) 變得更容易操作。
(B) 重量減輕。
(C) 速度更快。
(D) 性價比高的產品。

正確答案為 (A)

〈注意細節─特定事項〉
本題關鍵字為 improve，文中提及該詞彙後，提到改善後的基本功能和內建應用程式在使用上會更加順手，因此答案要選 (A)。

73. What will the listeners probably do next?
(A) Ask questions
(B) View package designs
(C) Create the advertisement
(D) Call a client's office

聽者接下來可能會做什麼事？
(A) 提出問題
(B) 查看包裝設計
(C) 製作廣告
(D) 打電話到客戶辦公室

正確答案為 (B)

〈注意細節─未來〉
本題詢問聽者下一步要做的事，通常會在段話後半段提及。後半段說話者提到，要讓大家先看看幾個有關包裝設計的初步構想，因此答案為 (B)。

Test 04

4_74-76　美式女聲

Questions 74-76 refer to the following speech.

Thanks to the University of St. Andrew for hosting tonight's event. It's my great privilege to accept the Edger Prize on behalf of Edinburgh Institute, where I've had the opportunity to collaborate with some of the most gifted linguists in the country. They are certainly in a class of their own. Special thanks go to the Research Foundation, which provides the majority of the funding for our study, and, of course, the panel of judges for selecting the Edinburgh Institute for this honor.

問題 74-76 題參考以下演講。

74 感謝聖安德魯大學舉辦今晚的活動。 **75** 我非常榮幸能代表愛丁堡學院得到艾爵獎， **76** 多虧愛丁堡學院，我才有機會和全國天賦異稟的語言學家一起合作，他們都極為優秀。我想特別感謝研究基金會提供了我們絕大部分的研究經費，同時我也要感謝評審委員們選擇愛丁堡學院，讓我獲得這份殊榮。

字彙　**host** 主辦（活動）　**privilege** 特權、殊榮　**accept** 接受、同意　**on behalf of** 代表　**opportunity** 機會　**collaborate with** 合作、共同工作　**gifted** 有天賦的　**linguist** 語言學家　**in a class of one's own** 獨一無二、出眾的　**majority** 多數、大多數　**funding** 資金；提供資金　**the panel of judges** 評審團　**honor** 榮耀

74. What is the purpose of the speech?
(A) To request funding
(B) To report research findings
(C) To accept an award
(D) To welcome guests

此場演講的目的是什麼？
(A) 尋求募款
(B) 報告研究結果
(C) 獲頒獎項
(D) 歡迎賓客

正確答案為 **(C)**

〈確認基本資訊－目的〉
本題詢問本段對話的目的，開頭通常就會出現相關答題線索。說話者簡單問候完後，說出得到 Edger Prize 艾爾獎的感言，因此答案要選 (A)。

75. Where is the speech probably taking place?
(A) At a university
(B) At a firm's auditorium
(C) At a city's arena
(D) At a town center

此場演講可能是在哪裡舉行？
(A) 大學
(B) 公司會議廳
(C) 市立運動場
(D) 城鎮中心

正確答案為 **(A)**

〈確認基本資訊－地點〉
談話開頭處談到目的之外，也會提到與地點相關的資訊。第一句提到感謝聖安德魯大學舉辦今晚的活動，因此答案選 (A)。第 **74** 題和第 **75** 題分別考目的和地點，兩者的答題線索皆出現在談話的一開始，因此聆聽一段談話時，請務必提前做好準備，一次選出兩題的答案。

字彙　**arena** 運動場

76. What does the speaker mean when she says, "They are certainly in a class of their own"?
(A) Some of the researchers are excluded.
(B) Several of the colleagues are exceptional.
(C) Some of the instructors teach only one class.
(D) Several students contributed their ideas.

說話者說「他們都極為優秀」是什麼意思？
(A) 部分研究人員被排除在外。
(B) 幾位同事十分優秀。
(C) 部分講師只為一個班授課。
(D) 幾名學生貢獻了自己的點子。

正確答案為 **(B)**

〈關鍵句－說話者意圖〉
請務必先確認關鍵句的前後句，以掌握說話者的意圖。說話者說出關鍵句之前，先提到他和全國天賦異稟的語言學家一起合作，暗示他們是極為優秀的人，因此答案選 (B)。

字彙　**exclude** 不包括　　**exceptional** 優秀的

4_77-79　澳式男聲

Questions 77-79 refer to the following advertisement.

After more than ten happy years at its location in Lambeth, Skin Clear & Beauty Clinic is happy to announce it is relocating to new premises in the heart of Westminster. Our beautiful modern clinic opens tomorrow on the corner of Vincent Street and Grosvenor Avenue. Skin Clear & Beauty Clinic utilizes cutting-edge technology to help treat a variety of skin conditions caused by aging, sun damage and allergies. To celebrate our move, all customers who visit before the end of February will receive 30 percent off any treatment. To take advantage of this offer, or to make an appointment, call us at 934-555-0381.

問題 77-79 題參考以下廣告。

在此很高興宣布，77 皮膚清潔＆美容診所在蘭貝斯度過 10 年以上的愉快時光後，將搬遷至威斯特敏斯市中心。78 我們美麗時髦的診所將於明天開幕，位置就在文森路和格羅斯芬諾大道交會處。77 皮膚清潔＆美容診所運用最新尖端技術幫您治療因老化、日曬、或過敏所造成的皮膚問題。為慶祝搬遷開幕，79 2 月底前來診的客人，無論您接受哪一種治療，都能享有七折優惠。欲使用此項優惠或提前預約者，請撥打電話至 934-555-0381。

字彙　**clinic** 診所　　**relocate** 搬遷　　**premises**（公司或機構）經營廠址　　**utilize** 利用
cutting-edge technology 尖端技術　　**treat** 治療、處理　　**sun damage** 曬傷　　**allergy** 過敏
take advantage of 利用、善用

77. What type of business is being advertised?

(A) **A beauty clinic**
(B) A cosmetic company
(C) A stationery store
(D) A fitness center

本廣告是宣傳何種產業？

(A) **美容診所**
(B) 化妝品公司
(C) 文具店
(D) 健身中心

正確答案為 (A)

〈確認基本資訊—主旨〉

本篇為皮膚診所的廣告。前半段提到公司名稱，中段又提到治療皮膚一事，因此答案選 (A)。

78. What will happen tomorrow?

(A) A new product will be launched.
(B) A special offer will end.
(C) A consultation will begin.
(D) **New premises will open.**

明天將發生什麼事？

(A) 新產品上市。
(B) 特惠活動結束。
(C) 開始接受諮詢。
(D) **新的營業場所開張。**

正確答案為 (D)

〈注意細節—特定事項〉

請先抓出關鍵字 tomorrow，再仔細聆聽內容。發言開頭告知診所搬遷至新的地點以及明天即將開幕一事，答案選 (D)。

字彙   **launch** 推出新產品   **consultation** 諮詢

79. What is offered at a 30 percent discount?

(A) A consultation
(B) **Any treatment**
(C) A training session
(D) All products

以下何者提供七折優惠？

(A) 諮詢服務
(B) **任何療程**
(C) 訓練課程
(D) 所有產品

正確答案為 (B)

〈注意細節—特定事項〉

聽到廣告文時，與折扣相關的答題線索通常會出現在後半段當中。題目中的 30 percent discount 為答題線索，而後半段提到只要在 2 月底之前來診所的客人，無論接受哪一種治療，都可以享有七折的優惠，因此答案要選 (B)。

Test 04

4_80-82 英式男聲

Questions 80-82 refer to the following news report.

In business news today, Advanced Electronics has announced its acquisition of Lunar Printer. The decision to sell Lunar, best known for its popular line of color printers, comes only three months following the retirement of the company's founder, Glen Lunar. Reportedly, negotiations have been taking place throughout the week and a deal was finalized on Wednesday, when Lunar directors agreed to an improved offer from Advanced Electronics. When asked to comment, Mr. Lunar supported the move, saying Advanced Electronics' wide distribution network would help introduce Lunar products to new customers.

問題 80-82 題參考以下新聞報導。

以下是今日商業新聞。⑧⓪ 先進電子公司宣布收購路拿印刷，路拿印刷以彩色印刷聞名，其公司創辦人葛蘭路拿退休後，⑧① 於短短 3 個月決定賣掉路拿印刷。根據消息指出，內部進行為期一週的協商後，公司董事們一致同意先進電子公司提出的改善案，並於週三做出決議。被問到其看法時，路拿先生表示支持。⑧② 他認為先進電子公司的廣泛銷售網絡，有助於將路拿的產品推廣給新客戶。

字彙　**electronics** 電子業　**acquisition**（企業）收購、買進　**retirement** 退休　**founder** 建立者、創立者
reportedly 根據傳聞　**negotiation** 協商、交涉　**take place** 發生、進行　**throughout** 自始自終；遍及
finalize 完成、結束　**comment** 發表意見

80. What is being reported?　　　　　本篇報導內容為何？
　(A) A stock offering　　　　　　　　(A) 股票上市
　(B) A retirement event　　　　　　　(B) 退休慶祝會
　(C) A construction project　　　　　(C) 建設計畫
　(D) A business take-over　　　　　**(D) 企業接管**

正確答案為 (D)

〈確認基本資訊—主旨〉

主旨通常會出現在開頭處。說話者開頭報導先進電子公司宣布收購路拿印刷的消息，因此答案為 (D)。

換句話說 **acquisition**（企業）收購 → **take-over** 接管（公司）

> 字彙　**take-over** 接管

81. What did Glen Lunar do three months ago?　　3 個月前葛蘭路拿做了什麼事？
　(A) He founded a new company.　　　　　(A) 創立新公司。
　(B) He opened a new store.　　　　　　　(B) 開設新商店。
　(C) He retired from his career.　　　　　**(C) 從職業生涯中退休。**
　(D) He launched a new line of products.　　(D) 推出一系列新產品。

正確答案為 (C)

〈注意細節—特定事項〉

題目關鍵字為 Glen Lunar 和 three months，因此請特別留意文中提及相關內容之處。當中提到公司創辦人葛蘭路拿退休後，在 3 個月後決定賣掉公司，因此答案要選 (C)。

82. What does the speaker mean when he says,　　說話者說「路拿先生表示支持」是什麼意思？
　"Mr. Lunar supported the move"?　　　　　**(A) 路拿先生同意這項決定。**
　(A) Mr. Lunar approved of a decision.　　　(B) 路拿先生想調回總公司。
　(B) Mr. Lunar wanted to relocate the headquarters.　(C) 路拿先生提供了財務上的支援。
　(C) Mr. Lunar provided financial assistance.　　(D) 路拿先生拒絕了提案。
　(D) Mr. Lunar rejected the offer.

正確答案為 (A)

〈關鍵句—說話者意圖〉

請務必確認關鍵句前後句，以推測出正確答案。說話者說出本關鍵句之後，提到先進電子公司擁有廣範圍的銷售網絡，助於將路拿的產品推廣給新客戶。這表示他支持被收購的決定，因此答案為 (A)。

4_83-85 美式男聲

Questions 83-85 refer to the following announcement.

Good afternoon, everyone. As you all know, we are relocating to a new facility next week, and working there will be much more efficient with the state-of-the-art production equipment that has been installed. So, put all your belongings into boxes. Take as many boxes as you need from the supply room. And remember, the company will be closed for Monday and Tuesday, but if you need to work on those days, please consult with your managers so that we can assign you to a temporary workstation in the new building.

問題 83-85 題參考以下通知。

各位午安，大家都知道 ⑧③ ⑧④ 下週我們將搬遷至新的機構。那裡設有最先進的生產設備，將能有效提升工作效率。因此，請各位將隨身物品裝箱，器材室中的箱子可以盡情取用。另外，請記得週一和週二公司沒有開門，⑧⑤ 如果想在這兩天工作的人，請先與你的經理商量，我們才會同意讓你暫時於新大樓的工作站內工作。

字彙　**efficient** 效率高的　**state-of-the-art** 最先進的　**install** 安裝、設置　**belonging** 隨身物品
supply room 器材室　**consult** 商量　**assign** 指派　**temporary** 暫時的　**workstation** 個人工作站

83. Who most likely are the listeners?
(A) Department heads
(B) Fitness instructors
(C) Marketing representatives
(D) Factory workers

聽者最有可能是誰？
(A) 部門負責人
(B) 健身教練
(C) 行銷代表
(D) 工廠工人

正確答案為 (D)

〈確認基本資訊一聽者〉
開頭處通常會提及與聽者有關的資訊。説話者於開頭提到下週將搬遷至新的地點，那裡設有最先進的生產設備，將能提升工作效率。當中有提到生產設備，因此答案應選 (D)。

84. What will happen next week?
(A) The company will move to a new building.
(B) Some employees will be recruited.
(C) The budget will be shortened.
(D) New tasks will be assigned.

下週將發生什麼事？
(A) 公司將搬遷至新大樓。
(B) 將僱用一些新員工。
(C) 將刪減預算。
(D) 將指派新的業務。

正確答案為 (A)

〈注意細節一特定事項〉
請從提及關鍵字 next week 之處找出正確答案。開頭告知下週將搬遷至新的地點一事，因此答案要選 (A)。第 83 題和 84 題的答題線索皆出現在談話的開頭處。請特別留意，**題目中提及「時間」或「地點」時，屬於較為單純的關鍵字，答題線索通常會一併出現。**

字彙　**recruit** 招聘、招募

85. What are some listeners requested to do?
(A) Contact their supervisors
(B) Put in extra hours
(C) Submit their report
(D) Assign a task

部分聽者被要求做什麼事？
(A) 聯絡他們的主管
(B) 延長工作時間
(C) 繳交報告書
(D) 指派任務

正確答案為 (A)

〈注意細節一要求〉
後半段通常會出現與要求相關的答題線索。本文後半段中提到如果想在特定日子工作，要先與經理商量，因此答案為 (A)。

換句話說　**consult with your managers** 與經理商量 → **contact their supervisors** 聯絡主管

Questions 86-88 refer to the following excerpt from a meeting.

In today's meeting we're going to look at how we can improve our service performance as hotel receptionists. We know that many guests, whether overseas tourists, company CEOs, or married couples, feel tired when they arrive to check in. They may be suffering jet lag from a long international flight, or may have been on the road for several hours. In your folder, you'll find our hotel's employee handbook and a questionnaire that I will ask you to complete later today. Now I'm going to play a short video clip. I'd like you to make some notes about the things our employees did well, and the things that you feel they should have done differently. After the video is finished, I'd like you to share your ideas, and then we'll take a short break.

問題 86-88 題參考以下會議摘錄。

86 今天會議要探討作為一名飯店接待員，該如何提升服務表現。我們知道有許多賓客，無論是外國觀光客、公司執行長、或是已婚夫婦，在辦理入住時早已疲憊不堪。他們可能是因長途飛行而有時差、或是因長時間車程感到不適。87 各位手上的資料夾有飯店員工指南以及問卷，稍晚要請各位填寫。現在我將播放一段短片，88 希望各位可以寫下我們員工的優良表現和尚待改善之處。影片播畢後，請分享你的看法，之後我們會有休息時間。

字彙　**improve** 改善、變得更好、提高　　**receptionist** 接待員　　**overseas** 國外　　**suffer** 遭受、經歷　　**jet lag** 時差

86. Who is the announcement intended for?　本篇通知的對象是誰？
(A) Restaurant servers　(A) 餐廳服務生
(B) Hotel employees　**(B) 飯店員工**
(A) Married couples　(C) 已婚夫婦
(D) Overseas tourists　(D) 外國觀光客

正確答案為 **(B)**

〈確認基本資訊─聽者〉
本題詢問聽者的身分，因此請從開頭處找出答題線索。說話者在第一句話提到要探討作為飯店接待員，應該如何提升
服務表現，這表示聽者為飯店接待員，因此答案選 (B)。

87. According to the speaker, what is contained in the folder?　根據說話者，資料夾裡包含什麼？
(A) An employee ID card　(A) 員工識別證
(B) A floor plan　(B) 樓層平面圖
(C) An employee manual　**(C) 員工手冊**
(D) A wage slip　(D) 薪資明細

正確答案為 **(C)**

〈注意細節─特定事項〉
請先抓出關鍵字 in the folder，再找出答題線索。說話者在中間部分提到資料夾內有飯店員工指南和問卷，答案選 (C)。
換句話說 **employee handbook** 員工指南 → **employee manual** 員工手冊

字彙 **wage slip** 薪資明細

88. What does the speaker ask listeners to do next?　說話者要求聽者接下來要做什麼事？
(A) Evaluate staff members　**(A) 對員工進行評價**
(B) Take a short break　(B) 休息一段時間
(C) Work in groups　(C) 分組進行工作
(D) Complete a questionnaire　(D) 完成問卷填寫

正確答案為 **(A)**

〈注意細節─請求〉
本題詢問要求事項，且使用關鍵字 next，答案通常出現在後半段。說話者在中間部分請聽者寫下員工的優良表現和尚
待改善之處，最適當的描述為 (A)。

4_89-91　英式男聲

Questions 89-91 refer to the following telephone message.

Hello, Ms. Gray. This is Frank from Cleveland Services. I'm calling to confirm that my team members and I will be getting to your house between 10:00 and 11:00 A.M. tomorrow with the refrigerator that you ordered from us. We'll place the new unit in the same wall where your old refrigerator is now. We can take that one away and dispose of it for you if you'd like. Also, I got your message asking if you needed to pull the sofa and table away from the window. Don't worry about it. We'll move them ourselves tomorrow morning. See you then.

問題 89-91 題參考以下電話留言。

哈囉，葛瑞小姐，我是克里夫蘭服務的法蘭克。我打來是要向妳確認，我和我的團隊預計於明天上午 10 點至 11 點之間帶著 89 妳向我們下訂的冰箱過去。90 我們會將新冰箱放在原本擺放舊冰箱的位置。如果妳同意的話，我們可以幫妳把舊冰箱帶走並處理掉。另外，我有收到妳的訊息，說想將沙發和桌子從窗戶旁移開。別擔心，91 明天上午我們會一起搬。到時見。

字彙　**confirm** 確認　　**dispose of** 處理掉、丟棄

89. What type of company does the speaker probably work for? 　說話者最有可能在什麼類型的公司工作？
　(A) A moving company 　　　　　　　　　　(A) 搬家公司
　(B) A real estate agency 　　　　　　　　　(B) 房屋仲介公司
　(C) An appliance dealer 　　　　　　　　**(C) 家電經銷商**
　(D) A cleaning service 　　　　　　　　　　(D) 清潔服務公司

正確答案為 **(C)**

〈確認基本資訊—說話者的工作地點〉
本題詢問說話者工作的地點，答題線索通常會出現在談話一開始。說話者簡單問候完對方後，告知明天預計於某段時間內，帶著聽者下訂的冰箱登門拜訪一事，因此答案要選 (C)。**遇到詢問人物的職業或工作地點，需先區分清楚問的是聽者的還是說話者的。**

> 字彙　**real estate agency** 房仲　　**appliance** 家電　　**dealer** 經銷商

90. What does the speaker offer to do tomorrow? 　說話者建議明天要做什麼事？
　(A) Dispose of old equipment 　　　　　　**(A) 處理掉舊設備**
　(B) Repair a product 　　　　　　　　　　　(B) 修理產品
　(C) Give a brochure 　　　　　　　　　　　(C) 提供說明手冊
　(D) Call before his arrival 　　　　　　　　(D) 抵達前電話通知

正確答案為 **(A)**

〈注意細節—特定事項〉
本題關鍵字 tomorrow 與第 89 題的答題線索有關，從中可以得知明天就是登門拜訪的日子。而下一句話提到如果聽者同意的話，可以幫忙把舊冰箱處理掉，因此答案選 (A)。

91. What does the speaker imply when he says, 　說話者說「別擔心」是什麼意思？
　"Don't worry about it"? 　　　　　　　　　　(A) 他的員工不會毀損任何東西。
　(A) His staff will not damage anything. 　　　**(B) 他們團隊會完成任務。**
　(B) His team will take care of a task. 　　　(C) 他能夠出售家具。
　(C) He will be able to sell the furniture. 　　(D) 他將收到估價單。
　(D) He will get an estimate.

正確答案為 **(B)**

〈關鍵句—說話者意圖〉
請務必確認指定句前後的情境，再來掌握說話者的意圖。說話者說出本指定句之前，先提到聽者提問的事項，表示聽者不用擔心這件事，並說明天會一併處理。因此這句話指的是說話者將會處理好事情，答案要選 (B)。

> 字彙　**damage** 損害　　**estimate** 估價單

4_92-94　英式女聲

Questions 92-94 refer to the following radio announcement.

Milkyway Cereal has issued a recall for its "Coco Oatmeal" brand cereal, after it was reported yesterday that some of the cartons did not contain their 450 gram capacity. Researchers of the production quality indicated a packing equipment failure, which has since been corrected. Affected batch numbers are from CP243 to CP390. These numbers appear on the carton label. If you have one of these cartons, you can exchange it for a free new box at any participating retailer. Milkyway offers its sincere apologies for any inconvenience this may have caused.

問題 92-94 題參考以下廣播通知。

92 銀河玉米穀片公司在昨日被報導其部分產品的內容物未達 450 公克後，宣布召回「可可燕麥片」品牌的玉米穀片。 93 品管調查人員指出其包裝設備故障，目前已恢復正常。受影響的產品批號為 CP243 至 CP390。外盒上皆有產品批號，94 如果您購買了前述批號的產品，請前往指定店家免費更換新品。造成您的不便，銀河在此致上最深的歉意。

字彙　**issue** 發布、公布　**recall** 收回、召回　**carton** 紙盒、紙箱　**capacity** 容量、容積　**indicate** 指出、表明　**batch number** 生產批號　**label** 標籤　**inconvenience** 不便

92. What is the problem?
(A) Some cereal cartons have wrong information.
(B) Some products have been mislabeled.
(C) Some cereal cartons are not full.
(D) Some products are of poor quality.

發生什麼問題？
(A) 部分玉米穀片的外盒上印有錯誤資訊。
(B) 部份產品貼錯標籤。
(C) 部分玉米穀片容量未達標準。
(D) 部份產品的品質不佳。

正確答案為 (C)

〈注意細節—問題點〉
詢問問題點的題目出現在第一題時，通常就是等同主旨，因此答題線索會出現在開頭處。 本文開頭提到某家公司因玉米穀片產品未達一定重量，宣布召回產品，因此答案為 (C)。

93. What is mentioned about the packing equipment?
(A) It is no longer malfunctioning.
(B) It will be replaced next month.
(C) It had been repaired before the incident.
(D) It will be inspected regularly.

下列何者符合包裝設備的描述？
(A) 不會再發生故障。
(B) 預計於下個月更換。
(C) 事件發生前已修好。
(D) 往後將定期維護。

正確答案為 (A)

〈注意細節—提及內容〉
請從提及關鍵字 packing equipment 的片段中找出答案。通知中段提到品管調查人員指出其包裝設備故障，目前皆已恢復正常，因此答案選 (A)。

字彙　**malfunction** 故障　　**incident** 事件　　**inspect** 檢查

94. What will customers who return cartons receive?
(A) A new box of cereal
(B) A refund
(C) A complimentary gift
(D) A discount coupon

顧客歸還產品後將會收到什麼東西？
(A) 新的玉米穀片產品
(B) 退款
(C) 免費贈品
(D) 折價券

正確答案為 (A)

〈注意細節—特定事項〉
說話者在後半段提到前往指定店家可以免費更換新產品，因此答案要選 (A)。

字彙　**refund** 退款

4_95-97　美式女聲

Questions 95-97 refer to the following announcement and graph.

I have one last thing to announce before we wrap up the meeting. As we all know, at the end of the last quarter, we asked our customers to send us their feedback on the new flavors they would like to add to our ice cream range. We narrowed down these proposals to four different flavors that would appeal to the widest range of consumers. We carried out nationwide taste tests last week and, overall, the melon flavors we produced were popular across the country. However, mango taste was people's favorite in Florida and banana was the best flavor in California.

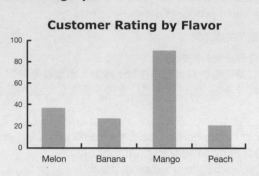

Customer Rating by Flavor

問題 95-97 題參考以下通知和圖表。

會議結束之前，我還有件事要宣布。如同各位所知，上一季末 ⑨⑤ 我們請顧客提供意見回饋，告訴我們希望增加的冰淇淋口味。綜合所有的建議後，我們精選出 4 種口味，以吸引更廣大的消費族群。⑨⑥ 上週我們在全國舉辦了試吃活動，整體而言，我們所生產的哈密瓜口味在全國各地大受歡迎。但是 ⑨⑦ 芒果口味主要受到佛羅里達州的歡迎，香蕉口味則是加州最喜歡的口味。

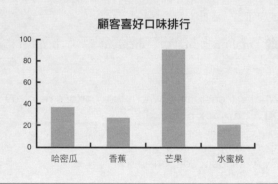

顧客喜好口味排行

字彙　**wrap up**（會議）結束　**feedback** 意見回饋　**flavor** 口味　**narrow down** 縮小、減少　**wide range of** 廣泛的
carry out 執行、實行　**nationwide** 全國性的

95. What does the speaker's company produce?
  (A) Canned fruit
  (B) Milk
  (C) Bottled drinks
  (D) Ice cream

說話者的公司生產什麼東西？
  (A) 水果罐頭
  (B) 牛奶
  (C) 瓶裝飲料
  (D) 冰淇淋

正確答案為 **(D)**

〈注意細節—特定事項〉
公司名稱中通常會包含公司生產的產品名稱，但是若文中未提及公司名稱時，請務必聽清楚當中提及產品名稱之處。說話者在開頭提到請顧客告知希望增加什麼口味的冰淇淋，因此答案為 (D)。

96. According to the speaker, what did the company do last week?
  (A) Conducted product trials
  (B) Added a new facility
  (C) Reduced a product price
  (D) Launched an advertising campaign

根據說話者，公司上週做了什麼事？
  (A) 進行產品測試
  (B) 增加新的設施
  (C) 調降產品價格
  (D) 推出廣告活動

正確答案為 **(A)**

〈注意細節—特定事項〉
請從文中提及關鍵字 last week 之處找出答案。談話中間提到上週在全國舉辦試吃活動，因此答案要選 (A)。
換句話說 **carry out taste tests** 舉辦試吃活動 → **conduct product trials** 進行產品測試

97. Look at the graphic. Where most likely is the result of this graph relevant?
  (A) California
  (B) Florida
  (C) Texas
  (D) Colorado

根據圖表，此長條圖最有可能是哪個地方的結果？
  (A) 加州
  (B) 佛羅里達州
  (C) 德州
  (D) 科羅拉多

正確答案為 **(B)**

〈注意細節—圖表相關〉
這類的解題重點在於先掌握題目選項和圖表的關係，但本題圖表中並沒有看到選項列出的地名，因此請務必仔細聆聽談話中提到地名和長條圖示呈現內容的關係。說話者在談話後半段提到佛羅里達州人最愛芒果口味、加州人最愛香蕉口味，而圖表中最長的長條圖示為芒果口味，表示此圖表是佛羅里達州的調查結果，答案選 (B)。

4_98-100 澳式男聲

Questions 98-100 refer to the following speech and table.

Before we enjoy this lovely meal, let's remember that we're here to honor Henry Williamson and his two decades of amazing service to M&T Developer. When Mark and I founded this company in 1998, Henry was our very first employee. We were two landscapers who knew a lot about plants but not much about the industry, and Henry had good communications with people. He answered the phones, negotiated contracts, and dealt with all of our clients. As we grew, he grew too, eventually becoming our general manger and overseeing the more than 50 employees who work for M&T today. We couldn't have become what we are today without him, and although we're sad that he's retiring, we wish him nothing but the best in the future. Let's raise our glasses to Henry Williamson, everyone!

The Future Conference Center		
Friday, June 18		
Hall Name	Event	Time
Apollo Hall	Employee Workshop	6:00 P.M. – 9:00 P.M.
Dominion Hall	Product Launching event	7:30 P.M. – 10:00 P.M.
Empire Hall	Retirement Party	6:30 P.M. – 9:30 P.M.
Warner Hall	Award Ceremony	8:00 P.M. – 11:00 P.M.

問題 98-100 題參考以下演講和表格。

在享受這頓美味佳餚之前，98 100 不要忘記我們聚集在此是為了向在 M&T 開發者服務了 20 年的亨利威廉森致敬。1998 年我和馬克創立公司之際，亨利是我們公司的頭號員工。99 當時我們倆是只懂植物的園藝設計師，對這個行業懵懵無知。亨利是一位善於與人溝通的人，他負責接聽電話、洽談合約、與客戶們打交道。他跟隨公司一同成長，最後成為公司總經理，現今管理超過 50 名在 M&T 工作的員工。沒有他，就沒有我們今天的成就。100 雖然他的退休令人感傷，但是我們還是要祝福他朝向更美好的未來。讓我們共同舉杯，敬亨利威廉森！

未來會議中心		
6 月 18 日星期五		
會議室名稱	活動	時間
阿波羅廳	員工研討會	下午 6:00 - 9:00
多明尼恩廳	產品發布會	下午 7:30 - 10:00
100 帝國廳	退休派對	下午 6:30 - 09:30
華納廳	頒獎典禮	下午 8:00 - 11:00

字彙　**decade** 十年　**landscaper** 園藝設計師、景觀設計師　**industry** 產業　**eventually** 最終　**deal with** 處理
　　　oversee 監督、管理　**raise** 舉起；增加

98. Why is the speaker delivering this speech?
(A) To introduce a celebrity
(B) To celebrate a company's anniversary
(C) To introduce a new employee
(D) To recognize an employee's service

為何說話者要發表這場演講？
(A) 介紹知名人士
(B) 歡慶公司紀念日
(C) 介紹新進員工
(D) 認可員工的服務

正確答案為 **(D)**

〈確認基本資訊─主旨〉
主旨通常會出現在談話的一開頭。說話者第一句提到不要忘記我們聚集在此的目的是向為 M&T 開發者服務 20 年的亨利威廉森致敬，這表示他想認可為公司效力的特定人士，因此答案選 (D)。

字彙　**recognize** 認可；承認　　**celebrity** 名人

99. What kind of services does M&T provide?
(A) Landscaping
(B) Product development
(C) Accounting
(D) Retail management

M&T 公司提供什麼樣的服務？
(A) 園藝設計
(B) 產品開發
(C) 會計
(D) 零售管理

正確答案為 **(A)**

〈注意細節─特定事項〉
當題目詢問公司是做什麼的，答題線索通常會出現在公司名稱當中。但是本篇文章提到的公司名稱為 M&T 開發者，無法從中推測出答案，因此請找尋其他的答題線索。說話者在談話中間提到公司創立之時，自己和事業夥伴 Mark 皆為 landscaper 園藝師，因此答案選 (A)。

100. Look at the graphic. Where is the event taking place?
(A) Apollo Hall
(B) Dominion Hall
(C) Empire Hall
(D) Warner Hall

根據圖表，此活動在哪個地方舉行？
(A) 阿波羅廳
(B) 多明尼恩廳
(C) 帝國廳
(D) 華納廳

正確答案為 **(C)**

〈注意細節─圖表相關〉
請務必先掌握選項和圖表間的關係。選項列出了表中的活動地點，可知談話中應該會提到活動或時間的相關答題線索。此場活動的目的為慶祝員工退休，而表中顯示退休派對是在 Empire Hall 內舉行，因此答案為 (C)。

101. The owner of Casper Airline announced that ------- is negotiating a deal with Super Jet to buy new airplanes.
(A) him
(B) he
(C) his
(D) himself

卡斯帕航空的老闆宣布，他正在與超級飛機公司協商購買新飛機一事。

正確答案為 **(B)**

〈代名詞格〉that 子句缺少主詞，因此答案要選主格 (B)。反身代名詞不能作為主詞使用，因此不能選 (D)。

字彙　**negotiate a deal** 協商談判

---

102. ------- the last ten years, Madison City's population has grown by about 30 percent.
(A) As
(B) Again
(C) During
(D) Below

過去 10 年來，麥迪遜市的人口成長了 30% 左右。

正確答案為 **(C)**

〈介系詞〉空格要放入可以與 the last ten years「一段時間」連用的介系詞，答案為 (C)，during 指「在～期間」。

字彙　**population** 人口

---

103. ------- to all the facilities is included with your stay at the Grand Plaza Hotel.
(A) Access
(B) Accessed
(C) Accessing
(D) Accessible

入住大廣場飯店的旅客可以使用所有的設施。

正確答案為 **(A)**

〈詞性〉空格為主詞的位置，應填入名詞。access 可以當名詞，答案選 (A)。

字彙　**facility** 設施　**access** 進入　**accessible** 可以進入的

---

104. Ms. Chalmers will help with the final draft, so it is not necessary to do all the editing by -------.
(A) yours
(B) your
(C) you
(D) yourself

查爾摩斯小姐會協助你完成最終稿，所以你不需要一個人編輯所有內容。

正確答案為 **(D)**

〈代名詞格〉by oneself 的意思為「獨自」，為常見的反身代名詞用法，答案為 (D)。

字彙　**final draft** 完稿　**editing** 編輯

105. Because humidity can ------- iron, the climate in materials storage units must be controlled.
(A) damage
(B) damaging
(C) damaged
(D) damages

因為濕氣會造成鐵變質,所以必須控管儲藏室內的溫濕度。

正確答案為 (A)

〈動詞〉空格位在助動詞 can 後方,應填入原形動詞,因此答案為 (A)。

字彙　**humidity** 濕度　**climate** 氣候

106. Mr. Bukowski is reviewing the training manual to see if updates -------.
(A) have need
(B) needing
(C) are needed
(D) to be needed

布考斯基先生正在查看培訓手冊,確認是否需要更新。

正確答案為 (C)

〈時態〉空格位在 if 子句的動詞位置,前方有複數主詞 updates,且後方並沒有受詞,因此答案要選被動語態 (C)。

字彙　**manual** 使用手冊、指南

107. After working in France for ten years, Georgina Garcia has ------- to Madrid to plan the opening of a fancy restaurant.
(A) visited
(B) returned
(C) occurred
(D) related

在法國工作 10 年後,喬治娜加西雅回到馬德里,計畫開一家高檔餐廳。

正確答案為 (B)

has 後方要接過去分詞表達過去完成式。空格應填入不及物動詞,搭配後方介系詞 to 一起使用,加上後方出現地點 Madrid 馬德里,因此答案選 (B)。

字彙　**fancy** 高檔的、特級的　**occur (to)** 想到

108. The city council approved the bill to increase funding of its road improvement -------.
(A) statement
(B) permission
(C) ability
(D) project

市議會批准法案,同意增加道路改善計畫的資金。

正確答案為 (D)

句中提到要增加修路的資金,根據題意,空格適合填入 (D) project。

字彙　**bill** 法案　**funding** 資金　**improvement** 改善　**statement** 聲明、陳述　**permission** 許可　**project** 計畫

109. After interviewing Mr. Finch personally, the company president ------- the committee's decision to hire him as Vice President.

(A) confirmed
(B) designed
(C) hosted
(D) created

親自面試完芬奇先生後，公司董事長證實委員會的決定並且聘用他為副董事長。

正確答案為 (A)

空格要填入適合搭配受詞 decision 的動詞，答案為 (A)。

字彙　**personally** 親自　**committee** 委員會　**host** 主持

110. Once the most recent update is installed, the tablet's platform will ------- longer support this software.

(A) not
(B) none
(C) no
(D) nowhere

一旦更新到最新版本，平板的系統平台便不再支援該軟體。

正確答案為 (C)

片語 no longer 的意思為「不再」，答案為 (C)。

111. Each sales team must ------- the result of its annual sales report by the end of the month.

(A) provide
(B) match
(C) reach
(D) earn

每個銷售團隊都必須在這個月底前提供年度銷售報告的結果。

正確答案為 (A)

空格要填入動詞，且後方有受詞 the result，符合題意的答案要選 (A)。

字彙　**reach** 聯繫上　**match** 相配　**earn** 賺得

112. South Central School's district managers are retired executives with a ------- of expertise across a wide range of industries.

(A) fame
(B) height
(C) labor
(D) wealth

南部中央學校的區經理皆是曾位居要職的退休人員，他們具備豐富的專業知識，其範圍橫跨各行各業。

正確答案為 (D)

expertise「專業知識」一字可以用 a wealth of expertise「具備豐富的專業知識」表示，因此答案為 (D)。wealth 原意為「財富」，因此 a wealth of 指「大量的、充裕的」。

字彙　**expertise** 專業知識或技術　**labor** 勞動、勞工　**a wealth of** 大量的、充裕的

113. The first step of airport construction will be building a runway capable of ------- midsize commercial airplanes.
(A) handling
(B) handler
(C) handles
(D) handle

機場建設的第一步為建造一條可供中型商用客機起降的跑道。

正確答案為 (A)

〈詞性〉空格位在介系詞 of 後方，因此要選擇名詞或動名詞。空格後方是名詞 midsize commercial airplanes，因此答案要選動名詞形態的 (A)。

字彙　**runway** 跑道　**capable of** 能夠～　**handle** 處理

---

114. Sonja Pakov is one of the most popular musical artists in South America, ------- only the Wright Band in record sales.
(A) toward
(B) except
(C) among
(D) behind

松亞帕格為南美最受歡迎的音樂家之一，其專輯銷售量僅次於萊特樂團。

正確答案為 (D)

空格要選擇介系詞的位置，且能帶出與 Wright Band「萊特樂團」作比較的功能，因此答案選 (D)。behind only 原意為「除了後方的那個之外」，也就是「僅次於」。

字彙　**behind only** 僅次於　**toward** 朝向　**except** 除了～之外

---

115. Operating instructions are posted above the copy machine so that you can ------- refer to them.
(A) consequently
(B) standardly
(C) namely
(D) easily

操作說明書張貼在影印機上方，方便你隨時參考。

正確答案為 (D)

空格要填入適合強調 refer to 的副詞。根據題意，答案為 (D)。

字彙　**consequently** 結果　**standardly** 一般地　**namely** 也就是　**easily** 容易地

---

116. The team's contributions to Narumi Skincare's marketing plan were very ------- acknowledged.
(A) favor
(B) favorably
(C) favorable
(D) favored

該團隊為鳴海護膚公司的行銷計畫所做出的貢獻廣獲肯定。

正確答案為 (B)

〈詞性〉空格位在副詞 very 和分詞 acknowledged 之間，因此答案要選副詞 (B)。

字彙　**contribution to** 對～的貢獻　**acknowledge** 認可、承認　**favor** 善意、贊同　**favorably** 善意地、順利地

117. The figures we received last week ------- need to be entered into the digital database.
(A) lately
(B) evenly
(C) ever
(D) still

我們上週收到的數據還需要輸入到數位資料庫中。

正確答案為 (D)

空格要填入適合修飾 need to 的副詞，答案為 (D)，表示「仍舊、還是」之意。

字彙　**lately** 最近　**evenly** 平等地　**ever**（用於問句）究竟；（修飾形容詞）從來

118. Contract holders may terminate their contract at any time, ------- notification is given in writing at least 14 days in advance.
(A) along with
(B) according to
(C) provided that
(D) regardless of

契約持有者可隨時終止合約，但應當提前 14 天以書面形式通知。

正確答案為 (C)

空格後方有主詞 notification 與動詞 is，為完整子句，因此答案要選可以接子句的連接詞 (C)。其他選項皆為介系詞，不能接子句。

字彙　**terminate** 終止　**at any time** 隨時　**notification** 通知　**in writing** 以書面形式　**in advance** 提早、事先　**along with**（介系詞）連同　**provided that**（連接詞）假如　**regardless of**（介系詞）無論；儘管

119. Choosing the best solution to elimination of computer viruses is rarely simple, ------- it is important to seek expert advice.
(A) why
(B) then
(C) nor
(D) so

要找出清除電腦病毒的最佳解決方式並不簡單，因此尋求專家的意見很重要。

正確答案為 (D)

〈連接詞〉空格的作用為連接逗點前後的子句，要填入對等連接詞，因此答案為 (D)。nor 是否定連接詞，後方的子句須倒裝，不適合填入空格中。

字彙　**elimination** 除去　**rarely** 很少、幾乎不　**seek** 尋找　**expert** 專家　**advice** 建議

120. Samuel Jenkins' original manuscript was published last year after Sylvon Publishing Company obtained his family's -------.

席利凡出版社獲得塞繆爾傑金斯家人的許可後，於去年出版了他的原始手稿。

(A) permission
(B) suggestion
(C) comparison
(D) registration

正確答案為 (A)

空格要填入可以當動詞 obtain「獲得」的受詞，根據題意，表示「得到家人的許可」最為適當，答案為 (A)。

字彙　**manuscript** 手稿　　**comparison** 比較　　**registration** 註冊

121. Mr. Lai's draft of Sientech Industries' new mission statement expresses the company's goals -------.

賴先生在西恩科技業的新使命宣言的草稿中，準確表達公司的目標。

(A) precise
(B) more precise
(C) preciseness
(D) precisely

正確答案為 (D)

〈詞性〉空格前方為一個結構完整的句子，因此答案要選能修飾整個句子的副詞 (D)。

字彙　**industry** 業界；工業　　**precise** 準確的　　**precisely** 準確地

122. Yoon Station, provider of premium television content, welcomes ------- ideas for improving our services.

頂級電視供應商尹站公司歡迎您提供具體建議，以改善我們的服務。

(A) specifics
(B) specifies
(C) specific
(D) specify

正確答案為 (C)

〈詞性〉空格要填入形容詞修飾名詞 idea，答案為 (C)。

字彙　**provider** 供應商、公司　　**content** 內容　　**specifics** 詳情、細節　　**specific** 具體的　　**specify** 具體說明

123. Jarman Food Company has attributed its recent popularity with consumers to changes in its recipes ------- its new packaging.

賈曼食品公司將近期廣受消費者歡迎的原因歸功於烹調方式的改變，而非其新包裝。

(A) as for
(B) even so
(C) rather than
(D) after all

正確答案為 (C)

空格填入 (C) 後，呈現前方 recipes 和後方 packaging 相互對比的語意，故為正確答案。

字彙　**attribute A to B** 把 A 歸因於 B　　**popularity** 人氣、受歡迎的程度　　**rather than** 而不是　　**after all** 終究、畢竟

Test 04

124. The assembly line will continue to run unless a problem requires ------- attention.
(A) bright
(B) fluent
(C) gentle
(D) urgent

正確答案為 (D)

空格要填入形容詞來修飾名詞 attention，符合題意的是 (D)。

除非有需要緊急關注的問題，否則生產線將持續運轉。

字彙　**assembly** 組裝　**fluent** 流利的　**gentle** 輕柔的　**urgent** 緊急的

125. As the lease agreement with Charat Properties is set ------- soon, the available office space can be advertised.
(A) expired
(B) to expire
(C) will have expired
(D) expiring

正確答案為 (B)

本題考的是片語 be set to 的用法，意思為「開始、著手」，因此要選不定詞 to，答案為 (B)。

查拉特不動產的租約快到期了，空出的辦公室空間可以開始刊登廣告。

字彙　**lease agreement** 租賃契約書　**office space** 辦公空間

126. Any furniture purchased at Green Company throughout November will be delivered ------- five business days.
(A) since
(B) between
(C) within
(D) above

正確答案為 (C)

〈介系詞〉空格要填入適合放在「5 天」前方的時間介系詞，答案為 (C)。

任何在 11 月份於綠色公司購買的家具，都會在 5 個工作日內送達。

字彙　**throughout** 遍及

127. Chung & Cho auto shop requires mechanics to contact a supervisor ------- if they notice any signs of wear on edges of belt.
(A) very few
(B) finally
(C) somewhat
(D) right away

正確答案為 (D)

空格要填入副詞來修飾前面的動詞 contact，因此答案為 (D)。finally 和 somewhat 會放在動詞或形容詞前方使用，不能放在子句的最後。

鍾&趙氏汽車維修廠要求修理工一旦發現皮帶邊緣有任何磨損，就要立即通知主管。

字彙　**auto shop** 汽車維修廠　**mechanic** 修理工　**notice** 注意　**signs of wear** 磨損的跡象　**somewhat** 有點、稍微

128. ------- First Carey Bank's parking area is now open to the public, a section has been reserved only for the bank's VIP customers.
(A) **While**
(B) When
(C) But
(D) For

僅管第一凱瑞銀行的停車位目前已對外開放，但是銀行仍為他們的 VIP 客戶預留了一個停車區域。

正確答案為 (A)

空格要填入從屬連接詞，根據題意，應使用表示讓步的連接詞來引導副詞子句，因此答案為 (A)。

129. The contract for the Ricci Complex project will be awarded to ------- construction firm submits the most energy-efficient design.
(A) which
(B) **whatever**
(C) each
(D) those

力士社區大樓的建案合約將會交給能提出最佳節能設計的建設公司。

正確答案為 (B)

〈關代〉空格前方有介系詞 to，後方有完整的名詞子句，因此空格應該填入具有連接詞功能的代名詞，答案要選複合關係代名詞 (B)。

字彙　**award** 給予、授予

130. Both Mr. Cresson's payment history and the amount ------- on his loan will be considered in his application for refinancing.
(A) interested
(B) **owed**
(C) joined
(D) occupied

克雷森先生申請再融資，他的過往償還紀錄和欠款金額都會納入考量。

正確答案為 (B)

空格要填入適當的過去分詞，放在 amount「總金額」後方作修飾。根據題意，空格後方出現 his loan「他的借貸」，應表示「欠款金額」最為適當，因此答案為 (B)。

字彙　**amount** 總金額　　**loan** 借貸　　**refinancing** 再提供資金　　**owe** 欠（錢）

Test 04

Questions 131-134 refer to the following e-mail.

To: jhewittt@mailday.co.uk
From: customerservice@powerprotection.com
Date: October 10
Subject: Product Review

Dear Ms. Hewitt:

Thank you for your recent -------. We hope you are enjoying your Power Protection software. In
        131.
the unlikely event that you ------- any problems, please call customer service at 034-555-3746.
        132.
Our technicians are ready to help 24 hours a day.

If you are happy with your product, please consider writing an online review by visiting
www.powerprotection.com/yourvoice. -------. They inform ------- customers and help us grow
        133.   **134.**
our business so we can expand our line of high-quality software.

問題 131-134 題參考以下電子郵件。

收件人：jhewittt@mailday.co.uk
寄件人：customerservice@powerprotection.com
日期：10 月 10 日
主旨：產品使用心得

親愛的休伊特小姐：

感謝您於近日 ㉛ 購買我們的產品，祝您使用電源保護軟體愉快。如您 ㉜ 遇到任何預期之外的問題，請撥
打客服專線 034-555-3746，我們有技術人員 24 小時為您提供協助。

若您對購買商品感到滿意，請至 www.powerprotection.com/yourvoice 線上填寫使用心得。㉝ 從很多方
面來説，我們十分感謝使用者分享的心得。這不僅能提供資訊給 ㉞ 潛在的顧客，有助於我們事業的發展，
如此我們才得以擴充生產線，產出高品質的軟體。

字彙　**unlikely** 預期之外的　**inform** 通知　**expand** 擴張　**line** 產品線

131. (A) production   (A) 生產
      (B) purchase   **(B) 購買**
      (C) application   (C) 應用
      (D) research   (D) 研究

正確答案為 (B)

由空格後方的內容，可以得知此封電子郵件是寄給購買軟體的消費者，因此答案要選 (B)。

132. **(A) experience**
      (B) experiencing
      (C) should have experienced
      (D) were experienced

正確答案為 (A)

〈in the (unlikely) event that〉指「如果、萬一」，是假設未來可能會發生的事，因此副詞子句內的動詞要使用現在式代替未來式，答案選 (A)。

133. (A) I just want to remind you about our monthly volunteer project.
      (B) Our promotion just started when we offered discounts on all appliances.
      (C) Construction will begin in about three months as scheduled.
      (D) Such reviews are appreciated in several ways.

(A) 再次提醒您，我們每個月會有一次的志工計畫。
(B) 促銷活動已經展開，所有品項皆有提供折扣。
(C) 按照原定計畫，將於 3 個月後開始施工。
(D) 從很多方面來說，我們十分感謝使用者分享的心得。

正確答案為 (D)

〈插入句〉
空格前方的句子提到 online review「線上使用心得」，後方句子也應提到與線上使用心得相關的內容，因此答案為 (D)。(D) 的句子也使用了 such review 指前面提過的 online review，也與前一句呼應。

字彙   **as scheduled** 按照原定計畫

134. (A) selective   (A) 有選擇性的
      (B) required   (B) 必須的
      (C) potential   **(C) 潛在的**
      (D) beneficial   (D) 有益的

正確答案為 (C)

空格用來修飾 customers，表示「潛在的顧客」較為適當，因此答案為 (C)。

Questions 135-138 refer to the following e-mail.

From: Jane Fisherman
To: All staff
Date: May 1
Subject: New branding guidelines
Attachment: Document.pdf

------- to this e-mail is an abbreviated version of our corporate branding guidelines, including
   135.

information on a new logo, font, and color palette. These guidelines, which are now -------, have
                    136.

also been posted on our internal employee Web site.

We are still working on revising the print and electronic publicity to reflect these new standards.

-------. A complete form reflecting the changes -------.
 137.   138.

Please let me know if you have any problems or concerns.

問題 135-138 題參考以下電子郵件。

寄件人：珍費雪曼
收件人：全體員工
日期：5 月 1 日
主旨：新產品命名指南
附件：文件 .pdf

本封電子郵件 ⑬⑤ 附上我們公司產品命名指南的簡略版，當中包含新的商標、字體和色彩表。此份指南自即刻起 ⑬⑥ 生效，同時發布在員工內部網站上。

我們還在修改紙本與電子的宣傳品以符合新的規範，⑬⑦ 希望能在本月底前完成。反映變更的完整表格 ⑬⑧ 稍晚會分發下去。

如有任何問題或疑慮，請讓我知道。

字彙   **abbreviated** 簡略的   **corporate** 公司的   **branding** 為產品命名   **including** 包含   **palette** 用色表
       internal 內部的   **publicity** 宣傳   **standard** 規範   **reflect** 反映

135. (A) Attach
(B) Attached
(C) Attaching
(D) Attaches

正確答案為 (B)

本句的主詞為 an abbreviated version，使用分詞構句的被動語態，將動詞置於句首倒裝，因此答案為 (B)。

136. (A) out of date　　　　　　　　(A) 過時的
(B) in effect　　　　　　　　**(B) 生效的**
(C) beside the point　　　　　　(C) 離題的
(D) on purpose　　　　　　　　(D) 故意地

正確答案為 (B)

空格位在形容詞子句中，形容詞子句中有用來代替 These guidelines 的關係代名詞 which 當作主詞，也有 be 動詞 are，因此空格應填入形容詞。根據題意，表達「指南生效」的 (B) 最適合。

137. (A) I'm pleased to inform you that our application for a grant was approved.
(B) Please talk to your manager to join the program.
(C) We hope to have the process finished by the end of this month.
(D) We're going to renovate one of our branches for a modern appearance.

(A) 很高興通知您補助金申請已獲得批准。
(B) 如欲參與計畫，請先告知你的經理。
(C) 我們希望能在本月底前完成。
(D) 我們打算將其中一家分店整修成現代風的外觀。

正確答案為 (C)

〈插入句〉

前方句子出現 still working「仍在作業中」，因此應選擇語意上有承接的 (C)，表達希望在某時間前完成。

字彙　**grant** 補助金　**approve** 核准

138. (A) to distribute　　　　　　　(A) 去分發
(B) had distributed　　　　　　(B) 已經分發
(C) was distributing　　　　　(C) 過去正在分發
(D) will be distributed　　　**(D) 即將被分發**

正確答案為 (D)

空格放在句子的動詞位置，且動詞 distribute 後方沒有受詞，因此答案要選被動語態 (D)。

字彙　**distribute** 發送、分配、分發

Questions 139-142 refer to the following information.

IMPORTANT! ------- 139. . Make sure that your new Power Tech 340 washing machine is installed on a foundation that is strong ------- 140. to support its weight when it is fully loaded. In order to prevent noise and vibration, the appliance should be leveled. This is done by ------- 141. the height of the small feet at the bottom corners of the machine. Be sure to attach the water-supply hoses at the back of the machine ------- 142. to the hot and cold water valves.

問題 139-142 題參考以下資訊。

重要！⑬ 操作洗衣機之前，請仔細閱讀以下說明。新型 Power Tech 340 洗衣機要安裝在 ⑭ 足夠支撐水滿位時的總重量的地基上。為避免機身晃動產生噪音，洗衣機需保持水平。透過 ⑭ 調整洗衣機下方 4 個底腳的高度，能保持機身平穩。請務必將機器後方的供水水管 ⑭ 牢牢地連接至冷熱進水閥。

| 字彙 | foundation 基礎、建立　fully loaded 滿載的　vibration 震動　level 弄平　be sure to 務必
hose 軟水管　valve 水閥 |

139. (A) I believe that technology will contribute to improving our customers' experience.
(B) We're famous for our speedy and efficient process.
(C) I don't know exactly how many people will turn up.
(D) Carefully read the following instructions before operating your new washing machine.

(A) 我們相信科技發展將對改善顧客體驗有所貢獻。
(B) 我們以速度和效能著稱。
(C) 我不太清楚會有多少人出現。
(D) 操作洗衣機之前，請仔細閱讀以下說明。

正確答案為 **(D)**

〈插入句〉
空格出現在第一句，可以看後面一句找到線索，後方提到了安裝洗衣機的操作說明，因此本資訊應該是操作說明書，答案為 (D)。

> 字彙　**turn up** 出現、到來

140. (A) enough
(B) very
(C) so
(D) hard

正確答案為 **(A)**

空格要能搭配後方的不定詞 to 一起使用，且可以修飾前方的 strong，因此答案要選副詞 (A)。

141. (A) adjusting　　　　　　**(A) 調整**
(B) examining　　　　　　　　(B) 檢查
(C) recording　　　　　　　　(C) 記錄
(D) describing　　　　　　　　(D) 敘述

正確答案為 **(A)**

根據前後文意，安裝洗衣機時，可藉由「調整」底腳高度來保持機身的平穩度，答案為 (A)。

142. (A) are secured
(B) securely
(C) secures
(D) security

正確答案為 **(B)**

空格後面的 to 是搭配前面的 attach 而來，attach A to B 指「把 A 接上 B」，因此答案要選能夠修飾動詞的副詞，也就是 (B)。

> 字彙　**secure** 使～安全、保衛　　**security** 安全

Questions 143-146 refer to the following article.

As flu season ------- once again, people wonder what they can do to keep from contracting the
143.
miserable virus. Getting vaccinated is the best solution, but there are many other ------- that can
144.
be taken!

Remember to wash your hands well and often. -------. If you feel sick, don't be a hero — go
145.
home and rest! ------- you don't feel too bad yet, it's often in the earliest stages of illness that you
146.
can spread your flu.

問題 143-146 題參考以下報導。

隨著流感季節再次 143 到來，人們想知道如何避免感染可怕的病毒。施打流感疫苗是最好的方式，但還有很多可以預防流感的 144 方法！

記得勤洗手。145 攝取充足維他命 C 有助於維持免疫系統。生病了就回家休息，不要逞英雄！146 即使你尚未感受到不適，仍有可能處於流感初期，具有傳染力。

字彙　**flu** 流行性感冒　**wonder** 想知道　**keep from** 阻止　**contract** 感染　**get vaccinated** 預防接種
spread 蔓延　**illness** 疾病

143. (A) approach
(B) approaches
(C) approached
(D) approaching

正確答案為 (B)

空格前方有連接詞 as，為副詞子句，時態要與主要子句動詞 wonders 一致，應填入現在式第三人稱單數型，因此答案為 (B)。

144. (A) warnings   (A) 警告
(B) symptoms   (B) 症狀
(C) precautions   **(C) 預防措施**
(D) communities   (D) 社區

正確答案為 (C)

空格所在的句子前方提到預防感染的方式。根據文意，空格填入 precautions「預防措施」最為適當，答案為 (C)。

145. (A) They give employees up to ten days of sick leave.
(B) The flu is spreading across borders through the area.
(C) Keep your immune system strong with plenty of vitamin C.
(D) Some people remain symptom-free for several years.

(A) 他們同意員工最多可以請 10 天病假。
(B) 流感正在該區域蔓延。
(C) 攝取充足維他命 C 有助於維持免疫系統。
(D) 有些人多年來都未出現症狀。

正確答案為 (C)

〈插入句〉

本句前一句與後一句都提到預防病毒感染的方法，因此答案要選同樣是預防流感的方法 (C) 才符合邏輯。

字彙   **up to** 多達   **sick leave** 病假   **across border** 跨越邊界   **immune system** 免疫系統   **symptom-free** 無症狀的

146. **(A) Even if**   **(A) 即使**
(B) As if   (B) 彷彿
(C) In case of   (C) 假如
(D) Rather than   (D) 而不是

正確答案為 (A)

根據題意，整句要表示「即使你尚未感受到不適，仍有可能處於流感初期」，因此應填入表示轉折的連接詞，答案為 (A)。

Questions 147-148 refer to the following flyer. 傳單

Seattle Movie Club

The Seattle Movie Club is proud to present our first Bollywood Festival. From September 18 through November 6, a total of eight contemporary and classic movies by Bollywood filmmakers will be shown at Coleman Theater near Lloyd Mall. The free movies, shown with Spanish and English subtitles, will begin at 7:00 P.M. each Saturday. To view the complete program, please visit our Web site at seattlemovieclub.org.

問題 147-148 題參考以下傳單。

西雅圖電影俱樂部

(147) 西雅圖電影俱樂部很榮幸能舉辦第一屆寶萊塢影展。從 9 月 18 日起自 11 月 6 日止，預計於羅伊德購物中心旁的科爾曼劇院播放 8 部由寶萊塢電影製片人拍攝的當代與經典電影。免費電影會提供西班牙文和英文字幕，並於每週六晚間 7 點開始放映。(148) 如欲查看完整場次資訊，請至網站 seattlemovieclub.org。

字彙　**contemporary** 當代的　**filmmaker** 影片製作人　**subtitle** 字幕　**program** 節目表

147. What is being announced?
(A) **The opening of a film festival**
(B) An interview with a Bollywood actor
(C) A film production
(D) A movie series

本文告知什麼內容？
(A) **影展開幕**
(B) 寶萊塢演員的訪談
(C) 電影製作
(D) 電影系列作品

正確答案為 (A)

題目詢問文章主題內容，通常可以在開頭找到線索，第一句寫 The Seattle Movie Club is proud to present our first Bollywood Festival，因此答案為 (A)。

148. According to the flyer, what can be found on the Seattle Movie Club Web site?
(A) Free tickets to a new film
(B) Directions to Coleman Theater
(C) **A list of events**
(D) Biographies of movie directors

根據傳單，西雅圖電影俱樂部的網站上可以看到什麼內容？
(A) 新片的免費票券
(B) 前往科爾曼劇院的路線
(C) **活動列表**
(D) 電影導演傳記

正確答案為 (C)

提到網址的最後一句寫 To view the complete program, please visit our Web site at seattlemovieclub.org，答案是完整節目表的 (C)。

字彙　**direction** 路線圖　**biography** 傳記

Test 04

Questions 149-150 refer to the following notice. 通知

Air Gold

Air Gold offers special meals, free of charge on all flights lasting three hours or more. Whether you reserved your flight with Air Gold or through an authorized agency, please call our customer service hotline at 121-555-0987 at least 24 hours before your scheduled flight departure to request a special meal. Travelers with any dietary concerns or restrictions may wish to call the hotline. Our catering staff will do its utmost to accommodate your needs. For a list of special meals, sample dishes or common ingredients, visit our Web site, www.airgold.com.

問題 149-150 題參考以下通知。

黃金航空

150 黃金航空免費為 3 小時以上的飛行提供特殊餐點。 149 向黃金航空或航空公司授權的旅行社預訂機票時,請於班機起飛前至少 24 小時,撥打客服專線 121-555-0987 完成訂餐。 150 有特殊餐飲需求或限制的旅客,請事先打客服電話告知,餐飲服務人員會盡力滿足您的需求。特殊餐飲列表、餐食樣品照、常用食材表請參閱網頁 www.airgold.com。

 字彙　**free of charge** 免費　**authorized** 經授權的　**agency** 旅行社　**dietary** 飲食方面的　**restriction** 限制
catering 外燴餐飲服務　**do one's utmost** 竭盡全力　**accommodate** 接納、接受;容納
ingredient 食材、原料

149. For whom is the advertisement most likely intended?
(A) Tour guides
(B) Travel agents
(C) Airline passengers
(D) Flight attendants

此篇文章最有可能的廣告對象是誰？
(A) 導遊
(B) 旅行社員工
(C) 飛機乘客
(D) 空服員

正確答案為 (C)

詢問文章訴求對象的訊息，多半可以在開頭找到答案。第一段提到 Whether you reserved your flight with Air Gold，會預定飛機的是乘客，因此答案為 (C)。

150. What is the purpose of the notice?
(A) To advertise a benefit of a membership program
(B) To give information about dining options
(C) To announce the hiring of aircraft pilots
(D) To suggest some healthful eating guidelines

本篇通知的目的為何？
(A) 宣傳會員制度福利
(B) 告知餐飲選擇資訊
(C) 公告招募飛機機師
(D) 提供健康飲食指南建議

正確答案為 (B)

詢問文章的主旨，答案通常會在第一段就出現。文章第一句提到提供機上飲食的訊息，接著針對餐飲服務進行說明 Our catering staff will do its utmost to accommodate your needs，因此答案為 (B)。

字彙　**benefit** 福利

Questions 151-153 refer to the following advertisement. 廣告

 Grand Opening Celebration!

Ashland Brothers Company

54 Thompson Plaza (Next to Kathryn's Bakery)
San Diego, CA 94789
512-555-0090

Grand Opening Specials:
30% off all desks and chairs
25% off sofa (leather only)
15% off any dining tables

Offers good from July 3 to August 3
(Free cleaning products with purchase of $30 or more: Thompson Plaza Store only)

Store hours 8:00 A.M. – 8:00 P.M.

Sign up for the Ashland Brothers Company membership — for just $25 per year, get an additional 10% off everything you buy at both our Thompson Plaza and Alina Mall store locations as well as online!

Visit our Web site at www.ashlandbrotherscompany.com.

This week only, order any bookcase online and get 40% off!

問題 **151-153** 題參考以下廣告。

🍽 **盛大開幕慶！**

亞什蘭兄弟公司

94789 加州聖地牙哥湯普森廣場 54 號（凱瑟琳麵包店旁）

512-555-0090

開幕特別活動：

151 桌椅全面七折

沙發（限皮革沙發）七五折

所有餐桌八五折

152A 優惠期間為 7 月 3 日至 8 月 3 日

（消費滿 30 美元以上，免費贈送清潔產品：僅限湯普森廣場店）

152B 營業時間：上午 8 點至晚上 8 點

申請加入亞什蘭兄弟公司會員，即一年消費滿 25 美元者，152D 於湯普森廣場店和愛麗娜購物中心店內消費時，可享有全品項九折的優惠，此優惠同樣適用於線上購物！

進入我們的網站 www.ashlandbrotherscompany.com

本週限定，153 線上訂購書櫃可享六折優惠！

字彙　**good** 有效的

151. What type of merchandise does Ashland Brothers Company sell?
(A) Electronics
(B) Office supplies
(C) Clothing
(D) Furniture

亞什蘭兄弟公司販售何種商品？
(A) 電子產品
(B) 辦公室用品
(C) 服飾
(D) 家具

正確答案為 (D)

文中中段寫到 30% off all desks and chairs, 25% off sofa (leather only), 15% off any dining tables，都是販賣家具品項，可以得知該公司為家具店，答案為 (D)。

字彙　**clothing** 服飾

152. What is indicated from Ashland Brothers Company?
(A) Its grand-opening specials are offered for only one week.
(B) It stays open until 10 P.M. on August 3.
(C) Its salespeople are highly trained.
(D) It has more than one location.

下列敘述何者符合亞什蘭兄弟公司？
(A) 開幕活動僅為期一週。
(B) 營業至 8 月 3 日晚上 10 點。
(C) 銷售人員皆接受嚴格的訓練。
(D) 分店數量超過一家。

正確答案為 (D)

開幕時間 Offers good from July 3 to August 3 不符合 (A)，營業時間 Store hours 8:00 A.M. – 8:00 P.M. 不符合 (B)，關於人員訓練文章中沒有提及。只有 (D) 的敘述符合文中的 both our Thompson Plaza and Alina Mall store locations。

153. For which item will the customers get a discount only when they purchase it by online?
(A) Baked goods
(B) Cleaning products
(C) Bookcases
(D) Leather items

下列產品中，何者僅限線上購買才享有優惠？
(A) 烘焙食品
(B) 清潔用品
(C) 書櫃
(D) 皮革

正確答案為 (C)

尋找關鍵字 online，最後一句提到 This week only, order any bookcase online and get 40% off!，答案為 (C)。

Questions 154-155 refer to the following text message chain. 文字簡訊串

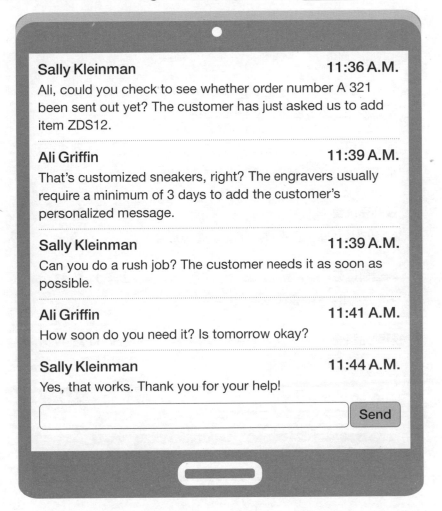

Sally Kleinman	11:36 A.M.

Ali, could you check to see whether order number A 321 been sent out yet? The customer has just asked us to add item ZDS12.

Ali Griffin	11:39 A.M.

That's customized sneakers, right? The engravers usually require a minimum of 3 days to add the customer's personalized message.

Sally Kleinman	11:39 A.M.

Can you do a rush job? The customer needs it as soon as possible.

Ali Griffin	11:41 A.M.

How soon do you need it? Is tomorrow okay?

Sally Kleinman	11:44 A.M.

Yes, that works. Thank you for your help!

Send

問題 154-155 題參考以下文字簡訊串。

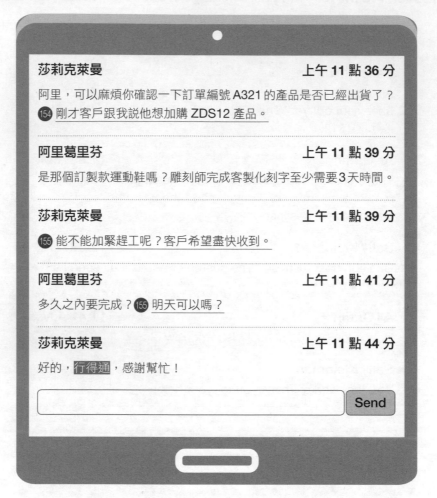

莎莉克萊曼　　　　　　　上午 **11** 點 **36** 分

阿里，可以麻煩你確認一下訂單編號 **A321** 的產品是否已經出貨了？
(154) 剛才客戶跟我說他想加購 **ZDS12** 產品。

阿里葛里芬　　　　　　　上午 **11** 點 **39** 分

是那個訂製款運動鞋嗎？雕刻師完成客製化刻字至少需要 3 天時間。

莎莉克萊曼　　　　　　　上午 **11** 點 **39** 分

(155) 能不能加緊趕工呢？客戶希望盡快收到。

阿里葛里芬　　　　　　　上午 **11** 點 **41** 分

多久之內要完成？(155) 明天可以嗎？

莎莉克萊曼　　　　　　　上午 **11** 點 **44** 分

好的，行得通，感謝幫忙！

| Send |

字彙　**customized** 客製化的　　**engraver** 雕刻師　　**rush job** 急事

154. What does the customer want to do?

(A) Add an item to the order
(B) Exchange a product
(C) Receive a refund
(D) Use a discount code

客戶想要做什麼？

(A) 加購產品
(B) 換貨
(C) 退款
(D) 使用折扣碼

正確答案為 (A)

莎莉克萊曼於上午 11 點 36 分撰寫的簡訊提到 customer，寫 The customer has just asked us to add item ZDS12，可以得知答案為 (A)。

155. At 11:44 A.M., what does Ms. Kleinman most likely mean when she writes "that works"?

(A) She plans to make a slide presentation at the meeting.
(B) She is informed that the equipment is repaired.
(C) The customer will be satisfied if the item is ready tomorrow.
(D) A shipping company will deliver the item by the end of the day.

上午 11 點 44 分克萊曼小姐寫「行得通」是什麼意思？

(A) 她打算在會議中用投影片做簡報。
(B) 她被告知設備已經修好。
(C) 若能在明天之前完成產品，客戶會很滿意。
(D) 物流公司會於今天之內將產品送達。

正確答案為 (C)

〈推測句意〉

詢問某句的意圖時，需要檢視其前後句並綜合考量。 莎莉克萊曼於上午 11 點 39 分撰寫的簡訊提到 Can you do a rush job? The customer needs it as soon as possible。對於她的提問，阿里葛里芬於上午 11 點 41 分回覆 How soon do you need it? Is tomorrow okay?，之後再接這一句話，因此答案選 (C)。

Test 04

Questions 156-157 refer to the following information. 資訊

Brilliant ideas for cutting electricity expenses.

There are some helpful suggestions for high office utility costs.

Environment: Pull up the shades and blinds for more natural light, whenever possible. Use bright wall paper to reflect more natural light.

Lighting: Replace incandescent light bulbs with florescent light bulbs, which have the same brightness and use less energy, without replacing light fixtures. Use motion sensors to reduce the usage of electricity in non-working areas where light is not constantly used, such as storage rooms or closets.

Office Equipment: Turn off printers and copiers when they are not in use. Use a power strip. It will be very convenient to turn off all office equipment with the flip of the switch. A screen saver is not an energy saver. Please turn off your monitor when you leave the office. Use an auto timer to turn off electricity when the office is not occupied.

問題 156-157 題參考以下資訊。

降低電費的智慧點子。

以下針對高昂的辦公室水電費提出幾項實用的建議。

環境：156 盡量拉開窗簾和百葉窗，讓更多自然光進入室內。使用亮色壁紙，反射更多的自然光。

照明：將白熾燈換泡成日光燈泡，便能在不更換燈具的情況下，使用較少的電量維持同樣亮度。在不需持續用電的非工作區域，如儲藏室或更衣室，裝設自動感應燈省電。

辦公室設備：印表機或影印機未使用時，請關閉電源。157C 善用電線排插，方便一次關閉所有電源。157B 螢幕保護程式並不具省電功能，離開辦公室時，請關閉你的電腦螢幕。157D 辦公室無人使用時，請使用自動定時器關閉電源。

字彙　**utility** 如水電瓦斯等公用事業費　**shade** 窗簾　**blind** 百葉窗　**incandescent** 白熾燈　**florescent** 日光燈的
light fixture 燈具　**motion sensor** 自動感應燈　**reduce** 減少、降低　**constantly** 持續地
power strip 電線排插　**flip of the switch** 按一下開關　**occupied** 已佔用的、有人使用的

156. According to the information, how can light at the workplace be maximized?

(A) By relocating light fixtures

(B) By installing motion sensors in work areas

(C) By using brighter lightbulbs

(D) By letting more daylight enter the room

根據本資訊，如何讓最多的光照進工作場所？

(A) 移動燈具位置

(B) 在工作區域裝設自動感應燈

(C) 使用亮度更高的燈泡

(D) 讓更多的陽光進入室內

正確答案為 (D)

第二段寫到 Pull up the shades and blinds for more natural light, whenever possible，可以得知答案為 (D)。

> 字彙　**maximize** 使～最大化

157. What is NOT mentioned as a way to limit energy consumption?

(A) Replacing office equipment with more efficient ones

(B) Turning off monitors instead of using screen savers

(C) Using power strips to turn off multiple devices

(D) Installing automatic timers

下列何者並非文中提及的節約能源方式？

(A) 換成效能更佳的辦公室設備

(B) 關閉電腦螢幕取代使用螢幕保護程式

(C) 使用電線排插來關閉多個電源裝置

(D) 裝設自動定時器

正確答案為 (A)

(C) 出現在第四段 Use a power strip. It will be very convenient to turn off all office equipment with the flip of the switch；(B) 出現在同段的 A screen saver is not an energy saver. Please turn off your monitor when you leave the office；(D) 出現在文章最後 Use an auto timer to turn off electricity when the office is not occupied。文中並未提及 (A) 的內容。

> 字彙　**energy consumption** 能源消耗　　**limit** 限制　　**replace A with B** 把 A 換成 B

Questions 158-160 refer to the following memo. 備忘録

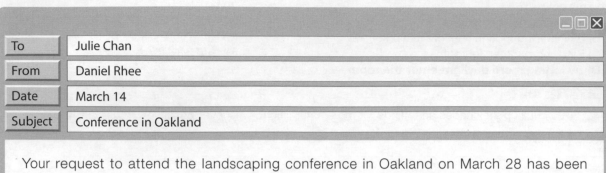

To	Julie Chan
From	Daniel Rhee
Date	March 14
Subject	Conference in Oakland

Your request to attend the landscaping conference in Oakland on March 28 has been approved by the vice president. In keeping with our travel policies, your plane ticket, rental car, and hotel room will be paid by the company in advance. –[1]–. Please plan to turn in receipts for meals, gasoline, and any other business-related expenses on your return. Please remember that company policy states that entertainment costs are not reimbursable. –[2]–.

A preliminary itinerary has you booked March 28 on Super Jet flight# 263, departing at 6:28 A.M. The return trip is for March 30 on flight 319, departing Oakland at 3:05 P.M. –[3]–. A compact vehicle has been reserved at Patel Autos at the airport; you can pick up the car there when you arrive. You will be staying at the Plaza Fisher Hotel on San Andreas Street. I hope all these arrangements meet with your approval. –[4]–. Please call me at extension 2326 between 9:15 A.M. and 4:30 P.M. tomorrow so that details can be finalized. I will email you a formal itinerary by the end of the week.

Thank you.

Daniel Rhee
Administrative Support Office

問題 158-160 題參考以下備忘錄。

收件人	茱莉陳
寄件人	丹尼爾李
日期	3 月 14 日
主旨	奧克蘭會議

158 您要求參加 3 月 28 日於奧克蘭舉行的景觀設計會議已獲得副總批准。 160 根據差旅規定，公司會提前支付您的機票、租車、飯店住宿費用。–[1]– 160 餐費、加油費、以及其他業務相關費用，請您於回國後繳交收據。請記得，按公司規定，娛樂費用不得報銷。–[2]–

依照預定行程表，已為您預訂 3 月 28 日上午 6 點 28 分出發的 Super Jet 航空 263 號班機，159C 回程為 3 月 30 日下午 3 點 5 分從奧克蘭出發的 319 號班機。–[3]– 159A 159D 我已向機場的帕特爾汽車公司預約了一輛小型房車，班機抵達後您可以直接取車。您將入住位於聖安地列斯街上的廣場漁人酒店。希望上述這些安排您會同意。–[4]– 請於明天上午 9 點 15 分至下午 4 點 30 分之間撥打分機 2326 給我敲定細節。我會在本週內以電子郵件將正式行程表傳送給您。

謝謝。

丹尼爾李
行政總務辦公室

字彙 **in keeping with** 與～一致　**reimbursable** 可報銷的　**preliminary** 初步的　**itinerary** 旅行計畫
compact vehicle 小型車　**arrangement** 安排　**meet with one's approval** 某人同意
extension 分機號碼　**administrative** 行政的

158. What is suggested about travel requests?
(A) They must have details about an itinerary.
(B) They must include a project proposal.
(C) They must estimate meal costs.
(D) They must be authorized by an executive.

下列有關出差的要求何者正確？
(A) 必須提供詳細的行程表。
(B) 必須同時附上企劃提案書。
(C) 必須估算餐食成本。
(D) 必須經高層主管授權。

正確答案為 (D)

信件開頭提到 Your request to attend the environmental law seminar in Oakland on March 28 has been approved by the vice president，由此可知答案為 (D)。

字彙　**authorize** 批准、授權

159. What is NOT stated about Patel Autos?
(A) It accepts reservations.
(B) It is on San Andreas Street.
(C) It has a location in Oakland.
(D) It rents small cars.

下列有關帕特爾汽車公司的敘述何者錯誤？
(A) 接受預約。
(B) 位在聖安地列斯街上。
(C) 有間位在奧克蘭的分公司。
(D) 出租小型車輛。

正確答案為 (B)

文章中提到 Patel Auto 帕特爾汽車的部份在第二段，A compact vehicle has been reserved at Patel Autos at the airport 當中提到 (A) 和 (D)；預約取車的地點為奧克蘭，因此 (C) 的敘述正確。位在聖安地列斯街上的是廣場漁人酒店，帕特爾汽車公司位在機場，因此答案選 (B)。

160. In which of the positions marked [1], [2], [3], and [4] does the following sentence best belong?
"You will be reimbursed for any additional expenses you incur while in Oakland."
(A) [1]
(B) [2]
(C) [3]
(D) [4]

在標示 [1]、[2]、[3]、[4] 的位置中，何者適合放入以下句子？
「您在奧克蘭出差期間所產生的額外支出將可報公帳。」
(A) [1]
(B) [2]
(C) [3]
(D) [4]

正確答案為 (A)

〈插入句〉

本題的關鍵句提到 reimburse「報銷費用、報公帳」，可見與報帳有關。[1] 後方的句子 Please plan to turn in receipts for meals, gasoline, and any other business-related expenses on your return 進一步提到報帳的方式，因此答案為 (A)。

字彙　**reimburse** 補貼、報公帳　　**expenses**（常用複數）支出、開銷　　**incur** 產生、招致

Questions 161-164 refer to the following e-mail. 電子郵件

From	Jane Kovar, President and CEO
To	All Bartel Financial Group Headquarters Staff
Date	February 3
Subject	Ellen Ortiz

After careful deliberation by the Bartel board of directors, I am pleased to announce that Ellen Ortiz, our current Director of Investor Relations, will take over as European Regional Manager when Andres Hildebrand retires next month. Ms. Ortiz's promotion comes at a time of increased emphasis on international markets. Working from our Rome office, she will oversee the continued growth of Bartel in Italy and its expansion into Germany and southwestern Europe.

Those of you who have worked with her know that Ms. Ortiz is an excellent choice for the job. After graduating from Kingston University in Dublin, she worked for Ostrava Finance in Italy for a number of years before joining Bartel over 20 years ago. She is a native Italian speaker and is fluent in several other languages. During her first years at Bartel, she worked in the Brussels office before being transferred to the Paris office, and finally to the headquarters here in London. Her outstanding leadership in investor relations has helped our client base grow by over 20 percent in the last 10 years.

Finally, to commemorate Mr. Hildebrand's many accomplishments during his years with Bartel, we have planned a farewell gathering for Friday, February 28, at the Prost Café near company headquarters from 6 P.M. to 8 P.M. For more information about the event, please contact my assistant Stan Milton at extension 1259. Any questions about these staffing changes should be directed to Bill Belmore, Director of Personnel, at extension 1286.

問題 161-164 題參考以下電子郵件。

```
┌─────────────────────────────────────────────────────────[_][□][X]─┐
│                                                                     │
│   ┌────────┐                                                        │
│   │ 寄件者 │  總裁兼執行長珍柯瓦爾                                   │
│   └────────┘  ──────────────────────────────────────────────────   │
│   ┌────────┐                                                        │
│   │ 收件人 │  巴特爾金融集團總公司員工                              │
│   └────────┘  ──────────────────────────────────────────────────   │
│   ┌────────┐                                                        │
│   │  日期  │  2 月 3 日                                             │
│   └────────┘  ──────────────────────────────────────────────────   │
│   ┌────────┐                                                        │
│   │  主旨  │  艾倫奧提茲                                            │
│   └────────┘  ──────────────────────────────────────────────────   │
│                                                                     │
└─────────────────────────────────────────────────────────────────────┘
```

經巴特爾董事會仔細考量之後，我很高興向各位宣布，現任投資人關係部總監 **(161)** 艾倫奧提茲將接替下個月退休的安德瑞斯希爾德布蘭，成為歐洲區經理。奧提茲小姐的升遷正好是國際市場日益受重視之時。她未來就任於羅馬辦事處後，將負責監督巴特爾於義大利的成長狀況，並將市場擴展至德國和西南歐。

曾與奧提茲小姐共事的人都知道，她接下此工作是極為正確的選擇。她從都柏林金斯頓大學畢業後，在義大利奧斯特拉瓦金融公司工作數年，接著於 20 年前正式進入巴特爾。**(162)** 她的母語為義大利文，並精通多種外語。剛進入巴特爾的前幾年，她在布魯塞爾工作，而後被調任至巴黎分公司，最後才派到 **(164)** 我們的倫敦總公司工作。她在投資人關係部門中展現傑出的領導能力，在她的協助下，過去 10 年間，公司客戶增加兩成以上。

最後，**(163)** 為了表揚希爾德布蘭先生在巴特爾工作期間創下的功績，我們計畫 2 月 28 日週五傍晚 6 點到 8 點，**(164)** 在總公司附近的普羅斯特咖啡廳為他舉辦歡送會。如欲了解該活動的詳細資訊，請撥打分機 1259 與我的助理史坦米爾頓聯繫。對於人事異動有疑問者，則請撥打分機 1286，直接聯繫人事部主任比爾貝爾莫。

字彙 **deliberation** 深思熟慮　　**emphasis on** 強調　　**transfer** 調職　　**headquarters**（固定用複數）總公司
client base 客戶群　　**by** 表數量的增減幅度　　**commemorate** 紀念　　**accomplishment** 功績
farewell gathering 歡送會　　**staffing change** 人事異動

161. What position does Mr. Hildebrand currently have?
(A) Chief Executive Officer
(B) Manager of Investor Relations
(C) Director of Personnel
(D) European Regional Manager

希爾德布蘭先生目前的職位是？
(A) 執行長
(B) 投資人關係部經理
(C) 人事部主任
(D) 歐洲區經理

正確答案為 (D)

可尋找電子郵件中提到 Hildebrand 希爾德布蘭的地方。第一段中提到 Ellen Ortiz will take over as European Regional Manager when Andres Hildebrand retires next month，可知答案為 (D)。

162. What is indicated about Ms. Ortiz?
(A) She lived in Brussels for over twenty years.
(B) She speaks several languages.
(C) She has a degree in International Business.
(D) She is leaving Bartel to work for a company in Germany.

下列敘述何者與奧提茲小姐相符？
(A) 她在布魯塞爾住了 20 年以上。
(B) 她會說好幾種語言。
(C) 她取得國際商務學位。
(D) 她將離開巴特爾前往德國的公司工作。

正確答案為 (B)

選項中提到許多有關 Ellen Ortiz 的經歷，詳述其經歷主要在電子郵件第二段，其中提到 She is a native Italian speaker and is fluent in several other languages，因此答案選 (B)。

163. What is the purpose of the event on February 28?
(A) To discuss potential replacements for Mr. Hildebrand
(B) To share investment opinions with prospective clients
(C) To announce Bartel's plans for a merger with a competitor
(D) To recognize Mr. Hildebrand's contributions to Bartel

2 月 28 日舉辦的活動目的為何？
(A) 討論接任希爾德布蘭先生的適合人選
(B) 與潛在客戶分享投資意見
(C) 宣布巴特爾與競爭對手合併的計畫
(D) 認可希爾德布蘭先生對巴特爾的貢獻

正確答案為 (D)

注意電子郵件中提到 2/28 這個日期的敘述，最後一段提到 to commemorate Mr. Hildebrand's many accomplishments during his years with Bartel, we have planned a farewell gathering for Friday, February 28，答案為 (D)。

字彙 **potential** 潛在的　　**replacement** 接替者、取代　　**prospective** 有希望的　　**merger** 合併

164. In which city will the event be held most likely?
(A) Brussels
(B) Paris
(C) London
(D) Rome

此活動最有可能在哪個城市舉辦？
(A) 布魯塞爾
(B) 巴黎
(C) 倫敦
(D) 羅馬

正確答案為 (C)

最後一段寫 at the Prost Café near company headquarters，指出地點位於總公司，再由前面文章得知總公司在倫敦，因此答案為 (C)。

Questions 165-167 refer to the following Web page. 網頁

http://easyservicestation.com

EASY SERVICE STATION

Easy Service Station owns and operates a large chain of truck stops and travel centers throughout Wisconsin. Our centers are conveniently located along most major highways and are open 24 hours a day, 365 days a year.

Easy Service Station center is equipped with fueling stations, a convenience store, a full-service restaurant and other amenities to make long-distance travel more comfortable.

• Automated teller machines are available 24 hours a day.

• Check cashing and money transfer services are available Monday to Friday, from 8 A.M. to 4 P.M.

• All locations have public laundries; some have public showers.

• Each location has an indoor lounge area with cable television and wireless Internet services.

• Hot food is available in our restaurants, and coffee and baked goods can be purchased in our convenience stores.

For a full list of Easy Service Station centers, click the link below.

www.easyservicestation.com/list

問題 165-167 題參考以下網頁。

http://easyservicestation.com

輕鬆服務站

165 輕鬆服務站在威斯康辛州經營多家大型連鎖卡車休息站和旅遊服務中心。服務中心大多設在主要高速公路旁，位置方便，24 小時營業全年無休。

輕鬆服務站設有加油站、便利商店、完全服務型餐廳、和其他便利設施，讓您在長途旅行中更加舒適。

• 自動櫃員機 24 小時全天候服務。

• 週一至週五上午 8 點至下午 4 點，提供支票兌現和轉帳服務。

• 所有服務站皆設有公共洗衣間，166 部分站點設有淋浴間。

• 各服務站設有室內休息區，提供有線電視和無線上網服務。

• 餐廳內提供熱食，咖啡和烘焙食品，可於便利商店內購買。

167 點擊下方連結，查看完整的輕鬆服務站地點清單。

www.easyservicestation.com/list

字彙 **be equipped with** 配備有、設有～　**fueling station** 加油站　**full-service** 有服務人員的
amenities（常用複數）便利設施　**automatic teller machine** 自動櫃員機　**cash** 兌現、換成現金

674

165. What does the Web page describe?

(A) **Roadside facilities**
(B) Car dealerships
(C) Relocation assistance
(D) Discounted hotels

該網頁在描述什麼？

(A) 路邊設施
(B) 汽車經銷商
(C) 搬遷服務
(D) 折扣酒店

正確答案為 (A)

本題詢問文章主題，通常可以在第一段找到答案。第一段提到 Easy Service Station owns and operates a large chain of truck stops and travel centers throughout Wisconsin. Our centers are conveniently located along most major highways，由此可知本文在介紹高速公路旁的休息站，因此答案選 (A)。

166. What do only some locations offer?

(A) **Shower rooms**
(B) A lounge area
(C) Hot meals
(D) Laundry rooms

僅限部分站點提供的是什麼？

(A) 淋浴間
(B) 休息區
(C) 熱食
(D) 洗衣間

正確答案為 (A)

文中提到 some have public showers，答案為 (A)。

167. What information can most likely be found by clicking the link provided?

(A) Room rates
(B) Service charges
(C) **Location information**
(D) Reservation details

點擊連結後最有可能出現哪些資訊？

(A) 房價
(B) 服務費
(C) 位置資訊
(D) 預約細節

正確答案為 (C)

網站連結出現在最後一句，提到 For a full list of Easy Service Station centers, click the link below，加上 Easy Service Station 是休息站，最有可能的答案是 (C)。

Questions 168-171 refer to the following article. 報導

Munich (March 22) – Munich-based Steinmeier announced plans on Tuesday to build a second processing facility. Currently, the company's sole facility is located near Frankfurt, about 480 kilometers from its Munich corporate headquarters. The new facility, which is expected to cost upwards of €30 million, is part of a corporate strategy to boost profits by expanding into overseas markets.

Executives hope the ambitious expansion to Shanghai in China will help the company to become a major competitor in the China market. Once completed, the two processing plants together will have the capacity to meet the demands of both the Chinese and European markets. –[1]–. "An added benefit is that we would be able to maintain essential production for both markets in the event that one of the facilities is temporarily shut down for maintenance work or repairs," said company president Daniel Hoffman.

Mr. Hoffman's father, Jeremy Hoffman, founded Steinmeier in 1979 after graduating from business school in Beijing. –[2]–. In its first year of business, the company managed to turn a sizeable profit, which grew by 47% the following year. Today, Steinmeier is an internationally recognized beverage brand distributed in 30 countries across Europe. Despite its enormous success, however, sales have slowed recently as market share has dropped, and a new management team under Mr. Hoffman is aggressively trying to turn the company around. –[3]–.

The full range of Steinmeier's existing beverage products should be available in 20 cities in China by the end of the summer, according to regional sales manager Amy Garrett. –[4]–. Ms. Garrett envisions launching a line of fruit-based baked goods such as cookies and cakes to complement the company's current product line. "Our hope is that we continue to grow and develop new items that our customers will love." she said.

問題 **168-171** 題參考以下報導。

慕尼黑（3 月 22 日）一總部位於慕尼黑的史坦麥爾公司在週二宣布設立第二個加工廠的計畫。目前，該公司唯一的廠房位於法蘭克福附近，距離慕尼黑公司總部 480 公里。新工廠預計耗資超過三千萬歐元，透過擴展海外市場來增加收益為企業戰略的其中一部分。

公司決策者 ⑯⑧ 希望擴展至中國上海的企圖，將有助於公司成為中國市場的主要競爭對手。一旦蓋好新工廠，兩個加工廠的產能將能同時滿足中國和歐洲市場的需求。–[1]– 公司總裁丹尼爾霍夫曼說道：「另一個好處是，如為進行維護或檢修，暫時關閉其中一間工廠時，仍能維持兩個市場所需的基本生產量。」

⑰① 霍夫曼先生的父親傑瑞米霍夫曼從北京商學院畢業後，於 1979 年創立了史坦麥爾公司。–[2]– ⑰① 公司營業第一年便創下極為可觀的利潤，第二年的獲利更成長 47%。今日，史坦麥爾公司成為一個備受國際認可的飲料品牌，流通於歐洲 30 個國家。⑯⑨ 儘管公司大獲成功，但隨著市佔率的下跌，近期的銷售量成長趨緩。霍夫曼先生所領導的新管理團隊正在積極嘗試扭轉公司的局面。–[3]–

根據區域銷售經理艾咪加雷特所述，史坦麥爾公司會於夏末前，在中國 20 個城市推出現有的全系列飲料產品。–[4]– ⑰⓪ 加雷特小姐打算推出一系列以水果為基底的烘焙食品，如餅乾和蛋糕，來補充公司目前的生產線。她說：「希望我們能持續發展並開發出顧客喜歡的新產品。」

字彙　**processing facility** 加工廠　**sole** 唯一的　**upward** 向上的　**strategy** 策略　**boost** 促進　**expand into** 擴展　**executive** 決策者、主管　**ambitious** 有野心的　**expansion** 擴展　**competitor** 競爭對手　**meet the demand** 滿足需求　**maintain** 維持　**essential** 必需的　**in the event that** 如果　**temporarily** 暫時地　**sizable** 相當大的　**enormous** 龐大的　**market share** 市佔率　**drop** 下降　**aggressively** 積極地、激烈地　**turn around** 革新、好轉　**full range** 全系列　**envision** 構想　**complement** 補充

168. Where will the new facility be located?
(A) Munich
(B) Frankfurt
(C) Shanghai
(D) Beijing

新的設施將設在哪裡？
(A) 慕尼黑
(B) 法蘭克福
(C) 上海
(D) 北京

正確答案為 (C)

文章第一段開頭提到即將興建第二間加工廠，接著第二段中提到 the ambitious expansion to Shanghai in China，因此答案選 (C)。

169. What is mentioned about Steinmeier?
(A) Its competitors sell less products than Steinmeier.
(B) It sells products only in Munich.
(C) Product sales have declined recently.
(D) It is planning to recruit new board members.

文中談及史坦麥爾公司的內容為何？
(A) 競爭對手的銷量低於史坦麥爾公司。
(B) 產品僅限於慕尼黑販售。
(C) 近期的產品銷量下跌。
(D) 招募新的董事會成員。

正確答案為 (C)

提到 Steinmeier 史坦麥爾公司的敘述，主要看第三段。第三段中提到 sales have slowed recently as market share has dropped，因此答案要選 (C)。

字彙　**decline** 下跌、衰退

170. What new type of product is Steinmeier planning to develop?
(A) Desserts
(B) Cosmetics
(C) Tableware
(D) Drinks

史坦麥爾公司計畫開發哪種新產品？
(A) 甜點
(B) 化妝品
(C) 餐具
(D) 飲料

正確答案為 (A)

第四段中提到 Ms. Garrett envisions launching a line of fruit-based baked goods such as cookies and cakes to complement the company's current product line，baked goods「烘焙食品」屬於 dessert「甜點」，答案為 (A)。

171. In which of the positions marked [1], [2], [3], and [4] does the following sentence best belong?

"Returning to northern German, he began selling fresh-squeezed fruit juice to restaurants and supermarkets across the region."

(A) [1]
(B) [2]
(C) [3]
(D) [4]

在標示 [1]、[2]、[3]、[4] 的位置中，何者適合放入以下句子？

「回到德國北部後，他開始販售現榨果汁給當地餐廳和超市。」

(A) [1]
(B) [2]
(C) [3]
(D) [4]

正確答案為 (B)

〈插入句〉

關鍵句提到回到德國一事，暗示前面有提及不在德國的狀況，[2] 前一句 Mr. Hoffman's father, Jeremy Hoffman, founded Steinmeier in 1979 after graduating from business school in Beijing 提到 Hoffman 曾經在北京念書並畢業，後一句 In its first year of business, the company managed to turn a sizeable profit, which grew by 47% the following year 則談到回國後的事業狀況，因此答案選 (B)。

字彙　**fresh-squeezed** 現榨的

Questions 172-175 refer to the following online chat discussion. 線上聊天討論串

Almed Abedi   _ X

Almed Abedi [4:30 P.M.]   I'd like to re-examine the way we are currently advertising our line of vitamin supplements.

Saori Iwamoto [4:31 P.M.]   Marina, since you are new to our company, let me give you some background. In order to improve sales, we started making vitamin supplements specifically designed for women.

Almed Abedi [4:32 P.M.]   We began selling these supplements a year ago, and we allocated a substantial budget to advertising in order to promote them.

Marina Jordan [4:33 P.M.]   Thanks for the detailed explanation. I think I saw the commercials on TV. I've also driven by the billboards on the side of the road. That must have helped a lot with sales.

Almed Abedi [4:34 P.M.]   That's true. I've analyzed the sales data. The results are about 20% higher than we had projected.

Saori Iwamoto [4:35 P.M.]   Because the sales are so high, I think it's time to stop paying so much to advertise it. We don't need to continue running such a big campaign anymore.

Almed Abedi [4:36 P.M.]   I agree. We can do without it. Clearly the product has responded to a need in the market. I think customers will continue to buy these supplements even if we do less marketing.

Marina Jordan [4:37 P.M.]   You're right. And I think we have to start an advertising plan for our next product.

Saori Iwamoto [4:38 P.M.]   Do you mean our newest line of vitamin supplements intended for seniors?

Marina Jordan [4:39 P.M.]   Yes. We will start selling them in about three months.

[   ]   Send

問題 172-175 題參考以下線上聊天討論串。

阿爾瑪德阿貝迪 [_ X

阿爾瑪德阿貝迪 [下午 4 點 30 分]	⑫ 我想重新審視一下我們目前的廣告維他命補充品系列產品的方式。
岩本彩織 [下午 4 點 31 分]	⑬ 瑪琳娜，因為妳剛進公司，我先介紹一下背景。為了提升銷量，我們開始製作女性專用的維他命補充劑。
阿爾瑪德阿貝迪 [下午 4 點 32 分]	一年前我們開始販售這些營養補充品。為了推廣產品，我們在廣告投下大筆預算。
⑬ **瑪琳娜喬丹** [下午 4 點 33 分]	謝謝你的詳細說明。我想我在電視上有看過廣告，也曾開車經過路邊的廣告看板。這種方式肯定會對銷量有很大的幫助。
阿爾瑪德阿貝迪 [下午 4 點 34 分]	沒錯，我分析了銷售數據，結果比我們原先預期高了 20%。
岩本彩織 [下午 4 點 35 分]	既然銷量已經增加，我認為差不多該停止投入大量金錢在廣告上了。我們沒有必要繼續進行這類大規模的宣傳活動。
阿爾瑪德阿貝迪 [下午 4 點 36 分]	我同意，我們可以不用再依靠廣告。⑭ 該產品反應市場有需求，我想就算我們減少廣告量，顧客仍會繼續購買該營養補充品。
瑪琳娜喬丹 [下午 4 點 37 分]	你說得對。我想我們應該開始進行下個產品的廣告計畫。
岩本彩織 [下午 4 點 38 分]	⑮ 妳是說為年長者設計的維他命補充劑新系列嗎？
瑪琳娜喬丹 [下午 4 點 39 分]	對，我們預計於 3 個月後開始販售。

Send

Test 04

字彙 **specifically** 專門地、專為 **supplement** 補充品、營養品 **allocate** 分配 **substantial** 大量的
billboard 廣告看板 **project** 預計 **campaign** 宣傳活動 **senior** 老年人

172. What is the purpose of the discussion?
(A) To assign specific duties
(B) To enhance employee productivity
(C) To write a budget proposal
(D) To modify a promotion strategy

討論的目的為何？
(A) 指派特定工作
(B) 提升員工工作效率
(C) 編寫預算提案
(D) 修改宣傳策略

正確答案為 (D)

看到詢問目的或主旨的題目，通常可以在文章開頭找到答案。下午 4 點 30 分，阿爾瑪德阿貝迪提到 I'd like to re-examine the way we are currently advertising our line of vitamin supplements，答案為 (D)。

字彙 **enhance** 加強 **duty** 職責、工作 **productivity** 生產力、生產效率 **specific** 特定的 **modify** 修改

173. What is indicated about Ms. Jordan?
(A) She is going to make a presentation.
(B) She is in charge of human resources.
(C) She has analyzed the sales data for the report.
(D) She has just started working at the company.

下列敘述何者與喬丹小姐相符？
(A) 她將要發表簡報。
(B) 她負責管理人力資源。
(C) 她分析了報告的銷售數據。
(D) 她剛進公司工作。

正確答案為 (D)

岩本彩織於下午 4 點 31 分的訊息中提到 Marina, since you are new to our company，此話可以得知答案為 (D)。

字彙 **in charge of** 負責

174. At 4:37 P.M., what does Ms. Jordan mean when she writes, "You're right"?
(A) She agrees it is time to develop a new product for women.
(B) She believes the product will sell well without less advertising.
(C) She thinks vitamins are essential for both women and children.
(D) She suggests that they start advertising on and off line.

喬丹小姐於下午 4 點 37 分的訊息寫「你説得對」，是什麼意思？
(A) 她同意現在正是為女性開發新產品的時候。
(B) 她相信就算減少廣告，產品仍會暢銷。
(C) 她認為維他命對女性和孩童來説是必需品。
(D) 她建議他們開始進行線上和實體廣告。

正確答案為 (B)

〈推測句意〉

遇到推測句意的題目，就要檢視該句的前後句。前一句阿爾瑪德阿貝迪於下午 4 點 36 分的訊息中寫 I think customers will continue to buy these supplements even if we do less marketing，喬丹小姐才説了 You're right，對此話表示同意，因此答案為 (B)。

175. What is true about the new products?
(A) They are specifically designed for women.
(B) They are easy to take.
(C) They are developed for older people.
(D) They must be consumed with food.

有關新產品的敘述何者正確？
(A) 專為女性設計。
(B) 容易服用。
(C) 為年長者所開發的產品。
(D) 必須與食物一同服用。

正確答案為 (C)

聊天串直到後半段才提到 the next product，岩本彩織於下午 4 點 38 分的訊息中提到 Do you mean our newest line of vitamin supplements intended for seniors? 由此可以得知答案為 (C)。現在正在宣傳的產品才是專為女性設計的產品，因此 (A) 並非答案。

字彙 **consume** 吃喝

Questions 176-180 refer to the following Web page information and e-mail. 網頁資訊／電子郵件

http://www.citizensfirstbank.com

CITIZENS FIRST BANK

| **ANNOUNCEMENT** | MY ACCOUNTS | FUNDS TRANSFER | EMPLOYMENT |

Introducing Special Savings Starting!

Citizens First Bank now offers a new account, Special Savings Starting. This account offers several advantages over our Choice Savings account including favorable interest rates and increased options for transferring funds.

For a limited time, we are inviting our customers to convert their Choice Savings accounts into Special Savings Starting accounts without our usual account conversion fees. In addition, customers who make the change now will enjoy a special operation fee of only $5 per month for the first 12 months. After 12 months, the rate will increase to the regular Special Savings Starting rate of $8.25 per month.

For further details or to take advantage of this offer, please speak to one of our account representatives at 800-555-0111.

問題 **176-180** 題參考以下網頁資訊和電子郵件。

http://www.citizensfirstbank.com

市民第一銀行

| 公告 | 我的帳戶 | 資金轉帳 | 就業 |

176 在此介紹 Special Savings Starting！

目前市民第一銀行正提供最新帳戶 Special Savings Starting。該帳戶比起原有的 Choice Savings 多了許多優勢，像是提供優惠利率，以及增加資金轉賬的選項。

179 我們想邀請我們的客戶將 Choice Savings 帳戶轉換成 Special Savings Starting 帳戶，限定期間轉換無需手續費。此外，177 現在進行帳戶轉換的客戶，前 12 個月使用，將享有每月 5 美元的營運維護費優惠。12 個月過後，費率將恢復正常價，每月 8.25 美元。

欲了解更多詳情或利用此項服務，請撥打 800-555-0111 向帳戶專員諮詢。

字彙 **account** 帳戶   **favorable** 良好的、有利的   **interest rates** 利率   **transfer** 轉帳
convert A into B 將 A 改成 B   **operation** 營運   **fee** 費用

To	customerservice@citizensfirstbank.com
From	jtownsend@blakeleyryecable.com
Subject	New Savings Account
Date	April 2

I recently opened a Special Savings Starting account, and it was my understanding that the balance of my Choice Savings account would be transferred into the new account automatically. However, when I log in to my online banking profile, I see that available funds listed are $0 for the Special Savings Starting account. Could you please tell me when the funds will be transferred to the new account?

Thank you for your assistance.

Jessica Townsend

收件人	customerservice@citizenfirstbank.com
寄件人	jtownsend@blakeleyryecable.com
主旨	新型存款帳戶
日期	4 月 2 日

⑰ 我最近開了一個 Special Savings Starting 帳戶，我原先以為 Choice Savings 帳戶的餘額會自動轉入新帳戶。但是 ⑱ 我登入網路銀行 ⑱ 簡介後，發現我的 Special Savings Starting 帳戶明細顯示的可用資金為 0 美元。麻煩告訴我何時才會將錢轉入新帳戶。

感謝協助。

潔西卡湯森

字彙 **savings account** 存款帳戶　　**balance** 餘額　　**automatically** 自動地

176. What is the purpose of the Web page information?
(A) To request customers for a payment
(B) To advertise a new type of bank service
(C) To review online banking procedures
(D) To report on the merger of two banks

該網頁資訊的目的為何？
(A) 要求客戶付款
(B) 宣傳新的銀行服務
(C) 審查網路銀行程序
(D) 告知兩家銀行合併

正確答案為 (B)

網頁開頭提到 Introducing Special Savings Starting!，由此可知本網頁要介紹銀行新的服務項目，因此答案為 (B)。

字彙　**procedure** 程序

---

177. What is stated about the operation fee?
(A) Customers can pay it in installments.
(B) It is offered at a discounted rate initially.
(C) It is lower than the fee at other banks.
(D) Customers can negotiate its due date.

下列何者為營運維護費的說明？
(A) 客戶可以選擇分期付款。
(B) 起初會提供優惠價格。
(C) 費用低於其他銀行。
(D) 客戶可以與銀行協調到期日。

正確答案為 (B)

關鍵字 operation fee「營運費用」出現在網頁第二段中：a special operation fee of only $5 per month for the first 12 months，可知答案為 (B)。

字彙　**in installments** 分期付款　　**initially** 最初　　**due date** 到期日

---

178. Why is Ms. Townsend concerned?
(A) Because her money has not yet been moved to the new account
(B) Because she has been overcharged for an operation fee
(C) Because she was unable to update her bank transaction
(D) Because her account has been accessed without her permission

為何湯森小姐表示擔憂？
(A) 錢尚未轉入新帳戶中
(B) 被收取過多營運維護費
(C) 銀行交易無法更新
(D) 有人未經她的許可登入帳戶

正確答案為 (A)

Townsend 的名字出現在電子郵件最下方的署名處，表示為寫信的人，信中提到 when I log in to my online banking profile, I see that available funds listed are $0 for the Special Savings Starting account，可知答案為 (A)。

字彙　**overcharge** 超收費用　　**transaction** 交易

---

179. What is most likely true about Ms. Townsend?
(A) She will close her account because of this inconvenience.
(B) Her operation fee has been increased.
(C) She will not be charged a fee for the account change.
(D) She is a new customer to Citizens First Bank.

有關湯森小姐的敘述何者正確？
(A) 因為感到不便，她決定結清帳戶。
(B) 她要繳交的營運維護費增加。
(C) 她不會被收取轉換帳戶手續費。
(D) 她是市民第一銀行的新用戶。

正確答案為 (C)

〈整合多篇文章資訊〉
電子郵件中寫 I recently opened a Special Savings Starting account, and it was my understanding that the balance of my Choice Savings account would be transferred into the new account automatically，表示她已轉換帳戶。而網頁中提到 we are inviting our customers to convert their Choice Savings accounts into Special Savings Starting accounts without our usual account conversion fees，表示轉用新帳戶的用戶免收轉換費用，因此答案選 (C)。

180. In the e-mail, the word "profile" in paragraph 1, line 3, is closest in meaning to?

(A) outline
(B) equality
(C) average
(D) stability

電子郵件中，第一段第三行的「profile」與以下何者的意思最為相近？

(A) 概要
(B) 平等
(C) 平均值
(D) 穩定性

正確答案為 (A)

〈推測字義〉

在 in my online banking profile，後方提到看到總金額為 0 元，推測可知道 profile 指「帳戶概要或明細」，可以讓用戶看到帳戶裡的金額，答案選 (A)。

Questions 181-185 refer to the following announcement and e-mail. 通知 / 電子郵件

International Business Reconstruction Association (IBRA)
Opportunities for Information Storage

IBRA invites you to participate in a live, online seminar entitled "Strategies for Raising Corporate Funds." The seminar focuses on essential information to include in a grant proposal that will ensure your organization receives financial or other support from local and international companies.

This event will be presented by Michelle Conner, development director at the Rosario Foundation. The seminar, which will take place on July 22 from 1:30 P.M. to 3:00 P.M. GMT, will be moderated by Virginia Ross, a reporter for the television program World Business Reports. Registration is required by June 30; please visit www.ibra.org.uk/seminar0722 for information about fees and additional details.

At the time of your registration, you will be given the opportunity to submit a question for Ms. Conner. She will be able to respond to a limited number of these during the seminar. However, her answers to all relevant questions submitted by participants will be posted by August 1.

問題 181-185 題參考以下通知和電子郵件。

國際商業重建協會（IBRA）
獲取資訊的機會

⑱ IBRA 邀請您參加名為「企業資金募集策略」的線上直播研討會。本研討會的重點在於說明募款企劃書中不可或缺的資料，保證讓您的公司獲得本地和國際企業在金錢上或其他方面的援助。

⑱ 本活動由羅薩里奧基金會開發總監蜜雪兒康納帶領。⑱ ⑱ ⑱ 研討會將於 7 月 22 日舉行，時間為格林威治標準時間下午 1 點 30 分到 3 點，由電視節目「世界商業報導」的記者維吉尼雅羅斯主持。活動報名期限至 6 月 30 日止。如欲了解費用和相關細節，請上 www.ibra.org.uk/seminar0722。

報名時，您有機會向康納小姐提問一個問題。研討會上她會針對部分問題進行答覆。不過，每位參加者提交的全部相關問題會全部於 8 月 1 日張貼回覆。

字彙　**live** 現場直播的　**seminar** 研討會　**entitled** 給予標題　**raise funds** 集資　**grant proposal** 募款企劃書　**ensure** 保證　**organization** 機構、團體　**present** 報告　**moderate** 主持　**relevant** 相關的　**participant** 參加者　**submit** 提交

```
○○○                          e-mail
```

From: mconner@rosariofoundation.org
To: keikomatusi@ibra.org.uk
Cc: swinkley@rosariofoundation.org
Subject: The Seminar
Sent: June 24

Dear Mr. Matusi:

I am very sorry to inform you that I am no longer able to fulfill my commitment to your organization. On the day I am scheduled to headline your event, I now, quite unexpectedly, need to travel to Barcelona on business. I have asked Smith Winkley, Associate Development Director, to present the seminar on my behalf as well as to participate in our video conference on July 31. He will be contacting you shortly by e-mail regarding these changes.

Mr. Winkley has planned and supervised fundraising campaigns for international firms for 25 years. Moreover, he is currently responsible for conducting our organization's online and in-person training sessions, so please rest assured that your seminar participants are in capable hands.

Again, my apologies for any inconvenience my cancellation causes.

Regards,

Michelle Conner

```
○○○                          e-mail
```

寄件人：mconner@rosariofoundation.org
收件人：keikomatusi@ibra.org.uk
副本：swinkley@rosariofoundation.org
主旨：研討會
寄件日期：6 月 24 日

親愛的松坂先生：

很抱歉通知您，我無法履行對您機構做出的承諾。我現在臨時發現，我負責活動的當天得前往巴塞隆納出差。**183** 我已經請開發副總監史密斯溫克利代替我出席研討會，並 **184** 參加 7 月 31 日的視訊會議。針對前述更動事宜，他會盡快透過電子郵件與您聯絡。

溫克利先生策劃和統籌募款國際企業活動已有 25 年的經驗。除此之外，**185** 目前我們公司是由他負責進行線上課程和面授培訓課程，所以請您放心，他會妥善帶領研討會參加者。

對於我失約所導致的不便，再次向您表達我的歉意。

蜜雪兒康納　敬上

字彙 **fulfill** 執行　**commitment** 承諾、保證　**headline** 帶領　**unexpectedly** 意外地　**present** 出席
on one's behalf 代替某人　**as well as** 而且　**in-person** 面對面的　**training session** 培訓、訓練課程
rest assured that 安心、放心　**in sb. capable hands** 由某人處理　**cancellation** 取消

181. What is suggested about the event on July 22?
(A) It has been paid for with money from a charity organization.
(B) It is intended for international students.
(C) It will give advice about joining international corporations.
(D) It will be broadcast live by a television station.

下列敘述何者與 7 月 22 日的活動有關？
(A) 活動費用由慈善機構支付。
(B) 該活動為國際學生所設計。
(C) 該活動提供加入國際企業的建議。
(D) 該活動將由電視台進行直播。

正確答案為 (D)

第一篇文章第一段中提到 a live, online seminar，第二段中提到 The seminar, which will take place on July 22 from 1:30 P.M. to 3:00 P.M. GMT, will be moderated by Virginia Ross, a reporter for the television program World Business Reports，由此可以得知答案為 (D)。

> **字彙** **charity organization** 慈善機構　　**be intended for** 以～為對象

182. What is indicated about seminar participants?
(A) They will receive professional development certificates.
(B) They should direct their questions to Ms. Ross.
(C) They must be members of the IBRA.
(D) They must sign up for the event in advance.

針對研討會參加者，文中提到了什麼？
(A) 他們將收到專業開發證書。
(B) 他們應該直接向羅斯小姐提問。
(C) 他們必須是國際商業重建協會的會員。
(D) 他們必須提前報名參加活動。

正確答案為 (D)

第一篇文中提到 The seminar, which will take place on July 22 和 Registration is required by June 30，表示需要事先報名，答案為 (D)。

> **字彙** **certificate** 證書　　**direct A to B** 把 A 提交給 B

183. What date will Ms. Conner go on a business trip?
(A) June 24
(B) July 22
(C) July 31
(D) August 1

康納小姐將於幾號出差？
(A) 6 月 24 日
(B) 7 月 22 日
(C) 7 月 31 日
(D) 8 月 1 日

正確答案為 (B)

〈整合多篇文章資訊〉
第一篇文章提到 The seminar, which will take place on July 22，表示研討會時間為 7 月 22 日。第二篇信件提到 On the day I am scheduled to headline your event, I now, quite unexpectedly, need to travel to Barcelona on business，表示她預計於那天出差，因此答案為 (B)。

184. What has Ms. Conner arranged for the event?
(A) To have a financial donation sent to the IBRA
(B) To meet with Ms. Matusi in Barcelona
(C) To have her presentation video recorded
(D) To have a colleague substitute for her

康納小姐為此事件安排了什麼？
(A) 捐款給國際商業重建協會
(B) 在巴賽隆納會見松坂先生
(C) 把她的演講錄製成影片
(D) 請同事代替她出席

正確答案為 (D)

電子郵件中提到 I have asked Smith Winkley, Associate Development Director, to present the seminar on my behalf，答案選 (D)。

> **字彙** **donation** 捐款、捐獻　　**substitute for** 代替～

Test 04

185. What is suggested about the Rosario Foundation?
(A) It offers online training opportunities.
(B) It is seeking a new development director.
(C) It has been in business for 25 years.
(D) It is regularly featured on World Business Reports.

針對羅薩里奧基金會，文中提到了什麼？
(A) 他們提供線上培訓的機會。
(B) 他們正在尋找新的開發總監。
(C) 他們經營了 25 年。
(D) 世界商業報導常報導他們。

正確答案為 (A)

〈整合多篇文章資訊〉
由第一篇文章可以得知康納小姐為羅薩里奧基金會的開發總監。又康納小姐在電子郵件中提到 our organization's online and in-person training sessions，因此答案要選 (A)。

字彙　**feature** 專題報導

Questions 186-190 refer to the following advertisement, e-mail and invoice. 廣告 / 電子郵件 / 發票

Get your dream car at Madison Autos.

If you want a nice car but don't want to spend a lot of money, then come to Madison Autos. We are in the business of buying and selling used vehicles. Our cars may not be brand-new, but we guarantee that they are in great condition. All vehicles are serviced when they arrive on our lot, and they are sold with a one-year warranty. We offer an extended two-year warranty with a purchase over $8,000. We also do repairs and order replacement parts right here on the lot.

Prices can be negotiated, so come visit Madison Autos and find your new car! Our address is 1807 Pine Street, Twin City, MN 00987.

問題 186-190 題參考以下廣告、電子郵件和發票。

在麥迪森汽車找到夢想中的汽車

如果你想要一台好車，卻又不想花大錢的話，來麥迪森汽車看看吧。186 我們從事二手車買賣，我們的車子雖然不是全新，但我們保證車況良好。所有來到我們車廠的汽車都會接受檢查，車輛售出時會提供一年保固。189 如車輛售價超過八千美元，則提供延長保固至兩年。我們這裡也提供維修和更換零件的服務。

價格有議價空間。請直接來麥迪森汽車，找到你的新車吧！我們的地址為 00987 明尼蘇達州雙子市松樹街 1807 號。

字彙 **used vehicle** 二手車　**in great condition** 狀況良好　**lot** 車廠、停車空間　**warranty** 保固（期）
replacement part 替換零件

Test 04

To	Marco Colombo <marcocolombo@madisonautos.com>
from	Sydney Payton <sidneypayton@gmail.net>
Date	March 21
Subject	A Car Purchase

Dear Mr. Colombo:

I am contacting you because one of my colleagues recommended your services. Apparently you have a reputation as a kind and patient salesperson. I am looking to purchase a vehicle because mine keeps breaking down these days. I'd like to replace it with a newer model. I was hoping that you would be able to help me find something suitable.

However, I'm on a tight budget, so I don't want to pay any more than $10,000 for a used vehicle. According to an advertisement I saw recently, your company has a few that might be suitable. I'd like to schedule a time to meet with you. Then you can tell me more about it.

Sincerely,

Sydney Payton

收件人	馬科可倫坡 <marcocolombo@madisonautos.com>
寄件人	希尼佩頓 <sidneypayton@gmail.net>
主旨	3 月 21 日
日期	買車

親愛的馬科可倫坡：

⑲ 我的一位同事向我推薦你們的服務，因此來信聯絡您。顯然你們的銷售人員以友善又有耐心打出好名聲。⑱ 近日我的車一直出問題，所以我打算買車。⑰ 我打算換台較新的車。希望您能幫我找到合適的車輛。

不過我的預算很緊，不想花超過一萬美元購買二手車。最近我看了廣告，發現貴公司似乎有些車蠻適合的。⑰ 想跟您約個時間碰面，麻煩您告訴我更多的細節。

希尼佩頓　敬上

字彙　**colleague** 同事　**recommend** 推薦　**reputation** 聲譽　**break down** 故障　**suitable** 合適的　**on a tight budget** 預算很緊

MADISON AUTOS

1807 Pine Street, Twin City, MN 00987

555-7465

INVOICE #:   123098
DATE OF SALE: March 30

Buyer INFO.

NAME: Sydney Payton
ADDRESS: 8912 South Hill Dr., Twin City, MN 00989
PHONE: 555-1423
LICENSE NUMBER: K500-2507-0902-00

Car INFO.

CAR: Prius Hybrid Z12
REGISTRATION: J87F09876SS
MILEAGE: 82,000
YEAR OF VEHICLE: 2013
SALES PRICE: $9,700
WARRANTY: Extended
METHOD OF PAYMENT: __√__ check _____ cash _____ credit

Signature of Seller: Marco Colombo
Signature of Buyer: Sydney Payton

Test 04

麥迪森汽車

00987 明尼蘇達州雙子市松樹街 1807 號

555-7465

發票號碼： 123098

銷售日期： 3 月 30 日

買家資料

姓名： 希尼佩頓

地址： 00987 明尼蘇達州雙子市南山區 8912 號

電話： 555-1423

車牌號碼： 500-2507-0902-00

車輛資料

車款： Prius Hybrid Z12

註冊號碼： 87F09876SS

里程數： 82,000

車輛年份： 2013

銷售價格： 189 9,700 美元

保固期： 189 延長

付款方式： ___√___ 支票 _____ 現金 _____ 信用卡

賣家簽名： 馬科可倫坡

買家簽名： 希尼佩頓

字彙　**mileage** 里程數

186. What is mentioned about cars in Madison Autos?
(A) They receive free servicing shortly after purchase.
(B) They can be paid for through financing plans.
(C) They were previously owned.
(D) They have the most popular features.

針對麥迪森汽車的車輛，文中提到了什麼？
(A) 購買後能馬上獲得免費服務。
(B) 接受用貸款方式購車。
(C) 車輛先前有主人。
(D) 具備最受歡迎的功能。

正確答案為 (C)

廣告文中提到 We are in the business of buying and selling used vehicles，used 這裡指「用過的、二手的」，也就是之前有車主轉手的，因此答案選 (C)。

字彙　**financial plan** 貸款、分期計畫

187. What is the purpose of the e-mail?
(A) To help design a car
(B) To distribute information
(C) To describe the process
(D) To ask for consultation

電子郵件的目的為何？
(A) 幫忙設計車輛
(B) 發布資訊
(C) 描述過程
(D) 尋求諮詢

正確答案為 (D)

電子郵件是表達有意購買車輛。第一段中提到 I was hoping that you would be able to help me find something suitable，以及最後一段提到 I'd like to schedule a time for me to meet with you，因此答案為 (D)。

字彙　**consultation** 諮詢

188. What is suggested about Ms. Payton's current vehicle?
(A) She bought it nearly 10 years ago.
(B) It is a four-door vehicle.
(C) She wishes to sell it to her colleague.
(D) It is not in perfect working order.

針對佩頓小姐目前的車子，文中提到了什麼？
(A) 購買至今將近 10 年。
(B) 車輛為四門車。
(C) 她想把車賣給同事。
(D) 車輛並非處於完美運轉的狀態。

正確答案為 (D)

在電子郵件中，佩頓小姐提到 mine keeps breaking down these days，答案為 (D)。

189. Why is Ms. Payton given an extended warranty?
(A) Because she spent over a certain amount of money
(B) Because she is a frequent customer
(C) Because she has joined a membership program
(D) Because Madison Autos is having a special event

為何佩頓小姐可以延長保固期？
(A) 因為她支付的款項超過特定金額
(B) 因為她是常客
(C) 因為她加入了會員
(D) 因為麥迪森汽車正在舉辦特惠活動

正確答案為 (A)

〈整合多篇文章資訊〉
廣告文中提到 We offer an extended two-year warranty with a purchase over $8,000，而發票上顯示的價格為 9,700 美金，因此可推測出答案為 (A)。其他選項在所有文章中都沒有提及。

190. What can be inferred about Ms. Payton?
(A) She paid for her vehicle with cash.
(B) Her colleague bought a car from Mr. Colombo.
(C) She chose a car that seats two people.
(D) She bought a Sport Utility Vehicle.

下列敘述何者與佩頓小姐有關？
(A) 她用現金買車。
(B) 她的同事曾跟可倫坡先生買過車。
(C) 她選了一輛兩人座車。
(D) 她買了一輛休旅車。

正確答案為 (B)

電子郵件中提到 one of my colleagues recommended your services，加上郵件寄信者是 Marco Colombo 可倫坡先生，可知答案為 (B)。

字彙　**Sport Utility Vehicle 即 SUV**，休旅車

Questions 191-195 refer to the following notice, e-mail, and article. 公告 / 電子郵件 / 報導

Fragment Master

If you have trouble getting rid of your old electronics, Fragment Master will come to you.

We are the region's largest recycler of electronic components. When you drop off your electronic devices, just put the materials in their proper place.

Box A: External hard devices, Miscellaneous
Box B: Monitors, Speakers, Laptop and Desktop computers
Box C: Keyboards, Accessories and Other devices

The current market for certain rare metals is strong. Therefore, for the time being, we will also be accepting small devices, including mobile phones, tablets, and hand-held video game systems through October 18.

We are here to help you. Please don't hesitate to ask for assistance at the service window.

問題 191-195 題參考以下公告、電子郵件和報導。

碎片大師

若您在丟棄老舊電子產品時遭遇到困難,請讓碎片大師來幫您。

191 我們是本地最大的電子零件回收商,若您要丟棄電子設備,請先分門別類。

箱子 A:外部硬體設備、雜項
箱子 B:螢幕顯示器、喇叭、筆記型電腦和桌上型電腦
箱子 C:鍵盤、配件、和其他設備

目前部分稀有金屬在市場上的行情 192 極佳,因此現階段到 10 月 18 日以前,我們仍收受手機、平板電腦、手持電子遊戲機等小型裝置。

我們是來幫助您的,請不要猶豫向服務窗口尋求協助。

字彙 | **get rid of** 擺脫、丟棄　**component** 零件　**drop off**（口）丟棄　**proper** 適當的　**accessory**（常數複數）配件　**external** 外部的　**miscellaneous** 混雜的、雜項　**rare** 稀有的　**for the time being** 暫且、現階段　**hand-held** 手拿的　**hesitate** 猶豫

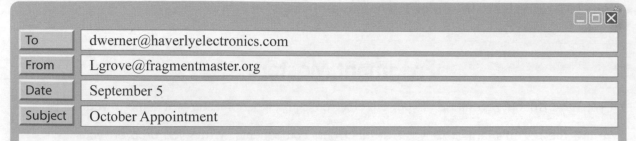

To	dwerner@haverlyelectronics.com
From	Lgrove@fragmentmaster.org
Date	September 5
Subject	October Appointment

Dear Mr. Werner:

I'm reminding you that a Fragment Master representative, Matt Lovito, will visit Haverly Electronics on the morning of October 19. Please have your scrap electronics sorted to expedite the evaluation process. Be prepared to negotiate the price at that time.

As you are aware, prices offered are subject to daily market conditions. Let me fill you in a bit about what we are currently experiencing. Prices on reclaimed plastic have been trending downward. Similarly, because supplies of copper and silver are high now, there has been downward pressure on prices for recycled sources. You will be pleased to learn, however, that demand for titanium is unprecedented. The price has already doubled this year. A manufacturer called Baxon Ltd. in Singapore has been willing to buy all we can provide in the short term.

It continues to be a pleasure doing business with you.

Sincerely,

Lucia Grove
Fragment Master

Singapore (Nov. 1) – Baxon Ltd. today announced the initial release of its newest model laptop computer, the Moonlight X10. The new product will be the fastest and lightest laptop in its class. These high-performance qualities are made possible by the use of newly designed rare-metal capacitors. The Moonlight X10 is also one of the first mass-produced laptops containing more than 50 percent recycled material, much of it salvaged from out-modeled consumer electronics. A limited number of model Moonlight X10s will be available tomorrow at the company's flagship store in Singapore. Although international customers must wait until November 30, Baxon plans to begin shipping the device to outlets throughout Singapore by November 10.

収件人　dwerner@haverlyelectronics.com

寄件人　Lgrove@fragmentmaster.org

日期　9 月 5 日

主旨　10 月碰面

親愛的沃納先生：

提醒您，碎片大師公司代表人麥特拉維多將於 10 月 19 日上午拜訪哈維利電子公司。請您先將報廢的電子產品分類，以加快評估過程。也請您到時準備好議價事宜。

如您所知，收購價格受到每日市場狀況而有所不同。我來說明一下目前我們所面臨的情況。再生塑料的價格持續呈現下降走勢，目前銅和銀的供應量過高，因此再生資源同樣也面臨價格下跌的壓力。不過值得高興的是，鈦的需求出現前所未有的增長，今年的價格已經翻倍。193 新加坡有間名為貝興有限公司的製造商一直樂於向我們購買近期所能提供的所有產品。

很高興能與您持續生意往來。

碎片大師
露西亞格羅夫　敬上

字彙　**representative** 代表人　**scrap** 廢棄物　**expedite** 加速執行　**negotiate** 協商　**aware** 察覺到的、明白的　**be subject to** 易受～影響的　**reclaimed** 回收利用的、改造的　**downward** 下降的　**pressure** 壓力、壓迫　**unprecedented** 史無前例的　**in the short term** 短期

新加坡（11 月 1 日）── 194 貝興有限公司今天宣布首次推出最新款筆記型電腦月光 X10。該新產品將會成為同級產品中速度最快、最輕薄的筆電。新的設計上使用稀有金屬加工成電容器，造就出高性能高品質的產品。193 月光 X10 同時是首批將回收的舊款消費性電子產品再利用的量產筆記型電腦，當中包含了五成以上的再生材料。明天公司旗下的新加坡旗艦店將會推出限定數量的月光 X10。195 海外消費者必須等到 11 月 30 日，但是貝興公司計畫在 11 月 10 日前，開始將裝置運送至新加坡各地的暢貨中心。

字彙　**high-performance** 高性能　**capacitor** 電容器　**mass-produced** 大量生產的　**salvage** 搶救　**out-modeled** 舊款的　**flagship store** 旗艦店

191. What does Ms. Grove most likely do for a living?
(A) Collect antiques for sale
(B) Sell computer accessories
(C) Develop software programs
(D) Run a recycling facility

格羅夫小姐最有可能從事什麼工作？
(A) 收集古董販售
(B) 販售電腦配件
(C) 開發軟體程式
(D) 經營資源回收公司

正確答案為 **(D)**

〈整合多篇文章資訊〉

從電子郵件可以得知 Ms. Grove 格羅夫小姐在碎片大師公司工作。第一篇公告也提到該公司是 the region's largest recycler of electronic components「當地最大的電子零件回收廠商」，因此答案為 (D)。

字彙　**antique** 古董

192. In the notice, the word "strong" in paragraph 4, line 1, is closest in meaning to
(A) brilliant
(B) athletic
(C) bright
(D) active

公告第四段第一行的「strong」與下列何者意思最為接近？
(A) 出色的
(B) 運動的
(C) 明亮的
(D) 活躍的

正確答案為 **(D)**

〈推測字義〉

提到 strong 的完整句子是 The current market for certain rare metals is strong，表示市場上的行情極佳，因此答案選 (D)。

193. What is probably true about Baxon Ltd.?
(A) It runs its own recycling center.
(B) It mainly manufactures external hard devices.
(C) It is Fragment Master's biggest customers.
(D) Some components of its latest laptops are from Fragment Master.

關於貝興有限公司，下列敘述何者正確？
(A) 資源回收中心由公司親自經營。
(B) 主要生產外部硬體設備。
(C) 該公司為碎片大師最大的客戶。
(D) 其最新的筆記型電腦有部分零件來自碎片大師。

正確答案為 **(D)**

〈整合多篇文章資訊〉

電子郵件中提到 A manufacturer called Baxon Ltd. in Singapore has been willing to buy all we can provide in the short term，指出貝興公司向碎片大師購買金屬。報導中接著提到 The Moonlight X10 is also one of the first mass-produced laptops containing more than 50 percent recycled material, much of it salvaged from out-modeled consumer electronics，表示貝興推出的新筆電中，有部分零件是使用碎片大師的再生材料，因此答案選 (D)。

194. What is the main purpose of the article?
(A) To explain the cost of manufacturing a product
(B) To question a change in product development
(C) To introduce a new product in electronics
(D) To report on a product malfunction

報導的主要目的為何？
(A) 說明產品生產成本
(B) 對產品開發過程中的變更提出疑問
(C) 介紹電子新產品
(D) 報告產品故障

正確答案為 **(C)**

文章的目的或主旨可以從開頭找到答案，在報導開頭提到 Baxon Ltd. today announced the initial release of its newest model laptop computer, the Moonlight X10，表示本報導重點為介紹新產品，答案為 (C)。

195. What can be suggested about the Moonlight X10?
(A) It has more features compared to competitors' products.
(B) It will not be sold outside of Singapore for some time.
(C) It is the lightest product ever in the market.
(D) It is made out of recycled materials only.

下列敘述何者與月光 X10 有關?
(A) 比競爭對手的產品具備更多功能。
(B) 有段時間不會在新加坡以外的地方販售。
(C) 是市場上最輕的產品。
(D) 全部用回收材料所製。

正確答案為 (B)

報導中提到 international customers must wait until November 30，因此答案選 (B)。文中並未提到競爭對手，因此不能選 (A)。文中提到 The new product will be the fastest and lightest laptop in its class，未與市場上所有產品比較，因此 (C) 的敘述並不正確。另外，由 containing more than 50 percent recycled material 可以得知 (D) 的敘述也不正確。

Questions 196-200 refer to following e-mails and schedule. 電子郵件 / 日程表

From	Scott Han <shan@dyscomventures.org>
To	All staff members of Dyscom Ventures
Date	January 9
Subject	Update
Attachment	deadline schedule.pdf

Dear colleagues:

Past editions of our company newsletter have focused only on developments in the IT industry and how they affect our company. This year I'd like to start including information about our employees in every issue. I have two features in mind.

The first will be announcements of professional achievements. If you have presented a paper in a conference, won an award, or completed a degree program, for example, please email me with your name and department and a description of your accomplishments in 40 words or less.

The goals of the second feature are to recognize employees who perform volunteer service in their communities and to bring attention to opportunities for community involvement. If you are a member of a local organization that needs help, please send me some information about the frequency and type of services and activities involved, whether they are one-time events like a charity golf tournament or more frequent events like volunteering in local schools. Attached is a complete list of the deadlines and publication schedules.

Sincerely,

Scott Han
Director, Internal Relations

DYSCOM VENTURES NEWSLETTER

Material	Deadline	For publication in
photo, illustrations articles, essays	February 8	March
photo, illustrations articles, essays	May 8	June
photo, illustrations articles, essays	August 8	September
photo, illustrations articles, essays	November 8	December

Any submissions that are received after the deadline will be published in the following issue. Please contact Scott Han at shan@dyscomventures.org if you have any questions.

問題 196-200 題參考以下電子郵件和日程表。

寄件人	史考特韓 <shan@dyscomventures.org>
收件人	迪斯康企業全體員工
日期	1 月 9 日
主旨	更新
附加檔案	截止日程表 .pdf

親愛的同仁：

過去我們公司的社內通訊僅關注資訊技術產業發展和對我們公司造成的影響。 196 197 今年我想開始在每期刊物中加入員工相關資訊。我想到兩個特色項目。

197 第一個是公告員工在專業上的成就。比方說，如果你曾在會議上發表報告、獲頒獎項、或是取得學位，請寄電子郵件給我，寫下你的姓名、所屬部門、並針對你的成就寫出 40 字以內的描述。

第二個特色目標是表揚在社區從事志工服務的員工，同時吸引大家關注社區參與的機會。如果你是地方團體的一員，需要為團體請求協助時，無論是像慈善高爾夫球賽這樣的一次性活動、或是本地學校的志工服務助這類次數較頻繁的活動，都可以把舉辦頻率、服務內容以及活動類型等相關資訊寄給我。附件是載有各期截止日和出版日的完整列表。

內部關係部主任史考特韓

字彙 **IT** 即 **information technology** 資訊科技　**edition**（印刷）版次　**issue**（雜誌）期、號
have in mind 想到、記住　**recognize** 認可、表彰　**volunteer** 志工　**involvement** 參與
bring to attention 使某人注意　**frequency** 頻率、次數　**involved** 有關的、牽涉在內的　**publication** 出版

迪斯康企業社內通訊

資料	截止日	刊登
照片、插圖 報導、短評	199 2 月 8 日	3 月
照片、插圖 報導、短評	5 月 8 日	199 6 月
照片、插圖 報導、短評	8 月 8 日	9 月
照片、插圖 報導、短評	11 月 8 日	12 月

199 截止日之後收到的任何資料，將刊登於下期。如有任何疑問，請發送郵件至 shan@dyscomventures.org 聯繫史考特韓。

字彙 **illustration** 插圖　**submission** 提交物　**following** 下一次的、隨後的

---

e-mail

FROM: David Greenberg <dgreenberg@dyscomventures.org>
TO: Scott Han <shan@dyscomventures.org>
DATE: February 28
RE: Upcoming Event
ATTACHMENT: photo.jpg

Hi, Scott:

Sorry I did not get this to you earlier.

The Zuengler Library is currently accepting donations of gently used books for its annual book sale that will be held on July 8 from 10 A.M. to 4 P.M. I will be coordinating volunteer efforts to organize the books the day before. We tend to receive large boxes full of books, and they must be sorted into different categories so that customers can easily find whatever type of book they looking for during the sale. It is a lot of work, so we need your help.

I am sending you a photo of me at last year's event for the newsletter. I hope this will raise awareness of this great event. Let me know if you need any more information.

Thanks.

David Greenberg
Research and Development

---

e-mail

寄件人：大衛格林伯格 <dgreenberg@dyscomventures.org>
收件人：史考特韓 <shan@dyscomventures.org>
(199) 日期：2 月 28 日
回覆：活動預告
附加檔案：照片 .jpg

嗨，史考特：

很抱歉沒能及早聯絡你。

(200) 祖恩格格圖書館在 7 月 8 日上午 10 點到下午 4 點將舉辦年度圖書銷售活動，目前正受理書況佳的二手書捐贈。我將協力安排活動前一天的書籍整理志工人力。(198) 我們到時會收到許多大箱書籍，得由志工將書籍分門別類，以便顧客在活動期間可以輕鬆找到想要的書。有很多事情要做，所以需要你的幫忙。

(199) 我把去年的活動照片發給你，希望能刊登在社訊上，提高大家對這項意義非凡活動的關注。如果需要更多的資訊，請再跟我說。

謝謝。

研發部大衛格林伯格

字彙　**coordinate** 協調　**raise awareness** 提升關注

196. What is the purpose of the first e-mail?
(A) To encourage Dyscom employees to submit papers for a conference
(B) To announce a job opening in the research department
(C) To explain procedures for the degree program
(D) To request information about Dyscom employees

第一篇電子郵件的目的為何？
(A) 鼓勵迪斯康的員工繳交會議報告
(B) 公告研究部門的職缺
(C) 說明學位課程的手續
(D) 要求迪斯康的員工資訊

正確答案為 **(D)**

第一封電子郵件第一段提到 this year I'd like to start including information about our employees in every issue，因此答案為 (D)。

197. What is NOT mentioned about the announcements?
(A) They are a new addition to the newsletter.
(B) They must be submitted by department supervisors.
(C) They honor award recipients.
(D) They can contain as many as 40 words.

下列何者是公告沒有提及的？
(A) 刊物中會加入新項目。
(B) 只能由部門主管提交。
(C) 他們會表揚獲獎者。
(D) 內容最多可達 40 個字。

正確答案為 **(B)**

電子郵件第一段提到 This year I'd like to start including information about our employees in every issue. 符合 (A)。第二段提到 The first will be announcements of professional achievements 符合 (C)。第二段接著提到 your name and department and a description of your accomplishments in 40 words or less 符合 (D)。因此答案是 (B)。

字彙 **recipient** 獲獎者

198. What is suggested about the book sale?
(A) It is held in the library of the local community center.
(B) It carries both new and used books.
(C) People donate a large number of books.
(D) The proceeds will be donated to the children's charity.

針對書籍銷售活動，文中提到了什麼？
(A) 活動於當地社區中心的圖書館舉辦。
(B) 同時販售新書和二手書。
(C) 人們捐贈大量書籍。
(D) 所有收益將捐給兒童慈善機構。

正確答案為 **(C)**

有關 book sale 的事情是在第二封電子郵件提到，其中提到 We tend to receive large boxes full of books，符合 (C)。

字彙 **proceeds**（固定用複數）收益

199. When will a photo of Mr. Greenberg most likely appear in the newsletter?
(A) March
(B) June
(C) July
(D) September

格林伯格先生的照片最有可能在何時出現在公司刊物上？
(A) 3 月
(B) 6 月
(C) 7 月
(D) 9 月

正確答案為 **(B)**

〈整合多篇文章資訊〉
第二封電子郵件中提到他發送去年的活動照片，郵件發送日期為 2 月 28 日。確認日程表後，符合的日期是第二行，預計於 6 月刊出，因此答案為 (B)。

200. What is Mr. Greenberg planning to do on July 7?

(A) **To organize materials that the Zuengler Library received**

(B) To participate in a sports competition

(C) To attend a lecture by an author at the Zuengler Library

(D) To write an article about the IT industry

格林伯格先生在 7 月 7 日有什麼計畫？

(A) **整理祖恩格圖書館收到的東西**

(B) 參加體育競賽

(C) 去祖恩格圖書館參加作家的講座

(D) 撰寫一篇有關資訊科技產業的文章

正確答案為 (A)

第二封電子郵件中提到 book sales that will be held on July 8 以及 I will be coordinating volunteer efforts to organize the books the day before，換言之，他在活動前一天 7 月 7 日要負責整理圖書館收到的書，因此答案為 (A)。

字彙 **author** 作家

Actual Test

05

中譯與解說

	答對題數	換算分數
聽力		
閱讀		

1. 5_01 美式男聲

(A) **A woman is gesturing at a white board.**
(B) A woman is handing out some papers.
(C) A woman is holding a cup.
(D) A woman is writing on a board.

(A) **女子正對著白板做手勢。**
(B) 女子正在分發紙張。
(C) 女子正拿著杯子。
(D) 女子正在板子上寫字。

正確答案為 (A)

問題選項的主詞皆為 woman，因此請特別留意女子的動作並仔細聆聽選項。(A) 描寫女子一邊發表一邊做手勢的樣子為最適當的答案。其他選項提到紙張、杯子、和板子，雖為照片中出現的物品，但皆與女子的動作無關，因此都不是答案。

字彙 **gesture** 做手勢 **hand out** 分配、發下去

2. 5_02 美式女聲

(A) Street performers are setting up their instruments.
(B) Equipment is being loaded into a van.
(C) **Pedestrians are watching a performance.**
(D) People are performing in an auditorium.

(A) 街頭表演者在架設他們的樂器。
(B) 裝備正被裝載到貨車上。
(C) **行人在觀賞表演。**
(D) 人們在禮堂表演。

正確答案為 (C)

本題為包含多個人物的戶外照片，請留意各個人物的動作。由照片可以確認有男子在街上表演，也有人們在觀賞表演，因此答案選 (C)。照片中有表演者，但是 (A) 選項描寫的動作不正確；照片中沒有出現貨車，因此 (B) 並非答案；(D) 與照片中的地點不相符。

字彙 **set up** 架設 **instrument** 樂器；儀器 **load** 裝載 **pedestrian** [pəˋdɛstrɪən] 行人 **auditorium** 禮堂

3. `5_03` 英式男聲

(A) A clipboard is being placed on a desk.
(B) The doors of the cabinet have been left open.
(C) Flowers have been put in a vase.
(D) Some cups of coffee are being served.

(A) 寫字板正被放在桌上。
(B) 櫃子的門開著。
(C) 花瓶放了一些花。
(D) 有人送上幾杯咖啡。

正確答案為 (C)

題目為無人的室內照片時，請務必認真聆聽各物品的名稱。(C) 正確描寫花瓶內插著花，故為正確答案。**(A) 和 (D) 皆以物品當作主詞，並使用被動進行式〈be being p.p.〉暗示有人做這些事情，不適用於本處的無人照片**；照片中的櫃子處於關閉狀態，因此 (B) 並不適當。

> 字彙　**clipboard** 寫字用的夾紙墊版　　**place** 擺放　　**cabinet** 櫃子

4. `5_04` 美式女聲

(A) A walkway runs along the beach.
(B) Two women are standing near one another.
(C) Railings line both sides of the path.
(D) A vendor is selling goods to the beachgoers.

(A) 沿著海邊有條步道。
(B) 兩名女子站得很靠近。
(C) 小路兩側有欄杆。
(D) 一名攤販正在販售商品給海邊常客。

正確答案為 (B)

(B) 描寫兩名女子彼此站得很近，為正確答案。照片中的道路並非在海邊；欄杆僅在道路的一側，因此 (A) 與 (C) 不正確；(D) 與照片中的動作不相符，並非答案。

> 字彙　**along** 沿著、向前　　**one another** 互相　　**railing** 欄杆、柵欄　　**path** 小徑　　**vendor** 攤販、供應商
> **beachgoer** 常去海邊的人

5. [5_05] [美式男聲]

(A) Some people are standing near an intersection.
(B) Some vans are parked on the street corner.
(C) Some trolley tracks run alongside a street.
(D) Some pedestrians are crossing the road.

(A) 一些人站在十字路口旁。
(B) 一些貨車停在街角。
(C) 電車鐵軌沿著道路延伸。
(D) 一些行人正在穿越馬路。

正確答案為 (C)

由照片可以確認電車鐵軌的狀態，因此 (C) 的描述最為適當。本題為無人的戶外照片，而 (A) 和 (D) 的主詞皆為人，描寫人物的動作，因此並非答案；(B) 街角沒有停放車輛，因此該敍述也不正確。

> **字彙**　**intersection** 十字路口、道路交叉處　**trolley** 電車、手推車　**track** 鐵軌　**run** 運行

6. [5_06] [英式男聲]

(A) The umbrella has been folded up.
(B) The chairs are being placed around the table.
(C) The shadow of the umbrella is being cast on a patio.
(D) Some bushes are being trimmed.

(A) 傘已經被收起來。
(B) 椅子正被放在桌子旁邊。
(C) 遮陽傘的影子投射在露台上。
(D) 灌木正在被修剪。

正確答案為 (C)

(C) 針對露台上的遮陽傘進行描寫，為最適當的答案。(A) 照片中的遮陽傘並非收起來的狀態，因此該敍述不適當；(B) 和 (D) 皆以物品當作主詞，**使用被動進行式〈be being p.p.〉暗示有人執行動作，不適用於無人照片。**

> **字彙**　**fold up** 折起　**cast** 投射（光影），三態同型　**patio** （可在上面擺桌椅的）露台　**bush** 灌木、樹叢　**trim** 修剪、修整

7. 5_07 〔美式男聲 / 美式女聲〕

Who's recording the meeting minutes today?
(A) She came in five minutes ago.
(B) It belongs to Ms. Wallace.
(C) Our assistant will.

誰負責記錄今天的會議記錄？
(A) 她 5 分鐘前到的。
(B) 這是瓦蘭絲小姐的東西。
(C) 我的助理負責。

正確答案為 (C)

本題為 Who 開頭的問句，詢問負責撰寫會議記錄的人。(C) 提到撰寫者的職稱，為正確答案。(A) 告知抵達的時間，適合用來回答 When 開頭的問句；(B) 提到第三者的名字，乍看之下可以用來回來 Who 開頭的問句，但是內容與題目無關。

> 字彙　minutes（固定用複數）會議記錄　　assistant 助理

8. 5_08 〔英式男聲 / 美式女聲〕

What will be the price to ship this package to Seattle?
(A) I have to know how much it weighs.
(B) Two hundred fifty dollars for a round-trip ticket.
(C) About a week or so.

這個包裹寄到西雅圖要多少錢？
(A) 我得先確認它的重量。
(B) 來回票為 250 美元。
(C) 大約一個星期左右。

正確答案為 (A)

本題為 What 開頭的問句，詢問 the price 費用。(A) 間接表示價格取決於重量多重，為正確答案。(B) 故意提到價錢，但前方提到的內容與寄送包裹的費用無關；(C) 回答時間，答非所問。

> 字彙　weigh 重達　　round-trip ticket 來回票

9. 5_09 〔美式女聲 / 美式男聲〕

Would you like to serve sandwiches at the reception?
(A) Everything was delicious.
(B) In Victoria Hall at 2.
(C) Cheese and crackers would be easier.

你打算在歡迎會上供應三明治嗎？
(A) 每樣東西都很好吃。
(B) 兩點在維多利亞廳。
(C) 提供起司和蘇打餅乾比較容易。

正確答案為 (C)

本題詢問是否要提供三明治。(C) 表示否定，並進一步提出其他種類的飲食為正確答案。(A) 用跟題目 sandwiches 有關的 delicious 想造成混淆；(B) 也使用聽到題目句的 reception 會聯想到的時間地點，但都與問題句無關。

> 字彙　serve 供應、準備　　reception 歡迎會；接待處

10. 5_10 〔美式女聲 / 英式男聲〕

Which location are you being transferred to?
(A) I'll get him on the line.
(B) I'm being sent to Montreux.
(C) The one next to the mirror.

你被調到哪一區？
(A) 我把電話轉給他。
(B) 我被送到蒙特勒。
(C) 鏡子旁邊的那個。

正確答案為 (B)

本題以 Which location 開頭，詢問對方被調到「什麼地方」。(B) 告知地點為最適當的回答。(A) 提到轉接電話，**故意使用到 transfer 的多種字義造成混淆**，請勿被誤導；題目的 transfer 指「調動職務」，(A) 的 transfer 則指「轉接電話」。(C) 單純告知某東西放置的位置，與調動地點無關，因此不是答案。

> 字彙　transfer 調動；轉接電話

11. `5_11` 英式男聲 / 美式男聲

I heard that Paul Martinez won the employee of the year award.
(A) That's great, I should do that.
(B) I heard that sound, too.
(C) I thought it was William Sanchez.

聽説保羅馬丁內茲獲得年度最佳員工獎。
(A) 太好了，我也應該那樣做。
(B) 我也有聽到那個聲音。
(C) 我以為是威廉桑奇茲。

正確答案為 (C)

聽到特定人士得獎的消息後，(C) 表示自己誤以為是另外一個人為最適當的回答。(A) 回答 That's great. 表示對於得獎消息感到開心，但是後方連接的內容與題目沒有關聯；(B) 重複題目開頭 I heard that. 讓人產生混淆，但 sound 指「聲音」，與題目的「消息」無關。

 字彙　**the employee of the year award** 年度最佳員工獎

12. `5_12` 美式男聲 / 美式女聲

How much do you think we should budget for the project?
(A) That sounds like a good amount.
(B) I definitely think we should.
(C) It's hard to say at this point.

你覺得應該要投入多少預算在企劃上？
(A) 聽起來是不錯的金額。
(B) 我認為我們勢必要做。
(C) 現階段還很難説。

正確答案為 (C)

本題為 How much 開頭的問句，詢問預算的金額。答案選 (C)，表示還很難説，非正面的回應。(A) 故意使用 amount 回答針對金額的提問，請勿被誤導；(B) 重複使用題目句中的 think，屬於陷阱選項。

 字彙　**budget** 預算　　**amount** 金額、數量　　**definitely** 肯定、明確地

13. `5_13` 英式男聲 / 美式女聲

Do you know when your train is due to arrive?
(A) From Oxford to New Castle.
(B) Yes, I will.
(C) Let me look at my ticket.

你知道火車何時抵達嗎？
(A) 從牛津前往新堡。
(B) 是，我會去做。
(C) 我確認一下我的車票。

正確答案為 (C)

本題為間接問句，詢問火車抵達的時間。(C) 表示要確認一下，屬於間接回答的方式，為最適當的答覆。(A) 提到地點，(B) 回答 Yes 表示知道時間，但是後方連接的補充説明答非所問。

 字彙　**due** 預期的

14. `5_14` 美式女聲 / 美式男聲

Are these the applications that we received today?
(A) No, those are yesterday's.
(B) Don't leave it behind.
(C) Mr. Miller sent them.

這些都是我們今天收到的申請書嗎？
(A) 不是，那些是昨天的。
(B) 別忘了帶走它。
(C) 米勒先生寄的。

正確答案為 (A)

本題詢問是否為今天收到的申請書。(A) 表示否定，並補充説明，為最適當的回答。(B) 回答內容與題目無關；(C) 回答是第三者寄來的，但是題目並非詢問誰寄送申請書，不適合作為答案。

字彙　**application** 申請書、報名表

15. `5_15` 美式女聲 / 英式男聲

Where will this afternoon's workshop be held?
(A) I'm sorry I can't make it.
(B) It's been put off until Friday.
(C) It's usually in the cabinet.

今天下午的研討會在哪裡舉辦？
(A) 抱歉，我可能沒辦法參加。
(B) 延期至星期五舉辦。
(C) 通常會放在櫃子裡。

正確答案為 (B)

本題為 Where 開頭的問句，詢問舉辦研討會的地點。(B) 表示研討會時間延期，自然延續對話，為最適當的回答。(A) 是婉拒邀約的回應，與題目無關。(C) 回答物品所在的位置，與題目詢問的研討會地點無關。

| 字彙 | **make it** 及時趕到　　**put off** 推遲、延期 |

16. `5_16` 美式男聲 / 英式男聲

Did you hear that Mr. Banks is planning to retire this month?
(A) I knew he was going to step down soon.
(B) I think he will be perfect for the job.
(C) He went out this morning.

你有聽說班克斯先生打算這個月退休嗎？
(A) 我知道他很快就要辭職了。
(B) 我認為他很適任這份工作。
(C) 他今天早上離開了。

正確答案為 (A)

本題為助動詞開頭的問句，詢問對方是否有聽說第三者要退休的消息。(A) 表示肯定的答覆，故為正確答案。(B) 和 (C) 的回答皆為答非所問，不能作為答案。

| 字彙 | **retire** 退休　　**step down** 退位、下台 |

17. `5_17` 美式男聲 / 美式女聲

How far have you progressed on your assignment?
(A) I'm nearly halfway through.
(B) About a ten-minute drive.
(C) No, I must have missed the sign.

你的工作進行到哪裡了？
(A) 完成將近一半了。
(B) 開車約 10 分鐘。
(C) 不，想必我錯過標誌了。

正確答案為 (A)

本題為 How far 開頭的問句，詢問「**工作進度**」。(A) 回答完成約一半，為最適當的答案。(B) 回答約 10 分鐘路程，適合用來回答以 How far 詢問「**距離多遠**」的問句，請勿被誤導。(C) 為 Yes/No 答句，不適合回答 wh 問句。

| 字彙 | **how far** 到什麼程度；（距離）多遠　　**progress** 進行　　**assignment** 任務、作業　　**nearly** 幾乎 **halfway** 在中途、到一半 |

18. `5_18` 英式男聲 / 美式女聲

Would you rather have Mr. Cabrera or Ms. Hernandez assist you?
(A) She is a very good assistant.
(B) I think I can do it on my own.
(C) He's right over there.

你想要卡布雷拉先生、還是赫南德斯小姐來幫你？
(A) 她是一位非常棒的助手。
(B) 我想我可以自己來。
(C) 他就在那裡。

正確答案為 (B)

本題詢問是否需要幫手。(B) 表示要由自己來，委婉拒絕對方，為最適當的回答。(A) 使用與題目句中 assist 有關的 assistant，請勿被誤導。(C) 的回答與題目內容無關。

| 字彙 | **would rather** 更願意、偏好　　**assist** 協助　　**on one's own** 獨自、獨立地 |

19. 5_19 〔美式女聲 / 美式男聲〕

How would you describe the new financial adviser?
(A) Please explain in detail.
(B) By calling the adviser.
(C) Quite friendly, I think.

你的新理財顧問如何？
(A) 麻煩你詳細説明。
(B) 打個電話給顧問。
(C) 我認為相當親切。

正確答案為 (C)

本題為 How 開頭的問句，詢問對某個人的看法。(C) 回答此人待人親切，故為正確答案。(B) 提出方法，適合用來回答 How 開頭的問句，不能作為本題的答案；(B) 僅重複使用題目句中的 adviser，並非答案。

> **字彙**　**describe** 敘述、描寫　　**financial adviser** 理財顧問

20. 5_20 〔美式女聲 / 英式男聲〕

These end-of-the-year sales performances are incredible.
(A) On the calendar.
(B) No, I don't work in sales.
(C) Yes, aren't they?

今年底的銷售業績相當驚人。
(A) 在月曆上。
(B) 不，我不在業務部門工作。
(C) 對，可不是嗎？

正確答案為 (C)

本題是敘述銷售業績良好的直述句。(C) 先表示同意，並反問對方表示相當認可，為最適當的回答。(B) 使用與題目 end-of-the-year 有關的 calendar，但答非所問。(C) 重複使用題目的 sales，也並非答案。

> **字彙**　**incredible** 難以置信的　　**end-of-the-year** 年底的　　**performance** 成果；表演

21. 5_21 〔英式男聲 / 美式男聲〕

When will the shipment of bulbs get here?
(A) They're sitting in my office as we speak.
(B) About this time last year.
(C) To the new branch office.

燈泡預計何時送達？
(A) 現在就在我的辦公室。
(B) 大約是去年這個時候。
(C) 送往新的分公司。

正確答案為 (A)

本題為 When 開頭的問句，詢問到貨時間。(A) 進一步表示早已送到辦公室，為最適當的回答。(B) 故意回答時間讓人產生混淆，不過時態錯誤，不能作為答案；(C) 適合回答 Where 開頭的問句。

> **字彙**　**shipment** 運送　　**bulb** 燈泡　　**sit** 位於（某處）　　**branch office** 分公司、分部

22. 5_22 〔美式男聲 / 美式女聲〕

The contents of this package are very fragile.
(A) About three hundred dollars.
(B) I think my schedule is flexible.
(C) I'll handle it carefully, then.

這個包裹的內容物為易碎品。
(A) 大約 300 美元。
(B) 我的行程很有彈性。
(C) 那我會小心搬。

正確答案為 (C)

本題為直述句，告知內容物易碎一事。(C) 表示會小心，自然延續對話，為正確答案。(A) 提到價格，答非所問；(B) 的回答與題目無關。

> **字彙**　**content** 內容　　**fragile** 易碎、脆弱的　　**flexible** 有彈性、可變通的　　**handle** 搬動；處理

23. 5_23 英式男聲 / 美式女聲

Whose marketing proposal was chosen for this week?
(A) Brian says it'll begin soon.
(B) Mr. Lansing's was, I think.
(C) Yes, I went there last week.

本週是誰的行銷提案獲選？
(A) 布萊恩說馬上就要開始了。
(B) 我以為是蘭辛先生。
(C) 對，我上週去過。

正確答案為 (B)

本題為 Whose 開頭的問句，詢問誰的提案被選中，題目使用到過去式。**(B) 提到第三者的名字，時態也一致**，故為正確答案。(A) 也使用人名，但是內容與題目無關，時態也不符。(C) 不能使用 Yes/No 回答 wh 問句。

字彙　**proposal** 提案、提議

24. 5_24 美式女聲 / 美式男聲

Haven't the tires for Mr. Sergio's car arrived yet?
(A) I'm not that tired.
(B) He's the head of marketing.
(C) You mean the ones for that sedan?

賽吉歐先生的輪胎還沒送到嗎？
(A) 我沒有很累。
(B) 他是行銷部門的主管。
(C) 你指的是那台轎車的輪胎嗎？

正確答案為 (C)

本題為否定疑問句，詢問輪胎是否已送達。(C) 提到特定的車子，並反問對方，為最適當的回答。(A) 使用 **tired**，僅與題目句中 **tires** 的發音相似，請勿被誤導；(B) 告知職稱，答非所問。

字彙　**arrive** 抵達、送達　　**sedan** [sɪˋdæn] 轎車

25. 5_25 美式女聲 / 英式男聲

Why weren't this year's profits as high as last year's?
(A) To meet important clients.
(B) Yes, it was profitable.
(C) Costs have increased.

為什麼今年的營收沒有去年高？
(A) 為了見重要的客戶。
(B) 對，有獲利。
(C) 成本增加了。

正確答案為 (C)

本題為 Why 開頭的問句，詢問營收降低的原因。(C) 說明原因為成本增加，為正確答案。(A) 選項使用的 to 不定詞可以用來回答 Why 疑問句，但是該句內容與題目無關；(C) 不能使用 Yes/No 回答 wh 問句。

字彙　**profit** 利潤、盈利　　**profitable** 有獲利的　　**increase** 增加

26. 5_26 美式男聲 / 英式男聲

Will you be working overtime this weekend?
(A) Yes, both days in fact.
(B) After lunch on Friday.
(C) He worked hard.

這個週末你要加班嗎？
(A) 對，兩天都要。
(B) 星期五午餐後。
(C) 他很認真工作。

正確答案為 (A)

本題為助動詞開頭的問句，詢問對方週末是否要加班。(A) 表示肯定，並補充說明週六週日都要工作，為最適當的回答。(B) 提到時間，但是內容與題目並不相關；(C) 重複使用題目句中的 work，並非答案。

字彙　**overtime** 加班、超時工作

Test 05

27. 5_27 美式男聲 / 美式女聲

You are working on your report, aren't you?
(A) Actually, I haven't even started.
(B) That's what Liam said.
(C) Nobody is working here.

你正在寫報告書,不是嗎?
(A) 其實我根本還沒開始。
(B) 那是利亞姆說的。
(C) 沒人在這裡工作。

正確答案為 (A)

本題為附加問句,確認對方是否正在寫報告書。(A) 回答還沒開始作為否定,為最適當的回答。(B) 提到與題目無關的第三者;(C) 重複使用題目句中的 working,並非答案。

> 字彙 **work on** 從事;致力完成

28. 5_28 英式男聲 / 美式女聲

Why don't you come to my office to go over this proposal?
(A) Sorry, I forgot to do it.
(B) Let me finish writing this e-mail first.
(C) Next year's budget proposal.

你可以來我辦公室對一下提案書嗎?
(A) 對不起,我忘記要做。
(B) 請先等我寫完電子郵件。
(C) 這是明年度的預算提案。

正確答案為 (B)

本題以 why not 開頭提問,為典型的提出建議問句,請對方到辦公室核對提案書。(B) 表示完成其他工作後就過去,為最適當的回答。(A) 回答 Sorry,表示鄭重拒絕對方的建議,但後方補充說明的內容與題目無關;(C) 重複使用題目句中的 proposal,並非答案。

> 字彙 **go over** 核對

29. 5_29 美式女聲 / 美式男聲

There's been a steady rise in demand for our products.
(A) I heard it's being held in Sydney this year.
(B) Let's check to see if he's available.
(C) Then we'll need to increase our production.

我們產品的需求維持穩定的成長。
(A) 聽說今年在雪梨舉辦。
(B) 我們看看他是否有空。
(C) 那麼我們要增加生產量。

正確答案為 (C)

本題為直述句,告知產品需求增加一事。(C) 回答需要增加生產量,為正確答案。(A) 提到活動地點,答非所問;(B) 回答 Let's check 表示要針對對方告知的消息進行確認,但是後方說明的內容與題目無關。

> 字彙 **steady** 穩定的 **rise in demand** 需求提升 **if** 是否 **available** 有空的、時間允許的

30. 5_30 美式女聲 / 英式男聲

Where can I buy something to drink during the break?
(A) Yes, they break very easily.
(B) Complimentary beverages will be provided.
(C) I didn't bring one.

請問休息時間要去哪裡買喝的?
(A) 是,它們很容易壞掉。
(B) 有免費提供飲料。
(C) 我沒有把它帶來。

正確答案為 (B)

本題為 Where 開頭的問句,詢問買飲料的地方。(B) 回答有提供免費飲料,等同於告知對方不需要購買,為正確答案。(A) 不能使用 Yes 或 No 來回答 wh 問句;(C) 與題目無關。

> 字彙 **complimentary** 免費贈送的 **beverage** 飲料

31. ⑤_31 英式男聲 / 美式男聲

Should we post the updates to the schedule on the Intranet?

(A) Not until they've been approved.

(B) I've already sent it by e-mail.

(C) I'm not sure he does.

我們要把最新的時程表公布在公司內部網路嗎？

(A) 等到被批准之後再說。

(B) 我已經以電子郵件的形式寄出了。

(C) 我不確定是不是他要做。

正確答案為 (A)

本題為助動詞開頭的問句，詢問是否要公告時間表。(A) 提到要先獲得批准才行，否定對方的詢問，為最適當的回答。(B) 乍看是可以的回答，**但回答中使用了單數受詞 it，與題目的複數受詞 updates 不符。**(C) 一開始用非正面答覆，但後方內容與題目無關。

字彙 **approve** 批准、許可   **intranet** 公司內部網路   **not until** 直到

Questions 32-34 refer to the following conversation.

W: Hi, Gabriel. I'd like to discuss the plans for the exterior work of Memphis House. Do you have a moment?

M: I'm sorry, not today. I'm taking a client to look at some apartments in West End area this afternoon.

W: I see, but we have to talk about this soon. I hope you're not planning on driving to West End. There's huge traffic congestion due to road repair work. You'd better take the subway.

M: Thanks for your advice, but I'll be okay. I'm going to leave an hour early, just in case.

問題 32-34 題參考以下對話。

女：嗨，加布里爾，㉜ 我想跟你討論一下夢菲思之家外部工程的計畫，你現在有空嗎？

男：抱歉，今天不行。㉝ 我下午要帶客戶去看西端區的幾間公寓。

女：了解，但是我們得盡快討論這件事。我希望你不是打算開車去西端，那裡正在進行道路施工，嚴重塞車。㉞ 你最好搭地鐵過去。

男：謝謝建議，但無所謂，我本來就打算提前 1 小時出發，以防萬一。

字彙　**discuss** 討論　**exterior** 外部的　**traffic congestion** 交通堵塞　**had better** 最好（表示建議）　**advice** 建議
just in case 以防萬一

32. What does the woman want to discuss with the man?   女子想和男子討論什麼事？
    (A) A remodeling project   **(A) 整修計畫**
    (B) An advertising strategy   (B) 廣告策略
    (C) An event plan   (C) 活動計畫
    (D) A traffic problem   (D) 交通問題

正確答案為 **(A)**

〈確認基本資訊—主旨〉
主旨通常會出現在對話開頭處，女子在第一句話提出她想和對方討論夢菲思之家外部工程的計畫，也就是 remodeling 改建工程，因此答案為 (A)。

換句話說 **exterior work** 外部工程 → **remodeling** 改建

33. Where does the man say he is taking a client?   男子提到他會帶客戶去哪裡？
    (A) To a manufacturing facility   (A) 生產設備
    (B) To a construction site   (B) 施工現場
    (C) To some properties   **(C) 幾間房子**
    (D) To a client's office   (D) 客戶辦公室

正確答案為 **(C)**

〈注意細節—特定事項〉
請先抓出關鍵字 taking a client，再仔細聆聽男子提及的內容。男子表示下午要帶客戶去看公寓，答案為 (C)。

換句話說 **some apartments** 幾間公寓 → **some properties** 幾間房子

字彙   **manufacturing facility** 生產設備   **construction** 施工   **property** 房地產；財產

34. What does the woman suggest?   女子建議什麼？
    (A) Calling a client   (A) 打電話給客戶
    (B) Checking the schedule   (B) 確認行程表
    (C) Taking public transportation   **(C) 搭乘大眾運輸工具**
    (D) Submitting a list   (D) 繳交清單

正確答案為 **(C)**

〈注意細節—建議〉
本題詢問女子建議的事項，須從女子的對話找出答案。女子告訴男子交通阻塞一事，建議他搭地鐵，**遇到詢問建議的問題時，可注意後半部對話使用到如〈had better〉、〈Let's ~〉或〈why not ~ ?〉表達建議的句子**。答案要選 (C)。

換句話說 **take the subway** 搭地鐵 → **take public transportation** 搭乘大眾運輸工具

5_35-37　美式女聲 / 美式男聲

Questions 35-37 refer to the following conversation.

W: Ryan, do you know if the new projector in Conference Room 203 is functioning? We're scheduled to have a meeting there next week.

M: Oh, Maintenance said they'll have it ready by Tuesday, including the new screen. Is that too late?

W: Well, I'm just worried I won't have enough time to try out the new projector beforehand. The presentation is on Wednesday morning, and I'd like to make sure I can operate it smoothly.

M: Well, I suppose we still have enough time to reschedule the presentation to Conference Room 201. It has an older projector and it's on the 5th floor. But on the other hand, the room is bigger and it's near the staff lounge.

問題 35-37 題參考以下對話。

女： 萊恩，203 會議室新的投影機現在可以用了嗎？我們下週要在那裡開會。

男： 噢，③⑤ 設備維修部門說週二前會用好，連同新的螢幕。時間上會太晚嗎？

女： 嗯，③⑥ 我擔心我沒時間提前測試新投影機。週三上午就要進行簡報，我想確保我可以順利操作機器。

男： 嗯，③⑦ 我想我們應該還來得及把簡報地點改到 201 會議室。雖然那裡的投影機比較老舊，又在 5 樓，但從另一方面來說，那間會議室的空間比較大，離員工休息室也很近。

字彙 **function**（機器）運轉　**schedule** 安排、預定　**maintenance** 維修、維修單位　**try out** 測試　**beforehand** 事先、提前　**presentation** 進行簡報　**operate** 啟動、操作　**smoothly** 流暢地　**suppose** 猜想、以為　**reschedule** 重新安排　**on the other hand** 另一方面

35. What are maintenance workers going to do by next Tuesday?
(A) Introduce the new system
(B) Install new equipment
(C) Clean the Conference Room
(D) Submit the form

維修人員在下週二前會做好什麼事？
(A) 介紹新系統
(B) 安裝新設備
(C) 打掃會議室
(D) 繳交表格

正確答案為 **(B)**

〈注意細節－特定事項〉
請從提及 maintenance workers 的對話中找出答題線索。男子告訴女子設備維修部門會在週二前安裝好投影機，選項中最為相符的描述為 (B)。

字彙　**install** 安裝、設置　**equipment** 設備　**submit** 提交

36. What is the woman concerned about?
(A) Testing a new device
(B) Meeting the deadline
(C) Using old equipment
(D) Rescheduling a presentation

女子擔心什麼事？
(A) 測試新機器
(B) 趕上截止日
(C) 使用舊設備
(D) 重新安排簡報時間

正確答案為 **(A)**

〈注意細節－擔心〉
請從女子提到問題或擔心的對話中找出答題線索。前半段對話，女子提到要開會一事。對話中段，女子表示她擔心沒有時間提前測試新投影機，因此答案要選 (A)。

換句話說 **try out the projector** 測試投影機 → **test a device** 測試機器

37. What does the man suggest the woman do?
(A) Send an e-mail
(B) Try a bigger screen
(C) Go to the staff lounge
(D) Use another place

男子建議女子做什麼事？
(A) 傳送電子郵件
(B) 改用更大的螢幕
(C) 前往員工休息室
(D) 使用其他地方

正確答案為 **(D)**

〈注意細節－建議〉
本題詢問男子建議的內容，因此請特別留意男子所說的話。後半段對話中，男子建議將地點改到 201 會議室，因此答案要選 (D)。

5_38-40 英式男聲 / 美式女聲

Questions 38-40 refer to the following conversation.

M: Hi. I'd like to return this tie that I bought here three days ago.

W: Certainly, sir. Do you have your receipt?

M: Yes, here it is.

W: Thanks. Can you tell me the reason for the return? Is there any problem?

M: No, the design is good and I really like it. But I got it as a gift for my coworker, and it turns out he already owns the exact same one. In fact, he bought it here.

W: It is a popular one. Would you like to have the money refunded to your card, or would you like a store credit instead?

M: I'll take the store credit. I shop here all the time.

問題 38-40 題參考以下對話。

男：妳好，㊳ 我想退掉 3 天前在這裡買的領帶。

女：沒問題，先生。㊴ 您有帶收據來嗎？

男：有，在這裡。

女：謝謝，方便請教您為什麼想要退貨嗎？這條領帶有什麼問題呢？

男：不是，它的設計很棒，我非常喜歡。我買來送給我同事，但他已經有一條一模一樣的領帶了。事實上，他也是在這裡買的。

女：這條領帶賣得很好。請問您希望將款項退回信用卡、還是換成消費抵用金？

男：換成店內消費抵用金。㊵ 我很常在這裡消費。

字彙 **return** 退貨、退回 　 **receipt** 收據 　 **exact** 確切的 　 **refund** 退款 　 **store credit** 消費抵用金

38. Why has the man come into the store?
    (A) To bring back an item
    (B) To get a gift
    (C) To apply for a job
    (D) To make a complaint

為何男子要來店裡？
(A) 為了退還商品
(B) 為了購買禮物
(C) 為了應徵工作
(D) 為了表達不滿

正確答案為 **(A)**

〈注意細節—特定事項〉
男子光臨店家的原因與對話主旨有關，請仔細聆聽前半段對話的內容。男子在第一句對話提到他想退掉三天前在店內購買的領帶，因此答案為 (A)。

字彙 **item** 物品 **complaint** 抱怨

39. What does the woman ask the man to provide?
    (A) Personal information
    (B) Proof of purchase
    (C) A gift voucher
    (D) A store credit

女子要求男子提供什麼東西？
(A) 個人資料
(B) 購買證明
(C) 禮券
(D) 消費抵用金

正確答案為 **(B)**

〈注意細節—請求〉
男子想要退還商品，女子問他是否有帶 receipt「收據」，因此答案選 (B)。
換句話說 **receipt** 收據 → **proof of purchase** 購買證明

字彙 **gift voucher** 禮券

40. What does the man let the woman know?
    (A) He doesn't like the item.
    (B) He is a regular customer.
    (C) He came with his coworker.
    (D) He lives near the store.

男子告訴女子什麼事？
(A) 他不喜歡這件商品。
(B) 他是店內的常客。
(C) 他和同事一起來。
(D) 他住在商店附近。

正確答案為 **(B)**

〈注意細節—特定事項〉
男子最後一句提到他很常來此消費，可以由此得知他是店內的常客，因此答案要選 (B)。

字彙 **regular customer** 常客

Questions 41-43 refer to the following conversation.

W: I was listening to the radio in the car and I heard that the tunnel construction in Midtown has finally been done.

M: Yes, I read that in the newspaper. The project was far behind schedule. I've been waiting for them to finish it since I moved here. The traffic down to Kingston Avenue should be much smoother from now on.

W: Absolutely! But it's going to cost us.

M: I know. It'll be free during August, but from September onward it's going to be $5 per vehicle.

問題 41-43 題參考以下對話。

女：我在車上聽廣播說 ㊶ 市中心的隧道工程終於完工。

男：對，我在報紙上看到消息。那項工程的施工進度大幅落後。我搬來這裡以來，就一直在等它完工。㊷ 從現在起，前往金士頓大道的交通應該會變得順暢許多。

女：理當如此！但是我們得多花錢了。

男：沒錯，㊸ 8 月還是免費的，不過從 9 月開始，每輛車通過隧道要支付 5 美元。

字彙   **tunnel** 隧道   **behind schedule** 進度落後   **onward** 向前的

41. What are the speakers discussing? 　　　　說話者在討論什麼事？
(A) The completion of a project　　　　　**(A) 工程完工**
(B) The commencement of the fiscal year　　(B) 會計年度開始
(C) The construction of a street　　　　　　(C) 道路施工
(D) The restoration of a bridge　　　　　　(D) 大橋整修

正確答案為 (A)

〈確認基本資訊－主旨〉
題目詢問對話主旨，請留意對話開頭。女子在第一句話告訴男子市中心的隧道工程完工的消息，因此答案要選 (A)。

> 字彙　**completion** 完成、完工　**commencement** 開始　**fiscal year** 會計年度　**restoration** 整修

42. What does the woman mean when she says, "Absolutely"?　女子說「理當如此！」是什麼意思？
(A) The tunnel should be renovated again.　　(A) 隧道需要重新整修。
(B) The transportation expenses will be increased.　(B) 交通費將會增加。
(C) Kingston Avenue will be closed in September.　(C) 9 月將封閉金士頓大道。
(D) There will be less traffic congestion.　　**(D) 塞車將會緩解。**

正確答案為 (D)

〈關鍵句－說話者意圖〉
詢問說話者說關鍵句的意圖時，請綜和檢視前後句的脈絡再回答。男子提到隧道工程完工後，前往特定道路的交通應該會變得順暢。接著女子對此話表達強烈的同意，因此答案要選 (D)。

> 字彙　**renovate** 整修　**expense** 支出、費用

43. According to the man, what will be offered in August?　根據男子所言，8 月將會提供什麼？
(A) Discount fare　　　　　(A) 費用折扣
(B) New bus routes　　　　(B) 新的公車路線
(C) Free usage　　　　　**(C) 免費使用**
(D) A travel card　　　　　(D) 交通卡

正確答案為 (C)

〈注意細節－特定事項〉
請特別留意男子提及關鍵字 in August 的內容。最後一句話，男子提到 8 月通過隧道不用收費，因此答案為 (C)。

> 字彙　**fare** 車費、車資　**route** 路線

5_44-46 美式女聲 / 英式男聲

Questions 44-46 refer to the following conversation.

W: Hey, Andy.

M: Good morning, Ms. Walters. The new shipment of women's summer clothing arrived this morning. Should I restock the section now?

W: No, Daniel called in sick, so I need you to fill in for him on register until Jasmine comes at noon.

M: Is Daniel okay? I remember he had a terrible headache yesterday.

W: I hope he gets well soon. You can get to the clothing this afternoon.

M: Sure. I did notice that we only have a couple of purses left on the shelf. We'd better put out some more.

W: That's a good idea. Do that right away while there aren't any customers in the store.

問題 44-46 題參考以下對話。

女：嗨，安迪。

男：早安，華特絲小姐。㊹ 夏季女裝今天上午新到貨了，要現在補貨上架嗎？

女：㊺ 不用，丹尼爾剛打電話來請病假，我需要你代替他站結帳櫃檯，直到潔絲敏來。

男：丹尼爾還好嗎？我記得他昨天開始就嚴重頭痛。

女：希望他能早日康復。衣服你今天下午再整理就好了。

男：好的。㊻ 我發現架上只剩下幾個手提包，我們最好再補上一些。

女：這個想法不錯，趁客人還沒來之前馬上完成。

字彙 | **restock** 補貨上架 　**call in sick** 打電話請病假 　**fill in for** 遞補、臨時接替 　**register** 收銀台 　**get to** 著手處理
notice 注意到、察覺 　**put out** 取出

44. Where do the speakers most likely work?
(A) At a restaurant
(B) At a travel agency
(C) At a retail store
(D) At a hospital

説話者們最有可能在哪裡工作？
(A) 餐廳
(B) 旅行社
(C) 零售店
(D) 醫院

正確答案為 **(C)**

〈確認基本資訊―地點〉
本題詢問説話者的工作地點，可以從對話開頭找尋答題線索。説話者彼此問候完畢後，針對衣服到貨一事展開對話，可以由此得知他們在販售衣服的地方工作，答案為 (C)。

字彙　**retail store** 零售店

45. What can be inferred about Daniel?
(A) He will handle the clothes.
(B) He is caught in traffic.
(C) He is out of town.
(D) He works as a cashier.

以下哪項對丹尼爾的推斷正確？
(A) 他會負責衣服。
(B) 他被困在車陣中。
(C) 他離開城市了。
(D) 他要當收銀人員。

正確答案為 **(D)**

〈注意細節―特定事項〉
請從提及關鍵字 Daniel 找答案。女子告訴男子丹尼爾請病假，並請他代替丹尼爾站在結帳櫃檯，因此答案要選 (D)。

字彙　**out of town** 出遠門　　**cashier** 收銀人員；收銀台

46. What will the man probably do next?
(A) Talk to Jasmine
(B) Restock some clothing
(C) Leave the office
(D) Put out some items

男子接下來可能會做什麼事？
(A) 跟潔絲敏説話
(B) 將一些衣服補貨上架
(C) 離開辦公室
(D) 取出一些商品

正確答案為 **(D)**

〈注意細節―未來〉
詢問男子下一步的行動，可以從對話後半段找線索。男子建議再多拿幾個手提包放到架上，女子對此表示同意，由此得知男子接著將取出要販售的商品，因此答案為 (D)。

5_47-49　美式女聲 / 美式男聲

Questions 47-49 refer to the following conversation.

W: Ian, did you hear that the marketing director decided to go ahead with his plan to open a branch in Brussels next month?

M: That's right. An analysis of market research conducted in Belgium last month revealed a high potential demand for our services there. At the moment, there aren't many Belgian companies in our industry now.

W: Then the marketing director's decision makes a lot of sense. We should quickly settle down there when the competition isn't fierce. I'd like to see the market survey you told me about. Is there any way I can have a look?

M: I am not the right person to answer that. You need to talk to someone in marketing about it.

問題 47-49 題參考以下對話。

女：㊼ 伊恩，你有聽說行銷總監決定在下個月推動設立布魯塞爾分公司的計畫嗎？

男：沒錯，上個月針對比利時的市調結果顯示，我們的服務在那裡有極大的需求量。㊽ 目前在比利時並沒有太多同業公司。

女：㊽ 那麼行銷總監的決定非常合理，我們得趁競爭還沒有那麼激烈的時候，盡快在比利時坐穩位置。我想看一下你剛說的市場調查內容，有什麼方法可以看到呢？

男：我不太適合回答妳這個問題，㊾ 妳可以問問行銷部門的人。

字彙　**marketing** 行銷　　**analysis** 分析　　**conduct research** 進行研究　　**reveal** 顯示、透露　　**potential** 潛在的　　**demand** 需求　　**Belgian**［ˋbɛldʒən］比利時的、比利時人　　**industry** 業界、行業　　**make sense** 合理　　**settle down** 安頓下來　　**competition** 競爭　　**fierce** 激烈的

47. According to the woman, what will happen next month?
(A) A regional office will open.
(B) A Belgian firm will be acquired.
(C) An analysis will be conducted.
(D) A decision will be made.

根據女子所言,下個月將會發生什麼事?
(A) 區域辦公室開張。
(B) 收購比利時公司。
(C) 進行某項分析。
(D) 做出某個決定。

正確答案為 (A)

〈注意細節—特定事項〉

請特別留意文中提及關鍵字 next month 的對話。前半段對話中,提到下個月要推動在布魯塞爾設立分公司的計畫,因此答案為 (A)。

換句話說 **branch** 分店、分公司 → **regional office** 區域辦公室

字彙 **acquire** 收購

---

48. What was the reason for the marketing director's decision?
(A) A lack of competition
(B) A certain industry regulation
(C) A shortage of hands
(D) An increase in efficiency

行銷總監做出此決定的原因是?
(A) 缺乏競爭者
(B) 某種產業規定
(C) 人力不足
(D) 提高效率

正確答案為 (A)

〈注意細節—特定事項〉

請仔細聆聽提及 marketing director's decision 的對話。對話中段,女子提到要趁競爭還沒有那麼激烈的時候,盡快坐穩位置,表示她認同總監的決定,因此答案選 (A)。

換句話說 **The competition isn't fierce** 競爭不激烈 → **A lack of competition** 缺少競爭者

字彙 **regulation** 規定 **shortage of hands** 人手不足 **efficiency** 效率、效能

---

49. What does the man mean when he says,
"I am not the right person to answer that"?
(A) He is unable to contact the CEO.
(B) He does not know the survey result.
(C) He is unable to answer the particular question.
(D) He is not in charge of the report.

男子說「我不太適合回答妳這個問題」是什麼意思?
(A) 他無法聯絡執行長。
(B) 他不知道調查的結果。
(C) 他無法回答特定問題。
(D) 他不負責管理這份報告。

正確答案為 (C)

〈關鍵句—說話者意圖〉

碰到詢問說話者意圖的題目時,請務必確認關鍵句前後句。女子先向男子詢問怎樣看到調查結果,男子以此句回答,並接著建議女子改向行銷部門的人確認,因此答案為 (C)。

字彙 **contact** 聯絡 **particular** 特定的、某個 **in charge of** 負責

New TOEIC 第五回

Questions 50-52 refer to the following conversation with three speakers.

W1: Isaac, do you have a minute? I was off on a business trip on Tuesday and Wednesday, and I'm behind schedule on the Rebecca Fashion ad campaign. Is there any way I can submit my work next Monday?

M: I'm sorry, Zoe, but it's not possible. I also have to send the copy to Rebecca by Friday evening. If you need help, I can assign part of it to someone else in your department.

W1: OK. Maybe I should ask someone else to join me.

W2: Sorry to interrupt, Zoe, but I just overheard what you were saying to Isaac. I could help out, if you like. I've worked with Rebecca before and I know her preferences.

W1: That's perfect, Sophia! Your help is needed.

W2: Is that okay with you, Isaac? If we work together, I'm sure we can complete it on time.

M: Why not? Go ahead. Let me know if you need anything.

問題 50-52 題參考以下三人對話。

女1： 艾薩克，你現在有空嗎？我週二和週三出差，所以我的蕾貝卡時尚廣告活動進度落後，**50** 有沒有可能把期限延到下週一呢？

男： 抱歉，佐伊，沒辦法。**52** 我也得在週五傍晚之前把影本傳給蕾貝卡。如果妳需要幫忙，我可以指派妳們部門的人幫妳分擔工作。

女1： 好，也許我應該拜託別人一起做。

女2： 抱歉打斷妳，佐伊。我剛不小心聽到妳跟艾薩克講話。**51** 如果妳不介意的話，我可以幫妳。我之前曾跟蕾貝卡共事過，很清楚她的喜好。

女1： 那太棒了，蘇菲亞！我需要妳的幫忙。

女2： 你也同意讓我幫忙嗎，艾薩克？如果我們同心協力，我相信一定能在時間內完成工作。

男： 當然好啊，就這麼做吧。如果有任何需要，請隨時跟我說。

字彙　**campaign** 宣傳行銷活動　**interrupt** 打斷　**overhear** 偶然聽到　**preference** 偏好、喜愛

50. What does Zoe ask of Isaac?
(A) If he can let her leave early
(B) If he can extend a deadline
(C) If he can give her a day off
(D) If he can buy her some new clothes

佐伊詢問艾薩克什麼事？
(A) 是否能讓她早點下班
(B) 是否能延長期限
(C) 是否允許她請假
(D) 是否能買幾件衣服給她

正確答案為 **(B)**

〈注意細節—請求〉
對話開頭，女子 1 和男子互相叫對方的名字，可以得知男子為 Isaac 艾薩克、女子 1 為 Zoe 佐伊。女子 1 向男子詢問能否將工作的完成期限延到下週一，因此答案選 (B)。**三人對話中經常會提及數個人名，若題目的關鍵字為人名時，請務必要確認該人名為該對話中的人物、還是對話之外的第三者。**

51. What does Sophia tell Zoe?
(A) She will take some time off.
(B) She can ask someone to help.
(C) She knows Rebecca.
(D) She knows Zoe's preferences.

蘇菲亞告訴佐伊什麼事？
(A) 她會休息一段時間。
(B) 她可以請別人幫忙。
(C) 她認識蕾貝卡。
(D) 她知道佐伊的喜好。

正確答案為 **(C)**

〈注意細節—特定事項〉
題目提及兩個人名，因此請仔細聆聽文中提及人名之處。女子 1 稱呼女子 2 為 Sophia 蘇菲亞，對她的話表示同意，由此可以得知女子 2 為蘇菲亞。而女子 2 表示要幫女子 1，並提到自己曾跟蕾貝卡共事過，因此答案選 (C)。

52. By when must the work be finished?
(A) Monday
(B) Wednesday
(C) Friday
(D) Sunday

他們要在哪天前完成工作？
(A) 週一
(B) 週三
(C) 週五
(D) 週日

正確答案為 **(C)**

〈注意細節—特定事項〉
女子 1 詢問男子是否能將工作的完成期限延至週一，而後男子回答要在週五傍晚之前傳給蕾貝卡，可知最晚要在週五前完成工作，答案為 (C)。

5_53-55 美式男聲／美式女聲

Questions 53-55 refer to the following conversation.

M: Okay, that's all I have to ask you. Do you have any questions about the job before we wrap up?

W: Thanks to your lucid explanation, if I was hired as a researcher, I would understand what to do. I have a question about the institution itself, though.

M: Feel free to ask me anything you'd like to know.

W: I was curious to know how your organization is funded. Is it mostly through government subsidy?

M: Partially, but not mainly. Personal donations are the highest percentage of our total funds. We also receive substantial contributions from corporate donors and various charities.

問題 53-55 題參考以下對話。

男：好，我已經問完所有的問題了，㊼ 結束前妳還有什麼工作上的問題想問嗎？

女：謝謝你的清楚說明，㊼ ㊼ 如果我受聘為研究人員的話，我會很清楚該做什麼了。不過，我還想請教一個有關機構的問題。

男：有任何想問的都歡迎提出。

女：我很好奇貴機構是如何籌措資金的？大部分是透過政府補助嗎？

男：一小部分是，但不是主要來源。㊼ 個人捐款是我們最大的資金來源。我們也會收到來自企業和慈善團體的大筆捐款。

字彙 **wrap up** 結束、收尾　**lucid** 清楚易懂的　**explanation** 說明　**institution** 機構　**feel free to** 無需拘束、隨意　**fund** 籌措資金；資金　**subsidy**（國家或機關提供的）補助金　**partially** 一部分　**donation** 捐款、捐贈　**substantial** 大量的　**contribution** 貢獻　**corporate** 公司的、企業的　**charity** 慈善團體

53. Who most likely is the woman?　女子最有可能是誰？
(A) A charity organizer　(A) 慈善工作主辦人
(B) An office administrator　(B) 辦公室主管
(C) A job candidate　**(C) 求職者**
(D) A research manager　(D) 研究經理

正確答案為 **(C)**

〈確認基本資訊—身分〉
男子在第一句話詢問女子針對工作是否還有其他問題想問，後方以聘用女子為前提展開對話，由此可以得知女子是來面試的人，因此 (C) 為最適當的答案。

字彙　**job candidate** 求職者

54. Where does the conversation most likely take place?　此段對話最有可能發生在何處？
(A) In a marketing office　(A) 行銷辦公室
(B) In an educational institution　(B) 教育機關
(C) At a research institute　**(C) 研究機構**
(D) At a fundraising event　(D) 募款活動

正確答案為 **(C)**

〈確認基本資訊—地點〉
女子為求職者，她提到聽完男子的說明後，讓她了解研究人員的職責，由此可以得知女子應徵的是研究人員一職，因此答案要選 (C)。

換句話說 **informative** 實用的 → **helpful** 有幫助的

字彙　**institute** 學校研究機關　**fundraising** 募款

55. According to the man, which group provides the most funding?　根據男子所言，哪個團體提供最多資金？
(A) Charitable organizations　(A) 慈善機構
(B) The government　(B) 政府
(C) Corporations　(C) 企業
(D) Private donors　**(D) 私人捐款者**

正確答案為 **(D)**

〈注意細節—特定事項〉
題目關鍵字為 funding，因此請從男子提及的相關敘述中找出答案。男子在最後提到最大的資金來源為個人捐款，因此答案為 (D)。

換句話說 **personal donations** 個人捐款 → **private donors** 私人捐款者

Questions 56-58 refer to the following conversation with three speakers.

W: Hi, guys. How's the layout of the advertisement for GS7 Automobiles coming along? Are you making any progress?

M1: Hi, Stephanie. We're running behind schedule. I doubt if we'll be able to finish on time. The clients have requested to have it done by next week.

M2: That's right. I have told them enough about the possibility of extending the deadline, but they didn't change their mind.

W: Well, they did. You're not going to believe this. They've just decided to push the due date back until the middle of October.

M1: Really? That's a relief. That will greatly reduce the pressure on us.

W: Yeah. As a matter of fact, they're having problems with their budget and cannot go ahead as planned.

M2: Thank you for the good news.

問題 56-58 題參考以下三人對話。

女： 嗨，各位。⑤⑥ GS7 汽車廣告設計如何，有什麼新進展嗎？

男1： 嗨，史蒂芬妮，我們工作進度落後，我懷疑無法在時間內完成。客戶要求我們在下週前做好。

男2： 沒錯，我已經跟他們談過延長期限一事，但是他們不打算改變心意。

女： 嗯，他們之前是如此。你們一定不會相信，⑤⑦ 他們剛決定把期限延長至 10 月中。

男1： 真的嗎？總算鬆一口氣。如此一來大大減輕了我們的壓力。

女： 是啊。⑤⑧ 事實上他們的預算出了點問題，無法按原定計畫走。

男2： 謝謝妳告訴我這個好消息。

字彙 layout（書、建築）設計、規劃　coming along 進展　progress 進展、進度　doubt 懷疑、不能肯定
request 請求　extend 延長　push back（時間、日期）推延　due day 期限　reduce 減低　pressure 壓力
as a matter of fact 事實上

56. What type of business do the speakers probably work for?　　說話者可能從事哪一種行業？
(A) An automobile company　　(A) 汽車公司
(B) A financial firm　　(B) 金融公司
(C) An advertising agency　　**(C) 廣告代理商**
(D) An electronic manufacturer　　(D) 電子製造商

正確答案為 **(C)**

〈確認基本資訊―地點〉
本題詢問說話者的工作地點，答題線索會出現在對話開頭處。女子在第一句話便提到 GS7 汽車廣告設計一事，因此答案要選 (C)。

字彙　**automobile** 汽車　　**financial firm** 金融公司　　**manufacturer** 製造商

57. Why does the woman say, "You're not going to believe this"?　　為何女子會說「你們一定不會相信」？
(A) 案子進展很快。
(A) A project has made much progress.　　**(B) 出現意外的決定。**
(B) An unexpected decision has been made.　　(C) 廣告活動非常成功。
(C) An advertising campaign was very successful.　　(D) 截止日將會提早。
(D) The deadline will be moved forward.

正確答案為 **(B)**

〈關鍵句―說話者意圖〉
請務必整合前後文內容來掌握女子的意圖。前一句男子表示他已經跟客戶談過延長期限一事，但是客戶並未改變心意，仍要求在期限內完成。而後女子說出此句，並告知客戶決定延長期限的消息，因此答案要選 (B)。

字彙　**move forward** 提前；前進

58. What does the woman say about the clients?　　女子提到了客戶的什麼事情？
(A) They are suffering from a lack of funds.　　**(A) 他們面臨經費不足的問題。**
(B) They recently started their business.　　(B) 他們最近展開新事業。
(C) They are having difficulty exporting.　　(C) 他們在出口上遭遇困難。
(D) They recently hired a new manager.　　(D) 他們最近雇用新的經理。

正確答案為 **(A)**

〈注意細節―特定事項〉
請仔細聆聽女子談及客戶的內容。後半段對話女子提到客戶預算出問題，無法按照原定計畫進行，答案為 (A)。
換句話說 **have problems with the budget** 預算上出問題 → **suffer from a lack of funds** 面臨經費不足

字彙　**suffer from** 遭遇（困難）　　**export** 出口

5_59-61 美式女聲 / 英式男聲

Questions 59-61 refer to the following conversation.

W: Good morning, Scott. Do you need any help putting together the data for the presentation on our car sales tomorrow?

M: I'm almost done, thanks, but there is something you could do for me. I still need to make some graphics to show last quarter's sales by branch. You're much better at using those chart programs than I am.

W: Sure, no problem. Actually, I made a very similar chart myself the other day. It'll be much faster if I update that with the new sales figures. Send me the data and I can do it right now.

W: That'd be a great help. Now I can finish up the sales projection, and we'll be ready by 6 o'clock.

問題 59-61 題參考以下對話。

女： 早安，史考特。㊾ 需要幫你彙整明天汽車銷售簡報上要用的資料嗎？

男： 謝謝，我已經做得差不多了。不過有件事要請妳幫我。我還需要把上一季的分店銷量做成圖表給大家看，我想妳比我更擅於使用圖表系統。

女： 好的，沒有問題。㏿ 其實我前幾天才做好一個類似的圖表，只要更新成新的銷售數字，就能迅速完成一份新的圖表。把資料寄給我，我馬上做。

男： 妳真的幫了我一個大忙。㏿ 那我來把銷售預估做完，預計 6 點前我們可以準備好。

字彙 **put together** 彙整、整合　　**graphic** 圖表（的）　　**quarter** 季度　　**chart** 圖表　　**figures** 數字、數據　　**projection** 預估、推測

59. What is the topic of the conversation?
(A) A meeting plan
(B) A retirement event
(C) A sales presentation
(D) The latest car model

本篇對話的主旨為何？
(A) 會議計畫
(B) 退休活動
(C) 銷售簡報
(D) 最新汽車模型

正確答案為 **(C)**

〈確認基本資訊一主旨〉
主旨的答題線索會出現在對話開頭處。女子在第一句話詢問對方是否需要幫忙彙整汽車銷售簡報上要用的數據，由此可以得知他們正在為簡報做準備，因此最適當的答案為 (C)。

60. What has the woman recently done?
(A) Designed a car
(B) Updated the figures
(C) Created a chart
(D) Attended a meeting

女子最近完成了什麼事？
(A) 設計汽車
(B) 更新數據
(C) 製作圖表
(D) 參加會議

正確答案為 **(C)**

〈注意細節一特定事項〉
本題詢問女子已完成的事情，因此請特別留意相關內容。對話中段，男子請女子幫忙使用圖表系統，女子表示她曾製作過類似的圖表，因此答案要選 (C)。

字彙 **attend** 參加、出席

61. What will the man do next?
(A) Contact a client
(B) Work on an estimate
(C) Revise data
(D) Attend a meeting

男子接下來將會做什麼事？
(A) 聯絡客戶
(B) 完成估算工作
(C) 修改數據
(D) 參加會議

正確答案為 **(B)**

〈注意細節一未來〉
回答未來做的事，要從對話後段尋找答案。後半段對話中，男子提到他要進行銷售評估工作，因此答案為 (B)。

字彙 **estimate** 估計；估價　**revise** 修改

Questions 62-64 refer to the following conversation and directory.

W: Douglas, I've just finished reviewing your report, and I've found some things that you need to change before you submit it to Mr. Moore. Some of the data you used is not accurate.

M: What do you mean? Do I have to start it over again? I've spent the whole week working on it.

W: No, you don't have to start over. You only need to revise the information regarding last year's second quarter. Somehow you entered the information from 2016 instead of 2017. It won't be difficult to correct the figures.

M: That's a relief. I think I can handle it then. Thanks for catching that for me. Mr. Moore would have been annoyed if I'd given him the report with faulty data.

Department Manager Directory		
Dept.	Manager	Extension No.
Advertising	Nicole Martinez	210
Human Resources	Erica Lopez	324
Maintenance	Ethan Cabrera	420
Accounting	Lewis Moore	518

問題 62-64 題參考以下對話和電話名冊。

女：道格拉斯，62 我剛看完你的報告，發現有些地方需要修改，才能提交給摩爾先生。裡頭有些資料有誤。

男：這是什麼意思？我得再次重做嗎？我花了一整個禮拜的時間才完成這份報告。

女：沒有，你不需要重做，只要修改有關去年第二季的資料就行了。不知道什麼原因，你把 2017 年的資料誤植成 2016 年。更正一下數字應該不會太難。

男：那我就鬆口氣了。我可以處理。63 64 謝謝妳幫我抓出錯誤。如果我把有錯誤數據的報告交給摩爾先生，他一定會很生氣。

部門經理電話名冊		
部門	經理	分機號碼
廣告	妮可馬丁茲	210
人力資源	艾莉卡洛佩茲	324
維修	依桑卡布雷拉	420
會計	路易斯摩爾	518

字彙　**review** 檢查、查看　**accurate** 正確無誤的　**start over** 重頭來過　**regarding** 關於
somehow 不知道什麼原因；以某種方式　**annoyed** 惱怒的　**faulty** 錯誤的

62. What is the main topic of the conversation?
(A) Plans for a seminar
(B) Adjustment of a document
(C) Ideas for a presentation
(D) Budgets for a project

本篇對話的主旨為何？
(A) 為研討會擬定計畫
(B) 修改文件內容
(C) 為簡報構思點子
(D) 案子的預算

正確答案為 **(B)**

〈確認基本資訊—主旨〉
本題詢問的是對話主旨，請留意對話開頭。女子在第一句話中提到她看過男子的報告，並指出需要修改後再交給上司，因此答案要選 (B)。

> 字彙　**seminar** 研討會　　**adjustment** 調整、修改

63. Why does the man thank the woman?
(A) She gathered some information.
(B) She gave him a ride.
(C) She noticed some errors.
(D) She sent an e-mail.

為何男子要感謝女子？
(A) 她彙整了一些資料。
(B) 她開車送男子一程。
(C) 她注意到一些錯誤。
(D) 她傳送了電子郵件。

正確答案為 **(C)**

〈注意細節—特定事項〉
請抓出關鍵字 thank，仔細聆聽男子向女子道謝的片段。後半段對話男子謝謝女子找出錯誤，因此答案為 (C)。

64. Look at the graphic. In which department do the speakers most likely work?
(A) Advertising
(B) Human Resources
(C) Maintenance
(D) Accounting

根據圖表，說話者最有可能在哪個部門工作？
(A) 廣告
(B) 人力資源
(C) 維修
(D) 會計

正確答案為 **(D)**

〈注意細節—圖表相關〉
題目選項列出部門名稱，剛好對應到圖表的部門，可推測對話應該會提到經理的名字或分機號碼作為答題關鍵，請特別留意相關內容。男子感謝女子找出錯誤後，提到如果他把有誤的報告交給摩爾先生，他一定會生氣。這表示摩爾先生為該男子的上司，而說話者們跟摩爾先生在同一個部門工作，因此答案選 (D)。

5_65-67　美式女聲 / 英式男聲

Questions 65-67 refer to the following conversation and chart.

W: Excuse me. I saw your ad in the newspaper that all of your air purifiers are on sale for 20% off this week, so I came to have a look.

M: You are at the right place. Are you interested in a high-capacity model for industrial use, or something for the home?

W: For family use only. And I'd like something made by Oscar Electronics.

M: Great choice. Oscar Electronics makes excellent machines.

W: I'd like to see whichever model is most efficient in terms of energy consumption.

M: Okay. Let me explain to you some details. The one with the highest efficiency rating is their most expensive model, but at the same time it's their best selling model.

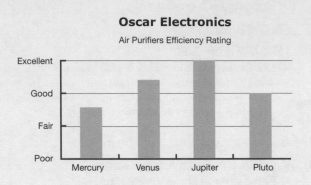

Oscar Electronics

Air Purifiers Efficiency Rating

問題 65-67 題參考以下對話和長條圖。

女：不好意思，㉞ 我在報紙上看到你們所有的空氣清淨機有八折優惠，所以過來這裡看看。

男：妳來對地方了。㉟ 妳想看高效能的工業用機型、還是家用機型呢？

女：家用的就可以。我想看奧斯卡電子製造的產品。

男：妳真的很會選，奧斯卡電子生產的機器很棒。

女：我想看看節能等級最高的機型。

男：好的，讓我為妳詳細說明一下，㊱ 效能等級最高的產品為價格最高的機型，但它同時也是最熱銷的機型。

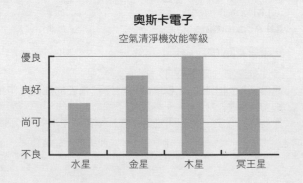

奧斯卡電子

空氣清淨機效能等級

字彙　**air purifier** 空氣清淨機　**efficiency rating** 效能等級、節能等級　**capacity** 容量、產能、生產力
industrial 工業的；產業相關的　**whichever** 無論哪個　**in terms of** 在～方面　**energy consumption** 能源消耗

65. According to the woman, how was the sale advertised?
(A) On the Web site
(B) In the newspaper
(C) On the television
(D) On the radio

根據女子所言，她透過什麼管道得知優惠廣告？
(A) 網站
(B) 報紙
(C) 電視
(D) 廣播

正確答案為 **(B)**

〈注意細節─特定事項〉
請先抓出關鍵字 sale，並仔細聆聽女子所說的話。女子在第一句話便提到她是看了報紙廣告後才過來的，因此答案要選 (B)。

66. What does the man ask about?
(A) Where the item is displayed
(B) When a shipment will be made
(C) Whether a discount coupon is valid
(D) How a product will be used

男子問什麼問題？
(A) 產品的展示位置
(B) 產品的配送時間
(C) 優惠券是否有效
(D) 產品的用途為何

正確答案為 **(D)**

〈注意細節─特定事項〉
請從男子向女子提問的片段中找出答題線索。女子表示她來此購買產品，接著男子問她想要工業用還是家用的機型，因此答案為 (D)。

字彙　**display** 展示　**discount coupon** 折價券　**valid** 有效的

67. Look at the graphic. Which model does the man say is the most expensive?
(A) The Mercury
(B) The Venus
(C) The Jupiter
(D) The Pluto

根據圖表，哪一款是男子所述最貴的機型？
(A) 水星
(B) 金星
(C) 木星
(D) 冥王星

正確答案為 **(C)**

〈注意細節─圖表相關〉
題目選項列出圖表下方的產品名稱，這表示對話中會提到圖表側邊的性能、或是長條圖的高低，因此請仔細聆聽相關答題線索。對話最後，男子提到效能等級最高的產品為價格最高的機型，而等級最高的產品為 (C)，為正確答案。

5_68-70 | 美式女聲 / 英式男聲

Questions 68-70 refer to the following conversation and layout.

W: Thanks for coming in today, Mr. Jonson. You had a meeting with the mayor last night, didn't you? How did it go?

M: It went well. I was asking her to promote our museum more on the city's Web site and she gave me positive answers. Anyway, what was it you wanted to discuss?

W: You know, I don't think the collection of statues should be kept in Room 2. All of the exhibits on that side of the museum are related to Greek art. I think the statues are more related to Egyptian art.

M: That makes sense. Let's move them to the room near the entrance beside the Egyptian art.

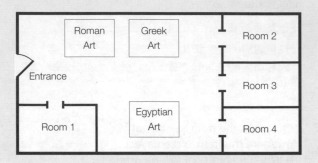

問題 **68-70** 題參考以下對話和平面圖。

女：強森先生，謝謝你今天過來。❽ 昨晚你和市長開過會了吧？結果如何呢？

男：非常順利。❾ 我向市長請求在市府網站上加強宣傳博物館，她也同意這件事。先不說這個，妳想跟我談什麼事？

女：我想你應該知道，雕像收藏品好像不太適合放在 2 號展示室，那邊的展示品都跟希臘藝術有關。我覺得雕像更偏向於埃及藝術。

男：妳說得有道理。❼⁰ 那我們把雕像移到入口處的埃及藝術旁。

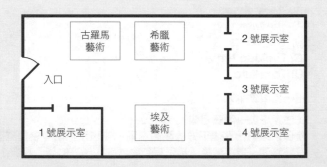

字彙 **mayor** 市長 **promote** 促銷、宣傳 **positive** 正面的 **statue** 雕像 **exhibit** 展示品、展出
relate to 與～有關、涉及

68. Who did the man meet yesterday?
(A) A museum director
(B) A town official
(C) A tour guide
(D) A department manager

男子昨天跟誰見面？
(A) 博物館館長
(B) 市府官員
(C) 導遊
(D) 部門經理

正確答案為 (B)

〈注意細節一特定事項〉
請務必仔細聆聽提及關鍵字 yesterday 的片段。女子向男子詢問昨晚和市長開會的狀況如何，這表示男子昨天跟市長見過面，因此最適當的答案為 (B)。

換句話說 **mayor** 市長 → **town official** 市府官員

69. How would the man like to promote the museum?
(A) In a newspaper
(B) On the television
(C) On the Web site
(D) On a street banner

男子想用什麼方式宣傳博物館？
(A) 刊登報紙
(B) 電視宣傳
(C) 網站宣傳
(D) 街頭看板

正確答案為 (C)

〈注意細節一特定事項〉
請從男子提及關鍵字 promote 之處找出答題線索。男子表示他在會議中提出在市府網站上宣傳博物館的要求，因此答案選 (C)。

70. Look at the graphic. Where will the collection of statues most likely be placed?
(A) In Room 1
(B) In Room 2
(C) In Room 3
(D) In Room 4

根據圖表，雕像收藏品會被放置在什麼地方？
(A) 1 號展示室
(B) 2 號展示室
(C) 3 號展示室
(D) 4 號展示室

正確答案為 (A)

〈注意細節一圖表相關〉
選項列出了平面圖中的展示室，可推測對話應該會提及平面圖中的其他資訊，因此**請聽清楚與 Roman Art, Greek Art, Egyptian Art 有關的答題線索**。女子提到題目關鍵字 collection of statues，並建議更換展示地點。而後男子同意將雕像移到入口附近的埃及藝術旁，因此答案選 (A)。

Questions 71-73 refer to the following talk.

Thank you for joining the tour of our food processing facility. I'm Melissa Grey, your guide today. Natural Catering has been providing ingredients for Auckland restaurants for ten years now. We're currently the main suppliers of vegetables to more than 20 percent of the eateries in Auckland. We're starting the tour here in the storage facility because I'd like to show you the fresh vegetables being delivered and taken directly to our processing area. We start preparing the vegetables minutes after they arrive to ensure that they're fresh when they reach your restaurants. At the end of the tour, I'd like to offer each of you an apron with the Natural Catering logo on it. I hope you will all like them. Let's get started.

問題 71-73 題參考以下談話。

感謝各位來參加食品加工設備的參觀行程，我是今天的導覽員梅麗莎葛雷。自然餐飲一直為奧克蘭的餐廳提供食材，至今已有 10 年的時間。現在我們成為主要蔬菜供應商，供應給奧克蘭兩成以上的餐廳使用。72 第一站我會帶各位參觀儲藏設備，因為我想向各位展示我們的新鮮蔬菜是直送加工區域。71 蔬菜送達幾分鐘內我們會立即處理，確保送到各位的餐廳時是新鮮的狀態。73 行程最後，我會送給各位印有自然餐飲商標的圍裙，希望你們會喜歡。那我們現在就開始吧！

字彙　**food processing** 食品加工　**catering** 餐飲、外燴　**ingredient** 原料、成分　**currently** 現在、當前　**supplier** 供應商　**eatery** 飲食店、餐館　**storage facility** 儲藏設備、儲存裝置　**ensure** 保證

71. Who most likely are the tour participants?
(A) Natural Park tourists
(B) Restaurant owners
(C) New interns
(D) Local residents

誰最有可能參加導覽行程？
(A) 自然公園的遊客
(B) 餐廳老闆
(C) 新的實習人員
(D) 當地居民

正確答案為 **(B)**

〈確認基本資訊—聽者〉
開頭處通常會提到與聽者資訊有關的答題線索。本文開頭提到 catering 和 restaurant，中間部分又提到他們會盡快處理蔬菜，以確保能新鮮送達各位的餐廳，因此答案要選 (B)。

字彙　　**tourist** 旅客　　**owner** 物主、擁有者　　**intern** 實習生　　**local resident** 當地居民

72. Where will the tour begin?
(A) At the main entrance
(B) In the manufacturing facility
(C) In the warehouse
(D) In the marketing office

參觀行程從哪裡開始？
(A) 大門入口
(B) 生產設備
(C) 儲藏室
(D) 行銷辦公室

正確答案為 **(C)**

〈注意細節—特定事項〉
請先抓出關鍵字 tour begin，並仔細聆聽相關片段。説話者於中間提到第一站要參觀儲藏設備，答案為 (C)。
換句話說 **storage facility** 儲藏設備 → **warehouse** 儲藏室

73. What will participants receive at the end of the tour?
(A) An item of clothing
(B) Food samples
(C) A carrier bag
(D) A booklet

參觀結束後，參加者會收到什麼東西？
(A) 一件衣物
(B) 食物樣品
(C) 購物袋
(D) 小冊子

正確答案為 **(A)**

〈注意細節—特定事項〉
請留意關鍵字 end of the tour 之處找出答案。後半段提到導覽行程最後會贈送印有公司商標的圍裙，答案為 (A)。

Questions 74-76 refer to the following news report.

And for today's local news, Finsbury City Council announced yesterday that it has approved the construction of the proposed Square One multiplex cinema and shopping mall complex located in the northwest of Bedford County. The project will cost an estimated two million dollars and is expected to take three years to complete. Controversy has swirled around the project, as many citizens wanted the land to remain protected open space. However, the Mayor of Finsbury argued that once completed, the complex will bring in millions of dollars in revenue for the city every year. "This development will be a boon to our city," he said. The groundbreaking ceremony for the complex will take place next Tuesday at 11 A.M.

問題 74-76 題參考以下新聞報導。

接下來是今天的地方新聞。74 芬斯伯里市市議會昨天宣布，預定於貝德福德縣西北部興建第一廣場影城兼購物中心的建案已獲得核准。此建案預估耗資兩百萬美元，預計 3 年完工。75 圍繞此建案的爭議不斷，許多居民希望把該土地保留為公共開放空間。76 然而，芬斯伯里市市長主張，一旦完工，該複合建築每年能為本市帶來數百萬美元的收入。他表示：「此開發案會為我們的城市帶來益處。」工程動土典禮預計於下週二上午 11 點舉行。

字彙　**council** 議會　**announce** 宣布　**multiplex cinema** 影城　**complex** 複合式、多功能建築　**controversy** 爭議　**swirl around** 圍繞～打轉、旋轉　**revenue** 收入　**boon** 提昇生活品質的好處　**groundbreaking ceremony** 動土典禮

74. What was announced yesterday?
(A) **A proposal has been approved.**
(B) A protest is going to be held.
(C) A new business has opened.
(D) A construction project has been completed.

昨天宣布了什麼事情？
(A) **提案獲得批准。**
(B) 即將舉行抗議活動。
(C) 即將展開新事業。
(D) 工程建設已完工。

正確答案為 (A)

〈注意細節—特定事項〉
請從文中提及關鍵字 yesterday 之處找答案。文中報導芬斯伯里市市議會於昨天宣布核准於貝德福德縣西北部建設購物中心一案，因此答案選 (A)。

字彙　**protest** 抗議

75. What can be understood from the report?
(A) Construction has already started.
(B) The shopping mall will be torn down.
(C) **Many residents are against the project.**
(D) The tax will be increased next month.

本篇報導可以得知什麼資訊？
(A) 已經開始進行施工。
(B) 購物中心即將拆除。
(C) **許多居民反對此項提案。**
(D) 下個月將調漲稅金。

正確答案為 (C)

〈注意細節—特定事項〉
本題題目中並未提及明確的關鍵字，因此聆聽時請特別留意當中出現各選項內容的片段。報導中段提到許多居民希望將建設用的土地保留為公共開放空間，所以圍繞此項建案的爭議不斷。綜合前述，答案要選 (C)。

字彙　**tear down** 拆除　**be against** 反對

76. What did the Mayor of Finsbury mean when he said, "This development will be a boon to our city"?
(A) The tax increase will be worth it.
(B) **The project will generate more income.**
(C) The land should remain as open space.
(D) The construction will cost a lot of money.

芬斯伯里市市長表示「此項開發案會為我們的城市帶來益處。」是什麼意思？
(A) 調漲稅金是值得的。
(B) **此項建案能增加更多收入。**
(C) 土地應保留為公共開放空間。
(D) 此項工程將會花費大筆金錢。

正確答案為 (B)

〈關鍵句—說話者意圖〉
請務必確認指定句前後的情境，來掌握說話者所謂的「有好處」是什麼意思。芬斯伯里市市長主張建設完工後，每年能帶來數百萬美元的收入，因此答案適合選 (B)。

字彙　**be worth it** ～是值得的　**generate** 產生　**income** 收入

5_77-79 美式女聲

Questions 77-79 refer to the following excerpt from a meeting.

Let me introduce myself. I'm Jade Larkin, and I'm in charge of the accounting department here at JAC recruitment. In a few minutes, I'll address how to get your business travel costs reimbursed, but first, did you all get the workshop pamphlet? Let's look at the front page. There you'll see a list of expense guidelines as well as price limits. For example, receipts are not required for meals or public transportation reimbursement unless the prices exceed the stated cost limits. Please use this information as a general planning guide when scheduling your travel. The second page includes a form to record your travel expenses. Now let's move on to page three, which details the official reimbursement procedure.

問題 77-79 題參考以下會議摘錄。

我來介紹一下我自己。 77 我叫嘉德拉琴，負責管理 JAC 人力招募的會計部門。稍後 78 我將説明如何報銷出差費用。首先各位手上都有研討會手冊了嗎？ 79 請看到第一頁的清單，上面列出報銷説明和費用限制。舉例來説，若餐費和交通費未超過規定上限時，就可以不用提供收據。各位在安排行程時，務必善用手冊資訊作為基本規劃指南。第二頁有差旅費表格。現在翻到第三頁，上面詳細説明公司規定的報銷步驟。

字彙 **recruitment** 招聘、招募 **address** 發表演說；處理（問題） **business travel cost** 出差費、差旅費
reimburse 報銷費用、報公帳 **pamphlet** 冊子 **exceed** 超過 **state**（文件中）陳述 **record** 紀錄

77. Who most likely is the speaker?
(A) A travel expert
(B) A personnel manager
(C) A recruitment officer
(D) A department head

說話者最有可能是誰？
(A) 旅遊專家
(B) 人事經理
(C) 招聘人員
(D) 部門主管

正確答案為 **(D)**

〈確認基本資訊—說話者〉
開頭通常會提到說話者的身分。說話者於開頭自我介紹，表示自己負責管理 JAC 人力招募的「會計部門人員」，答案選 (D)。這裡需注意，談話中雖提到公司名稱為 JAC "recruitment"，但 recruitment 是公司名稱，而非職稱，不要將說話者誤認為招聘官。

78. What is the talk mainly about?
(A) Employee benefits
(B) Paid vacations
(C) Business travel expenses
(D) Travel schedules

本篇談話主要在談論什麼？
(A) 員工福利
(B) 有薪假
(C) 出差費用
(D) 旅遊計畫

正確答案為 **(C)**

〈確認基本資訊—主旨〉
請從開頭處找出與主旨相關的答題線索。說話者於開頭處提到她會為大家說明報銷出差費用的方法，答案為 (C)。

字彙　**benefit** 福利　　**paid vacation** 有薪假

79. What is on the first page of the booklet?
(A) A hiring contract
(B) An accounting report
(C) A set of rules
(D) A dress code

手冊第一頁的內容是？
(A) 僱用契約書
(B) 會計報告
(C) 一套規範
(D) 服裝規定

正確答案為 **(C)**

〈注意細節—特定事項〉
請留意說話者提及關鍵字 first page 的片段。當中提到手冊第一頁 front page 上有報銷說明和費用限制，答案選 (C)。
換句話說　**a list of expense guidelines** 費用說明清單 → **a set of rules** 一套規範

Test 05

5_80-82　美式男聲

Questions 80-82 refer to the following announcement.

Good food costs less at Freshisland! We always offer you the best deals. Today's specials include our food and beverage department; get three liters of fresh-squeezed orange juice for only ten dollars! Our meat department is featuring the best quality beef for just a dollar nineteen per 100 grams. Look for a host of yellow-marked items throughout the store. And don't forget our delicatessen. Our soups and made-to-order sandwiches are perfect for a fresh, hot lunch on the go. This week, our chicken sandwich and vegetable soup set is an amazing half off. Remember, you can always find the best deals here at Freshisland.

問題 80-82 題參考以下通知。

在新鮮島嶼，您可以用划算的價格買到美食。我們隨時為您提供最棒的價格。⑧⓪ 今日優惠為食品區及飲料區商品，您只要花 10 美元，就能買到 3 公升的現榨果汁！肉品區主打高品質牛肉，100 克只要 19 美元。您可以在店內找到許多貼有黃色標籤的商品。⑧① 別忘了我們還有熟食專賣店。我們的湯品和現點現做的三明治是相當適合忙碌生活的新鮮午餐組合。⑧② 本週的驚喜半價優惠為雞肉三明治和蔬菜濃湯組合餐。請記住，您隨時都能在新鮮島嶼找到最優惠的價格。

字彙　**the best deal** 撿便宜、價格最優惠　　**squeeze** 榨出　　**feature** 以～為特色　　**a host of** 許多的
delicatessen [ˌdɛləkə`tɛsən] 熟食店，簡稱 **deli**　　**made-to-order** 現點現做的　　**on the go** 非常忙碌的

80. What does the speaker imply when he says, "Look for a host of yellow-marked items throughout the store"?
    (A) Expiry dates are organized by color.
    (B) Shoppers must go to the service desk.
    (C) The store will be renovated soon.
    (D) There are many bargain items.

說話者說「您可以在店內找出眾多貼有黃色標籤的商品」暗指什麼意思？
(A) 有效期限依顏色分類。
(B) 購物者必須前往服務台。
(C) 這家店即將進行翻修。
(D) 店內有許多特價商品。

正確答案為 **(D)**

〈關鍵句—說話者意圖〉
先確認此指定句的前後句，綜合判斷後再來推測答案。說話者在指定句前面介紹各種實惠商品，根據語意適合的答案為 (D)。

字彙　**expiry date** 有效期限　　**bargain item** 特價品

81. Where can shoppers get lunch?
    (A) In the deli department
    (B) In the vegetables and fruit section
    (C) In the food and beverage department
    (D) In the meat and fish section

購物者可以在哪裡買到午餐？
(A) 熟食區
(B) 蔬果區
(C) 食品飲料區
(D) 肉類和鮮魚類區

正確答案為 **(A)**

〈注意細節—特定事項〉
特別留意文中提及關鍵字 lunch 的片段。說話者提到熟食專賣店為忙碌的人準備了湯品和三明治的組合，答案為 (A)。

82. What item is fifty percent off?
    (A) Beef
    (B) Today's fish
    (C) Lunch set
    (D) Orange juice

以下哪種商品提供五折優惠？
(A) 牛肉
(B) 今日鮮魚
(C) 午間套餐
(D) 柳橙汁

正確答案為 **(C)**

〈注意細節—特定事項〉
請從說話者提及關鍵字 fifty percent off 之處找出答案。後半段說話者提到適合作為午餐的選擇，並介紹本週提供的半價餐點為雞肉三明治和蔬菜濃湯的組合餐，因此答案為 (C)。

換句話說　**half off** 半價 → **fifty percent off** 五折優惠

5_83-85 澳式男聲

Questions 83-85 refer to the following telephone message.

Hello, Ms. Blair. This is Will Mackenzie. I've almost got your tax return ready; it looks like you'll be getting a healthy refund this year. Congratulations! I need a few more things though, to complete your file. For the work you completed at your apartment, we'll deduct Internet fees, phone bills, and even a portion of your rent from your taxes. If you could scan and send me copies of those three bills today, that would be very helpful. I also need you to sign a couple of documents. I'll be in Liverpool on Monday from 10 A.M. to 6 P.M., so I could either stop by your place or we could meet at a coffee shop. You can reach me on my mobile at 805-555-0307 and let me know which you'd prefer.

問題 83-85 題參考以下電話留言。

嗨，布萊兒小姐，我是威爾麥肯齊。84 我差不多完成妳的所得申報書了，看來妳今年可以收到一筆可觀的退稅，恭喜妳！83 不過我還需要一些東西才能完成這份文件。由於妳是在自家公寓辦公，所以我們會從所得稅中扣除網路費、電話費、還有一部分租金。如果妳在今天掃描並寄出這 3 份帳單的影本給我，將有助於完成這件事情。85 還有幾份文件需要妳的簽名。星期一早上 10 點到傍晚 6 點我會在利物浦，可以順道過去妳家，或是約在咖啡廳見面。我的手機號碼是 805-555-0307，麻煩妳再跟我聯絡，告訴我妳怎樣方便。

字彙　**tax return** 所得申報書　　**healthy**（數量）多的　　**deduct** 扣除、減除　　**a portion of** 一部分的　　**stop by** 順路造訪

83. Why has the speaker made the call?　　　　說話者打這通電話的原因為何？
(A) To arrange an interview　　　　　　　　(A) 為了安排面試
(B) To find out when taxes are due　　　　　(B) 為了確認稅金繳納期限
(C) To share work assignment　　　　　　　(C) 為了分攤工作任務
(D) To obtain more information　　　　　　**(D) 為了取得更多資訊**

正確答案為 **(D)**

〈確認基本資訊─目的〉
開頭提到對方可以收到一筆可觀的退稅，而後表示需要對方再提供一些資料，因此答案要選 (D)。

84. Who most likely is the speaker?　　　　　說話者最有可能是誰？
(A) An accountant　　　　　　　　　　　**(A) 會計師**
(B) A customer service representative　　　　(B) 客服代表
(C) A secretary　　　　　　　　　　　　　(C) 祕書
(D) A store clerk　　　　　　　　　　　　(D) 店員

正確答案為 **(A)**

〈確認基本資訊─說話者〉
開頭通常會提到說話者的身分。本文開頭提到快完成所得申報書，表示說話者從事與所得申報有關的工作，答案為 (A)。

85. What does the speaker let the listener know?　　說話者告訴聽者什麼事？
(A) His taxes are completed.　　　　　　　　(A) 他已完成繳稅。
(B) He lives in Liverpool.　　　　　　　　　(B) 他住在利物浦。
(C) He needs her signature.　　　　　　　　**(C) 他需要她的簽名。**
(D) He owns a coffee shop.　　　　　　　　(D) 他擁有一家咖啡廳。

正確答案為 **(C)**

〈注意細節─特定事項〉
本題題目並未使用明確的關鍵字，因此請注意聆聽提及選項的片段。後半段說話者提到他需要聽者的簽名，答案為 (C)。

字彙　　**signature** 簽名

Questions 86-88 refer to the following talk.

This year marks the 10th anniversary for us, and the celebration banquet begins in three hours. We have a lot of preparation to do, so we need all hands on deck. First, we don't have enough seats in the hall to accommodate the 300 guests we're expecting, but Ravensdale Publishing next door has agreed to loan us some chairs. We've already got 150 in place, so we need to carry the other half from their building to ours. Dave and Nathan, I'll assign that task to you. Amy and Daniel, could you please go to the fifth floor, get the printed programs, and bring them down here? While you're doing that, Charles and I will get started on arranging the place settings on the banquet tables. The caterers are expected to arrive at half past six.

問題 86-88 題參考以下談話。

今年是我們成立十週年紀念，慶祝會將於 3 小時後開始。86 我們有很多的準備工作要做，所以需要大家同心協力完成。首先，宴會廳的座位數不夠容納我們預計的 300 名賓客，不過隔壁的雷文斯代爾出版社已經同意把椅子借給我們。87 88 我們已經有 150 張椅子就緒，所以我們需要從他們大樓再搬另外一半數量的椅子過來。88 戴夫和娜珊，你們負責這份工作。艾咪和丹尼爾，可以請你們到 5 樓把印好的節目單拿過來這裡嗎？大家動作的這段時間，我和查爾斯會開始進行宴會桌的擺設工作。外燴服務餐點預計於 6 點半抵達。

字彙　**mark** 紀念　　**banquet** 宴會　　**all hands on deck** 所有人齊心協力　　**accommodate** 容納　　**loan** 借出
caterer 外燴業者

86. What does the speaker mean when she says, "we need all hands on deck"?
(A) The listeners should applaud now.
(B) The event will be held on the ship.
(C) Everyone should work together.
(D) The listeners should submit the reports.

説話者説「需要大家同心協力完成」是什麼意思？
(A) 聽者應於此刻鼓掌。
(B) 活動將於船上舉行。
(C) 大家應該要分工合作。
(D) 聽者應該要繳交報告。

正確答案為 (C)

〈關鍵句—説話者意圖〉
請務必確認關鍵句的前後句，掌握説話者的意圖。説話者在前一句提到有很多準備工作要做，答案選 (C)。

字彙　**applaud** 鼓掌

87. How many more chairs should the employees carry?
(A) 50
(B) 100
(C) 150
(D) 300

員工們應該要再搬多少張椅子？
(A) 50
(B) 100
(C) 150
(D) 300

正確答案為 (C)

〈注意細節—特定事項〉
留意説話者提及椅子數量之處。當中提到目前宴會廳內有 150 張椅子，要從隔壁搬剩下一半的椅子過來，答案為 (C)。

88. According to the speaker, what task will Nathan take on?
(A) Moving the chairs
(B) Printing the programs
(C) Preparing the tables
(D) Greeting the guests

根據説話者，娜珊負責什麼工作？
(A) 搬椅子
(B) 印出節目單
(C) 準備桌子
(D) 迎接賓客

正確答案為 (A)

〈注意細節—特定事項〉
仔細聆聽關鍵名字 Nathan 娜珊相關的片段。説話者提到搬椅子一事，接著請戴夫和娜珊負責這份工作，答案選 (A)。

Test 05

755

5_89-91　美式女聲

Questions 89-91 refer to the following advertisement.

Are you seeking fast, effective relief from your seasonal allergies? Allegra has been used for years to treat allergy symptoms from sneezing and nasal congestion to itchy throat. A single dose of Allegra relieves symptoms for 24 hours. It comes in both a capsule, and a child-friendly liquid in two different flavors: orange and strawberry. It has never been easier to get your kids to take their medicine! Allegra also produces none of the unpleasant side effects that many other allergy medications do, such as drowsiness, dry throat, or a cough. Get Allegra to help manage your health. It can make a huge difference in your life.

問題 89-91 題參考以下廣告。

89 你是否正在尋找快速有效緩解季節性過敏的方法？多年來，艾來錠一直被用來治療打噴嚏、鼻塞、喉嚨癢等過敏症狀。服用一顆艾來錠，便能緩解症狀長達 24 小時。90 艾來錠有膠囊和藥水兩種包裝，後者有柳橙和草莓口味，適合孩童服用，沒有任何藥能比它更容易讓孩子吃下去！91 艾來錠不會產生其他過敏藥會產生的不適副作用，如嗜睡、喉嚨乾、咳嗽等。請使用艾來錠來管理你的健康，它會為你的生活帶來巨大變化。

字彙　**seasonal** 季節性的　**allergy** 過敏　**symptom** 症狀　**nasal congestion** [ˋnɛzəl kənˋdʒɛstʃən] 鼻塞　**itchy** 癢的　**dose** 一劑藥量　**relieve** 減輕、緩和　**side effect** 副作用　**drowsiness** 昏睡

89. What is Allegra's intended use?
(A) To treat back pain
(B) To stop coughing
(C) To ease allergy symptoms
(D) To help with sleeping problems

艾來錠的用途為何？
(A) 治療背痛
(B) 停止咳嗽
(C) 緩解過敏症狀
(D) 改善睡眠問題

正確答案為 **(C)**

〈注意細節一特定事項〉
請留意提及關鍵字 Allegra 的片段。本題問藥物用途，類似主旨，應該能在文章開頭找到。開頭推薦使用艾來錠解決過敏，因此答案為 (C)。

90. What is true of the medication?
(A) It is available in two flavors.
(B) It is not for children.
(C) It only comes in capsules.
(D) It has been discontinued.

下列何者為符合該藥物的說明？
(A) 有兩種口味。
(B) 不適合孩童食用。
(C) 只有膠囊包裝一種。
(D) 已經停產。

正確答案為 **(A)**

〈注意細節一特定事項〉
本題題目中並未出現明確的關鍵字，因此請注意聆聽各選項的片段。中間提到藥品分膠囊和藥水，藥水有兩種口味，適合孩童服用，因此答案為 (A)。

字彙　**discontinue** 停產

91. What does the speaker say about Allegra?
(A) It will be available soon.
(B) It causes no side effects.
(C) It is good for long-term use.
(D) It should be taken three times a day.

針對艾來錠，說話者說了什麼？
(A) 很快就會上市。
(B) 沒有副作用。
(C) 適合長期服用。
(D) 一天要服用 3 次。

正確答案為 **(B)**

〈注意細節一特定事項〉
廣告後半段中提到艾來錠沒有任何副作用，因此答案選 (B)。

Test 05

Questions 92-94 refer to the following talk.

Congratulations on joining us at Telpod Network. We're glad to have you all in our team. The first thing you should know is that due to the sensitivity of our clients' information, we have very strict safety measures in place. All of you will be expected to show your employee badge every time you enter or exit the premises. This rule applies at all times, for every employee. If for some reason you don't have your badge and need to come in or leave, you should get help from the guards. They will verify your identity and sign you in or out. At the end of this orientation session you'll each be issued your own badge. Keep the badge in a very safe place when it is not being worn as you will need to pay a fee of $100 to replace your badge if it somehow becomes lost.

問題 92-94 題參考以下談話。

92 恭喜各位加入泰帕網路公司。很高興能邀請各位加入我們的團隊。93 首先各位需要明白,有鑑於客戶資料的敏感性,我們公司採取極為嚴密的安全措施。各位進出大樓時,務必出示員工識別證。此項規定適用於任何時間以及每一位員工。94 欲進出大樓者,若基於某些理由未攜帶識別證時,請尋求警衛協助。他們會驗證你的身分,並進行出入登記。本場教育訓練結束後,你將會拿到專屬的識別證。識別證未配戴時請務必妥善保管。若不慎遺失識別證,需支付 100 美元手續費申請補發。

字彙 **sensitivity**(話題)敏感;(人)多愁善感 **strict** 嚴格的 **safety measure** 安全措施 **in place** 就位 **badge** 識別證 **premises**(公司或機構)經營廠址 **verify** 驗證 **orientation session** 員工培訓課程

92. Who most likely are the listeners?
(A) Security guards
(B) New employees
(C) Department heads
(D) Visitors

聽者最有可能是誰？
(A) 保全人員
(B) 新進員工
(C) 部門主管
(D) 訪客

正確答案為 (B)

〈確認基本資訊—聽者〉
文章開頭通常會提到與聽者身分有關的答題線索。本文開頭祝賀加入公司的人，並表示很高興能一起工作，答案為 (B)。

93. What aspect of the firm does the speaker emphasize?
(A) Its strong security
(B) Its generous pay
(C) Its friendly managers
(D) Its talented workers

說話者特別強調公司的哪個部分？
(A) 保安嚴密
(B) 薪資優渥
(C) 友善的主管
(D) 才華洋溢的員工

正確答案為 (A)

〈注意細節—特定事項〉
請留意說話者向新進員工強調的內容。開頭提到聽者最先需要知道的是公司採取極為嚴密的安全措施，答案選 (A)。

換句話說 **strict safety measure** 嚴密的安全措施 → **strong security** 保安嚴密

94. What should listeners do if they temporarily misplace their badge?
(A) Call a guard
(B) Pay a fine
(C) Use a main entrance
(D) Request a receipt

聽者一時忘記攜帶識別證時，該怎麼做？
(A) 呼叫警衛
(B) 支付罰金
(C) 從正門進出
(D) 索取收據

正確答案為 (A)

〈注意細節—特定事項〉
請抓出關鍵字 temporarily misplace their badge，並仔細聆聽前後的內容。中間部分提到欲進出大樓者，若基於某些理由未攜帶識別證時，請尋求警衛的協助，因此答案要選 (A)。後半段則提到遺失識別證時，需要付錢申請補發。這邊請特別注意，切勿將補發費用當成罰金。

字彙 **misplace** 亂放 **fine** 罰金

Test 05

Questions 95-97 refer to the following advertisement and schedule.

I have one last thing to tell you. We are planning a seminar by Chloe Adams, one of the most successful marketing entrepreneurs in our country. When she was a university student, she started her first business and turned it into a multi-million-dollar company within a few short years. Now, Chloe devotes her time to helping others follow in her footsteps. Her two-day seminar will show you how to analyze markets, identify opportunities, and think strategically so that you too can establish and develop a successful business. Chloe will be leading her two-day seminar here in Zurich the first weekend in September at the Hotel Montana. So please visit her Web site at chloeadamsevent.com and register today.

Hotel Montana – Event Bookings	
Event Date(s)	Venue
September 1-4	The Euros Room
September 2-4	The Zepiros Room
September 5&6	The Notos Room
September 6	The Boreas Room

問題 95-97 題參考以下廣告和時間表。

最後還有一件事要告訴各位，我們正在為克羅伊亞當斯策畫研討會，她是國內最成功的市場行銷企業家之一。95 她大學的時候開創了她的第一份事業，短短幾年內，這間公司的市值便高達數百萬美元。現在，克羅伊將她的時間投注在協助他人複製自己的成功模式。96 為期兩天的研討會中，她將傳授如何進行市場分析、辨識機會、以及戰略性的思考方式，讓你也能建立並發展成功的事業。97 克羅伊將於 9 月的第一個週末，在蘇黎世蒙塔那酒店進行為期兩天的研討會。現在就請前往她的網站 chloeadamsevent.com 報名參加。

蒙塔那酒店 ── 活動預定	
活動日期	地點
9 月 1 日至 4 日	歐羅斯廳
9 月 2 日至 4 日	仄費羅斯廳
9 月 5 日和 6 日	諾托斯廳
9 月 6 日	玻瑞阿斯廳

字彙 **entrepreneur** [ˌɑntrəprəˋnɜ] 企業家   **devote** 投注（時間、金錢、努力）   **footstep** 步伐
identify 確認、鑑定（身分）   **strategically** 戰略上   **establish** 建立、設立

95. What did Chloe Adams do when she was a university student?
(A) She married an entrepreneur.
(B) She studied abroad.
(C) She created a software program.
(D) She founded a company.

克羅伊亞當斯大學時期做過什麼事？
(A) 嫁給一位企業家。
(B) 出國留學。
(C) 製作軟體程式。
(D) 成立一間公司。

正確答案為 **(D)**

〈注意細節―特定事項〉
請特別留意文中提及題目關鍵字 **university student** 之處。前半段介紹該名女子在念大學時，開創了自己的第一份事業，因此答案為 (D)。

96. What skill does Chloe Adams teach at her seminar?
(A) Software development
(B) Strategic thinking
(C) Decision making
(D) Risk analysis

克羅伊亞當斯將在研討會上傳授什麼技巧？
(A) 軟體開發
(B) 戰略性思考
(C) 決策
(D) 風險分析

正確答案為 **(B)**

〈注意細節―特定事項〉
請留意聆聽關鍵字 **seminar**。談話中間介紹研討會將針對建立和開發事業，傳授市場分析、辨識機會、以及戰略性思考的方法，因此答案要選 (B)。

97. Look at the graphic. In which venue will Chloe Adams' seminar probably be held?
(A) The Euros Room
(B) The Zepiros Room
(C) The Notos Room
(D) The Boreas Room

根據圖表，克羅伊亞當斯的研討會可能會在哪個地方舉行？
(A) 歐羅斯廳
(B) 仄費羅斯廳
(C) 諾托斯廳
(D) 玻瑞阿斯廳

正確答案為 **(C)**

〈注意細節―圖表相關〉
選項列出了活動預定表中的地點，因此可以推測出談話中應該會提到活動日期。後半段提到 9 月的第一個週末將會舉辦為期兩天的研討會。而表格中連續兩天的預定為 5 日和 6 日，因此答案為 (C)。

5_98-100 澳式男聲

Questions 98-100 refer to the following announcement and map.

Employees of Plasto Accounting who make use of the Number 46 bus to come to work will no longer be able to get off the bus at the bus stop across from the office. We have been informed that beginning Wednesday next week, the bus will be stopping at the newly renovated Millton Hotel instead. We have decided to provide a shuttle bus from the hotel once in the morning and once in the evening. The departure times will be decided based on a survey of employees to be conducted on Thursday afternoon.

問題 98-100 題參考以下通知和地圖。

98 利用 46 號公車上班的普拉斯托會計師事務所員工們，往後你們不能在辦公室對面的公車站下車。99 我們接獲通知，下週三開始，公車將改停在全新整修的米爾頓酒店。我們已決定提供往返於飯店與公司間的接駁巴士，早晚各一次。100 週四下午對員工進行意見調查之後，會決定發車時間。

字彙 **departure** 出發、離開　**survey** 調查　**conduct** 實施

98. Look at the graphic. Which bus stop will no longer be available?
(A) G1
(B) H2
(C) H4
(D) I5

根據圖表，往後將取消停靠哪一個公車站？
(A) G1
(B) H2
(C) H4
(D) I5

正確答案為 (B)

〈注意細節―圖表相關〉
遇到圖表相關題，請先查看圖表並對照選項，以推測出答題線索。本題的圖表為地圖，因此答題線索可能是與位置相關的描述。開頭告知普拉斯托會計師事務所的員工們，往後不能在辦公室對面的公車站下車。這段話表示取消停靠的是普拉斯托會計師事務所對面的公車站，答案為 (B)。

99. When is the change scheduled to occur?
(A) On Tuesday
(B) On Wednesday
(C) On Thursday
(D) On Friday

何時會開始產生變動？
(A) 星期二
(B) 星期三
(C) 星期四
(D) 星期五

正確答案為 (B)

〈注意細節―特定事項〉
注意聽時間相關的關鍵字。談話中間部分提到公車將於 Wednesday next week 下週三開始停靠其他地方，因此答案要選 (B)。

100. What are employees asked to do?
(A) Hand out some forms
(B) Renew their contracts
(C) Attend a conference
(D) Give their opinions

員工被要求做什麼事？
(A) 分發表格
(B) 更新合約
(C) 參加研討會
(D) 提供意見

正確答案為 (D)

〈注意細節―要求〉
最後一句提到會對員工進行意見調查，以決定接駁巴士的發車時間，等同於要求員工參與意見調查，答案為 (D)。

字彙　**renew** 更新　　**opinion** 意見

Test 05

101. When attaching company contracts to an e-mail, keep these documents ------- by password-protecting them.
(A) secure
(B) security
(C) securely
(D) securing

在電子郵件加入公司合約附檔時，請以密碼加密保護文件安全。

正確答案為 (A)

〈特殊動詞〉空格要填入動詞 keep 的受詞補語，keep 為連綴動詞，要使用形容詞補充說明受詞 documents，答案選 (A)。

字彙　**attach A to B** 將 A 附加至 B　**secure** 安全的　**securely** 安全地

102. Reasons for the increase in computer sales throughout the nation are not ------- clear.
(A) smoothly
(B) entirely
(C) justly
(D) tightly

電腦在全國銷量增加的原因目前還不清楚。

正確答案為 (B)

根據題意，要選出最適合修飾形容詞 clear 的副詞，因此答案為 (B)，表示「尚未完全弄清楚」。

字彙　**throughout** 遍及　**entirely** 完全地　**justly** 正當地　**tightly** 牢固地

103. Mr. Sherman is organizing the company banquet, so please let ------- know if you are able to attend.
(A) he
(B) his
(C) him
(D) himself

謝爾曼先生正在規劃公司宴會，可以參加的人請告知他一聲。

正確答案為 (C)

〈代名詞格〉空格要填入動詞 let 的受詞，此受詞也要可以表示前面的 Mr. Sherman，因此答案為 (C) him。

字彙　**organize** 安排　**banquet** 宴會

104. Before laying the new carpet, make sure the surface beneath it is completely -------.
(A) flat
(B) flatly
(C) flatter
(D) flatten

鋪設新地毯之前，先確保地毯下方地面是否完全平整。

正確答案為 (A)

〈詞性〉空格要填入 be 動詞的補語，且可以用副詞 completely 修飾，因此答案要選擇形容詞 (A)。

字彙　**lay a carpet** 鋪地毯　**surface** 表面　**beneath** 在～下方　**flat** 平坦的　**flatly** 斷然地　**flatten** 擊倒

105. Customer service representatives are expected to respond within two hours to callers ------- leave a voice message.
(A) who
(B) they
(C) their
(D) when

客服人員應於兩小時內回覆留下語音留言的來電者。

正確答案為 (A)

〈關代〉空格位在名詞 callers 和動詞 leave 之間，要填入關係代名詞主格，才能同時扮演主詞和連接詞的角色，答案為 (A)。

字彙　**service representative** 客服人員　**respond** 應答

106. Oldbrook Town's annual fashion fair helps residents learn about current trends while ------- having fun.
(A) formerly
(B) ever
(C) lastly
(D) also

歐德布洛克鎮的年度時裝展覽會讓居民在同樂之餘，還能了解流行趨勢。

正確答案為 (D)

空格要填入副詞。主要子句中的 learn about current trends 和空格後方的 having fun 為同時發生的事，因此答案要選 (D)，表示「也」的概念。

字彙　**formerly** 以前　**lastly** 最終地

107. At Copper Ltd., there are ------- opportunities for professional advancement.
(A) plenty
(B) each
(C) every
(D) many

古柏有限公司提供許多升遷機會。

正確答案為 (D)

〈數量詞〉空格要填入可用來修飾 opportunities 的數量形容詞。(D) 可以修飾複數名詞，故為正確答案。plenty 要搭配 of 一起使用，才能修飾複數名詞。each 和 every 後方則要連接單數名詞。

字彙　**advancement** 升遷

108. Herman Printing Services uses higher quality paper ------- its competitors do.
(A) what
(B) that
(C) such
(D) than

赫爾曼印刷公司所使用的紙張品質比同業要好。

正確答案為 (D)

〈比較級〉空格前方出現比較級 higher，因此答案要選比較級句型中會出現的 than，答案選 (D)。

字彙　**competitor** 競爭者

109. Because of the unfavorable weather, the painters are not finished ------- the north side of the building.
(A) with
(B) out
(C) from
(D) of

由於天候不佳，油漆工無法順利完成建築北側的粉刷。

正確答案為 (A)

本題考片語 be finished with 的用法，意思為「尚未完成」，因此答案為 (A)。

字彙　**unfavorable** 不利的

110. Patients must sign an authorization form ------- medical records can be transferred to new insurance providers.
(A) except
(B) before
(C) instead
(D) rather

病患簽署授權書後，才能把病歷移交給新的保險公司。

正確答案為 (B)

〈連接詞〉空格前方有主詞 Patients 與動詞 must sign，為完整句，後方也是完整句，有主詞 medical records 與動詞 can be transferred，表示空格要填入連接兩個句子的連接詞。符合題意的答案要選 (B)。instead 和 rather 當副詞皆表達「轉折」的語意，但後方要先接逗點才能接句子。

字彙　**authorization** 授權　　**medical record** 病歷　　**insurance provider** 保險公司　　**except** 除了～之外　　**rather** 相當

111. For security reasons, visitors to the Green Bay Science and Technology Research Institute must be ------- at all times.
(A) displayed
(B) estimated
(C) conferred
(D) escorted

基於安全考量，訪問綠灣科技研究院的人全程須有人員隨行。

正確答案為 (D)

空格位在 be 動詞後方，要填入過去分詞。查看選項後，可以得知本題要選出適當的被動式動詞。根據題意，最適合搭配主詞 visitors 的動詞為 (D) escorted「護送」。display「展示」和 estimate「評估」語意上皆不適合。confer「商談」為不及物動詞，要與 with 一起使用，因此不能填入本題的空格中。

字彙　**display** 展示　　**estimate** 評估、估價　　**confer (with)** 商談　　**escort** 護送

112. The laboratory manual details our procedures for handling materials as ------- as possible.
(A) safety
(B) safely
(C) safer
(D) safest

實驗室指南詳細載明盡可能安全處理材料的步驟。

正確答案為 (B)

〈比較級〉〈as ~ as〉為同等比較的用法，因此空格應填入形容詞或副詞的原級。空格填入副詞，用來修飾動詞片語 handling materials 較為適當，答案選 (B)。

字彙　**detail** 詳細說明　　**procedure** 步驟

113. In Ms. Bukowski's -------, the shift supervisor is in charge of the restaurant.
(A) duty
(B) absence
(C) instance
(D) event

布考斯基小姐缺勤時會出值班主管代理管埋餐廳。

正確答案為 (B)

本題考的是 in one's absence 的用法，意思為「某人不在時」，因此答案為 (B)。

> 字彙　**shift** 輪班　**in charge of** 負責

114. Call Perrybridge Office Furniture representatives ------- immediate cost estimates over the phone.
(A) to receive
(B) receiving
(C) will receive
(D) receives

聯絡佩里橋家具的代表，就能馬上透過電話收到估價。

正確答案為 (A)

〈動詞〉本句是以動詞 Call 開頭的命令句，後方已有受詞，而空格後方又出現名詞 cost estimates 當受詞，表示空格需選擇另一個動詞，因題目的前後兩個子句之間缺少連接詞，因此選擇不定詞 to 來表示打電話的目的：call to + 原形動詞，答案選 (A)。

> 字彙　**immediate** 立即的　**cost estimate** 估價

115. We are ------- to discuss your remodeling needs in detail via e-mail or telephone.
(A) delighting
(B) delighted
(C) delights
(D) delight

我們很樂意透過電子郵件或電話跟您詳談裝修需求。

正確答案為 (B)

本題考的是 be delighted to 的用法，意思為「樂意去做～」，因此答案為 (B)。

> 字彙　**remodel** 改建、整修　**in detail** 詳細地　**via** 透過

116. The Kerton Town Council ------- receives project proposals, so applicants should expect to wait several months for a decision.
(A) quickly
(B) recently
(C) regularly
(D) similarly

科頓市議會經常收到計畫案，因此申請者得等上數月才能得到結論。

正確答案為 (C)

空格放在動詞 receives 前方，應填入可修飾動詞的副詞。動詞使用現在式，因此答案選 (C) 最為適當，表示「經常會收到」。(B) recently 不會與現在簡單式連用。

> 字彙　**expect** 預期　**recently** 最近　**regularly** 經常地　**similarly** 相似地

117. ------- Jung's Burger opened its newest franchise, the first 100 customers were given a free soda.
(A) Now
(B) When
(C) As if
(D) After all

鍾氏漢堡的最新連鎖店開幕時，提供前 100 名消費者一瓶免費汽水。

正確答案為 (B)

空格適合填入副詞子句連接詞，根據題意，答案選 (B)，表示時間的概念。Now 應該與現在進行式連用，時態不對。After all「畢竟」表達轉折語氣的副詞，語意上不合邏輯。As if「彷彿」通常會用在假設語氣。

字彙 **after all**（副詞）終究、畢竟　　**as if**（連接詞）彷彿

118. Please include the serial number of your product in any ------- with the Customer Service Department.
(A) corresponds
(B) correspondence
(C) correspondingly
(D) correspondent

任何與客服部往來的信件，請附上所購買的產品序號。

正確答案為 (B)

〈詞性〉空格位在 any 後方，所以應填入名詞。(B) correspondence 有「信件」的意思，為語意上最適合的答案。

字彙 **serial number** 產品編號　　**correspond** 與～一致　　**correspondingly** 相應地　　**correspondence** 通信、信件　　**correspondent** 通訊記者、特派員

119. Fisher & Phillips Insurance Company offers coverage to ------- and commercial property owners in Barcelona.
(A) habitual
(B) residential
(C) necessary
(D) settled

費雪＆菲利浦斯保險公司為巴塞隆納的住宅與商用建築所有人提供保險。

正確答案為 (B)

空格後方有對等連接詞 and 和形容詞 commercial，因此要填入語意上能與 commercial「商用的」最相應的形容詞，(B) residential「住家的」最適當。

字彙 **coverage** 保險項目　　**property** 房地產、建築物　　**habitual** 習慣的　　**residential** 居住的　　**settled** 固定的

120. Heike Construction Company is seeking a heavy equipment ------- with at least two years of related experience.
(A) operational
(B) operating
(C) operator
(D) operate

海克建設公司正在尋找至少有兩年相關經驗的重型機械營運商。

正確答案為 (C)

〈詞性〉空格前方出現冠詞 a 和不可數名詞 equipment，表示空格要填入單數可數名詞，因此答案為 (C)。

字彙 **related** 相關的　　**operational** 經營上的　　**operator** 經營者

121. A blue label indicates a package containing extra virgin olive oil, ------- a green label indicates it contains balsamic vinegar.
(A) whereas
(B) whether
(C) both
(D) about

藍標為特級初榨橄欖油包裝，綠標則為巴薩米可醋包裝。

正確答案為 **(A)**

〈連接詞〉空格前後各連接一個完整子句，所以要填入副詞子句連接詞。根據題意，答案要選 (A)，表示前後對比。

字彙　**indicate** 指出、表示　　**contain** 包含　　**whereas** 但是、儘管

122. If the Vogel Marathon is canceled, ------- who prepaid the registration fee will receive a full refund.
(A) those
(B) which
(C) them
(D) whichever

如果沃格馬拉松活動取消，預先繳交報名費者可獲得全額退款。

正確答案為 **(A)**

〈關代〉空格後方的 who 為關係代名詞主格，空格應填入 who 的先行詞，表示不特定的多數，因此答案為代名詞 (A)。

字彙　**prepay** 預付　　**registration fee** 報名費　　**full refund** 全額退款

123. Orangedale Publishing's Chief of Staff meets regularly with the staff to ensure that procedures ------- correctly.
(A) to be performed
(B) would have performed
(C) had been performed
(D) are being performed

奧蘭治代爾出版社主管會定期和員工會面，以確認他們有確實按照流程做事。

正確答案為 **(D)**

〈時態〉空格位在 that 子句中的動詞位置，動詞 perform 後方並未連接受詞，因此要使用被動語態。(C) 和 (D) 皆為被動語態，而空格與主要子句動詞 meets 的時態要相同，因此答案為 (D)。

字彙　**chief of staff** 幕僚長、參謀長　　**ensure that** 保證

124. Technicians are trying to determine exactly ------- caused the building's power failure.
(A) what
(B) that
(C) whose
(D) those

技術人員正試圖找出大樓停電的確切原因。

正確答案為 **(A)**

〈關代〉空格要填入動詞 determine 的受詞，而其後方出現動詞 cause，應選擇一個可以引導名詞子句的疑問詞，同時扮演連接詞和名詞的角色，因此答案為 (A)。

字彙　**determine** 確定、找出　　**power failure** 停電

Test 05

125. ------- the popularity of our new wireless speaker, production will be increased fivefold next year.
(A) **As a result of**
(B) On behalf of
(C) Moreover
(D) Assuming that

由於新的無線藍牙喇叭廣受歡迎，明年生產量將增加 5 倍。

正確答案為 (A)

空格位在名詞片語的前方，應填入介系詞。根據題意，能表達出因果關係較為適當，因此答案為 (A)。

> 字彙　**popularity** 受歡迎　**fivefold** 五倍的　**as a result of** 由於　**on behalf of**（介系詞）代表　**moreover**（副詞）此外　**assuming that**（連接詞）假設

126. ------- having the support of local officials, the Highbrook Library renovation project experienced numerous setbacks.
(A) Conversely
(B) Otherwise
(C) Whether
(D) **Despite**

儘管獲得當地官員支持，海特布魯克圖書館的整修計畫仍經歷許多阻礙。

正確答案為 (D)

空格後方為動名詞片語，因此答案要選介系詞 (D)。

> 字彙　**official** 官員　**setback** 阻礙、挫折　**conversely**（副詞）相反地　**otherwise**（連接詞）否則、不然

127. Blakeley Architects noted that the community center ------- a one-story building for maximum accessibility.
(A) that remains
(B) **should remain**
(C) to remain
(D) remaining

布拉克利建築師事務所指出，應保留社區活動中心的一層樓，將空間做到最有效的利用。

正確答案為 (B)

〈詞性〉空格位在 note 後方所接的 that 子句中，須填入動詞，因此答案為 (B)。

> 字彙　**note** 提到、注意到　**community** 社區　**one-story** 一層樓的　**maximum** 最大化　**accessibility** 取得、利用

128. Nelson Groth Institute offers an ------- of professional services to meet the needs of students.
(A) **array**
(B) entity
(C) article
(D) item

尼爾森葛斯學院提供一系列的專業服務，以滿足學生的需求。

正確答案為 (A)

本題考的是 an array of 的用法，意思為「一系列、大量的」，答案為 (A)。

> 字彙　**entity** 實體

129. ------- events this year in the second and third quarters caused profits to differ significantly from the original projection.
(A) Total
(B) Marginal
(C) Representative
(D) Unforeseen

今年的第二季和第三季發生了意外事件，導致獲利和原先預期相去甚遠。

正確答案為 (D)

空格要填入形容詞修飾 events。根據題意，表示「原先未想到的」較為適當，因此答案為 (D)。

字彙 **significantly** 顯著地　　**projection** 預測　　**marginal** 微小的、不重要的　　**unforeseen** 沒有預料到的

130. Mr. Hendley ------- authority to his most trusted employees in an emergency.
(A) aligned
(B) exercised
(C) delegated
(D) nominated

亨得利先生在緊急情況下，將權限委任給他最信任的員工。

正確答案為 (C)

本題考的是 delegate authority to 的用法，意思為「授權給～」，因此答案要選 (C)。

字彙 **authority** 權力　　**trusted** 受到信賴的　　**align** 校準、排成一直線　　**exercise** 運用、行使　　**delegate** 委任
nominate 任命；提名

Questions 131-134 refer to the following notice.

At Household Superstore, we sell major appliances from top brand names. We're the only store in the area that stocks replacement parts for all of our appliances. Parts ------- by phone at 032-555-2938 or online. Registration is not ------- for online orders. However, it will make the process faster the next time you shop with us. -------. As a result, your order might arrive in several shipments. ------- will increase your shipping charges.
131. 132. 133. 134.

問題 131-134 題參考以下公告。

居家超級商店販售頂級品牌的家電產品。本區僅有我們一間有備齊店內所有家電的替換零件。零件可透過電話 032-555-2938 或網路 ⑬ 訂購。無 ⑬ 需註冊即可於線上選購,但若註冊為會員,下次購物時能加速購物流程。⑬ 為加速訂單配送流程,零件皆由供貨廠商直接出貨。因此,您所訂購的商品可能會分批出貨,運費也將⑬ 隨之增加。

字彙　**appliance** 家電　**stock** 存貨　**replacement part** 替換零件　**registration** 註冊　**shipment** 貨運、運送

131. (A) should have ordered
(B) **may be ordered**
(C) were ordered
(D) to order

(A) 應該已經訂購
(B) **可被訂購**
(C) 已被訂購
(D) 去訂購

正確答案為 (B)

空格位於動詞的位置，且後方沒有連接受詞，應使用被動語態。空格要填入表示可能性的概念，因此答案為 (B)。

132. (A) advisable
(B) available
(C) **required**
(D) renewable

(A) 明智的
(B) 可得的
(C) **必需的**
(D) 可更新的

正確答案為 (C)

空格後方的句子為 However, it will make the process faster the next time you shop with us. ，根據文意，答案要選 (C)，表示註冊並非必要之事。

> 字彙　**advisable** 明智的　**renewable** 可更新的

133. (A) **To expedite delivery of your order, parts are sent directly from different suppliers.**
(B) The company is currently interviewing candidates for the position.
(C) We offer all the supplies you need to prepare for any event.
(D) Please inquire at the service desk if it will be permitted on your flight.

(A) **為加速訂單配送流程，零件皆由供貨廠商直接出貨。**
(B) 公司正在面試職位候選人。
(C) 我們提供準備活動時所需的必需品。
(D) 請向服務台詢問飛機上是否可以使用。

正確答案為 (A)

〈插入句〉
插入句要檢視空格前後句，綜合語意再選擇。 空格後方的句子提到分批出貨一事 in several shipments，(A) 句子也有提到供貨商 different suppliers，**語意上有承接**，為正確答案。

> 字彙　**expedite** 加速執行　**delivery** 發貨　**supplier** 供貨商　**inquire** 詢問　**permit** 允許

134. (A) They
(B) Both
(C) Some
(D) **This**

正確答案為 (D)

空格指的是前面一整句所提及的情況，因此答案要選 (D) This，代替前面一整句。

Questions 135-138 refer to the following e-mail.

To: Karen Karl
From: Liz Steinhauer
Subject: Special Project
Date: April 2

Good morning, Ms. Karl.

I have a list of special projects that must be completed, and I would like to assign you the job of ------- our collection of informational brochures. This will be one of your ongoing responsibilities
135.
because these pamphlets are revised periodically, and only the ------- versions are available to
136.
library patrons.

-------. Anything dated before February of this year should be replaced with the revised
137.
document, which can be printed from the library's internal Web page. Please complete this task
------, as a number of the brochures are quite outdated.
138.

Thank you.

Liz Steinhauer
Head Librarian

問題 135-138 題參考以下電子郵件。

收件人：凱倫卡爾
寄件人：利茲史坦豪爾
主旨：特別企劃
日期：4 月 2 日

早安，卡爾小姐。

我有一份特別企劃清單必須完成，而我想把 ⑬ 更新宣傳手冊的工作交派給妳。這份工作將會成為妳日常進行的職責之一，因為這些手冊需定期修訂，只需提供 ⑬ 最新版本給圖書館讀者即可。

⑬ 請檢查位在圖書館入口處以及借還書櫃檯的資訊展示架。凡今年 2 月之前的任何文件都應該換成修訂後的文件，文件可以從圖書館內網列印出來。請 ⑬ 儘快完成這份工作，因為多數手冊已經相當老舊。

謝謝。

利茲史坦豪爾
圖書館館長

 字彙 **assign** 分派　**periodically** 定期地　**patron** 老顧客　**be replaced with** 取代　**internal** 內部的　**outdated** 過時的　**librarian** 圖書管理員

135. (A) writing
(B) copying
(C) updating
(D) mailing

(A) 撰寫
(B) 複製
(C) 更新
(D) 郵寄

正確答案為 (C)

空格所在句的後方提及 revised periodically 定期修訂，且空格後方接名詞 collection，因此空格應填入 (C)，前後句內容才有所呼應。

136. (A) initial
(B) current
(C) duplicate
(D) draft

(A) 最初的
(B) 當前的
(C) 複製的
(D) 草案

正確答案為 (B)

空格要填入可以修飾 versions 的形容詞。前方句子提到 revised periodically，空格填入「當前的、最新的」較為適當，因此答案為 (B)。

137. (A) Thank you for becoming a member of our library organization.
(B) Check the information displays at the library entrance and the checkout desk.
(C) Our remodeled offices are due to open in April as scheduled.
(D) Your support has enabled us to improve our office products.

(A) 感謝您成為圖書館的會員。
(B) 請檢查位於圖書館入口處和借還書櫃檯的資訊展示架。
(C) 整修後的辦公室將如期於 4 月開放。
(D) 多虧您的支持，讓我們得以改善辦公室用品。

正確答案為 (B)

〈插入句〉
空格後面一句提到需換掉日期較舊的文件，唯一有提到與文件相關的句子為選項 (B)。

字彙　**entrance** 入口　**checkout desk** 借還書櫃檯　**be due to** 預期的　**enable** 使能夠

138. **(A) promptly**
(B) prompting
(C) prompted
(D) prompt

正確答案為 (A)

空格出現在完整句後面，本句不缺主詞與動詞，適合選擇可修飾動詞 complete 的副詞，因此答案要選 (A)。

字彙　**promptly** 迅速地

Questions 139-142 refer to the following article.

Windom Pharmacy Makes Prescription Orders Easier for Customers.

By Daniel Banaszek

Seattle (July 12) — Windom Pharmacy is about to make life easier for its tech-savvy customers.
-------. Customers will be able to receive a text message ------- a prescription is ready for pickup.
  139.   **140.**
The previous notification system required pharmacy staff to make time-consuming phone calls.

"The old system was not very -------," CEO Jessica Windom said in a press release.
                                     141.

"People don't always listen to their voice mail in a timely manner. Text notifications will begin on

July 15. -------, customers who prefer phone calls still have the option," Ms. Windom noted.
    142.

問題 139-142 題參考以下文章。

溫頓藥局讓領藥變得更容易。

丹尼爾班納柴克

西雅圖（7 月 12 日）── 溫頓藥局正準備讓善用科技的顧客生活能更輕鬆。 **139** 這家人氣連鎖藥局近日將提供手機通知領藥服務。 **140** 當藥局備好處方藥，顧客便會收到文字簡訊通知領藥。先前的通知方式需要藥局員工耗費時間撥打電話。

「先前的方式實在不夠 **141** 有效率。」執行長潔西卡溫頓於報導中所述。

「人們通常不會即時聽取語音留言。文字簡訊通知將於 7 月 15 日起實施。 **142** 但是習慣電話通知的顧客還是能選擇電話通知。」溫頓小姐補充。

字彙　**pharmacy** 藥局　**prescription** 處方箋　**tech-savvy** 精通科技的　**pickup** 領取　**notification** 通知
time-consuming 費時的　**press release** 新聞稿　**in a timely manner** 及時

139. (A) Though we are now quite busy, my staff can handle the workload.
(B) I am writing to let you know that I have told all my friends about the service.
(C) One of these is creating a new line of women's vitamin supplements.
(D) The popular drugstore chain will soon offer mobile alerts for prescription orders.

(A) 雖然我們現在很忙，但是員工還是可以完成工作。
(B) 我寫信是要告訴你，我有跟我的所有朋友提及這項服務。
(C) 其一是生產新的女性專用維他命營養品系列。
(D) 這家人氣連鎖藥局近日將提供手機通知領藥服務。

正確答案為 **(D)**

〈插入句〉

空格後方的句子出現 to receive a text message，表示與簡訊服務有關，因此答案要選 (D)。

字彙　**workload** 工作量　　**supplement** 補充品、營養品　　**alert** 通知

140. (A) sooner
(B) despite
(C) when
(D) though

(A) 更快地
(B) 儘管
(C) 當
(D) 即使

正確答案為 **(C)**

空格應填入適當的副詞子句連接詞，連接前後兩個子句。根據前後文意，答案要選 (C)，表示時間概念。

141. (A) fair
(B) efficient
(C) profitable
(D) clarifying

(A) 公平的
(B) 有效率的
(C) 有利潤的
(D) 澄清

正確答案為 **(B)**

空格要填入形容詞，描述啟用簡訊通知前所使用的方式。而空格前方出現 not，表示「沒有效率」最符合文意，因此答案要選 (B)。

142. (A) As a result
(B) Therefore
(C) However
(D) Likewise

(A) 因此
(B) 因此
(C) 然而
(D) 同樣地

正確答案為 **(C)**

空格前後內容為相反的概念，因此填入 (C) 最符合文意。

Questions 143-146 refer to the following e-mail.

To: All members
From: Vanessa Kwan
Date: August 21
Subject: Good News

Balmer Theater at the Durian Art Center is pleased to share good news with season subscribers.

The construction of an annex to the main building is almost finished and should be ready for the September 20 opening.

Last fall, the Durian Art Center ------- to add a studio to the theater auditorium so it can create
                                      143.
sets for drama productions. The new ------- allows our theater to expand current events for all
                                        144.
audiences. -------, it will be the home for classes and summer camps. -------.
              145.   146.

Sincerely,

Vanessa Kwan
Art Director, Balmer Theater

問題 143-146 題參考以下電子郵件。

收件人：所有會員
寄件人：關凡妮莎
日期：8 月 21 日
主旨：好消息

榴槤藝術中心的巴默劇場很開心能和季度用戶分享一個好消息。位在主要建築旁的附屬大樓即將完工，並準備於 9 月 20 日開放。

去年秋天，榴槤藝術中心 143 決定在劇場內增設一間工作室，如此便能在製作戲劇用布景。新的 144 空間讓本劇院可以為觀眾擴大現有的活動規模。145 同時還能當做課程和夏令營場地。146 感謝各位的支持，也期待向各位展現我們的新設施。

關凡妮莎
巴默劇場藝術導演

字彙　**subscriber** 用戶、訂閱者　　**annex** 附屬大樓　　**auditorium** 禮堂　　**set** 布景

143. (A) will decide
(B) decides
(C) decided
(D) has decided

(A) 即將決定
(B) 會決定
(C) 決定了
(D) 已經決定

正確答案為 (C)

空格要填入正確的動詞時態，前方出現過去時間 Last fall，可知時態要用過去式，答案要選 (C)。

144. (A) report
(B) space
(C) donor
(D) leadership

(A) 報告
(B) 空間
(C) 捐贈者
(D) 領導地位

正確答案為 (B)

空格是前句提及的 studio「工作室」，要填入同樣能表示空間的選項，因此答案為 (B)。

145. (A) In spite of this
(B) On the contrary
(C) Additionally
(D) Nevertheless

(A) 儘管如此
(B) 相反地
(C) 而且
(D) 儘管如此

正確答案為 (C)

空格後一句進一步補充説明前一句內容，因此答案要選 (C)。

146. (A) I have attached a list of events that will take place at this year's trade fair.
(B) Located just an hour from busy downtown, we are an ideal destination for you.
(C) Please review the open positions at our Web site and contact me for further information.
(D) We thank you for your support and look forward to showing you our new facilities.

(A) 附檔為今年於貿易博覽會舉行的活動清單。
(B) 我們這裡距離繁忙的市區僅一小時車程，是您最理想的選擇。
(C) 請於我們的網站上查看職缺內容，如需更多資訊，請再與我聯絡。
(D) 感謝各位的支持，也期待向各位展現我們的新設施。

正確答案為 (D)

電子郵件的主要內容是告知新建設施，因此最後一句應填入 (D) 較為適當。

字彙　**attach** 夾帶檔案　**take place** 發生　**trade fair** 博覽會　**destination** 目的地

Questions 147-148 refer to the following information. 資訊

This is to certify that

Jennifer Lloyd completed a series of three training sessions entitled
"Issues of Online News Reporting: Neutrality in Economic and Political Stories"
on May 25 at the Lamnan Professional Development Center.

Her series of sessions was rated very good by the course participants.

Mark Linksky, Training Director

Lamnan Professional Development Center

問題 147-148 題參考以下資訊。

本證以茲證明

 珍妮佛羅伊德完成以下培訓系列課程的三堂課
系列課程為「線上新聞報導議題：經濟和政治新聞的中立性」
於 5 月 25 日在拉姆南專業發展中心完成。

她在系列課程的表現獲課程學員評定為優等。

培訓主任　馬克林克思開

拉姆南專業發展中心

字彙　**certify** 證明　**entitle** 下標題　**neutrality** 中立性　**rate** 評等　**participant** 參加者

147. What did Ms. Lloyd do on May 25?
(A) She delivered a lecture.
(B) She underwent a training course.
(C) She appeared in a newspaper.
(D) She reported a technical problem.

5 月 25 日羅伊德小姐做了什麼？
(A) 發表一場演説。
(B) 完成培訓課程。
(C) 出現在報紙上。
(D) 提出一個技術問題。

正確答案為 (B)

注意關鍵字 May 25，本篇提到 Lloyd completed a series of three training sessions entitled "Issues of Online News Reporting: Neutrality in Economic and Political Stories" on May 25 完成培訓課，因此答案為 (B)。

字彙　**deliver a lecture** 發表演說　**undergo training** 受訓

148. Who most likely is Ms. Lloyd?
(A) A Web site designer
(B) A software developer
(C) A director of a development center
(D) A journalist

羅伊德小姐最有可能是誰？
(A) 網站設計師
(B) 軟體開發人員
(C) 發展中心主任
(D) 新聞工作者

正確答案為 (D)

課程名稱為 Issues of Online News Reporting: Neutrality in Economic and Political Stories，與新聞業者有關，可推測羅伊德小姐為新聞工作者，答案為 (D)。

字彙　**journalist** 新聞記者

Test 05

Questions 149-150 refer to the following warranty card. 保固卡

Quentin Power Tools Inc.

WARRANTY CARD

Quentin Power Tools Inc., repairs, at no cost to our customers, any defective products, within a designated period of time. This warranty extends to the original purchaser of the product and lasts up to three weeks from the purchase date. If we are not able to repair the product, we may replace it with a comparable item.

The warranty does not cover any consumer negligence or accidental damage. It also does not cover part failure when someone other than a Quentin employee attempts to repair the product.

When sending an item for repair or replacement, you must include your name, street address and phone number for us to assist in returning shipment. It is recommended (although not required) to enclose a note explaining the problem you had using the item.

Once we receive your shipment, it normally takes 14 to 21 business days until we respond.

If you have further questions about product warranty or repair information, please call our Warranty Information Line at 1-800-555-4455.

Revised November 10

問題 149-150 題參考以下保固卡。

坤庭電動工具公司

保固卡

於指定期間內,坤庭電動工具公司會免費為顧客維修任何瑕疵產品。保固對象適用於產品原購買者,保固時間為購買日起的三週內。無法維修之產品,將會更換成其他同等級產品。

若因消費者人為疏忽、意外導致的損壞,則不適用保固維修。同時坤庭公司員工以外的人自行維修引起的零件故障,亦不在保固範圍內。

(150) 欲將產品送修或換貨時,請提供您的姓名、地址和電話,以便協助我們寄回產品。建議可以附上紙條(非強制性),說明您使用時遇到的問題。

(149) 我們收到您的貨件後,通常需要 14 到 21 個工作天才會回覆。

如果您對產品保固或維修資訊有任何疑問,請撥打我們的保固資訊專線 1-800-555-4455。

11 月 10 日修訂

字彙 | **warranty** 保固　**at no cost** 無償　**defective** 有缺陷的　**designated** 指定的　**extend to** 提供給(某對象)
comparable 可相比的　**cover** 承保　**negligence** 疏失　**attempt to** 試圖～　**enclose** 附上、封入
normally 通常

149. What information is stated on the warranty card?　保固卡中提到了什麼資訊？
(A) Names of dealers that provide replacement parts　(A) 供應替換零件的業者名稱
(B) A list of tools that are covered　(B) 提供保固的工具清單
(C) Costs of specific types of repairs　(C) 特定維修項目的費用
(D) An estimation of the time needed to complete repairs　**(D) 預估維修所需的時間**

正確答案為 (D)

保固卡中僅提到 Once we receive your shipment, it normally takes 14 to 21 business days until we respond，符合 (D)。

字彙　**dealer** 經銷業者　**cover** 包含　**specific** 特定的　**estimation** 估計

150. According to the warranty card, what must be included with a request for repair services?　根據保固卡，申請維修服務必須提供的東西是什麼？
(A) A copy of the warranty　(A) 保固卡副本
(B) A photo of the product　(B) 產品照片
(C) Shipping information　**(C) 送貨地址**
(D) A note explaining problems　(D) 問題說明紙條

正確答案為 (C)

請在保固卡中找尋關鍵字 **include**，第三段提到 you must include your name, street address and phone number for us to assist in returning shipment，答案選 (C)。問題說明紙條 not required，表示非必須的，因此不能選 (D)。

Questions 151-153 refer to the following article. 報導

Local Company Is Recognized

by Walter Vine

Milwaukee — In its December edition, *Adventure Wilderness Magazine* rated the Milwaukee-based Quest Out Tour Agency at number seven on its list of Top Ten Travel Companies for the upcoming year.

According to *Adventure Wilderness Magazine*, Quest Out made the list because it demonstrated a strong commitment to offering tour participants a rewarding and memorable experience. They range from canoeing, hiking, and cross-country skiing, to bird-watching, whale-watching, and dog sledding. Quest Out has developed fun-filled activities for every type of outdoor adventure.

The owner of Quest Out, Campbell Hargrove, was delighted to find out that his company had made the list. In a statement the company released yesterday, he said, "We are honored to be recognized as one of the preeminent travel companies in the country, alongside popular companies like Igloo Ice Explorer and Eco-World Travel Company, which have been in the eco-adventure business much longer than we have."

問題 151-153 題參考以下報導。

本地企業獲認可

華特韋恩撰寫

密爾瓦基──《冒險荒野雜誌》12 月號將 152B 密爾瓦基的向外探索旅行社評選為新年十大旅行社第七名。

根據《冒險荒野雜誌》的報導，151 向外探索旅行社之所以上榜，是因為他們堅持承諾提供旅客有意義且難忘的體驗，152C 項目涵蓋獨木舟、健行、越野滑雪、賞鳥、賞鯨、狗拉雪橇等活動。向外探索旅行社持續開發出各種充滿樂趣的戶外探險活動。

152D 向外探索旅行社的老闆坎貝爾哈葛羅夫對於公司上榜一事感到高興。他於昨日發布的公司聲明中表示：「153 我們很榮幸能與冰屋探險家和綠色世界這兩家知名公司一起被評為國內最卓越的旅行社之一。這兩家旅行社比敝社在生態冒險旅遊產業經營更長時間。」

 字彙　**edition** 出版版次　**make the list** 上榜　**demonstrate** 展示、示範　**commitment** 承諾、保證　**rewarding** 值回票價的　**memorable** 難忘的　**sledding** 滑雪橇　**statement** 說明、陳述　**release** 發表　**be honored to** 對～感到光榮　**preeminent** 卓越的　**alongside** 連同

151. Why was the Quest Out Tour Agency selected by *Adventure Wilderness Magazine*?
(A) It is one of the most popular travel companies in the region.
(B) It is more committed to the environment than its competitors.
(C) It offers more outdoor activities than other travel companies.
(D) It organizes tours that are likely to be remembered for a long time.

為何向外探索旅行社會被《冒險荒野雜誌》選中？
(A) 它是該地區最受歡迎的旅行社之一。
(B) 它比起競爭業者更加致力於環境保護。
(C) 它比其他旅行社提供更多的戶外活動。
(D) 它一直規劃更令人難忘的旅遊。

正確答案為 **(D)**

第二段提到獲選的原因 offering tour participants a rewarding and memorable experience，因此答案為 (D)。

字彙　**region** 地區　　**be committed to** 致力於

152. What is NOT indicated about the Quest Out Tour Agency?
(A) Its trips cost a lot.
(B) It is based in Milwaukee.
(C) It takes travelers on ski trips.
(D) Its owner is Campbell Hargrove.

針對向外探索旅行社，何者文中並未提及？
(A) 行程費用極高。
(B) 位在密爾瓦基。
(C) 提供旅客滑雪行程。
(D) 老闆為坎貝爾哈葛羅芙。

正確答案為 **(A)**

(B) 出現在 Milwaukee-based Quest Out Tour Agency 中；(C) 出現在 They range from canoeing, hiking, and cross-country skiing, to bird-watching, whale-watching, and dog sledding 中；The owner of Quest Out, Campbell Hargrove 與 (D) 相符，文中並未提到 (A)。

153. What is suggested about Eco-World Travel Company?
(A) It takes travelers to destinations outside the country.
(B) It has been in operation for quite a while.
(C) It does not offer outdoor activities.
(D) It is not as popular as the Quest Out Tour Agency.

針對綠色世界旅行社，文中提到什麼？
(A) 帶旅客至國外旅遊。
(B) 經營了很長一段時間。
(C) 未提供戶外活動。
(D) 受歡迎的程度比不上向外探索旅行社。

正確答案為 **(B)**

最後一句提到 Eco-World Travel Company, which have been in the eco-adventure business much longer than we have，因此答案為 (B)。

字彙　**in operation** 營運　　**quite a while** 一段時間

Test 05

Questions 154-155 refer to the following online chat. 線上聊天室

Sean Renault [2:30 P.M.] I'm setting up the conference room for the board meeting but can't find the cable for the laptop.

Natalie Albright [2:32 P.M.] I'm not sure which cable you mean.

Sean Renault [2:35 P.M.] The one that hooks up a computer to the projector. I think it's missing.

Natalie Albright [2:37 P.M.] That has happened before. I'll bring one down in a few minutes. Anything else?

Sean Renault [2:39 P.M.] I think there's also a remote for the projector. I can't find that either.

Natalie Albright [2:43 P.M.] I'll grab that as well.

Sean Renault [2:45 P.M.] Thanks a lot.

Send

問題 154-155 題參考以下線上聊天室。

尚雷諾 [下午 2 點 30 分] ❶❺❹ 我正在會議室布置董事會會議，但是我找不到筆電的電線。

娜塔莉艾布萊特 [下午 2 點 32 分] 我不確定你說的是哪種線。

尚雷諾 [下午 2 點 35 分] ❶❺❺ 連接電腦和投影機的線，我猜應該是不見了。

娜塔莉艾布萊特 [下午 2 點 37 分] 之前也發生過同樣的事。❶❺❺ 我馬上帶一條過去。還有其他問題嗎？

尚雷諾 [下午 2 點 39 分] 我記得還有一個投影機遙控器，我找不到。

娜塔莉艾布萊特 [下午 2 點 43 分] 我會一併帶去。

尚雷諾 [下午 2 點 45 分] 非常感謝。

Send

字彙　**set up** 安裝、布置　**board meeting** 董事會會議　**hook up** 連接　**in a few minutes** 立刻、馬上　**remote** 遙控器　**grab** 抓住、取得　**as well** 也

154. Why is Mr. Renault contacting Ms. Albright?
(A) To confirm the date of a board meeting
(B) To discuss a meeting agenda
(C) To ask for help with a piece of equipment
(D) To verify the event venue

為何雷諾先生會聯繫艾布萊特小姐？
(A) 確認董事會的開會日期
(B) 討論會議議程
(C) 針對某項設備尋求幫助
(D) 核對活動場地

正確答案為 **(C)**

本題詢問對話的主題，在對話一開頭就看到雷諾先生於下午 2 點 30 分寫道 I'm setting up the conference room for the board meeting, but can't find the cable for the laptop，由此可以得知答案為 (C)。

字彙 | **confirm** 確認　**agenda** 議程　**verify** 確認、證實　**venue** 活動場地

155. At 2:37 P.M., what does Ms. Albright mean when she writes, "That has happened before"?
(A) She knows why the equipment is replaced.
(B) She knows which cable Mr. Renault needs.
(C) She thinks the computer is out of order.
(D) She acknowledges her mistakes.

艾布萊特小姐於下午 2 點 37 分的訊息中寫「之前也發生過同樣的事」是什麼意思？
(A) 她知道為什麼要更換設備。
(B) 她知道雷諾先生需要哪一種線。
(C) 她認為是電腦故障。
(D) 她承認自己的錯誤。

正確答案為 **(B)**

〈推測句意〉
要推測關鍵句的意圖，就要檢視關鍵句的前後句，前面一句雷諾先生提到電腦連接投影機的線不見，後面一句艾布萊特則回應 I'll bring one down in a few minutes，因此答案為 (B)。

字彙 | **out of order** 故障　**acknowledge** 承認；認出來

Questions 156-157 refer to the following text message. 文字簡訊

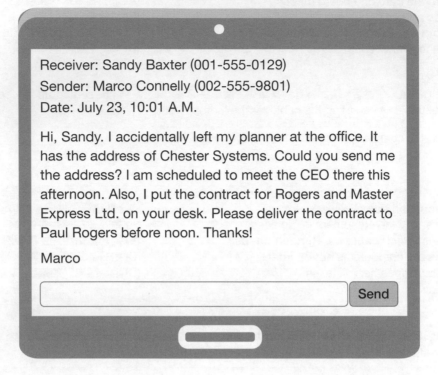

Receiver: Sandy Baxter (001-555-0129)
Sender: Marco Connelly (002-555-9801)
Date: July 23, 10:01 A.M.

Hi, Sandy. I accidentally left my planner at the office. It has the address of Chester Systems. Could you send me the address? I am scheduled to meet the CEO there this afternoon. Also, I put the contract for Rogers and Master Express Ltd. on your desk. Please deliver the contract to Paul Rogers before noon. Thanks!

Marco

Send

問題 156-157 題參考以下文字簡訊。

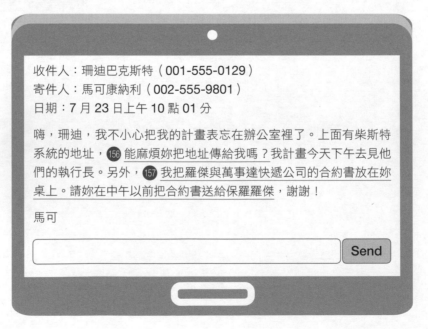

收件人：珊迪巴克斯特（001-555-0129）
寄件人：馬可康納利（002-555-9801）
日期：7 月 23 日上午 10 點 01 分

嗨，珊迪，我不小心把我的計畫表忘在辦公室裡了。上面有柴斯特系統的地址，156 能麻煩妳把地址傳給我嗎？我計畫今天下午去見他們的執行長。另外，157 我把羅傑與萬事達快遞公司的合約書放在妳桌上。請妳在中午以前把合約書送給保羅羅傑，謝謝！

馬可

Send

字彙 **accidentally** 偶然地　　**planner** 時間表、計畫表

156. What is the main purpose of the message?
(A) To cancel a meeting
(B) To ask for information
(C) To request a new planner
(D) To schedule an appointment

這封簡訊的主要目的為何？
(A) 取消會議
(B) 要求資料
(C) 要求新的時間表
(D) 安排預約

正確答案為 (B)

簡訊中提到 Could you send me the address?，可知答案為 (B)。

157. What should Ms. Baxter do?
(A) Send a message to a client
(B) Go to the office of Chester Systems
(C) Write a contract for Mr. Rogers
(D) Give someone a document

巴克斯特小姐應該要做什麼？
(A) 傳訊息給客戶
(B) 前往柴斯特系統的辦公室
(C) 為羅傑先生擬一份合約書
(D) 給某人一份文件

正確答案為 (D)

簡訊中提到 Please deliver the contract to Paul Rogers，因此答案為 (D)。

Questions 158-160 refer to the following memo. (備忘錄)

To	All employees
from	Linda Meyerson, President, Meyerson Lighting Company
Subject	Office Relocation
Date	April 30

Meyerson Lighting Company has experienced phenomenal growth over the last two years, and while that is good for business, it also means that we have outgrown our original space here in the historic Creston Building. –[1]–. As discussed at the company meeting on March 29, we were in negotiation to purchase the recently renovated Barnet Building. I am happy to announce that we reached an agreement with the seller on April 14. The Barnet Building facility is almost double the size of our current location, providing additional offices, conference rooms, and much-needed manufacturing space. –[2]–.

The Barnet Building is just two kilometers away from our present location. We have contracted Kalamar & Murray Commercial Mover to assist us when we move on Thursday, May 16. –[3]–. Next week we will be providing all employees with a special packet containing information about the move, including a description of what each person will be responsible for packing and a comprehensive timeline for the week of the move. –[4]–. New office assignments and sketches of the Barnet Building that show the layout of offices, meeting rooms, and production space will also be provided. On May 13, all employees are welcome to visit the new building to become acquainted with the interior. Our goal is to resume work as soon as possible.

I look forward to seeing you all in our new facility.

問題 158-160 題參考以下備忘錄。

收件人	全體員工
寄件人	邁爾森照明公司總裁琳達邁爾森
主旨	辦公室搬遷
日期	4 月 30 日

158 邁爾森照明公司在過去兩年來經歷驚人的成長。儘管以商業角度來說是件好事，但這也意味著我們原本的地點，歷史悠久的克雷斯頓大樓已經容納不下我們所有員工。–[1]– 如同 3 月 29 日於公司會議上討論的結果，我們正在協商買下翻修完畢的巴尼特大樓一事。我很開心宣布，我們已於 4 月 14 日與賣方達成協議。160 巴尼特大樓的空間是現在大樓的兩倍，將提供更多的辦公室、會議室、以及我們急需的生產作業空間。–[2]–

巴尼特大樓距離我們目前的位置僅兩公里遠。我們已經與卡拉馬＆莫瑞商業搬家公司簽訂合約，他們會在 5 月 16 日搬遷時提供我們協助。–[3]– 159 下週將會提供全體員工搬遷資訊的特別資料包，當中包含各位負責打包的東西與搬遷當週的完整時間表。–[4]– 159 還會提供新辦公室的配置圖和巴尼特大樓的略圖，展現辦公室、會議室、和生產空間的規劃。5 月 13 日這天歡迎所有員工來參觀新大樓，熟悉室內的裝潢。我們的目標就是盡快重新開始工作。

期待在新的大樓內見到各位。

字彙 **phenomenal** 驚人的 **outgrow** 長大（而不再需要） **historic** 有歷史意義的 **negotiation** 協商 **reach an agreement** 達成協議 **much-needed** 急需的 **present** 目前的 **contract** 簽約 **mover** 搬家公司 **containing** 包含 **description** 描述 **be responsible for** 對～負責 **packing** 打包行李 **comprehensive** 全面的 **timeline** 時間表 **layout** 格局、設計 **become acquainted with** 熟悉～ **resume** 重新開始

Test **05**

158. What is suggested about the Creston Building?
(A) It was renovated to have more space.
(B) It was sold to another lighting company in April.
(C) It is where Meyerson Lighting Company first started doing business.
(D) It was originally intended to be a storage facility for Meyerson Lighting Company.

針對克雷斯頓大樓，文中提到什麼？
(A) 為增加更多空間而進行翻修。
(B) 4 月份時被賣給另一家照明公司。
(C) 邁爾森照明公司首次創業的地方。
(D) 原本打算作為邁爾森照明公司的倉庫使用。

正確答案為 (C)

第一段中寫道 we have outgrown our original space here in the historic Creston Building，因此答案為 (C)。

字彙　**originally** 原先　**storage facility** 儲藏設備、倉庫

159. What is NOT mentioned as being included in the packet that employees will receive?
(A) Instruction for packing
(B) Detailed schedules
(C) A diagram of a building
(D) Directions to the new location

針對員工收到的資料包，何者文中並未提及？
(A) 打包指示
(B) 詳細時間表
(C) 大樓示意圖
(D) 新位置路線圖

正確答案為 (D)

仔細尋找提到關鍵字 packet 的段落，第二段提到 what each person will be responsible for packing and a comprehensive timeline for the week of the move，符合 (A) 與 (B)。(C) 出現在 sketches of the Barnet Building that show the layout of offices 中。文中並未提到 (D)。

字彙　**diagram** 圖表

160. In which of the positions marked [1], [2], [3], and [4] does the following sentence best belong?
"We will now be able to increase production to meet the rapidly growing demand for our custom-designed lightings."
(A) [1]
(B) [2]
(C) [3]
(D) [4]

在標示 [1]、[2]、[3]、[4] 的位置中，何者適合放入以下句子？
「我們現在將能增加產量，以滿足快速成長的訂製款照明設備需求。」
(A) [1]
(B) [2]
(C) [3]
(D) [4]

正確答案為 (B)

〈插入句〉

本插入句提到增加產量的事情，因此要尋找前後有提到相關內容的地方。[2] 前一句提到 The Barnet Building facility is almost double the size of our current location, providing additional offices, conference rooms, and much-needed manufacturing space，提到新大樓新增了生產空間，能接續插入句提到增加產量一事，因此答案選 (B)。

字彙　**rapidly** 迅速地　**custom-designed** 訂製的

Questions 161-164 refer to the following e-mail. 電子郵件

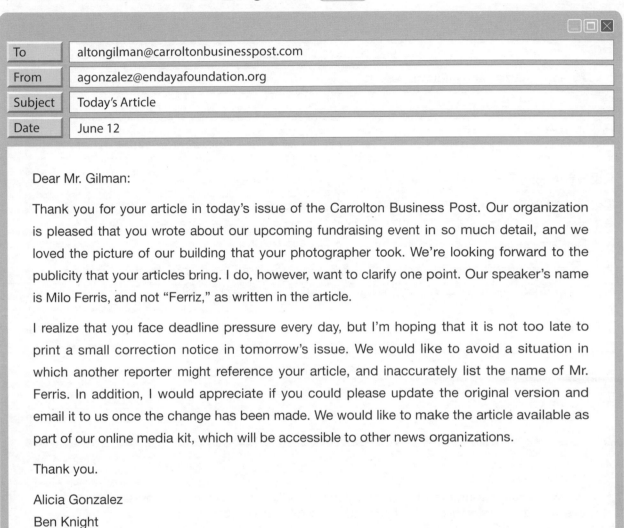

To	altongilman@carroltonbusinesspost.com
From	agonzalez@endayafoundation.org
Subject	Today's Article
Date	June 12

Dear Mr. Gilman:

Thank you for your article in today's issue of the Carrolton Business Post. Our organization is pleased that you wrote about our upcoming fundraising event in so much detail, and we loved the picture of our building that your photographer took. We're looking forward to the publicity that your articles bring. I do, however, want to clarify one point. Our speaker's name is Milo Ferris, and not "Ferriz," as written in the article.

I realize that you face deadline pressure every day, but I'm hoping that it is not too late to print a small correction notice in tomorrow's issue. We would like to avoid a situation in which another reporter might reference your article, and inaccurately list the name of Mr. Ferris. In addition, I would appreciate if you could please update the original version and email it to us once the change has been made. We would like to make the article available as part of our online media kit, which will be accessible to other news organizations.

Thank you.

Alicia Gonzalez
Ben Knight

問題 161-164 題參考以下電子郵件。

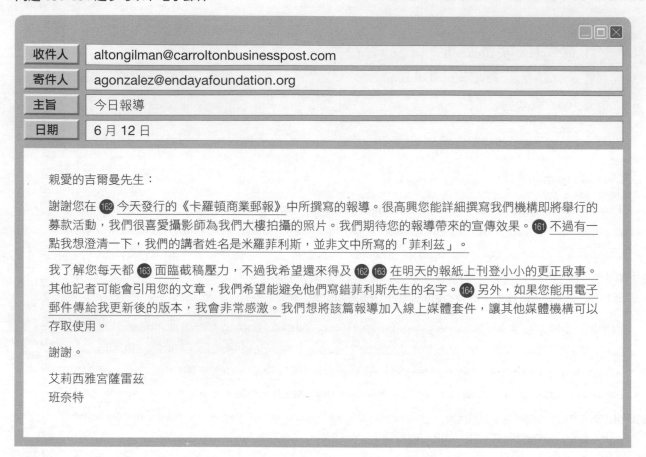

收件人　altongilman@carroltonbusinesspost.com
寄件人　agonzalez@endayafoundation.org
主旨　今日報導
日期　6 月 12 日

親愛的吉爾曼先生：

謝謝您在 162 今天發行的《卡羅頓商業郵報》中所撰寫的報導。很高興您能詳細撰寫我們機構即將舉行的募款活動，我們很喜愛攝影師為我們大樓拍攝的照片。我們期待您的報導帶來的宣傳效果。161 不過有一點我想澄清一下，我們的講者姓名是米羅菲利斯，並非文中所寫的「菲利茲」。

我了解您每天都 163 面臨截稿壓力，不過我希望還來得及 162 163 在明天的報紙上刊登小小的更正啟事。其他記者可能會引用您的文章，我們希望能避免他們寫錯菲利斯先生的名字。164 另外，如果您能用電子郵件傳給我更新後的版本，我會非常感激。我們想將該篇報導加入線上媒體套件，讓其他媒體機構可以存取使用。

謝謝。

艾莉西雅宮薩雷茲
班奈特

字彙　**issue** 期號　**fundraising** 募款活動　**publicity** 宣傳　**clarify** 澄清　**realize** 明白　**pressure** 壓力
correction 修正　**reference** 參考　**inaccurately** 不準確地　**accessible** 可使用的

161. What is the purpose of the e-mail?
(A) To cancel a subscription
(B) To request a correction
(C) To promote an upcoming event
(D) To recommend a new organization member

此封電子郵件的目的為何？
(A) 取消訂閱
(B) 要求更正
(C) 宣傳即將舉行的活動
(D) 推薦新的組織成員

正確答案為 (B)

文章目的通常會在第一段提到，第一段中段提到 I do, however, want to clarify one point. Our speaker's name is Milo Ferris, and not "Ferriz," as written in the article，加上第二段中提到 I'm hoping that it is not too late to print a small correction notice in tomorrow's issue，因此答案為 (B)。

字彙　**cancel** 取消

162. What is probably true about the *Carrolton Business Post*?
(A) It has a reader's column.
(B) It recently funded a charity event.
(C) It is published daily.
(D) It releases information on business events.

有關《卡羅頓商業郵報》的敘述何者正確？
(A) 有讀者專欄。
(B) 最近為慈善活動提供資金。
(C) 每天都會發行。
(D) 上面會刊登商業活動資訊。

正確答案為 (C)

文章第一句提到 your article in today's issue，第二段提到 Tomorrow's issue，可知答案為 (C)。

字彙　**column** 專欄　　**fund** 提供資金；資金

163. The word "face" in paragraph 2, line 1, is closest in meaning to
(A) confront
(B) feature
(C) oppose
(D) overlook

第二段第一行的「face」與下列何者意思最為接近？
(A) 面對
(B) 以～為特色
(C) 反對
(D) 忽略

正確答案為 (A)

〈推測字義〉
整句是 you face deadline pressure every day 中，這裡的 face 當動詞，指「面臨、面對」，因此答案選 (A)。

字彙　**oppose** 反對　　**overlook** 忽略

164. What does Ms. Gonzalez request by e-mail?
(A) A revision of the publication guideline
(B) A list of media organizations
(C) A reference letter
(D) A copy of an article

宮薩雷茲小姐要求透過電子郵件發送什麼？
(A) 出版指南修訂版
(B) 媒體機構清單
(C) 推薦信
(D) 報導的文件副本

正確答案為 (D)

注意看提到關鍵字 by email 的段落，第二段中段提到 I would appreciate if you could please update the original version and email it to us once the change has been made，請對方傳給他更正後的報導，因此答案選 (D)。

字彙　**revision** 修訂版　　**guideline** 指南　　**reference letter** 推薦信

Questions 165-167 refer to the following information.

Drayton Music Festival

Interested in donating some of your time while enjoying all kinds of great music? Then volunteer at the fifteenth annual Drayton Music Festival! This year's festival runs from October 25 to 31 at the county fairgrounds in Drayton and features music from more than 50 talented groups, including local favorites Starroad Pop Band, Jazz Heroes, and Jackson's String Quartet.

Volunteers are needed to

- help with publicity — designing and posting a flyer and sending press release — starting in October.
- greet the musicians and help them locate their housing assignments from October 23 to 29. All out-of-town musicians will be hosted by area families.
- operate the ticket booth, direct guests to the parking areas during the festival, and provide general information.

In appreciation, each volunteer will receive a limited edition Drayton Music Festival T-shirt and four complimentary tickets.

If you are interested in volunteering, please contact Justin Brown at justinbrown@draytonmusicfest. org by September 17.

問題 165-167 題參考以下資訊。

德雷頓音樂節

您有興趣在享受各種美妙音樂之餘,貢獻出一點時間嗎?請成為第 15 屆德雷頓音樂節的志工吧!今年的活動時間為 10 月 25 日至 31 日,在德雷頓的露天廣場舉行。屆時將有超過 50 組才華洋溢的音樂團體帶來表演,165 包含當地人氣的星路流行樂團、爵士英雄、以及傑克森弦樂四重奏。

志工需要做的事情為:

- 協助宣傳 —— 167D 設計並張貼傳單,並發送新聞稿 —— 從 10 月開始。
- 迎接音樂家,並幫他們安排 10 月 23 日至 29 日的住處。166 所有外地的音樂家們將會寄宿於當地的家庭。
- 167A 167B 看管售票亭,活動期間引導客人前往停車場,提供一般資訊協助。

為表示感激,每位志工將獲得德雷頓音樂節的限量版 T 恤和 4 張免費門票。

如果您有興趣成為志工,請在 9 月 17 日前聯繫賈斯丁布朗 justinbrown@draytonmusicfest.org。

 字彙　**volunteer** 自願服務　**annual** 每年的　**fairground** 露天廣場　**string quartet** 弦樂四重奏　**locate** 找出、確認位置　**housing** 住房　**out-of-town** 外地的　**operate** 營運　**direct A to B** 指引 A 去 B　**in appreciation** 感謝、感激　**ticket booth** 售票亭　**complimentary** 贈送的

165. What is indicated about the event?
(A) It will take place on October 1.
(B) It features a variety of music types.
(C) It is run by a professional musician.
(D) It may be rescheduled because of rain.

下列敘述何者與本活動相符？
(A) 將於 10 月 1 日舉行。
(B) 以各式各樣的音樂類型為特色。
(C) 由一名專業音樂家開辦。
(D) 下雨的話，有可能會改期。

正確答案為 (B)

第一段中寫道 features music from more than 50 talented groups, including local favorites Starroad Pop Band, Jazz Heroes, and Jackson's String Quartet，因此答案為 (B)。

字彙　**a variety of** 各式各樣的　　**run** 經營

166. What is suggested about some of the performers?
(A) They will be donating used instruments.
(B) They will be providing funds to the event.
(C) They will be staying at homes in Drayton.
(D) They will be receiving a major award at the event.

針對一部分表演者，文中提到什麼？
(A) 他們將捐出二手樂器。
(B) 他們將為活動提供資金。
(C) 他們將寄住在德雷頓的住家。
(D) 他們將在活動中獲得重要獎項。

正確答案為 (C)

文中針對志工要做的工作提到 All out-of-town musicians will be hosted by area families，因此答案為 (C)。

字彙　**used instrument** 二手樂器　　**major** 重要的

167. What task will NOT be done by volunteers?
(A) Selling tickets for festival performances
(B) Taking musicians to the fairground
(C) Giving audience directions to the parking area
(D) Distributing publicity materials

下列何者並非志工必須完成的工作？
(A) 販售活動表演門票
(B) 帶音樂家到露天廣場
(C) 引導觀眾前往停車場
(D) 發放宣傳資料

正確答案為 (B)

文中針對志工要做的工作提到 operate the ticket booth，符合 (A)。direct guests to the parking areas during the festival 對應至 (C)。designing and posting a flyer and sending press release 對應至 (D)，文中並未提到 (B)。

Questions 168-171 refer to the following text message chain. 文字簡訊

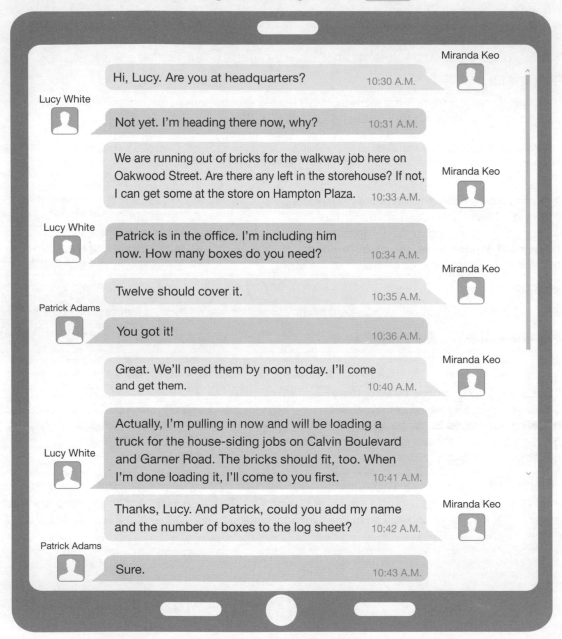

Miranda Keo
Hi, Lucy. Are you at headquarters? 10:30 A.M.

Lucy White
Not yet. I'm heading there now, why? 10:31 A.M.

Miranda Keo
We are running out of bricks for the walkway job here on Oakwood Street. Are there any left in the storehouse? If not, I can get some at the store on Hampton Plaza. 10:33 A.M.

Lucy White
Patrick is in the office. I'm including him now. How many boxes do you need? 10:34 A.M.

Miranda Keo
Twelve should cover it. 10:35 A.M.

Patrick Adams
You got it! 10:36 A.M.

Miranda Keo
Great. We'll need them by noon today. I'll come and get them. 10:40 A.M.

Lucy White
Actually, I'm pulling in now and will be loading a truck for the house-siding jobs on Calvin Boulevard and Garner Road. The bricks should fit, too. When I'm done loading it, I'll come to you first. 10:41 A.M.

Miranda Keo
Thanks, Lucy. And Patrick, could you add my name and the number of boxes to the log sheet? 10:42 A.M.

Patrick Adams
Sure. 10:43 A.M.

問題 **168-171** 題參考以下文字簡訊。

米蘭達基奧

嗨,路西,你現在在總公司嗎? 上午 10 點 30 分

路西懷特

我還沒到,現在正要過去那裡,怎麼了? 上午 10 點 31 分

168 170 奧克伍德街走道工程用的磚塊都用完了,倉庫還有剩嗎?如果沒有的話,我可以去漢普頓廣場的商店買一些。 上午 10 點 33 分

米蘭達基奧

路西懷特

派翠克在辦公室裡,我現在把他加進對話。
169 妳需要幾箱? 上午 10 點 34 分

169 12 箱應該夠。 上午 10 點 35 分

米蘭達基奧

派翠克亞當斯

這裡有! 上午 10 點 36 分

太好了,今天中午前會用到它,我現在過去拿。 上午 10 點 40 分

米蘭達基奧

路西懷特

其實我正在停車,正在卡爾文林蔭大道和迦納路上的房屋外牆工程這裡上貨。應該還放得下磚塊。
170 裝運完畢後,我先過去找妳。 上午 10 點 41 分

謝謝妳,路西。還有,派翠克,**171** 可以請你把我的名字和箱子數量加進日誌表中嗎? 上午 10 點 42 分

米蘭達基奧

派翠克亞當斯

沒問題。 上午 10 點 43 分

字彙 **headquarters**(固定用複數)總公司 **head** 前往 **run out of** 用完 **walkway** 走道 **storehouse** 倉庫
pull in 停車 **load** 裝載 **house-siding** 房屋外牆 **fit** 符合 **log sheet** 日誌表

168. Where does Ms. Keo probably work?
(A) At an architecture firm
(B) At a delivery service
(C) At a construction company
(D) At a home improvement store

基奧小姐可能在哪裡工作？
(A) 建築公司
(B) 快遞公司
(C) 營造公司
(D) 居家裝潢店家

正確答案為 (C)

米蘭達基奧於上午 10 點 33 分的簡訊中寫道 We are running out of bricks for the walkway job，由此可以得知答案為 (C)。architecture firm 為建築公司，是負責房屋結構設計，接下來的施工工程則會發包給營造公司（construction company）執行，請勿混淆。

> 字彙　**construction company** 施工單位、營造公司　**home improvement** 居家修繕裝潢

169. At 10:36 A.M., what does Mr. Adams most likely mean when he writes, "You got it"?
(A) The traffic is running smoothly.
(B) He is free to help at noon.
(C) The truck Ms. White needs is available.
(D) There is enough material for the work.

亞當斯先生於上午 10 點 36 分的簡訊中寫「這裡有！」代表什麼意思？
(A) 交通順暢。
(B) 他中午有空幫忙。
(C) 懷特小姐可以使用卡車。
(D) 有足夠的材料可以用在工程上。

正確答案為 (D)

〈推測句意〉
路西懷特於上午 10 點 34 分的簡訊中提到 How many boxes do you need?，接著米蘭達基奧於上午 10 點 35 分的簡訊中回覆 Twelve should cover it，而題目關鍵句便是針對此句話反應，表示有 12 箱，因此答案要選 (D)。

170. Where does Ms. White say she will go?
(A) To Oakwood Street
(B) To Hampton Plaza
(C) To Calvin Boulevard
(D) To Garner Road

懷特小姐說她會去哪裡？
(A) 奧克伍德街
(B) 漢普頓廣場
(C) 卡爾文林蔭大道
(D) 迦納路

正確答案為 (A)

路西懷特於上午 10 點 41 分的簡訊中提到 When I'm done loading it, I'll come to you first.，通知基奧小姐。查看基奧小姐於上午 10 點 33 分的簡訊後，可以得知她在奧克伍德街，因此答案為 (A)。

171. What does Ms. Keo ask Mr. Adams to do?
(A) Explain the directions to Ms. White
(B) Submit a request for time off
(C) Keep an accurate record of the items
(D) Calculate how much to bill a customer

基奧小姐要求亞當斯先生做什麼事？
(A) 向懷特小姐說明路線
(B) 繳交休假申請書
(C) 準確紀錄品項
(D) 計算向客人收費的金額

正確答案為 (C)

米蘭達基奧於上午 10 點 42 分的簡訊中寫道 could you add my name and the number of boxes to the log sheet?，告知亞當斯先生，因此答案為 (C)。

> 字彙　**time off** 請假　**accurate** 準確的　**keep a record of** 紀錄　**calculate** 計算　**bill** 請款

Questions 172-175 refer to the following article. 報導

TIME TO LET MAYHEN BANK GO

Dublin (July 1) – Mayhen Bank, located in Broadstone, only a short distance from Dublin's central business district, will close its doors on August 31 after over 50 years of being in business. –[1]–.

Mayhen Bank has served as the primary financial institution for thousands of customers since its opening. –[2]–. However, about 10 years ago, the bank began to see a significant decline in customers as many left the single-branch institution in favor of larger ones in the area that offered more branch locations and services.

Mayhen Bank will not be gone for good, though, as it has successfully negotiated a merger with Ireland's First Bank, a multicity corporation offering a variety of personal and commercial banking services. "We look forward to providing all Mayhen Bank customers with a positive banking experience, and we are happy to have them as clients," said Adam Petrovich, chief operating officer of Ireland's First Bank. –[3]–.

Former Mayhen Bank customers will have the availability of several new products and services after the merger, including expanded options for banking accounts and loans. –[4]–. The merger will be completed at the end of next month when Mayhen Bank's 500 remaining customers switch to the Ireland's First Bank location of their choice.

問題 172-175 題參考以下報導。

是時候該送走梅罕銀行了

都柏林（7 月 1 日）一梅罕銀行位於布拉斯通，鄰近都柏林中心商業區。在經營 50 餘年後，將於 8 月 31 日吹熄燈號。–[1]–

梅罕銀行自開業以來，一直是數千名客戶的主要金融機構。–[2]– 然而 173 約 10 年前，僅此一家別無分行的銀行大量流失客戶，因為這些客戶轉而支持該區其他提供更多分行據點與服務的大型銀行。

172 話雖如此，梅罕銀行並不會永遠消失。因為它已經成功與愛爾蘭第一銀行談成合併案。愛爾蘭第一銀行為一家擁有多個據點的企業，提供各式各樣的個人和商業銀行服務。愛爾蘭第一銀行的首席營運長亞當彼托維奇表示：「我們期待提供正面的銀行體驗給梅罕銀行的所有客戶，也很高興能迎接他們成為我們的客戶。」–[3]–

175 合併之後，梅罕銀行的舊用戶將能使用多種新產品和服務，包括銀行帳戶和貸款上將增加更多的選項。–[4]– 172 174 預計下個月底完成合併，屆時梅罕銀行剩下的 500 名客戶會轉到自己所選的愛爾蘭第一銀行據點。

字彙 **business district** 商業區 **close one's door in business** 停業 **serve as** 擔任 **primary** 主要的、首要的 **institution** 機構 **single-branch** 僅此一家、別無分行的 **in favor of** 支持、贊同 **for good** 永久 **negotiate** 協調 **multicity** 多個城市 **corporation** 企業 **commercial** 商業的 **operating officer** 營運長 **former** 先前的、前任的 **merger** 合併 **expanded** 擴大的 **option** 選項 **remaining** 剩下的 **switch** 轉換、交換

172. What is the purpose of the article?
(A) To announce the opening of a bank
(B) To request consumer reviews of local businesses
(C) To report on new policies affecting customers
(D) To publicize the merger between two businesses

本篇報導的目的為何？
(A) 宣布銀行開幕
(B) 對當地企業要求消費者評估
(C) 報導影響客戶的新政策
(D) 公布兩家公司的合併

正確答案為 **(D)**

本篇報導針對梅罕銀行合併的過程進行說明，最後寫 The merger will be completed at the end of next month，答案選 (D)。

字彙　**affect** 影響　　**policy** 政策　　**publicize** 公布、告知

173. Why did Mayhen Bank lose a lot of customers?
(A) Because it charged too many fees
(B) Because it has too few locations
(C) Because its employees are not well trained
(D) Because it is closed too early on weekdays

為何梅罕銀行會失去很多客戶？
(A) 收取過多服務費
(B) 銀行據點過少
(C) 員工並未受過良好的訓練
(D) 平日太早關門

正確答案為 **(B)**

第二段提到梅罕銀行倒閉的原因，many left the single-branch institution in favor of larger ones in the area that offered more branch locations and services，single-branch 指「別無分行的」，後面也提到客戶轉而支持其他有分行的大銀行，因此答案為 (B)。

字彙　**employee** 員工　　**well trained** 訓練有素的　　**weekdays** 平日

174. What is stated about Mayhen Bank?
(A) It has about 500 customers.
(B) It opened 10 years ago.
(C) Its president will resign soon.
(D) It was formerly called Ireland's First Bank

針對梅罕銀行，文中提到什麼？
(A) 約有 500 名客戶。
(B) 10 年前開幕。
(C) 董事長即將辭職。
(D) 以前被稱作愛爾蘭第一銀行。

正確答案為 **(A)**

最後一句提到 Mayhen Bank's 500 remaining customers，因此答案為 (A)。第一段提到 over 50 years of being in business，因此 (B) 的敘述有誤，而文中並未提到 (C) 和 (D)。

字彙　**resign** 辭職

175. In which of the positions marked [1], [2], [3], and [4] does the following sentence best belong?
"Additionally, all Mayhen customers will receive a complimentary $40 gift card from Ireland's First Bank as a welcome gift as soon as their accounts are transferred."
(A) [1]
(B) [2]
(C) [3]
(D) [4]

在標示 [1]、[2]、[3]、[4] 的位置中，何者適合放入以下句子？
「此外，梅罕銀行的客戶在轉移帳戶後，將會收到愛爾蘭第一銀行贈送的 40 美元禮物卡作為歡迎禮。」
(A) [1]
(B) [2]
(C) [3]
(D) [4]

正確答案為 **(D)**

〈插入句〉
本插入句開頭寫 Additionally，表示是前一句的補充說明，加上內容提到舊用戶轉到新用戶的事，適合放在最後一段。[4] 前一句提到合併後的好處，放在此句後方最符合文意，因此答案選 (D)。

字彙　**additionally** 此外　　**transfer** 轉移

Questions 176-180 refer to following memo and form. 備忘錄 / 表格

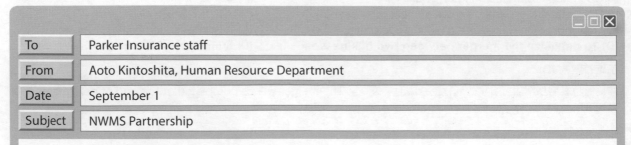

To	Parker Insurance staff
From	Aoto Kintoshita, Human Resource Department
Date	September 1
Subject	NWMS Partnership

As a part of its employee appreciation program, Parker Insurance Agency has partnered with New Way Mobile Service (NWMS) to offer employees discounted mobile phone service. Staff members who change to open either an individual or family service plan with NWMS will save 20% and 25%, respectively, off telephone charges for the first month of their subscription. Additionally, the account service charge will be waived. Subscription plans are for one year and will be automatically renewed for another year unless service is cancelled.

Employees wishing to take advantage of this offer should contact the NWMS Customer Service Department at 321-555-0123. Applications are also accepted electronically at www.nwms.com/corpsaving. To start the subscription process, employees must provide a work e-mail address and employee number. In addition, be ready to submit a valid credit card number as well as a government-issued document, such as a driver's license or passport, that carries a unique identification number.

NWMS CUSTOMER COMPLAINT FORM

Customer Details
Name: *Edward Boulanger*
Account Number: *BA834-1*
Date: *December 3*
E-mail address: *eboulanger@parkerinsurance.com*

Details of Complaint

Last October I opened a mobile phone plan account after learning about the special offer for Parker Insurance Agency employees. According to the promotional material distributed by my employer, I should not have been charged an account service charge to start the service. The NWMS representative I spoke with on the phone when I signed up also confirmed this. Nevertheless, the charge appeared on my first billing statement, dated November 30. Please remove the erroneous charge from the bill and send me an amended version. Of course, the new bill should continue to reflect a 25% discount on phone charges.

Thank you.

問題 176-180 題參考以下備忘錄和表格。

收件人	帕克保險公司全體員工
寄件人	人力資源部木下奧多
日期	9 月 1 日
主旨	NWMS 共同合作

⑰⑥ 作為員工感謝計畫的一部分，帕克保險公司與新方行動服務公司（NWMS）合作，提供員工手機服務優惠。⑰⑨ 員工只要更換成 NWMS 的個人或家庭服務方案，便能在訂閱首月，分別享有電話費八折和八五折的優惠。⑰⑦ 此外免收帳戶服務費。訂閱方案為期一年，如未取消服務，則會自動續約一年。

欲利用此優惠的員工請撥打 321-555-0123 聯繫 NWMS 的客服部，或是採線上申請的方式 www.nwms.com/corpsaving.。⑰⑧ 員工必須提供工作用的電子郵件地址和員工編號，才能啟用訂閱服務。除此之外，請備妥一組有效的信用卡號，和政府核發之身分證明數字的文件，如駕照或護照。

> **字彙** **partnership** 合作 　**appreciation** 感激 　**partner with** 與～合夥 　**individual** 個人 　**respectively** 各別地 **waive** 免除 　**charge** 費用；索費 　**subscription** 訂閱、訂購 　**automatically** 自動地 **take advantage of** 利用 　**electronically** 透過電子手段、線上 　**government-issued** 由政府發行的 **carry** 運送、攜帶、備有 　**identification number** 身分證數字

NWMS 客戶投訴單

客戶資料

姓名：愛德華布蘭格

帳戶號碼：BA834-1

日期：12 月 3 日

電子郵件地址：eboulanger@parkerinsurance.com

投訴細節

去年 10 月在我得知提供給帕克保險公司員工的特別優惠後，便申辦了手機。根據我的雇主所發的促銷資料，啟用服務時不會向我收取帳戶服務費。申辦時我也在電話上向 NWMS 的人員確認過這一點。但是這筆費用卻出現在我第一筆 11 月 30 日的帳單上。⑱⓪ 請從帳單中刪除有問題的費用，⑰⑨ 重新寄給我修正過後的版本。而新的帳單中同樣也要給我八五折的電話費優惠。

謝謝。

> **字彙** **customer complaint** 客訴 　**special offer** 特惠活動、折扣 　**promotional** 宣傳的、促銷的 **distribute** 分配、分發 　**employer** 雇主 　**sign up** 申請 　**nevertheless** 然而 　**billing statement** 帳單明細 **erroneous** 有問題的、錯誤的 　**amended** 修正後的

176. What is the memo mainly about?
(A) **The addition of a benefit for employees**
(B) Use of company phones for work purposes only
(C) The renewal of a mobile phone subscription
(D) Requirement for employees to register with NWMS

備忘錄主要的內容為何？
(A) **新增的員工福利**
(B) 公司電話僅用於工作目的
(C) 手機續約
(D) 要求員工在 NWMS 註冊

正確答案為 (A)

詢問文章主題的答案多半會在文章開頭出現，備忘錄第一句提到 As a part of its employee appreciation program，表示為感謝員工的計畫，接著提到 Parker Insurance Agency has partnered with New Way Mobile Service (NWMS) to offer employees discounted mobile phone service，因此答案為 (A)。

字彙 **benefit** 福利　**renewal** 續約　**register** 註冊

177. What is indicated about the account service charge?
(A) It can be paid in installments.
(B) It will be refunded if an account is cancelled.
(C) It usually costs $25.
(D) **It will be complimentary.**

下列敘述何者與帳戶服務費相符？
(A) 接受分期付款。
(B) 帳戶被取消時，將提供退款。
(C) 通常要支付 25 美元。
(D) **將會免費贈送。**

正確答案為 (D)

請在文章中尋找關鍵字 account service charge，備忘錄提到 the account service charge will be waived，waive 指「免除」，因此答案為 (D)。

字彙 **in installments** 分期付款

178. What is NOT required for the NWMS application?
(A) An employee number
(B) **A postal code**
(C) A credit card number
(D) An e-mail address

申請加入 NWMS 不需要的東西為何？
(A) 員工編號
(B) **郵遞區號**
(C) 信用卡號碼
(D) 電子郵件地址

正確答案為 (B)

備忘錄最後一段提到申請時需要的東西 employees must provide a work e-mail address and employee number「電子郵件」與「員工編號」，符合 (A) 與 (D)。be ready to submit a valid credit card number as well as a government-issued document, such as a driver's license or passport, that carries a unique identification number「信用卡號」，符合 (C)，並未提到 (B)。

179. What can be inferred about Mr. Boulanger?
(A) He works in Mr. Kintoshita's department.
(B) **He has subscribed to the family service plan.**
(C) He opened his account through the Parker Web site.
(D) He learned of NWMS' offer from one of his family members.

下列哪個敘述與布蘭格先生相符？
(A) 他在木下先生所屬的部門工作。
(B) **他申辦家庭服務方案。**
(C) 他在網站上開通自己的帳戶。
(D) 他從家人那得知 NWMS。

正確答案為 (B)

〈整合多篇文章資訊〉
備忘錄中提到 Staff members who change to open either an individual or family service plan with NWMS will save 20% and 25%, respectively, off telephone charges。而客訴提到 the new bill should continue to reflect a 25% discount on phone charges，表示 Mr. Boulanger 布蘭格先生申請的是家庭方案，因此答案選 (B)。選項 (A) 文章無特別提及；客訴表中提到 The NWMS representative I spoke with on the phone 表示是透過電話申請，(C) 不對；而客訴表第一句提到是透過雇主得知，(D) 也不對。

180. What does Mr. Boulanger request that NWMS do?
    (A) Cancel his monthly plan
    (B) Make changes to the revised company policy
    (C) Send him a corrected billing statement
    (D) Extend his discount to his friends

布蘭格先生要求 NWMS 做什麼？
(A) 取消他的月付方案
(B) 更動修改後的公司政策
(C) 寄給他更正過的帳單
(D) 將優惠範圍擴大到他的朋友

正確答案為 **(C)**

投訴表中提到 Please remove the erroneous fee from the bill and send me an amended version，答案選 (C)。

字彙	**corrected** 修正的

Test 05

Questions 181-185 refer to following schedule and e-mail. 時間表 / 電子郵件

Connelly Publishing House Presents Randy Carmichael's *The Art of Daydreaming*
National Book Tour
Southwestern Region - May Public Appearances

Thursday, May 10, 6 P.M.

Jessie's Book Haven – 500 Oak Terrace, Tucson, AZ 02116

A meet-and-greet with Mr. Carmichael will take place at 5 P.M.; by invitation only.

The reading session starts at 6 P.M. and is open to the public.

Saturday, May 12, 5 P.M.

Barnes and Nomads – 218 Maynard Street, Austin, TX 78704

Book reading begins at 5 P.M., followed by the book signing at 6 P.M. Due to a scheduling conflict, Mr. Carmichael will not be able to take questions at this presentation.

Wednesday, May 16, 6 P.M.

Café Reynolds – 685 Cherry Tree Avenue, Houston, TX 19103

Limited seating. Please visit www.cafereynolds.com to register for the event.

There is a $5 advance ticket fee. Tickets sold at the door will be $8.

Monday, May 21, 6 P.M.

Jefferson Public Library – 400 Jefferson Avenue, New Orleans, LA 21202

Attendees will have the opportunity to ask questions.

Afterward, a dinner reception for all attendees will be held in the library conference center.

Additional notes:

• All dates, times, and locations are subject to change.

• Unless otherwise indicated, Mr. Carmichael will read excerpts from *The Art of Daydreaming*, sign copies, and answer questions from the audience at each appearance.

• Copies of *The Art of Daydreaming* will be available for purchase at all venues.

• On June 1, future tour dates and cities will be announced on the publisher's Web site and in local newspapers.

To request an appearance by the author, please contact Cecilia Haywood at chaywood@connellypublishing.com.

問題 181-185 題參考以下時間表和電子郵件。

⑱ 康奈利出版社為蘭迪卡麥可的《白日夢的藝術》 舉辦全國書籍巡迴 西南部地區—5 月份公開活動

⑱ 5 月 10 日星期四下午 6 點
傑西的圖書避風港 —— 02116 亞利桑那州土桑市橡樹街 500 號
卡麥可先生的見面會將於下午 5 點舉行，僅限受邀者參加。
朗讀會將於下午 6 點開始，開放一般大眾參與。

5 月 12 日星期六下午 5 點
巴恩斯和流浪者 —— 78704 德州奧斯丁市梅納德街 218 號
下午 5 點開始進行朗讀會，接著於下午 6 點舉辦簽書會。礙於時間關係，本場活動中卡麥可先生不接受提問。

5 月 16 日星期三下午 6 點
⑱ 咖啡雷諾德 —— 19103 德州休斯頓櫻桃樹大道 685 號
座位有限，請上 www.cafereynolds.com 報名參加活動。⑱ 預購門票為 5 美元，現場購票為 8 美元。

5 月 21 日星期一下午 6 點
傑佛森公共圖書館 —— 21202 路易斯安那州紐奧良市傑佛森大道 400 號
參加者將獲得提問的機會。
活動後將為所有參加者準備晚宴，於圖書館會議中心舉行。

補充說明：
- 日期、時間、地點可能會有所變動。
- 除非另有說明，否則卡麥可先生每場活動都會節錄《白日夢的藝術》中的一小段進行朗讀與簽書，並接受讀者提問。
- 所有活動地點均可購買到《白日夢的藝術》一書。
- 6 月 1 日將會在出版社網站和當地報紙上公布後續巡迴的日期和城市。

如欲邀請作者出席活動，請由 chaywood@connellypublishing.com. 聯繫賽西麗雅海伍德。

字彙　**book tour** 書籍巡迴　　**public appearance** 公開見面活動　　**meet-and-greet** 見面會　　**invitation** 邀請
book signing 簽書會　　**scheduling conflict** 時間衝突　　**advance** 事先的、預先的　　**attendee** 參與者
afterward 之後　　**reception** 招待會　　**be subject to** 視～狀況而定　　**otherwise** 否則、不然　　**excerpt** 摘錄

To	Cecilia Haywood <chaywood@connellypublishing.com>
From	Jason King <jasonking@tucsonuniversity.com>
Date	May 25
Subject	Mr. Carmichael's Book Tour
Attachment	Inquiries.doc

Dear Ms. Haywood:

I want to thank Connelly Publishing for bringing Mr. Carmichael to Tucson and for inviting me to the private reception that preceded the public event. It was my honor to have an opportunity to meet one of my favorite authors in person and to exchange some words. I am planning to use *The Art of Daydreaming* in my introductory psychology class and had some questions for him. Since there was not enough time to discuss them all, he suggested I forward them to you. (See attached documents.) And I also want to speak with you about the possibility of having Mr. Carmichael visit my class to talk to my students. I try to bring in one guest lecturer each semester, and I think Mr. Carmichael is perfect. I hope to hear from you soon.

Sincerely,

Jason King

收件人	賽西麗雅海伍德 <chaywood@connellypublishing.com>
寄件人	傑森金恩 ⑱ <jasonking@tucsonuniversity.com>
日期	5 月 25 日
主旨	卡麥可先生的書籍巡迴
附件	提問 .doc

親愛的海伍德小姐：

⑱ 我要感謝康奈利出版社請卡麥可先生到土桑市，還邀請我參加公開活動前的私人招待會。我很榮幸能有機會親眼見到我最喜歡的作家，並和他小聊一下。⑱ 我計畫於我的入門心理學課上使用《白日夢的藝術》一書，向他提出了一些問題。由於當時沒有足夠的時間討論，他建議我把問題轉交給您（詳見附件）⑱ 另外我還想跟您談談卡麥可先生到我的課堂上和學生交流的可能性。每學期我都會試著邀請一位客座講師，我認為卡麥可先生是適當的人選。期待能盡快得到您的回應。

傑森金恩　敬上

字彙 **precede** 先於 **it's one's honor to** 是某人的榮幸能～ **in person** 親自 **introductory** 入門的 **psychology** 心理學 **forward** 轉發 **semester** 學期

181. What is suggested about the book tour?
(A) All venues have a seating capacity of over 100.
(B) Invited guests will receive a copy of Mr. Carmichael's book.
(C) It will conclude on May 25.
(D) It is organized by Connelly Publishing.

針對書籍巡迴，文中提到什麼？
(A) 所有場地皆有超過 100 個座位。
(B) 受邀嘉賓將獲得卡麥可先生的書。
(C) 於 5 月 25 日結束。
(D) 由康奈利出版社籌劃。

正確答案為 **(D)**

時間表的標題為 Connelly Publishing House Presents Randy Carmichael's The Art of Daydreaming National Book Tour，因此答案選 (D)。(A) 與 (B) 文章無特別提及，最後一場巡迴時間是 May 21，(D) 不正確。

字彙　seating capacity 座位數量　conclude 結束

182. What location requires an admission fee?
(A) Jessie's Book Haven
(B) Barnes and Nomads
(C) Café Reynolds
(D) Jefferson Public Library

哪個場地需要支付入場費？
(A) 傑西的圖書避風港
(B) 巴恩斯和流浪者
(C) 咖啡雷諾德
(D) 傑佛森公共圖書館

正確答案為 **(C)**

時間表中有提到入場費的 There is a $5 advance ticket fee. Tickets sold at the door will be $8 出現在 Café Reynolds，答案為 (C)。

字彙　admission fee 入場費

183. What is the purpose of the e-mail?
(A) To give instructions about publishing a book
(B) To ask for assistance with making an arrangement
(C) To provide information on a psychology course
(D) To inquire about tours by other authors

電子郵件的目的為何？
(A) 提供出版書籍的相關說明
(B) 要求對方協助安排
(C) 提供心理學課程的資訊
(D) 詢問其他作家的巡迴

正確答案為 **(B)**

文章的目的通常會在開頭提到，不過本篇電子郵件是先讚美活動成功，才提到來信目的 I also want to speak with you about the possibility of having Mr. Carmichael visit my class to talk to my students，答案為 (B)。

字彙　instruction 說明、指示

184. What date did Mr. King meet Mr. Carmichael?
(A) May 10
(B) May 12
(C) May 16
(D) May 21

金恩先生在哪天見到卡麥可先生？
(A) 5 月 10 日
(B) 5 月 12 日
(C) 5 月 16 日
(D) 5 月 21 日

正確答案為 **(A)**

〈整合多篇文章資訊〉

電子郵件的第一句提到 I want to thank Connelly Publishing for bringing Mr. Carmichael to Tucson and for inviting me to the private reception that preceded the public event，表示他參加的是在土桑市舉辦的巡迴場次，查看時間表的日期後，可以得知答案為 (A)。

185. Who most likely is Mr. King?
(A) A textbook publisher
(B) A bookstore owner
(C) A university professor
(D) A newspaper correspondent

金恩先生最有可能是什麼人？
(A) 教科書出版商
(B) 書店老闆
(C) 大學教授
(D) 報社記者

正確答案為 (C)

電子郵件中提到 I am planning to use The Art of Daydreaming in my introductory psychology class，且金恩先生的電子郵件地址為 jasonking@tucsonuniversity.com，由這兩點可以得知答案為 (C)。

Questions 186-190 refer to the following memo, advertisement, and e-mail. 備忘錄 / 廣告 / 電子郵件

To	All Multiflex Gym Specialists
from	Donald Warren
Date	April 22
Subject	Promotion

As you know, many Dover College students stay in town during the summer, so we will be offering the yearly 30 percent summer discount for students who enroll during the first two weeks of June. However, Multiflex Gym is also considering offering two special discounts to new and continuing members during the upcoming summer season (June 1~August 1).

We would like to hear from our staff before making a final decision about the two possible offers. The first option would be to offer a family discount. This would mean that any current member could add a household member (age 16 or older) to his or her current membership for 20 percent less than the normal membership fee.

The second possible offer would be that Gold-level members could bring a friend for free from 6 A.M. until 4 P.M. on Tuesdays and Wednesdays. These friends would have access to the entire gym, including the yoga rooms. However, the driving range for golfers would be off limits to ensure that our members do not have to wait longer than they already do for their availability.

Please reply by May 3 with the promotion that you think would be most beneficial for our members.

Thank you for your help in making this decision.

Test 05

Don't Miss Out on Our Special Offers Only for Dover College Students!

Sign up between June 1 and August 1 to receive a 30% discount on your summer membership at any level and get your own personalized water bottle for free.

Bring a friend on Tuesdays and Wednesdays:
Beginning June 1, all Gold- and Platinum-level members can bring a friend for free during their fitness visits on Tuesdays and Wednesdays. Friends must sign in and show a valid ID to the receptionist to use our facilities.

Multiflex Gym

問題 186-190 題參考以下備忘錄、廣告、和電子郵件。

收件人	多方健身房的所有教練
寄件人	唐納德沃倫
日期	4 月 22 日
主旨	促銷活動

大家都知道，⑱ 夏季有許多德佛大學的學生會留在市區，因此我們將提供一年會員七折的夏季優惠給 6 月前兩週入會的學生。然而，多方健身房也考慮在即將到來的夏季（6 月 1 日至 8 月 1 日）提供新舊會員兩項特別優惠。

⑱ 在做出最後決定之前，我們想聽聽工作人員對於兩項方案的想法。第一個選項可以當做家庭優惠，也就是任何現任會員皆可以增加一名（16 歲以上）家庭成員到他原有的會員制度中，會費是 ⑱ 一般會員的八折。

第二個方案則 ⑱ 針對金級會員，他們可以在週二及週三上午 6 點到下午 4 點之間免費帶一位朋友同行。這些同行友人可以使用整個健身房，包含瑜伽教室。⑱ 不過不包含室內高爾夫練習場，這是為了保障我們的會員不要花上比原先更久的等待使用時間。

請在 5 月 3 日前回覆你認為對會員最有利的促銷活動。

謝謝各位協助我做出決定。

字彙 **specialist** 專家　**enroll** 註冊、入會　**consider** 考慮　**continuing** 連續的、續約的　**household** 家庭　**have access to** 可以使用～　**driving range** 高爾夫練習場　**beneficial** 有益的

千萬不要錯過專屬於德佛大學生的特別優惠！

在 6 月 1 日至 8 月 1 日期間，任選等級入會者，皆能享有夏季會員的七折優惠，並免費獲贈個別訂製的水瓶。

週二和週三請帶朋友過來：

⑱ 從 6 月 1 日起，所有的金級和白金級會員，皆能在週二和週三免費帶朋友上健身房。朋友必須簽名，並向櫃檯人員出示有效身分證件，便能使用我們的設施。

多方健身房

字彙 **personalized** 個人化的　**facility** 設施

To: Kevin Diego <ksukel@bvgfitness.com>
From: Bill Pullman <avelez@bvgfitness.com>
Date: August 2
Subject: Re: Numbers

Dear Kevin:

As always, thank you for sending the report. I was thrilled to see that the numbers of Gold- and Platinum-level members have each increased by 18 percent since the start of the summer promotion.

The large number of students from Dover College who have signed up for Gold-level memberships has led us to consider that we might want to offer the student discount again when classes begin in the fall. I have also heard that the fitness facility of the college is going to be remodeled over the next school year, which means students will be looking for alternative options. Even better, our main competitor is 10 kilometers farther from the school. So, we are looking into collaborating with the college to provide shuttle buses to help students get to and from the gym. This would hopefully encourage more students to choose Multiflex Gym.

I will keep you posted.

Bill Pullman, Sales Manager
Multiflex Gym Corporate Office

收件人：凱文迪亞哥 <ksukel@bvgfitness.com>
寄件人：比爾普爾曼 <avelez@bvgfitness.com>
日期：8 月 2 日
主旨：回覆：成員數

親愛的凱文：

謝謝你如往常一樣傳送報告書給我。⑱ 自從推出夏季促銷活動以來，看到金級和白金會員的數量皆增加了 18%，令我振奮不已。

大量的德佛大學生申請加入金級會員，這讓我們得考慮，是否要在秋天開學時再次提供學生優惠。⑲ 我還聽說學校的健身中心預計於下個學年重新裝修，這代表學生將會尋找其他的替代方案。更棒的是，主要競爭對手距離學校有 10 公里之遙。因此，我們正在打聽與學校合作的方法，以提供學生往返學校和健身房之間的接駁車，希望這麼做能夠鼓勵更多的學生選擇多方健身房。

我會持續跟你報告最新進展。

業務經理　比爾普爾曼
多方健身房公司辦公室

字彙　**be thrilled to** 感到興奮激動的　　**alternative** 替代的（方案）　　**farther** 更遠地　　**collaborate** 合作
to and from 往返於　　**keep posted** 持續更新消息

186. What is the purpose of the memo?
(A) To announce the hiring of new instructors
(B) To remind gym members of closing days
(C) To thank employees for their service
(D) To ask employees to give feedback

備忘錄的目的為何？
(A) 公布雇用新講師
(B) 提醒健身房會員閉館日
(C) 對員工服務表達感謝
(D) 要求員工回饋意見

正確答案為 (D)

備忘錄第二段中提到 We would like to hear from our staff before making a final decision about the two possible offers，答案為 (D)。

187. In the memo, the word "normal" in paragraph 2, line 4, is closest in meaning to
(A) standard
(B) average
(C) natural
(D) unusual

備忘錄中，第二段第四行的「normal」與下列哪一個的意思最為接近？
(A) 一般的
(B) 平均的
(C) 自然的
(D) 不尋常的

正確答案為 (A)

〈推測字義〉

normal membership fee 指「一般會員費用」，答案選 (A)。

188. What is implied about the driving range?
(A) It will be converted into yoga rooms.
(B) It has popular features.
(C) It is located in a separate building.
(D) It will be temporarily unavailable during the summer.

下列何者敘述與高爾夫練習場相符？
(A) 將被改成瑜伽教室。
(B) 受到歡迎。
(C) 位在另一棟大樓裡。
(D) 夏季暫時無法使用。

正確答案為 (B)

請在文章中找關鍵字 driving range，備忘錄提到 the driving range for golfers would be off limits to ensure that our members do not have to wait longer than they already do for their availability，提到會員使用時要等待，表示高爾夫場很受歡迎，因此答案為 (B)。

字彙　convert into 轉換成～　separate 分開的　temporarily 暫時地

189. What is indicated about Multiflex Gym?
(A) It offers free snacks on Tuesdays and Wednesdays.
(B) Every family member can get a discount.
(C) Platinum-level members can get T-shirts when they join.
(D) Many students were able to bring friends during the summer.

針對多方健身房，文中提到什麼？
(A) 週二和週三提供免費點心。
(B) 每個家庭成員都可享有優惠。
(C) 加入白金級會員可以獲贈運動衫。
(D) 夏季有許多學生帶朋友前來。

正確答案為 (D)

〈整合多篇文章資訊〉

電子郵件中寫道 the numbers of Gold- and Platinum-level members have each increased by 18 percent since the start of the summer promotion，當中 summer promotion「夏季促銷」可以對應至廣告的 all Gold-and Platinum-level members can bring a friend for free during their fitness visits on Tuesdays and Wednesdays，答案為 (D)。

190. What will probably happen at Dover College?
    (A) The sports competition will begin in the summer.
    (B) Fitness specialists will be hired.
    (C) The fitness facility will be renovated.
    (D) Fitness classes will be provided to the community.

德佛大學可能會發生什麼事？
(A) 於夏季展開體育競賽。
(B) 雇用健身教練。
(C) 重新翻修健身中心。
(D) 提供社區健身課程。

正確答案為 (C)

注意關鍵字 college 與同義詞，電子郵件提到 the fitness facility of the college is going to be remodeled over the next school year，答案為 (C)。

Questions 191-195 refer to the following advertisement and e-mails. 廣告 / 電子郵件

Come and Visit Carolina Apartments Open House

Carolina Apartments are having an open house this Friday and Saturday, March 1 and 2. After two years of construction, Carolina Apartments are almost complete. So people will be able to move in at the beginning of May. There are still more than 100 units available for purchase or rent. These include apartments with two, three, and four bedrooms. There are both furnished and unfurnished apartments available. All furnished apartments are only available to rent, though. The facilities at Carolina Apartments are top-notch, and the complex is located near outstanding schools and the main shopping district in London. Anyone is welcome to attend the open house. Tours of the available apartments will be given, and visitors will be shown around the entire building as well. Call 023-555-4321 for more information and to get directions to the open house.

問題 191-195 題參考以下廣告和兩封電子郵件。

來參加卡羅來納公寓的開放看屋活動

195 卡羅來納公寓將於本週五、六，也就是 3 月 1 日和 2 日開放看屋。193B 歷經兩年的建設後，卡羅來納公寓即將完工。預計能在 5 月初入住。目前仍有超過 100 間公寓可供購買或出租，有兩房、三房、和四房的公寓，附家具和無家具兩種都有，附家具的公寓僅限出租。卡羅來納公寓具備一流的設施，193A 位置臨近倫敦的名校和主要商圈。無論是誰都歡迎前來看屋。191 我們將提供公寓導覽服務，同時會帶訪客參觀周邊環境。請撥打 023-555-4321 了解更多資訊，並取得前往看屋的路線指示。

字彙　**open house** 開放看屋　　**unit**（公寓）一間　　**furnished** 附家具的　　**top-notch** 頂尖的、一流的
complex 複合式建築　　**shopping district** 商圈

To	inquiries@krausrealestate.com
From	teresawalters@gmail.net
Subject	Carolina Apartments
Date	March 6

To whom it may concern:

I attended the open house at the Carolina Apartments last Saturday. My sons and I were impressed with what we saw, and we have agreed that we would like to live there. We are going to move to London in June, and we intend to live in the city for the next three years. After that, I will be relocated to my company's headquarters in Manchester. That's why I am not interested in buying an apartment but would instead prefer to rent one. I would like to have a three-bedroom apartment so that each of my sons can have his own room.

I'm currently in Edinburgh, but I can arrange to fly to London whenever you need me to sign a contract. So please inform me of the availability of the apartments.

P.S. I have learned that the rent on a three-bedroom unit is £1,200 a month. Is it still in place?

Sincerely,

Teresa Walters

收件人	inquiries@krausrealestate.com
寄件人	teresawalters@gmail.net
主旨	卡羅來納公寓
日期	3 月 6 日

敬啟者：

⑲⑤ 上週六我參加了卡羅來納公寓開放看屋的活動。我跟我兒子對於看到的公寓印象深刻，一致同意要住在那裡。我們預計於 6 月搬到倫敦，打算未來 3 年住在這座城市裡。之後將搬到曼徹斯特的總公司。這就是為什麼我不打算買公寓，寧可選擇承租的原因。我想要承租三房公寓，如此我的每個兒子都可以擁有自己的房間。

雖然我現在人在愛丁堡，但我隨時可以安排飛往倫敦配合簽約。因此麻煩告訴我是否能承租公寓。

附註：據我所知，⑲③Ⓓ 三房公寓的租金為每月 **1,200** 英鎊，現在還 ⑲② 算數嗎？

泰瑞莎華特絲　敬上

字彙　**To whom it may concern** 敬啟者，為非指定信件的常見正式開頭用語　　**be impressed with** 對～印象深刻
relocate 搬遷　　**prefer** 偏好　　**sign a contract** 簽約　　**in place** 有效的、可行的

E-Mail Message

To: teresawalters@gmail.net
From: lindakraus@krausrealestate.com
Date: March 7
Subject: Re: Carolina Apartments

Dear Ms. Walters:

Thank you for inquiring about Carolina Apartments. Like you, many people are very pleased with how the apartments look, so it's one of the most popular properties in the region. Due to that fact, there are no longer any three-bedroom units available. The last three-bedroom apartment was just sold this morning. As a result, we have only a few four-bedroom apartments still available to rent. Of course, the rent for these apartments is a bit higher. It costs £600 more a month to rent a four-bedroom unit than it does to rent a three-bedroom unit. If you are still interested, please let me know immediately, and once I receive a nonrefundable payment of £100, I can reserve one for you until you are able to fly here to sign a contract. If you are no longer interested in Carolina Apartments, I can introduce you to several other properties in the same neighborhood that I'm sure you would approve of.

Regards,

Linda Kraus
Kraus Real Estate Agency

電子郵件訊息

收件人：teresawalters@gmail.net
寄件人：lindakraus@krausrealestate.com
日期： 3 月 7 日
主旨： 回覆：卡羅來納公寓

親愛的華特絲小姐：

感謝您詢問卡羅來納公寓。很多人像您一樣，對公寓的外觀相當滿意，因此它是該地區最受歡迎的房子之一。也因為這樣，目前已經租不到三房公寓了。今天上午才剛賣掉最後一間三房公寓，因此我們只剩幾間四房公寓可供出租，而這幾間公寓的租金當然會稍高一些。193D 與三房公寓相比，四房公寓的租金每月會多 600 英鎊。如果您仍有興趣承租，請盡快通知我。194 一旦我收到不可退款的訂金 100 英鎊，便會為您預留公寓到您飛來簽約。如果您對卡羅來納公寓不再有興趣的話，我可以為您介紹同個社區其他您應該會滿意的房子。

克勞斯房屋仲介公司　琳達克勞斯

 字彙　**nonrefundable** 不可退款的　　**reserve** 保留　　**real estate agency** 不動產仲介

191. According to the advertisement, what will happen at the event?
(A) **Visitors will be given tours.**
(B) A film will be shown to the public.
(C) Contracts will be signed.
(D) Negotiations will be conducted.

根據廣告所述，活動中會發生什麼事？
(A) **提供訪客導覽服務。**
(B) 公開放映電影。
(C) 簽署合約。
(D) 進行協商。

正確答案為 **(A)**

廣告文中寫到 Tours of the available apartments will be given，因此答案要選 (A)。

192. In the first e-mail, the word "in place" in P.S., is closest in meaning to
(A) appropriate
(B) invalid
(C) efficient
(D) **good**

第一封電子郵件的附註中，「in place」與下列何者意思最為接近？
(A) 適合的
(B) 無效的
(C) 有效率的
(D) **有效的**

正確答案為 **(D)**

〈推測字義〉
Is it still in place? 一句中，it 指的是前一句的 rent，意思為此租金現在是否還有效，因此答案選 (D)。**形容詞 good 搭配合約書或條件使用時，意思為「有效的」。**

字彙　**appropriate** 合適的　**invalid** 無效的、失效的　**efficient** 有效率的　**good** 有效的

193. What is NOT mentioned about Carolina Apartments?
(A) It is conveniently located near a school.
(B) It is currently being constructed.
(C) **It is a twenty-story building.**
(D) Its rent for a four-bedroom apartment is £1,800.

針對卡羅來納公寓，何者文中並未提及？
(A) 鄰近學校，交通方便。
(B) 目前正在建設中。
(C) **它是一棟 20 層樓的建築。**
(D) 四房公寓的租金為 1,800 英鎊。

正確答案為 **(C)**

廣告文中提到 the complex is located near outstanding schools 和 After two years of construction, Carolina Apartments are almost complete，提到 (A) 和 (B)。第一封電子郵件中寫道 the rent on a three-bedroom unit is £1,200 a month，而第二封電子郵件中寫道 It costs £600 more a month to rent a four-bedroom unit than it does to rent a three-bedroom unit，由此可以算出四房公寓的租金為 1,800 英鎊。文中並未提到 (C)。

194. What does Ms. Kraus suggest to Ms. Walters?
(A) **Paying a fee to guarantee that she gets an apartment**
(B) Flying to London this coming weekend
(C) Considering buying an apartment instead of renting one
(D) Getting a smaller apartment for a lower price

克勞斯小姐向華特絲小姐提出什麼建議？
(A) **付費以確保她能取得一間公寓**
(B) 這個週末飛往倫敦
(C) 考慮買下公寓，而非承租
(D) 以較低的價格購買較小的公寓

正確答案為 **(A)**

第二封電子郵件中寫道 once I receive a nonrefundable payment of £100, I can reserve one for you until you are able to fly here to sign a contract，因此答案為 (A)。

195. What is implied about Ms. Walters?
(A) **She visited to the Open House on March 2nd.**
(B) She has already sent her rental fee to Ms. Kraus.
(C) She is moving into a three-bedroom apartment next month.
(D) She is relocating to Manchester in two years.

下列敘述何者與華特絲小姐相符？
(A) **她於 3 月 2 日參加開放看屋活動。**
(B) 她已支付租金給克勞斯小姐。
(C) 下個月她將搬進一間三房公寓。
(D) 兩年內她將搬到曼徹斯特。

正確答案為 **(A)**

〈整合多篇文章資訊〉
廣告文中寫道 Carolina Apartments are having an open house this Friday and Saturday, March 1 and 2，而電子郵件中寫道 I attended the open house at the Carolina Apartments last Saturday，因此答案選 (A)。

Test 05

Questions 196-200 refer to the following flyer, Web page, and letter. 傳單 / 網頁 / 信件

PLEASE SUPPORT THE STEWART DANCE COMPANY.

The Stewart Dance Company has been at the forefront of Australian Dance for 40 years. We offer great variety in repertoire and present more than 100 performances annually. To enable us to keep up the good work, your help is needed. Your financial support will allow us to maintain low ticket prices and keep dance performances accessible to everyone.

When you give to the Stewart Dance Company, we give back to you. The more you give, the more we return. For a complete list of our membership program, visit our Web site, www.stewartdancecompany.com. You can also view our performance schedule for this year.

問題 196-200 題參考以下傳單、網頁、和信件。

請資助史都華舞蹈公司。

40 年來，史都華舞蹈公司一直站在澳大利亞舞蹈界的第一線。我們提供 **197** 各式各樣的演出節目，每年舉辦超過一百場的表演。為了讓我們能夠繼續提供優質演出，我們需要您的幫助。**196** 您經濟上的支持，能讓我們維持低票價，並確保每個人都能看到舞蹈表演。

若您願意資助史都華舞蹈公司，我們會回饋給您。您給得越多，我們就能回饋越多。欲了解完整的會員制度表，請上我們的網站 www.stewartdancecompany.com，也能查看今年的節目時間表。

字彙 | **forefront** 最前線 **repertoire** 表演節目單 **present** 呈現 **annually** 每年 **keep up** 保持
financial 經濟上的 **maintain** 維持 **accessible** 可接近的、可得到的

www.stewartdancecompany.com

| Our history | Schedule | **Membership Program** | Contact |

Silver $49

<u>Benefits</u>: Receive tickets to our weekend matinee performances once a month, and a one-year subscription to the dance magazine *Movement* (published four times a year).

Gold $99

<u>Benefits</u>: Receive tickets to our weekend matinee performances once a month, a 20% discount on all weekday evening performances and a one-year subscription to the dance magazine *Movement*.

Platinum $199

<u>Benefits</u>: Receive Gold-level benefits, specially reserved seating, tickets to opening night performances, and the opportunity to dine with renowned choreographer Tom Roman, who directed the performance for our award-winning modern dance, *Dubliners*, at the annual Stewart Dance Company banquet.

You can send your donation to Elena Gibson, fund-raising manager, Stewart Dance Company, 199 Chestnut Street, Sydney.

www.stewartdancecompany.com

| 我們的故事 | 時間表 | **會員制度** | 聯絡我們 |

銀級　49 美元

福利：每月會收到一次白天場的表演門票、以及為期一年的舞蹈雜誌 ⑳ 《舞動》（每年出刊四次）。

⑲ **金級　99 美元**

福利：每月會收到一次白天場的表演門票，平日晚間表演皆可享有八折優惠，以及為期一年的舞蹈雜誌《舞動》。

⑲ **白金級　199 美元**

福利：享受與金級會員同等的福利，還有專屬指定座位、⑲ 首演夜的表演門票、並有機會 ⑲ 在史都華舞蹈公司的年度晚會，與指導獲獎的現代舞《都柏林人》的知名編舞家湯姆羅曼一同用餐。

您可以將捐款寄到雪梨市栗樹街 199 號史都華舞蹈公司，給募款經理艾琳娜吉普森。

字彙　**matinee** 白天場　**reserved** 預訂的、預留的　**dine** 用餐　**choreographer** 編舞家　**direct** 指導、指揮
award-winning 獲獎的　**donation** 捐獻

199 Chestnut Street, Sydney

Dear Ms. Gibson:

As always, it is pleasure that I have the opportunity to support the Stewart Dance Company this year. I have enclosed a donation in the same amount of $199 as last year.

My colleagues, Karen Myers and Justin Copperfield, who are currently working in our travel agency, showed interest in supporting the Stewart Dance Company. They will contact you in the near future and you will be receiving donations of $99 from both of them.

I will definitely attend the Stewart Dance Company's banquet this year since I had a great time in joining last year's event. I look forward to another season of fine performances.

Yours sincerely,

Amy Hollister
Hollister Travel
187 Howell St. Birmingham, Sydney

雪梨市栗樹街 199 號

親愛的吉普森小姐：

一如既往，我很高興今年也有機會支持史都華舞蹈公司，**199** **200C** 隨信附上與去年相同金額的捐款 199 美元。

199 **200A** **200C** 目前在我們旅行社工作的同事凱倫麥爾和賈斯丁科波菲爾表示有興趣資助史都華舞蹈公司。不久之後他們會與您聯繫，您將會收到兩份 99 美元的捐款。

200B 我去年參加活動相當開心，所以今年我一定會參加史都華舞蹈公司的宴會，我很期待這一季的精彩表演。

霍利斯特旅遊
艾咪霍利斯特
雪梨市豪威爾街伯明罕 187 號

字彙　**colleague** 同事　**currently** 現在　**travel agency** 旅行社　**in the near future** 不久後　**attend** 參與

196. What is the main purpose of the flyer?
(A) To encourage people to go to dance performances
(B) To ask the public for donations
(C) To announce a release of a new dance magazine
(D) To invite people to an awards ceremony

傳單的主要目的為何？
(A) 鼓勵人們參加舞蹈表演
(B) 向大眾募款
(C) 宣布發行新的舞蹈雜誌
(D) 邀請人們參加頒獎典禮

正確答案為 (B)

文章目的可以在文章開頭中找到。傳單第一段中提到 Your financial support will allow us to maintain low ticket prices and keep dance performances accessible to everyone，因此答案為 (B)。

197. In the flyer, the word "variety" in paragraph 1, line 2, is closest in meaning to
(A) diversity
(B) difference
(C) entertainment
(D) change

傳單第一段第二行的「variety」與下列何者意思最為接近？
(A) 多樣性
(B) 差異
(C) 娛樂
(D) 變化

正確答案為 (A)

〈推測字義〉
offer great variety in 的意思為「提供各式各樣的～」，因此答案為 (A)。

字彙　**diversity** 多樣性

198. What is implied about the Stewart Dance Company?
(A) It runs a dance performance twice every day.
(B) It recently hired a choreographer, Tom Roman.
(C) It hosts a banquet every year.
(D) It will hold a performance to raise funds.

下列敘述何者與史都華舞蹈公司相符？
(A) 每天舉行兩次的舞蹈表演。
(B) 最近雇用了一位編舞家湯姆羅曼。
(C) 每年都會舉行宴會。
(D) 將要舉辦募資活動。

正確答案為 (C)

網頁上寫道 the annual Stewart Dance Company banquet，annual 表示「年度的」，可以得知答案為 (C)。

199. What benefits will Ms. Hollister receive that Ms. Myers will not?
(A) Discounted admission prices
(B) Free tickets to opening-night performances
(C) A subscription to a magazine
(D) Tickets to weekend matinee performances

霍利斯特小姐享有，麥爾小姐沒有的福利為何？
(A) 入場費優惠
(B) 首演夜表演的免費門票
(C) 雜誌訂閱
(D) 週末白天場的表演門票

正確答案為 (B)

〈整合多篇文章資訊〉
請從文章中找到這兩個名字，信件中提到 I have enclosed a donation in the same amount of $199 as last year，表示霍利斯特小姐為白金級會員；以及 they will contact you in the near future and you will be receiving donations of $99 from both of them，表示麥爾小姐為金級會員。查看網頁中金級會員和白金級會員的差別，會發現兩種會員皆有週末白天場的表演門票，但是首演夜的表演門票是白金會員的專屬福利，因此答案要選 (B)。

200. What is NOT true about Ms. Hollister?
  (A) She is working with Ms. Myers.
  (B) She has attended the Stewart Dance Company's banquet before.
  (C) She donates more money than Mr. Copperfield.
  (D) She will receive the magazine *Movement* every month.

針對霍利斯特小姐的敘述，下列何者有誤？
  (A) 她和麥爾小姐一起工作。
  (B) 她曾參加過史都華舞蹈公司的宴會。
  (C) 她比科波菲爾先生捐更多錢。
  (D) 她每個月都會收到《舞動》雜誌。

正確答案為 (D)

信件中寫道 My colleagues, Karen Myers and Justin Copperfield，符合 (A)；since I had a great time in joining last year's event 符合 (B)；I have enclosed a donation in the same amount of $199 as last year 和 you will be receiving donations of $99 from both of them 可以對應至 (C)。根據網頁內容，《舞動》雜誌一年只發行四次，因此答案選 (D)。

Actual Test 1 字彙 & 片語

- **a good value at**
  價格划算
- **Absolutely.**
  （表贊同語氣）當然。
- **accept**
  接受、同意
- **access**
  取得、到達
- **accommodate**
  接納、容納
- **accommodation**
  住宿
- **accordingly**
  依照、相應地
- **accurate**
  精確的
- **addition**
  添加、增加物
- **address the issue**
  解決問題
- **address**
  演講、對～說話、處理
- **adequate**
  充足的
- **admission fee**
  入場費
- **advancement**
  晉升
- **advantage**
  優點
- **advertise**
  刊登廣告、宣傳
- **advice**
  建議
- **advisor**
  顧問
- **afford**
  負擔得起
- **affordable**
  價格實惠的
- **agreement**
  協議、協定
- **ahead of time**
  提早
- **ahead of**
  提前
- **aid**
  幫助、援助
- **allegedly**
  據說
- **alternative**
  替代的
- **ambitious**
  有野心的
- **amenities**
  便利設施
- **analyze**
  分析
- **apologize**
  致歉

- **appeal**
  提出訴求、異議
- **appealing**
  吸引人的
- **appliance**
  家電
- **applicant**
  申請者
- **apply for**
  申請
- **apply to**
  適用於、應用於
- **appointment**
  任命
- **appreciate**
  感激
- **approach**
  方法
- **appropriate**
  適當的、恰當的
- **approve**
  核准、通過
- **arrange**
  安排、擺放
- **art gallery**
  畫廊
- **artwork**
  藝術作品
- **as chance would have it**
  湊巧、碰巧
- **as stated**
  如上所示、按照規定
- **as usual**
  照例、一如往常
- **as well**
  也、同樣地
- **assignment**
  分配、任務
- **at no charge**
  免費
- **attend**
  參加
- **attendant**
  服務員
- **attendee**
  參加者
- **attraction**
  觀光景點
- **attribute**
  特質
- **audit**
  審計
- **automatically**
  自動地
- **available**
  有空的；可用的
- **award**
  獎

- **award-winning**
  得獎的
- **away from**
  遠離
- **baggage claim tag**
  行李提領標籤
- **ban**
  禁止
- **banner**
  橫布條、橫幅標語
- **based on**
  基於
- **be advised to**
  被建議
- **be aware that**
  意識到、知道
- **be elevated to**
  晉升到（某職位）
- **be eligible for**
  符合～的條件
- **be involved in**
  涉及到～
- **be known as**
  以～著稱、被稱作～
- **be known for**
  因～而聞名
- **be likely to**
  有可能～
- **be nominated as**
  被提名為、獲選為
- **be prone to**
  易～的
- **be referred to**
  被推薦
- **be transferred to**
  轉調到
- **be unclear about**
  不確定
- **be up to**
  準備好～
- **be willing to**
  樂意、願意
- **behavior**
  行為
- **behind schedule**
  進度落後
- **benefit**
  有益的
- **bid on**
  投標、競價
- **bill**
  帳單
- **bitter**
  嚴寒刺骨的
- **blame**
  責備
- **blizzard**
  暴風雪
- **bottom line**
  底線、最重要的點

- **branch**
  （公司）分行
- **break down**
  故障
- **browse**
  瀏覽
- **budget**
  預算
- **bulletin board**
  公布欄
- **bundle**
  優惠方案
- **business day**
  營業日
- **business district**
  商業區
- **by-law**
  章程、細則
- **café**
  簡餐廳
- **calculate**
  計算
- **campaign**
  宣傳活動
- **cancel**
  取消
- **candidate**
  應徵者、候選人
- **catering**
  餐飲、外燴
- **cathedral**
  大教堂
- **CEO**
  執行長
- **chain**
  連鎖店
- **challenging**
  具挑戰性的
- **charge**
  收費；費用
- **charger**
  充電器
- **charity**
  慈善事業
- **check**
  帳單
- **chief**
  （階級、職務上）首領、首長
- **civic**
  市民的
- **civil engineer**
  土木工程師
- **claim**
  聲稱、主張
- **closing address**
  閉幕演講
- **colleague**
  同事
- **combination**
  組合

- **combine**
  結合～
- **commercial**
  商業的、營利的
- **common space**
  公共空間
- **community**
  社區
- **compare to**
  與～相比
- **competent**
  能幹的、稱職的
- **complaint**
  抱怨
- **complete range**
  完整產品種類
- **complete**
  完成、完畢
- **completion**
  完成
- **complex**
  複合式建築
- **complimentary**
  贈送的、免費的
- **composed of**
  由～組成
- **condominium**
  公寓
- **conduct an interview**
  進行採訪
- **confusion**
  混亂
- **connecting flight**
  轉機
- **consider**
  考慮
- **consult**
  諮詢、查閱
- **consumer survey**
  消費者問卷調查
- **container**
  容器、貨櫃
- **content**
  內容
- **contract**
  合約
- **contribution**
  貢獻
- **convene**
  召集
- **convert**
  轉換
- **convincing**
  有說服力的、令人信服的
- **cooling**
  冷卻
- **corporate**
  企業的

- **cost reduction**
  降低成本
- **counter**
  櫃檯
- **coupon**
  優惠券
- **courteous**
  彬彬有禮的、謙恭的
- **cousin**
  表或堂兄弟
- **cover**
  代理職務
- **coverage**
  （保險、賠償）涵蓋範圍
- **craft**
  精巧地製作、打造
- **craftspeople**
  工藝家
- **critic**
  評論家
- **crowded**
  擁擠的
- **current**
  目前的
- **currently**
  目前
- **customarily**
  通常、習慣上、照例
- **customize**
  量身訂做
- **customized**
  客製化的
- **damage**
  損害
- **deadline**
  截止日、交件日
- **dealer**
  經銷商
- **decade**
  十年
- **decision committee**
  決策委員會
- **decoration**
  裝飾
- **defer**
  延後、延期
- **definitely**
  當然、肯定地
- **degree**
  度
- **deliver the message**
  傳遞訊息
- **delivery**
  運送
- **depart**
  離開、出發
- **department**
  部門
- **depend on**
  根據、取決於

- **dependent**
  依靠的
- **deposit**
  支付押金；存款
- **description**
  說明
- **deserve**
  應得、值得
- **deterioration**
  惡化、退化
- **development**
  開發（案）；發展
- **device**
  裝置
- **dietary request**
  餐飲要求
- **directly**
  馬上、立刻
- **discard**
  丟棄
- **disregard**
  忽視
- **disrespectful**
  無禮的、不敬的
- **distribute**
  發行、發放、分配
- **district**
  區域、地方
- **do one's banking**
  辦理銀行業務
- **doctorate**
  博士學位
- **doubt**
  懷疑
- **draft**
  草稿
- **drop**
  將～排除在外、放棄
- **dual**
  雙的、雙倍的
- **economical**
  實惠的
- **efficiently**
  有效地
- **elaborate**
  精心製作的、精巧的
- **elect**
  選舉
- **election**
  選舉
- **electrical grid**
  供電系統
- **embark on**
  著手、開始
- **emphasize**
  強調
- **employee handbook**
  員工手冊

- **enclose**
  隨信附上
- **ensure**
  保證
- **enterprise**
  企業、公司
- **entrance fee**
  入場費
- **equipped with**
  配有
- **establish**
  建立、設立
- **estimate**
  估價、估計
- **evaluation**
  評價
- **eviction**
  逐出
- **exclusive right**
  獨家授權
- **exclusive**
  獨有的、獨家的
- **executive**
  主管；執行單位
- **existing**
  目前的、現有的
- **exit**
  離開
- **expect**
  期待、預期
- **expectation**
  期待、預期
- **expense**
  支出、開銷
- **expire**
  到期
- **express shipping**
  快遞
- **expulsion**
  開除、退學
- **extend**
  延伸、擴展、擴大
- **extensive**
  整體的、廣泛的
- **extremely**
  非常、極其
- **facade**
  正面、外觀
- **facility**
  設備、設施
- **faculty**
  師資
- **family matter**
  家庭事務
- **fare**
  車資
- **feasibility**
  可行性
- **feature**
  特點；以～為特色；專題報導

- **feedback**
  回饋意見
- **feet**
  英呎
- **fill in for**
  替～輪班、遞補～
- **fill out**
  填寫
- **finalize**
  最終確定、定案
- **financial**
  財務金融的、經濟上的
- **firm**
  公司
- **flight crew**
  機組人員
- **floor plan**
  平面圖、藍圖
- **fog**
  霧
- **follow up**
  追蹤、繼續進行
- **food wrapper**
  食品包裝
- **footbridge**
  人行橋、天橋
- **for a day or two**
  一到兩天
- **forecast**
  天氣預報，當動詞時三態同型
- **formally**
  正式地、形式上
- **formerly**
  過去、以前
- **forthcoming**
  即將來臨的
- **found**
  創立、建立
- **foundation**
  基金會
- **frequency**
  頻率、次數
- **garbage pickup**
  收垃圾
- **gem**
  寶石、珍寶
- **general public**
  一般大眾
- **general**
  一般的、普遍的
- **generalization**
  一般化
- **generalize**
  使～一般化
- **generally**
  通常、一般地
- **get back to**
  再聯絡、回覆
- **get over**
  去到（遠方）、跨越～

- **go through**
  通過
- **gradually**
  逐漸地
- **grant**
  補助金
- **grassy area**
  草地
- **pile**
  一堆
- **ground rule**
  基本法則
- **handle**
  處理、負責
- **happen to**
  偶然
- **hardware store**
  五金行
- **hassle**
  麻煩、麻煩的狀況
- **have good access to**
  接近～
- **hazard**
  隱憂、潛在危險
- **head to**
  前往
- **help oneself to**
  自行取用（食物等）
- **historical**
  歷史有關的
- **hit**
  打擊
- **honor**
  向～致敬、尊敬
- **housekeeping**
  客房部、客房服務
- **housing cost**
  住屋費用
- **identification card**
  識別證；身分證
- **illegal**
  非法的
- **impact**
  影響、衝擊
- **implement**
  實施、執行
- **improvement**
  改善
- **in ~ condition**
  處在～狀況
- **in detail**
  詳細地
- **in line with**
  與～一致
- **in person**
  親自
- **in place**
  準備就緒的
- **in the distance**
  遠處

- incentive
  獎勵
- inconvenience
  不便
- inconvenient
  不便的
- individual
  個人的、個別的
- individually
  個別地
- industrial-grade
  工業等級的
- inexpensive
  廉價的
- incomplete
  不完全的
- in-flight magazine
  機上雜誌
- influx
  流入
- in-house
  公司專屬的、內部的
- initial
  最初的
- inquire about
  詢問、打聽
- inspect
  檢查
- institution
  機構
- Internet service provider
  網路服務供應業者
- interrupt
  打斷、中斷
- interruption
  中斷
- introductory course
  入門課程
- invaluable
  貴重的
- invoice
  發票
- issue
  發行、發給
- itemize
  逐條列明
- itinerary
  活動日程表
- jar
  寬口罐
- job description
  職務說明
- join
  加入、參加
- jot down
  概略寫下、草草記下
- journalist
  記者、新聞工作者

- keen
  敏捷的、敏銳的
- keep a close eye on
  密切關注～
- keynote address
  主題演講
- knowledgeable
  博學多聞的
- lab equipment
  實驗室設備
- landmark
  地標、里程碑
- lead through
  通往
- lead to
  導致、引起
- lease
  租約
- leave ~ behind
  留下～、遺留
- lecture
  講座、講課
- length
  長度
- local
  當地的
- lodge
  小屋、山莊
- lodging
  房舍、住宿的地方
- look through
  瀏覽
- maintain
  維持
- maintenance
  維護
- make a copy
  複製、備份
- make an exception
  破例
- make sure to
  務必、確保
- malfunction
  故障
- manual
  使用手冊、說明書
- manually
  手動地
- manufacture
  大量生產、製造
- manufacturer
  製造商
- manufacturing
  製造業
- mark
  紀念、標記、記號
- marvel
  奇蹟
- massive
  大量的

- mayor
  市長
- mechanical
  機械方面的
- meet needs
  滿足需求
- memo
  備忘錄、內部通知
- merchandise
  商品
- minimize
  使～降到最低
- minus
  零下的
- moderate
  溫和的、中等的
- modification
  修改
- moisture
  濕氣
- monthly rates
  月租
- mural
  壁畫
- nationwide
  全國性的
- nearby
  附近的
- negative effect
  負面影響
- newsletter
  時事通訊
- not A until B
  直到 B 才 A
- notify
  通知
- nuisance
  麻煩事
- number
  （數量）多達
- despite
  （介系詞）儘管
- obediently
  順從地
- object
  物件
- of interest
  對～感興趣的
- on behalf of
  代表
- on display
  展示中
- on leave
  休假中
- on the road
  旅行或移動途中
- once
  一旦
- opponent
  對手

- optical
  光學的
- option
  選項
- organize
  組織、籌劃
- original
  原本的
- ornate
  華麗的、裝飾的
- out of town
  （因出差等）不在、出遠門
- outage
  斷電
- outreach
  推廣服務（活動）
- outstanding
  傑出的
- overcome
  克服
- overlook
  俯瞰、眺望
- overseas
  海外地、海外的
- package
  方案
- paper feed
  （影印機）送紙匣
- parasol
  陽傘
- parking meter
  停車計時器
- parking spot
  停車位
- partially
  部分地
- pass along
  傳遞、轉達
- pass on
  傳承
- pass
  通行票券
- passenger
  旅客
- payment
  付款
- payroll
  工資單
- peak season
  旺季
- penalty
  罰鍰
- pending
  待辦的、未決定的
- per person
  每一人
- permission
  許可
- permit
  許可、准許

- personnel
  人事
- pharmaceutical
  製藥的
- phase
  階段
- place an order
  訂購、下單
- plant
  工廠
- plasterwork
  石膏製品
- point out
  指出
- point to
  指向
- policy
  政策、方針
- position
  職位
- post
  張貼、告示
- postpone
  延後
- potential
  可能性、潛力
- practical
  實用的、實際的
- precise
  精確的
- preciseness
  精確、嚴謹
- precision
  精確度、精準
- prepaid
  預付的
- preregistered
  提前登記的
- present
  提出、出示
- presentation
  上台報告
- preserve
  保存
- president
  總裁、董事長
- press release
  新聞稿、聲明稿
- price range
  價位
- pricing agreement
  價格協議
- prime
  主要的
- prior to
  在～之前
- privilege
  特權
- proceeds
  收入、收益

829

- **process**
  處理
- **produce**
  農產品
- **productive**
  有生產力的、有成效的
- **prohibit**
  阻止、禁止
- **promising**
  有希望的、有前途的
- **promote**
  推銷、晉升
- **promotion**
  促銷宣傳；晉升
- **promotional strategy**
  促銷策略
- **promotional**
  促銷的
- **promptly**
  立即地
- **property**
  不動產、財產
- **proposal**
  提案
- **publication**
  出版物
- **publicize**
  公布
- **purchase**
  購買、購買之物
- **qualify for**
  符合資格
- **questionnaire**
  問卷調查
- **raise the capital**
  籌募資金
- **rate**
  評等、評價；費用
- **rather than**
  寧可～也不願
- **raw material**
  原物料
- **reach**
  聯繫、聯絡
- **reception**
  歡迎會；接受
- **recognize**
  認可、肯定
- **recommend**
  推薦
- **record**
  創記錄
- **recruit**
  新成員；招募、招聘
- **reduced price**
  優惠價格
- **reflect**
  反射、倒映

- **refrigeration**
  冷凍、冷藏
- **refund**
  退款
- **regarding**
  關於
- **regional**
  地區的
- **regionally**
  區域性地
- **register**
  報名、註冊
- **regular customer**
  常客
- **reimbursement**
  核銷、報公帳
- **reject the claim**
  駁回主張
- **relaxing**
  令人放鬆的
- **relay**
  傳達
- **release**
  推出、發行
- **relevant**
  相關的
- **relocation**
  搬遷
- **remind**
  提醒
- **remote**
  偏遠的
- **remove**
  移除
- **renovate**
  改建
- **renowned**
  知名的
- **rent**
  租金
- **rental agreement**
  租賃合約
- **repeat business**
  再次光臨
- **repeatedly**
  反覆地
- **repetitive**
  重複的
- **replace**
  替代
- **replacement**
  替換品、替代
- **represent**
  代表
- **representative of**
  代表～的
- **representative**
  有代表性的
- **reserve**
  預約

- **residence**
  居住地
- **resident**
  居民
- **residential**
  住宅的
- **resolve**
  解決
- **resource room**
  資料室
- **restoration**
  修復
- **restorative**
  恢復的
- **restore**
  修復
- **retirement**
  退休
- **retreat**
  靜修會（指工作期間的休閒聚會）；撤退
- **retrieve**
  取回
- **return one's favor**
  回報某人恩惠
- **returning student**
  在學生，泛指新生之外的在學生
- **review**
  評論、評價；查看
- **revise**
  修正、修改
- **revised**
  修訂的
- **revive**
  復興、復甦
- **round-trip**
  往返
- **run**
  行經；營運
- **runway**
  飛機跑道
- **sales figures**
  銷售數字
- **satellite**
  衛星
- **sb. be off**
  某人不在、離開的
- **scarcely**
  幾乎不
- **scenery**
  風景、景色
- **scenic**
  風景優美
- **schedule**
  排定
- **screen**
  篩選
- **seating**
  座席、座位

- **secure the right to**
  確保權利
- **security deposit**
  保證金
- **select**
  選擇、挑選
- **seminar**
  研討會
- **session**
  （一系列）課程
- **set up an appointment**
  安排會面
- **set up**
  建立、設立
- **sewer**
  下水道
- **sewing factory**
  縫紉工廠
- **shareholder**
  股東
- **shift**
  輪班
- **ship**
  運送
- **shore**
  岸邊
- **shoreline**
  海岸線
- **shortage**
  缺乏
- **shortly**
  立即、馬上
- **shove around**
  推來推去
- **showcase**
  作品展示
- **shut down**
  關閉、停工
- **sign a contract**
  簽訂合約
- **sign up (for)**
  申請、報名
- **significant**
  重要的
- **significance**
  意義、重要性
- **signify**
  意味著
- **similarly**
  相似地
- **since**
  自從
- **sincere apology**
  誠摯道歉
- **situated**
  位於～的
- **skillful**
  熟練的

- **so far**
  到目前為止、目前
- **solicit**
  徵求、請求給予
- **souvenir**
  紀念品
- **specialize in**
  擅長、專門做
- **specify**
  詳細說明
- **speculation**
  推測、猜測
- **spokesperson**
  發言人
- **sponsorship**
  贊助、資助
- **staff lounge**
  員工休息室
- **stand**
  攤子、攤位
- **state-of-the-art**
  最先進的
- **status**
  狀態
- **strategy**
  策略
- **stream**
  流出、流經
- **striking**
  顯著的、突出的
- **sturdy**
  結實的、堅固的
- **submit**
  提交、繳交
- **subscriber**
  訂戶
- **suit**
  適合
- **suitable**
  合適的
- **suite**
  套房
- **summon**
  召集
- **sunbathe**
  做日光浴
- **supervisor**
  主管
- **supplies**
  補給品、日用品
- **surface**
  表面
- **suspend**
  暫時中止
- **suspension**
  暫停、中斷
- **sweeping**
  徹底的、廣泛的
- **take a step**
  採取措施訂戶

- **take action**
  採取行動

- **take advantage of**
  利用

- **take notes**
  做筆記

- **take off**
  起飛、出發

- **take on**
  承擔（工作）

- **take place**
  發生；舉行

- **technician**
  技術人員

- **tenant**
  承租人、房客

- **terms of the contract**
  合約條件

- **That makes two of us.**
  我也是這麼認為。

- **this month's issue**
  本月號

- **thoroughly**
  徹底地

- **throughout**
  遍及；從頭到尾

- **time off**
  休假

- **time-consuming**
  耗時的

- **tolerate**
  忍受、默許

- **tough**
  困難的

- **tour agency**
  旅遊業者

- **trade agreement**
  貿易協定

- **traffic congestion**
  交通堵塞

- **trail**
  小徑

- **training center**
  訓練中心

- **transfer from A to B**
  從 A 轉（帳）到 B

- **transfer**
  調任

- **transport**
  移動、運送

- **treasured**
  珍貴的

- **treasury**
  財政部

- **trial**
  審判、試驗

- **tunnel**
  隧道

- **turn in**
  繳交

- **ultimate**
  最終的

- **unacceptable**
  不能接受的

- **undecided**
  未定的

- **under negotiation**
  談判中、協商中

- **under warranty**
  保固內

- **undergo**
  歷經

- **understandable**
  可以理解的、合乎情理的

- **undertake**
  從事、承擔

- **uniquely**
  獨特地

- **unit**
  小機器、機件

- **upkeep**
  維修保養

- **used to**
  曾做過～

- **utility**
  公共設施（水電等）相關費用

- **valid**
  有效的

- **vary**
  多樣

- **vendor**
  攤販、商人

- **venue**
  活動地點

- **verify**
  確認

- **violence**
  暴力

- **virtually**
  事實上、幾乎

- **volunteer**
  自願、義務去做

- **wade**
  涉水而行

- **wait tables**
  餐廳服務生上餐

- **waive the fee**
  減免收費

- **wide range of**
  各式各樣的

- **with conditions**
  有條件地

- **workflow**
  工作流程

- **working order**
  正常運轉狀態

- **workload**
  工作量

- **yet**
  已經（用於疑問句）；還、仍然（用於否定句）

- **You bet.**
  當然。（贊同許可之意）

831

- **a handful of**
  少數的
- **a shortage of**
  短缺～的
- **abruptly**
  突然地
- **access**
  使用
- **accessible**
  易接近的；可進入的
- **accessory**
  配件
- **accompany**
  伴隨、陪同
- **accountant**
  會計師
- **achieve**
  達成
- **acquire**
  收購
- **acquisition**
  收購
- **additional**
  額外的
- **administration**
  管理、行政業務
- **admission**
  入場、入會
- **admit**
  承認
- **advance ticket**
  預售票
- **affect**
  影響
- **agree with**
  同意～看法
- **agriculture**
  農業
- **aircraft**
  飛機
- **airfare**
  飛機票價
- **aisle**
  走道
- **alert**
  警報
- **all year around**
  一整年
- **alleviate**
  減輕、緩解
- **alongside**
  並肩、在旁邊
- **alter**
  更改、修改
- **analysis report**
  分析報
- **angle**
  角度
- **anniversary**
  紀念日

- **announce**
  宣布、公布
- **annual**
  年度
- **appeal**
  呼籲、訴求
- **appealing**
  吸引人的
- **appoint**
  任命
- **approaching**
  接近的
- **approval**
  許可
- **approximate**
  大約的
- **approximately**
  大約地
- **approximation**
  近似值
- **apron**
  圍裙
- **architect**
  建築師
- **architecture**
  建築
- **as to**
  至於、說到
- **aside from**
  除～以外
- **assembly**
  裝配
- **asset**
  資產
- **assist sb. in sth.**
  協助某人做某事
- **assistant**
  助理
- **astronaut**
  宇宙航行員
- **at all times**
  隨時
- **at will**
  隨意
- **athlete**
  運動員、選手
- **attach**
  連接、使附著；隨信附上
- **attempt to**
  試圖
- **attractive**
  有吸引力的
- **auction**
  拍賣
- **audit findings report**
  審計結果報告
- **auditorium**
  禮堂

- **available**
  可購買的、可使用的
- **awards ceremony**
  頒獎典禮
- **aware of**
  意識到
- **baked**
  烘焙的
- **be capable of**
  有能力去～的、能勝任～的
- **be committed to**
  致力於
- **be compatible with**
  與～相容
- **be considered**
  被納入考慮
- **be entitled to**
  有～的資格
- **be exposed to**
  暴露於～
- **be good for**
  利於、有益於
- **be interested in**
  感興趣、有意願
- **be limited to**
  僅限於
- **be located**
  位於
- **be opened to the public**
  對大眾開放
- **be pleased to**
  樂於、對～感到高興
- **be reluctant to**
  不願意、不情願做～
- **be satisfied with**
  對～感到滿足的
- **be supposed to**
  應該
- **beneath**
  在～下方
- **between A and B**
  介於 A、B 之間
- **beverage**
  飲料
- **billing mistake**
  帳單錯誤
- **blockbuster**
  賣座電影
- **board chair**
  董事會主席
- **board of directors**
  董事會
- **board**
  搭乘（車、船、飛機）
- **book reviewer**
  書評家
- **bound for**
  開往

- **brainstorming**
  腦力激盪、集思廣益
- **broadcast**
  廣播
- **broadcasting station**
  廣播電台
- **broadly**
  概括地
- **brochure**
  （廣告）小冊子
- **budget reduction**
  預算刪減
- **bulk order**
  大宗訂單、大量訂購
- **by oneself**
  獨自、親自
- **caddie**
  高爾夫球童
- **call off**
  取消、撤回
- **capability**
  能力
- **capacity**
  容量；能力
- **car**
  （列車）車廂
- **cargo terminal**
  貨運轉運站
- **cast a vote**
  投票
- **cast**
  卡司、演員群
- **cavity**
  蛀牙
- **celebration**
  慶祝
- **certificate**
  禮券、證明
- **certified**
  有資格的、被證明的
- **chairperson**
  主席、議長
- **check**
  託運行李
- **clerical work**
  文書工作
- **clinic**
  診所
- **closely**
  緊密地
- **collaborate**
  合作
- **come by**
  順道過來
- **come to a decision**
  做出決定
- **command**
  命令

- **comment on**
  對～發表評論
- **commercial space**
  商業空間
- **commission**
  委託、委任
- **commitment**
  付出
- **committee**
  委員會
- **comparable**
  可比較的、相當的
- **compete**
  競爭
- **competition**
  競賽
- **complain about**
  抱怨
- **complement**
  補足
- **complete**
  完全的
- **comprise**
  包含、由～組成
- **conference**
  會議
- **confirm**
  確認
- **confirmation**
  確認
- **connect**
  連結
- **construction site**
  建築工地
- **construction work**
  施工工程
- **correction**
  改正、修正
- **correspondent**
  撰稿人、外派記者
- **council**
  議會
- **course**
  高爾夫球場
- **courtyard**
  庭院、院子
- **cover**
  行走
- **covering**
  帷幕、遮棚
- **creativity**
  創造力、創意
- **credential**
  資格證
- **crew**
  工作人員
- **critical**
  重要的
- **custom-made**
  客製化的

- **cutting-edge**
  先進的、尖端的
- **damaging**
  有破壞性的
- **deal with**
  處理
- **dealership**
  經銷商
- **debate**
  辯論
- **decor**
  室內裝潢
- **defective**
  有缺損的
- **deliver**
  運送、投遞
- **deli**
  熟食店
- **deluxe bed**
  豪華雙人床
- **demand**
  需求
- **demonstrate**
  展示、證明
- **departure**
  離開
- **despite**
  （介系詞）儘管
- **destination**
  目的地
- **determine**
  決定
- **direction**
  方向、路線
- **director**
  總監、主管
- **discontinue**
  中斷、停產
- **division**
  部門
- **do not honor**
  不配合特定行銷行為
- **documentary**
  紀錄片
- **downtown**
  市中心（的）
- **draft**
  草擬；草稿
- **dramatically**
  劇烈地、顯著地
- **draw up**
  草擬、起草
- **draw**
  吸引
- **durable**
  耐用的
- **duration**
  期間
- **ease**
  減輕、緩和

- **eatery**
  餐飲店、飯館
- **editorial**
  社論
- **efficiency**
  效率、效能
- **electrical work**
  電力作業
- **electrician**
  電工
- **eliminate**
  排除、消除
- **emerge**
  浮現、顯現
- **emotional**
  情感上的
- **emphasis**
  強調
- **employee orientation**
  員工訓練
- **enable**
  使能夠
- **end up**
  最終成為
- **endeavor**
  努力
- **enhance**
  加強、提昇
- **enroll**
  入學
- **entertainment**
  娛樂、消遣
- **enthusiastic**
  熱情的
- **entity**
  團體、組織
- **entry**
  參賽作品
- **equipment**
  設備
- **exact**
  確實的
- **exactly**
  確實地、完全準確地
- **exactness**
  正確、精確
- **exceed**
  超出
- **excerpt**
  摘錄、節錄
- **exclude**
  排除
- **exclusion**
  排除
- **excursion**
  （團體）短程出遊、遠足
- **exhibit**
  展出

- **exhibition**
  展覽
- **exotic**
  異國的
- **expand**
  擴張
- **expectation**
  期望、預期
- **expert**
  專家
- **expertly**
  熟練地、專業地
- **explore**
  尋找、探索
- **fairway**
  （高爾夫球場開球區和果嶺之間的）球道
- **farewell ceremony**
  歡送會
- **favor**
  贊同、青睞
- **festivity**
  慶祝活動
- **few**
  很少、不多
- **figures**
  數據、數字
- **fill the position**
  遞補職缺
- **filmmaker**
  電影製作人或公司
- **financial report**
  財務報表
- **fine dining**
  精緻餐飲
- **former**
  以前的
- **forward**
  轉寄、轉達
- **free food tasting**
  免費食物試吃
- **free of charge**
  免費
- **frequent-flyer program**
  常客飛行計畫
- **full fare**
  全額票價
- **full-time**
  正職的
- **fully-furnished**
  全套裝潢的
- **function**
  運作
- **gallery**
  畫廊
- **go ahead**
  著手進行；前進
- **go over**
  仔細檢查

- **good**
  有效的
- **graph**
  圖表
- **gross margin**
  毛利
- **guarantee**
  保證（書）
- **gum**
  牙齦
- **hard currency**
  強勢貨幣
- **hardhat**
  安全帽經營權
- **have a difficult time**
  做～經歷困難
- **have in mind**
  考慮、想到
- **headquarters**
  總部
- **high-end**
  高階的、高級的
- **highlight**
  強調
- **high-profile**
  知名度高的、高調的
- **host**
  主演；款待
- **human resource**
  人資
- **humidity**
  濕度
- **improve**
  改善
- **improvise a speech**
  進行即興演說確切的
- **in advance**
  預先、提前
- **in effect**
  生效
- **in progress**
  進行中
- **in public**
  公開
- **in stock**
  在貨的、有庫存的
- **in the meantime**
  同時間
- **in time**
  及時
- **inasmuch as**
  （連接詞）由於、因為
- **inaugural**
  開幕的
- **inclement weather**
  險惡天氣
- **include**
  包括
- **incorrect**
  錯誤的

- **indicate**
  表明、指出
- **ineligible**
  沒有資格的
- **inform**
  通知
- **innovative**
  創新的
- **insider**
  內部人員、知情者
- **insight**
  洞察力
- **inspector**
  檢查員
- **inspire**
  激發靈感
- **install**
  安裝、設置
- **installment**
  （系列中的）部分；分期
- **instance**
  實例
- **instead**
  作為替代
- **institute**
  教育機構、學院
- **instruction**
  指示；指導
- **intend**
  打算、計畫
- **interim**
  中間的、暫定的
- **interior decorator**
  室內設計師
- **inter-relationship**
  相互關係；人際關係
- **interview**
  訪談
- **inventory**
  存貨清單、產品目錄
- **investor**
  投資者
- **jersey**
  球衣、隊服
- **job opportunity**
  工作機會
- **journal**
  期刊、學術刊物
- **judge**
  評審委員
- **keep ~ handy**
  隨身攜帶～
- **label**
  標籤
- **laboratory**
  實驗室
- **land**
  降落
- **lead**
  指揮、帶領

- **leave out**
  遺漏
- **librarian**
  圖書館員
- **licensing office**
  牌照辦公室
- **lie with**
  取決於
- **located**
  位於～的
- **long-term**
  長期的
- **look forward to**
  期待
- **low-income**
  低收入的
- **loyalty-club member**
  忠實顧客會員
- **luxurious**
  豪華的
- **mailroom**
  收發室
- **major**
  主要的、大的
- **make a purchase**
  購物
- **make an agreement**
  達成協議
- **market share**
  市佔率
- **material**
  材料、素材
- **maximize**
  最大化
- **mechanic**
  技師
- **meet the standard**
  達到標準
- **merchant**
  商人
- **merger**
  合併
- **metropolitan area**
  大都會區
- **minor**
  少的；次要的
- **multiple**
  多數的
- **native**
  本地的、土生土長的
- **natural resources**
  天然資源
- **nearly**
  幾乎
- **night shift**
  夜班
- **not-for-profit**
  非營利的

- **notice**
  公告、通知
- **now that**
  由於
- **obtain**
  獲得
- **obviously**
  顯然地
- **occasion**
  特殊場合或活動
- **occupied**
  使用中的
- **occur**
  發生
- **official**
  正式的
- **officiate**
  主持、行使職務
- **omit**
  遺漏
- **on another note**
  另一方面
- **on hand**
  方便的、在手邊、在場
- **on track**
  進行中的
- **one another**
  彼此、互相
- **ongoing**
  持續進行的
- **open-access**
  開放存取的
- **open-air**
  戶外的、露天的
- **operate**
  操作；經營
- **opinion**
  意見
- **opposite**
  相反的、對面的
- **or so**
  大約
- **ordinary**
  普通的
- **orientation session**
  員工培訓課程
- **originate**
  起始、發源
- **out of stock**
  無庫存、缺貨
- **oversee**
  監督、管理
- **overtime rate**
  超時工作費、加班費
- **ownership**
  物主、所有權
- **ownership**
  經營權
- **panel**
  評審團

- **parcel**
  包裹
- **participate in**
  參加
- **password**
  密碼
- **patient**
  病人
- **patron**
  老主顧
- **pattern**
  圖案、圖樣
- **permanent**
  永久的、常任的
- **pet care**
  寵物照護
- **photocopy**
  影印
- **plastic bag**
  塑膠袋
- **platform**
  月台
- **plenty of**
  充裕的～
- **plug in**
  插上電源
- **plumbing**
  水管設施、管道工程
- **positive**
  正面的
- **feedback**
  回饋意見
- **poverty**
  貧窮
- **practically**
  實際上
- **praise**
  讚許
- **preferably**
  偏好地
- **preferred customer**
  貴賓客戶
- **presence**
  存在
- **press official**
  媒體工作者
- **prestigious**
  頗富盛名的
- **price quote**
  報價單
- **price tag**
  標價
- **primarily**
  主要地
- **print**
  書面、平面
- **proceed to**
  前往～
- **production facility**
  生產設備

- **proficient**
  精通的
- **profile**
  簡介
- **progress**
  進展；前進
- **project director**
  專案經理
- **promo code**
  優惠代碼
- **proximity**
  鄰近
- **public reading**
  公開朗讀會
- **publicist**
  宣傳人員
- **publisher**
  出版商
- **pursue**
  追求
- **put on**
  穿戴上
- **qualification**
  資格條件
- **qualified**
  合格的
- **quarterly**
  季度的
- **rare**
  稀有的、罕見的
- **read through**
  看完
- **real estate agent**
  不動產仲介
- **realty**
  房地產
- **rear**
  後方的、後面的、後門的
- **reasonable**
  合理的
- **receipt**
  收據
- **receptionist**
  接待員
- **recipient**
  受獎人、接受者
- **recount**
  詳述
- **recycle**
  回收利用、再生
- **reduce costs**
  降低成本
- **reflective**
  反射的
- **refurbish**
  翻新、整修
- **regardless of**
  不管、無論
- **region**
  地區

- **registration fee**
  註冊費、登記費
- **registration**
  登記、註冊
- **regret**
  遺憾；後悔
- **reluctance**
  （名詞）不情願
- **remark**
  談論
- **remodeling**
  整修
- **renovation**
  裝修、整修
- **reporter**
  記者
- **representative**
  代表人
- **reschedule**
  重新安排
- **research**
  研究、調查
- **resort**
  度假村
- **rest**
  剩餘
- **restriction**
  限制
- **resume**
  重新開始、恢復
- **resurface**
  重鋪路面
- **retail store**
  零售商店
- **retailer**
  零售商
- **retire**
  退休
- **retroactively**
  事後追補、溯及既往
- **right away**
  立即、馬上
- **rigorous**
  嚴格的
- **routine**
  日常的
- **row**
  （劇院座位）排
- **rug**
  地毯、踏墊
- **sales opportunity**
  銷售機會
- **satisfaction rate**
  滿意度
- **save**
  節省、儲蓄
- **schedule conflict**
  行程衝突、撞期
- **sculpture**
  雕塑

- **seasoned**
  經驗豐富的、老練的
- **seek**
  尋找
- **selection**
  選擇、挑選
- **serial number**
  產品編號、序號
- **serve**
  招待、服務、供應
- **setting**
  環境
- **setup**
  安裝
- **several**
  幾個的
- **severe**
  嚴重的、劇烈的
- **SF**
  科幻小說
- **short notice**
  臨時通知
- **short on**
  短缺
- **showcase**
  展示
- **sideline**
  （運動場地）邊線
- **signature**
  簽名
- **site supervisor**
  現場主管
- **sneak peek**
  搶先看、先睹為快
- **sophisticated**
  精密的；老練的
- **spacious**
  寬敞的
- **specific**
  具體的
- **specifically**
  明確地、具體來說
- **specification**
  規格
- **specified**
  詳細說明的、具體列出的
- **spice up**
  增添趣味
- **stack**
  堆
- **statement**
  帳單、清單
- **stay off**
  遠離
- **steady**
  穩定的
- **step down**
  辭職、退位
- **stop by**
  順道拜訪

- **storage**
  儲藏
- **stretch**
  一段路
- **student loan**
  就學貸款
- **submission**
  提交；提案書
- **subsequence**
  接續、持續
- **substantially**
  大量地
- **eventful**
  多事的、特別的
- **sudden**
  突然的
- **supplier**
  供應商
- **suppose**
  猜想、認為
- **surpass**
  超出
- **switch**
  更換
- **tape ~ shut**
  用膠帶密封～
- **technical support**
  技術支援
- **temporary**
  臨時的
- **terminal**
  終點站；航廈
- **textile**
  紡織品
- **the month after next**
  兩個月後
- **the weather clears up**
  天氣好轉
- **though**
  然而、不過
- **thrilling**
  令人興奮的、激勵人心的
- **timeline**
  時間表
- **to be honest**
  老實說
- **To whom it may concern**
  敬啟者
- **tournament**
  錦標賽
- **transaction**
  交易
- **transfer**
  移轉
- **transition**
  過度、轉變

- **treatment**
  診療
- **triple**
  成長三倍
- **turnout**
  參加人數
- **turnover**
  離職率
- **ultimately**
  最終、最後
- **under construction**
  施工中
- **under new ownership**
  換人經營
- **undergo**
  經歷
- **unemployment**
  失業率
- **unfold**
  打開
- **unless**
  除非
- **upcoming**
  即將到來的
- **variation**
  變化、差異
- **vehicle**
  車輛
- **vigorous**
  活力充沛的
- **visual aid**
  （圖表等）視覺輔助
- **voice**
  表達、發言
- **volunteer**
  志工；志願做
- **water purifier**
  淨水器
- **waterfront**
  水畔
- **welcome reception**
  歡迎會
- **well furnished**
  家具陳設得當
- **well-being**
  福祉、福利
- **wholesaler**
  批發商
- **widespread**
  大批的、廣泛的
- **wireless Internet connection**
  無線網路連接
- **wonder**
  想知道
- **work on**
  從事；對～起作用

  wrap 包裝

- **year-end function**
  年尾活動、尾牙

Actual Test 3 字彙 & 片語

- **a deluge of**
  大量的
- **abide by**
  遵守
- **acclaimed**
  受到讚揚的
- **account**
  帳戶、帳單
- **acquaintance**
  熟識的人
- **add to**
  加入
- **adjust**
  調整
- **adopt**
  採用
- **advance deposit**
  預繳押金
- **advanced degree**
  （碩博士等）高等學歷
- **advanced**
  高級的、進階的
- **advertisement**
  廣告，簡稱 ad
- **advertising rates**
  廣告價格
- **after all**
  畢竟、終究
- **agenda**
  議程
- **agent**
  代理人、仲介
- **ahead of schedule**
  提前
- **aim at**
  瞄準
- **alike**
  相似的、相同的
- **ancient**
  古代的
- **anthology**
  選集
- **apart from**
  除～之外、此外
- **apparel**
  服裝、服飾
- **apparently**
  似乎、看來
- **application**
  申請（表）
- **appropriately**
  適當地
- **architectural**
  建築學的
- **arise**
  發生
- **artisan**
  工匠
- **as a result**
  因此

- **as long as**
  （連接詞）只要
- **as of**
  自～起
- **as soon as**
  一旦
- **as well as**
  也
- **aspiring**
  有抱負的
- **assessment**
  評定、評估
- **assign**
  指派
- **assistance**
  協助
- **associate editor**
  副編輯
- **assortment**
  分類、各種各樣
- **assume that**
  假設、假定
- **at a minimum**
  最低限度
- **at one's convenience**
  在某人方便的時候
- **at the latest**
  最遲、最晚
- **attached**
  附加的
- **attest to**
  證實
- **attractive**
  吸引人的、有魅力的
- **audit committee**
  審計委員會
- **availability**
  可用、可取得
- **average**
  平均的
- **award ceremony**
  頒獎典禮
- **baggage carousel**
  機場行李送帶
- **balance**
  收支平衡
- **banquet**
  晚宴
- **bash**
  派對
- **be honored to**
  很榮幸～
- **be in line with**
  符合、適合
- **be new to**
  新來的
- **be required to**
  被要求、必須

- **be responsible for**
  對～負責
- **beloved**
  心愛的
- **best known**
  最知名的
- **beyond the scope of**
  超出～範圍
- **bilingual**
  雙語的
- **billboard**
  看板
- **boarding pass**
  登機證
- **book signing**
  簽書會
- **bother**
  打擾
- **brew**
  醞釀、形成
- **bring along**
  帶～來、攜帶～
- **bring in**
  帶來
- **by mistake**
  錯誤地
- **cabinet**
  陳列櫃、櫥櫃
- **capable of**
  有能力做～
- **certainly**
  當然、無疑地
- **certification**
  資格、檢定
- **challenge**
  挑戰
- **check in**
  報到、登記、辦理手續
- **choreographer**
  編舞家
- **circulation**
  （新聞雜誌）發行量
- **classical**
  古典的
- **clerk**
  櫃檯人員
- **clutter**
  混雜、壅塞
- **cluttered**
  雜亂的
- **commuter**
  通勤者
- **companion**
  同伴、朋友
- **comparably priced**
  同等價格的
- **competitor**
  競爭對手

- **compromise**
  妥協、讓步
- **conclude**
  總結、下結論
- **consequently**
  結果、因此
- **considerably**
  大幅地、相當
- **construct**
  建設
- **construction**
  建設、工程
- **consult with**
  和～商量
- **consultant**
  顧問、諮商師
- **consultation**
  諮詢
- **contact**
  聯絡
- **continuing-education**
  進修教育
- **contribute to**
  致力於、貢獻
- **contributor**
  撰稿者；捐助者
- **convention**
  會議
- **cooperation**
  合作
- **copier**
  影印機
- **couch**
  長沙發
- **countless**
  無數的、數不盡的
- **credit**
  貸款
- **crucial**
  重要的、決定性的
- **culinary**
  烹飪的
- **currency**
  貨幣
- **customer survey**
  顧客意見調查
- **customer**
  顧客
- **cylinder**
  圓筒、圓柱體
- **damp**
  潮溼的
- **data analysis**
  數據分析、資料分析
- **deactivate**
  使失效
- **decline**
  拒絕

- **deftly**
  熟練地、巧妙地
- **delay**
  延期、耽擱
- **delegate**
  代表
- **delightful**
  令人愉快的
- **demonstration**
  示範、展示
- **depart**
  出發、離開
- **designated**
  指定的
- **desirable**
  令人滿意的
- **detour**
  改道
- **dining**
  用餐的
- **discharge**
  排放、流出
- **displace**
  取代、代替
- **dispose of**
  丟棄
- **dispute**
  辯論、爭論
- **donation**
  捐贈
- **double-check**
  再三確認
- **drawing**
  抽出、抽籤
- **drop by**
  順道拜訪
- **eager**
  渴望的、熱切的
- **edition**
  出版版次
- **editor-in-chief**
  總編輯
- **electricity**
  電、電力
- **electronics**
  電子產品
- **elevator**
  電梯
- **elsewhere**
  在別處
- **empty of**
  缺乏
- **enchanting**
  迷人的
- **enclosed**
  隨函附上的
- **encourage**
  鼓勵、獎勵
- **end product**
  成品

836

- **energy usage**
  能源使用
- **enter into**
  輸入、進入
- **enthusiasm**
  熱情
- **enthusiast**
  愛好者
- **entire**
  全部的、整個的
- **entrance**
  入口
- **entrant**
  參賽者
- **entrepreneur**
  企業家
- **entry form**
  參加申請表
- **evaluate**
  評估
- **eventually**
  終究、最終
- **exceed one's expectation**
  超乎～的期待
- **exceptional**
  非凡的
- **exhibitor**
  參展者
- **expedition**
  探險
- **expenditure**
  支出、費用
- **expertise**
  專業
- **explanation**
  說明
- **express mail**
  快遞
- **extension (phone)**
  分機
- **fabric**
  織物
- **facilitate**
  幫助、使容易
- **financial situation**
  財務狀況
- **fit into**
  適合、符合
- **fitting room**
  試衣間
- **flat**
  平坦的
- **flexible**
  有彈性的、靈活的
- **follow the process**
  依照程序
- **followed by**
  隨後、接著

- **for a while**
  暫時、一會兒
- **forbid**
  禁止
- **forceful**
  強而有力的、有魄力的
- **foreign exchange**
  外幣兌換
- **formally**
  正式地
- **founder**
  創建者
- **freeze**
  當機
- **further**
  更進一步、更深入
- **garage**
  車庫、停車場
- **gathering**
  聚會
- **generate**
  產生
- **generous**
  慷慨大方的
- **get a credit for**
  獲得信用（點數）
- **get rid of**
  擺脫
- **get through**
  處理
- **given that**
  考慮到～
- **go (on) well**
  很順利
- **go up**
  上漲、漲價
- **govern**
  管理、控制
- **grab a bit**
  吃點東西
- **graduate**
  畢業生
- **gripping**
  扣人心弦的
- **grocery**
  食品雜貨
- **growing demand**
  持續增加的需求
- **hair treatment**
  頭髮護理
- **half an hour**
  半小時
- **hand out**
  分發
- **handy**
  手邊的、方便的
- **hardly ever**
  幾乎不
- **have ~ in common**
  有～的共同點

- **have got to hand it to**
  相當佩服～
- **head office**
  總公司
- **health insurance**
  健保
- **highly ranked**
  名列前茅的
- **highly**
  非常
- **hire**
  雇用者；聘用
- **hiring committee**
  招聘委員會
- **historic**
  具歷史意義的
- **honor**
  名譽
- **ideal**
  理想的
- **identical**
  同樣的、完全相同的
- **identifiably**
  可辨識的
- **illustration studio**
  插圖工作室
- **impression**
  印象、感想
- **in a minute**
  立即、馬上
- **in addition to**
  此外
- **in an effort to**
  致力於
- **in compliance with**
  符合
- **in contrast to**
  與～做對照
- **in operation**
  營運
- **in order to**
  為了～
- **in terms of**
  在～方面
- **inclusion**
  包含
- **increase**
  增加
- **industry**
  產業、工業
- **inherit**
  繼承
- **input**
  意見、想法
- **installation**
  安裝、裝置
- **instead of**
  代替、而不是～

- **instruction manual**
  使用說明書
- **instructor**
  講師、指導者
- **insufficient**
  不足、缺乏
- **insurance**
  保險
- **intended feature**
  預期的特性、原來的特性
- **intern**
  實習生
- **intersection**
  交叉路口、十字路口
- **intranet**
  內部通訊網
- **introduction**
  說明書、介紹
- **investigation**
  調查
- **investment**
  投資
- **issue**
  （雜誌、書籍）期號；議題
- **It drives sb. up the wall.**
  使某人大怒。
- **it's a shame**
  可惜～
- **joint**
  共同的、聯合的
- **journalism**
  新聞業
- **keep sb. up**
  讓某人保持清醒、無法睡覺
- **keynote speaker**
  專題主講人
- **kneel down**
  跪下、跪坐
- **landscaper**
  景觀設計師
- **last-minute**
  最後一刻的、緊要關頭的
- **launch**
  推出
- **law firm**
  法律事務所
- **layout**
  平面圖、格局
- **left-over**
  剩下的
- **lighthouse**
  燈塔
- **likeness**
  相似之處
- **limited**
  有限的
- **live**
  現場的

- **location**
  地點
- **make a point of**
  重視、強調
- **make a reservation**
  預約
- **management**
  經營管理
- **manufacturing facilities**
  生產設備
- **match for**
  與～匹配
- **measure**
  測量
- **meet a demand**
  滿足需求
- **misdirect**
  迷路
- **miss out**
  錯失
- **moderate**
  主持
- **modify**
  修改
- **much more worth the price**
  物超所值
- **near-term**
  近期的
- **negotiate**
  協商、談判
- **nominate**
  提名
- **nominee**
  被提名者
- **occupation**
  職業
- **occupy**
  佔據
- **off the coast**
  鄰近海岸
- **off the lot**
  離開停車場
- **offer**
  提供
- **on a regular basis**
  定期地、經常地
- **on schedule**
  如期地
- **on-site**
  現場的
- **operating hours**
  營業時間
- **opportunity**
  機會
- **organizer**
  主辦者、承辦人
- **otherwise**
  否則、不然

- **out of luck**
  運氣不好
- **out of service**
  停止運行
- **out of the question**
  絕不可能的
- **outline**
  大綱、概要
- **overcharge**
  超收費用
- **overtime**
  加班
- **own**
  擁有、持有
- **pace**
  步調、進度
- **packaging**
  包裝
- **panel**
  座談小組
- **participant**
  參加者
- **performance review**
  績效考核
- **periodically**
  定期地
- **persuasive**
  有說服力的
- **place on a list**
  列入清單
- **playhouse**
  劇場
- **popularity**
  受歡迎
- **portfolio**
  作品集
- **positive**
  積極的、肯定的
- **preference**
  偏好、傾向
- **preferred**
  優先的、首選的
- **presenter**
  做簡報的人
- **previous**
  以前的
- **previously**
  以前
- **pricey**
  昂貴的
- **prize**
  獎金
- **profitable**
  有利潤的
- **proof of purchase**
  購物證明
- **proper**
  適當的

- **publicity**
  宣傳、輿論關注
- **put on**
  上演
- **put together**
  裝配、組合、擺設
- **qualifying**
  具資格的
- **random**
  隨機的
- **rate**
  費用
- **rather than**
  而不是
- **rating**
  評價、評分
- **reach**
  達到
- **reading material**
  讀物、閱讀資料
- **rearrange**
  重新安排
- **receive**
  接收
- **receptacle**
  容器
- **recline**
  斜躺、倚靠
- **recognize**
  表揚、嘉獎；認可、承認
- **recover**
  復原
- **recreational**
  休閒的、娛樂的
- **redo**
  重做
- **reduce**
  減少、降低
- **refer A to B**
  介紹 A 給 B
- **refreshment**
  點心
- **refundable**
  可退費的
- **registration form**
  註冊表
- **regular price**
  定價
- **regulation**
  規定
- **reliable**
  可靠的、可信賴的
- **relic**
  遺跡、文物
- **relocate**
  搬遷
- **renew**
  更新
- **reputation**
  聲望、名譽

- **request**
  請求
- **required**
  必要的
- **research and development**
  研究開發
- **resign**
  辭職
- **retention**
  保留
- **revenue**
  收入
- **revolutionary**
  革新的
- **rewarding**
  值得的、有所收獲的
- **royal**
  皇家的
- **rush hour**
  尖峰時間
- **rush**
  匆促
- **safety**
  安全
- **secure**
  保護
- **security**
  保安
- **seldom**
  （否定頻率副詞）很少、幾乎不
- **sensible**
  合理的
- **separate**
  各自的、單獨的
- **settle**
  定居、安頓
- **shrink**
  縮小、縮水
- **shuttle bus**
  接駁公車
- **sidewalk**
  人行道
- **slight**
  些微的
- **so that**
  以便～
- **soak**
  浸泡
- **social gathering**
  聯誼會
- **solar panel**
  太陽能板
- **solely**
  唯一地
- **somehow**
  不知何故、不知怎麼地
- **somewhat**
  多少、有點

- **sophistication**
  熟練
- **sound**
  健全的、堅固的
- **specialist**
  專家
- **sponsor**
  贊助
- **standard**
  標準
- **story**
  樓層
- **straighten**
  整平
- **subscription**
  （文化活動的）長期票
- **substantial**
  相當大的、可觀的
- **sufficient**
  足夠的
- **superior quality**
  卓越品質
- **surplus**
  盈餘
- **tag**
  標籤
- **take the stairs**
  使用樓梯
- **take**
  搭乘；花時間
- **talented**
  有才華的
- **target**
  把～視為目標、瞄準（某群體）
- **teardown**
  拆除
- **testament**
  證明
- **texture**
  質感、質地
- **the public**
  公眾
- **thesis**
  論文
- **throne**
  王位
- **through**
  透過
- **time frame**
  時間範圍
- **timely**
  及時地
- **tiny**
  很小的
- **tour conductor**
  領隊、導遊
- **tour**
  旅遊行程

- **remarkable**
  非凡的
- **transparent**
  透明的
- **trap up**
  捕捉、陷入
- **travel expense**
  差旅費、出差費用
- **trial period**
  試用期
- **twist**
  轉折
- **typically**
  通常、一般來説
- **underway**
  進行中的
- **unlike**
  和～不同、不像
- **unloading area**
  卸貨區
- **unpack**
  打開包裹
- **value**
  重要性
- **various**
  各種各樣的
- **vegetarian**
  素食者
- **via**
  經由
- **Visitor Bureau**
  觀光局
- **volume**
  音量
- **warehouse**
  倉儲
- **waste removal**
  清除垃圾
- **widely**
  廣泛地
- **wipe**
  擦拭
- **without damage**
  沒有損壞
- **workshop**
  工作坊
- **workstation**
  個人工作站
- **year-round**
  整年的

Actual Test 4 字彙 & 片語

- **misplace**
  亂放、放錯地方
- **a variety of**
  各式各樣的
- **a wealth of**
  大量的、充裕的
- **abbreviated**
  簡略的
- **access**
  存取（資料等）；進入
- **accommodate**
  接納、接受；容納
- **accomplishment**
  功績
- **accounts office**
  會計事務所
- **acknowledge**
  認可、承認
- **across border**
  跨越邊界
- **administrative**
  行政的
- **afterwards**
  之後
- **agency**
  旅行社
- **aggressively**
  積極地、激烈地
- **allergy**
  過敏
- **allocate**
  分配
- **along with**
  連同
- **alternative**
  替代方案
- **analysis**
  分析
- **antique**
  古董
- **app**
  應用程式
- **arena**
  運動場
- **arrangement**
  安排
- **as if**
  彷彿
- **as scheduled**
  按照原定計畫
- **aspect**
  方面
- **at any time**
  隨時
- **at once**
  馬上、立即
- **attribute A to B**
  把 A 歸因於 B
- **authorize**
  批准、授權

- **author**
  作家
- **auto shop**
  汽車維修廠
- **automatic teller machine**
  自動櫃員機
- **award**
  給予、授予
- **balance**
  餘額
- **batch number**
  生產批號
- **be equipped with**
  配備有、設有～
- **be featured in**
  刊登～為特集
- **be intended for**
  以～為對象
- **be subject to**
  易受～影響的
- **be sure to**
  務必
- **be told to**
  被告知
- **behind only**
  僅次於
- **belonging**
  隨身物品
- **beside the point**
  偏題的
- **beneficial**
  有益的
- **benefit**
  福利
- **beside the point**
  離題的
- **bill**
  法案
- **biography**
  傳記
- **blind**
  百葉窗
- **board**
  公布欄
- **boost**
  促進
- **branding**
  為產品命名
- **brasserie**
  小餐館
- **broad**
  廣大的
- **built-in**
  內建的
- **by**
  表數量的增減幅度
- **can afford to**
  能負擔～

- **cancellation**
  取消
- **capacitor**
  電容器
- **cargo ship**
  貨船
- **carpet layer**
  鋪設地毯人員
- **carry out**
  執行、實行
- **carton**
  紙盒、紙箱
- **cash**
  兌現、換成現金
- **Castalian Spring**
  希臘聖泉
- **celebrity**
  名人
- **certain**
  確信、無疑的
- **certificate**
  證書
- **client base**
  客戶群
- **client**
  客戶
- **climate**
  氣候
- **clothing**
  服飾
- **collaborate with**
  合作、共同工作
- **collide**
  相撞、碰撞
- **come along**
  發展
- **commemorate**
  紀念
- **commence**
  開始
- **commercial**
  （電視或廣播）廣告
- **commitment**
  承諾、保證
- **compact vehicle**
  小型車
- **comparison**
  比較
- **component**
  零件
- **concentrate on**
  集中、全神貫注
- **conduct**
  帶領；執行
- **constantly**
  持續地
- **consumer review**
  用戶評價
- **consume**
  吃喝

- **contemporary**
  當代的
- **contract**
  感染
- **convert A into B**
  將 A 改成 B
- **coordinate**
  協調
- **crane**
  起重機
- **croissant**
  可頌
- **cyclist**
  單車騎士
- **decline**
  下跌、衰退
- **deliberation**
  深思熟慮
- **describe**
  敘述
- **dietary**
  飲食方面的
- **direct A to B**
  把 A 提交給 B
- **discount**
  折扣
- **dispatch**
  派遣、發送
- **do one's utmost**
  竭盡全力
- **dock**
  碼頭
- **downward**
  下降的
- **drop off**
  （口）丟棄
- **drop**
  下降
- **due date**
  到期日
- **duty**
  職責、工作
- **earn**
  賺得
- **easily**
  容易地
- **editing**
  編輯
- **efficient**
  效率高的
- **elimination**
  除去
- **emphasis on**
  強調～
- **empty**
  清空
- **energy consumption**
  能源消耗

- **engraver**
  雕刻師
- **enormous**
  龐大的
- **enrollment**
  註冊、入學
- **entitled**
  給予標題
- **envelope**
  信封
- **envision**
  構想
- **erect**
  設立、建立
- **escalator**
  手扶梯
- **essential**
  必需的
- **even if**
  即使
- **evenly**
  平等地
- **eventual**
  最終的
- **ever**
  （用於問句）究竟；
  （修飾形容詞）從來
- **examine**
  檢查
- **except**
  除了～之外
- **exhausted**
  精疲力竭的
- **expansion**
  擴展
- **expedite**
  加速執行
- **external**
  外部的
- **extra**
  額外的、另外收費的
- **fancy**
  高檔的、特級的
- **favorable**
  良好的、有利的
- **favorably**
  善意地、順利地
- **favor**
  善意、贊同
- **fee**
  費用
- **figure out**
  想出、理解
- **final draft**
  完稿
- **financial plan**
  貸款、分期計畫
- **financial service**
  金融服務

- **flagship store**
  旗艦店
- **flavor**
  口味
- **flip of the switch**
  按一下開關
- **florescent**
  日光燈的
- **flu**
  流行性感冒
- **fluent**
  流利的
- **fly direct**
  （班機）直飛的
- **following**
  下一次的、隨後的
- **for the time being**
  暫且、現階段
- **fresh-squeezed**
  現榨的
- **fueling station**
  加油站
- **fulfill**
  執行
- **full range**
  全系列
- **full-service**
  有服務人員的
- **fully loaded**
  滿載的
- **gather**
  收集
- **gentle**
  輕柔的
- **get vaccinated**
  預防接種
- **gifted**
  有天賦的
- **go well**
  進展順利
- **grant proposal**
  募款企劃書
- **guideline**
  方針、規範
- **hand-held**
  手拿的
- **hanger**
  衣架
- **headline**
  帶領
- **hesitate**
  猶豫
- **high-performance**
  高性能
- **hose**
  軟水管
- **illness**
  疾病
- **illustration**
  插圖

- **immune system**
  免疫系統
- **in a class of one's own**
  獨一無二、出眾的
- **in a rush**
  趕時間
- **in case of**
  假如
- **in charge of**
  負責
- **in installments**
  分期付款
- **in keeping with**
  與～一致
- **in one's opinion**
  某人覺得
- **in sb's capable hands**
  由～處理
- **in the event that**
  如果
- **in the short term**
  短期
- **in writing**
  以書面形式
- **incandescent**
  白熾燈
- **incur**
  產生、招致
- **indefinitely**
  無限期
- **industry**
  產業
- **ingredient**
  食材、原料
- **in-person**
  面對面的
- **interest rates**
  利率
- **internal**
  內部的
- **invention**
  發明
- **jet lag**
  時差
- **keep from**
  阻止
- **labor**
  勞動、勞工
- **lately**
  最近
- **laundry**
  待洗衣物；洗衣店
- **layover**
  飛行中途暫停留
- **leaflet**
  傳單
- **leak**
  漏水

- **lease agreement**
  租賃契約書
- **leave off or the day**
  下班
- **level**
  弄平
- **light fixture**
  燈具
- **limit**
  限制
- **line**
  產品線
- **linguist**
  語言學家
- **loan**
  借貸
- **lot**
  車廠、停車空間
- **mail**
  郵件
- **maintenance work**
  維修工作、設備保養
- **majority**
  多數、大多數
- **make a photocopy**
  影印
- **manuscript**
  手稿
- **mass-produced**
  大量生產的
- **match**
  相配
- **meet with one's approval**
  某人同意
- **mileage**
  里程數
- **miscellaneous**
  混雜的
- **mobile device**
  行動裝置
- **motion sensor**
  自動感應燈
- **namely**
  也就是
- **narrow down**
  縮小、減少
- **negotiate a deal**
  協商談判
- **negotiation**
  協商、交涉
- **nephew**
  姪子、外甥
- **no point + Ving**
  做～沒有意義的
- **notice**
  注意
- **notification**
  通知

- **occur (to)**
  想到
- **office hours**
  營業時間、辦公時間
- **office space**
  辦公空間
- **on a tight budget**
  預算很緊
- **on business**
  出差
- **on most days**
  大多時候、一般而言
- **on one's behalf**
  代替某人
- **on one's own**
  獨自、獨立地
- **on purpose**
  故意地
- **on the other hand**
  另一方面
- **on time**
  準時
- **opening**
  職缺
- **operation**
  營業、運作、操作
- **organization**
  機構、團體
- **out of date**
  過時的
- **outing**
  短程旅遊、郊遊
- **out-modeled**
  舊款的
- **owe**
  欠（錢）
- **palette**
  用色表
- **pass out**
  分發
- **perform**
  執行、履行
- **personally**
  親自
- **phone directory**
  電話簿
- **physician**
  （內科）醫生
- **population**
  人口
- **power strip**
  電線排插
- **precisely**
  準確地
- **preliminary**
  初步的
- **premises**
  （公司或機構）經營廠址
- **prescription**
  處方籤

- **present**
  出席；做簡報
- **pressure**
  壓力、壓迫
- **procedure**
  程序
- **processing facility**
  加工廠
- **product trial**
  產品測試
- **productivity**
  生產力、生產效率
- **program**
  節目表
- **project**
  提案；預計
- **prospective**
  有希望的
- **provided that**
  假如
- **provider**
  供應商、公司
- **public relations**
  公關活動
- **pull ahead of**
  領先
- **quite a bit of**
  相當多的
- **rack**
  掛物架
- **raise awareness**
  提高認知度
- **raise funds**
  集資
- **raise**
  舉起；增加
- **rarely**
  很少、幾乎不
- **rather than**
  而不是
- **recall**
  收回、召回
- **reclaimed**
  回收利用的、改造的
- **refinancing**
  再提供資金
- **regulation**
  規定
- **reimbursable**
  可報銷的
- **reimburse**
  報銷費用、報公帳
- **related to**
  與～有關
- **renter**
  房客、承租人
- **replace A with B**
  把 A 換成 B
- **replacement part**
  替換零件

- reportedly
  根據傳聞
- rest assured that
  安心、放心
- résumé
  履歷表
- run out of
  用完、耗盡
- rush job
  急事
- salvage
  搶救
- savings account
  存款帳戶
- say
  （口）假設、舉例來說
- scrap
  廢棄物
- selective
  有選擇性的
- senior
  老年人
- session
  會議、集會
- shade
  窗簾
- shelter
  遮蔽處
- shorthanded
  人手不足的
- sick leave
  病假
- signs of wear
  磨損的跡象
- sizable
  相當大的
- slide
  投影片
- So that's all.
  原來如此。
- sole
  唯一的
- specifics
  詳情、細節
- specific
  具體的、特定的
- Sport Utility Vehicle
  即 SUV，休旅車
- spread
  蔓延
- staffing change
  人事異動
- standard
  標準規範；標準的
- standardly
  一般地
- stationery
  文具
- station
  配置、位於
- stock
  進貨
- stopover
  飛行中途停留
- stuff
  東西、物品
- subscription
  訂閱（費用）
- substitute for
  代替～
- subtitle
  字幕
- suffer
  遭受、經歷
- sun damage
  曬傷
- supplement
  補給品、營養品
- supply room
  器材室
- suspend
  懸掛、吊
- symptom-free
  無症狀的
- take effect
  生效、實施
- take-over
  接管
- temporarily
  暫時地
- terminate
  終止
- the panel of judges
  評審團
- tidy
  整潔、整齊的
- toward
  朝向
- training session
  培訓、訓練課程
- transfer
  調職；轉帳
- travel along
  沿著～行走
- treat
  治療、處理
- try on
  試戴、試穿
- turn around
  革新、好轉
- turn up
  出現、到來
- turn
  依次、照順序
- unexpectedly
  意外地
- unit
  （公寓大樓的）單間套房
- unlikely
  預期之外的
- unprecedented
  史無前例的
- up to
  多達
- updated version
  最新版本
- upward
  向上的
- urgent
  緊急的
- used vehicle
  二手車
- utilize
  利用
- vacant
  空的
- valve
  水閥
- vessel
  （大型）船、艦
- vibration
  震動
- wage slip
  薪資明細
- warning
  警告
- warranty
  保固（期）
- wide range of
  廣泛的
- wind
  （道路或河川）蜿蜒、曲折前進
- wire
  電線、鐵絲
- workforce
  人力
- wrap up
  （會議）結束
- yet
  （用於問句）已經

841

- **delegate**
委任

- **a host of**
許多的

- **a portion of**
一部分的

- **accessibility**
取得、利用

- **accidentally**
偶然地

- **acknowledge**
認出

- **additionally**
此外

- **adjustment**
調整、修改

- **advance**
事先的、預先的

- **advisable**
明智的

- **air purifier**
空氣清淨機

- **align**
校準、排成一直線

- **all hands on deck**
所有人齊心協力

- **along**
沿著、向前

- **amended**
修正後的

- **amount**
金額、數量

- **annex**
附屬大樓

- **annoyed**
惱怒的

- **annually**
每年

- **apartment**
公寓

- **applaud**
鼓掌

- **appreciation**
感激

- **arrive**
抵達、送達

- **as a matter of fact**
事實上

- **assist**
協助

- **at no cost**
無償

- **authority**
權力

- **authorization**
授權

- **automobile**
汽車

- **badge**
識別證

- **bargain item**
特價品

- **be against**
反對

- **be due to**
預期的

- **be impressed with**
對～印象深刻

- **be replaced with**
取代

- **be subject to**
視～狀況而定

- **be thrilled to**
感到興奮激動的

- **be worth it**
～是值得的

- **beachgoer**
常去海邊的人

- **become acquainted with**
熟悉～

- **beforehand**
事先、提前

- **billing statement**
帳單明細

- **bill**
請款

- **board meeting**
董事會會議

- **book tour**
書籍巡迴

- **boon**
提昇生活品質的好處

- **bulb**
燈泡

- **bush**
灌木、樹叢

- **business travel cost**
出差費、差旅費

- **call in sick**
打電話請病假

- **capacity**
容量、產能、生產力

- **carry**
運送、攜帶、備有

- **cashier**
收銀人員；收銀台

- **cast**
投射（光影）

- **caterer**
外燴業者

- **certify**
證明

- **chart**
圖表

- **checkout desk**
借還書櫃檯

- **chief of staff**
幕僚長、參謀長

- **clarify**
澄清

- **close one's door in business**
停業

- **column**
專欄

- **commencement**
開始

- **comprehensive**
全面的

- **conduct research**
進行研究

- **confer (with)**
商談

- **contain**
包含

- **continuing**
連續的、續約的

- **controversy**
爭議

- **conversely**
相反地

- **corporation**
企業

- **correspond**
與～一致

- **correspondence**
通信、信件

- **correspondingly**
相應地

- **cost estimate**
估價

- **cover**
補償、承保

- **custom-designed**
訂製的

- **customer complaint**
客訴

- **deduct**
扣除、減除

- **delegate**
委任

- **delicatessen**
熟食店，簡稱 deli

- **deliver a lecture**
發表演說

- **departure**
出發、離開

- **designated**
指定的

- **detail**
詳細說明

- **devote**
投注（時間、金錢、努力）

- **diagram**
圖表

- **dine**
用餐

- **direct**
指導、指揮

- **discount coupon**
折價券

- **discuss**
討論

- **display**
展示

- **diversity**
多樣性

- **donor**
捐款者

- **dose**
一劑藥量

- **driving range**
高爾夫練習場

- **drowsiness**
昏睡

- **due day**
期限

- **due**
預期的

- **duplicate**
複製的

- **edition**
出版版次

- **efficiency rating**
效能等級、節能等級

- **electronically**
透過電子手段、線上

- **employer**
雇主

- **end-of-the-year**
年底

- **ensure**
保證

- **entirely**
完全地

- **entity**
實體

- **erroneous**
有問題的、錯誤的

- **escort**
護送

- **estimation**
估計

- **exercise**
運用、行使

- **expanded**
擴大的

- **expiry date**
有效期限

- **export**
出口

- **extend to**
提供給（某對象）

- **exterior work**
外部工程

- **fairground**
露天廣場

- **farther**
更遠地

- **faulty**
錯誤的

- **feel free to**
無需拘束、隨意

- **fierce**
激烈的

- **financial adviser**
理財顧問

- **financial firm**
金融公司

- **fine**
罰金

- **fiscal year**
會計年度

- **fit**
符合

- **fivefold**
五倍的

- **flatly**
斷然地

- **flatten**
擊倒

- **flat**
平坦的

- **fold up**
折起

- **food processing**
食品加工

- **footstep**
步伐

- **for good**
永久

- **forefront**
最前線

- **fragile**
易碎、脆弱的

- **full refund**
全額退款

- **function**
（機器）運轉

- **fund**
提供資金；資金

- **fundraising**
募款

- **furnished**
附家具的

- **gesture**
做手勢

- **get to**
著手處理

- **gift voucher**
禮券

- **government-issued**
由政府發行的

- **grab**
抓住、取得、有效率的

- **graphic**
圖表（的）

- **groundbreaking ceremony**
  動土典禮
- **habitual**
  習慣的
- **had better**
  最好（表示建議）
- **halfway**
  在中途、到一半
- **have access to**
  可以使用～
- **healthy**
  （數量）多的
- **home improvement**
  居家修繕裝潢
- **hook up**
  連接
- **household**
  家庭
- **house-siding**
  房屋外牆
- **how far**
  （距離）多遠；到什麼程度
- **identification number**
  身分證數字
- **identify**
  確認、鑑定（身分）
- **if**
  是否
- **immediate**
  立即的
- **in a few minutes**
  立刻、馬上
- **in a timely manner**
  及時
- **in appreciation**
  感謝、感激
- **in favor of**
  支持、贊同
- **in place**
  準備就緒的；有效的、可行的
- **in the near future**
  不久後
- **inaccurately**
  不準確地
- **income**
  收入
- **incredible**
  難以置信的
- **industrial**
  工業的；產業相關的
- **instrument**
  樂器；儀器
- **insurance provider**
  保險公司
- **introductory**
  入門的
- **invalid**
  無效的、失效的

- **invitation**
  邀請
- **it's one's honor to**
  是某人的榮幸能～
- **itchy**
  癢的
- **item**
  物品
- **job candidate**
  求職者
- **just in case**
  以防萬一
- **justly**
  正當地
- **keep a record of**
  紀錄
- **keep posted**
  持續更新消息
- **lastly**
  最終地
- **lay a carpet**
  鋪地毯
- **load**
  裝載
- **locate**
  找出、確認位置
- **log sheet**
  日誌表
- **lucid**
  清楚易懂的
- **made-to-order**
  現點現做的
- **major**
  重要的
- **make it**
  及時趕到
- **make sense**
  合理
- **make the list**
  上榜
- **marginal**
  微小的、不重要的
- **marketing**
  行銷
- **matinee**
  白天場
- **medical record**
  病歷
- **meet-and-greet**
  見面會
- **memorable**
  難忘的
- **minutes**
  會議記錄
- **moreover**
  此外
- **move forward**
  提前；前進
- **mover**
  搬家公司

- **much-needed**
  急需的
- **multicity**
  多個城市
- **multiplex cinema**
  影城
- **nasal congestion**
  鼻塞
- **negligence**
  疏失
- **neutrality**
  中立性
- **nevertheless**
  然而
- **nonrefundable**
  不可退款的
- **normally**
  通常
- **note**
  提到、注意到
- **official**
  官員
- **on the go**
  非常忙碌的
- **one-story**
  一層樓的
- **onward**
  向前的
- **open house**
  開放看屋
- **operating officer**
  營運長
- **operational**
  經營上的
- **operator**
  經營者
- **oppose**
  反對
- **originally**
  原先
- **out of order**
  故障
- **outdated**
  過時的
- **outgrow**
  長大（而不再需要）
- **out-of-town**
  外地的
- **overhear**
  偶然聽到
- **overlook**
  忽略
- **owner**
  物主、擁有者
- **packing**
  打包行李
- **paid vacation**
  有薪假
- **pamphlet**
  冊子

- **particular**
  特定的、某個
- **partner with**
  與～合夥
- **partnership**
  合作
- **path**
  小徑
- **patio**
  （可在上面擺桌椅的）露台
- **pedestrian**
  行人
- **performance**
  成果；表演
- **periodically**
  定期地
- **personalized**
  個人化的
- **pharmacy**
  藥局
- **phenomenal**
  驚人的
- **pickup**
  領取
- **planner**
  時間表、計畫表
- **power failure**
  停電
- **precede**
  先於
- **preeminent**
  卓越的
- **prefer**
  偏好
- **present**
  呈現；目前的
- **primary**
  主要的、首要的
- **profit**
  利潤、盈利
- **projection**
  預估、推測
- **protest**
  抗議
- **psychology**
  心理學
- **public appearance**
  公開見面活動
- **public transportation**
  大眾運輸工具
- **pull in**
  停車
- **push back**
  （時間、日期）推延
- **put off**
  推遲、延期
- **put out**
  取出

- **quarter**
  季度
- **quite a while**
  一段時間
- **railing**
  欄杆、柵欄
- **rapidly**
  迅速地
- **rather**
  相當
- **reach an agreement**
  達成協議
- **realize**
  明白
- **recently**
  最近
- **reception**
  歡迎會；接待處
- **record**
  紀錄
- **recruitment**
  招聘、招募
- **reference letter**
  推薦信
- **reference**
  參考
- **refund**
  退款
- **register**
  收銀台
- **regularly**
  經常地
- **related**
  相關的
- **relieve**
  減輕、緩和
- **remaining**
  剩下的
- **renewable**
  可更新的
- **renewal**
  續約
- **repertoire**
  表演節目單
- **respectively**
  各別地
- **respond**
  應答
- **restock**
  補貨上架
- **return**
  退貨、退回
- **reveal**
  顯示、透露
- **revision**
  修訂版
- **rise in demand**
  需求提升
- **route**
  路線

- **safety measure**
  安全措施
- **seasonal**
  季節性的
- **securely**
  安全地
- **secure**
  安全的
- **sedan**
  轎車
- **semester**
  學期
- **sensitivity**
  （話題）敏感；（人）多愁善感
- **serve as**
  擔任
- **service representative**
  客服人員
- **setback**
  阻礙、挫折
- **settled**
  固定的
- **set**
  布景
- **shipment**
  運送
- **shopping district**
  商圈
- **shortage of hands**
  人手不足
- **side effect**
  副作用
- **significantly**
  顯著地
- **single-branch**
  僅此一家、別無分行的
- **sit**
  位於（某處）
- **sledding**
  滑雪橇
- **smooth**
  順暢的
- **special offer**
  特惠活動、折扣
- **squeeze**
  榨出
- **start over**
  重頭來過
- **state**
  （文件中）陳述
- **storage facility**
  儲藏設備、倉庫
- **store credit**
  消費抵用金
- **storehouse**
  倉庫
- **strategically**
  戰略上

- **strict**
  嚴格的
- **string quartet**
  弦樂四重奏
- **subscription**
  訂閱
- **subsidy**
  （國家或機關提供的）補助金
- **survey**
  調查
- **swirl around**
  圍繞～打轉、旋轉
- **symptom**
  症狀
- **tax return**
  所得申報書
- **tear down**
  拆除
- **tech-savvy**
  精通科技的
- **the best deal**
  撿便宜、價格最優惠
- **the employee of the year award**
  年度最佳員工獎
- **ticket booth**
  售票亭
- **tightly**
  牢固地
- **to and from**
  往返於
- **top-notch**
  頂尖的、一流的
- **tourist**
  旅客
- **track**
  鐵軌
- **trade fair**
  博覽會
- **transfer**
  調動；轉接電話
- **travel agency**
  旅行社
- **trim**
  修剪、修整
- **trolley**
  電車、手推車
- **trusted**
  受到信賴的
- **try out**
  測試
- **undergo training**
  受訓
- **unfavorable**
  不利的
- **unforeseen**
  沒有預料到的
- **used instrument**
  二手樂器

- **waive**
  免除
- **walkway**
  走道
- **weekdays**
  平日
- **weigh**
  重達
- **well trained**
  訓練有素的
- **whereas**
  但是、儘管
- **whichever**
  無論哪個
- **would rather**
  更願意、偏好

Vocabulary Test

Actual Test 01	Actual Test 02	Actual Test 03	Actual Test 04	Actual Test 05
1. address	1. accessible	1. agenda	1. misplace	1. amount
2. afford	2. acquire	2. assessment	2. alternative	2. authorization
3. benefit	3. auditorium	3. be in line with	3. balance	3. comprehensive
4. budget	4. board of directors	4. considerably	4. be equipped with	4. confer (with)
5. colleague	5. certificate	5. decline	5. boost	5. correspondingly
6. dealer	6. confirm	6. entrance	6. commercial	6. delegate
7. evaluation	7. defective	7. gathering	7. dispatch	7. ensure
8. expense	8. eliminate	8. impression	8. exhausted	8. negligence
9. faculty	9. enroll	9. nominate	9. favorable	9. overhear
10. formerly	10. excursion	10. industry	10. in installments	10. patio
11. grant	11. in effect	11. instructor	11. in the event that	11. precede
12. honor	12. inspector	12. investment	12. majority	12. profit
13. implement	13. inventory	13. negotiate	13. notification	13. reception
14. in place	14. make a purchase	14. out of service	14. preliminary	14. recruitment
15. issue	15. orientation	15. persuasive	15. premises	15. register
16. lease	16. permanent	16. recognize	16. provided that	16. relieve
17. malfunction	17. price quote	17. required	17. reimburse	17. respectively
18. number	18. qualified	18. resign	18. specific	18. shortage
19. outreach	19. reschedule	19. surplus	19. supplement	19. smooth
20. permit	20. turnover	20. warehouse	20. terminate	20. waive

| Answer Keys |

Actual Test 01

1. **address**
演講、對～說話、處理

2. **afford**
負擔得起

3. **benefit**
有益的；獲益

4. **budget**
預算

5. **colleague**
同事

6. **dealer**
經銷商

7. **evaluation**
評價

8. **expense**
支出、開銷

9. **faculty**
師資

10. **formerly**
以前

11. **grant**
補助金

12. **honor**
向～致敬、尊敬

13. **implement**
實施、施行

14. **in place**
準備就緒的

15. **issue**
發行；議題

16. **lease**
租約

17. **malfunction**
故障

18. **number**
數量多達；數字

19. **outreach**
推廣服務

20. **permit**
許可

Actual Test 02

1. **accessible**
易接近的、可進去的

2. **acquire**
收購、併購

3. **auditorium**
禮堂

4. **board of directors**
董事會

5. **certificate**
禮券；證明

6. **confirm**
確認

7. **defective**
有缺損的

8. **eliminate**
排除

9. **enroll**
入學

10. **excursion**
短程出遊、遠足

11. **in effect**
生效

12. **inspector**
檢查員

13. **inventory**
存貨清單、產品目錄

14. **make a purchase**
購物

15. **orientation**
員工培訓

16. **permanent**
永久的、常任的

17. **price quote**
報價單

18. **qualified**
合格的

19. **reschedule**
重新安排

20. **turnover**
離職率

Actual Test 03

1. **agenda**
議程

2. **assessment**
評定、評估

3. **be in line with**
符合

4. **considerably**
大幅地、相當

5. **decline**
衰退、下跌；拒絕

6. **entrance**
入口

7. **gathering**
聚會

8. **impression**
印象

9. **nominate**
提名

10. **industry**
產業；工業

11. **instructor**
講師、指導者

12. **investment**
投資

13. **negotiate**
協商、談判

14. **out of service**
停止運行

15. **persuasive**
有說服力的

16. **recognize**
表揚；認可、承認

17. **required**
必須的

18. **resign**
辭職

19. **surplus**
盈餘

20. **warehouse**
倉庫

Actual Test 04

1. **misplace**
遺失、找不到

2. **alternative**
替代方案；替代的

3. **balance**
盈餘；平衡

4. **be equipped with**
設有～、備有～

5. **boost**
促進

6. **commercial**
多媒體廣告

7. **dispatch**
派遣、發送

8. **exhausted**
筋疲力竭的

9. **favorable**
有利的、良好的

10. **in installments**
分期付款

11. **in the event that**
如果

12. **majority**
多數

13. **notification**
通知

14. **preliminary**
初步的

15. **premises**
（公司或工廠）經營廠址

16. **provided that**
假設

17. **reimburse**
報銷費用、報公帳

18. **specific**
具體的

19. **supplement**
補給品、營養品

20. **terminate**
終止

Actual Test 05

1. **amount**
金額、數量

2. **authorization**
授權

3. **comprehensive**
全面的

4. **confer (with)**
商談

5. **correspondingly**
相應地

6. **delegate**
代表；委任

7. **ensure**
保證

8. **negligence**
疏失

9. **overhear**
偶然聽到

10. **patio**
（可在上面擺桌椅的）露台

11. **precede**
先於

12. **profit**
利潤、營利

13. **reception**
歡迎會；接待處

14. **recruitment**
招聘、招募

15. **register**
收銀台；註冊、報名

16. **relieve**
減輕、緩和

17. **respectively**
個別地

18. **shortage**
不足、短少

19. **smooth**
順暢的

20. **waive**
免除